# Other books by Fred Patten

Best in Show: Fifteen Years of Outstanding Furry Fiction (2003)
Reprinted as:
Furry! The World's Best Anthropomorphic Fiction! (2006)

Watching Anime, Reading Manga:
25 Years of Essays and Reviews (2004)

Already Among Us; An Anthropomorphic Anthology (2012)

The Ursa Major Awards Anthology:
A Tenth Anniversary Celebration (2012)

What Happens Next: An Anthology of Sequels (2013)

Five Fortunes (2014)

Funny Animals and More: From Anime to Zoomorphics (2014)

Anthropomorphic Aliens: An Interstellar Anthology (2014)

The Furry Future : 19 Possible Prognostications (2015)

An Anthropomorphic Century: Stories from 1909 to 2008 (2015)

Cats and More Cats: Feline Fantasy Fiction (2016)

Gods with Fur: And Feathers, Scales,… (2016)

Furry Fandom Conventions, 1989-2015 (2017)

Dogs of War (2017)

Symbol of a Nation (2017)

# Dogs of War II

## Aftermath

*Edited by Fred Patten*

# Dogs of War II Aftermath

Production copyright FurPlanet Productions © 2017
Cover artwork copyright © 2017 by Teagan Gavet

**Published by FurPlanet Productions**
Dallas, Texas
www.FurPlanet.com

Print ISBN 978-1-61450-397-2
Electronic ISBN 978-1-61450-418-4

First Edition Trade Paperback December 2017
Second Edition Trade Paperback September 2018

To

# Lethargos

## The earliest known war dog

The Greek city-states of Magnesia and Ephesos in Ionia went to war in the mid-7th century B.C. According to *Dogs in Ancient Warfare* by E. S. Forster (Cambridge University Press, May 1941), the Magnesian horsemen were each accompanied by a war dog and a spear-bearing attendant. The dogs were released first and broke the enemy ranks, followed by an assault of spears, then a cavalry charge. According to *Early Greek Warfare: Horsemen and Chariots in the Homeric and Archaic Ages* by P. A. L. Greenhalgh (Cambridge University Press, May 1973), Callinus of Ephesus (active ca. 650 B.C.) mentions an epitaph recording the death in battle of a Magnesian horseman named Hippaemon, "who was buried with his horse Podargos, his dog Lethargos, and his squire Babes."

The epitaph does not record whether Hippaemon, his dog, his horse, and his spearman all fell in battle, or whether his dog, horse, and spearman (probably a slave) were slaughtered to be buried with him, as was common in the 7th-century B.C.

# Table of Contents

# Introduction

## *by Fred Patten*

Is war "popular"?

It must be, or there wouldn't be so much of it. The history of mankind is the history of warfare. Neanderthal man versus the Cro-Magnons. Upper Egypt versus Lower Egypt. The Achaeans versus the Trojans. Whether the Trojan War is real history or myth is still debated, but nobody doubts that warfare between circa-1500 B.C.E. city-states and between migrating tribes and the settled lands they migrated into was well-established. Warfare from then until now has been almost constant. Wars between nations. Civil wars. Wars against minorities.

Do animals other than humans fight? Are you kidding? Look at "dog vs. dog" and "dog vs. cat". Eagles steal fish from other eagles. Some say that animals fight only for food, but consider a rabbit warren or a henhouse when a fox gets into it. In 1987 a pack of three coyotes got into the flamingo enclosure at the Los Angeles Zoo and slaughtered 47 birds. The use of animals in human warfare is documented back to at least 700 B.C.E., and much earlier if you consider men riding horses into battle. Animals haven't seemed to mind being pressed into service in mankind's wars.

When animals are bioengineered into human-level intelligence, or evolve into intelligence, will they become too intelligent to fight? Ha-ha-ha! No more than humanity has become too intelligent to fight. Predictably the only major difference is that animals will start using the tools of warfare such as swords and guns as well as their natural teeth and claws.

When FurPlanet Productions announced warfare as the theme for *Dogs of War*, we hoped to get about 20 stories. Instead we got 43 stories; well over 340,000 words. *Dogs of War,* with the first half of these stories, went on sale at Further Confusion 2017 and sold out there.

*Dogs of War II Aftermath* is the other half of the 43 stories. War is popular, so enjoy!

*There are different ways to consider intelligent dogs for future warfare. In "Dog, Extended" the increased intelligence can be turned on and off.*

*What does an intelligent person think about becoming unintelligent again if he's successful?*

# Dog, Extended

## *by Cairyn*

I run.
Stony ground.
Jump, jump, catch disc.
I run.
I fetch. I give.
Master throws.
Far, far. I run. Jump.
Air hot, dusty. I breathe.
Catch disk.
Lamp glows, siren howls.
Master looks back.
I drop disk.
I expect.
Master calls.
I come. Disc stays.
Through door. Down hall. Master coughs.
In room. Prep room. Boxes here.
Master gives harness.
Master gives Box

\* \* \*

and I am back to completeness, as if waking from a pleasant dream. The desert heat assaults me, although I am aware that it had been there all along. Just as a dog I don't seem to feel it all that much. Being a dog means more focus; you remain aware of your surroundings, but you are not oppressed by it. I suppose it is a necessity for a hunter species.

Murat starts talking right away. He puts a lot of trust in my ability to switch context. Of course, the Box helps keeping things straight. As long as it is not connected, it keeps its internal state—frozen thoughts waiting to be finished. I shake a little to settle the harness and the Box, and the cables along my neck wriggle around.

"Could you secure the cords, please?" I interrupt Murat.

He notices that the neck belt of the harness is not properly closed, and tidies it up, fixing the push-buttons that hold the cables in place. The jacks in my head have clips that prevent the plugs from slipping out, but put enough pull on it, and they will break. I have seen it before. Wouldn't do if I lose the better part of my mental capacity in the middle of a combat situation. Even if I'm only there for the sniffing.

"The satellite scans confirm troop movement, and we pick up data streams," Murat continues. "Not a lot of it, but Command suspects high-ranking officers are involved. Signatures match. It is possible that we found Al'Adeed's last hideout."

Al'Adeed, "the scholar". The current face, voice, and supreme leader of the ITAA, formerly PISL, formerly IS or Da'esh, formerly... oh, the names change, but the cause continues. Nevertheless, Al'Adeed's capture or demise would be another huge blow for the extremists' propaganda machine, and since the media is where the war is truly fought, the 37th would make it possible. (I am secretly glad they didn't call us the K9th. Dog puns, I hate them with a passion.)

We set out in the trusty flatbed transporter along with the rest of the battle squad as soon as commands have been issued and the strategy is laid out. The target is about two hundred kilometers away, far east of the glowing ruins of Aleppo in the middle of, well, nothing. There is a lot of nothing in Syria these days.

I'm a sniffer, not a strategist, but I am aware that a massive airstrike may do the job. Command wants Al'Adeed alive if possible, though, and they want the ITAA tech, and all info that they can get hold of. The hackers still haven't been able to get into their current network, so Command needs a foot in the door.

The landscape goes by, mostly flat, mostly gray. Dogs can't see red shades, so anything yellow is just a bright gray with a hint of green, and anything orange is mostly gray, and anything red is really really gray. Our passive camouflage is desert colored too, which means patterns of dull gray, for my eyes. The absence of true spectral green does nothing to improve my mood. I like the green forests and crystal lakes. After a few months of desert, even the cloudless blue sky seems to gray out with dust.

Buddy howls in excitement although any action is still hours ahead. Nobody reprimands him; in the middle of nothing, no one can hear him anyway. He's a border collie, quite a bit smaller than me. His black and white fur is dusty already, but not enough to keep him from standing out. The Box seems larger on him than it feels on me—pouches to the right and left of his chest, strapped to his body with a harness. Each pouch has a size of about twenty centimeters by ten by five, and looks faux leathery and rather ordinary; no outward controls, just four cables winding their way to the back of Buddy's head. The Kevlar lining and additional cushioning protect the organic matter inside.

I remember that Boxes have been offered on the free market some years ago. They weren't exactly a raving success; I don't know the reason. Maybe the cables and jacks in the head are putting people off. Looks too much like a cruel lab experiment, although there is no pain for the dog, I can testify. Maybe the idea of having a dog with human intelligence makes humans uncomfortable. Or the Boxes were just too expensive, who knows.

Dog, extended. The police have some, private security firms have some, even some rich people have some, so it's not just the military career. But here I am. Nobody asked me anyway. A Box doesn't come with citizen rights.

The convoy thunders along the street (euphemism for compressed dust), seven vehicles in a hurry to meet the enemy. First is the scanner jeep, sensing for mines, movement, heat signatures, occupied frequencies, whatever there is to scan for. Then the troop transporter, carrying sixteen humans. After that a Beast—huge tank-like vehicle with four towers at the corners, sprouting automatic guns and cannons. It runs on tires, not tracks, so it can keep up with the convoy easily enough, storming the desert rumbling like a mad elephant.

I have never seen an elephant.

We follow at some distance, a high-walled flatbed transporter with the dogs (three), dog masters (three), and a Box technician. Normally the Boxes don't need maintenance, but Gustav is along for the ride just in case. He's a good guy but not as smart as you may expect from a specialist for organic, nanotech-enabled neural networks. Well, he's in the desert with us; what can you say.

Behind us, the command jeep, the drone controller, and finally the carrier with the Hyenas. Not real hyenas, other than us real dogs. A Hyena is actually the size of a medium pony. Robotic animals with weirdly bent legs and neither head nor tail, they are controlled by a military AI and carry medium weaponry. Dogs have never been entrusted with offensive weapons, although that may have something to do with size and weight. Hyenas are strong and can withstand severe punishment, and they come in handy as first line of attack.

"Hyena" is not an acronym, in spite of the military's unrelenting love of acronyms. I do remember that the first versions of the walking machines were called "dogs", which I personally consider rather unflattering. Heck, a biological hyena might consider the current moniker unflattering, too.

Most of the vehicles have air conditioning, but the dog transport just has a tarpaulin to protect us from the sun and the head wind. Cheapskates. At home I like to stick my head out of a window and enjoy the air stream; here the dust would batter my eyes so I keep my head inside.

A hundred kilometers away from the target, we stop. The drone controller extends its satellite uplink arms and fires off one of the jet propelled drones. Murat talks to Command and gets back to us with a prominent frown.

"They apparently have scanned that area before," he explains. "No results then. Whatever they have found now, it must be a completely new enemy camp. We have no reliable info, but Command suspects they will not have dug in very deeply in the meantime." He alludes to the Afghanistan cave systems: deep dark tunnels partly natural, partly artificial. Lots of good dogs lost to booby traps. Good to hear that it will not be like that, but who knows. "Bad news is they will see us coming from kilometers away. We cut all their satellite links, destroyed the stratospheric balloons, and grounded their last planes, but even with no aerial support, they can easily spot our trek." By the dust cloud, I suspect.

Buddy wags a little. "That means a lot of shooting. We're not in for the shooting."

"We may not be needed at all," Murat confirms. "The Beast will break into whatever defenses they have set up, then the troops go in. Command hopes they won't completely destroy their tech in the meantime." Wish upon a star, I think, but don't say it aloud.

"They are doomed," Rocket exclaims. He's named after some animated character from way back, a raccoon or something who got three solo movies and a series. Occasionally, Rocket makes dogs and people watch them, as if he's proud of his namesake. He bears no resemblance to a raccoon though, not even in species—he's a golden retriever. "We have cut apart their network, taken their resources, and got their supporters to denounce them. They have nowhere to go. They will fight tooth and claw."

"We are sniffers," I state. "The troops will take care of the battle."

Gustav nods. "Can't say I'll be sad."

The other two handlers—Kurt, caring for Buddy, and Jareer, working with Rocket—don't comment. Kurt is a veteran who knows how quickly plans and expectations go up in flames. Jareer rarely says anything. When he and Rocket joined the team, some grunt joked that Al'Adeed had cut out Jareer's tongue. Jareer broke his nose, so there was perhaps more truth spoken that day than anyone cared for.

We talk strategy for a while, which is bull talk because Command wouldn't ask us for an opinion. Then Murat suggests that we should run around and play for a few minutes. He knows what we need. Dogs relieve tension with exercise; also, I need to pee. Murat takes the box harness off my back and disconnects

\* \* \*

I stand still.

I wait.

Master allows.

I jump.

Buddy jumps.

We run.

Sun hot.

I mark stones.

I topple Buddy. I am strong. Joy.

We race.

Stretch, good.

Breathless. Hot.

Sniff scorpion. Bitter smell. I shy.

Sit and look. Stones.

Master calls.

"Rex!" My name. My name!

I go back.

Buddy goes back.

Jump.

Master has Box.

Master gives harness.

Master gives Box

\* \* \*

and the consciousness returns to full clarity for both of us, complexity, speech. Neither of us can stand the heat for too long, so we lie down under the tarp, sip a little water, and pant. Exhausted, yet refreshed: I wonder whether dogs would have a word for that if we had a language of our own.

Rocket didn't join in. The temperatures are even worse for him. I am a short-haired Belgian Shepherd so I'm better suited for the climate than either him or Buddy, even though I'm never truly comfortable here. My light brown coat matches the desert, Murat once said.

The trek goes on. The drone controller keeps its communicative array deployed, which makes for an awkward and slow drive. I watch it sway in the wind for a while, then lie down and sense the rumbling of the road.

"It will all end," Rocket says. It sounds more like an attempt to convince himself. "We can go home, be dogs."

"There will be others," I remind him. "Humans fight a lot. If not here, it'll be somewhere else."

"I am tired."

"Humans need us, and we follow. We're their dogs; it's been that way for millennia."

"Ours is not to reason why, ours is just to do and die," Rocket declares. I know it's a quote, I have heard it before, although I can't quite remember the source. I would look it up on the internet, the Box has WiFi access, but the accessible uplink has been taken down while we are on the road.

"Maybe we can go home after all," I suggest soothingly.

"Live without Boxes?"

"Maybe. I would expect that a smart dog comes in handy for many things, but if you want to be just a dog, I'm sure the humans will find a place for you." I wonder how many lies I have just spoken—none, one, or two?

"Raccoons could use Boxes. Raccoons have hands. They could go far with a Box. Have the humans ever tried to give a raccoon a Box?"

"They did." I remember reading about the experiments. The humans had tried a whole lot of animals, some with better results than others. In the end, they went with dogs. They always do.

"What happened?"

"Boxes are too large for them, and they didn't get them miniaturized any further. Remember, raccoons are quite small. And they were not really suitable anyway. Different mindset."

"Opportunistic?" Rocket sounds hopeful, almost... admiring, as if he wanted to be more opportunistic himself.

"Raccoons have no loyalty," I phrase, and regret it. He turns away, sulking.

Loyalty, well. I have thought about loyalty before. It's in our nature as dogs. Of course, evolution has imprinted us with that sense of loyalty, because wolves are pack hunters, they need each other, they cannot exist in a social void. A lone wolf is a sad, sad thing. So, it's in our genes, and as dogs, we have transferred that loyalty to humans over a very long period of time. It's not really a decision, it's a part of our nature, so deeply anchored that even the enhanced intelligence of the Box cannot overcome it.

Humans love that, humans call it noble. But truly, is it something else than the attempt to fight the dumb desperation of not belonging?

\* \* \*

We are still a long way off the target. I am lost in thoughts—about the Box, about being dog, about Rocket and raccoons and faith and loyalty—when the world ahead of us goes up in flames. For a moment, I am too shocked to react; short-lived fire blossoms around us, thunderous explosions, wreckage is flying, but the tarp is blocking my sight to the front. The transporter veers off the street. I hear the Beast's secondary engines power up. I imagine its turrets swinging towards any target that presents itself. The troop transporter comes into view, jolting across the desert ground, as we do. Every turn of the wheels feels like being hit by a giant, dusty fist.

Our vehicle sways, and I can see the street and what's left of the scanner jeep. A smoldering ruin topped by skeletal metal fingers, burning out in bright and hot flames. I cannot see anything inside, but no one comes out. The drone controller has already started a swarm of small helicopter drones, surveying the area, but the Beast's turrets turn aimlessly and do not strafe any lurking enemy with death and devastation, so apparently the drones provide no usable intel.

Do and die, but there is nothing to do for us, so we look over the wall and strain our poor short-sighted dog eyes to make sense of the situation. No more explosions follow, the human troops move out in silence—actually, their helmets are transmitting commands—and we stay put and don't bark, so the only sound is the rumble of engines and the crackle of flames. Whoever attacked the convoy is nowhere to be seen; the spectacle of threat-and-response unfolds like a well-rehearsed play where a significant part of the actors is missing.

No enemy. After a while, Command orders the troops to collect evidence. We are sent out to pick up scent trails, moving very carefully, but find nothing but metal and more metal and some bitter remains of fuel and explosives. Buddy notices strange prints in the sand, as if a big lizard has run across the desert, but here too only a hot metal smell lingers over the sand, so it was no animal that left the tracks.

It takes a while to sort out the disaster.

"Mines," Gustav suggests during a break. "Thousands of them around, probably from some earlier war."

"The scanner should have picked them up," Murat argues.

"Whatever it was, it must have been automated," Rocket claims. "If it was a remote with feedback, the ITAA would have followed up with a full-scale attack."

I'm not so convinced; needle-prick attacks are not unknown around here as a guerrilla tactic, but I don't have anything better to offer, so I keep my muzzle shut. They'll tell us sooner or later. Probably later; dogs aren't their first priority.

When the troops over at the drone controller start to grumble and throw their hands up in despair, I guess they found the source of the attack, and they don't like it. Murat joins them and comes back with the news, the expression on his face saying 'they give us only the bare necessities but we know anyway'.

"SAM." He throws the acronym at us like an old bone and leaves it to us to gnaw on it.

Strategic Ambulatory Mine, so that's what it was. A nasty little device that moves on tiny legs, carrying three miniaturized rockets. Controlled by an AI, it is deployed along roads; the things move into position on their own, identify targets matching their strategic goals, and wait off the street outside of scanner radius to hit the enemy. When they're out of rockets, they can even return to a rendezvous point to be collected and re-equipped again.

Thing is, the ITAA doesn't have any. Their mines are old-fashioned cheap boom devices that kill indiscriminately. This SAM was one of ours, probably left over from the second Syrian war. It must have worked with old codes, or lost the proper codes over the years when some chips failed, and it was missed during the deactivation phase after the war. Hello, SAM, nice to meet you again.

So we had been hit by friendly fire—from a different war, to boot.

I am not a comedian. I do not find it funny. Neither do the others. We settle down and sulk.

* * *

There is a reason why dogs are equipped with Boxes. Reliable AIs are huge. The servers that run IBM's Watson Squared take up three levels in their Detroit computing center. Google's Empirical Brain is almost as large. The Japanese have another, I keep forgetting its name, but I'm sure it's not any smaller. (There are quite a few closet-sized quantum computers around too, but they are more or less specialists for breaking encryption.) The singularity has come, but its children are immobile giants that think weird thoughts.

So they have dogs. A dog provides a brain, basic instinct, a bit of knowledge, and a pleasant personality. The Box provides the extension: gray matter, if you want to call it that; processing power, as Gustav would say. A fundamentally higher level of cognitive abilities, the architects blathered, but I am cognitive enough without a Box, thank you.

Although...

Sometimes I do not know what I am. To what extent I am myself. Where I end, and the Box starts. I like being smart. I am aware that I am not so very smart without the Box. I may be more me, but less of an intelligent being. Rocket likes it better being just himself. I... am not sure. A Box learns when I learn. A Box is not a notepad, it's a hugely complex neuronal network. It develops. It molds after my brain. It provides more than just processing power, it becomes a part of what I am.

To a degree, I am the Box. I couldn't speak without the Box (literally—when I talk, my voice comes from speakers built into the Box, since a dog's muzzle cannot form human words). I couldn't grasp complex concepts. A great deal of the abstractions that I understand are actually patterns inside the Box, not in my brain.

My Box. Me. The borders have blurred over the years. One might think it's easy to see the difference when the Box is disconnected, when I am just dog, but when I am just dog, I'm not able to comprehend the issue any more.

The Box isn't me, either. Without the dog, a Box becomes unusable. Pure neuronal networks are what drives SAMs and Hyenas. They are not intelligent, in the sense that humans understand. They are missing what a dog has to add to the mix. They don't have personality, they don't have empathy, they don't have loyalty. They are incomplete.

All of this is me.

Taking away the Box leaves the dog. I'm a good dog, I believe. I once was just a dog. But other than Rocket, I do not yearn for the olden days. Thinking in this complex, convoluted way beyond instinct and survival and games of fetch just suits me fine.

I want to be all of me.

* * *

We have to wait. Command has asked for a new scanner jeep because going on without one would be too dangerous. (A fat lot of good it did to have one in the lead. I shouldn't question Command, but I do. All soldiers do. They keep their muzzles shut, of course.)

Murat offers to take off the Box while we are just sitting there. I refuse though; I want to think. Lately, I do more and more thinking. I sleep better without the Box, and the dreams are more pleasant, but outside of service with thinking time of my own, I seem to grow mentally. The sun is setting quickly, a starry sky becomes visible, and my thoughts expand to envelop the horizon.

War is a lot of waiting between frantic bursts of activity, and with time, you learn to occupy yourself during that waiting time. I can see movies on the web as long as the uplink is active, or browse a little, but right now the ether is dead for all of us. No matter, I have enough things on my mind to last the night.

I think of the SAM and what havoc it wrought to us in just a second (and we were lucky that it had just one rocket left). Just another relic from a time that politicians like to forget. There are millions of things just like it, many still loaded with destruction. Yet here we are, perpetuating the tradition with more weapons and more violence. This is the point where I understand Rocket's desire to get away from it all. Even from the Boxes, from a mind. Loyalty, we have it. But you cannot help musing whether the loyalty is placed upon the right humans.

Murat just sits there, too. He has a player in his pocket but doesn't use it. He probably has thoughts of his own.

Murat is German by birth, but his grandparents came to Germany from Syria as refugees during the first war. There was some hope by then to recover from the conflict, which was later lost entirely in the devastation of the second war. Murat's grandparents and parents never went back. The global players waged their proxy war in Syria until their interests moved elsewhere. There was nothing to return to. Does Murat feel some loyalty toward the country of his ancestors? Or toward the country where he was born as a citizen, as a stranger? Germany did not enter the war until after the Merkel Arcology firebombing. Under different circumstances, Murat might never have seen Syria at all.

I wonder whether I should talk to him. About loyalty, about belonging. But his mind is elsewhere.

The dumb desperation of not belonging, he knows it well enough.

* * *

The droning staccato sound of a helicopter cuts the night. We all look up; it's a transport carrying the required jeep. Someone higher up is in a hurry, we're supposed to continue during the night. Command instructs the new crew. I listen intently from a distance. Humans tend to forget how good dogs can hear.

Two other battle squads have cut off Al'Adeed's likely escape routes in the north and east. Satellites have been positioned to survey the area. Backup for us is being assembled. If we fail to capture him, Al'Adeed will be killed under any circumstances. The higher-ups want proof to exploit in their propaganda, but if push comes to shove (they call it measured response), they will settle for total destruction. Those other "responses" (nee mid-range missiles) are on standby.

But still, we're the vanguard. The honor of the first assault. Sarcasm can be learned; it doesn't come with the Box.

Onward we go. The dust gives way to reveal rock, limestone formations. I see grooves and ditches in the stone, washed out eons ago by water long vanished. Still no vegetation to speak of. The convoy goes off-road and follows an ancient river bed, dry now, smoothed by millennia of unrelenting wind. I can't smell anything noteworthy on the air, even with my nose up in the head wind. The terrain makes for a slow and uncomfortable ride; at least we're not dragging a dust cloud behind any more.

We receive the standby command through the Boxes. It's not really necessary, the sound of the vehicle engines already changes, telling us all we need. The only sign of the target is a modest plain-rock hill ahead, half hidden by cottage-sized boulders that line our path of approach. The Beast roars and passes by the lead vehicles; a monster of fury and determination. No hint of the enemy yet, but it's only a question of minutes. I am not authorized to link into the local tactical network now, but doubtlessly, Al'Adeed has prepared his defenses already, which will equally doubtlessly be smashed by the Beast. Behind us, the command vehicle, the drone controller, and the Hyena carrier stop and spread out. The four Hyenas are deployed—their carrying arms swing outwards and down; Hyena legs start twitching even before they touch the ground, then they get released and gallop ahead.

I hear explosions, fire blossoms, projectiles howl. We stay in place; we're the sniffers, the fighting is for the troops. Shouts in Arabic (I guess), a roar of rapid gunfire. I dare a look over the wall of the transport, which may be a bit risky but the vehicle is not armored anyway, and the tarp will not protect us from direct strafing, so I know we're not parked in the fire zone. Gustav looks a bit white around the nose though.

The troop transport has stopped quite a bit ahead of us, and the last two soldiers are disembarking; not mere grunts but specialists in powered armor. The exosuits secure the area from behind. Boulders are protecting our position but keep me from observing the action directly. Once, I glimpse the Beast passing by halfway up the hill. Seems we are making quick progress.

Behind us, the retractable automatic cannons of the command jeep swivel nervously, but it seems as if Al'Adeed's men never had a chance to get around and attack from the other side. I have no clue about the enemy's numbers. Closing my eyes, I try to get information by scent, but the wind dissipates the unpleasant smells and mixes what's left so I only get the impression of tumultuous battle.

Rocket has closed his eyes and pants. I do not disturb him.

* * *

Explosions abate, battle sounds die down, and silence once more engulfs the desert. Without any further information from Command, the vehicles move again, half around the hill and upwards. I can see bodies and the remains of guns and rusty trucks; not even a proper bastion or emplacement. The battle plays out in my mind, but most likely it's a Hollywood version heavily influenced by the movies I've seen. Us dogs rarely get into these first encounters, so I'm lacking the experience and the expertise. I do notice that two Hyenas are down, so Al'Adeed's defenses have not been as weak as they now seem after their defeat. None of our men have fallen though, and when we join the Beast, it's still growling and grumbling, as if awaiting the next strike.

The hill is much more ragged than first impressions suggested, with clefts everywhere, and the top seems to be split along the middle like bread crust. Due to an earthquake that lifted the area, I guess, but I'm no geologist. What I can see is a narrow ravine leading into the hill. A Hyena stands on guard in front of it (the second remaining one probably on the other side), trembling, machinery huffing, ceaselessly stirring its legs. The entrance of the cleft is barely two meters wide, too narrow for it to enter because of its protruding weapon arrays right and left. It has a searchlight directed at the gorge so when we leave the transporter and join it, we can look right down the passage.

Murat receives orders through his helmet. "Seems that Command was wrong about Al'Adeed not digging in. We've got a whole cave system ahead of us."

"How deep?" Buddy wants to know.

"Unknown. There is no data at all. Seems these caves were unearthed only a short time ago, or someone kept them secret for quite a while."

Local tactical network becomes available; time for us to shine.

The cleft leads us steeply downward, the stars still visible above us, until we arrive at a hole in the rock face on our right. An exosuit guards it. Behind, a tunnel leading even farther down, cutting off the sky.

Great, so it's Afghanistan all over.

Water has washed out these caves from the limestone in ancient times, but the rock is dry as bone today. Down, down to where the tunnel widens into a cave—like the stomach of an animal, I imagine. Five soldiers and the second exosuit have set up an emplacement here; it seems like the last defensible position against a sally. Beyond this post, the cave branches out into more tunnels and clefts, a jagged labyrinth that beckons the unwary into a trap.

This is not a comfy stone-age family dwelling cave, nor the regular plan of a mining operation—we stand in a chaotic place formed by the unpredictable forces of nature. There are no stalactites and stalagmites due to the lack of a constant water supply in higher rock layers. Part of the walls have been smoothed and washed out when there still was a river running through; others were later damaged by geological forces and turned into a hard-edged broken mess. I can see which tunnels formed the erstwhile subterranean river bed (most likely to lead to habitable deeper hollows) and which were just ripped open and broken out of the rock.

We get to work before the new soldier scents start to overpower the older tracks. Checking out the entrance of each tunnel and the whole cave bottom, we map the trails in time and intensity. Here, this tunnel was definitely used but not in recent days. There, a crack in the wall is suspiciously smelly, there's something behind it. Metal for weapons caches, explosive bitterness for booby-traps. We find it all, and determine the most promising vector for the advance.

Time is of the issue. With this extensive cave system, we cannot say whether there are more exits above ground. The other battle groups are blocking the surface escapes in some distance but the newfound topology here might tunnel below their position, leading to another failure to capture Al'Adeed and his stalwart men. The satellites might still be able to follow them but… I do not desire the shame and blame for a mission gone awry.

Deciding on a tunnel, we move on. A pathfinder robot takes the lead, just in case of an ambush that we dogs don't scent out. It's a small six-legged disposable unit that transmits video and infrared. Then one dog follows, Buddy in this case. Then an exosuit and the rest of the soldiers, conga lining down the corridor. Rocket, me, and the dog handlers bring up the rear, sniffing out the details that the vanguard misses, ready to take the lead position which changes every few minutes.

We're deeper down than the average surface now; the tunnel reaches a dip and winds upwards again until it disappears behind a curve. Air is stale and motionless, ground is brittle and rough.

"There is something here," Buddy warns. "Hot copper, can't identify it."

A sharp hissing sound hurts my ear. Buddy starts to scream and turns around and around as if hunting his tail. No gunfire, nothing but this eerie hiss. Pathfinder remains unaffected; the exosuit raises his weapons in the vain attempt to lock on a target, and Kurt runs forward, snatches Buddy up in his arms, and retreats again.

Rumbling replaces the hiss, and now I smell flames. Something rolls around the corner ahead, and down the tunnel. The exosuit fires; soldiers assume their battle stance; we dogs retreat. Sniffing, not fighting. I scent the nature of the trap and bark a warning before I race up our side of the tunnel; two soldiers hear me and break ranks.

The trap explodes behind us, sucking the air out of the tunnel and our lungs, then bursting into a spray of fire and heat. The pressure of the explosion pushes us forward, my ears hurt even more, and the only thing that saves us from being killed right away is the interconnectedness of the cave system where the effects of the detonation dissipate into the cracked jumble of stone.

The enemy does not follow us out of the caves.

Neither do our men.

\* \* \*

Later, we report to Command. The trap was primitive yet effective enough, some kind of incendiaries in large plastic balls thrown down the tunnel. Anything more sophisticated would have been picked up by the scanners; classic low-tech against high-tech scenario. Normally we have adapted to that, it was working only because circumstances and topology favored Al'Adeed's men. The corner kept the trap out of sight of the pathfinder until the last moment; the slope of the tunnel allowed the explosives to roll; the ground was just smooth enough not to slow down the balls; and still, typically the lead dog would have sniffed the fire and recognized the trap for what it was, allowing us to retreat quickly back to higher ground. Hitting Buddy with whatever the hot copper smell is—that had been the last straw that confused us just long enough and robbed us of our intel.

Four men dead—the exosuit driver and the three soldiers that stood their ground—one badly wounded, and one survivor. The latter two are the ones that I managed to warn. The pathfinder is lost. And Buddy, we still don't know what's up with him.

Command says it was a necessary risk, and we're to be commended for surviving, and we need to go in again.

* * *

There are too many attack vectors—fire, poison gas, explosives, automated guns, pressure, water, sound, acid, immobilization foam, laser, each coming in variants—so we need to find out what the new threat is before we start a new approach. The element of surprise, feeble from the start, is lost anyway, so Command's only hope is to catch Al'Adeed and his staff alive for a show trial and five hundred years of rotting in Pakavodia.

Still night, but the tech people have set up bright lamps all over the makeshift camp. We join Gustav, Kurt, and Buddy for a muzzleful of kibble, a bowl of water, and information.

Buddy seems to be fine, but Gustav has taken off his Box and is working on it, prodding the thing with sensors. So, Buddy is in dog mode and sniffs my ass, wagging. Then he walks away and rolls on the ground. Kurt catches him before he gets funny ideas.

"No response from the network," Gustav says. "It's dead as a doornail." I want to growl at him, that's half of Buddy's brain he's talking about, but he seems as tired as we are so I keep my teeth off his throat.

"Do you know what hit it?" Murat asks.

"Can only guess. Some pulsed microwave device, I'd say, but we'd need a lab to tell. The Boxes are EMP-hardened; they should withstand quite a lot of overload. No accident or side effect. Whatever it was, it was a weapon specifically designed against Boxes."

"Are you able to regenerate it?"

"Tough luck. This is not a digital processor that we could exchange for a new one, it's an organic neuronal network. The data is part of the net. Fry the neurons, and you can't just update it with a backup." Gustav goes into explaining mode. "The Boxes have to be trained, they must learn. Static connection, dynamic response, and there is the dog brain that controls it and uses it… Most of the gray matter in here"—he pokes the Box—"has died off, and all its stored knowledge has died with it. It's done. And I think that part of Buddy's jacks have been killed too; we use the same patterned neuronal cells for the brain interface, so even if we had a fresh Box to use, we couldn't attach it any more. I don't know whether the damage could be repaired on the interface, but even if…"

Even if, the new Box would be a baby, with no information and no training, that would require years of learning cycles and adaption. I know, I wear a Box, I've gone through all of that. And the knowledge in Buddy's old Box cannot be replicated or saved. The new Box would start all over again. Half of what Buddy was is gone, forever.

I don't know what to say.

Kurt slowly strokes Buddy. It should be okay, it should be fine. Buddy is alive. Buddy is a good dog, he still has all his limbs, all he was born with. He's alive. Kurt still cries.

* * *

We make another attempt and push forward to the next cave. More tunnels. I find one of the anti-Box weapons by smell, hot copper, easy to identify actually if you know what to sniff for. The techs salvage it without blowing it up (or themselves), and Rocket and I are all over it to learn the scent.

It's either Korean or Chinese in the basic design. Work for hire? Gustav gets online and does research. We haven't seen anything like it in the past. Gustav's first idea turns out to be true, it's targeting Boxes on purpose. It's not very effective, I can sniff the things out, and then the humans can just destroy them or deactivate them. They reek of a new development that has too many kinks to be of practical use.

Murat thinks that Al'Adeed is throwing everything at us that he still can get his hands on. "I'd say with a few years of development, they could make these things quite deadly. Enhance the reach, cover up the smell, add a self-destruct mechanism. He probably didn't want to play his hand that early."

"He knows he's dead no matter what he does," I conclude. "No point in holding back. I wonder why he hasn't blown up the whole cave system yet, just to take us with him."

"I haven't talked to the psychology strategists. Maybe Al'Adeed still hopes to get away. What would you do in his place?"

I am a dog, not a religious fanatic, so I don't know. It's not a fair question either; when it comes to extreme situations, you never know how you'd react until you've actually been in one. I've never been cornered by an enemy bent on eradicating me and all I stand for. Admittedly, I don't stand for a lot of things. I'm property, an extended animal, and the part of me that might think about it and philosophize and rationalize and wish and hope and dream—that part is not even in my body.

So, if I would stand for anything... if I had any beliefs or goals greater than me...

Beyond sniffing and rolling in the dust and being rewarded with treats for a job well done...

"I suppose I would want my cause to go on... my purpose."

Murat nods. "That's pretty deep."

"For a dog?"

He laughs. For a moment I feel the affection between us, like on the best of days. Then we are called in again.

\* \* \*

The hours drag on, outside the sun rises to burn the dust some more, and we map out the cave and tunnel system piecewise. This turns out to be more difficult than expected; our location systems are obviously not working ten or twenty meters under the desert ground. The pathfinders are measuring distances and turns but as soon as the ground gets too jagged, they lose traction and produce some incoherent information. Automatic signal triangulation breaks off too often. We can do it, of course, but it takes too much time.

There are enough traps of any kind as well to slow down our advance, and a few instances of direct contact with the enemy. We don't fall for it a second time. They die.

The techs are working on reconfiguring the Hyenas so they may fit into the tunnel system, but we have already found passages that are too narrow even for the exosuit so a fat lot of good that will do. Labyrinthine, dark, broken: the subterranean world makes a terrible battlefield.

There is a distinct unease in the air. We do not know what else Al'Adeed is able to throw at us, and there is the very real possibility that he just may decide to end it and blow up himself and us, or incinerate the hill and its surroundings, depending on what destruction he still can muster.

Maybe he's all out of explosives, huddled in a corner, awaiting capture.

Maybe he's already dead. We have no confirmation of any sort. The satellites are watching the surface and give no indication that anybody has escaped the caves.

"I wonder if the tunnels even have some exit," Murat muses. "The water might have drained away into a deeper stratum. Or the continuation of the river bed could be buried today."

As if on cue, we discover a blocked tunnel. This is a recent slide, and I smell traces of explosives that linger in the stale atmosphere. "They collapsed it," I explain. "Fairly recently too."

Two more rock falls close by cause excitement in Command. It looks as if Al'Adeed has shut himself in; his last stand, so to speak. We're hot on his trail. A tech is brought down to examine the rubble and to check the stability of the ceiling; Command wants to blow open the way but the limestone is fragile.

The tech recommends careful digging instead, which is news that Command doesn't want to hear. While they speculate about getting a Hyena down here and re-equip it for digging, I and Rocket survey the vicinity. There are several crevasses leading into or maybe through the walls, most of them too narrow for even a dog without Box. A few seem passable for me or a human to wriggle through. I am not sure whether they reconnect with the tunnels on the other side. They are not even booby-trapped. Dead ends most likely; they smell like dust and petrification.

Except, one of them smells differently.

I call Rocket to confirm: it's fresh air, only a feeble whiff of it, but this gap is leading somewhere. Just large enough for me to wriggle through despite the Box. Maybe a human could squeeze into it as well, but of course Command sends me. Expendability is a factor.

The rock cuts into my paws, legs, and belly while I am crawling into the crevasse. It gets dark, and I don't have a light attached on the Box, but my night sight helps. Occasionally a stray beam brightens the path when the humans in the cave behind me move around. I wonder what will happen if I get stuck and need to be rescued. Normally I don't suffer from claustrophobia, but I am not accustomed to spelunking either, and it is a really narrow place. My paws stir up pebbles that probably haven't been moved in ten thousand years. Every now and then, the Box snags on the rock and needs a careful tug to break free. Some sharp edges have cut through the fur, and I am bleeding a little.

I snake around a corner, and there is light again. The crevasse does not widen; if anything, it feels as if it's getting even narrower. I need to tilt the Box a little to manage it through. Okay, so a human would not have made that after all.

The exit leads into a cave that seems packed with equipment. Crates and barrels, cages and skeleton containers, even shelves with cardboard boxes. Lots of smells as expected from a storeroom. Human stench too, but nothing that would announce their immediate presence.

Outside of the cave, behind a low entrance framed in timber, there is a larger grotto. Here, the fresh air scent is readily apparent; it comes from a number of cracks in the wall. Light, too, but I can't look outside, the natural vents are too high up. I look around. There is the other exit of the collapsed tunnel. Desks and chairs of various size and nature. Computers and other tech everywhere. Weapons, from pistols to submachine guns, ammo in boxes. Another tunnel sloping upward, and yet another down, and I realize the smell of something big, something metal, something chemical. Like a huge vehicle, but also different. A mortar of considerable size maybe, waiting outside (shouldn't the satellites pick that up?). Or a rocket-throwing tank, ready for attack. Why hasn't Al'Adeed used it against us yet? Maybe it was one of these last-effort things, like the anti-Box weapons, not quite ready to be used.

Good. May it rot here with all of Al'Adeed's men.

And then Al'Adeed himself steps out of one of the open tunnels, a huge unkempt gray-bearded man rather undeserving of the moniker "scholar", and certainly not huddled in a corner. I recognize him from the files, even though he seems older and harder and radiates a hatred that was never as palpable in any image. He wears an active camo suit; I see the pattern changing as he walks but it is damaged and doesn't properly replicate the environment. I don't bark but attack, unthinkingly—he may still have some of his men around.

He sees me lunging at him and sprints down to the other open tunnel. With a few powerful leaps I am almost close enough to dig my teeth into him, but then I smell hot copper and immediately break off the assault, yowling when I feel a jab in the brain, jumping away from the tunnel entrance.

Al'Adeed is gone, out of reach. Down the tunnel he moves, around a bend and into the open air that wafts into the cave, carrying the large and threatening smell with it.

The anti-Box keeps me from following. So close, so close I was and yet the scholar has escaped. That is mortifying and unbecoming of a good dog. Yet I have no options—I can't unplug the Box and leave it behind, continuing the pursuit as dog; the design of the harness does require human help. I can't pass through the corridor without destroying the

Box and myself. I can't disable the anti-Box weapon, not even with all the artillery lying around—I have no hands to operate the guns, and I am unarmed with anything I can actually use. Sniffing, not fighting, and up to this minute I had no real qualms about that. I can't take another route; a short look confirms that the tunnel Al'Adeed came from only leads up to some kind of study. No exit there.

Obviously, I will have to wait until the humans have dug through the rubble and can join me, destroy the hot copper reeking thing and give pursuit. I could crawl back through the crevice but that would be fairly pointless.

So I try to send a message on the relays we had installed for the local tactical network—no success though, the Box doesn't even connect; it seems some jammer is installed here—and wonder why the satellites have not noticed another opening from above, or at least a cleft in the rock. There is light outside; too bright to be artificial I think; must be a chasm that opens right up to the sky. Command could send the Beast around on the surface, or perhaps a Hyena if the techs haven't disassembled them to uselessness yet.

There is no way Al'Adeed can escape now; unless he has a teleporter waiting for him, or a similarly improbable piece of sci-fi tech, even for the Koreans these days.

I am curious though, and do not want to wait for Command reprimanding me for not being fast enough, so I decide on some recon. I move a table over to the vents, and then heave a plastic chair up on the table which is rather difficult with no hands, even if the chair is light. Standing on my hind legs on the chair, I manage to get high enough to squeeze my head into the vent and peer outside.

It does not take much more than two seconds to realize that I found a long range nuclear missile arsenal mounted outside.

* * *

A decade ago, even before the Korean reunification, the North Korean Disarmament Treaty promised to destroy a large cache of strategic nukes stationed near Kanggye. It was always rumored that part of these arms had disappeared before their scheduled elimination, but even thorough investigation never found a proof.

I have no doubt that the evidence is right before my nose. Four missiles possibly equipped with several nuclear warheads each, from a time when NK did little else but construct these things and let its citizens starve. How did they wind up in ITAA hands? Considering the diligence of the international weapon smuggling trade, I am not totally surprised, but it must have been a bitch (no pun) to get all the parts here and reassemble them. Probably took years and many dead specialists to keep it secret, practically under the nose of everybody with a vested interest in the country or the conflict.

The missiles sit in a framework of steel trussing, wedged into a gorge. I can't read Korean but the characters painted on the hulls are definitely CJK, not Arabic. Far up, covering the gorge's opening to the sky, I see a thin irregular silver net glistening; bright blue rings are slung around some junctions of the web. Never seen anything like it, but it must be the cause why the satellites can't see the true topology of this area. You probably have to stumble over the gully to notice it, and for all I know the ITAA may have installed holographic deceptors on the surface, which would account for the drones not detecting anything with their purely optical sensors.

This is bad. This is bad on a nightmare level.

I do not know whether the missiles are in working order. But the fact that Al'Adeed has blown up all access tunnels to this place and sacrificed apparently all of his men to delay our progress tells me that it is not an idle installation, no retreat to quietly lay down and die.

This is his last coup, his last strike at the enemy.

I would want my cause to go on, I told Murat. And I am merely a dog with no cause to speak of.

Al'Adeed probably wants no less. And what could be a greater beacon to rally all leftover fanatics sympathetic to the ITAA than a score of burning cities? With the organization dying, this level of devastation could rekindle the idea at least in the mind of zealots, and perhaps lead to a new generation of extremists.

And if it doesn't have any lasting effects, the direct impact alone will be dreadful. Even if only one missile works, even if only one warhead finds its target, the number of immediate victims will go into the millions.

Al'Adeed wants to take all he has, and set the world on fire.

I can't reach Al'Adeed, so I jump down, race into the storeroom, and bark down the crevice to rouse the humans. The speakers on the Box are not very powerful but at least Rocket's ears should pick up my human-voice once they understand the gravity of the situation and listen.

There is no response. They are gone; I don't know why, maybe they are looking for the jammer, or are trying to restore the network, or have cleared out because they decided to blow up the blockage after all, or a booby-trap forced them to retreat. It doesn't matter. I am cut off, I am alone, I am trapped.

I return to the table and the chair and the vent. Can't see anything on the ground level; there must be a control station somewhere, and Al'Adeed will be there to initiate the launch.

There is only one exit, and it has an anti-Box.

My mind tries to retreat into speculations—what happens on the surface, why hasn't Al'Adeed used the missiles long ago, won't the launch destroy the grotto, but the rationality flowing through the Box recognizes these thoughts as mere escape from the single necessity I'm facing. Second by honey-thick second ticks by.

There is only one exit.

There is only one dog who knows what's going on.

While I watch, the silver net parts in the middle, and the halves fall down. Launch will follow within minutes. What's the countdown? I am not even sure that I can stop it. Still, I dread to act. It is not my life, but it is my mind, and in a way, the loss will be worse.

An AI, be it a pathfinder or a Hyena, would not hesitate. It has no sense of self-preservation though. Self, what a concept.

In the end, loyalty lies at a dog's core. Can I do anything less than a Hyena? Can I do anything less than a human? I belong.

I want to think a meaningful, huge last thought, just because I can.

But it's a borrowed mind anyway.

Three leaps take me to the tunnel

\* \* \*

Hiss. Pain! Sharp. Run!
Fuel scent. Open air. I see sky.
Find man. Bad man!
Much noise.
Bad man! Bang. Hurts more.
I run. I jump.
Bite!
Bite, bite!
Bad man rolls. I roll.
I tear throat. Bite!
I pant.
Hurt, much pain.
No command. I wait.
Stay, Rex.
Stay.

\* \* \*

Green grass. Like home. Feel good.
No dust. I breathe.
Cool air.
I jump. I fetch! Shake disc.
I give. Master throws.
I run.
Rocket looks.
Looks smart. Looks sad.
Look Rocket look.
I play.

The British invented concentration camps during the Boer War. In "Remembrance", they invent using canid soldiers for World War I—not dogs, Blackbacks. (Black-backed jackals.)

It takes a while for even the human Tommies to get used to them.

# Remembrance

## by Alice "Huskyteer" Dryden

Harry squeezed into the narrow shelter, curled his tail around himself, and sat down. His sergeant, Chander, who was eating something ghastly out of a mess-tin, flicked his ears but did not look up.

"What are you eating?" Harry asked, shaking the wet from his own ears. The rain that fell here might not drench like a monsoon, but it was cold and it seeped through his fur.

"Rat," Chander said, still chewing.

"You know what rats eat."

"The rats eat my comrades. I eat the rats. I fall. The rats eat me…" He rested the tin on his knee while he made a sacred and complicated gesture with his paws.

"Well, thank God I'm not religious," Harry said.

Chander grinned at that, revealing a row of long teeth. Harry sat beside him in the shelter, a short tunnel dug into the side of the trench, so the two Blackbacks were shoulder to shoulder. It kept them warm, at least. While Chander ate, Harry removed his shirt and began the tricky business of burning the lice from the seams with a candle. He'd comb his fur later, before he slept, and perhaps enjoy a few precious hours free of itching before the bloody things bred again.

Harry smelled the approaching officer before he heard him, and pulled his shirt back on, hiding the strip of charcoal fur after which his Tribe had named itself long ago. The two scrambled upright, bushy tails swinging for balance.

"Lieutenant. Sergeant." Captain Salt waved them back down. He had very blue eyes, and freckles that made him look, even to inhuman eyes, younger than he was. Despite his innocent appearance, he had a decade's service behind him. Salt was all right. An old colonial hand, he had commanded a Blackback company before. He had even bothered to work out that his lieutenant's name was Ari, not 'Arry, but by then the mistake was so ubiquitous that it had stuck.

"Your presence is requested for the wiring party tonight. Report to me at dusk."

"With that lot?" Chander asked, jerking his muzzle downwind to where their neighbors, a Tommy battalion, were posted. The Tribes had been eradicated across this whole continent by the late Middle Ages, and the Tommies and *poilus* were, Harry sometimes thought, more frightened of the Blackbacks than they were of the Germans.

"Yes, with that lot. And behave yourself. I know your idea of a joke and it could get you shot."

"We don't need them to hold our paws! We can manage a little cutting job!" Chander protested.

"No doubt," Salt said, diplomatically. He reached out to give Chander a soft tap on the underside of his jaw; something else he had learned in his previous command. Chander lowered his large ears.

"You have no idea how many conferences and arguments in Whitehall it took to bring you into this war," the Captain said. "We could have had the whole lot over and done with by now if we'd had you from the start, in my opinion. But someone had to decide whether it was sporting to turn you loose on the Germans, and vouch that you wouldn't eat your allies. So don't mess about," he finished, raising his voice to its usual level and giving his usual smile.

"You need me and my ears, don't you?" Chander smirked.

"And Harry and his brain," the Captain told him. "Between the pair of you, you just about make up a half decent soldier. Good grief, Chander, you might have cut the tail off," he finished, and was gone.

Chander, stretching himself out as long as he could in the confined space, pulled a crumpled pack of cigarettes from his pocket, lit one, and stuck it in the side of his mouth.

"What are you doing? What about your nose?" Harry wrinkled up his muzzle.

Cigarettes, like chocolate, arrived in their rations, and were kept to trade with those Tommies brave enough to venture along the Lines to where the Queen's Own Blackbacks were posted. So much of what they were given was useless, or almost useless—like the gas masks, meant for a flat and snub-nosed face, or the helmets that squashed their ears uncomfortably. They couldn't wear the boots, and spent much of their limited free time cleaning between their toes.

Chander took a defiant puff. "Listen, Lieutenant, the less I smell around here the better."

"You won't catch many rats like that."

"I can still hear them, can't I? Best ears in the company, me. And not smelling them makes them easier to eat."

Harry shook his head. "What you need," he said, "Is vegetables. We've got a couple of hours. I'm going to see if I can scrounge some cabbages."

"The French villagers will shoot you like a fox in the henhouse. They'll think you're after their babies."

"And *that's* why you shouldn't eat rats in front of the humans."

"Old Salty doesn't count," Chander said, swallowing the last of his meal. "Shall I catch you one while you're out?"

"No thanks." Harry wriggled out of the shelter and brushed the mud from his tail.

"I'll get some kip, then. Those badgers down below kept me awake again earlier."

"You can't hear badgers. Don't show off." Harry slung his gas mask and kit over his shoulder.

"Remember!" Chander called after him. "You don't ask for cabbages—you ask for shoes!"

"Shoes." Harry shook his head and padded off along the slippery duckboards. Chander was already lying back, eyes shut and whiskers twitching as he dozed.

\* \* \*

"*Choux,*" Harry said. He smiled what he thought of as his European smile, the one where his lips stayed over his teeth. Peasants like this woman had never seen anyone like him outside a circus or travelling exhibition, and he wanted her to help him as a favor, not out of fear.

The young woman in the doorway looked silently up at him. Harry was tall, and his large ears heightened the effect. He had quickly learned to stoop—except around officers, who would snap at him to stand up straight and not slouch, man… or whatever you are. He dropped into a crouch in the barnyard, lowered his ears, and swung his tail up onto his knee. Europeans seemed to like tails.

This farm behind the lines had little left. The cavalry had taken the horse, and a shell had taken the barn. The crops had been trampled by marching feet, and most of the hens scared out of laying by the sound of bombs. Harry noted each new privation and hole, and felt it as though the farm, his discovery, was his own property.

He didn't like to beg, but they simply had to supplement the daily ration with an occasional fresh egg, or a rabbit, or something green. Corned beef and biscuit wasn't enough to keep eyes, ears and teeth sharp.

Finally, the woman said something rapid in French that was far beyond Harry's skills. It sounded like a question, and he thought he made out the word '*bébé*'.

"No!" Harry said at once, shaking his head so his ears flapped. His paws made quick movements of denial, almost like one of Chander's religious gestures. The woman frowned and went back inside, but the door stayed open. Harry waited. Just because she hadn't shot him yet, didn't mean today wasn't the day.

Perhaps he should have sent Chander, who seemed to get on better with people the less effort he made. He ate rats, bared his fangs, and claimed to hear things he couldn't possibly hear, yet they liked him. Harry tried so hard to fit in, and was shunned. But it was restful to see someone out of uniform, getting on with their ordinary life as best they could. The houses here, the clothes, the faces and voices, were memories he wanted to take home with him, despite the stares and the risks.

The woman returned with a small sack. It smelled of corn, but also of cabbages, and he felt two firm, round lumps inside.

He should offer something in return. He tried, every time he came, but was always refused. Maybe she just didn't understand.

"*Je... aider?*" he said, and mimed chopping firewood with an axe.

The woman shook her head decisively. Maybe he should have acted out something less violent.

"*Merci, madame! Merci beaucoup!*" With another European smile, Harry took the sack and walked away.

His return journey took him through the reserve trenches and the support line. Soldiers loafed, or wrote, or cooked meals only slightly less awful-smelling than Chander's. Some were too tired to pay attention as Harry walked past, while others gave him the familiar, silent stare. One gripped the collar of a little terrier, which fixed bright eyes on Harry and bristled all the way along its back. Its tail was wagging, at least, which made it the friendliest creature Harry had met since leaving his own company.

When he had first arrived, Harry had tried saying "Good morning!" and "Hello!" as he passed through the trenches. He still called out greetings as he moved along, but he no longer hoped to get an answer.

He spoke because if he spoke, and spoke English, he was less likely to find himself bayonetted by his own side.

"What you got there, then? Is it a baby?"

"Baby-eater! Let's see!"

Neither of the two boys standing in front of him reached up to Harry's chest, and he was amazed they had passed the physical exam. That was the trouble, he thought—most Tommies hadn't been born into a warrior caste, but grabbed for the Front from all sorts of jobs. Teachers; factory workers; coal miners, though most of those worked as sappers, not soldiers. No wonder they had no sense of who and what Harry was.

"No, look," he said. "Cabbages! Just cabbages!"

He rolled one out to show him, and the boy snatched it from his paw. His ears, Harry noticed, stuck straight out, and were very pink.

"Dogs don't eat cabbages!" he said. Harry, torn between *Yes, they do* and *We're not dogs*, said nothing.

He said nothing when the boy and his friend began kicking his cabbage back and forth like a football, scattering greenish leaves. He said nothing when they jostled close to him, smelling of sweat and dirt, grabbing his paws to examine the pads and the claws. He only moved away when one of them tried to snatch a button from his coat. That was what you did to dead Germans, not living allies.

"Go on," the boy pleaded. "Give us one. Souvenir."

If he had been a boy himself, Harry could have taunted and shoved back, but his strength and teeth were too dangerous. No matter how much he was provoked, retaliation was strictly forbidden. He couldn't even growl.

He took cigarettes from his coat, two packs, three, as many as he had stuffed in there thinking they would come in useful, and thrust them into the outstretched, grubby hands. Like street children at home, he thought. But street children could be dispersed with a snap of teeth and a few curse words, all the while knowing they were in no danger and laughing back at him.

Harry returned to his own trench with one cabbage, no cigarettes, and an intact uniform. He decided this counted as an overall victory. Certainly the London papers would have painted it that way.

\* \* \*

"Chander, I know you're proud of your lugholes, but lay them flat before you get them blown off, will you?" Captain Salt said in an undertone. Obediently, the sergeant folded his ears back against his skull.

There were six of them in the party: Harry, Chander, the Captain, and three lads. They crouched around the Captain and studied the map on his knees, which showed their theoretical journey to a circled target in neat pencil lines with arrows.

Salt hadn't drawn a route back. Return journeys tended to be hurried and disorderly, if they were made at all.

"Learn to trust Chander's ears," Salt told the three strangers. "A lot of nonsense might come out of his mouth, but he's pretty useful when he shuts up and listens."

One of the boys gave a quiet, nervous laugh.

"I can hear the badgers scratching down in the earth," Chander said, swiveling his ears to demonstrate. For dramatic effect, he swiveled his eyes, too, and gestured with his paws.

"No, he can't," sighed Harry.

"I can! They keep me awake!"

Harry nudged him hard in the ribs, and he subsided. They were strange and foreign enough already, without his sergeant giving them supernatural powers on top.

"We'll be cutting the wire in front of the enemy positions here and here," Salt's pink finger stroked the map.

"Why?" Chander asked. Harry showed him a flash of teeth, quick enough for the humans to miss it in the dark, but the captain didn't seem upset by this insubordination.

Salt let Chander get away with murder, and Salt outranked Harry, but Harry was directly responsible for keeping Chander in line. The captain was not making this job any easier.

"You don't need me to tell you there's a big push coming," Salt said. "Our sappers have been tunneling under the enemy's position to set mines. Tomorrow the whole lot goes sky high, and we mop up whatever's left."

Harry imagined the soldiers toiling in the dark, the yawning space beneath the trench, and the explosion underground that would kill or maim or bury alive. He rolled his shoulders forward so his neck disappeared into its ruff of fur, and shifted his bare feet for the reassurance of solid earth beneath them.

"Any more questions? Good. Let's go."

Harry was careful to keep his ears tucked back as he climbed the ladder and emerged from the trench. The landscape, with its craters, tracks and occasional blasted trees, bore little resemblance to Salt's map. Harry stared out across No Man's Land, trying to align the landmarks he could make out with his memory of the terrain. The wind ruffled the fur of his neck, in the gap between jacket and helmet. It almost always blew towards the enemy lines, making him feel exposed. But there was nobody on the other side to smell him; the enemy held no territory where the Tribes could be conscripted or recruited.

Cutting the enemy's barbed wire meant an attack was coming within the next few days. Parties like this one went out, night after night, to repair their own wire and cut the other side's. Give your soldiers a clear passage to the enemy, and block the enemy's path to you. Like a game.

To reach the enemy wire, they first had to navigate their own. Harry stooped, crouched and lifted, losing a tuft of fur from his neck on one of the barbs. Chander moved up beside him, gliding along the ground with a boneless crawl that even Harry found unnerving.

"Bleeding," he observed, and put his tongue to Harry's neck to staunch the blood and cover its sharp scent. Harry pulled away. Soldiers didn't do that; not in Europe.

"No time," he justified himself to Chander's hurt expression. "Just a scratch."

"You must feel at home here, eh, Backy?" one of the boys whispered. He smelled of shaving. "Seeing as it's No *Man's* Land. Get it?"

"Quiet, Jones," Salt said, adding, "I imagine he's heard that one, lad."

Harry had, but he was grateful the boy had spoken to him.

A star shell exploded above them, flooding the field with light. Harry shut his eyes to prevent the reflective glow that could give their position away. When he opened them, Salt and the lads, who had flattened themselves to the ground beside him, were lying still to rub their eyes. Harry couldn't see perfectly, but his sight worked better in the dark than theirs, and he could use his nose, too. Salt made a slight movement with his hand, urging Harry into the lead.

He moved one limb after the other, pausing to listen as each paw set. He disliked going on all fours, because it looked too doglike, but here both Blackback and human must crawl or die. Big guns were firing in the distance, and the vibration trembled his whiskers. Somewhere an owl called, because not far away there were woods and fields still whole, with small creatures to hunt. His nose told him the sudden rustle to his left was only a rat, but Salt and the soldiers he'd brought all froze at the sound. He beckoned them on, and the procession continued its slow passage to the wire.

A single shot. The kind a bored sentry fires into the night.

After all the stillness and the listening, the noise shocked Harry into a bare-fanged growl. Jones—the one who had made the No Man's Land joke—paused on hands and knees, then sank forward and down. Harry

43

covered the ground in a moment to crouch at his side, though he had smelled the brain mixed in with his blood and knew there was little hope, but one of the others shoved him back.

"Get away from him!" he shrieked.

So much for silence. Harry went sprawling, and another bullet whined over his head. With Chander close behind, he slithered into the slight depression where a shell had landed. Cold, muddy water soaked through his uniform to his belly and thighs, but he was only interested in keeping skin and flesh intact.

There were more shots, then silence. Whoever had been firing obviously thought they'd hit their target. Harry poked his muzzle over the lip of the crater, and sniffed. Salt and the others were both still alive, at least. He let out a low bark, designed to reach as far as Salt's ears but not the enemy trench beyond. One of the soldiers flopped into the hole, then the captain joined them, half-dragging the other. The five lay awkwardly huddled together. The boy who had shouted at Harry lifted his head to see where his friend lay, and Salt pushed it back down.

"He's dead, lad. Harry, tell him."

"It's true." Harry didn't elaborate, because what good would it do the boy to know that a Blackback nose could tell living from dead at this distance, or that Chander's ears were keen enough to pick up even faint, shallow breaths? Chander had found a wounded officer that way, saved his life, but Harry had told him to say he'd stumbled across the casualty by accident.

"So. Jerry's woken up," Salt said, "but that wire needs cutting tonight."

Neither Tommy spoke. It was left to Harry, the eater of babies and now, apparently, bodies, to take the lead. He constructed a European smile: cheerful, but not too cheerful, acknowledging the loss of Jones. There was no reaction. They couldn't see him, of course.

"We'll cut it, sir," he said.

"*À l'attaque*, then!" With these words, Salt scrambled back out of the hole.

"I don't know any French," Chander protested, staying still. Harry gave him a shove. The Tommies just stared, and Harry couldn't resist showing off to them. He'd bet they didn't know any French themselves, while Harry shared that gift with the officer. The *other* officer, he reminded himself, although the lowliest Tommy lieutenant held authority over the highest-ranked Blackback.

"Yes, you do. What about 'souvenir', like all those bits and bobs you pinch when we take an enemy trench, or pick up in the villages? That's

French. It means a memento, a remembrance." He eyed his sergeant. "You don't know what those words mean, either, do you?"

Chander shrugged, and swiped Harry's face with his tail as he crawled after the captain.

\* \* \*

The wires sprang apart under Harry's cutters. To him, the click of the blades carried like a shot, and the uncoiling metal sang. He used his coat to muffle the sounds, but he couldn't cover the heavy breathing of the two lads. Salt crouched, holding his pistol, and Chander had his head close to the wire, clipping away with apparent enjoyment.

Harry placed his paw on Chander's shoulder and his muzzle to his ear.

"You're supposed to be listening out," he mouthed into the furry triangle. Chander flicked his ear away.

"Doing both," he growled under his breath.

Harry was still deciding how to respond to that when the German soldier loomed out of the night beside him.

The wind—the bloody prejudiced wind that always blew towards the enemy—had betrayed their ears and noses, or they had got distracted. Whether the grey-clad soldier had been out on a wiring party of his own, was returning from some other mission or had simply got lost, he had not expected to find two Blackbacks in his way. His eyes opened very wide, and he drew breath for the shout that would bring the enemy up and out and upon them. But before he could make a sound, Harry's fangs were clamped around his throat.

He twisted as they fell, so the corpse was cushioned by Harry's lithe, soft body. Then he rolled out from under it and spat away his mouthful of chewed flesh. Panting, wide-jawed, he plunged his muzzle into the filthy water of a shell-hole to rinse it, catching a brief reflection of his wild, yellow eyes and bloody maw. The other four watched him rise to his knees. Salt still held his gun at the ready, and Harry wasn't entirely sure who for. He shook himself, and glared at the terrified Tommies, daring them to speak.

Captain Salt rolled the body over with his foot, concealing the gaping wound at the throat, and kicked it away so the head was submerged in the shell-hole. He gestured with his pistol, back the way they had come.

Silently, rapidly, they made their way across No Man's Land, through their own barbed wire defenses and down into the trench. The two surviving Tommies turned towards their station without saying a word.

"Goodnight," Salt called after them. To Harry, who knew Salt well, his voice had a hard edge.

"Goodnight, sir," one of the boys replied, and added, after a hesitation, "All right, Backy."

"See you, Backy," muttered the other.

They moved off down the trench with the sloped backs and dragging feet of the utterly weary.

"It's a strong word, 'atrocity'," Salt said, "but if they bring in that body, they'll use it."

"Why is it different from using a bayonet? Or a gun, come to that?" It was more honest, to kill with the teeth, and tidier than scattering brains everywhere the way the bullet had done to Jones.

"It's not, Harry, and I know that as well as you do. But the people at home won't. Still, can't be helped now. Very prompt action. Well done."

"Think they'll talk?" Chander asked, looking past Salt into the blackness where the Tommies had disappeared.

"No. If I did, I'd have shot them both. Night." Salt jerked his arm in a half-hearted salute and left for his dugout, which was, by trench standards, first class accommodation.

Harry leaned back against the wall and looked upwards, to where the sky was lightening. He folded his paws in his lap and let his eyes close.

"I saved everyone's lives," he said.

"Maybe you'll get a pretty medal," Chander yawned. "That'll be nice."

"There was no time to do anything else, and a shot would have been noisy."

Chander's only answer was another yawn.

"We're all just 'Backy' to them," Harry continued.

"They're mostly all just Tommy to us."

He heard the scrape and hiss as Chander lit a match, concealing the spark behind cupped paws. The burning tobacco reached his nose a few moments later, along with the noise of slow, contented breaths.

"I hope those badgers don't keep me awake again," Chander mumbled. "There's a whole family of them. All scratching away."

"Shut up." Harry wriggled his shoulders, trying to find a comfortable resting place for them against the muddy earth. The regular wheeze of Chander's breath told him that the sergeant had dropped off already, but Harry could not. His muscles refused to relax, and his feet twitched in the mud. His closed eyelids acted as a cinema screen for endless footage of soldiers crawling, soldiers shooting, soldiers falling. He drifted close to the edge of sleep, only for a frame of his mental movie to startle him back into half-consciousness with a jerk of paw or knee. In sepia shades of mud, he watched stooped men tunneling underground. Digging. Burrowing. *Scratching.*

"Chander!"

The sergeant's eyes snapped open. He was too well-trained to move until he knew where he was—many a soldier had sleepily risen and stretched, only to be picked off by a sniper—but the fur visible on his neck and tail fluffed up and settled only slowly as he glared at Harry.

"Get out of the way. I want to listen to your badgers."

Ruffled and with one ear inside-out, Chander looked as if he wanted to argue, but when he saw Harry's expression he closed his muzzle with a click.

Harry placed his head exactly where Chander's had been, and tilted his ears back. His sense of hearing might not be as acute as the sergeant's, but as he held his breath he could make out a faint scratching, far below. He sat back upright.

"Tell Captain Salt I need to see him," he said. "Now."

\* \* \*

"*Oeufs,*" Harry said. "Please?"

From the look the woman gave him, he thought he must have got the wrong word and asked for pineapples, or top hats. She held up one finger and disappeared into the farmhouse.

He had left Chander sitting in the shelter like a king, holding court as a stream of visitors from their own and the neighboring companies dropped by to congratulate and thank him.

Nobody else could have heard the enemy miners beneath their position, let alone pinpointed their precise depth and the direction of their digging. That had enabled the British sappers to dig into the tunnel and lay an explosive charge. Harry and Chander had felt it under their feet as they sat side by side in the shelter, Harry teaching Chander the French words for his favorite foods.

The Tommies had started touching Chander's ears, as a good luck charm. He bore it patiently, and had even begun to give away his cigarettes rather than smoking them. He'd been offered gifts himself, of course, and politely refused the inappropriate ones.

"We don't eat chocolate," he explained, and got respectful nods and apologies.

Not every soldier who came to marvel at Chander stopped to talk to Harry, or the others in his unit. But enough did that they had begun to make friends, and to teach each other card games. The boy with the sticking-out ears had come; he hadn't recognized Harry, but he had persuaded a couple of the Blackback privates to play football with him. With a proper, leather ball.

Chander had offered to come to the farmhouse today, try out his new language skills, but Harry wanted to see the farmer's wife again. Still waiting on the step, he was uncomfortably aware that farmers kept guns, for shooting foxes. But when the woman returned, she carried a baby in her arms. It was barefoot, like Harry, and kicking as much as it could manage through several layers of frilly clothing.

"I really don't eat..." Harry was beginning, when the baby was placed in his arms. He cradled it uncertainly while the mother watched, all smiles. Its clean scents of soap and powder, and its softness, were so unlike anything he experienced in the trenches that he rested his chin on its head to breathe it in, and licked the small, curved ear, no longer afraid that his motives would be misunderstood.

The woman held up her finger again, and went back inside. Harry, not sure what was expected of him, jiggled the baby, who reached up to grab a handful of the soft fur spilling over his shirt collar.

This time, when she returned, the woman was holding a box camera. Still smiling, she raised it to her face.

"*Souvenir,*" she said.

Harry's ears flicked at the word, but he realized he didn't mind it when it came with a smile and was requested, not grabbed. He was part of the strangeness of the times she lived in; a part she valued and wanted to preserve. There were surely many she would rather forget. Harry guessed he had become the Frenchwoman's Blackback, as she was *his* farmer's wife.

She cooed to the baby, to attract its attention. It turned at the sound, and its fist tightened in Harry's fur. The baby had no teeth, and no comprehension of how to smile for the camera anyway, but Harry showed every one of his.

*Warfare between the stags and the wolves. Or is it between the stags themselves?*

*A far-distant people have the saying, "The enemy of my enemy is my friend". Faramund learns it the hard way.*

# Scars

## *by Televassi*

It was a challenge.

"I dare you!"

Faramund pushed his way out from the gaggle of scruffy fawns wrestling with each other. He didn't heed their goading; he didn't believe what they said about him, or his father. He could only have been a warrior. That showed on the fawn's fur, which despite his youth had already begun to turn a deep, rusty red. Before midsummer he had shed the white spots from his coat, whilst his scent had matured, growing pungent and earthy like that of a full-blooded stag. Already the swelling buds of his horns burst through the messy mop of hair between his ears, leading even wise old Etjar to predict he'd have twenty-one points to his antlers before long. There wasn't a surer sign of good breeding than that. It made Faramund deaf to all their taunts.

Father would've been proud.

The young buck straightened his back, looking ahead at the empty hall. That evening it would be full, the adults hunched over the tables—feasting, exchanging golden gifts for their brave deeds, telling stories, boasting how many battles they'd fought through. Bards would travel many miles up from the south to sing the songs of great warriors, and learn a new tale or two to be told. Faramund spent the nights propped against the barred doors, tapping his hooves against the floor. Maybe, someone would sing of him one day. That was the ultimate goal of a warrior, to have such renown that the herds would speak his name, and he would be remembered.

Behind him the mob's hooves clattered about as they jostled with each other for a good view, having given up on their name-calling. They never were inventive, and the insults were always the same. The tall fawns pushed to the front, whilst those caught behind them hopped from foot to foot, clambering upon their peers' backs for a good view, forcing their legs to wobble like a newborn's. They were a raucous bunch, their cries of excitement a garbled mess.

"I bet he can't touch the thane's sword!" a bullish voice roared above the others. It was Jorvnir's. Faramund doubled his pace, eager to shut him up. Jorvnir was the son of Hrothgar—he'd always had it easy. It showed; he still had thick, fatty cheeks, wielded a hefty rump on him, and fine silk clothes to tuck it under. He hadn't had to fight anyone; no one dared call him weak, a coward, a runt, a bastard. Such was Hrothgar's reputation with blade in hand.

Faramund ruffled the fur on his chest, his muscles showing more through hardship than good eating. The young stag strode out, dwarfed by the benches. The smell of stale mead made his stomach turn and stuck to his hooves as he crossed the floor. The others laughed and wrestled with each other as they jostled for a good position, succeeding only in making more of a racket. Faramund kept moving, deaf to the mob behind him.

None of them were this brave, though. No one dared to touch Hrothgar's sword, not even Jorvnir. The pious ones who cut their horns whispered it was a gift from the pale gods. Faramund snorted at such superstitious nonsense—the pale gods died out a long time ago. The predations of the wolves were real enough; a ruthless, savage breed, with no loyalty to even their kith and kin. Hrothgar had supposedly seized the blade from them, but it was more than a trophy. Every warrior skilled enough to take a wolf's sword swore that they never wielded anything better; theirs were made from pattern-welded steel, an art still unknown to even the herds' best smiths. There was some truth in it, for Hrothgar had taken so many lives that if he held the sword right, the steel shone with a pink tinge.

In the gloom the blade glimmered, propped up against the throne. Faramund felt his nerves flutter in his chest—he swallowed hard and clenched his fists. He quickened into a brisk trot, no longer caring how the sound echoed about the hall. Too much noise had been made anyway, but he'd show them before they were caught. He'd suffer the indignity of his punishment gladly because it would show them up.

Pride surged in Faramund's blood, pushing him up the steps. They were wrong about him. Father was a warrior. Only the thane's closest companions were allowed up the steps of Hrothgar's silver throne, and here he was! He'd show them—he'd be standing there before long. Jorvnir could watch, green-eyed, all he wanted. He would be the first to stand there, to have Hrothgar inspect his horns and give him a place at his table for his good breeding; for that was a sure sign of good deeds to come.

The sword rested across the arms of the throne like a bar, forbidding anyone from sitting there. Now that he was this close, Faramund could see it was huge—almost as long as he was tall! He certainly couldn't lift it... However! He pulled up... wiggled a bit... And—Aha! He squirmed his way around, and there he was, sitting on the throne! He paused for a moment to lap up the anticipation of the mob, watching as the sword lay over his lap. For a brief moment, Faramund felt that this is what it must be like to be a king; everyone beneath your feet, in awe of your every action. For a son of an unwedded doe, it was strange to think what it would be like to give orders, but it sounded good.

As Faramund sat there figuring out how to lift the blade, its scabbard caught his eye. It was decorated with abstract figures that seemed to shift in the light. It was strange; if he leaned one way they were stags, but if he looked another way, they became wolves. The budding stag remembered the old stories of the world; of the pale gods, all beings' four-legged past, and the Dark Age. He felt the long hairs of his mane prickle, but he brushed the thought away.

Faramund paused, gazing down on the others. They were crouching, watching with hands over their mouths, vainly trying to stay quiet. Faramund licked his lips; he hadn't noticed his mouth was dry. Then placed his hands on the scabbard and with a great push—lifted it off the throne! The mob entirely forgot themselves, turning on Jorvnir like wolves. "Beaten by a bastard!" they cackled. "He's a better son than you!" Jorvnir stalked off with a face like thunder. Faramund felt his pride swell in his chest, a great smile beaming across his face as the sword became strangely light in his grip—

"*Faramund!*"

His arms quivered, wobbled, and then buckled. The sword clattered down on the floor with an alarming ring. Instantly the mob scattered, melting away on the four winds as Gerwis, the wet nurse, tried to grab hold of them, but they ducked, curved, and wiggled out of her grasp. Her heart wasn't really in it though—her eyes were fixed on Faramund. She stormed down the hall towards him. There wasn't any point in running.

His ears stung as she grabbed hold, and with them, wrenched him off his feet. With the other hand she picked up the sword and put it over her back, as if it were a feather. Faramund heard her rant and rave dimly, as he heard—and felt—his ears crunch as she tugged him along. She was a nurse—a low born who'd been refused the right to breed; deemed unworthy of bearing a child of her own. Not even a stag with a handful of points to his rack would look at her! But here she was putting the fear of the gods into him.

Down the corridors they went, through doors that opened when she shouted her name. Some she pounded with her fist until they opened, and continued onward. They were going down passages the young buck had never seen, deeper into the back of the hall complex—Hrothgar's private quarters.

It was for the sake of his ears alone that Faramund felt relief when she flung him forward. He steadied himself, leaping to his feet, giving his ears a consoling rub. He heard the rush of blood throb through them with each heartbeat, but he wouldn't cry. He took a moment to look around.

They were somewhere at the back of the hall, in a small courtyard. Underneath the roiling plumes of cloud in the sky above two deer clashed with each other, the splintered remains of their spears lying about in the sand. Each time they darted to the side they cast up clouds of dust that made Faramund's eyes smart, while their exertions mixed up their scent beyond recognition. They fought before the seat of a hulking grey stag, surrounded by a small group of attendants. Among them he spied old Etjar whispering into Hrothgar's ear, and Ada, a white fawn, busily applying poultices to two bloodied warriors as she continued her apprenticeship under the stern eye of the healer. Faramund shot his half-sister a brief grin in reply to her puzzled look.

"I'm busy, Gerwis!" the grey stag barked, flicking the nurse away with his hand, like one would do with a buzzing fly. Faramund had never seen Hrothgar so close; he was used to seeing him far away, sitting on his throne. He was huge! Faramund counted the twenty-one points on his antlers with a slack jaw, envying how his muscles bulged from underneath his thick fur, and the thick, ropey scars on his body—wounds from heroic deeds, no doubt.

"My lord, I caught—"

"Then you punish them. I am busy," he growled, swinging his head towards her. He seemed wolfish in his anger. For a brief moment, the two deer paused in their fight. Faramund looked at them briefly, but gave up when he couldn't recognize them for all their armor. "Did I tell you to stop?" Hrothgar demanded. The clash of steel rang out again.

Gerwis knelt, kissing the thane's hand. "I caught the fawns misbehaving. Faramund was sitting on your throne. He dropped your sword." Hrothgar tilted his head to the side, reaching out to touch the ruff of fur under Gerwis' neck. Faramund couldn't understand why he would lower himself to touch her like that. They paused for a moment.

Then he nodded and she went on her way—the field of war was not her concern.

Without looking at the fawn, Hrothgar pointed and beckoned him to approach. Faramund tried to appear strong. He reminded himself he'd have twenty-one points too one day, though the thought didn't stop his stomach from fluttering about. Fear brought back all his worries; that he was a mistake that was allowed to be kept, one that Etjar said to leave to fend for itself. Hardship makes a warrior, and if it broke the bastard of a pleasure-doe, then there would be nothing to mourn. Weakness couldn't be tolerated when the wolves come. Every winter they'd sneak out of the forests and make war upon the herds. Their campaigns were unlike that of the quarrels between the herds; they never fought for reputation, treasure, or glory—instead only with the aim of bringing death and destruction to the plains.

Hrothgar held his palm out, motioning for the young stag to stop. He pointed at the floor. Faramund sat in the dust, blanching his russet fur, as he waited at the foot of the grey stag.

They stayed in silence as the two deer went on fighting, neither yet managing to draw blood. Sometimes, the stag got his sword past the tan doe's shield, only for her to twist her body away from the blow. Any blow she replied with merely slid off the stag's armor—it didn't seem like she'd last long.

"Your son insulted me," Hrothgar said. Her ears flicked towards the sound, but she didn't look—weathering a chain of blows on her shield. A couple of splinters flew into the air. Faramund's heart wrenched—he'd snuck off this morning thinking she'd be satisfying another stag.

It was fast. The stag's sword flashed. Faramund's mother was crouched on the floor. Her sword lay in the dirt beside her. Faramund saw blood and something white and shiny in the middle. The stag swung his sword, angling in for a fatal blow.

Faramund darted out before Hrothgar could stop him, deftly picking up the blade.

"Wait, Brodgar," Hrothgar laughed. "Maybe it wasn't a mistake to let a pleasure-doe hold a sword," he sneered, watching Faramund intently. Brodgar snorted and held his sword in mid-air, flicking his ears in irritation.

"Faramund thinks he can too." Hrothgar grinned at Brodgar. "Go," Hrothgar said, turning to Faramund. "Prove you're better than your breeding."

"My lord please—whatever he meant," his mother began, cradling her arm—

"Silence!" Hrothgar roared.

Faramund was frozen to the spot. He didn't realize how heavy the blade was. His ears were roaring as his blood rushed through his head, heart pumping madly.

Brodgar laughed and swung his sword wildly, while Faramund tried to lift up his sword to parry—but let out a high-pitched scream. He tumbled to the ground; the tip of Brodgar's sword catching his muzzle, carving a long, red groove across his face. The fawn scrambled around in the dirt gasping, gritting his teeth, rubbing his eyes madly as he felt blood trickle down from his forehead. He couldn't see.

Yet somehow, he'd kept the sword in his hand. Hrothgar stopped laughing as Faramund scrambled to his feet, swinging the blade about. The white stag laughed and kicked him, his hoof smacking the fawn square in the chest, knocking out his breath. Something cracked, leaving him wheezing.

"You couldn't even touch me if you tried," Brodgar sneered, somewhere above him. Dazed, Faramund's ears flicked about in opposite directions.

"Faramund!" his mother shouted. Hrothgar remained silent for a moment, and then he sighed and lay back in his seat, pouring himself another cup of wine.

The young stag didn't listen to his mother. Instead his foe's laughter filled his ears. He felt his unknown father's blood surging through his veins. He was not a weakling. He was a warrior—this was what the word meant. He would not surrender so easily.

He swung the blade again. Truth be told, Faramund couldn't see what he was doing. He felt it sail through the air, light, as if an extension of his arm, and then—crack! He hit something. Brodgar screamed, swinging his blade blindly at Faramund, who by sheer luck leapt out of the way. There was no respite though; the white stag lunged after the fawn, stamping his hooves on his thin legs.

"Enough!" Hrothgar thundered. Brodgar's hands trembled with fury as he raised his sword above his head—he let off another scream and threw his sword into the dirt, stalking off. His breath trailed out of his muzzle like smoke. For a moment there was silence as Faramund waited for Hrothgar to speak. He felt his mother tending to him, washing the blood out of his eyes. Except for the cut on his face, he'd suffered worse in fights before, but oddly this time his mother didn't clip his ears and scold him. When his vision returned, Faramund saw the grey stag resting his head on a hand, twirling a braid of fur underneath his chin, and Brodgar storming off towards his attendants. A thick red line ran across the white stag's body from the top of his neck, across his breast, finally tapering off at his waist.

"Come here," Hrothgar commanded. Faramund obeyed. Hrothgar stood up, entirely dwarfing the fawn. His antlers, all twenty-one points, towered above him, their shadow casting over Faramund like the branches of a tree. "You have some guts, for a young one," Hrothgar said quietly, tapping the swollen buds of bone on his head. "You just gave Brodgar, prince of the Cavanii, his first scar. Do you know he's to be high king one day? He's the best warrior our people have ever seen; no one has beaten him." He chuckled briefly. "But..." He lifted his hand—and punched. Hard.

He heard Hrothgar laugh as he lay sprawled on the ground.

"Consider that a warning. Do not, ever, disrespect me again."

Faramund clung to his muzzle, setting his jaw. He couldn't stop the blood, but he did not cry as Ada rushed over and stitched his face together. When it was done, she kissed him on the cheek, and whispered how brave he had been. Faramund learnt two lessons about being a warrior that day. Never suffer an insult. Never shy away from a fight. Faramund clenched his teeth and vowed not to forget. He would never be a forgotten undesirable like Gerwis.

\* \* \*

The roll of seasons passed over the world. The healer managed to set his mother's arm, but feeling never came back to it. She always held it close to her body like a crooked wing, never able to straighten it out. Her fighting days were over—any prestige she had won evaporated overnight like the morning dew, leaving her without a hope of bettering herself.

Faramund didn't forget the scar that ran across his muzzle. The skin grew over black and shiny whenever it caught the light, but the russet fur didn't grow back, always reminding him of his failure at Brodgar's hands. He came of age quickly, winning his first spar when he was twelve, and every single one since then. Only Brodgar could claim to have beaten him. It was hardly a fair fight they said, and Ada kept reminding him, but it was no consolation.

Hrothgar, meanwhile, wasted away, his grey pelt losing its shine, becoming white at the tips. When Faramund was twenty, the old lord took his sword and went deep into the woods at sunset, as was custom. Everyone heard the howling that night, but by morning there was silence. It was clear only Faramund could be his successor; unlike Jorvnir, he proved himself to be the best warrior. He was received on the throne with few grumbles—even Jorvnir held his tongue.

* * *

"This is not a wise idea," Etjar hissed, pulling Faramund aside. The old stag bowed his head, showing respect to his lord, but still he held him fast. His grip was surprisingly sure, but Faramund didn't flinch. "You're offering the High-King the perfect excuse—"

Faramund cursed and pushed his companion aside. "You're a coward, to think that I'd balk at the thought of Brodgar coming here." The years had weathered him; he'd grown tall and wise, experience helping to temper his relative youth. Handsome curls of hair tussled his mane, his eyes had taken on a darker hue, his face had broadened, but more to his concern, his horns had grown well, a full rack of sixteen points, and no less before his twentieth year. Even Etjar, who was well admired by the females in his prime, couldn't boast that.

"Why should I fear welcoming the High-King into my hall?" Faramund retorted, seating himself on his throne. "A lord doesn't refuse the king when he asks for hospitality—without such laws, we're no better than the wolves."

Etjar snorted, turning his lips up to show his crooked, yellowed teeth. "I know the law. You still can refuse—it's just your pride. It's not wise to invite your enemy into your hall."

"Etjar speaks true," Jorvnir said, catching Faramund's eye. As the years had passed over Hrothgar's son he proved his mind was as sharp as any sword, though he was just no good with a blade in hand. "Though," he shrugged, "a lord who shuts up his doors doesn't stay a lord for long. One does not insult the High-King and expect to get away with it." Etjar shot him a venomous look, infuriated by his refusal to take a clear side.

"I'm not a coward," Faramund growled, his hands curling into fists. "If Brodgar draws his blade against me, I'll welcome the chance to avenge his insult!"

"You are too full of pride for your own good," Etjar replied sourly. "It's deceitful of you to welcome your king when you only wish to avenge an old insult." The old stag paused for a moment to regain his breath. In his youth he had fought through many battles, so even when his strength fled and tradition dictated that he go alone into the woods to die, younger lords kept him in exchange for his wise counsel.

"It is the law of the gods to give hospitality when one asks of it. It is also their law to protect those who offer their homes," Faramund countered, snorting. "Your mind, bitter with anger, sees plots where none exist." He shook his head mockingly. "It's this unseasonal weather that's to blame for his petition. We are the closest house in the north that can answer Brodgar's call, now that the wolf of winter has come early," Faramund finished.

"I doubt Brodgar is happy about the situation either," Jorvnir added, fidgeting with belt loop where the hilt of his sword would be. "To be caught out at the turn of the season, and to cry to you for shelter, from you no less… Even he would fancy your company over the wolves."

"A good liar makes any plan look like coincidence," Etjar countered, but Faramund just grinned and shook his head.

"A good lord doesn't make enemies needlessly."

"That is true," Jorvnir shrugged, tapping his hoof against the floor. He furrowed his brow. "Mind you, if you desire the destruction of your enemies, you level them in one single blow." He held up his hands in apology to Faramund, who glared at him in reply.

"I won't offer anyone the opportunity to call me a coward by refusing him," Faramund replied.

"You really think you can trust that brute in your hall?" Etjar pressed again.

"Brodgar would not be so arrogant, or so foolish," said Faramund. "You may think him a beast, but it takes a sharp mind to make its way to the top, more so to stay there, may I remind you!" He growled, grinding his teeth in frustration. He looked like he'd lower his antlers and charge, trying to gore him like a feral beast. "My mind is set," he huffed, rolling his head back. "Your pathetic mewling wearies my ears—leave me."

"They are weary," the old stag snapped, "because their head refuses to heed wise council," he finished, lips trembling in his fury. He stalked off, refusing to bow or say another word.

Jorvnir nodded, faintly smiling, as if he was delighted with Faramund's decision despite his own lack of commitment either way. He made a quick exit, giving a low bow, leaving Faramund alone. He felt a hot flush as anger bubbled up from his stomach. Brodgar had broken his mother's arm and ruined her reputation. It was his blade that had marked Faramund—that scar had never healed, and while it made quite the imposing mark, none of the does would look at him affectionately from that side. It was a reminder of failure, rather than triumph, and if Brodgar placed his hoof out of step, Faramund would be delighted to avenge himself. The wolves could be damned.

Curiously, the clatter of his hooves didn't fade. Instead, they grew louder, until Ada stepped through the door. Since it was her, Faramund didn't snap his fingers for her to go. He'd never openly admit it, but he had a soft spot for the doe. She was the apprentice of the healer who'd tended to his face, and thanks to her, Faramund could at least say it could have been worse. The healer refused to tend to a bastard's injuries. As a result, he was protective of her, rejecting each and every advance of a stag who mistakenly thought they were worthy of her.

"Brodgar's summons weighs on your mind," Ada said, gently brushing his arm. Faramund shivered; her touch was feather-light, yet he remembered how swift she'd used her sword. In years gone by they had sparred together whenever she had a free moment, but now that she had succeeded her teacher, mixing poultices and setting bones demanded her full attention. Faramund sighed, leaning forward to reciprocate her touch.

"I'd rather talk about something else," Faramund murmured.

"You shouldn't avoid the subject," Ada replied. Her insistence was delicate. "You don't have to fight everyone."

"You're good at reminding me that," he smiled, giving her a faint kiss.

"Just because you think that scar makes you only fit for war, doesn't mean you have to think that way," she said, kissing him gently on the exposed flesh.

"You don't need to—"

"Brodgar is old. You are brave and strong, but testy and foolish. I know how you won't suffer an insult, but such an absolute is not the right way to rule," she smiled, kissing him delicately on the cheek, imploring him to listen. "With the wolves coming, it's better to secure an alliance. Your pride won't let you, so I'll do the wise thing for you." She sighed. "Brodgar is after all, without a mate."

Faramund sat up in alarm. "No! You'd be away from this hall, from all of us—he'd keep you as spoil, never letting you go out to fight and cover yourself with glory—"

"You're sweet, but we shouldn't fight among ourselves for the sake of your pride," Ada said in a hushed tone.

"But I'd rather die than let you prostitute yourself to him!" he pleaded.

"Keep that sentiment for the battlefield." She sighed. "There'll be plenty of those this winter. With the wolves growing bolder, it's pointless to fight among ourselves."

"I forbid you from doing this!" Faramund shouted, but he knew he could never force her. This was no longer about his pride, it was about his heart. "I can't stand to lose you," he whispered.

"I still love you," she replied, sighing into his ear. She took hold of him and they embraced warmly. Faramund closed his eyes—which trembled underneath his eyelids. "That's why I have to do this—I won't let you harm yourself with this mistake."

It was true, and though Faramund wished otherwise, he knew it couldn't be so. "Don't go where I cannot protect you," he whispered instead.

"Faramund," She smiled sadly. "Don't you see it's my turn?"

* * *

The great hall hummed with activity. Every single inch of space on the mead-benches was crammed full of deer; from aging warriors with blunt antlers, to yearlings who sat in the laps of their mothers crying for milk. It was quite a sight, seeing the entire strength of the herd swelled up under one roof. Knowing he had risen from their number, Faramund felt a little proud; the nameless mass all knew him for his battle-deeds.

He looked across at the High-King's party; a grizzled and motley array of stags. Some of them had lumps cut out of their shoulders, fingers cut off, and eyes missing. It had always been a great boast that the breeding of the High-King's line was second to none, but Faramund found himself unimpressed—scars were the marks of survivors, victors bore none.

The most scarred of them all was Brodgar himself. Thick, leathery lines ran down his body—reminders of terrible wounds. The greatest of them was visible for all to see; a dark pit on the side of his face where an eye used to be. It was just as well that the High-King ate and drank readily, otherwise Faramund would have believed he was no living being, but a wight brought back from the beyond.

Instead, Faramund ate nothing. He barely drank, and his servants seemed confused, busying themselves with any minor task, topping up the mead so they did not appear idle. The truth was, seeing Ada with Brodgar stole all the joy out of his life. Every warm smile that broke across Brodgar's twisted muzzle was an insult he couldn't bear, and every time he leered forward towards his half-sister, he clenched his jaw.

However, Ada was right, and that alone stayed his hand. At first Brodgar and his companions had sat in silence, their amber eyes, reflecting the hearths, glowering inside their sockets. The rich, fruity wines lay untouched, the golden mead undrunk, and the glistening platters growing cold. Ada went up and bowed with a sly wink to her eye, and began working her charm. The stony-faced High-King melted before her, finally bringing him out from the cold.

"I suppose I should be happy," Faramund huffed, turning to Jorvnir, who stood behind him in his mail, watching. "It was her plan after all, and she seems to have spotted an opportunity where I would have given him the sword," he relented, fiddling with his sword. Sighing, he picked up a goblet and with a grimace, drained it.

He winced as he heard another bellow of laughter from Brodgar—who now had his hand firmly around Ada's breasts—like they were another course served up for him to eat.

"Brodgar will leave with her come the morning, and I guess the next time I see Ada, that brute will have put a fawn in her." Faramund growled, pushing away his goblet. Though he hadn't drunk much, he was feeling light-headed, and the lack of food didn't help. Jorvnir was dutiful with the wine though—he kept shooing off the servants, insisting on waiting on his lord personally. He pointed out every suspicious glance the High-King made to his troops, whispering how he didn't believe Ada's plan was working, that it was shameful for her to treat herself so for the sake of an alliance. Instead Faramund sat there in silence, focusing his attention on draining another cup.

"Another drink?" Jorvnir asked, stepping forward to push the cup towards Faramund, who took it and drank deeply, leaving the goblet half empty.

"My Lord," Faramund snapped, reminding him to be respectful. "Gods," he spat "that's foul wine—get me something better. Now!" Wordlessly, Jorvnir nodded, glancing to the side as both stags caught sight of Brodgar muttering to one of his troops, who promptly excused himself from the hall.

"At least you've given me a good excuse to follow," Jorvnir whispered as he left in a hurry, his stubby white tail flashing as he turned the corner.

Faramund thought it was the drink, his head was buzzing. Perhaps he should eat something, but then the sight of Brodgar turned his stomach, and he drank some more—out of spite, and in part out of hope it would mellow his mood.

"My lord, you—" Faramund jumped, surprised at Etjar's presence.

"Look at him, look at how he treats her—like she's some common whore—like it's only coins that open her legs. How can I stand still and watch this, knowing how easily she wields her sword—he does this to mock me."

Etjar stood silent, his brow creased as he tried to figure out what to say. Faramund took this as a vindication—how could it not be? He winced as he heard Ada gasp, but she did nothing to hit Brodgar. What a brute—using his position so that he could—

"Faramund," Etjar said firmly, grasping him on the hand. "You do not look well. You should retire for the night." His ears stood back at such a suggestion.

"I would never—"

"Your eyes are glazed, one of your ears flicks about without the other," Etjar said sternly. "You are not well."

"But Ada—"

"She can take care of herself."

"Then why does she let—"

"Enough!" Etjar hissed. "You'll attract the attention of the High-King. Retire to your chambers, you need to rest."

"Brodgar would think it amiss if I left," Faramund huffed, the noise of the hall thankfully hiding their speech.

"I don't believe he'd notice," Etjar replied.

Faramund paused for a moment. He felt like a fawn again; his back tingled as if he could feel the white spots forming on his coat. He looked over at Ada, who now was crooning into Brodgar's ear like some sort of hypnotic bird.

"Make an excuse for me then," Faramund replied. The next thing he remembered was being alone in his room, heaving his stomach out into a bucket. The stench was thick and acidic; it hurt his throat and burnt his nostrils.

* * *

Faramund woke, his mouth completely dry. His head was throbbing. He smelt smoke.

The flames had already claimed the thatch—they were shooting down to the ground. Like a beast, the inferno roared, its hungry tongues lapping across the beams. The wood creaked and groaned, while the heat prickled between his fur. Faramund blinked away the tears as his eyes stung. Still weak, he stumbled to the floor and out into the hall—stomach clenching, but nothing came up. He didn't waste time, scrambling across the stone floor. Others rushed with him. He heard the clatter of their hooves but no one recognized him; their eyes flashing by wide and white. Under one of the benches he saw a fawn; wide-eyed, lip trembling. Someone pushed by, wrenching the child away, disappearing into the smoke.

Ahead, Faramund glimpsed Ada by the hall's open doors, dragging Etjar. He was unconscious; a bloody stump from his missing antlers. Panic lent Faramund strength; he scrambled to his feet and rushed towards the darkness and the snow falling through the open doors.

Then the smoke shifted and Brodgar appeared from the darkness. He was laughing. With an arm, he wrenched Ada over his shoulder and kicked Etjar in the face with his hoof. Faramund saw a tooth shine as it flew out into the night. But the doorway gave a heaving groan before it buckled, fire swirling down, sealing Faramund inside the inferno. He howled. He would rather die sword in hand than burn.

Someone rushed towards Faramund. He saw their lips move, and knew he had to follow. He felt their hands lift him to his feet; he felt—claws—to their grip. But he couldn't see. Maybe it was a trick of the flames, but as he followed, a dark tail seemed to swish behind him, far too long and bushy to be a deer. But he kept following, further back, into thicker smoke. Away from Ada. Away from Brodgar. Away from his foe.

Faramund fell to the ground as his hooves gave way on the soft sand. They'd arrived in the courtyard where Hrothgar made him fight Brodgar, many years ago. Fortunately, the flames had not caught here—it was dark, except for the wavering glow of the inferno behind him. It wouldn't be for long, though; soon the fire would swallow the surrounding outbuildings, trapping Faramund once again.

The fresh air helped clear the stag's head, but he couldn't see a way out. The walls were sealed up with stone, and neither could he see a way to climb out. Rushing forward, Faramund searched for a way out among the overturned tables. The servants had run off carrying whatever they could, but how? In the back of a storeroom he saw one of the stone slabs had been hauled aside with great effort—it was covered in claw marks. Where the slab once lay was a tunnel. The flames catching in the rafters behind him burnt away his uncertainty. Without a moment's hesitation, Faramund jumped into the darkness.

\* \* \*

It was cold and wet. Damp lingered in the air, soothing Faramund's throat with each breath. A faint orange glow flickered behind him, urging him deeper, until everything faded into darkness.

Feeling with his hands, Faramund crept through the tunnel. In some places, his hooves slipped in the mud, and in others his antlers caught on the ceiling. Part of him hoped to bump into someone, just so the silence would end. Part of him hoped that he would not—as they would know his shame, that he had shown the white tail to his foes.

Being underground felt smothering. The earth muffled any sound, ate up any scent, and the darkness mocked his feeble attempts to find the way. Faramund couldn't shake off the fear that the walls were closing in, that the dirt was slowly swallowing him up in some strange, macabre parody of birth.

To his relief, the moist earth began to crunch underfoot, full of ice. The darkness lifted, and his sensitive eyes glimpsed flakes of snow drifting past him on a growing wind. Relief flooded him as he clambered upward, until he heaved himself out of the hole, letting his limp body roll down through the snow. It soothed his burns and calmed his weary senses. For a while he lay there, watching his breath trail out from his muzzle.

Only once his limbs started to grow numb did the stag gather his bearings. The tunnel had opened up underneath the roots of an old oak tree, and to any eye, it seemed like a badger's sett. The forest surrounded him, a maze of disorientating shapes in the darkness. Faramund recognized nothing, and overhead the branches reached out into a dark sky.

The stag cursed. Without the stars he couldn't get his bearings. He was lost, unsure of which way led him towards Brodgar. Resigned to waiting until dawn, he slunk back among the roots of the oak tree, finding some shelter there among the earth. At least Brodgar did not get the satisfaction of killing him, but it was scant consolation.

\* \* \*

Faramund barely slept. He felt like a fawn, curled up in the tree, hiding from the world—from his mistakes. When daylight crept over the world, it revealed his cowardice—his fur was singed in places, bloodied in others, and his hooves ached, but it was superficial. He was still alive. Faramund tried not to think what his father would have said of him.

He froze, hearing movement outside. Laughter echoed between the tree's boughs. Fear gripped him, and vainly he cast the air for scents—he didn't smell any other deer, but then again, his people weren't renowned for their sense of smell.

"Lost in the woods... All alone..." The words drifted past his ears. He crawled out from between the roots and scanned the dense forest. "It has no sword!" The laughter came again, bubbling up as if from the earth. Faramund tried to hold himself, but he felt unsteady. Was it the smoke? Had he breathed in too much? His stomach twisted painfully, reminding him that he hadn't eaten.

"It smells of shame," it snapped behind him. Faramund spun around, but was knocked off his feet. He felt a clawed hand grip his throat, and another wrench his face upright.

"Stinks."

The wolf spat. Its large, yellow eyes made him feel sick. They never stayed still, always twitching at every subtle movement. Faramund quivered instinctively, vainly trying to swallow as the tips of its claws pushed down. He started to wheeze. The wolf stuck its tongue out, licking its bloody tongue across the stag's lips. Clearly it had eaten recently.

"Not hungry." It snickered. Faramund wasn't sure how it knew his people's tongue, but being a wolf, it wouldn't make anything easy. He watched as thick beads of saliva dripped from the corners of its red maw, shivering as he felt its hot breath on his lips.

It let him go, laughing as he tried to spring to his feet. The brute lunged at him, forcing him to jump back and run, only for it to nimbly rush around and appear in front of him, snapping its jaws. Every time Faramund tried, the wolf ran circles around him with its slender legs, prancing about with laughter.

"Too easy, it gives up," it chided, champing its fangs in front of him. Again it angled its head low, trying to catch his gaze with that evil eye. "Faramund." It smirked, fangs poking out from between its black lips.

"How do you know my name?"

"Know the many and much," it growled, mincing out the words. "Names. Gods. Secrets. I tell it." The wolf wagged its dark tail and leapt out of the way.

"What do you want?" Faramund asked, hoping that at least it might not want to eat him. Yet.

"Little deer asks what little deer doesn't know." It laughed, skittering away again, skulking about inside the undergrowth, throwing its voice here and there. "I know how to help. I know how to hinder."

"You wouldn't help me," Faramund called after it.

"Wolf helps deer make more dead deer. Wolf eats again. All things help wolf in the end." It laughed, bursting out from the gorse, scattering the needles across the snow. Inside its mouth it held the blade of Faramund's sword—charred and warped out of shape. It spat it out onto the snow, stamping down on it with its paws.

"But it needs a sword. I know one better." It spoke cryptically, taunting Faramund. "Steel shall sing again," it grinned. "Will Faramund be brave?" The sword under its paws gave a groan as it scraped its claws against it, then a sharp screech as it sheared into two. Faramund felt the fur on the back of his neck turn stiff.

"I can show," the wolf said. "Deer will need to be brave," it laughed, enjoying how Faramund grew angry at its taunts. "Must be brave. If it not follow wolf close, another will eat him." Without waiting for a response it slunk off into the undergrowth. "Come..." The word murmured about beneath the shadows of the trees, the movement of the branches appearing like lips.

For a moment, Faramund hesitated—he'd already been betrayed once already. Why should he trust a wolf? His options were few. He couldn't run. The uneven ground, twisting boughs, and snaking tree roots would trip him—he would never outrun the wolf. If it was toying with him, then there was nothing he could do. But if what it said was true... then even in this weakened state, he could make Brodgar pay. The stag wasn't yet ready to believe the tales; that their best blades almost knew what to do to win. Right now he needed a good sword, and he was out of options.

So Faramund followed. The branches and brambles scratched at the scabs on his pelt, causing the burns to weep. He tried to stay upright, but the low branches pushed him lower, bending forward until he crawled, on hands and knees, on all fours like the wolf before him. Sometimes ahead he saw a pair of amber eyes watching from behind the leaves, saying nothing.

"So slow," it laughed, its claws skittering across the ground ahead, "Many ways to run yet."

It was a lie. The trail began to relent. The trees pulled back, the branches spaced out. Faramund was able to crouch along, and then stand. The wolf was nowhere to be seen—as if the forest had breathed back in its earthy pelt. As he searched about he began to make out shapes in the trees. Their broad trunks twisted together, forming walls. The empty branches meshed together overhead into a roof, illuminated by the sun above. The earth was covered with a light dusting of snow that swirled about his every step. Like his eyes adjusting from the light to the dark, he began to see. The roots tangled together and flattened, forming ornate, weird patterns on the floor. Nestled in the holes between them lay pile after pile of bones—some yellowed and green with moss, others white and shining.

In the center stood a great tree. Its branches were thick, its trunk more than any could lay their arms around. It had leaves, of red, green and gold, despite the winter. Emerging from behind it, an old wolf stood. Its hair was long and silver, glossy even as it caught the light in the gloom. It had many scars across its body and only one eye. In its hand, he saw Hrothgar's sword. The old wolf walked up to the tree and buried the blade inside the trunk, as easily as one would slip underwater. Then the wolf spoke, glaring at Faramund hungrily.

"Whoever draws this sword shall receive it from me as a gift, and shall prove to all that never have they carried a better sword than this one," the old wolf spoke. He was fluent, unlike the other—none of his words chewed up, no snarling, and no growling. As he slunk back, a younger wolf appeared, growling at the yellow eyes gleaming from the alcoves. He stood up, speaking in some quick tongue to his kind, pointing accusingly at Faramund, before approaching the trunk.

Setting his paws on it, he pulled. It did not move. Then he pulled again, gripping so tightly that his claws sank into his palms, and still it did not budge. There was a chorus of laughing howls as another wolf leapt, grabbing the scruff of the young one's neck in its jaws and flinging him. The newcomer tried a different way, clamping his teeth across the handle, but it did not move. Then a third came, seeming confident in himself, snapping at the weaklings who cowered before him. The old wolf smirked, watching as with each pull he seemed to waste away, until that proud wolf collapsed at the foot of the trunk—old, withered becoming grey dust that settled among the bones.

The yellow eyes turned to Faramund. The stag shifted from hoof to hoof on instinct, uneasy at having so many wolves stare at him. It was more than that, though, it was having to willingly walk towards what might be his death. Of course he'd faced many foes before, but this was different. Yet... he had nothing to lose.

Faramund walked up to the tree. His legs trembled, muscles flexing in instinct, ready to run at a moment. So close to it, he realized it dwarfed everything. It had scars, broken branches, and warped twisted bark—even scorch marks from where lightning had hit it. It was an old creature; it had lived through countless lives. It had been there since the beginning, and would be there until the very end.

The stag turned to inspect the sword. The blade had sunk deeply into the trunk, but as he looked away from it, it seemed only a needle. A thick, sickly-smelling sap dripped about the wound, the heady scent making it hard to concentrate. In a swift movement, he grabbed hold. Then he pulled. At first he thought he'd lost his grip, but then he saw the glimmer of metal next to him. The wolves who had surrounded him faded away silently, disappearing into the leaves with only the flick of their tails to follow. Only the wolf-guide remained there, briefly laughing to himself before disappearing as well, leaving Faramund alone among the hall of bones.

\* \* \*

Faramund kicked the ashes with his hoof as he searched the ruins. A couple of embers glowered angrily at him, hissing and spitting as the snow fell on them. Here and there, he found a charred bone, or the warped, blackened shape of a blade. He couldn't tell how many had died or survived. Everything was gone—the flames had swept from the hall across the outbuildings, raising it all.

The russet stag gripped his sword tightly, enough for his knuckles to pop loudly. His anger didn't come from what he saw; he'd witnessed many battles and grown numb to death. The rage came from not knowing which way to turn. The snow surrounding the hall was all churned up, making it impossible to pick up a trail.

Faramund sat next to Etjar, who watched over the remains. A gleaming tip poked out from the back of his neck, curiously free of blood. His body sat there slumped, the spine propping it upright. The crows had already taken his eyes, but the empty sockets stared accusingly out towards the frozen plains. Leaning closer, they seemed to point at the trail of churned up snow that angled west. Faramund whispered a goodbye to his friend and trudged along that trail. Soon enough it turned south, in the direction of Brodgar's hall.

\* \* \*

Faramund circled Brodgar's party as they huddled around the fires. Like a wolf, Faramund had found the winter to be his friend. It had slowed his quarry, sapped their strength; they no longer seemed so full of spirit now that they had slept out in the cold.

The new moon had come with a darkness that was absolute. The stars lay blotted out behind roiling pillars of cloud that swept in with the dusk, landing the world into a realm of primordial stillness, except for the fires flickering up from the valley before him. Compared to the night, they were nothing but brief candles, waiting to be snuffed out.

He watched the sentries, eyes shining blindly as they reflected the firelight, ears flicking about in vain to pinpoint the crunch of snow under his hooves. If he had had a bow and a dozen arrows, he could have stuck them all with shafts and left them for the snow. But his pride demanded that he see Brodgar die up close. For a warrior, it could be no other way.

"Who's there?" a black stag hollered. His mane was tangled into a bunch of messy braids, a thick scar across his snout, and a set of mismatched horns sprouted from his head. The sweat and grime of his fur glowed amber as it caught the flames. "Speak, or I'll stick you," he said, levelling his spear towards the sound of Faramund's steps.

Faramund let the firelight answer as he stepped out of the shadows; his pelt was unkempt, fur matted and tangled into knots. He no longer looked like a warrior. The patches of burnt, bare skin had hardened and scabbed over with a yellow crust that cracked every time his flesh moved. He looked nothing like the pampered lord of days ago; torso gaunt, limbs thin, and weary eyes that were hooded and dark. If he were to have walked into his hall in this state, none would have recognized him. To the stag before him, he seemed only a weary beggar, shuffling forward underneath a ragged cloak.

"You see me now," Faramund replied, "Will you now share your fire with me, as is ancient law?"

The black stag snickered as he ran his eyes up and down the stranger. "It's not my place to break the Gods' Law," he nodded, deciding the beggar was no threat to able bodied warriors. With that, he threw his cloak down onto the snow, and offered Faramund to sit while he dug through his pack. "Here's some food and some wine; a soldier's rations aren't sweet, but they'll keep you going."

Silence fell between them as Faramund chewed. It was hard and salty, the wine coarse and acidic, but he felt it lend him strength. About him, the other deer went about their business, laughing and joking as they sat about the fires. Occasionally, a shout went up as two warriors brawled with each other, or a chorus of whistles when a pair tried to creep off into an empty tent. Every so often the black stag frowned at Faramund and flared his nostrils, as if he recognized his scent, only for the sentry to huff and go back to chewing his ration. For once, Faramund thanked the pale gods for his people's poor sense of smell. A good distance away from the other warriors stood three large tents around a towering pyre. There two warriors struggled, grunting and sweating as they wrestled with each other. Even in the darkness he recognized Brodgar, the silhouette of his twenty-one points casting weird shadows as he threw down anyone who stood before him.

"What goes on over there?" Faramund pointed, curling his cloak about him so the stag wouldn't see the hilt of his sword, pressed close against his thigh.

"The High-King Brodgar," the black stag snorted, "and another of his amusements. Once he's beaten them all in wrestling, he'll insist on swordplay," he said gruffly.

"And then?" Faramund asked.

"He'll beat them all." The stag shrugged, narrowing his eyes as Faramund laughed. "What?"

"Of course he will! Who would be fool enough to best their king?"

"What would you know of it?" The black stag demanded, but Faramund shook his head, stalking off towards the shadows. The stag didn't bother to stop him; he snatched back his rations, muttering what possibly could a cripple do?

Faramund felt his heart stutter and thud as he stalked through the snow. He didn't think of how he would challenge Brodgar, or even what he would say. He simply felt the heat of the fire prick his fur, smelt the smoke, heard the groaning of the wooden beams around him. When he stepped through the circle, he let his cloak fall down from his body, and cast his scabbard into the fire.

Brodgar said nothing for a moment. His eyes widened in recognition, then he laughed; a long, loud, mocking bellow, like one does when confronted with something ridiculous. "I've been looking forward to this," he replied, drawing his blade. "I've been waiting a long time for a good fight."

Then Brodgar fell upon him. He was quick, quicker than Faramund expected from an old, hulking, scarred beast. He would tire soon. Faramund dodged and ducked, letting the blade swing through the air. They paused, trying to size each other up. Brodgar huffed and changed his stance, still smiling. "I'll enjoy hacking your antlers off." His breath trailed out of his muzzle in great clouds of smoke.

Faramund didn't bother to reply; he was busy searching for any weaknesses. This close, he could see most of Brodgar's scars were superficial, his thick muscles rolling underneath the exposed skin. His bare fur glistened as it caught the firelight, covered as it was with sweat from their wrestling. The one advantage Faramund had was Brodgar's missing eye; and the blade in his hand seemed to close in on that target as if with a thought of its own.

The young stag dashed forward, probing Brodgar's blind side—who stepped away, maneuvering so Faramund always stayed in sight. It wasn't perfect though—if Faramund struck quickly, his parry was slow and imprecise. Suddenly Brodgar cut back, his blade angled right for Faramund's neck. Caught off guard by the ruse, he ducked, but the steel caught the top of his antler, cleaving several points clean off.

Brodgar laughed, and his people laughed with him, but Faramund did not care. It was bone that he had struck, not blood, even if the force of the blow still hurt. Sensing his advantage, Brodgar advanced, slashing, stabbing—his blade hummed through the air. It was all he could do—all Brodgar let him do—to parry and dodge, and hope that Brodgar would tire. He didn't. His heavy breathing kept on; so did the blows. One poor step, one hasty parry, and that would be it.

Faramund caught sight of Ada, held by one of Brodgar's servants. A red mist descended over Faramund's vision; his ears roaring as his blood surged past them. This was no longer just about him. This brute was no good for her. Every fiber of his ruined body burnt with that belief, smothering any doubt. Faramund found time to counter Brodgar's attacks—a probing stab here, or a low slash to his legs. The blade in his hand began to hum as it caught the air, seeming to grow lighter, until it felt weightless. Then it found home. Faramund ducked and then thrust his blade up at Brodgar's thigh. It was on his blind side. He leapt back too slowly, sensing the danger but unable to see it. The blade gave a brief shudder as it nicked the bone, and then slipped past through his flesh. Brodgar roared, lashing out, but Faramund was no longer there. The ill-aimed counter sent the High-King off balance, allowing Faramund to sneak behind and bring his blade down, across Brodgar's back.

Blood fell onto the snow, the crimson catching the firelight. It was Faramund's turn to laugh as Brodgar recovered his guard, but it was no good. The blade in Faramund's hand found a way past Brodgar's guard every time, nipping through to take quick bites that would harry and tire its prey.

And tire Brodgar did. Faramund grew bolder, his strikes becoming heavier rather than quick. He was searching for that fatal blow, but Brodgar's scars were a testament to his strength. The High-King weathered the storm—and struck back. Faramund saw the steel gleam as it snuck under his guard. It was only a few seconds later that he felt pain. He dimly heard the cheers, but he was so focused on the blade in his hand that he did not stop.

Faramund let his blows fall in a flurry, quicker than he could think. With each, he felt Brodgar's parry become weaker. Then the steel in his hand sang—he saw Brodgar's sword fly out from his hand. Faramund buried the point of his blade square into Brodgar's chest. Cartilage crunched. Bone broke.

Faramund slipped off onto the ground, holding his side. His hands felt slick and hot. He looked up at Brodgar—who lay on the ground too, kicking his legs. He'd driven the blade home, right through Brodgar's breastbone, burying it to the hilt. There was silence all around as Brodgar lay there spluttering, coughing up blood, feebly clutching fistfuls of snow. His eyes went white and rolled around like a mad beast's; thrashing his head about like a swimmer in the sea, struggling to keep his head above water as he drowned in his own blood. Brodgar kept gurgling, on and on, until Faramund stood up, grasping Brodgar's own blade, and severed his head from his body.

There was silence from all the deer, except for their heavy breathing and the odd jingle of metal as they shifted uncomfortably from foot to foot. Faramund sank to his knees, the fire in his side awakening. He dropped his sword, pressing against his side, but his hands became slick with it, and it kept welling up around his hands. It didn't matter, though. He'd avenged his people, his mother, and his pride.

There was a shout then; next he knew, Ada was beside him, checking his wound, rummaging about and calling to a few others, who with a couple of hesitant glances, reluctantly came to her. Faramund's ears caught some of the murmurs that drifted through the air, but his mind was wandering, and he could pick nothing out. Dizzy, he half expected for them to fall upon him with their swords, but they never came.

A tall stag stepped forward, with black and grey fur and an impressive array of white antlers curling about the top of his head. He pulled out his sword and thrust it down into the snow.

"On the renown of Brodgar's name, and my name, and the names of my kin, we shall abide to the Gods' Law. An old insult is paid, though we grieve at his departure." He paused, turning away, but then added, "I thank you for giving mercy at the end."

Faramund blinked, his ears twitching. He didn't expect that—the courtesy enraged him. "Never mind the destruction of my people's home and the murder of innocents," he spat. Even though he was wounded and lying on the floor, the gob of spittle travelled well, landing square on the speaker's cheek.

"Yes, about that," the stag continued, wiping his face with a cool expression. "I assume you don't know about Jorvnir."

"I know he's dead like Etjar, and the others!"

"Maybe shortly," the stag huffed. He flicked his fingers for two warriors to appear, dragging a chained and blindfolded Jorvnir. Faramund opened his mouth to protest, but Ada silenced him with her hand before he could waste his breath.

"Listen, brother," Ada whispered. "Jorvnir's the one who wrought all this death upon us; he started the blaze, and did all he could to see you perish in it."

At these words Jorvnir's ears perked upward, tilting about as they tried to guess where Faramund was. "My lord! Don't listen to these cowards' lies!"

"Even when caught, the viper still wiggles its tail," the stag cursed, wrenching apart Jorvnir's jaws and grabbing hold of his tongue, which writhed and curled about like a fat worm inside his glistening mouth. "It shall gladden me to do some good," he continued, drawing a thin knife.

"Wait!" Faramund shouted.

The stag flicked his ears, his brow raised. "You held a snake to your bosom. This is the wretch who burnt down your herd's house, and had my kin hold the blame—"

"It's all lies my lord—they have no—" Jorvnir was silenced as one of his captors punched him hard in the belly, forcing the rest of his breath to come out as a wheeze.

The black and grey stag shouted back, lowering his horns. "None of us have to suffer the scorn of a godless wretch such as you." He pushed past the mailed stag, thrusting him onto the snow. "We have paid enough for your schemes. We found these on him," the stag said, plucking a small bag from his pocket and throwing it to Faramund. Ada caught it neatly for him and plucked open the drawstring. Inside lay a small gourd that, when uncorked, fizzed at the touch of the air with a foul aroma, and a set of flint and steel, the latter of which was freshly scratched.

"But I saw Brodgar kill Etjar, and drag you away," Faramund murmured.

"Brodgar was trying to stop me going inside to search for you," she sighed, "and Etjar, like you, thought Brodgar was behind it all."

"Brodgar noticed something was amiss." The black stag interjected. "Your aide, Etjar, said you had taken ill. It would seem that is the cause," he paused. "And the fire, too."

"Then why did I find Etjar left as carrion, with a sword through his gullet?" Faramund countered.

Ada bowered her head and answered, "I asked him to come with us, but Etjar was stubborn, and said he wouldn't leave until he found you." She sighed. "I don't know what happened to him."

"I don't understand. Why let me fight Brodgar then?" Faramund whispered, the pain from his wounds starting to bite.

The black and grey stag laughed. "Who are we to intervene in the personal quarrels of lords and kings? You two were set to fight; like kindling easily brought to flame. Your traitor recognized that, and used it to his own ends. It's fortunate Ada caught him."

Faramund felt his fury drain. Jorvnir, who had served him faithfully, whose advice had never let him astray—why? Sensing that there was nothing more he could do, Jorvnir laughed—long and loud. In the firelight, his eyes shone with a hopeless gleam, taking on an uncanny, yellow tinge. "Death is inevitable. No one remembers the great names. I'd rather have mead and a warm hearth than surrender it for an honorable death." He spat. "By your pride as a warrior, I challenge you, Faramund." A hush fell over the crowd. "Under the witness of the creators, fight me or break your vows and be called a coward. I shan't be robbed of the joy I'll get from butchering you."

"You should have let me cut out his tongue." The stag spat at Jorvnir, who just grinned manically back at him. "There's no need to do this fiend the honor—he's desecrated the same laws he calls upon now, he has no right to claim—"

Faramund shook his head, feeling his strength ebb from his side. His pride spoke for him. "I've never refused a fight, and I've never lost a fight. My reputation is more precious to me than my life, and I won't let this fiend sully it. Come then, let me make you a feast for the crows."

Snarling and without a sword, Jorvnir leapt free from his captors, dipping his head forward, sending the points of his antlers hurtling towards him. It seemed a mad, desperate move for someone to behave like a beast—but it was a cunning one. Eyes wide with hatred, he charged; a set of sixteen sharp points hurtling towards Faramund, who couldn't parry them. He had no shield and he couldn't run.

Instead, he pointed Brodgar's blade in front of him and waited.

Faramund's body shuddered, tumbling backwards as Jorvnir hit. For a strange couple of moments they tumbled, holding each other in a weird embrace. Then there was a crunch, and a sick, wet, slurping sound, followed by a sudden crack. Jorvnir's body slumped down onto the earth. Faramund followed; two thick shafts of antler lay embedded in his chest, one through a lung, the other through his heart.

He didn't hear Ada whisper her goodbyes; but that is the nature of death. All that mattered was that he could go to the house of death with his pride intact.

* * *

When dawn came, not even the crows came close. The wolf chuckled to itself, reuniting the sword with its scabbard from the burnt out fire. With a clawed hand, it plucked the antlers from Faramund's chest, and carried both corpses to the hall of bones. Without their High-King, winter would leave a lasting scar upon the herds.

*How intelligent should an animal-soldier be to be an effective fighter?*
*If it's too intelligent and can think for itself, how do its commanders control its loyalty?*

# The Surface Tension

## *by Dwale*

The trailer fishtailed on the sheet of ice covering the highway while the storm wailed and strove to get them sliding sideways. Inside was Erin, a panda in a jacket and drab canvas jumpsuit, sitting on the floor and using the wall-mounted folding chair as a stanchion. That was easier than trying to sit in it since the entire trip had been like this. As she clung there in queasy suspense, she entertained a daydream wherein some faceless person higher up in the chain of command scoffed and asked, "A seatbelt? When is she ever going to need *that*?"

"Five minutes," said grave and professional Lubin, henceforth referred to as Command, over the intercom. He was not in fact a decision-maker, but the one through whom her superiors relayed orders. Erin had never actually seen him since he was always seated at a terminal in the driver's cab.

"*The heated cab*," she recalled, hugging her jacket to herself and shivering before she decided to get up onto her knees and inch her way over to the loader. She took hold of a support while her breath formed short-lived wisps in the air, then hauled herself upwards with a groan, certain that the stiffness in her joints had to be abnormal for someone her age.

The inhaler was in her left inner pocket and would warm her up. There would be a tank of compound Q in the *waschbär*, but there was no reason she couldn't get a head start. She put the inhaler to her lips and pressed the canister down. The spray escaped with a hiss, astringent on her tongue and tasting of chemicals in all the worst ways. The flavor, if she'd been called on to describe it, was something like a combination of ammonia and "rotten salt." It could linger on the tongue for hours, but she and the drug cocktail were old friends, so while she couldn't be said to have acquired a taste for it, she accepted it as part of experience's toll.

Her hands and feet were already starting to go numb before she shlepped herself into the open hatch with one heavy, artless lunge, flopping into the cramped compartment in a manner that called elephant seals to mind, despite her panda phenotype.

Warmth, a pleasant heaviness, spread up from her extremities to her heart, then to her head. With compound Q in her system she could sit immobile in the pilot's compartment for twelve hours or more, though ideally she would get out to stretch her legs every two. She was perfectly at ease. Her thoughts were clear and sharp and she had no more of them than was needful.

The truck began to slow three kilometers ahead of the destination, as sudden breaking would not be possible on the slick roads. When they finally stopped, it wasn't two seconds before she heard the other vehicles disgorge their occupants just outside the trailer in which she had been riding. The rolling door to her left rattled its way up the tracks and the mountain winds came slashing in like a cloud of cold scythes. A pair of techs, raccoons, climbed into the trailer, one to strap her into the harness and one to work the loader. They were silhouettes against the white landscape. Erin's eyes watered as sleet flew into them, but she barely felt it.

"We made good time," said the intercom, "Kadesh is going to be in position in fifteen minutes. Communications says they've been sweet-talking her for the past hour."

Erin hadn't any notion why someone might need to sweet-talk a spy satellite, but wasn't curious enough to ask. Perhaps it was technical jargon.

Instead, she left her body behind, interfacing with the *waschbär*. She always did this when they started strapping the harness on because the technician had to reach in-between her legs for a buckle and it was embarrassing. The *waschbär* responded to her overture with an ultrasound pulse into the booster chip implanted in her brainstem. The chip made control a breeze, while the two pistol grips in the pilot's compartment were mainly there to give her something to hold. The OS's blue-grey top menu appeared in her mind's eye along with the two words, "Interface initiated."

The hatch closed. She sat in the confines with no more room to move then a Shingon Buddhist holy man in the final stage of self-mummification. Her view of the outside world was limited to what she could see through the translucent red visor. But that was only for a moment before the sensory feedback system engaged.

How would she have described the sensation of having five extra limbs and seven additional eyes? She wasn't sure. Both bodies felt equally her own.

"Hey, the loader would've torn this right off the wall," said a tech as he slammed the folding chair, the one she'd been using as a stanchion, shut with a clang. "Get it together!"

"Sorry," Erin said, though she knew he couldn't hear her. Someone hit the deployment switch and the motor behind her came to life, grinding as it launched the loading platform forward. It—she—went out after the scurrying silhouettes of the raccoons from the support team. Her outer body couldn't feel the blizzard hissing against her armor. Two of the *waschbär's* cameras were in back of the carriage, which was like having eyes in her shoulder blades. Ice blew in and settled on the loader's bare metal frame and drivetrain cover.

There was a mechanical crack and then she was being lowered. The motor hummed and the vibrations went through both her bodies. She called up yesterday's overhead shot of the compound and the image slid into her awareness. It was deemed unlikely that the terrorists were aware they were being monitored, so the layout was probably still the same. And it sounded as though she was going to have a live satellite feed from Kadesh any time now.

Erin, through the being of her walking armor, stood up, towering over the support crew from a height of three meters, scarcely aware of the dainty panda body sitting with legs folded in the cockpit.

"My left arm is a little unresponsive," she said as she worked the elbow. It must have been time to replace the actuators. That was a serious undertaking since parts had to be machined by hand. The factories that had once produced replacements had long crumbled back into the earth.

Rather than reply, Command gave her the rundown. For the time being, she was to proceed to point A, on the opposite side of the terrorist facility from the driveway where the defenses were concentrated. She and her team would take them from behind. They wouldn't know what had hit them until it was too late.

Their caravan consisted of six vehicles, two eighteen-wheeled trucks and four light armored carriers. The trucks were for launching and supporting the *waschbär* and the spider. The carriers held a dozen men each: three full special ops units and a field maintenance crew. One unit and the field crew would handle defending the caravan. The others would come along to provide close-in support for the walking armors that Erin and her sister were piloting.

The spider was coming around now. It was an older design than the *waschbär*, hexapodal and armless, but with an array of different armaments. They were all in a package about as small and low to the ground as an economy car. It didn't have a high top speed, but was nimble in ways no wheeled or tracked vehicle could ever be. It was said the thing could damn near do ballet. And of course, it could bring heavy fire support to terrain hitherto accessible only by foot or air: whether rocky crags and canyons, or through areas of dense vegetation, and places where either weather conditions or enemy defenses made the use of helicopters inadvisable. It was a niche combat role, but one nevertheless deemed important enough to warrant filling during the wars of former times. Now the spider, like her own armor, had become a symbol of the state's power. Old technology, half-forgotten by the world outside the city walls, they could climb down from their tractor-trailers and rain death onto the primitives like angry gods.

"Is that Erin?"

It was Ava, her sister's voice, coming not over the telecom, but directly into her head. It sounded so much like her own voice that Erin might have taken it for a passing thought instead of a communiqué.

"Yes, ma'am!" she replied.

"Ma'am?" Ava said, stifling laughter, "I'm only two years older than you! Anyway, just follow my lead and you'll be fine."

"Do not use this channel for socializing!" Command barked. Things quieted down after that. Erin could still hear the storm, but she could adjust the volume on the output as easily as she could flatten her own ears, and her second skin was nearly soundproof. The rhythms of her body, the sound of her breath and heartbeat, did not discomfort her. They let her know she was alive when she could barely feel them.

The ground troops were getting into position, chimerae of wolf stock in armored snowsuits, rifles at the ready, indistinguishable on account of their being clones. The scouts had already gone ahead, so next it would be her turn to march as soon as they synched with the AI on the orbital surveyor Kadesh. That was happening now, and the first words from Command were these:

"Oh, hell!"

That was apt because hell broke loose. The overhead from Kadesh's infrared showed that there were warm bodies all around them in the woods. The scouts took fire from riflemen in concealed pits. Simultaneously, there came a series of short, swooping noises from the south. The canisters, like little grey fire extinguishers, began to fall. One bounced off the shoulder of Erin's armor.

"Gas!"

People started firing into the trees. There was shouting, so much confusion that no one listened to Command's ordering all foot to charge through the poison clouds rather than stand there or go backwards.

"Ava," Erin shouted in her mind, "check your filters!"

"They're good, what about you?"

"Mine are on."

The spider's turret turned to face the south and fired a volley of six rocket-propelled grenades at their attackers. They flashed out of the launcher and were gone, so fast that the explosions seemed to occur at almost the same time. Erin heard bullets pinging off of her.

"Protocol C!" Command shouted, over and over. Most of the soldiers were on the ground, frothing and convulsing, but some made it to the vehicles and were starting to pull away. There wasn't time to load up Erin and Ava. They were being abandoned, along with men who might have been saved.

A crowd of figures in black ponchos and gas masks rushed out from the forest. Bipedal walking armors like Erin's could be knocked on their backs with nothing more than a lever and a little manpower. Some of these guys had long metal pipes with them. She growled when she saw them.

She realized that she and her team had been duped. The enemy had known every detail of their operation, right down to the range of their thermal sensors and the whereabouts of Kadesh. This was the same enemy her commanders had called "ignorant tier zeroes, little more than animals with rifles and clubs." "Ferals," they were called, but these had possessed a knowledge of chemistry potent enough to make nerve gas, as well as decryption abilities on par with the military's. And now they were coming to kill her and her sister.

The spider's close-in defense system was designed to intercept RPGs and wouldn't help Ava in this situation. Erin was in-between her sister and the black ponchos in a blink. The *waschbär's* left arm was a combination shield/battering ram, but there was an electrolaser mounted near the elbow. Too quick for the eye to follow, an ultraviolet laser under its protective dome ionized the air between it and its targets, then current passed through a series of amplifiers and was let out into the ion channel the laser had just created. Each shot surged and cracked like a lightning bolt. Precise aiming was unnecessary because the electricity would seek the path of least resistance and jump to its victim of its own accord.

The closest three ponchos went down. A fourth got zapped and the rest ran for it.

"Don't let them get away," said Command, the truck already on the road and moving. "Erin, engage."

The *waschbär*'s chain gun was what Erin thought of as her tenth limb. It fired 30mm gyroscopically-corrected explosive-tipped rounds; these were each roughly the size of the tube from a roll of paper towels and tended to disintegrate objects such as armored cars and reinforced concrete bunkers. It was a later addition, she'd been told. The main armament had at first been an air-gun that fired rubber balls. "Less lethal," her instructors mentioned, and "crowd control" when discussing the original design, though Erin felt pretty sure that her chain gun would control the *hell* out of a crowd.

She had them in her sights. All she had to do was think it, and the rounds would fly. But what they would do to flesh...

The *waschbär* took a step backwards and wriggled its right shoulder as though struck. It wasn't Erin who had initiated that movement; she had never been more sure of anything in her life. But neither had she been hit that she could see.

"Erin, engage!"

"I'll get it," Ava said, but the spider froze in place before it had a chance to aim.

"No," Command said, "she has to learn."

Red haze filled Erin's vision. She felt her brain issue commands to the chain gun, the same as if she had done it herself; but she hadn't done it and couldn't make it stop. As her gun took aim, she made to try and override it with the manual controls, only to find she couldn't move a muscle. The armor was not being remote-operated, she realized. She was.

"*No!*" she thought when the firing started, and would have screamed, but nothing she did would make either of her bodies obey her.

Her chain gun unloaded at the unspectacular rate of two rounds a second, but each one was havoc. 30mm shells sped through the air, whizzing away in spirals like supersonic fruit flies as they adjusted to compensate for the wind. A person didn't need to be struck directly, as the explosive force of each payload was lethal to a range of three meters. The fleeing terrorists detonated like fireworks stuffed with raw hamburger. Someone's arm spun away in an arc, hand still clutching a pistol, and landed a short time after the firing stopped. Not a single target had escaped.

"Protocol C," Command said one final time.

The first step was to commit to radio silence. Erin and Ava made for the trees to the northeast. It seemed to her that the terrorists must have withdrawn on realizing that they weren't equipped to take down walking armors; but whatever the case, the fighting was over for now. After all the gunfire, the quiet weighed on them like a wet woolen shroud. And so it went for the next six hours.

Protocol C was simple enough: locate a defensible position and conceal yourself there to await further instructions. Walking armors handled the snow better than most tracked or wheeled transit; in a storm like this, even infantry would be unable to keep pace. Erin had plenty of time to relive the invasion; Command taking her bodies away from her, and turning those foreigners into bloody kibble with the chain gun that was like her own limb. Some of them had been so much smaller than the others. She recalled through the numbness of shock that the terrorists were said to deploy children as soldiers.

It was midwinter and the days were short. They had just finished using the spider's winch to get them up the far side of a ravine when Ava stopped and put her armor into passive mode. The steep climb would be nearly impossible without special equipment, so this place was more defensible than most. They were getting out to find shelter on foot, Erin realized, hopefully close by.

"*Did Ava see something?*" she wondered.

A cold, sleet-heavy wind rushed in when Erin opened the hatch. The spider let its operator out right at ground level, but Erin would have benefitted from a two-meter stepladder like they had on the truck. One of her boots went out from under her when she made to jump down. The next thing she knew, she was buried face-first in the snow with her feet poking out like a tent-peg. Flailing her legs, she thrashed ineffectually until Ava pulled her up and free.

Ava dusted Erin's hair off, though that might have been redundant given the fact that the younger panda was blushing so hard that her ears steamed.

"*I looked like a fool in front of* her!"

Ava and Erin shared the same face, though Erin's was lankier, less filled-out on account of the age difference. Among the armor pilot clones, where identity crises were common as breathing, Ava's hairstyle was remarkable only in its plainness. She wore it shoulder length and kept it brushed, that was all. Erin's was cut short on the left side and her tips were dyed purple. Of a sudden, she was seized with a crazy certainty that her own fashion sense was frivolous. It was a level of self-consciousness that made her wish so much that she could crawl under a rock for an extended stay. But at that moment, both of their hairstyles looked more like the flailing of a wounded animal, whipped in every direction at once by the terrible storm.

Words were exchanged, their shouts reduced to whispers by the deafening rush. Ava gesticulated until Erin took her meaning, which struck her as odd since the impromptu sign-language hadn't conveyed much of anything. Ava would unpack the emergency supplies from the spider (and how Erin envied her that storage space) before the two pushed on for the cavern Ava had spotted, which was not far.

They were freezing by the time they got inside; but as they walked, they realized that the snow was melting a ways in. A little farther and it was warm enough to remove their jackets. The cavern smelled of mud and mildew. She detected the notes of biological waste from somewhere deeper in. They both had little LED flashlights, so they ended up swinging their beams around without spotting much of interest, until they illumed a stack of white boxes in a chicken-wire enclosure. There were tracks all around it, bipedal but with a caniform morphology. They had been made when the floor was damp or partially flooded; it was dry as dust now.

"Well," Ava said, and clicked her tongue. "What have we here?"

Erin followed on her heels. Secreted around one corner, there was a pile of blankets and a pillow, too, and a broadband receiver with cables trailing off, away and out of sight.

"That's a MEHS-42," Ava said. "They would have needed to use the decryption, which means they also have code sets. So *that's* how they got the jump on us. Their command and control structure is a lot more sophisticated than we thought."

If Erin's memory served, then the MEHS-42 was from the same series of computer relays as the ones they used in their armors, but it had to be military-grade equipment either way since the civilian models tended not to have advanced cryptographic software.

Ava stopped so short that Erin almost walked into her. Without turning, she said, "A lot of us freeze up the first time we're asked to fire on a live target. The electrolaser's not always lethal, so that's different. But…"

"I feel sick," Erin said. "When he took over, it felt so…"

"Dirty?"

Erin nodded, which Ava seemed to realize even though she hadn't seen her do it, being herself preoccupied with the wood-and-wire construct they'd found.

"That's why you'll do it yourself next time." She knelt beside the chicken-wire cage and examined the padlock. Erin stood there, hugging herself.

"When I went to shoot, the *waschbär* seemed to… I don't know. It was like it flinched."

Ava gave the padlock a few hard yanks, to no effect. It wasn't coming off that way. "Yeah, the spider does that too. When you're hit with that anxiety, the system reads it. The movement data from pilot after pilot, all dreading what's about to happen. The OS remembers."

It was true. This was Erin's third mission; the previous two had been riot control. In those, the crowds had dispersed on seeing the *waschbär* take its place behind a row of infantry. There hadn't been any fighting on her part.

"It's why they paired you," Ava said. She'd got a screwdriver from somewhere and was working the chicken-wire loose from the frame, one peg at a time. "Otherwise this would have been a one-person job, excepting the ambush. We're lucky to find this store. I can't wait to see what's in these boxes. Could be drugs, counterfeit net cards…"

Erin remembered that she'd been paired with another armor on her first two deployments as well, which meant that talk about it being "a mere show of force" had been misleading, with Command ready and willing to fire for the whole duration. A mere show of force indeed!

For the moment, she set those thoughts aside to concentrate on more immediate matters. As she seated herself on the pile of blankets, she couldn't help but marvel at Ava's stamina. After today, with Command's intrusion into her being, the massacre at the roadside and the long, lonely march through the blizzard, she just wanted to lie down and cry. Not Ava, though. Even out of her armor, one did not think of her as being susceptible to things like sentiments or bullets. She was calm and confident and her movements possessed an indolent grace, whereas Erin was always nervous and prone to knocking things over on accident. While Erin took stock of her feelings about this older version of herself, she found envy and admiration in almost equal measure, and something else besides, something she could not yet name.

"What you did back there," Ava said, "when they came to tip our armors over, you saved me. Thank you."

Erin had been too deep in thought to notice Ava turn, but now that she registered Ava's eyes shining green with reflected light, she shivered, and it wasn't from the cold. She was so caught off guard that she stammered.

"Oh, n-no! Ma'am!"

"*Smooth...*" she thought.

Ava went back to work on the wire. Erin sighed and decided to kill some time scanning the broadband receiver. But first, she wanted a hit of compound Q. The inhaler should have been in her left inner pocket, but when she reached in, her eyes went wide and her mouth fell open.

"My inhaler!"

"You must have dropped it when you face-planted earlier."

Erin was on her feet. "We have to go back, we have to -"

"In all that snow, with the sun going down? You'll be antsy tonight, but you won't start withdrawing until tomorrow. I'll give you a pull from mine in the morning. There's still a canister in each of our armors, too. The bigger worry is that they'll come to collect what's in these boxes."

"Then I'll help," said Erin, resigning herself. "I'll go crazy just sitting here. Is there another screwdriver?"

"Yeah, there's a toolkit, some canned vegetables... But no, don't come here yet. Switch on that receiver and put it in scan mode. Set an alarm for any signal with Command's ID tag. That'll keep us from having to constantly check our armors."

As Erin punched in the necessary commands, she wondered that such equipment could end up in the hands of foreign terrorists. Certain persons, it was said, within the uppermost levels of society were not subject to the rules imposed on the dual populations of East Nine; both the registered, "tiered" chimerae on one side of the walls, and the feral inhabitants of the shanty-megalopolis on the other. The ones who made the decisions for all the rest were interested solely in their own pursuits. It must have been so, for how else could they profit on the misery of the powerless? But what responsibility could be lain on those who arm the enemy when their influence puts them above the law?

She sighed and tried to refocus. The receiver wouldn't be picking up much in that storm, so the younger panda got to work on the cage. The pegs came out easy enough with a little jostling, so it wasn't the sort of work that demanded Erin's full attention. Her mind drifted again.

"Ava. Ma'am."

"Just 'Ava' will do."

"The ones before us. When I thought about them, their imprints in my control system... How many batches came before us?"

"They won't tell us," Ava said, grim as midwinter, "but we put our heads together and worked out some things. We were probably the ninth, which would make *you* -"

"What else were you able to work out?

Erin hadn't meant to interrupt, but she was so hungry to learn anything about her origins after so many years of being kept in the dark. Ava wasn't from her nursery, she was a transfer. Maybe restrictions had been lighter at that other nursery, giving the batch of clones more time to collude.

Ava had stopped working and fixed her gaze on Erin, who felt the blood go to her ear-tips like the gauge of a thermometer in boiling water.

"Because our brain structures are so similar," Ava said, turning back to her task, "we've all had a lot of the same thoughts. We don't know everything, but… Here, pull down and we're in."

"Please," Erin said while she fumbled with the ungainly spread of wire. "Anything you found out. We can compare notes."

"Later. Right now, these boxes… damn, they're heavy!"

The two of them heaved out one of the boxes, which they saw now were filthy with mud, but were waterproof. Ava had to strain to get the lid off, the seal on it was so tight.

"Paper?"

"Inktext. It would be."

Without hesitation, Ava had one of the pamphlets in hand and began to read:

"The prophet Malachi was the greatest orator the world has ever seen. His rhymes were both fresh and dope and destroyed haters with ease. This is evidence the verses are divine, as the mortal mind simply lacks the capacity to always provide such sick burns in freestyle. He was unbeaten in a thousand debates."

By the time Ava was done reading, Erin was laughing so hard she had tears in her eyes while even Ava, a habitual stoic, couldn't help but crack a smile. "I think they must have learned English from old movies," she said.

"Do you think?" Erin was still tittering, but that died when she saw Ava open up the pamphlet and look inside. "Hey, don't…"

"Just a peek. Let's see, 'Pronunciation guide for Buraziiyan Portugaiz'? Oh, they have it in another language under the English script. 'Think not that the people preceding you are better, when you were made to replace them. No! You come through them but are not of them. In truth, all praise is for God, The Clement! It is He who wills that you free your brethren from the oppressors. It is He who bestows life, and He knows best the fate of disbelieving folk.' It must lose something in translation," she muttered. "Still…"

Ava tossed the flier back into the box. "Right now, everyone outside the walls of East Nine is hoping to get in. But if they get it into their heads that the system is evil, they'll have a reason to try and overrun us. They'll call themselves liberators, but all the while they'll be thinking, 'We can take this place over and have their technology for ourselves.' It's dangerous."

Erin nodded. There was no question who the "oppressors" were meant to be in that dichotomy. The terrorists meant to distribute these to the slums. They were calling for a revolution. Even someone with as restricted an upbringing as herself could see it.

"We have to burn these," Ava said. "We can't just leave them."

"Agreed. As soon as we get -"

"-our orders."

"Hey, don't-!"

"-finish your sentences?"

"Do you think -"

"-that our booster chip signals are intermingling? No."

"Ah... Well, what about -"

"It's not telepathy."

"Ah."

And Erin sat there feeling foolish because towards the end of that exchange not even she was sure which of them had been the one speaking, nor even if the whole conversation had been in her head. She watched Ava check to see how the receiver was coming along, fidgeting. Finally, she blurted out just to break the silence.

"The Original. What was her -"

"Christine. That was her name. She wasn't chosen for her coloration, as you have assumed, but because she was instrumental in redeveloping the code that drives our armors. That, incidentally, must be the reason they continue to clone her even though they know half of us won't shoot the first time we're asked. That would have been unacceptable for a purpose-built soldier, so it seems that whether intentional or not, she had become too much a part of the OS after her work on it. None of their other programmers could undo what she had done."

The assumption about coloration to which Ava referred was the one Erin had held in answer to the question, "Why a panda?" Up until now, she'd thought they'd chosen the panda phenotype because back in the days when the police and the military had been separate entities, black and white had been the colors of the police. Designer chimerae had been cheap and readily available back then, so color-coordination wasn't so frivolous a proposition as to be out of the question. And a bear's sense of smell would have made them even more effective than police dogs. But no, it seemed The Original had been a person named Christine, and a computer genius? That couldn't be right.

"I was stunned, too," Ava said, "to think that sort of potential existed in me. In a freer world, I might have...!"

There came over the two a mixture of elation and fear in the formless knowing of what they might achieve, if only they had some control over their destinies, if only they weren't slaves of the state. No, they were lower even than slaves. They were attack dogs.

"But we can't." Ava's face darkened. She was showing teeth, white and sharp. "They have us. For now, they have us. You know about it, right? The kill-tack?"

"No, I..."

"Yeah, they put it in when they installed your booster chip. It's just a little plastic explosive and a detonator. You act out, or some bean-counter decides you're too expensive to feed, and 'Pop!' You're gone."

"I don't want to think about that!" Erin covered her ears and screwed her eyes up tight. "How could anyone want to think about that?"

"If you die by getting hit by a bus, say," Ava explained, her tone low and edged with severity: "The material that makes up that bus already exists. That matter has been making its way through time and space, from the beginning of the universe, to be dug up and processed and fabricated just to become the means of your demise. You could be shot tomorrow, or drown in fifteen years, or die any number of other deaths. It's like that for everyone. The fact that we know about this changes nothing."

"They wouldn't put something like that in us. I don't believe it," Erin said. "I can't."

"That's one way of coping. But I'm telling you this because you have a right to know." Ava shrugged and bent back to the receiver.

* * *

"We're lucky we found this place," Erin said after a while. Her boredom had tangled with her unease and come up triumphant.

"No luck about it, I saw this cave on the satellite view. You know, the one we were supposed to memorize?"

"Ah..."

Ava chuckled. "Anyway, the takeaway from all this is that it's important to -"

"-live in the moment." Erin finished.

Ava smiled in response. "We should eat and try to, uh, answer the call of nature. It'll be easier as the compound Q wears off. But after that, do you want to play?"

"Play." Erin stared at Ava's cocked eyebrow, uncomprehending.

"Like the other girls, back in the nursery…"

"Oh," Erin said as the meaning sank in, then squeaked a surprised, "Oh! No, I…"

"We all do it," she said, crawling towards Erin on all fours, green eyes glinting in the dark. Erin had been propositioned like this before and was aware that sort of thing occurred. In the small family to which she belonged, they weren't even allowed to apply for a coupling license until they'd put in six years of service, and they were segregated from the rest of society. Such happenings were to be expected, but apart from some youthful experimentation, Erin had kept herself apart from it.

"We can't," Erin whispered. She backed away, but made it only a meter before her shoulder-blades touched wall. "We're sisters."

Ava's muzzle was only inches from her own. "We're not sisters, we're clones. And who would know you better? Outside. Inside. Everyone should do what you're thinking of doing."

Erin shut her eyes and shook her head. She sat that way, trying to control her quickened breath and heartbeat. When next she dared to look, she saw Ava back at the receiver, playing with the controls as if nothing had happened.

"I need a hit of Q," Erin said with quivering voice. Ava frowned in response.

"Not until morning. We don't know how long we're going to be here, so we have to conserve it. Trust me, the withdrawal is no joke."

Erin was half-certain Ava was only withholding on account of the incident a moment earlier, but was in no position to complain either way. Later, they would eat a sparse meal of canned bamboo shoots ("Is this ironic?" Ava had wanted to know) and rest in their underwear together in the nest of blankets. At one point Ava, sleepily and without awareness, threw her arm around Erin's waist, whose heart began to beat so hard she was amazed her sister could sleep through it.

\* \* \*

It was shortly after dawn (according to Ava's watch, as they couldn't see the sky) when Erin's nose began to run. A feeling at once hot and cold spread out over her body, like the inside of her skin had been rubbed down with menthol. The muscles in her limbs kept constricting like they wanted to curl in on themselves. She trembled and couldn't get comfortable no matter what she tried. It was when Ava noticed the pacing that she produced the inhaler and offered it.

"Only one," Ava warned. Erin took a long, grateful drag and settled back. Within five seconds, the muscle spasms had stopped; another ten and her nostrils dried.

"So that's the withdrawal," Erin mused. "You weren't kidding. That sucked."

"Only the preliminary stages. A few more hours and you'd have been begging to die."

Erin regarded her sister with glazing eyes as a pleasant fuzziness took hold of her nerves and her body faded to the edges of her awareness. "Aren't you going to take a hit?"

"No, I use as little as I can. One hit a day is enough for me."

"I see," Erin said. "I guess I should start doing that, too, then. Any idea what that stuff is?"

"We figured out some of the constituents. The chief ingredient is an analog of gabapentin, but it also contains morphine, eszopiclone, and lisdexafetamine: everything you need to ignore your body for a few hours. We think there are other drugs in it as well."

Ava had apparently finished checking the receiver. "Nothing from Command yet," she announced, though that wasn't news since they would have heard the notification they'd set.

"The caravan might have been attacked again farther up the road," Erin said, lips puckering into a dour pout, "in which case -"

"-In which case they'll be sending a sizable force to extract us. There's no cause for panic yet. There." Ava pointed with her muzzle towards a pail she'd found. "We need water, so take that up and fill it with clean snow. Pack it down as hard as you can, but be quiet and keep your head down. Your spots will stand out if anyone's looking."

As Erin made her way up the slope towards the cave's entrance, she reflected that Ava's demeanor had not changed in light of the pick-up attempt the night before. If it had been the other way 'round, with Erin as the aggressor, she would have been embarrassed enough to die and certainly wouldn't have been able to play it cool the next morning. It was at times like this that she half-doubted sharing any genetic information with her sisters, despite being physically identical. There was no way, she reasoned, that someone like her could become Ava in only a couple of years. And yet, she knew that the differences in their respective upbringings could result in only minor neurological divergence. Regardless of any quirks, tics, or idiolectic variance, she and her sisters were, broadly speaking, interchangeable.

*"Why, then?"* She wondered as she surveyed the blank winter scene of the world above. The *waschbär* and spider stood a short distance away, a

pair of fantastical sentries so glazed with ice they seemed made of frosted glass, and shone like galaxies in the bright morning sunlight.

*"Why do I feel so self-conscious around her?"* But dredge her mind though she might, it produced no answer except the one she knew already: that Ava projected a combination of confidence and competence to which Erin aspired. She was attracted to it, to *her* with the surety of magnetism; she who was forever making mistakes, the clumsy and shy girl who had plumbed her own heart over a thousand sleepless nights, seeking assurance, but always come up lacking. There was no use hiding the truth from herself any longer. Life was too short. That went double if what Ava had said about their having explosives in their skulls was true. Sighing, she shoveled snow into the pail with her numb, paw-like hands. At least the storm had passed.

Bears have some of the sharpest noses in nature, so even a human/panda chimera like Erin had no difficulty discerning the cooking meat as she made her way back down to the cavern. She soon found Ava busy at the camping stove (part of the survival kit she'd had on the spider), searing a lump of heavily processed flesh in its own juices. Erin's stomach growled as she joined her sister.

"I wanted to apologize," Ava said, not looking up. "I'm sorry if I made you uncomfortable last night."

"No, it's fine. I…" Erin paused to gather her thoughts. "If I was going to 'play' as you call it, I think I would want it to be with you."

"I know. You've been watching me since the day we met."

To that, Erin had no response apart from a blush mercifully concealed beneath her fur.

They ate in silence. There was little to do but wait and watch the receiver for any sign of a transmission from Command. None came, so they whiled away the morning in chit-chat and idle musings.

The terrorists must, they reasoned, have had multiple such receivers, else they would not have left this one unguarded. There were probably other caches such as this, too, scattered throughout the area. The extensive cave system allowed them to move personnel and contraband without anyone being the wiser. They may well have been infesting this region for months or even years before wind of it finally got to the authorities.

Around noon, Erin's nose started to run again, so Ava let her take another pull from her inhaler. A couple of hours later, however, Erin's body, being cheated of its usual dosage, protested with hot and cold flashes, with restlessness and a serious case of the jitters.

"I need another hit," she said.

"No, I'm sorry. I know it feels bad, but you'll thank me if we end up stuck here a while."

Erin huffed and was tempted to march out into the daylight to dose from the canister in the *waschbär*, but thought better of it. The on-board operating system was configured to release compound Q over an extended period, and every hour she spent there was a drain on the fuel cells. It wouldn't do to have her armor run down before they reached safety. So, she busied herself instead, first through pacing, then after that wore thin, by familiarizing herself with the terrorist propaganda.

She poured through the boxes to discover there were eight different pamphlets, all told, and their content affirmed what she and Ava had judged on reading from the first. There were verses glorifying God, and exhortations to righteousness and charity which seemed so innocuous that, out of context, she might have wondered why the powers that were took such umbrage with printed text, religious in particular. For example, there was this verse:

"You who would be forgiven must become vessels of forgiveness,

And you who would receive mercy, first be merciful to your fellow men.

Be just, and fear the Day of Judgement, if you have good sense,

For ill works shall be weighed against your remembrance."

She thought that was fairy-tale nonsense, but dangerous? Not so much. But there were other, darker currents amongst the phrases as well, words like, "The autocrats do but sow wicked seeds, watered with your brothers' blood. They reap an evil fruit, how then shall they harvest virtue? Arise, for your Lord is with you! Arise and destroy the tyrants!" Even so…

"I don't understand how people get taken in by this crap," she said. She had been so engrossed that she jumped a little when she noticed that her sister had come up next to her and joined in the research.

"Unity," Ava said simply, "the drive to be a part of something greater. It's a bulwark against the loneliness."

Erin peered at the words again, but her dubious regard must have been so obvious that Ava was able to pick up on it, because she began to elaborate without being prompted.

"Loneliness is part of being alive," Ava said, sending her literature back into its box with a wrist-flick. She stared at Erin, who became aware of a sort of subdued intensity in her sister's words. Ava continued:

"We come into the world and form this armor around ourselves. We have to, because it's in our nature to harm one another, and once we've been hurt we feel like we can never again be naked and vulnerable. But we still yearn for connection.

"It's about being understood, I think. For some people, that means adopting a creed. Believing the same thing means thinking some of the same thoughts. Others create art, exposing their hearts like castaways writing in the sand in hope of rescue. Some try to dispense with the connection altogether, to endure the loneliness because their fears outweigh their longing. Whatever the case, we find ways to cope. And how are you coping, Erin?"

"Poorly." The word had formed spontaneously, as though her throat had issued it without first consulting her brain. She clamped her hand over her mouth like she meant to force that truth back into her voice box, but it was too late. The question had caught her off guard and she had answered it.

Her strategy in life had been to keep her head down and try not to think too much about her troubles. The drugs aided her in this, numbing her both inside and out, but that was a treatment, not a cure. It was not until that moment that she realized the depth of her emptiness. Her eyes turned to her older sister. She held her breath, waiting for the reply.

"My offer is still on the table," Ava said, voice gentle as mist. "You can connect with me, if you want."

"Connect? But you said -"

"What is it, then, if not connection?" As Ava spoke, her eyes seemed to cloud over. A faint but unmistakable smile bloomed at the corners of her mouth. She continued.

"Through that intimacy, the armor falls away. We break the surface tension called 'self' and merge, like rain on the ocean. We become naked and vulnerable again. That isn't the loss of innocence, but its reclamation. You like me, don't you?"

"Y-yes, but..." Erin stammered, shuddering. Although she didn't understand it, her libido, so long suppressed by medication and social conditioning, was now, in the absence of those factors, flowering to life like a seed in the warmth of spring.

"It's ok," Ava said, leaning in to plant a light kiss on Erin's cheek. "I'll be here when you're ready."

* * *

Evening came and went without any word from Command, and a survey aboveground had detected no enemy pursuit. The two pandas lay on their sides in the absolute darkness, the elder's arm encircling her younger sister's waist. Erin was not, Ava had explained, in full withdrawal, but adjusting to the decreased dosage. This entailed shivering and endless nervous twitches that were not exactly painful, but unpleasant in some extreme yet indefinable way.

"*If this isn't full withdrawal,*" Erin thought, "*I'd hate to see what is!*"

Ava stirred behind her. "Can't sleep?"

"No…" A powerful tremor tore through Erin's body and she whimpered.

"I know a trick that might help," Ava said. "Do you want me to try?"

"Anything!" She had an inkling of what was about to happen, but was too miserable to refuse anything that might ease her predicament. And so Ava went to work, nuzzling Erin's neck while playing her most delicate place with the deftness of a concert violinist. To Erin, feverish and dysphoric amidst the bedlam of her vacillating internal chemistry, the sweet tingling of her sister's touch was like a pleasant day-dreamt island floating on a sea of nightmares. Mixed up in all this was an acute awareness of her sister's arousal. Though there was nothing tactile to suggest its existence; she just knew somehow, and the knowing pleased her.

At last, kneaded to the point of release for the first time in her life, she cried out wordlessly into the subterranean night, her voice rebounding in ever-fainter echoes until it joined with the silent earth. Panting, she allowed herself to be soothed by Ava's cooing. She had expected that the spasms would pass after that, but was disappointed when they returned full force in less than a minute.

"I thought you said I would sleep," she complained.

"A few more times," Ava said, chuckling, "and you will."

* * *

The alarm sounded just after midnight and that meant action. Ava was first on her feet, so eager to check the receiver that she almost went over without switching the lantern on first. Erin was on her heels.

"It's from Dobbins," Ava announced. The Dobbins base had been the staging point of their operation. It was one of the most secure facilities for thousands of kilometers, so they could be sure any transmission with that ID tag was legit.

In light of recent events, Command was not messing around with the encryption: a standard-issue receiver like this one couldn't even pretend to decipher the information it was gathering. In this instance, that was because the string of numbers constituted a set of instructions for an ultrasound projector made to interface with a living brain. Such technology was in extreme scarcity; there was no way terrorists would have anything like it. Ava and Erin did, though, and it was parked right outside, ready to go.

They both understood, without having to discuss it, that they would have to mobilize soon, perhaps even immediately. That left only the matter of the inktext, those pamphlets which were doubly contraband on account of being both non-electronic (and therefore unregulatable) and religious, which would have to be burned in the name of duty. But when they locked eyes there was an exchange, neither verbal nor of body language, but as though understanding passed between them on invisible wisps of aether.

"We'll say we were afraid the smoke would give away our location," Ava said.

Erin executed a stiff nod. "We agreed they're dangerous," she replied, bemused.

"They are words that contain ideas, and any idea can be dangerous if people make it so. Does that give us the right to take their choice away?"

They exited the cave, the earthen womb that had kept them safe and warm in the face of the storm. It was still dark outside, but a gibbous moon shone down from the western sky, reflecting off the blanched panorama of hills and trees. The cold bit into Erin's nostrils and the insides of her ears.

Ava climbed into the spider to get their orders while Erin dug for the inhaler she'd lost in the shadow of the *waschbär*. It took some effort, but when she found it, she was able to put it into her pocket without using it.

"They want us to rendezvous with the caravan over on seventy-six," Ava said. "We can make it by dawn if we hurry."

Erin, seized with a sudden impulse, went to her sister and leaned in through the armor's hatchway, kissing her on the lips before recoiling with a start, like she'd just realized she had important business elsewhere. She stood there, fidgeting and frowning at the thought imposing itself into her newly minted contentment.

"I don't want to hurt anyone," she said. "I won't. I'll find a way."

"Maybe you will," Ava said, composed and mild. "I never did. One more for the road?"

Erin's response to this was to squeeze her eyebrows together and cock her head like a dog receiving an unfamiliar command.

"Radio silence," Ava said. "We don't know how long until we're alone together, either."

With that, meaning flooded into Erin's awareness like a preview of the dawn some scant hours in the future. Once more, she bent her body so that she might taste her sister's mouth, which she did with such fierce hunger, growling, scissoring her jaw, that she half-frightened herself. It was true that she didn't know how long it would be until she could be alone with Ava again. All she could do was hope it would be soon.

Later, it began to snow. It was not like the vicious, sleet-laden stuff blown in on a blizzard's storm-winds, but light and slow-falling, like strands of fine lace. The snowflakes settled like weary congregants into the hollow footprints the two had left behind. By sunrise, it would have been impossible to say whether they had come that way at all.

*Cortraire Cunor faces the twin problems of nepotism—or of reverse-nepotism; being denied a merited advancement because of having a famous name, and it would look like nepotism—and of being in the shadow of a more popular sibling. Here is how he gets out of them.*

*"My Brother's Shadow" takes place in the fox nation of Expermia on the anthropomorphic world of Clorth, the same setting as Anglin's "On the Run from Isofell" in* Gods with Fur. *See also Anglin's five* Silver Foxes *books; especially the third,* Prelude to War *(CreateSpace, October 2013).*

# My Brother's Shadow

## by M.R. Anglin

"I don't understand." Cortraire stood with his hands behind his back. "I'm more than qualified. I have the hours. And you denied my promotion anyway?"

"That's about the size of it." The Grand Councilwoman, Lirai Cunor, sat in a mahogany chair behind the oak desk in her office. Both the chair and the desk had been carved with various Expermian animals, but the traiungo, a lizard-like mammal, had the most presence. In fact, the Cunor family seal featured two traiungai, one gold and one silver, fighting in such a way that they formed a circle. That seal had been carved on the front of the Grand Councilwoman's desk and mounted on the white stone wall. The walls also had the Expermian gods and goddesses carved all over them.

The Grand Councilwoman herself had her own sort of presence. Her graying brown hair peeked out from under a green cloche hat with an emerald embedded on the front. Like all Expermians her hair turned a different color at the ends, and Cortraire saw the bluish-green tips on the edges. Her brown fur had also started graying, but she wore it with an air of dignity that dared anyone to say anything disparaging about it. Her ears—as long as the length of her head—drooped a bit at the ends, showing her age, but her olive eyes shone bright—accentuated by the wrinkles that formed around her eyes when she smiled. By all accounts, she was a beautiful vixen, and age had only enhanced that. She sat with her slender hands clasped on the table and her chin raised, a picture of the leader of Expermia's Grand Council.

Beside her stood General Cunor, the highest ranking military officer in the Expermian army. Like Cortraire, he wore the black, blue, and silver uniform of the Expermian military, but his came complete with a variety of medals on his chest. Cortraire's only had the insignia depicting his rank as Private 3rd class. The General's stomach also had a paunch to it. Cortraire couldn't remember the last time he had done any type of exercise.

Cortraire ran his hands through the brown hair he had inherited from the Grand Councilwoman. His hair, however, turned a shade of blonde at the ends. "*Grammai*, I—"

"Ah, ah, ah," The Grand Councilwoman wagged her finger in the air. "That's Mrs. Grand Councilwoman."

"Excuse me?"

The Grand Councilwoman gave him a smile that could silence a crying baby and set him giggling.

Cortraire clenched his teeth. "Okay, then, *Mrs. Grand Councilwoman*. Can you at least tell me why I won't be promoted to Corporal? This is the third time my application has been denied. My commanding officers have all recommended me, and—"

"Aw, honey, this isn't about your qualifications as a soldier." She stood, revealing an iridescent green and blue dress. It had two splits up either side. Underneath, she wore a skirt that flowed onto the ground. Long pieces of cloth called *toagae* hung from her shoulders held in place with pins that had the family seal carved on it. The flurry of fabric flitting as she moved dazzled Cortraire's eyes. "This is about your qualifications as a Cunor."

Cortraire started. "Excuse me?"

"We Cunors have a name to uphold, a reputation that goes back generations." The Grand Councilwoman turned to the window behind her desk. She beckoned to Cortraire to stand beside her. "When you climb military ranks, you're putting yourself in front of the public. High ranking Cunors need to have Expermia's complete confidence." She looked out on the scene below her office.

Her office had been built on the top floor of the western spire of the government complex. The view overlooked the main courtyard where the Silver Fox fountain stood in the center of the lawn. People milled around below, taking pictures or heading down the sidewalk along on their way.

"My issue with you is how you conduct yourself." The Grand Councilwoman turned to Cortraire. "How can I possibly trust your judgment when you chose that..." she paused to find the right word, "... low class citizen to be your wife?"

Cortraire let his ears angle back. "Is this about Annais?"

"This is about your ability to make sound decisions as is exemplified in your choice of Annais." The Grand Councilwoman batted her eyes.

"Don't you know that every decision you make is scrutinized? And I did try so hard to warn you away from her."

"You can't be serious!" Cortraire swung around to his father. "*Papai...* sir, I mean... is that really the reason?"

General Cunor nodded. "It is."

"There, see?" The Grand Councilwoman crossed the room to pat her son's cheek. "I am trying to preserve our family name, Cortraire. You had the option of joining me on that quest by choosing from a variety of good Expermian families for your wife... or even from families with a high SF index... but you had to stoop for a Kirion."

"I didn't *stoop* for anyone." Cortraire let his ears fall flat. "The Kirion family is a lovely, proud, intelligent set of people, and you'd know that if you spent the time to get to know them."

"I don't need to know anyone from *that* family." The Grand Councilwoman took her seat, "Particularly after what happened at the wedding."

"So they had a good time." Cortraire shrugged. "They're a big family, and they get loud—"

"I hate big families."

"You came from one."

"That's why I hate them." The Grand Councilwoman laced her fingers and rested her chin on them. "Unless a couple has a high SF index which precipitates them to keep trying until they have a Silver Fox—a thing I believe will only happen with Marviot and Karalaina—I don't see a reason for an upstanding Expermian family to have more than one child." She eyed the General.

Cortraire stifled a growl that threatened to roll out of his throat. He was the younger of the General's two sons.

"Good morning, *Grammai!*" The door burst open. Marviot, Cortraire's older brother, walked in wearing the Expermian military uniform. He had red fur and green eyes that he had inherited from their deceased grandfather. His brown hair faded to a shade of blue at the ends.

"Marviot!" The Grand Councilwoman glided over to hug Marviot. "How are you this morning, my dear? Have you heard anything from Karalaina?"

"Apparently, her schoolwork has prevented her from coming home for spring break." Marviot sniffed.

"Again?" The Grand Councilwoman frowned. "I don't like this. She hasn't been home since she left for that Cultural Exchange Program. The girl is a Dúcume and has a 98% SF index rating. She's practically guaranteed to have a Silver Fox child once she gets married. I don't like that she's in an Outsider country for so long. She should be here where we can keep an eye on her."

"Never mind, *Grammai*." Marviot patted her shoulder. "I have it all under control. Make sure you don't forget about the meeting we're having this weekend with her parents. Once the paperwork is in process, I'll have her home in no time."

"I hope so." The Grand Councilwoman laced her fingers. "I can't wait to start planning your wedding. It will be the biggest celebration Expermia has ever seen."

Cortraire narrowed his eyes. She had barely showed any concern over planning his wedding.

"You will get to it soon, *Grammai*, but in the meantime, what's going on in here?" Marviot turned to Cortraire. "Your face could sour milk, Cortraire."

"He's upset because I won't approve his promotion to Corporal." The Grand Councilwoman waved her hand.

"You're not Corporal, yet?" Marviot's raised an eyebrow. "I thought you got promoted last year."

"It was denied." Cortraire bit his lips together to avoid saying anything he'd regret.

"Denied?" Marviot frowned. "Why?"

Cortraire's tail bristled, "Because of Annais."

"Cortraire, it has nothing to do with her." The Grand Councilwoman resumed her seat. "The fact of the matter is that you haven't acted in accordance with the Cunor name. You don't look like a Cunor, live like a Cunor, make decisions like a Cunor…" She sighed. "You lack that ambitious fire that all we Cunors have. So until you act in accordance to your name, I will not approve your promotion. Simple as that."

"That's not your decision to make, *Grammai*." Marviot sat on the corner of her desk. "You shouldn't have the power to promote or demote people in the military. It's outside of your jurisdiction."

"The only reason I asked to see you is because the General wouldn't talk to me unless you were present." Cortraire felt his fur settle.

"So what do you have to say for yourself, *Papai*?" Marviot turned to the General.

The Grand Councilwoman narrowed her eyes at him. "Yes, Nairon. What do you have to say?"

The General cleared his throat. He loosened his collar and glanced at his mother. "Until you act in accordance with your name, I will not approve your application." He grinned at her.

"You see?" The Grand Councilwoman folded her hands on the desk.

Marviot chuckled. "You're a vile, conniving, little cur, *Grammai*."

"You only say that because you love me." The Grand Councilwoman patted Marviot's hand.

Cortraire clenched his teeth together so hard, they squeaked. It took all he had in him not to explode. "If that's the end of it, I would like to be excused."

"Go ahead." The Grand Councilwoman waved him off.

Cortraire gave a stiff salute, swung around, and marched out of the office. He strode down the hall, muttering to himself.

"Cortraire, wait. Cortraire!" Marviot chased after him.

Cortraire waited until Marviot caught up with him. "What is it, Marviot?"

"Look, I know you're upset." Marviot put a hand on his shoulder. "Why don't you let me handle it? I'll go talk to them. You'll get that promotion in no time."

"I don't want you to do that." Every strand of fur on Cortraire's body bristled. "This isn't just about the promotion. This is about how they treat me. It's like they think I'm not good enough for the family."

Marviot inhaled through his teeth. "Well…"

Cortraire let his ears drop. "Don't tell me you agree with them, Marviot."

"When it comes to qualifications, Cor, there's no contest." Marviot threw up his hands. "Heck, you could even outrank me with the amount of work you do."

"Outrank you… you know, that reminds me. Why are you still the same rank as me?" Cortraire eyed Marviot. "You've been in the military three years longer than I have, and you're the golden child. Why aren't you a general by now?"

"That's exaggerating a little, Cortraire. I wouldn't be general by now." Marviot scratched his chin. "Major, maybe."

"I'm serious, Marviot."

"It's because I don't do the work." Marviot shrugged. "I'm too busy being Expermia's poster child… perfect family, perfect looks, perfect fiancé. I'm at openings, interviewed on TV, going on special assignments… secret missions."

"Secret missions?"

"Let me level with you, Cortraire. I could use a sounding board." Marviot's voice dropped to a whisper. "This does not go beyond us, but I've been on the trail of someone in the Council that's trying to undermine Expermia."

"What?"

"It's true." Marviot looked Cortraire in the eye. "This person is working with our enemies. I believe he has contacts with Outsiders and is trading weapons with them. I need to take them out ASAP." He clapped Cortraire on the back as his voice rose to a normal level. "The game's afoot, little brother. And I intend to win it. If you can help me out, I'd be grateful."

"How?"

Marviot shrugged. "If you hear something suspicious let me know. But mostly, keep it in the back of your mind. Sometimes you come up with things that I overlook."

"I see." Cortraire nodded.

"So with all that going on, I don't have time to do... whatever it is you all do at the base. It'll be too obvious if they promote me with no qualifications. However." Marviot held up a finger in the air. "Once all this is over and I marry Karalaina, I'll put my nose to the grindstone and surpass you in no time."

"Seems like that will be easy with them calling the shots." Cortraire glared over his shoulder at the closed office door. "I don't know what they want from me."

"They want you to stand up and act like a man, buddy." Marviot smacked Cortraire's chest with the back of his hand. "You're too soft-hearted, Cortraire. You have to show them you have what it takes to live up to our glorious name."

"And how am I supposed to do that?"

"I dunno." Marviot threw an arm over Cortraire's shoulder. "But I'll keep my eyes open. You do too. I'm sure an opportunity will present itself soon."

"Fine." Cortraire shrugged his brother's arm off. "I'll do that, but in the meantime, I have a bigger problem." He ran his hands over his hair. "I don't know what I'm going to tell Annais about this."

\* \* \*

Cortraire pulled up to his house tucked away in the Paimal District, a neighborhood nestled in among the poorer side of the wealthy set. He put his car in park and gazed up at the house. Palm trees shaded the front door and walk, and a lush garden tucked the house away from prying eyes. Annais had been excited to move here, but his father and grandmother had frowned at his choice. The house he had grown up in had open terraces, columns, large gardens, fountains, six bedrooms, and seven and a half bathrooms. But this house had only two bedrooms and two bathrooms. He could have gotten a bigger house… but perhaps he had a bit of snobbery in him. He couldn't see himself raising a family in a lesser neighborhood, but at the same time he couldn't justify spending more than he could afford to get a bigger house. But this… this place met all his needs—comfy, shaded from the desert heat, far enough from the city to be quiet, but close enough for an easy commute.

He shook his head as he got out of the jeep. "Even my choice of homes doesn't match up with the Cunor standard." He paused as he shut his door. His jeep was practical and easy to care for. "Or my choice in cars." He chuckled to himself as he walked up the walk. "I'm about as far removed from a Cunor as anyone could be." He walked into the house.

A washrag sailed through the family room and smacked the wall beside his head. He froze. Shouting and cheering welled up from the kitchen.

"Stop that, Andrais!" Annais' voice rocketed over all the noise. "You can't do that when Cortraire comes home."

Cortraire smiled. Looks like some of his in-laws had stopped in for a visit. Funny, he hadn't noticed another car in the driveway. He peeked out of the sidelight. Yup. There was Andrais' car—a tan, older model vehicle parked beside his jeep.

"I must have been more distracted than I thought." Cortraire picked up the rag and closed the door harder than usual—his way of announcing his presence without being too obvious. But shouting drowned out the door's slam.

"Don't get mad because your reflexes are dull, Ani," came Andrais' voice.

"My reflexes are fine." Annais sounded a bit out of breath. "You shouldn't be throwing things in the house."

"Oh, relax. I'll go get it." A vixen about Cortraire's age walked out of the kitchen. She had brown hair that flipped up at the ends revealing orange tips. She hesitated when she saw Cortraire. "Look who's here. The man of the house."

She, like most Expermian women, wore a traditional Expermian outfit—a long flowing dress with two high splits up the side and skin-tight pants worn underneath. She had her *toagae* wrapped around her waist.

"Good afternoon, Isa." Cortraire nodded at her. Isa wasn't her real name, but Cortraire never heard what her real name was.

"Formal little stiff, ain't cha?" Isa snatched the rag out of his hand. "When are you going to relax around me? And why are you standing at the door?"

Cortraire glanced around. He hadn't moved since he walked into the house. "I have no idea."

Isa gave a smirk. "Hey, Ani! Hubby's home!"

"Cortraire." Annais thrust her head out of the kitchen. "You're home already? Is it that late?"

"Yeah." Cortraire followed Isa to the kitchen. "I see we have some company." He waved at the two men sitting at the dining room table—two of Annais' brothers. They had the same brown hair that flipped up at the ends, but the tips of Andrais' hair turned violet at the ends, and Namone's turned green.

"Company, he says." Namone pounded and gave a raucous laugh. "Since when is family company?"

"Since Ani decided to marry a fancy-pants, rich Cunor." Isa tossed the rag in the sink. "Now she's all manners and raised pinkies." She plopped herself in a seat at the table.

"I haven't changed at all since I've been married." Annais turned from the sink, revealing her big stomach. "Have I?"

Cortraire sat at the table, his eyes fixed on Annais. He loved watching her. Like the rest of her family, Annais had brown hair that flipped up at the ends, but her hair turned a shade of pink at the ends—a pink Cortraire grew to love more each day. He loved her hazel eyes and the way her snout was a bit too big for her face. And he loved her tiny nose at the end of it. But most of all, he loved her growing stomach with their first child developing inside. He loved every single curve, strand, and line on her.

"Are you seriously asking if you've changed while you're wearing those designer clothes of yours?" Isa rested her cheek on her fist.

Annais slammed the bowl she had been washing in the sink. "I would love to go bargain hunting like I used to, but the Grand Councilwoman forbade me from going to the places we used to shop."

"You have private conversations with the Grand Councilwoman?" Andrais snickered. "Nope. You haven't changed at all."

"Would you guys stop it?" Annais threw the sponge in the sink. "I— oooh!" She rubbed the side of her stomach.

Cortraire hopped to his feet. "Annais, are you okay?"

"The baby is kicking right underneath my ribs. Look at this! I'm getting a bruise." Annais lifted her dress to show him.

By reflex, Cortraire looked away. Big mistake. Andrais and Isa burst into laughter.

"What are you looking away for, Cortraire?" Namone pounded his fist on the table. "You've already seen everything!"

"Unless there's something you and Ani aren't telling us..." Isa's tail flicked playfully.

Annais smacked her on the back of the head. "Stop being crude. Cortraire is... a gentleman. It wasn't that long ago we were practically strangers. We're... still getting used to each other." She rubbed her arm as color came to her cheeks.

Cortraire could have kicked himself. Even though his grandmother hadn't taken an interest in fixing him up with a wife like she had with Marviot, Cortraire hadn't taken the time to get to know Annais before he married her, a thing not uncommon among Expermian marriages. Cortraire adored Annais, but if he was honest with himself, her pregnancy was the result of duty—duty to Cortraire's family and Expermia to produce an heir to the Cunor name, duty to himself to be a man and provide a child, and duty to Annais to make her a mother. Now that he had fulfilled that duty... Cortraire felt a lump rise in his throat... maybe she wouldn't want him to touch her anymore. After all, his father and mother had never been affectionate. And when his father did hold her, his mother always showed a pained expression as if she didn't want him to touch her. Cortraire couldn't stomach the thought of Annais giving him that look.

"Wow. The fun got sucked out of this room real quick." Isa reached over to yank Annais' tail. "Come sit down, Ani. You've been standing since we got here." She vacated her seat.

"I can't." Annais pulled her tail from Isa's grasp. "I haven't even started dinner yet."

"It's not like we weren't distracting you at every moment." Isa pushed Annais into the chair.

"Don't worry about dinner, Annais." Cortraire stood to get the phone. "With this many guests, it'll be easier to order something tonight."

"Must be nice to be able to order food whenever you like." Isa snatched the phone from him. "Let me do it. This family has sophisticated tastes."

"In other words, they're picky." Annais nudged Isa with her toe. Isa stuck her tongue out at her.

"So, Cortraire, I hear you're up for a promotion." Andrais leaned close to him.

"How did you hear that?" Cortraire said.

"Sorry, I couldn't resist saying something." Annais clasped her hands. "So how'd it go?"

Cortraire averted his eyes. "I got passed over."

"What?" Annais dropped her hands. "Why'd they pass over you again?"

Cortraire shrugged. "I'm not qualified enough."

Annais stared at him with her eyes narrowed a bit. Cortraire stifled a shudder. In the short time he'd known her, he became well acquainted with that look. It meant, "I don't buy your bullcr—"

"That's too bad, Cor." Andrais clapped Cortraire's back, winding him. "But you gotta do better than that. You need to keep providing for our sister, you know."

"The military isn't like the rest of Expermia, Cortraire." Namone tapped his finger on the table. "You can't use your name to skate through."

Cortraire stared at his hands. If only he knew…"I'll have to try harder. Sorry I let you down."

"I know you can do it." Isa cupped her hand over the phone. "Just apply yourself like Marviot. Oh, man! Do I wish I was Karalaina. She is so lucky… Oh, hello?" She went back to the phone.

"Yeah, well… we can't all be Marviot." Cortraire leaned back in his chair. Annais caught his attention. She watched him with that same expression, but now her mouth pinched together. There would be no peace in the house tonight until she got to the bottom of this.

Cortraire cursed silently and closed his eyes. Would nothing go right today?

\* \* \*

"Bye, Andrais. Bye, Namone. Later, Isa!" Annais hopped a bit as she waved at her family.

"Drive safely!" Cortraire stood beside her and waved.

"See you later!" Isa leaned out of the window as they drove off. She kept waving as they went down the road.

"Your family is so much fun." Cortraire chuckled at the neighbor's wondering eyes looking after them.

"Noisy, though." Annais turned back into the house. "It's always so quiet when they leave."

"But at least they tidy up after themselves." Cortraire walked into the house. Everything gleamed in the fading light.

"Makes the house seem emptier than it is." Annais smoothed down her hair.

Cortraire shut the door. It echoed across the house, announcing that he and Annais were alone together. A lump grew in his throat—

He shook his head. She was his wife. No need to be nervous around her. He glanced at her out of the corner of his eye. Annais ran her hand through her hair over and over, trying to get her flyaway ends to stay down.

"Stop that." Cortraire gently slapped her hand out of her hair.

"Nervous habit." Annais took a deep breath. "Be honest with me, Cortraire. Do you mind when my family visits?" She took to rubbing her stomach.

"Why would I mind?" Cortraire watched her. He would have loved to touch her stomach, to feel his son or daughter bump and jump around in there, but… all he could see when he imagined touching her was his mother's pained expression. He turned away from Annais.

"It's just that… your family seems to take issue with them." Annais stretched her back.

"My family takes issue with everything." Cortraire returned his gaze to her stomach. "How are your ribs?"

"Sore. Very, very sore." Annais rubbed the place in question. "Honestly, this kid does not want to settle down. Every time I think he's fallen asleep, he starts up again on the other side."

"He? Annais, did you look at the gender report?" Cortraire sighed. "I thought we decided not to."

"I didn't look, but he's so active that I figure he must be a boy. Maybe we should check to see if I'm right." Annais edged to the side table where they had stashed the report. A smile played at her lips.

"Oh, no you don't." Cortraire caught her hand. He laughed as he pulled her close to him. "Don't you dare, you little…" He trailed off. He held her so close to him that he felt the baby kick. Annais gazed into his face with an expression he'd never seen before. He let her go. "Sorry…" he muttered.

"Cortraire, you don't have to—ow!" Annais massaged her stomach.

Cortraire's ears perked. "Are you okay?"

"He kicked me right in the sore spot." Annais leaned on the back of the couch. "Man, this hurts."

"Um… do you want some tea? I can make you some Caronine tea. It's supposed to be calming. Maybe it will get the baby to relax."

"I'll try anything." Annais allowed Cortraire to help her into the kitchen. He set her down at the table and went to the cupboard. "I've never heard of Caronine tea."

Cortraire took five of the tea canisters from the cabinet above the sink. "It's a blend of five different teas. My mother used to be a professional, certified tea sommelier before *Papai* made her quit. Apparently, my grandfather didn't like tea." He scooped a bit of each into a tea infuser.

"She loved this. She used to drink it all the time." He dropped the infuser into a mug of hot water from the kettle.

"I can imagine to deal with your family." Annais rested her cheek on her hands. "They're a bit stiff and stuffy for my tastes."

"But it's still my family." Cortraire smiled at Annais over his shoulder.

"I guess they can't be all that bad if they raised you."

Cortraire turned back to his task. Once the tea had infused into the water enough, he mixed in some honey and set it before Annais.

"No milk?"

"Try it first."

She took a sip. "Mmm... this is good."

"Glad you like it." Cortraire washed out the infuser in the sink.

"So." Annais took another sip. "You want to tell me the real reason you didn't get the promotion?"

Cortraire's ears twitched. He thought she had forgotten about that. "I told you, Annais. I'm not qualified—"

"Oh, please, Cortraire. Everyone knows you're an overachiever. You'd do anything for Expermia. You don't meet qualifications, you exceed them." Annais tapped her finger on the table like her brother had earlier. "To say you're not qualified is a bold-faced lie, and I hate when you lie to me, Cortraire. So tell me the real reason before I get angry."

Cortraire turned off the faucet and wiped the counter before sitting beside her at the table. "My grandmother doesn't believe I'm enough of a Cunor to warrant a promotion."

"What is that supposed to mean?" Annais slammed her mug on the table. Surprisingly, none of the tea splashed on the table.

"I'm good enough for my family, I suppose."

"And what, pray tell, are the requirements of being a Cunor?" Annais crossed her arms.

"I'm too soft-hearted according to Marviot."

"How is that a bad thing? You're fair to everyone, regardless of who their family is or their SF ranking."

"I'm not ambitious enough."

"In other words, you're not ruthless." Annais raised her mug for another sip of tea.

"And my grandmother takes issue with my life choices."

"What do you mean by that?"

"You know... where I chose to live, what I drive, who I marri—" Cortraire clamped his mouth shut.

"Who you're what?" Annais set down her cup. "Wait... who you *married?*"

Cortraire closed his eyes and felt his ears fall. He hadn't mean to go there.

"Is the Grand Councilwoman punishing you because of me?"

"No, Annais." Cortraire waved his hands. "She said it has nothing to do with you."

"That's BS, and you know it." She slammed her palm on the table, but it lacked the power that she had before. "I can't believe that old crone!"

"Annais, please calm down." Cortraire patted her hand.

"Don't tell me to calm down." Annais jerked her hand from his grasp. She drank some more tea. Her fur settled. After a few more sips, she tilted her head to the side. Her eyes closed slightly—as if she wanted to sleep.

"I'm sorry, Annais." Cortraire hung his head. A Cunor wouldn't have made such a dumb mistake.

"Cortraire." Annais placed her hand on his. "Don't beat yourself up. You'll get a chance to show them what you're made out of. Just wait. Your time is coming."

Cortraire forced a smile. "Marviot said the same thing."

"I can't believe we agree." Annais ran her finger around the lip of the mug. "But we always seem to agree when it comes to you." She yawned. "You have an effect on us... or is it affect? Why do those words sound so similar?" Her words started to run together.

Cortraire gazed at her. "Are you okay? How's the tea working?"

"This stuff is amazing." Annais stretched out on the table. "I feel great."

"Did the baby stop kicking?"

"I think he's kicking harder." Annais rested her head on her arm. "But I'm so relaxed right now, I don't even care." She poked her stomach. "Kick harder, little guy. I can take it."

"*Mamai* never acted like this after drinking that tea." Cortraire inhaled though his teeth. "Maybe I used too much sanpan in the blend."

Annais reached up to stroke Cortraire's cheek. "You know something, Cortraire, you are a handsome, handsome fox." She let her hand drop. "So very handsome."

"Yeah... too much sanpan." Cortraire took the mug from her reach and emptied out the rest of the tea. Next time, he'd have to adjust the recipe a bit—if he ever made it for her ever again.

\* \* \*

The Expermian government's Capitol building had been built with four spires, each one dedicated to the different branches of the government. One spire held the Grand Council's offices and the Grand Councilwoman's residence. Another housed a special temple that allowed members of the Grand Council and their families to worship the separate Expermian gods in private. Yet another had been dedicated to Expermia's justice system and housed the country's Supreme Court. And the last spire held the country's military headquarters.

Cortraire gazed up at the building as he made his way to Tempagole, the capital's military base. He never got enough of those spires rising into the air or of the stained-glass windows depicting scenes from Expermia's volatile history. He found the Capitol beautiful beyond words.

His pants vibrated. Cortraire fished his phone from his pocket. "Hello?"

"Where are you, Cor?" Marviot said over the line.

"I'm heading to the Temp." Cortraire kept walking. "I'm passing the Capitol. Why?"

"Stay right there, I'm coming out."

"But I've got training soon. I—hello?" Marviot had hung up. Cortraire slipped the phone back in his pocket. "I better not be late." He leaned on the gate surrounding the Capitol and waited.

"Cortraire!" Marviot jogged out of the Capitol to greet him. "Glad I caught you. Today is your lucky day!"

"What's up, Marv?" Cortraire pointed in the direction he had been going. "I can't stop for long. I've got training soon, and I have to change."

"Forget about that." Marviot threw his arm around Cortraire's shoulder. "I have a proposition for you... an opportunity, if you will." He held up an envelope in two fingers. "This is an official order for you to participate in an important military assignment." He dangled it in front of Cortraire's face.

"What?" Cortraire snatched the envelope. "But I've never received an assignment like this before. They only ever ask someone like you."

"I know." Marviot tickled his whiskers. "I had to pull a lot of strings. Say thank you."

"Thank you, Marviot. Thank you!" Cortraire ripped open the envelope. "I can't believe this is happening. I—" He paused to read the order. "Marviot, this is addressed to you."

"That is true, but I can't do it." Marviot released Cortraire. He walked in circles around him. "I made plans to go see Karalaina this weekend. And when I get back, I have to get back to the 'game'... you know the one. So I want you to go instead."

"That's not how it works, Marviot." Cortraire stuffed the order back in the envelope.

"It works that way if I say it does."

"Marviot…"

"Cortraire, get off your high horse and think. This is an opportunity for you… an opportunity to show you are 100% Cunor stock." Marviot wrapped his arm around Cortraire's neck. "Look at this." He pulled the order out of the envelope. "This is addressed to Private 3rd Class Cunor. That could be you as well as me."

"It says Private 3rd Class Cunor, M.," Cortraire tapped the name. "Besides, you don't go by Private 3rd Class. You said, and I quote, 'I don't care if *Lance Corporal* is a depreciated term. Lance Corporal sounds more distinguished than Private 3rd Class.' You required everyone to call you that. You even got *Papai* to implement it all around."

"All except in official papers like this one, and that worked out well for me. And for you because now all we have to do is white out the 'M.'"

"Do you know how much trouble we can get into?"

"I'll get *Papai* to sign off on it." Marviot dropped his arms. "It's not that big a deal, Cortraire."

"Marviot, I don't like this…"

"I'll level with you." Marviot stood in front of him to look him in the eye. "I have to go see Karalaina this weekend. Her fascination with Outsiders is getting out of hand, and her parents don't seem to have any control over it. I have to go remind her about what's important and snap her out of it before she ruins her life. Besides, this favor isn't only for me. This is your chance to repay me." He patted Cortraire's cheek.

"Repay you for what?"

"When you decided to marry Annais… for whatever reason you decided to marry her… I stood up for you. I bore the brunt of *Grammai's* wrath so you could get what you wanted."

"Marviot…"

"You will never get a chance like this. If you do well, *Grammai* won't be able to deny your worth to this family. You'll be promoted in no time."

"Well…"

"And what about Annais? Don't you want to rise through the ranks for her? To show her the finer things in life that she wouldn't experience otherwise?" Marviot held the order in front of Cortraire. "This could propel you forward down that road."

That did it. Cortraire reached out and took the paper.

"That's my bro." Marviot clapped Cortraire on the back. "All you have to do is show up, do what you're told, and smile for the cameras when you get back. One more thing…" He tapped the order. "Briefing's in 30." He walked off, waving as he went.

When he was gone, Cortraire held the order up to the light. He grinned. Finally. His first special assignment. Opportunity had graced him with this chance, and in thirty minutes, he—

Cortraire read the order then glanced at his watch. "Marviot, you moron! The briefing's not in 30. It's in five!" He charged into the government building and darted to the elevator. He had to make it to his commanding officer's office in time or they'd never take him seriously again.

\* \* \*

Cortraire barreled down the hall toward Colonel Bain's office. Soldiers and civilian staff members stared as he sprinted past them. He skidded to a halt outside the office and glanced at his watch. One minute to spare. He smoothed down his hair, straightened his jacket, and paused to take a deep breath before he knocked.

"Come."

Cortraire entered. "Private 3rd Class Cunor reporting, sir." He saluted.

The office had a long table with three officers sitting behind it. In the middle sat Colonel Bain, to the left Major Tairan, and to the right Lt. Colonel Devaine. The window behind their seats overlooked the training field where soldiers ran obstacle courses, jogged laps around the base, or exercised in neat rows with a training officer barking at them.

"Ah, Private Cunor." Colonel Bain stood. His voice had a rich, deep quality that impressed Cortraire. The way he pronounced his words—so carefully and with such majesty struck a chord with him. Bain demanded attention, focus, and respect without having to say so. "What a pleasure it is to meet... wait. You're not Marviot Cunor."

Crap. Cortraire knew this wouldn't work. But he was in too deep now. "No, sir. My given name is Cortraire."

"But I thought we were getting Private Cunor." Bain sank into his chair. "You're not Cunor."

"I am, sir. Private Cortraire Cunor, sir." When he saw the confusion in his face, he added. "I'm Marviot's brother."

"Cunor has a brother?" Tairan angled one of his ears. He had black hair that faded to white at the ends and a scar across his cheek.

"He's not too well known." Devaine said. He had red hair that faded to orange at the end.

Cortraire narrowed his eyes. "Apparently, my grandmother keeps my existence quiet."

"I can see why." Tairan rested his head on his hands. "You don't have that Cunor presence."

Cortraire clenched his teeth to keep from saying anything.

"I was looking forward to meeting Marviot Cunor." Bain ran his hand over his hair—blonde with robin's egg blue tips. "How did I make that mistake?" He opened his file. "Oh, look at that. It really does say, 'Private 3rd Class Cunor.'"

Cortraire's ears pricked. Marviot must have gotten all this changed before he had even approached Cortraire. The sneak… as manipulative as their grandmother.

"Easy mistake to make." Devaine sat straight. "But Marviot prefers 'Lance Corporal.'"

"Isn't that a depreciated term?" Bain sat tall and still.

"In Expermia, at least," Devaine folded his hands on the desk. "I think Outsiders use it in some branches of their military."

"Let's get back to the point." Tairan slapped his hand on the table. "If they sent him along, he at least must be qualified."

"I can vouch for that." Devaine drummed thumbs on the table. "He's served under me a couple of times. Diligent, disciplined, conscientious… honestly, I can't say why he's still a private."

"Maybe they don't want him to overshadow his brother." Bain studied Cortraire. "Marviot is set to be the next Grand Councilman."

"Could be." Devaine laced his fingers. "If Marviot spent more time in training rather than doing PR, he'd be Captain by now."

"Gentlemen, we are not here to discuss Marviot's training schedule." Tairan snorted. "We are here to finish this briefing."

"Quite right." Bain reviewed his file. "Here's the crux of it, Cunor. The terrorists are… for lack of a better word… terrorizing the citizens in the desert areas near the Expermian border to Itzputza."

"They've been running around, killing people, kidnapping women, and attacking the local government areas." Devaine clenched his fists on the table.

"We have taken out many of their bases, but they keep popping up." The corner of Tairan's lip rose. "We can't even identify which of the Outsiders' nations have sent them, and none of them will claim responsibility for their attacks."

Cortraire nodded. The terrorist threat in the Western Desert had dampened textile commerce with the Western Desert Clan. According to news reports, the government had the attacks under control, but deep down, everyone knew better. No civilian wanted to go drive down there to pick up the goods and transport them back to the capital.

"We got a tip that their leader is located in a new base." Devain slid a map in front of Cortraire. "We've located it here." He tapped the map.

"Your team will go in and eradicate that base and anyone in it." Bain's voice fell into a deep bass.

"Sounds simple enough." Cortraire took the map.

"You'll be with a section of troops." Tairan read from his paper. "Sergeant Kollan will be your commanding officer."

Bain leaned forward to Cortraire. "Those terrorists must be completely wiped out. I can't stress that enough. They are dangerous— amassing weapons that could destroy whole cities if we let them."

"I understand, sir," Cortraire said. "Only…"

"Go ahead," Bain said.

"Any particular reason why we're not sending troops from the Orantaine base to handle this?" Cortraire studied the map. "It's right there next to the target. It seems to me, sirs, that it would be a waste to send troops from the capital there when there are already troops stationed there."

Silence fell. Devaine and Tairan turned to look at Bain whose ears fell slightly. Perhaps this had been a source of previous discussion among them. Bain's eyes narrowed a bit and his mouth pressed together. It felt like a shadow descended on the office.

Cortraire stepped back. "Did… I ask a question I shouldn't have?"

"Not at all." Bain shook his head. The shadow passed over. "The truth of the matter is… I have long believed that a member of the military stationed at that base is in cahoots with the terrorists. How else could they continue to evade us? That stays within this room, by the by."

"Of course, sir," Cortraire said.

"Orantaine is my base, Cunor." Bain leaned forward. "I finagled my way over to the Capitol to get help in figuring out what's going on there. We keep bombing the terrorists' hideouts, and the same group keeps popping up. I am determined to sort this out."

Cortraire swallowed hard. Marviot had mentioned the same thing a few weeks ago. "I understand fully, sir. I'll keep my eyes open and report anything suspicious."

"Good lad." Bain patted the table in front of him. "When the threat is eliminated, your triumph will be broadcast all over Expermia. You, sir, will become a hero in the people's eyes… much like your brother."

Cortraire couldn't stop the smile from coming on to his face. "That sounds good, sir."

"Excellent." Bain tapped his hands on his desk as he straightened up.

Cortraire slid the map back to the officers. "But, um, if I may, sirs…"

"Go ahead," Bain said.

"This is my first time on this type of assignment, and I want to know… is it usual for you to brief privates like this?" Cortraire held his hands behind his back.

"Yes, well, you're not just a private, are you?" Devain smiled. "You're a Cunor."

Cortraire nodded. "Yes, sir."

"You will be leaving this weekend." Bain stood. "May Hamatan, king of battles, grant you success." The other two stood.

Cortraire saluted.

"You're dismissed," Bain said.

Cortraire clicked his heels, turned, and marched out. Once he closed the door behind him, a smile spread across his lips. This was it… his chance to be seen as a hero to all of Expermia. His smile spread from ear to ear.

Wait until Annais heard about this.

\* \* \*

Cortraire eased the front door open and cocked his ears. He expected to hear the raucous laughing of his in-laws, a sound he needed a moment to process. Every day during this past week, one or more of Annais's siblings had come to visit her—her parents had even come to visit yesterday. They all seemed excited about something or other, but no one told him what they were celebrating. But today silence greeted him.

He walked into the house with his ears swiveling. He heard nothing. No laughter, no cheering, no screaming, no shouting. They must not have come over today. That meant he'd be alone with Annais this afternoon. His heart fluttered even as his stomach knotted.

"Get over yourself, Cortraire!" Cortraire slapped his cheeks. "She's your wife! You know, your father would have mastered this household by now. Your brother too. Heck, Marviot's even going over to the Outsider's country to handle his fiancée." He stopped in front of the front mirror hanging near the front door. "Everyone's right about you. You, sir, are no Cunor. Well, no more! From this moment on, you will start acting like a Cunor. You are going to go into that kitchen, grab your wife, kiss her all over her adorable face, and get over whatever fear is controlling your life! It doesn't matter what she says, you are going to take control!" He nodded to himself. "Right!"

"Annais!" Cortraire marched into the kitchen. Empty. "Annais?" He glanced out at the backyard where she liked to lay out sometimes.

Nothing. Then looked into the basement where the laundry room was and in the downstairs bathroom. *Nada.*

"Annais!" He shouted. No response.

"She must be out." Cortraire chuckled to himself. "I decide to behave like a Cunor, and there's no one around to practice on. Story of my life." He climbed the stairs. Best to get into more comfortable clothes before she came home.

He climbed the stairs and glanced at the nursery in his way to the Master Bedroom at the end of the hall. Annais stood in the center of the nursery gazing at the empty crib.

"Annais, there you are." Cortraire stepped in.

"Cortraire?" Annais swung around. "When did you get home?"

"Just now. I was calling for you. Didn't you hear me?"

"I was caught up in my thoughts. Sorry." Annais smoothed her hair down.

"Would you stop that?" Cortraire caught her hand and set it by her side. "What are you doing in here? Nesting?"

"I was, but there's nothing more to do." Annais tapped her elbows. "You know, Cortraire, I think this house might be a little small for our family."

Cortraire flicked his ears back. "I admit the house isn't the biggest in the world, but it'll do for the baby."

"I'm not so sure…"

"How much room can one kid take up, Annais?"

"What about our second?"

"Two kids can share this room." Cortraire wandered around inside of it. "It's big enough. And when the time comes, we can find a bigger place."

"That time might come sooner than you think, Cortraire."

Cortraire let his ears flatten. "I thought you liked this house, Annais. You gushed about it and about this neighborhood when we negotiating the price."

"I do like it. But I think that we may need more room than we originally anticipated."

Cortraire threw up his hands. "I don't believe this!"

"Don't believe what?"

"First my family, then the military, now you?" Cortraire clutched his hair. "No one thinks I can do anything! And now you think I can't provide a good enough house for my family?"

Annais stared at him a moment. "What are you talking about?"

"Forget it!" Cortraire marched out of the nursery. "This assignment couldn't have come at a better time."

"What assignment?" Annais followed after him. "Cortraire, come back!"

Cortraire marched into his bedroom. He tried to unbutton his uniform jacket, but his fingers fumbled at the buttons. He threw up his hands with a yell and plopped on the bed. Silence hovered over the house.

"I have never seen you so agitated." Annais leaned on the doorway, watching him.

Cortraire snorted.

"I wonder if this is what motherhood is going to be like," Annais muttered. She walked in and unbuttoned his jacket for him. "Go change your clothes." She patted his back.

Cortraire marched for the attached bathroom.

"So you want to explain to me what all this bluster is all about?" Annais followed him. "What assignment did you get?"

"I got orders today to go on a special military exercise." Cortraire threw off his jacket.

"Cortraire, that's great!" Annais clasped her hands. "I knew you'd get an opportunity!"

"You say that now."

"And what's that supposed to mean?"

"I have enough pressure from my family to measure up." Cortraire flung the jacket into the hamper. "I don't need you implying that I can't provide a good enough house for my children!"

"When did I say—oh, you mean when I… ugh!" Annais blew her bangs from out of her eyes. She took a deep breath through her nose. "I'm sorry, Cortraire. I didn't mean it that way. Honestly, I love this house. I don't want to move."

"Then why were you complaining that it's too small?"

All of Annais' hair rose. "Because I—" She halted and took a deep breath. Then she took another. And another. "Deep breath, Ani. Deep breath." She took one more and released it through her nose. "Okay." She turned her eyes to Cortraire. "Let's leave that alone for a moment. I can see you're upset about this. I'm sorry I said that. It's not what I meant. Let's leave it at that." She placed a hand on his cheek. "Okay?"

At her touch, all Cortraire's anger and frustration melted away. He placed his hand on hers. "Okay."

"So tell me about your assignment. Where are you going? What are you doing?"

"It's incredible, Annais. Wait till you hear." Cortraire paused to gather his thoughts. "This morning, Marviot came to me and—"

"Marviot?" Annais shook her head. "They give him so much leeway. What, do they have him giving the orders now?"

"Well, no. See, it was his assignment, and he passed it to me—"

"What? He can't do that."

"Apparently, he can. So anyway—"

"You can't take that assignment, Cortraire." Annais crinkled her nose like she did when she got angry. "This is Marviot's opportunity, not yours."

"What's the difference?"

"The difference is that you need to make them see *your* potential, not your brother's." Annais poked his chest. "You can't move up by hiding in his shadow."

Cortraire stiffened. Shadow? He wasn't hiding in anyone's shadow. "Annais, listen…"

"I don't need to listen. You can't take an assignment that was meant for someone else. It's wrong."

"I know, but—"

"This isn't like you, Cortraire." Annais narrowed her eyes slightly. "You're not this blindly ambitious."

"Would you let me finish a sentence?" Cortraire blurted. His heart pounded in his ears. "My goodness, woman, don't you shut up?"

Annais' eyes widened. Her mouth dropped open.

"I'm sorry you feel that way, Annais, but it's already done. I've accepted, been briefed, and I leave this weekend. That's it! You clucking about it is not going to change anything!" Cortraire pushed past her, stormed out of the bedroom, down the stairs, and out the front door. He slammed it behind him as hard as he could. Then he stood out in the hot air and panted through his teeth.

The heat of the afternoon sun tickled his skin. He scratched his scalp and sank onto the front step. "What is wrong with me?" He clutched his hair. In all his life, he had never been so angry. And he'd never blown up at Annais before. But her words… they stung. They punched him in the gut and left him winded. Under her scrutiny, his opportunity to impress her deflated like a balloon.

He buried his face in his hands. "Why do I fail so hard at life?"

"You don't fail at life."

Cortraire picked up his head. Annais eased herself down beside him.

"At least, you don't fail when you're not trying to be someone else." She inhaled through her teeth. "Calm down in there." She rubbed her stomach. "I'm having a moment with your father."

Cortraire averted his eyes. He couldn't bring himself to look at her.

"Cortraire, is there anything I can say to talk you out of going on this assignment?"

"No."

"Then at least promise me one thing." Annais placed a hand on his chest. "When the time comes, show them what *you* can do. Don't go out there trying to prove you're good enough to be a Cunor. Prove to them that they are lucky to have you in the Cunor family."

Cortraire dared to look at her. Her deep, wise eyes met his without faltering. He nodded.

"One more thing." Annais shoved him. "Don't you ever speak to me that way again! '*Clucking*'? 'Don't you ever shut up, woman'? Are you serious?" She poked his chest with her nail. "I'm your wife, but that does not give you the right to disrespect me. You got that?"

Cortraire stared at her. Her hair stood on end, waving and dancing in the wind. A laugh slid out of his mouth before he could stop it.

"Are you laughing at me?"

"No, no, no. I'm not." Cortraire waved his hands. "I promise I'm not. It's just… you've never hesitated to call me out. I really appreciate that about you." He took her hands. "I'm sorry about what I said. It won't ever happen again."

"It better not." Annais pressed her lips together. "You are so lucky you are cute." She smoothed down his hair then tapped his chin. "A little rumpled, but adorable."

"If getting rumpled is all that's happened after getting into an argument with you, I'm lucky."

"You're right." Annais hefted herself to her feet. Cortraire jumped up to help her. "Cortraire, there's one more request I want to make of you: please come home safely." She pushed her stomach out a bit. "I want these kids to know their father, okay?"

"Of course I'll come home, Ani." Cortraire shrugged. "I've been trained for this. I'll be fine."

Annais stared at him a moment. "Boy, hints fly right over your head, don't they?"

Cortraire turned to her. "Huh?"

"Never mind." Annais smirked. "I'm going to have so much fun with this. Now if you'll excuse me, I'm going to price twin-sized beds." She walked into the house.

"Why? We have plenty of beds."

Annais snickered at him. "Right over your head." She walked to the kitchen. "I'll start dinner."

Cortraire hesitated in the entryway. Hints? What hints? He shut the door and sighed. One day, maybe he'd be able to understand his wife.

\* \* \*

"Bye, Annais." Cortraire tossed his things into the back of his jeep.

"You stay safe, okay, Cortraire?" A dry breeze fluttered through Annais' hair and flitted the dress that hugged her curves before draping off of her growing stomach. The rising sun tinted her hair with gold. Cortraire bit his bottom lip. Boy, she looked nice today. It almost made him want to skip the mission and stay home.

"Are you going to be okay while I'm gone?" Cortraire scratched his hair. "I know you like to overextend yourself, and—"

"Jazzie's coming to help me while you're gone, so don't worry." Annais clasped her hands together. "I can't wait to spend time with my baby sister."

"Okay… but don't push yourself too hard." Cortraire pressed his hand on one of hers. "Take it easy while I'm gone. I told Marviot to look out for you. He'll be gone this weekend, but he should be back by the beginning of the week."

"I know that, Cortraire. You told me already."

"Okay, but if anything happens, call him." Cortraire reached for the car door. "Oh, and before I forget… when we were younger and *Papai* had to go away, he gave us a keyword. All we had to do was say it to anyone in the military, and they'd get him a message to contact us as soon as possible. I've set one up for you with Marviot. If there's an emergency, tell him 'krakken.' If you send him a written message, make sure you spell it with two 'k's. You don't have to tell him what the emergency is, but if he hears the keyword, he'll find a way to contact me no matter where I am."

"Would you stop worrying about me, Cortraire?" Annais rolled her eyes. "You're the one who's going off to war. I should be worrying about you."

"It's not war, Annais." Cortraire shook his head. "Marviot's told me about these types of missions. It's easy; you go in; you follow orders; you come back and smile for the cameras when they interview you. Simple."

"That doesn't make me worry less." Annais bit her lips together. "Promise me you'll stay safe, and you won't do anything stupid."

"I won't. I mean, I will... I mean..." Cortraire took a deep breath. "I'll come back to you fine. Nothing will keep me away."

Annais wrapped her arms around him and buried her face in his uniform—desert camouflage this time. Cortraire froze a moment before wrapping his arms around her. Her scent wafted up into his nostrils—a pleasant mix of lemon cleanser, milk, honey, and lilac perfume.

"Remember what I told you," she whispered in his ear. "This is your time to shine."

"I will." Cortraire pulled away from her. "I should go."

"Call me when you're leaving the base, okay?"

Cortraire got in the jeep. "See you in a few days."

Annais waved at Cortraire as he took off down the road. He watched her in the rearview until she faded out of sight. Man, he missed her already.

When he got to the city, he parked in the secure lot across the street and headed to the briefing room he had been assigned to.

A group of 24 soldiers—both foxes and vixens—had converged in the room. They all wore the same desert colored camouflage, and all had a duffel bag with their personal items inside. They stood in groups talking, laughing, and murmuring. Cortraire slipped in and sat in a corner on one of the many benches in the room. He chuckled to himself. This felt remarkably like secondary school. He was always the quiet kid. It took a lot of courage for him to walk over and talk to Annais for the first time.

The door opened and a soldier walked in. He had red hair that faded to a shade of green at the ends. Cortraire recognized him as Sergeant Kollan, one of Marviot's acquaintances.

Cortraire groaned. As the first person to see him, he had to call the group to attention. He stood and called in a loud voice, "At ease, soldiers!"

The entire group quieted. They turned to the door and waited for the sergeant to speak.

"Good morning. Glad to see you all awake and alert." Kollan stood in the front of the room with his hands behind his back. "When I looked through our orders, I noticed that most of you have served with me on similar missions in the past. I look forward to serving with you again. Seeing as though you all know how this works, we'll skip the official briefing... unless there's someone who wants it?" His eyes scanned the crowd.

Cortraire stood still. He had been briefed already and had gotten the rundown from Marviot, so he didn't need a refresher. But... one soldier—a skinny fox with black hair that faded to blonde—shifted as he stood. The way he stood, a little shaking but tight, told Cortraire this may be his first assignment ever.

"Excuse me." Cortraire raised his hand. "I wouldn't mind a brief rundown, if you don't mind."

Everyone turned to him. Some snickered.

"Ah, yes." The sergeant narrowed his eyes at Cortraire, trying to see his nametag. "I'm sorry; I don't recognize you. You are…"

"Private 3rd Class Cunor." Cortraire stood at attention.

"Cunor?" Kollan's ears pricked. "You're not Marviot."

Cortraire stifled a curse. "I'm his brother, Cortraire."

"Cortraire? Ah. I haven't seen you since you were in school. Filled out a bit, didn't you? Ugh! I thought I would be working with Marviot today. This is annoying." Kollan glared at Cortraire. "Well then, since *Cunor* here needs a refresher, I suppose we'll have to waste time indulging him. This assignment…"

Cortraire sighed as Kollan went over their objective. What a perfect way to start the day.

"You really put your foot in it, Cunor." A vixen whispered to him. Her nameplate read, "Artis." She had dark eyes, and short black hair that faded to blue at the ends. "You should have kept your mouth shut."

"I know that," Cortraire whispered back.

"Then why didn't you?"

Cortraire motioned to the skinny soldier. "Something tells me he had no idea what was going on."

"Really?" Artis narrowed her eyes at the soldier. "And what does that have to do with you?"

"Not a thing." Cortraire shook his head. Marviot was right; he was too soft-hearted. He should have kept his mouth shut and let the kid take care of it himself. But then, this wasn't a game. Going out there without knowing what was happening could be deadly. "I'm such a sucker," Cortraire muttered.

"And that's the crux of our assignment." Kollan tapped the map behind him. "Any questions, Cunor?"

"I'm good," Cortraire said.

"Then suit up. Get your equipment from the armory, and let's get going." Kollan clapped his hands. "Move!"

The entire group started moving and gathering their things.

"Kirion." Kollan called across the room over the noise of the crowd. "You ready for this?"

A soldier, older than most in the room, nodded. "I'll have everything ready by the time we leave."

"Good man." Kollan left the room.

"Kirion…" Cortraire gazed across the room at him. Kirion was Annais' maiden name. Was he a part of her family?

Artis clapped a hand on Cortraire's shoulder. "Kirion is Kollan's go-to weapons expert. He's better than most experts with a higher rank, in my opinion. Then again, most of the soldiers in this room are the best. Look over there." She pointed to a fox and a vixen standing together. "He's Tannor, and she's Chall. You want to find out anything about a location, get him to do a scan. He can tell you everything down to the population of ants in the area. And Chall's our communication's girl. She can connect to, hack into, or block any signal, anywhere. Yup, we're all the best here, which is why we thought we were getting Marviot."

"And what do you do?" Cortraire picked up his bag while keeping an eye on Kirion.

"Sharpshooter or close range marksman, whatever the case may be." Artis made like she was shooting her finger. "I can shoot a bird on the wing straight in the eye."

"I see." Cortraire kept studying Kirion. He didn't look too familiar, and Cortraire couldn't place him at his and Annais' wedding. Maybe he didn't have any relation to Annais at all.

"Excuse me?"

Cortraire turned. The skinny soldier stood in front of him. His nametag read, "Artis."

"You're Cortraire Cunor, right?"

"Yeah." Cortraire shouldered his bag.

"It is an honor to meet you." He shook Cortraire's hand. "Call me Mal. Thanks for what you did."

"Not a problem."

"Except it is." Artis narrowed her eyes. "I thought I told you to keep a low profile and keep your mouth shut."

"I thought I was." Mal ducked, his ears dropped a bit.

"Do you know each other?" Cortraire said.

"He's my little brother." Artis sniffed. "A ball of nerves if ever I saw one. But he has the potential to be one of the best stealth fighters in the world. He can get you in and out of anywhere at any time. I had him volunteer for this assignment hoping to introduce him to Marviot… sort of fast-track his career, but all we got was you. No offence."

"None taken," Cortraire said.

"But this is even better, sis!" Mal balled up his fists. "I've been wanting to meet you for a long time—ever since I saw you on TV escorting the Expermian Ambassador to that Outsider nation… um, Drymairad, was it? I remember seeing you standing unafraid even though you were surrounded by Outsiders. You're an inspiration to me."

"It's not that big a deal." Cortraire shrugged. "Non-Expermians aren't anything scary. Once you start fearing them, that's when they get power over you."

"Wow." Mal saluted. "It's an honor to serve with you."

"Why are you doing that? I'm not your superior."

"But…"

"No, buts." Cortraire clutched his bag. "Have you gotten your weapons from the armory, yet?"

Mal stiffened. "Not yet."

"Then?" Cortraire shooed him away. "You don't want to be the one everyone's waiting for."

Mal saluted and darted away.

"And stop saluting me." Cortraire called after him. "What is his problem?"

"You'd better get your weapons too." Artis smacked his back. "You don't want to be the one everyone's waiting for."

"Yes, Corporal."

"I was wondering when you'd notice."

"I noticed a long time ago."

"So what should I call you then? You like 'Lance Corporal' like Marviot, or…"

"Let's go with Private Cunor." Cortraire rubbed the back of his neck. "Using a depreciated title because it sounds nice seems… pretentious."

Artis snickered. "That's one thing we agree on… but don't tell Marviot I said that."

Cortraire smirked. "I won't."

\* \* \*

"We're leaving now," Cortraire said over the phone. He plopped himself down in the passenger seat at the head of the convoy. "Once we get started you won't be able to contact me. We'll have jamming signals going just in case… Okay… bye… What? No… you can't… alright, but I'm serious when I say don't overwork yourself, Annais. Rest. And let Andrais do all that… fine. Bye." He pushed the button to hang up. "That girl is going to give me a heart attack. Now she wants to rearrange the house? What part of don't lift heavy things does she not understand?"

"Annais was always an active one." Kirion got into driver's seat. "As tough as nails, though, and with a mouth to match."

"That's her, alright. I—" Cortraire's ears pricked. "So you do know her. You're her... what, uncle..."

"I'm her eldest brother." Kirion furrowed his brows. "I was at your wedding."

"Oh! I... don't remember." Cortraire sank low in his chair. "There was a lot of people there."

"I'm not as loud as other members of my family." Kirion snorted through his nose. "Compared to them, I'm easily forgettable."

"But wait... Annais' eldest brother is 25 or 26."

"That's right."

"Then shouldn't you be a sergeant or something by now?"

"He should, but he doesn't have a fancy pants name like you and me." Artis jumped over the door and landed in the back of the jeep.

"What?" Cortraire turned to her. "He's not getting promoted because of his name? That's—that's insane!"

"It's military code." Kirion cleared his throat. "And I quote, 'All officers should be upstanding Expermian citizens, respected among both civilians and his fellow military personnel.' Unquote."

"But that has nothing to do with family rank," Cortraire said.

"It does to the brass." Artis threw herself back. "They promote good families like ours first, and the rest when there is space left."

Cortraire turned to his brother-in-law. "Kirion..."

"Doesn't bother me." Kirion shrugged. "I love this country, and my time for promotion will come. Besides, I don't want to deal with the politics of being a commissioned officer... at least, not for a while yet."

"Well, I do." Cortraire crossed his arms. "I can't believe the amount of favoritism I've seen in the past few days."

"Favoritism you're a part of." Artis poked his shoulder.

"What?" Cortraire turned to her.

Artis leaned forward to thrust her head between Kirion and Cortraire. "I know for certain that Marviot was assigned to this mission, but here you are in his place. They don't bend rules like this for just anyone. They wouldn't even do it for me."

Cortraire's heart dropped. "I... I mean..."

"Ah, no worries." Artis waved her hands. "It's how things are done around here. You want to make it up the ranks, you get there any way you can, am I right?"

Cortraire slid low in his seat. Annais was right. He shouldn't have taken this assignment. Now he was a part of the problem.

"Don't feel so bad, Cunor." Artis smacked Cortraire's shoulder. "Everyone gets favors to move up faster. Those who don't end up being Corporal for seven years like Kirion here."

Kirion raised his chin. "And proud of it."

Cortraire shut his eyes. That's it. This was the last time he used his name or connections to bend the rules. He didn't want a promotion because of tricks. He wanted to earn it. After all, Annais wouldn't be happy with anything less.

* * *

"Hey! Hey, wake up, sleepyhead." Artis smacked Cortraire on the back of the head. "Get up! We're here."

Cortraire snorted awake. Sand dunes stretched as far as the eye could see, interrupted by the occasional scrubby bush in the distance. The horizon shimmered in the heated air.

Cortraire blinked. He must have fallen asleep between their last stop and here. He stretched, shook his head as hard as he could, and slapped his cheeks with both hands. He blinked again and got out of the car.

"Marviot does that when he wakes up after a long trip, too." Artis stood with her hand on her hips.

Cortraire pressed his lips together. "Let's not bring up those who aren't here." He glanced around. The convoy had parked at the base of a sand dune. Most of the soldiers sat in the cars talking, but about five or so... including Kirion and Kollan... had perched on the top of the dune. In their camos, they were nearly invisible. Kirion had set up a four-missile launcher below the dune's edge to hide it. He tinkered with the mechanism. Chall and Tannor had their equipment out, but instead of looking at the readouts, they spoke with their heads close together. Chall giggled every once in a while.

"What's our status?" Cortraire headed for the sergeant. "I must have missed the orders..."

"Would you relax?" Artis leaned on the jeep. "We're not doing much. We wait for them to confirm the target, aim the missiles, obliterate the base, and then we go home."

Cortraire lowered his ears. "Doesn't seem like we're doing much for such an exclusive assignment."

"That's what makes it exclusive." Artis smirked. "You don't think they'd send Marviot on a *dangerous* mission, do you? He's our future Grand Councilman."

Cortraire turned up his nose. "Marviot would go on any mission he chooses, dangerous or not." He headed up the dune where Kollan had stationed himself. He walked halfway up before dropping to his belly and army crawling the rest of the way.

"Finally awake, Cunor?" Kollan sat below the edge of the dune.

"Sorry about that. Won't happen again."

Kollan chuckled. "You are nothing like Marviot, I'll tell you that."

Cortraire angled his ears back but didn't say anything. "Would it be alright if I took a look at the target? I've never seen a terrorist base in real life. I'm a bit curious."

"Knock yourself out." Kollan handed him some binoculars. "But it's not anything to write home about."

"Thanks." Cortraire peered through the binoculars.

A small settlement... no more than 100 buildings strong... greeted him. The buildings were made out of sand colored brick, but most of them had some sort of damage to them. One of them had a chunk missing from the roof with scorch marks marking the hole. Laundry and long pieces of colored cloths hung on clotheslines all around the settlement. Men milled around the place, painting scorched walls, rebuilding burnt homes, and repairing broken windows. Old women and young men carried furniture, baskets of clothes, or other things out of the houses. Some of the items were broken beyond repair. Those, they tossed into a large pile in the street.

Cortraire narrowed his eyes as he studied the scene. Outsiders... non-fox species like coyotes, lizards, and the like... helped with the repair. But the Expermians didn't bat an eye at them. Further—Cortraire studied each and every person he saw—there were no young ladies in the group. None... neither Outsider nor Expermian.

"Sarge." Cortraire lowered his binoculars. "This doesn't look like a terrorist base."

"And what did you expect, Cunor?" Kollan yawned. "A big sign that says 'Terrorists 'R' Us'?"

"No, but this looks like—" Cortraire looked through the binoculars again. "This looks like one of those textile settlements the Western Clan uses. It's a civilian settlement."

"And what makes you think terrorists wouldn't *use* a civilian settlement as their base?" Kollan shook his head. "We have orders, Cunor. Destroy the base at this location—"

"With all due respect, our orders are to locate the terrorist base and destroy that." Cortraire motioned to the settlement, though without his binoculars he couldn't see it. "It says nothing about harming civilians."

"Civilians? Look at it!" Kollan threw his hand in the air. "The place is crawling with Outsiders."

"That doesn't mean they're terrorists!"

Kollan snorted through his nose. "I'm beginning to see why you haven't been promoted. You don't know when to keep your mouth shut."

Cortraire fell silent.

"Look, Cunor, Outsiders have no place in Expermia." Kollan flicked his tail. "If they are congregating like that, they must be up to something nefarious. Can we at least agree on that?"

Cortraire lowered his eyes. He had a choice to make. He could fall silent and let them destroy this settlement as per their orders... a thing Marviot surely would do... or he could attempt to drag things out in order to be sure of the situation—despite the possibility of saving the lives of Outsiders in the process. But if he spoke up, it could reflect negatively on his career, particularly if he turned out to be wrong. What to do? What to do... ?

"Are we ready, Kirion?" Kollan turned to him.

"In a minute." Kirion tinkered with the missile launcher.

"You're taking longer than usual to set this up." Kollan crossed his arms.

"I have to be sure that I hit the right target." Kirion looked at Cortraire out of the corner of his eye.

Cortraire met his eyes—the same eyes that Annais had—bright and clear without a hint of deceit. Annais... Cortraire found himself smiling at the thought of her. If she were here now, she'd yell at him for being so indecisive. She'd crinkle her nose at him for bowing down to pressure. He chuckled to himself. He'd never be able to look her in the eyes again if he buckled now.

"No, Sarge, I don't agree with you." Cortraire turned to Kollan.

"That's too bad, Cunor, because I'm the one calling the shots here." Kollan turned to Kirion. "Are we ready?"

Kirion nodded.

"Please wait, Sarge." Cortraire caught his shoulder. "What if this is a civilian settlement, and we wipe it off the face of the map? That's not going to sit well with the Expermian people or the Grand Council."

"And what proof do you have that it is a civilian base other than it doesn't look like a terrorist one? Eh, Cunor?"

"Um, Sarge." Tannor raised his hand. He had headphones on his ears and peered at his scanner's screen. "Cunor might be right about this."

"What are you talking about, Tannor?" Kollan narrowed his eyes at him.

Tannor lifted the headphones off his ears. "When Cunor first raised the question about this being a civilian settlement, I ran a scan on their weapons. There are none."

Kollan's ears shot up. "What?"

"They have no weapons, not even what they'd need to scare off the local wildlife." Tannor looked in the settlement's direction. "It's possible that they're jamming our scans, but—"

"That's not possible." Chall sat up. "I've got anti-jamming jammers going—the best in the business. If they've got weapons good enough to take out entire cities and Tannor can't find them, they're either shielded real well, they're in another location, or they're non-existent."

"Then it might not be a terrorist base." Kollan snatched the binoculars from Cortraire. He peered through them. "Then what are Outsiders doing there?"

"We should send someone to find out," Cortraire said.

"And would you volunteer to go?" Kollan looked at him out of the corner of his eyes.

Cortraire shrugged. "Sure."

Kollan stared at him a moment. "Fine. Anyone else want to go with Cunor?"

"I will!" Mal raised his hand.

Cortraire jumped. Mal stood right behind Cortraire. He hadn't seen or heard him approach.

"I'll go too." Tannor gathered his equipment. "I want to get a more in-depth scan of the place. If they've weapons there, I'm going to find them."

"I'll watch your back." Chall gathered her equipment as well.

Three other soldiers volunteered.

"Guess I'm coming too." Artis slipped her hands in her pockets. "Someone needs to make sure you all don't get shot in the back while you're busy investigating."

"Fine, Cunor. I'll leave it up to you." Kollan smacked Kirion on the shoulder. "I'm going to have Kirion keep his hand on the button. If anything goes wrong, I'll have him fire even if you're not back yet. Clear?"

"Understood." Cortraire slid down the dune. "Let's get all our stuff loaded." He jumped into the driver's seat.

"Slide over, Commander." Artis leaned in through the window.

"Huh?"

"Kollan put you in charge of this little excursion." Artis shoved him over. "We don't let Commanders drive. But don't fall asleep." She patted the seat. "Mal."

Mal scurried up to climb into the driver's seat. He sat beside Cortraire and bounced in the seat. His grin stretched from ear to ear.

"Reign it in there, sweetie." Artis patted Mal's shoulder as she got into the car.

"Look, Artis. I'm not trying to undermine your command." Cortraire turned to her as Tannor and Chall got in the car. "I'll be more than happy to defer to you since you outrank me."

"What are you talking about?" Artis hopped in the back seat. "You're a Cunor. That's all the ranking you need."

Cortraire exhaled through his nose. That again, huh? "Alright, then. Let's go."

Mal started the jeep and put it in gear. The car with the other soldiers in it pulled in behind them. Cortraire snorted as they topped the dune. The more he heard his last name, the less he liked it. But he had to put that behind him. Here at the top of the dune, the soldiers stood in full view of any enemies surrounding them. Cortraire hoped he had made the right choice.

\* \* \*

Cortraire's jeep pulled into the village and down one of the streets. The villagers stopped and stared as they passed. Those in their way made room for them, picking up obstacles that blocked their path and allowing them to pull into the middle of the village where a mosaic tile circle had been laid. Cortraire got out of the jeep and studied the mosaic. The grout had been filled with sand, and the tile had been covered with dirt and had faded so much that Cortraire couldn't tell what it used to depict.

The settlement's damage looked worse up close than it had from afar. Scorch marks marred each and every building. The smell of smoke hung in the air. Bullet holes riddled the walls.

The other soldiers got out of the car and congregated around Cortraire, guns at the ready. Tannor and Chall stayed in the car with their equipment. Cortraire had his rifle hanging from his shoulder and his laser pistol in his hostler, but he didn't take hold of either. Instead, he surveyed the gathering crowd. Like when he had spied them through the binoculars, the group consisted of mostly men, old women, and children… no young ladies to be found. But unlike before, the Outsiders in the group had conveniently disappeared.

One of the villagers walked forward to greet Cortraire. He had yellowish fur, brown hair that faded to white at the end, and wore an Expermian tunic weaved with iridescent colors, metallic threads, beads, and patterns—actually, all of the villagers did. The Western Clan was famous for its rich textiles. The villager stopped a respectable distance from Cortraire and held out his hands palm up to show he was unarmed. He bowed slightly, but his mouth was set in a line. The corners of his eyes and mouth wrinkled as he narrowed them.

"Greetings." Cortraire held up a hand in response. "My name is Private Cunor of the Expermian Armed Forces." He winced. He shouldn't have used his last name. But the name didn't elicit a response from the villagers. He charged ahead. "I would like to speak to the person or persons in charge of this village on an urgent matter."

"So, you've finally come for us, huh?" The villager grunted through his nose.

Cortraire glanced at his fellow soldiers. They all slightly shrugged. "I beg your pardon."

"Don't act dumb." The villager motioned to the sand around them. "It's all around the surrounding settlements how you all come in and destroy our villages with no warning."

"We destroy terrorist bases, not settlements." Artis stepped forward. "We wouldn't destroy a civilian settlement unless they were harboring, aiding, and abetting terrorists."

The villager thrust a finger in her direction. "And I'm saying you're dirty, rotten liars!"

"You little ingrate!" Artis strode forward, her fur on end. "I ought to—"

"Wait, wait, wait…" Cortraire stepped in between them. "Let's start at the beginning. Who are you?"

The villager sniffed. "You can call me Nef. I'm the leader of this textile settlement."

"Mr. Nef." Cortraire bowed slightly. "Rest assured that the Expermian military only destroys places that they deem are nests of terrorist activities. That's why I'm here today. We received a report that this village is a terrorist base, so we came to investigate."

"This place?" Nef roared with laughter. "We are no terrorists. But if you came to get that gang of rogues that passed through here, you're too late. They're already gone."

"So they were here?" Cortraire surveyed the village.

"Were you aiding them?" Artis adjusted her rifle in her hands.

"Aiding them? Are you serious? Look at what they did!" Nef motioned around him. "They came in demanding that we help them, but once we found out what they were about, we refused. They took everything over. They stole our weapons, took our food, burned our town, destroyed our livelihood, murdered those who tried to resist them, and… and they…" He faltered. His lips trembled, and his ears fell. "They kidnapped our girls… 10 of them."

"That's terrible." Cortraire gazed around the village.

"That might not seem like a lot to you, but we're only a community of 30 families." Nef thrust his face into Cortraire's. "That's one third of us that lost a sister or daughter or mother or wife!"

The word "wife" caught Cortraire by the throat. His mind turned to Annais. If anything happened to her, he wouldn't know what to do with himself.

Cortraire stepped back. "Mr. Nef, believe me when I say, we are committed to wiping out the scoundrels who did this to you."

Nef's ears pricked. A light came to his eyes. "Then go follow them. They went that way… to the east. We will help you. We're not great fighters, but we can track them, and—"

Cortraire held up a hand. "I have my orders. This place was marked as a terrorist camp, and I have to make sure it's not true before I can do anything else. Your cooperation on this matter will make my investigation go quicker and smoother."

"Then what do you want us to do?"

"Bring everyone out to the village center." Cortraire crossed his arms. "I'll put everyone under guard while we search your village to make sure you're not hiding anyone or anything."

"Fine." Nef put his fingers to his mouth to whistle, but hesitated. "There's one thing…"

"What's that?" Cortraire said.

"We're not terrorists." Nef kept his hands close to his mouth. "Remember that… no matter what some of us look like."

Cortraire furrowed his brows. "I understand," he said, though he really didn't. "No one will shoot unless I give the order. Clear?" He eyed Artis.

"Clear," the soldiers said in unison.

"Fine." Artis lowered her rifle.

Nef gave a loud, piercing whistle that made Cortraire's ear twitch.

Expermians poured out of every building in the vicinity, and then… Cortraire stifled a gasp… Outsiders appeared. He felt Artis stiffen, but she didn't make a move to fire. The Expermians stood around each family of Outsiders. When they gathered in front of Cortraire, they stood so that the Outsiders were huddled in the middle of the group.

"I knew it." Artis clicked the safety on her gun.

"Hold your fire." Cortraire held up a hand. He turned to Nef. "Explain what Outsiders are doing here."

"Out here in the Western Clan's territory, we meet lots of Outsiders close to the border." Nef motioned to the group. "Most we meet got lost in the desert while running from something. Those are as vicious, cruel, disgusting, and vile as we've been taught. But some are simply creative and curious who have heard about our textiles and have come to learn our manufacturing and dyeing techniques. Who are we to say we can't improve Outsiders' lives by nurturing that creativity? We run a… what do they call it in the other country… a trade school for them. But we screen all our Outsiders before we allow them into our clan. In fact, they fought the hardest when we tried to resist the scoundrels who came in. Their girls as well as ours got kidnapped. I cannot allow you to hurt them."

"This is an unusual set of circumstances." Cortraire scratched his hair. "But I've always held that just because you're an Outsider doesn't make you a terrorist. Artis."

"What's up?"

"You and the rest keep an eye on them. Don't let anyone leave until I'm finished searching, but don't shoot unless you have to. And…" Cortraire leaned close to her. "If you have to shoot, use non-lethal force."

Artis narrowed her eyes. "Fine."

"Mal, you're with me." Cortraire turned to the truck. "How's it going, Tannor?"

"I'm not getting anything." Tannor removed his headphones. "The place is clear of any weapons."

"Can you walk with your scanner?" Cortraire asked.

"Yup."

"Then come with me." Cortraire beckoned him. "Help me scan for bodies."

"Gotcha." Tannor hopped out of the jeep with a portable scanner in his hands.

Cortraire, Tannor, and Mal searched the buildings one by one. First Tannor scanned the interior to see if he could find a heat signature. Once he cleared it, Cortraire and Mal would go in to visually confirm. After that, they moved on to the next.

While Cortraire waited for Tannor to finish scanning last building, his eyes drifted to the dunes outside the village. The border separating Expermia from the Outsiders lay a few miles in that direction. He'd been to an Outsider country before and found the people strange, but not too bad. But to live in such close proximity to them… to willingly live among them and work with them for extended periods... Cortraire shuddered. He didn't think he could do it.

His ear twitched. Cortraire swung around to face a gutted building. Its doors had been ripped off of its hinges, and its windows broken.

"I got something." Tannor raised his scanner toward the building.

"I heard it." Cortraire kept his eyes on the building. "Cover me." He entered.

It had been a house. The kitchen lay straight ahead, and an open space... the family room, maybe... stretched to the right. Cortraire went room by room, searching. He emerged with a "clear." But he didn't let his guard down. He knew he had heard something...

Something bumped from the kitchen. Cortraire swung around to face it.

"Whatever it is, it's in the kitchen." Mal appeared behind him.

Cortraire jumped. It took all of his self-control not to swing around and shoot Mal. The kid needed a bell or something.

Tannor stepped forward with his scanner in hand. Cortraire and Mal walked behind him, Mal keeping an eye on things behind them. They entered the kitchen. Tannor pointed his scanner to the ground.

"There," Tannor pointed to the ground.

Cortraire studied the floorboards he had indicated. There was nothing there.

"I got it." Mal squatted. He lifted up a small square of wood that hid a gap large enough to fit four fingers through.

"It's a latch. Probably leads to a cellar." Cortraire narrowed his eyes. "But why so well hidden?"

"Not hidden. It's a root cellar." Mal motioned to it with his gun. "My great-gran has one of these. It's ergonomic because you don't want a big hole in the floor to trip over."

"Okay, then. But anything could be in there." Cortraire slipped his fingers into the latch. "Ready?"

Mal took aim. Tannor stood back.

Cortraire flung the hidden door open. "Freeze!" He pointed his gun at the space.

It had been a cellar... jars of preserved fruit and vegetables had been set on shelves all around. A ladder led up from the dark ground. A single Expermian fox—about 15 years old—looked up at him from the darkness. "Don't shoot!" He held up his hands. "Please. I give up!"

"Get out here." Cortraire stepped back so the kit had room to climb out. "Keep your hands where I can see them."

The fox climbed the ladder.

"Turn around." Cortraire shoved him around with the end of his gun. "Let's go. Walk slowly outside and toward the village center. Don't try anything."

"I won't. I won't." The kit complied.

Cortraire shoved the kit out of the building and toward the villagers in the center of the town. "What is this?" He shoved the young fox in the dirt in front of Nef. "I found him hiding in one of your cellars."

Nef stared at him. His top lip rose, exposing very sharp teeth. The young man cowered on the ground in front of him.

"He was one of them!" Nef approached him slowly. "One of those miscreants that took my granddaughter away."

The entire village turned to the young man. Snarls and murmurs ascended from the crowd.

"I'll rip him limb from limb!" Nef charged at him.

Cortraire stepped in between them. He caught Nef and threw him to the ground. "Hold on a minute, Gramps."

"Hold on nothing! He's one of them!" Nef scrambled to his feet. His tail bristled. "He shot up our peaceful town!" He charged at him again, but Cortraire held him back. "Let me go! Let me get a chunk of him. Where's my granddaughter, you little maggot?"

The villagers turned their attention to the young man. They grumbled and closed in on them. Cortraire stiffened his whiskers. Riot mentality had reared these people up to the point where they forgot they were surrounded by armed soldiers. He used his body as a shield for the young kit while trying to hold back Nef. "Now wait. Calm down, everyone."

A laser shot blasted right at the crowd's feet. A piece of grass caught on fire. The villagers stopped.

Artis walked in between them and snuffed out the fire with her shoe. "Let's not forget your situation here. We still haven't cleared you as non-terrorists." She nodded at Cortraire.

"Thanks." Cortraire turned to the fox. "What do you have to say for yourself, kit?"

"I'm sorry; I'm sorry." The young fox cowered on the dirt. He held his hands over his head and rocked back and forth. "I'm sorry. Please don't hurt me."

"Not so tough now that you don't have a gun pointed at us, eh?" Nef spat at him. "Let me go. I want a piece of him. You can shoot me afterward."

"Calm down, I said." Cortraire shoved Nef into the crowd. "Or I'll have you tied up." He glanced to the young fox. "State your name and start explaining."

"My name is Aphain. I… I was a part of them, but I don't want to be anymore." Aphain looked up at Cortraire through wide eyes. "Those guys are crazy."

"Liar!" Nef said, though he didn't charge again.

"It's true!" Aphain's eyes welled with tears. "The only reason they're not after me now is because they told me to stay behind. They put me in the cellar and said I was supposed to hide out there and report to them when the military wiped out the village."

"But that doesn't make sense." Cortraire peered at him. "If you were down there when we fired, you'd be dead too."

"I think that was the idea." Aphain ducked his head. "I started asking questions I shouldn't have. I wanted to run as soon as they left, but they locked me down there. I couldn't escape until you let me out."

"That's stupid. If they wanted you dead, there's a real simple way to do it." Artis pointed her gun at his head. "One laser to the head is all it would take."

"Who knows how these terrorists think?" Cortraire pushed her gun down. "Probably thought it would be poetic justice to have the military kill one of theirs that they didn't trust."

"Don't tell me you believe him!" Nef snorted at Aphain. "You were one of the worst ones, strutting around like an alpha traiungo."

"I acted that way because I didn't want to get killed." Aphain clutched his ears. "But I'm telling you, they're insane. Why else would I risk it all and tip off the feds they were coming here?"

"You tipped them off?" Cortraire's peered at Aphain.

"About two weeks ago when Mortaine, our leader, decided to come to this place to prepare the attack." Aphain swallowed hard. "When I signed up, he said that he got a message from the great god, Rophim, that it was time for Outsiders to die. But he's nuts! He's trying to wipe out the Expermian base… um, Orantaine, I think the name was."

"Orantaine?" Cortraire's ears pricked. "That's our most important base in this sector. If they took that out, Expermia would be vulnerable to Outsider attack."

"And they can do it too." Aphain stood on his feet. "He 'n' Boss got weapons from Outsiders. Mortaine says the Expermian government isn't doing enough about the Outsider problem, so he 'n' Boss's want to take out the Grand Councilwoman. Those terrorist bases you've been hitting… it's all a part of his plan, a distraction so he can move undetected. Once he takes out the base, he'll launch an attack on Itzputza. Of course, they'll counterattack, and Expermia will be pulled into war. In the chaos, Boss'll take over Silver Sait and kill the Grand Councilwoman. Thousands of Expermians will die. I'm telling you, they're nuts!"

"There's a big hole in those plans." Artis turned up her nose. "There's no way Mortaine'll be able to get to the Grand Councilwoman once war breaks out. He'll be too busy fighting here."

"You're not listening!" Aphain bared his teeth. "Mortaine is the one who wants to fight the Outsiders, but Boss is the one who'll take out the Grand Councilwoman."

"So you're talking about two people?" Cortraire held up two fingers. "This Mortaine guy, and someone else?"

"Yes!" Aphain said.

"Someone in the military…" Cortraire gazed in the direction Silver Sait, the capital, would be.

Chall stepped forward. "If that's the case, we need to contact Orantaine, and—"

"They've already infiltrated your communications." Aphain tugged on his ears. "If you try and contact them, you'll be talking to him. That's how he got rid of the other soldiers they sent after him."

"We'll see about that." Cortraire beckoned to Chall. He led her a short distance away. "Is what he's saying possible? Can they hack into a military signal?"

Chall waved her hand. "It's nearly impossible once we have our jamming signals going."

Cortraire lowered his voice. "What if it was an inside job?"

"An… inside…" Chall's ears lowered. "Are you serious?"

"Just listing possibilities."

Chall gazed at him a moment. "If one of ours were responsible, it's entirely possible."

"Could you find out if they have?"

Chall scratched her hair. "I could try, but if it is an inside job, they'd be using our own signals. I don't know if I'd be able to catch it."

"See if you can. In the meantime, we need to report to Sarge." Cortraire let his voice return to normal. "How secure would wireless communications among our group be?"

"If the scenario you're painting is true, I wouldn't trust it," Chall said.

Cortraire nodded. "Mal."

"Yes." Mal trotted over to him.

"Go back to Sarge, and tell him that we have a big problem here. Tell him not to use our communications and to get down here as soon as possible."

"Understood." Mal headed to the jeep. He jumped in and took off.

"What do you want us to do with him?" Artis jerked a thumb at Aphain.

Cortraire took a deep breath. "Tie him up and set him on the mosaic there. That will assure the villagers that he's not going anywhere. While we're waiting for Sarge, let's help them clean up a bit. These people have been through a lot."

Artis chuckled. "Alright."

"What's that smirk about?"

"I was thinking that you're nothing at all like Marviot." Artis shrugged. "He would have come in, figured out everything, and been gone by now… if he even set foot in the village at all. He certainly wouldn't be helping with cleaning up."

"I see."

"I was also thinking that you not being like Marviot might not be a bad thing." Artis winked at him before turning to repeat his orders.

Cortraire watched her walk away. Maybe she was right. After all, Annais had said the same thing. And he started to realize that Annais was hardly ever wrong.

* * *

Cortraire had been up on a ladder painting the side of a building when the jeep with Mal and Sergeant Kollan pulled up. He climbed down the ladder, handed the brush to another soldier, and went to greet him.

"I see you've taken the urgency of the situation to heart." Kollan slammed the car door shut.

"I thought we should help the people here while we were waiting for you to arrive. We have a big problem—"

"Mal briefed me on the situation." Kollan clicked his tongue. "What a mess this is. And we can't even contact HQ for further orders."

"Not if what Aphain here says is true." Cortraire led Kollan to Chall. "I thought we could test it. Chall says she'll try to see if the signal is compromised."

Chall put her headphones on. "But I can't guarantee anything. You'll need to keep them on the line as long as possible so I can try my scans. I'm ready when you are. The frequency's set up."

"Fine." Kollan picked up the radio receiver.

"If I may…" Cortraire reached for the receiver. "I've been thinking about this situation, and I think I have an idea that can help."

Kollan studied him for a moment. "It seems you were right about everything so far." He handed him the receiver.

Cortraire took a deep breath and let it out in a steady stream. He closed his eyes, cleared his throat, raised the receiver to his mouth and said, "Orantaine base, come in." Cortraire dropped his voice lower, allowing the bass to boom in his throat. He pronounced his words with authority—short and to the point. Just like Marviot.

Kollan and Chall gazed at him.

Mal's mouth dropped open. "You sound like Marviot."

Cortraire held a finger to his lips.

Static erupted from the radio before a deep voice said, "Orantaine military base, Corporal Landai speaking."

"This is Lance Corporal Cunor speaking. I'm part of an anti-terrorist squad that was sent to the Western Desert. We've finished eliminating the terrorist base, and I'm confirming our scheduled arrival tomorrow morning at 8:30 a.m., over."

"One moment, please, over," Corporal Landai said.

Kollan furrowed his brows, but kept his mouth closed. His eyes remained glued to the radio.

Landai returned. "Arrival time confirmed, Lance Corporal. We're happy to have the future Grand Councilman down for a visit."

Cortraire paused. His hand dropped for a moment before he caught himself. "We're moving out now. Over and out." He hung up.

"That wasn't nearly enough time for me to scan." Chall removed her headphones.

"No need. Aphain's right. They have intercepted the signal." Cortraire's voice cracked. He cleared his throat. "Imitating Marviot hurts my voice."

"And how do you figure that they've intercepted it, Cunor?" Kollan crossed his arms.

"First of all, we're not scheduled to go to that base. They should have known that." Cortraire let his ears fall back. "Second of all, he thought that Marviot Cunor was coming, and he didn't bat an eye. I've seen the way people react to my brother... the way you all reacted when you discovered I came instead of him. They should have been crapping their pants to hear he was on his way for a surprise visit, but—"

"Nothing. I figured that's what you were doing." Kollan clenched his teeth.

"It's not definitive proof, but it's in line with what we have so far." Cortraire turned to Aphain. "And if he's right about this, he could be right about everything else. They could have the weaponry to take out the base and cause a war Expermia is not prepared for."

"We have to stop them." Kollan smacked his fist in his palm. "This was supposed to be an easy assignment."

"There's something else." Cortraire led him away from the others. "When I was getting briefed for this assignment, Colonel Bain told me something disturbing. I'm not supposed to say anything, but I believe it has bearing on this assignment."

"What is it, Cunor?"

"He said that he believed that there is a traitor in the military. Marviot also said something similar to me a few weeks ago."

"I don't believe this." Kollan tugged on his ears. "Any idea who it is?"

Cortraire shook his head. "But Aphain's story seems to support this. He mentioned someone he called 'Boss' in addition to Mortaine, the leader of this terrorist cell... or perhaps I should say gang leader. Or maybe they're insurgents? I'm not even sure what to call them now."

"This keeps getting better and better." Kollan blew a breath. "Think this kit knows where they're headed?"

"I'm pretty sure he does." Cortraire looked over his shoulder. "Hey, kit!"

Aphain looked up from where he had been tied up. They had set up a tarp over his head to keep the sun off, and Artis stood beside him with her gun at the ready—both to keep him from trying to escape and to stop the villagers from attacking him.

Cortraire walked over to him. He stooped in front of him. "Do you know where your group is going to strike from?"

"I don't know off-hand, but I could point it out on a map." Aphain nodded toward the east. "They're attacking from a point three miles from the base at sunrise tomorrow morning."

"Three miles outside of the base..." Kollan stroked his chin fur. "We'll have to drive all night to make it there before sunrise."

"And we'll need time to rescue the hostages," Cortraire stood.

"Then we need to get going. Get everyone ready, Cunor. We're leaving in thirty." Kollan caught Aphain by the collar. "You're coming with us." He shoved him to the jeep.

"Alright, everyone!" Cortraire clapped his hands. "Let's pack up! Mal, go on and tell Kirion to pack up his equipment."

After Mal left, Cortraire walked around repeating the message to everyone who hadn't heard. Only after they had headed out from the village did Cortraire realize what had happened. Kollan had given him an order to relay to the rest of the team. He had given him authority, and it had nothing to do with his name or his brother or anything else.

Cortraire grinned. Annais would be so proud when she heard about this.

* * *

Cortraire didn't fall asleep this time. The urgency of the situation weighed down on him. Instead he studied the landscape, watched as the sun set behind him and as the moon rose in the sky. He saw the stars come out and the night animals skitter around on the distance dunes. And he noted when the moon set and the stars started to disappear.

"It's nearly sunrise." Aphain said from the back seat where Artis had set him. His hands remained tied. "We're too late."

"We're not too late." Cortraire checked the map that Aphain had marked. "We should stop here, Sarge. We don't want them to see us coming. The point marked is a half-a-mile up."

Kollan nodded. He ordered the convoy to halt. "Kirion." He marched over to him as soon as he got out of the car. "Can you hit your target from here?"

Kirion looked out over the landscape. "Get me the coordinates, and I can hit it."

"Right. Come with me." Kollan shoved Aphain toward one of the soldiers once Artis got him out of the car. "And keep an eye on this one. If anything goes wrong, we have him to blame."

"I told you everything," Aphain trembled in the soldier's grasp. "Believe me, I want this to stop."

"If you're telling the truth, you have nothing to worry about." Cortraire clapped Aphain's back.

"Let's take a look and what we're up against, Cunor." Kollan climbed the dune and peered through his binoculars. Cortraire, Kirion, and Artis followed him. "What do you make of it, Kirion?"

"In my opinion, any doubt the kit was lying is gone." Kirion snorted through his nose. "They've got a lot of weaponry. Tannor would be able to tell you how much, but from what I see they've got enough to blow Orantaine off the map."

"But they don't look like they're getting ready to attack." Artis peered through her scope. "They look like they're… waiting for something."

Cortraire looked through his binoculars. In the center of camp, he spotted a tent with two guards stationed outside of it. A third shoved a vixen into it. Cortraire clenched his teeth… perhaps that's where they held the kidnapped girls. No telling what they were doing to them.

Another fox, this one dressed in a blue tunic, emerged out of a tent nearby. He made his way to a table with a radio set up on it. A tarp had been stretched over it. The fox sat at the table, picked up the receiver, and spoke into it.

"We could easily figure out what they're up to." Cortraire grinned at the figure through the binoculars. "They're not the only ones who can intercept a signal."

"Good call." Kollan beckoned to Chall. Once she understood what was happening, she had her equipment set up in seconds. They also brought Aphain to identify who was speaking.

"Here we go." Chall pushed a button.

"… push back the attack," someone said through the radio.

"That's Mortaine," Aphain said.

"Why?" came a gravelly voice in reply.

Cortraire's ears pricked. That voice…

Artis shoved Aphain. "Who's that?"

"That's the Boss," Aphain said. "I don't know who it is, but Mortaine's always talking to him."

"We found out that Marviot Cunor is scheduled to come to the base at 8:00 this morning," Mortaine said.

"Marviot, huh? I hadn't heard about that." The voice snorted. "That must be the reason he sent that idiot on his assignment in his stead."

Cortraire ignored the insult and instead closed his eyes to concentrate. That voice… he knew it from somewhere… a rich, deep quality that couldn't be hidden. But there was interference—voice altering technology, maybe…

"I know you want him, Boss, so I figure I can catch him for you," Mortaine said. "I can ship him over to you before we attack the Outsiders, or I can take him out myself. Choice is yours."

"Catch him alive, but not necessarily unharmed," Boss said. "Be careful, though. He's wily, violent, and slippery."

Cortraire stifled a snicker… unsuccessfully. That was a great description of Marviot if he'd ever heard one.

"By the way, I'll be shipping out a little present to you along with Cunor… one of the feminine variety. They're even some… uh…" Mortaine's voice took on a disgusted tone. "… exotic varieties that you favor so much in there."

The voice chuckled. "You know me too well. Don't linger. This is our moment."

"No prob, Boss," Mortaine said.

Chall clicked off of the radio. "There you have it."

"Then we have more time," Kollan said. "Cunor—"

"One second, Sarge." Cortraire held his knuckles against his forehead. That voice… something about it felt familiar to him. If only he could get rid of the distortion. "Chall, do you have that recorded?"

"Of course," Chall said.

"Play it back for me." Cortraire cocked his ears toward it as Boss' voice came out of the speaker. "Can you erase that gravel?"

"Sure." Chall did so.

"And get rid of the distortion."

Chall did so. The voice became a more recognizable but not quite clear yet.

"And now up the tenor a bit and reduce the bass."

And then, clear as day, Bain's voice erupted out of the speaker. "You know me too well. Don't linger. This is our moment."

Cortraire cursed.

"What the hell?" Kollan fell back onto his tail. "That's the Colonel."

"This is insane!" Artis clutched her hair. "He's in the top tier of the military. He has access to the Grand Councilwoman."

"And with him monitoring our airwaves we can't warn anyone. Dammit." Kollan slammed his fist on the sand.

Cortraire bit his lip. "Chall, how secure are text messages?"

"Text messages?" Chall furrowed her brows.

"Yes." Cortraire pulled out his phone. "I want to text my wife. If I can get a message to her, she can get it to Marviot. He might be able to do something over there."

"I can make that as secure as you want." Chall shrugged. "But Bain has our decryption technology. You might as well be sending him the message."

"True, but why would he care if I send a personal note to my wife?" Cortraire typed a text on his phone.

Hey, Annais. We got a chance to send messages home so I thought I'd send you one. I miss you so much. This assignment is turning out much differently than I thought it would. It's tougher than battling a krakken. Like Marviot said to me a few weeks ago, "the game's afoot." Speaking of, Marviot's name proceeds me everywhere I go. Honestly, his reputation is the BANE of my existence. Take care of yourself, Ani. Can't wait to see you.

"That is a bit of a risk, Cunor." Kollan read what he had written. "What if she doesn't know to give it to Marviot? Or what if he doesn't understand what you're trying to say? Or what if Bain intercepts, and he *does* understand what you're trying to say?"

"Do we have a choice?" Cortraire said.

Kollan shook his head. "Do it, Chall."

Chall extended her hand. "Let me have the phone." She plugged it into her machine. "Here we go. Sent."

"Good." Kollan checked his watch. "It's 5:45 now. Visibility will be about 5 miles once the sun rises so that mean we have until about 7:30 until they realize Marviot's not coming. We need to take them out before them."

"What about the hostages?" Cortraire gazed at the camp. "We can't let them get caught in the cross-fire."

"I can't risk them attacking the base, Cunor." Kollan looked him in the eyes. "But if you think you can do it, go get them. But I won't postpone our attack for you. We're firing at 7:15 the latest. If you're not out by then…"

"I understand." Cortraire looked at Artis. "Is there any way I can convince you to come with me?"

"As if you could stop me." Artis patted her rifle. "I'm dying for action."

"I'll go," said another soldier.

"Me too," said yet another.

"I want to come too." Mal raised his hand.

"I'd be happy to have you," Cortraire said.

"Ah, no." Artis stood between them. "You stay here where it's safe, Mal."

"We're going to need him, Artis." Cortraire grinned. "He can get in and out of anywhere, remember?"

"Ugh. Fine. But if anything happens to him…" Artis poked Cortraire's neck with a sharp nail. "I'm putting a laser through your throat."

"Fair enough." Cortraire rubbed his neck. "Let's move."

\* \* \*

Cortraire darted from shadow to shadow, pausing long enough for Mal to signal the rest of the team to follow. Cortraire shook his head as he ducked into the shadows at the side of a tent. Though he tried to keep his eyes on Mal, the soldier had a remarkable ability to disappear into the background. Even now, Cortraire lost him among the shadows. He sat back and waited, scanning the darkness for any movement from Mal or the enemy.

A clicking sound came to his ears—Mal's signal. Cortraire peered in its direction until he found Mal's silhouette. Mal held up a hand for the team to stop where they were and darted off to investigate the tent where Cortraire suspected they kept the girls.

Cortraire crouched in his hiding spot. Behind him, Artis and the others watched his back. He held his breath and remained as still as he could. This camp had no good hiding places. If the enemy looked in the right place…

A slight click reached Cortraire's ears. Mal had appeared again. He made hand signals to indicate that this tent was indeed the target. Cortraire nodded. He gave signals for Mal to wait. Then he turned to Artis. He nodded, and she nodded in response. Together they crept close to the entrance of the tent where two of the enemy stood guard.

Cortraire counted down on his fingers… three… two… one…

He pounced on the first guard and knocked him on the back of the head with his rifle. Artis tackled the other. She whipped his head to the side so fast, Cortraire heard a crack. He fell, neck broken.

Cortraire winced but saw the logic in her actions. After all, he'd have to do something to deal with his own unconscious guard. He tied the guy's hands, stripped him to his underwear, and fastened him to one of the tent posts.

That done, he joined Artis where Mal had been hiding.

"Mal, stay hidden and keep watch. Warn us if anyone is coming." Cortraire used hand signals to the rest of the team to follow Mal's lead. "When we send the girls out, make sure you and the rest get them to safety."

"Understood," Mal said.

Cortraire and Artis glanced at each other and slipped into the tent.

Nine girls—six foxes, one coyote, a serval, and a lizard—slept on the floor of the tent. They huddled together, trembling even though the air wasn't cold. But one of them, a vixen, sat up at the back of the tent, wide awake. Her eyes widened when she saw them. Her mouth opened to scream.

"Shh!" Cortraire put a finger to his lips. "We're here to rescue you. We're military."

The girl kept her mouth open, ready to scream. But her eyes roved over them.

Cortraire glanced around. "Can you help me wake your friends up quietly? We're about to bomb this place, and we need to get you out before that happens."

"I… think I've seen your face somewhere before… maybe on TV." The vixen squinted in the dim light. Her eyes roved over his nametag. "Cunor? Are you Marviot Cunor?"

Cortraire shook his head. "That's my brother."

"Then you're… Cortraire?"

Cortraire nodded.

"I saw you and your brother singing at the Silver Crescent Moon Festival on TV." A smile spread across her lips. "They really sent you to rescue us?"

"Keep quiet, and get a move on." Artis stationed herself at the entrance. She peered out. The sun's starting to rise."

Cortraire held a finger to his lips. "We have to hurry." He reached for the girl closest to him. "Help me."

The vixen shook a young serval next to her. "I'm Caira."

"Nice to meet you." Cortraire laid his hand on one of the vixens' mouth. Her eyes snapped open. She kicked and screamed in a muffled voice.

"It's okay. It's okay, Alaina." Caira placed her hand on the vixen's shoulder. "He's going to help us."

Alaina looked from Cortraire to Caira. Her breath came in short gasps, but she stopped struggling. Cortraire sent her from the tent where Mal snatched her into the darkness. He sent her to another member of their team who ferried her away to safety. They repeated the process with each of the girls.

"Other than Caira, that's the last one." Artis sent out another girl into the darkness.

"Come on, Caira." Cortraire took her hand. "It's time to get you—"

A click. Cortraire froze.

"We got trouble." Artis ducked into the tent. "One of the enemy is outside. Crap! I hope he doesn't see—"

"Hey!" came a voice from outside. "That's one of the girls!"

Artis cursed. She jumped out of the tent and opened fire.

"Let's go." Cortraire pulled Caira out. Artis followed, spraying the enemy with laser fire.

"The enemy has invaded the camp!" one of the enemy said.

"There they are," said another.

They converged on Cortraire and Artis. A slight click came to his ears. Cortraire swung around to see Mal peeking around one of the tents. He beckoned to Cortraire.

"Run! Run and don't stop!" Cortraire swung Caira in Mal's direction. "We'll cover you."

Caira ran, keeping her head covered as she did. She darted through two men who changed direction to nab her. Cortraire shot them where they stood. Mal snatched her arm and ran, disappearing into the vanishing shadows.

"Freeze!"

Cortraire glanced behind him. The enemy had converged on them. Artis had her hands in the air.

"Drop your weapon."

Cortraire turned and dropped his pistol on the ground. Then he shrugged off the rifle he carried. One of the enemy scooped up their weapons. His eyes fell on Cortraire's name tag.

"Well... well... look at this." He turned. "Hey, Mort! We found Cunor!"

"Is that so?" The fox who Cortraire had seen in the binoculars strode forward. He stood taller than the rest, his fur orange, and his hair blonde and fading to red at the edges. He had a scar across his lips. He held a rifle in his hands and had a knife strapped to his thigh. "You sneaky, little bastard. I should have known you'd pull something like... wait. You're not Marviot. Who the hell are you?"

"Private 3rd Class Cortraire Cunor. Why?" He smirked. "Were you expecting someone else?"

Mortaine snarled. He slugged Cortraire so hard his head spun.

"What the hell am I supposed to tell Boss now?" Mortaine clicked his tongue. "Kill them."

One of his followers took aim. "Bye, Cunor scum and friend."

Cortraire hissed in a breath. Poor Annais. What would she say when she heard that he'd been gunned down in the desert far from home? No, he couldn't let it end here. He had to get back to her somehow. He had to—

A flash of light blinded them. An explosion ripped through the south side of the camp. The ground rumbled beneath them, and fire and smoke belched into the air.

"What was that?" The fox about to shoot lowered his gun. "Bombs?"

"The military's attacking," yelled another.

Cortraire glanced at Artis who nodded. He leapt at the one with the gun, tackling him to the ground. He snatched it as he rolled to his knees and fired. Artis elbowed another in the face, snatched his weapon, and shot him with it. She opened fire on the rest.

"Come on, Artis." Cortraire darted past her. "We have to get out of here."

Another explosion rocked the air. This one was much closer. It blew nearby people off their feet and rattled the equipment scattered in the camp. Cortraire shielded himself from the blast of heat.

"I'm right behind you." Artis yelled over the noise. "I—ugh!" She dropped.

"Artis?" Cortraire turned to her. She had collapsed on her face. Blood seeped out between her shoulder blades.

"Oh, no!" Cortraire dropped to his knees beside her. He pressed a hand on the wound and felt for a pulse with the other hand. He found one. "I gotta get you to help."

"Think about yourself, Cunor!" Mortaine loomed over him. "You're going to need a lot more help than she will."

Cortraire snarled and fired. The shots hit Mortaine's chest, head, legs, and arms, but… nothing happened. Mortaine threw his head back in laughter.

"You like it?" Mortaine held out his hands. "Outsider technology… nullifies all laser-based weaponry. It's so much better than that weak body armor Expermians have."

"So it's true." Cortraire let his nose flare. "You are trading with Outsiders for weapons!"

Mortaine snorted. "One day, I will eliminate them all. But in the meantime, I'll use them for all they've got."

"And that gives you the right to betray Expermia?"

"Betray them?" Mortaine's fur rose. "If anyone's betrayed Expermia, it's the Cunor family!"

"What?"

"For the first time in centuries, the government's sent out Expermian citizens to an Outsider country for 'cultural awareness'!" Mortaine paced in front of Cortraire, clutching his hair. "They even sent Karalaina Dúcume, the only chance for a Silver Fox we're ever going to get!"

"We need to understand Outsiders if we are ever going to—"

"And the government is negotiating with them!" Mortaine went on. "Sending ambassadors." He pointed his gun at Cortraire. "You went as one of their bodyguards."

"I did, and I'm proud of it." Cortraire glared at him. "I don't like Outsiders any more than you do, but I'm doing my job to uphold Expermia's honor. But you—you might have issue with my family, but how dare you take the lives of Expermian civilians? How dare you attack our brave foxes and vixens who put their lives on the line on your behalf? You're worse than an Outsider, Mortaine. You're nothing but a dirty, rotten traitor!"

"That's it." Mortaine grinned at Cortraire. Cortraire heard his gun charge. "I am going to enjoy this. It's the beginning of the end of the Cunor family. Say good-bye."

Cortraire gripped some sand in his hand. He knew it was a bad idea—what Expermian growing up in the desert didn't know to shield their eyes in a fight? But he was desperate. He threw the sand into Mortaine's face.

Mortaine simply closed his eyes. When he opened them, he raised an eyebrow. "Really? That's all you got?"

"I was desperate. But I guess it did have some use." Cortraire launched himself at Mortaine. Mortaine pulled the trigger. Lasers whizzed by Cortraire. He felt a sting in his arm, leg, and side before he tackled Mortaine to the ground. Cortraire punched him over and over again. Mortaine snarled. He caught Cortraire's shoulder and threw him to the side. Cortraire wrapped his legs around Mortaine to keep from being separated from him. Only... his left leg felt strange and unresponsive.

No time to think about that now. Cortraire snatched the knife from Mortaine's thigh and plunged it into his neck. Blood spurted from the wound. Mortaine collapsed on the ground, convulsed, and lay still.

"Guess your fancy Outsider tech can't protect against that." Cortraire spat at him.

Another explosion rocked the ground. Secondary explosions rocked the air and erupted into a fireball that blazed to the sky.

"Kirion must have hit the weapons cache. I have to get Artis out of here." Cortraire turned to where she lay. He tried to walk to her, but his leg gave out. He dropped to his knees. A sticky substance drenched his uniform's leg. He pressed his hand against it and examined it. Blood. He glanced at his arm and his side. Blood soaked his uniform. "Crap!" He looked at Artis' still form.

"Killai!" Mal's appeared in front of them. He dropped beside Artis. "Oh, no. No! Killai!"

"Mal?" Cortraire grit his teeth. Now that he knew he was wounded, the pain set in. "What are you doing here?"

"My sister. She wasn't accounted for, and I—oh, crap!" Mal darted to him. "Not you too."

"Look, Mal. Artis is alive. But we have to get her to the base hospital." Cortraire tried to stand, but to no avail.

"We need to get both of you to a hospital!" Mal spoke into a radio at his hip. "I found them. We need a medic. They're both down."

Cortraire wavered on his hands and knees before collapsing on the ground. His head felt funny... lightheaded and dizzy. His eyes drifted closed. "No, no... you can't fall asleep here, Cortraire." He shook his head and slapped his cheeks. "You have to go back home to Ani. You promised."

"Calm down, Cunor. Please." Mal dragged him closer to Artis. "Help is on the way."

Cortraire squeezed his eyes shut. He had to focus... concentrate. He couldn't let the image of Annais fade from his mind. He had to stay awake so he could get back to her. Come on, Cortraire. Stay awake...

\* \* \*

Cortraire opened his eyes to a view of the hospital room's ceiling. He sighed. He was beginning to hate that view. He had been rushed here after Kollan and Mal had come to move him and Artis out of the fire zone. Cortraire had fought to stay conscious the entire time to the hospital and had succeeded until they put him under anesthesia to cauterize his wounds. Since waking, Cortraire had been treated to this bland view. He put his arm over his eyes and groaned. White, white, everywhere. White table, white curtains, white sheets, even white flowers in his room. Too much white.

"Boy, you screwed this assignment up pretty good."

Cortraire lifted his arm off his eyes. "Marviot?" He turned to the side.

Marviot sat at his bedside with his nose upturned. "It was supposed to be simple: go in, bomb a terrorist camp, get home, and brag about it to any news channel that would listen." He crossed his arms. "But you turn it into this whole song and dance—preventing your sergeant from blowing a civilian village off the face of the map, saving the base, rescuing kidnapped girls, destroying the terrorists that I've been trying to track down for years—which turn out not to be terrorists after all—and exposing the leader I've been trying to find for weeks." He smirked. "Nice job."

"So it worked." Cortraire beamed. "Annais got the message to you?"

"Yup." Marviot sniffed. "The girl called me all in a panic. I didn't understand anything until she mentioned 'krakken.' When she gave me the message and I understood what you were trying to say, I couldn't believe it. By the way, 'BANE of my existence'? Is that the best you could come up with?"

Cortraire shrugged. "I was under pressure."

"Thanks to you I got to Bain before he could try anything." Marviot twitched his ears. "I heard the story of how you figured it out from Chall.

I have to say, you've got good ears. I wouldn't have been able to recognize his voice from that recording."

"It's how he spoke." Cortraire clutched the edge of his sheets. "It's distinctive."

"You wouldn't believe some of the stuff we found in his house." Marviot ground his teeth together. "He had girls from the previous terrorist camps we've hit locked up in his basement. And there's an investigation going to find out if they were even really terrorist camps." He cursed. "He had us all fooled. Well, most of us." He smiled at Cortraire. "When do you get out of here?"

"Another few days or so." Cortraire laid his head back on his pillow. "I can't wait to go home. I miss Annais. How is she doing? Did you tell her about my injuries?"

"I had to." Marviot blew through his nose. "Ever since you sent her that message, she wouldn't stop whining about you. And when her brother got home, and you weren't with the team…"

"Poor Ani…"

"Poor Ani? Poor me." Marviot turned up his nose. "I had to put up with her—"

"What are you talking about? I'm tired of waiting." A feminine voice shouted from in the hall. "My husband's in there, and I'm going to see him."

Marviot narrowed his eyes. "Speaking of…"

Cortraire shot up in bed. "Annais is here?" He winced and clutched his arm.

"And loud wherever I take her." Marviot hefted himself out of the chair. He walked to the door and opened it.

Annais' voice barged in like a freight train. "I am not being belligerent; you're being belligerent! Get your hands off of me!"

"Hey!" Marviot spoke in a voice that, though soft, cut through all the commotion. "She belongs here. Let her in."

"That's right," Annais said, and Cortraire could picture a superior smile on her face. "Hands off! What kind of man puts his hands on a pregnant lady, anyway?" She walked in with her nose in the air. But when her eyes fell on Cortraire, all her defiance melted. "Oh, Cortraire!" She held her hands over her mouth.

"Annais!" Cortraire held his hands out to her.

"Cortraire!" She rushed to him, fell on top of him, and threw her arms around him. He winced in pain but didn't push her away.

"We're leaving in ten minutes, Annais. No longer. I'm taking you back to the city, and I have a schedule to keep." Marviot walked out without another word.

"I was so worried about you, Cortraire." Annais sobbed in his hospital gown. "I was scared that I lost you."

"I missed you so much." Cortraire inhaled her scent. It flooded his nostrils and made him feel as if he were home. "You were all I could think about while I was gone."

"My brother told me you were here. He drove me over, but they wouldn't let me come see you until Marviot came." Annais clutched to him. "What would I have done if you didn't come home?"

"I'm fine, Annais." Cortraire held her, ignoring the pain his arm, side, and leg.

"You are not fine!" Annais pulled away so she could look him in the eyes. "Look at you. You're lying in a hospital bed with bandages all over. You almost died!" Tears rolled down her face.

"Don't cry." Cortraire wiped the tears from her cheeks. "There's no way I could ever leave you. How's the baby?" He placed his hand on her stomach. He felt a bump push against his hand. "He or she is still as active as ever I see."

Annais wiped her eyes. "They're fine, Cortraire."

"I'm so glad."

Annais chuckled. "Still the hints go right over your head."

"What are you talking about?"

"Don't get mad, okay?" Annais took a tissue from the table and blew her nose. "I looked at the gender report."

"I thought we were going to wait."

"I couldn't help it, and I'm glad I looked. We would have had a big surprise if we made it all the way to delivery without knowing."

"Without knowing what? What are you going on about?"

"We're having boys… twin boys, Cortraire."

Cortraire stared at her a moment. "Wait, two of them?"

Annais nodded.

"Twins…" Cortraire laid his head back on the pillow. "Twins." He ran a hand through his hair. A laugh leapt out of him. "Twins! Ani!" He pulled her close to him and kissed her, right on the lips. It had been a long time since he had done that. He had forgotten how soft her lips were, even though they were a bit chapped. He ran his hands down her spine and to the base of her tail. Her curves felt smooth and natural under his hands.

154

"Wow." Annais said when he let her go. "You've never kissed me like that before."

"Does… it bother you?"

Annais shook her head. "Frankly, I wish you'd do it more often."

"Then your wish is my command." Cortraire held her close to him. "I'll be sure to do it as much as I can from now on."

"Cortraire… you…" Annais brushed down her hair.

"Stop that." Cortraire caught her hand. "Why do you always mess with your hair like that?"

"Oh!" Annais' ears lowered. "You know… no reason… nervous habit."

"Ani." Cortraire looked her in the eyes.

She sighed through her nose. "It's… it's so messy all the time." She smoothed down her hair. "My mother used to tell me that I'd never keep a man if with my hair a mess. I try to keep it neat but…"

"Ani, you don't need to worry about that. I love your flippy hair the way it is." Cortraire ran his hands through her hair. "The ends look like pink, crescent moons."

Annais looked at him. "Really?"

"It's one of the things I love about you. So stop messing with it, okay?"

"You're so sweet, Cortraire."

"Come over here." Cortraire pulled her close and kissed her again.

"It's time to go, Annais." Marviot barged in. "We have to—oh, really? Can't you two at least wait until you get home? This is a hospital, not some seedy motel. Have some restraint."

"No, no, no. No more restraint." Cortraire looked in Annais' eyes. "I am never letting go of her again."

Annais giggled.

"That's cute." Marviot rolled his eyes. "You're going to have to let her go for a little while at least, Cortraire. Let's go, Annais. I'm leaving."

"All right." Annais stood, rubbing her belly. "Come home soon, Cortraire."

"I'll be home before you know it."

Annais kissed his temple and ran her hand along his face before heading to the door. She paused in front of Marviot. "Thank you for letting me in here, Marviot."

"I didn't do it for you." Marviot smiled at Cortraire. "I did it for my brother." He winked at Cortraire before walking out behind her. The door closed.

Cortraire laid his head back on the pillow. Imagine. Boys... twin boys. Now he had another reason to hurry up and get better. Plus, he'd have to help redo the house to make room for one more baby. He grinned. He couldn't wait to get back to home.

\* \* \*

Cortraire's leg twinged in pain, but he shook it out as he walked into the Capitol building. He took in a deep breath. It smelled and looked the same as it had the last time he'd come here. With a smile that took up his face, Cortraire strolled across the lobby to the elevators.

"Private Cunor!" A voice called from down the hall.

"Do you mean me or my brother?" Cortraire turned to see who was addressing him.

"You, of course." Mal walked over to him.

"Mal! Good to see you." Cortraire caught sight of his insignia. "Oh, you're a Corporal now!" He saluted.

"What are you doing?" Mal smacked his hand out of the air.

"You deserve it after what you did for Artis and me." Cortraire placed a hand on Mal's shoulder. "It was brave of you to come back into the battlefield to look for us. How is she, by the way?"

"She's fine." Mal grinned. "She got back here faster than you."

"I'm sure she won't let me forget it, either." Cortraire chuckled.

"What are you doing here? I thought you weren't back on duty until next week."

"I couldn't stay still any longer." Cortraire smiled at him. "Three weeks is far too long to be stationary. I had some paperwork I wanted to file, so..."

"Overachieving as always. At least that's what my sister would say. By the way, I have a message from the Grand Councilwoman. She wants to see you. Marviot asked me to deliver it to your house, but since you're here..." Mal handed him the note.

Cortraire took the note. His stomach sank. "Oh, great."

"Isn't an invitation to visit the Grand Councilwoman supposed to be a good thing?"

"Well... it's... it's a family issue." Cortraire smirked. "Thank you for giving this to me, Mal." He saluted.

"Stop that!" Mal smacked his hand out of the air. "Besides, you'll be joining me in no time. You'll see." He strode down the hall, waving over his shoulder.

Cortraire watched him walk off. "You know, something, Mal. I think you're right. I won't let anything stop me." He studied the note. "Not even you, *Grammai*... or rather, Mrs. Grand Councilwoman." He continued his trek toward the elevators. Once he filed the paperwork, he'd go see her. Though, honestly, he could think of ten other things he'd rather be accomplishing that day, and eight of them involved Annais.

\* \* \*

Cortraire peeked into the Grand Councilwoman's office. "You wanted to see me, ma'am?"

"Yes, come in, Cortraire." The Grand Councilwoman stood with her back to the door.

Cortraire walked in. He saluted.

The Grand Councilwoman turned to face him. "Cortraire, I—why are you saluting me?"

"Considering our last encounter, Mrs. Grand Councilwoman, I didn't know how I should approach you."

"Mrs. Grand Councilwoman..." She chuckled to herself. "Call me *Grammai*, Cortraire." She took her seat.

"But you said—"

"That was before." The Grand Councilwoman rested her chin in her hands. She heaved a sigh. "I am an old, foolish vixen, Cortraire. Truly, truly, I am. When I heard that you had stopped your team from annihilating that settlement, I was proud of you. When I heard that you were the one who exposed Bain, I was floored. But when I heard that you were laying in a hospital near death... I... I was terrified." She gazed at her desk for a stretch. "All I could think of was how I could lose my grandson. I cried for days." She wiped her eyes. "Honestly, I didn't know I loved you that much."

"Neither did I," Cortraire said. "You never showed it much."

"Like I said, I'm an old, foolish vixen." The Grand Councilwoman bowed her head. "Forgive me, Cortraire. I'm so glad you're okay."

Cortraire smiled at her. "I'll gladly forgive you, *Grammai*."

The Grand Councilwoman snorted through her nose. "You're nothing like Marviot or myself. We would have held a grudge for ages." She opened a drawer on her desk.

"What's the point of holding grudges?"

"Power, I guess." The Grand Councilwoman pulled out a file. "You'll be happy to know that the Military Council has voted to reopen your promotion application, Corporal. Congratulations."

"That's great, *Grammai*, but..." Cortraire held up the paper he carried in his hands. "I came here today to file for a military name change."

The Grand Councilwoman furrowed her brows. "A name change? Cortraire, that's for military women who get married and want to change their last name."

"There's nothing that says a man can't file the paperwork." Cortraire jerked his thumb over his shoulder. "I just finished. It's stamped and everything. I'm officially Private Cortraire now, so I'm afraid that promotion may no longer valid."

"So let me get this straight." The Grand Councilwoman sat straight in her chair. "You don't want to be known by Cunor anymore?"

"No, I don't. Not in my military career, at least."

"Cortraire..."

"*Grammai*, your values for the Cunor name and how I conduct myself are completely different. We'd only continue to butt heads." Cortraire held his hands behind his back. "Besides, I decided that I don't want to get promoted or to receive special treatment because of my name. I want to earn them. And when I do make it up here—and I will make it up here, *Grammai*—I want to use the influence I earn to change some things."

The Grand Councilwoman studied his face. She pressed her lips together. "I will admit one thing, you are more popular with the common folk than either Marviot or myself." She took a deep breath. "You will still keep the name Cunor for legal documents and anything to do outside of the military?"

"Of course. I love my family. I don't want to leave it behind."

"Then I will allow it."

"Thank you."

"I still think you'll get your promotion, Cortraire." The Grand Councilwoman stood. "What you did when you saved those people and rescued those girls... and me... it's the least we can do." Her whiskers stiffened. "Even if you did save Outsiders in the process."

"Thank you, *Grammai*."

"By the way, congratulations." The Grand Councilwoman smiled at him. "I hear you're having twins."

"Yes, both boys."

"Twins..." The Grand Councilwoman turned her attention to the wall where a carving of a fox and a vixen holding hands and dancing had been carved. "Ania and Gorrtan truly seem to have their eye on you."

Cortraire turned to the carving. Ania and Gorrtan, the Expermian goddess and god of death, ruled the underworld together. It was said that when a person came close to death but survived, it was because Ania had pity on them and sent them away from the gates of death and back to the world of the living. Further, since Ania and Gorrtan were twins, all multiple pregnancies were a sign of the gods' blessing.

"Maybe they do. At least…" Cortraire clutched his chest. It had gotten tight for some reason. "… sometimes I feel someone has their eye on me."

"Well, then." The Grand Councilwoman turned to him. "Back home with you. Get some rest, and get well soon, Cortraire."

"Yes, *Grammai.*" Cortraire turned to leave. But before he did, he reached over the desk and gave his grandmother a kiss on the cheek.

"Oh!" The Grand Councilwoman touched her cheek. "No one's done that to me since your grandfather was alive."

"I hope I didn't overstep my boundaries."

She shook her head. "It was a nice surprise."

Cortraire gave a slight bow before leaving the room. He made his way back down to the lobby with a grin on his face. Time to head home with Annais.

\* \* \*

"I don't care what you have to do!"

Cortraire exited the elevator to Annais' voice resounding across the lobby. She stood at the reception desk with her tail bristling.

The receptionist stiffened his whiskers. "Ma'am, I'll need you to calm down—"

"Don't tell me to calm down! My husband could be lying on the floor bleeding from open wounds." She jabbed the receptionist in the chest. "Find him now!"

"Ani, what are you doing in here?" Cortraire approached her. "I thought you were going to wait in the car."

"Cortraire." Annais swung around. "You took so long I thought something happened to you. I shouldn't have let you out of the house. You might feel better, but you're not healed yet. Your injuries could have reopened or—"

"Alright, alright, Ani." Cortraire raised his hands. "But you can't go around threatening people to get your way."

"I've learned that when you don't have a name to back you up, you have to be tough." Annais crossed her arms.

"Ani." Cortraire let his ears angle back.

"Perhaps I did go too far." Annais grinned at the receptionist. "Sorry about that. I was worried about him." She pointed at her belly. "Blame it on pregnancy hormones."

The receptionist gave a nod and a smirk. Cortraire rolled his eyes. This story would spread all over the base. He wasn't going to hear the end of it when he resumed his duties next week.

"But you should be in bed, Cortraire." Annais pointed to the door. "To the car. Let's go."

"I'll give in since you're such a cute nurse." Cortraire kissed her behind the ears.

"Cortraire." Annais swatted at him. "You got so frisky since you came back."

"Life's too short to hold back." He leaned on her, pretending to need her help to walk.

Annais supported him out of the building and down the front path. The ends of her hair tickled his nose.

Cortraire smiled. This might not be the ideal lifestyle for a Cunor, but it was his. And he loved every minute of it.

*Revolutions seem to be a regular part of history. For thousands of years, the ethnic components of a country, of a supposedly united people, have revolted to become their own nation, to gain their own independence.*

*But what if the successful new nation subdivides again? If its peoples have a new revolution? What happens to former friendships?*

# Close to Us

## by Mikasi Wolf

Isla laughed as he chased Lensky, the wolverine's bulk making him stumble as he pursued the black-striped badger. Lensky leapt over a seesaw before him, and that was all Isla needed for an advantage. Bracing a footpaw against the center beam, the wolverine leapt, all four paws finding the badger as he landed. Lensky stumbled and twisted, only to collapse in a tangle of fur as Isla's weight and strength reigned victorious. He squealed as Isla jabbed his belly mercilessly with blunt, worn claws. The two youngsters lay on the rubber padding of the playground, bellies heaving hard.

"Nice technique," giggled Lensky. For a large guy, the wolverine was pretty agile in his own way.

"Old wolverine trick," said Isla proudly. His voice was accented with a Chekish slant. "Leap from higher ground and land on your target. Helped us many times when our forefathers fought the Ostravs." His stumpy ears twitched as he heard the distant ring of a bell. "Hey, want to get some ice cream?"

The badger sat up and brushed the dirt off his fur and clothes. "Sure. My name's Lensky, by the way. Lensky Schmander." He held out a black-furred paw.

"Isla Racovitch," replied the wolverine with a fanged grin, drawing Lensky into a hug. Lensky's eyes opened wide as he felt the paws of a complete stranger around him. "Traditional Chekish greeting. Hope you don't mind?" Isla raised his eyebrows with a smile as he stood.

"No, I don't," answered Lensky, briefly wondering what his parents would say if they saw. He accepted Isla's paw as he pulled him up.

\* \* \*

"So, where do you go to school?" asked Isla as the two cubs stuck their snouts into their cups of ice cream. "Never seen you around here before."

The wolverine was stocky for someone who was ten years of age, larger than most other Chekish kits. His fur was surprisingly well-kept for a wolverine, though several strands kept sticking out no matter how hard he smoothed them down. On the other paw, Lensky's fur was immaculately smooth and clean, a faint scent suggesting the use of fur conditioner.

"Jalen Junior School, about a half kilometer that way," said Lensky, gesturing with his muzzle. "Since Father allowed me to walk to school alone, he figured I'm old enough to go anywhere else by myself. The school holidays are on, so I thought I'll take a chance at the playground."

"Your father sounds strict," remarked Isla, wrinkling his strawberry-cream muzzle. "You're like what, 9 years old now?"

"That's right," Lensky slurped proudly, tongue curling through the recesses of the cup.

"No way!" exclaimed Isla, throwing his head back. "You waited that long for your freedom?"

"I beg your pardon?" asked Lensky with an eyebrow raised.

"In Chek society, everyone's free to go where they want by the time they're six!" exclaimed Isla. He smacked Lensky on the back, squashing dessert into his snout. "Think of the places you can be, the fun you're missing! You got any brothers or sisters?"

"No, I'm a single cub," said Lensky, swirling his tongue hard around his nose and muzzle. Cream bubbled out from a nostril.

Isla dropped his face into his other paw. "Ah, then you don't know what you're missing! Come play with me and my brother sometime. You come to this park often?"

Lensky thought about it for a moment. Isla seemed like an interesting guy. "No, but I'll like to meet you both."

Isla smiled. "Same time here tomorrow?"

Lensky clasped his paw. "Yes! See you then!"

\* \* \*

Lensky couldn't wait for tomorrow to come. It wasn't easy convincing his parents that he just wanted to have fun by himself, when asked if he could go to the playground. He would have told them he wished to meet a new friend, but then, his parents had never approved of Cheks. "They may have helped us win the war," Father had snorted as he drew back his pipe. "But they're still a rowdy, barbaric lot! Drinking parties after work from Monday to Friday? Not to mention bar brawls just for the fun of it! Stay clear from them, my son, and you'll have nothing to worry about. There're many other folks you can be friends with."

More than once, Lensky had asked what this war was and how anyone could ever wish harm upon another. Mother had then shushed him, saying that there was a time and place to explain. But that time never came. Not even the history lessons in school delved into it.

\* \* \*

"So what do your parents do for a living?" asked Isla as he and Lensky clawed their way onto the molded plastic roof. The badger had hesitated to take the risk, but Isla had encouraged him not to fear as long as he followed his lead. Tracing the makeshift footholds Isla had used was easily done, and the two mustelids soon sat at the highest point of the castle, undisputed Lords of the Playground. Isla's brother couldn't make it as he needed to help Grandpa with one of his errands.

"They're officials in the Ministry of Order," confirmed Lensky. "They help in making policies regarding what rules citizens have to follow, and liaise with their Chek counterparts on conflicting ones. What's yours?"

"Oh, Ma and Pa's dead," said Isla calmly. Lensky almost toppled off the roof, but the wolverine grabbed the scruff of his neck in time.

"That's horrible!" exclaimed the badger, composing himself in a dignified manner. Isla shrugged.

"Death is part of life. There is nothing to be sad about," answered Isla, resting his paws on his lap. His ears remained up. "It comes regardless of who you are, so what's there to worry? Ma and Pa died fighting the Ostravs as members of the Chekish Resistance, so we knew they died for a good cause. Having given their lives for my people, my relatives consider them heroes. We sing of their names whenever a toast is proposed!" The wolverine swung his fist forward as he stood, his figure silhouetted against the rising sun. "When I grow up, I wanna be a soldier or cop. Then I can protect my people as they did. What do you wanna do?" Isla sat back down, muzzle trained on Lensky. His light brown eyes were so bright Lensky couldn't tear his eyes from them.

"A little young to be thinking of a job, don't you think?" The badger stuttered. Isla sure saw things differently. Lensky hadn't spoken to any

Cheks in his neighborhood before, what with him having gone to an all-Mel school at his parent's behest and all.

Isla shook his head, flapping his paw. "It's your life. Is it ever too late to think about it?"

Lensky bit his lip. "Well, Father and Mother work in the Ministry, so I'll probably get a job in policy-making or law enforcement." His eyes brightened. "Hey, maybe we can join the United Law together! We can fight criminals side-by-side!"

"Sounds good, I plan on going as soon as I'm done with High School," said Isla, stretching himself out on the warm plastic roof. He closed his eyes as a patch of sun found his face, lighting up the different hues in his brown and black fur. "From what I've heard, you only need a leaving cert and to be eighteen to join."

"What about college?" said Lensky, his brow creasing. "Father says that you need that if you want to make a decent living."

"For now, relax, brother." said Isla with his eyes closed. "Chekish words of wisdom. 'Rest before suffering.' You'll have plenty of time to think about all that. Or not."

Lensky recalled how strong and confident Isla had looked when he stood earlier, so sure of life and his path through it. With the sun on him, he looked so happy, so carefree. The badger wanted very much to feel that way, to not have his parents' expectations weighing upon him. He lay back against the warm roof, and only then did he get what Isla had said.

This was the life.

* * *

He had lunch at Isla's house that day. Isla's Grandpa didn't care whether Lensky was there or not, as long as his boys got his lunch and vodka ready while he went to chat with a friend who just got off work. Lensky helped Ivor with the potatoes, hastening to help the younger wolverine lift a tureen half his size. Isla and Ivor were only ten and nine but the two had a certain independence absent in the upbringing Lensky was subjected to. Although the food was nothing fancy, what with the Racovitch's meals being provided out of veteran donations by the local chapter of Chek Veterans, there was enough to eat. Grandpa had hung up his service jacket for good after the Chekish Resistance disbanded five years back, with two medals for distinguished and long-term service. According to Isla, the war itself had lasted ten years, but Grandpa had been involved in Resistance Operations since he was 16. For close to eighty years, the Ostravs had ruled much of the continent through conquest, including the historic homeland of the Mels and Cheks. After years of preparation, the resistance finally happened, resulting in a full-blown war. The war had brought his son and daughter-in-law together, when Resistance members were sent to reinforce their comrades in the widely-contested capital. Lensky felt totally at home here, despite Mels rarely being in the company of Cheks. The two brothers threw wisecracks at each other so much like a conversation that Lensky was hesitant to join in, least he offended someone.

"Where do I set this?" asked Lensky as Isla hefted a large pot of some weird stew onto the creaking table.

"Just thereabouts," gestured Isla at the center of the table. "Take your seat, Lensky. We're going to give thanks before we start."

"What about your Grandpa?" asked Lensky as he sat next to Ivor. The younger kitten beamed at him and Lensky smiled back nervously. His fur was neater than his brother's, with a light brown patch on the front of his throat.

"Grandpa always has his lunch late. He'll take a while with his friend," Isla rolled his eyes. "Shall we?" Isla sat down on Lensky's other side as he gave him a wink.

The two wolverines each grasped Lensky's paw as they bowed over the table. Lensky followed their lead quickly, despite being taken by surprise.

"Thanks we give to those who came before, those who gave their lives and blood to feed, nourish, and nurture us," chanted Isla and Ivor together. "We thank you, dear Forefathers for sending a good friend our way, though he be of different fur. Praised be."

Isla and Ivor released their grip, words of the chant resonating through Lensky. When he blinked, there were tears in his eyes, his lip quivering at the words of the penultimate sentence. It was so personal, almost like it had been worded specially for the occasion. Never had he felt so welcome, with that sense of belonging radiating through him. He hastily drew the back of his paw across his eyes.

Isla smiled and placed a paw on his shoulder. "Tears are for times of sadness, brother, and not happy occasions. And we're both glad you can be with us. It is not often that good friends come our way, and Ivor agrees. What say we eat and drink to the start of friendship?"

And right at that moment, Lensky realized he didn't care what his parents thought. As one, he and his friends placed their glasses together and drank. A toast to family, friendship, and of better things to come. It was the first time he tasted alcohol.

\* \* \*

Lensky had always known he would go to police academy, but never did he think it would be without his parents' blessing. Two years after the Racovitch family had toasted in his honor, Father had discovered his friendship, spying the three of them seated together at a bench. He had yelled at the wolverines to go back and be good citizens, dragging Lensky back by the scruff of his neck. When he got home, Lensky was taken to his room and thrashed, each beating for every month he had presumably known the Racovitches. He was ordered to cease all dealings with Cheks, friend or otherwise. The fact that clashes between the Cheks and Mels were recent news meant that the good reputation of the Schmander family could have been besmirched, forget the fact that his "friends" were probably involved in those clashes some way or another. Ever since the Cheks and the Mels were united as one nation after the defeat of their oppressive Ostrav rulers, cultural and social differences between the two groups had been a constant cause for tensions. From what Lensky could gather, the Cheks did most of the actual fighting during the War, while the smaller-sized Melish were generally assigned to support roles. The Melish hated playing second-fiddle to their more outgoing counterparts, and it wasn't long after the war ended that they made their displeasure clear. But the Chekish culture of honoring their fallen during simple get-togethers at the bar and full-scale memorial days only further served to fuel the anger of the Mels', believing these served to remind the badgers of their superiority.

Lensky had a choice; cease all dealings with the Racovitches or be disowned. He humored his father, though by now he understood enough of Chekish culture to see past his parents' delusion. He could understand why others would see Cheks as unruly; they partied hard, believing life should be lived to the fullest. They belched after each meal to express their thanks to the Forefathers for providing for them. They had brawls to resolve disagreements, because only then could they truly let it all out. But all in all, they were still a respectable people worthy of their cultural heritage and pride.

Lensky agreed that his grades in school had been sliding; but Isla and Ivor had taught him things about society he wouldn't have learnt in a Mel-run school. They taught him how to think of life in its finer points, rather than in numbers and figures. They taught him how to respect people of different fur, such as the elderly Ostrav wolf couple who lived just a street away. Despite staying on after their people were driven out of the country by the victors, the Cheks in the neighborhood still gave them the dignity accorded to elders, allowing them to age gracefully in an otherwise hostile land.

So it came as no surprise that Lensky signed up as an officer of the United Law with Isla shortly after High School. Already eighteen, his parents no longer had any say in the matter. The two friends stood solemnly beside each other as they were sworn in before the two flags of the United Alliance, never alone even here. Where other enlistees had parents and family weeping after them as they marched, no one except Ivor saw the two friends off, solidifying their resolution in each other. They braved the same drills and morning parades. They covered for each other when the Parade Sergeant came by, and shouldered each other as the route marches wore onto them.

The unarmed combat training sessions began two weeks into their training. The instructor, a grizzled-furred Drill Sergeant named Pazca who had fought under the Melish resistance during the Ostrav Oppression paced before the seated recruits, sizing up the crop before him. He nodded approvingly at the proportional mix of Melish and Chekish greenhorns.

"Every apprehension of a suspect requires the use of unarmed combat!" barked Staff Sergeant Pazca, his intensity causing ears to flatten. "You may be armed with a truncheon or sidearm in your duties, but one won't always have such good friends by his side!" Nobody laughed. "Maybe you have your cuffs out; or worse, a troublemaker shows himself when you go off-duty! But with the right technique, every suspect can be overcome!"

Sergeant Pazca approached his larger badger assistant from behind. In a flick of a whisker, the corporal was down on the ground with the Sergeant bent over him, paw twisted behind his back. The way the Sergeant lay over the prone corporal with his teeth gritted piqued Lensky's interest as the corporal let out a groan. Something more tangible started creeping to his mind, but it was gone the instant Sergeant Pazca stood back up. The badger wondered if they would repeat that move again.

"I want two of you jokers to show me how it's done!" barked Staff Pazca. "Racovitch, Schmander, you're up!"

Lensky looked nervously at the recruits sitting behind him as he and Isla went up to the training mat. This wasn't the first time he had been called up, so perhaps the Sarge believed he had potential. He wondered who would be doing the restraining first. If Isla was, he had a point of reference to follow. Wolverine and Badger stood before one another, the eyes of their peers boring onto them. The size difference between the two species was yet another reminder of how different they were. The scent of badger lingered where the corporal had been.

Sergeant Pazca glared at them with his paws crossed. "You waiting for Year's End? Restrain one another!"

For a moment Lensky's mind turned blank. The instant Isla darted forward, he understood.

The badger ducked to the right, guessing that at that angle, Isla would stumble as he moved, making it easier to get behind him. For a split-second, that seemed to work, the next, 180 pounds of wolverine slammed atop him, Lensky's paws drawn behind his back. Isla's musk hit his nostrils and he struggled to fight against him, the pungent scent spurring him to greater exertion. The wolverine's strength prevailed, and the badger felt Isla slam back against him, his muzzle a mere nose-length away. Lensky was close enough to feel and smell Isla's breath coming in short pants, and his eyes widened.

"Well executed!" exclaimed Sergeant Pazca as he and the trainees clapped. Isla looked sheepish before standing back. Lensky remained on the training mat, his paws aching something awful. "I want everyone to pair off and follow Isla's example. Chop chop!"

"You okay?" asked Isla as Lensky got up slowly, the ache in his arms fading through his muscles. The badger's shorts suddenly felt much too uncomfortable as the wolverine's musk lingered on him, tantalizing yet teasing. Lensky turned away, readjusting his shorts as he did.

"I'm fine. Just need to catch my breath," he panted. Isla nodded and stepped back, stumbling slightly as he did.

\* \* \*

"So how long has it been?" asked Isla as he and Lensky stood outside their bunkroom at night. The argument from the other trainees over whose turn it was to sweep the bunkroom could be heard, but the wolverine knew no one would listen in on them.

Lensky placed his paws on the railing, looking at the parade square four floors down. Three flagpoles stood before it, bare of flags now that it was night. For years, he had seen his peers in school pair up, not always of the same fur, but always of the other gender. There were a few girls he had hung out with during recess, but he hadn't seen them as anything more than schoolmates. Tanja Heinz was always trying to chat him up, and he didn't understand why until a year later. By then, she was already with someone else. Lensky already knew he wasn't alone in this; he had heard of guys who liked other guys, such as Leo in the class next to his. But Leo's classmates had always given him a hard time, and once the school bully Leeds had beaten him for being seen with his brother.

Lensky had thus told himself he was straight like everyone else. But each time he thought he got over it, he was reminded otherwise whenever he met the Racovitches. The fact that he enjoyed the company of the brothers more than that of his school peers became a bigger cause for worry. Of the two of them, Isla put him most at ease, always there with an encouraging word. Those muscles of his were a bonus. Ivor was more of the quiet type, and was far less outspoken than his brother. He was also intellectual and thoughtful of society and life in its finer points. He could hold a conversation with Lensky about the Theory of Species Selection from noon to dusk, and Lensky had to admit that his smaller size gave him a certain cuteness Isla didn't have. The realization that he was different haunted him, and the badger had considered talking to the Racovitches about it. But who was to say that the strongest of friendships could not be broken by conflicting opinions? He wondered if Ivor knew about his being gay; the younger wolverine was too observant to not have.

"I guess it was some time after meeting the both of you," sighed Lensky, bracing for Isla's anger. "What about you?" he added tentatively.

"About three years?" Isla wrinkled his brow. "Not that I didn't like you earlier, but I didn't know what you made of it. Ivor thinks you're cute, but don't tell him I said that. You really think you can hide anything from your closest friends? It was pretty clear from the start."

"Oh my," Lensky felt giddy all of a sudden. "You knew before?"

Isla threw back his arms. "Sure we do! Why, you worried we'll squeal on you?" he laughed.

"No, it's just that…" Lensky's tongue seized up. "It's just that it feels so…strange. I don't know what to think of this."

"Don't think, just do," said Isla simply. "Looks pretty straightforward to me, if you'd pardon the expression. You like us. We like you. What's so hard about that?"

"But I can't decide who I want to be with." replied Lensky.

"No one's asking you to choose. There's enough of you for the both of us." Isla winked at the badger.

Lensky glared at him. "Come on, let's be serious here! Is everything really that clear-cut to you? I understand what you mean but I believe one should only share his life with one other. Otherwise it's bigamy."

"While the other lives his life in despair, waiting for his one true love," cooed Isla. He laughed as Lensky punched him in the shoulder. "Life isn't complicated, little badger. It's only the people in it that make it so." The wolverine stretched himself, the muscles on his exposed chest rippling. "Anyway, it's late. All you need is a good sleep, and it'll be better tomorrow. You'll see." The wolverine went back into the bunkroom,

Lensky growled in frustration, banging his paws on the railing. Everything to Isla seemed so simple, so straightforward. But the more he thought about it, the more he realized that all the good advice he had came not from his parents or society, but from the wolverines he grew up with. When had Isla ever gotten him into trouble despite his way of thinking things? Ivor would probably be cautious, like he was being, but would most likely agree that overthinking never helped anyone. Perhaps Lensky's only problem was his Melish upbringing, where everything had to be done by society's expectations and the law.

It was five minutes to lights out. Lensky took a look back before rushing to the loo. Man, just thinking how Isla looked, and he so needed that.

\* \* \*

Lensky could barely sleep that night, but the conversation he'd had with Isla had definitely given him a new perspective. It was all he could do not to think of Isla's form during training. Twice, he didn't hear his Drill Sergeant call him, and ended up doing push-ups as punishment. Fifty push-ups were hard on the arms, but Lensky could see Isla looking almost hungrily at him whenever his arms flexed up and down, his body buckling with the effort.

The weekends off saw the three of them meeting up for dinner and vodka, and it was then Lensky realized how good company the two brothers were. He really couldn't choose between the two of them. Each had their own unique quirks and personalities that he found attractive. By the ninth weekend after their training had concluded, Lensky received his first nuzzle. The three of them were sitting on a lookout point overlooking the Twin Capitals of the United Alliance, the cool evening breeze blowing onto their fur. They had driven up here straight from the academy. On the left lay Tasvous where most of the Cheks lived, and on the right was Belhinder. The lights on the Belhinder side were brighter, as Mels tended to work long hours in the office.

"So what are your plans for the future?" asked Ivor of Lensky and Isla. Despite the cool air, the younger wolverine wore cut-offs and a sports vest that exposed most of his fur.

"Well, we just finished our training, so all we can do for now is wait for our posting. A few years on the beat, then I'll probably opt to take the detective exam," answered Lensky. Isla gaped.

"Why would you do that? True protection of the people comes from the ground work!" the wolverine snorted.

Lensky's muzzle twitched. "Hey, detectives protect the people too, you know. You know, by working on cases? I don't want to be a patrolman my whole life."

"Kind of hard to understand the people when you'll be behind a desk, don't you think?" snorted Isla. "You remember Corporal Pavel who walks the beat near our house? He says the detectives only go out after the crime has already been committed. How useful is that? Me, I'm gonna be a patrolman. Then I can catch the perp before he does anything. With the public disturbances that keep occurring recently, I'm guessing there's going to be a lot to be done soon."

There was no reasoning with the wolverine when he spoke like this. "I guess," said Lensky. "What about you, Ivor? You're studying sociology at the University, so what do you want to be?"

Ivor was silent for a while. "A politician," he finally said.

"Why?" Ivor held a debate well, as he had proven during their conversations, but he didn't strike the badger as the strong, confident type. The way the politicians at United Hall yelled over one other on TV, one almost expected them to have experience putting people down. Perhaps from the Police or Army.

"You know the recent clashes between the Melish and Chekish youths?" began Ivor. Lensky nodded slowly. "I think the main reason why conflict exists is because each side doesn't understand enough about the other. If I'm a politician, I will be able to educate the people about this."

"My little bro, a politician?" Isla wrinkled his muzzle. "Next thing I hear is you becoming an activist."

Ivor scowled. "And what's wrong with that?"

"You ever see them parading around United Hall, calling for species equality, and marriage rights?" boomed Isla. "If what they did worked, well, we wouldn't have the social problems taking place right now, would we?"

"These things take time." Ivor's voice had an edge to it. Lensky had originally thought it had been nothing, but during the past year, the two brothers started arguing more often. More often than not, it occurred whenever Isla made comparisons over how those who didn't further their studies could go much further than those who did. The percentage of Chekish students accepted into institutions of higher learning were considerably less than that of the Melish, and Lensky knew how much getting into college meant to the younger wolverine. Isla was critical of what he called "The System", believing that the most fruitful way through life is to work alongside the people, rather than above them.

"Yeah, I know," huffed Isla. "A shitload of it."

Ivor stood up, his muzzle open in a snarl. "Well then, perhaps I should take my activist streak somewhere else? I'm heading back to the university." The younger wolverine stalked away from them.

"Hey, come back, Ivor!" called Lensky as he got up, but Isla pulled him back down onto the bench.

"Don't bother about him. Little kit's always going off in a huff when he can't win an argument." snorted Isla. "Seriously, calls himself a sociologist and lets me get the better of him?"

"You don't have to talk to him like that," said Lensky. "Getting into college means a lot to the little guy. You think putting him down's going to have him agree with you?"

"Little brothers should always respect their elders," said Isla. "And so should little badgers." He shifted closer and nuzzled Lensky's neck with a lick. The scent of the wolverine had gotten overpowering, and it was all Lensky could do not to flinch away. "Now that we're finally alone, I can think of a couple of things we can do…"

"Seriously, Isla, is that all you think about?" Lensky yelped as Isla's teeth grazed his neck.

"It's all I could after you held back on me all this while," growled Isla as his arm circled around Lensky's chest. "Come on, Ivor won't mind. There's no one here but us…"

Lensky had no idea what to do in such a situation. On one hand, his body wished to submit, the wolverine's insistence a strong encouragement. On the other, they were in a public space, and being caught doing something more than make out was a misdemeanor, enough to lose their badges for. This would mean that everything, from their high school education to the twelve weeks of training, would have been all for naught. The park wardens sometimes conducted surprise patrols, mainly for crime prevention. Isla would say they were "stopping people's fun".

"Come on, let's go back to my place," said Lensky pushing Isla away as coyly as he could. "It's got more than enough space for a big guy like you." The badger pulled away from Isla nibbling his ears.

"Forefathers! Did you just pull that line from 'Musk Detective'?" guffawed Isla, stumbling as he followed Lensky to the parking lot. The two of them got into the patrol car they had been issued, Lensky yelping as Isla squeezed his tail. The engine stalled five times before Isla could get it started. The car rolled down the hill's winding road faster than Lensky would have liked, and the badger could swear that it had more to do with impatience than anything else.

"This is Division 3, all units report in," crackled their car radio. Isla's ear flicked. Lensky grabbed the mouthpiece quickly as the car bumped over a curb.

"Car 11G, over," replied Lensky. "Come in, Division 3."

"Car 11G, proceed immediately to the corner of Henna and Braun," replied the operator. "Report to Captain Ira for your next orders. No sirens to be used en route."

Lensky frowned in confusion. "Division 3, please confirm. Officer Racovitch and I are currently on block leave from the Academy."

"All block leave was cancelled effective 2200hrs," replied the operator. "Failure to report for duty is a chargeable offense. Confirm your status, over."

Lensky looked furtively at Isla as he swallowed. "Car 11G heading to location. Over and out."

Isla growled as he swung his paw against the wheel. "Oh, fuck them! Let's go for a round first before seeing the Cap! I know a good place not five minutes from here."

"Whatever happened to 'Doing the ground work'?" snapped Lensky. "Put a sock in it. I'll make it up to you later, alright!"

They roared through the streets of Tasvous, making several sharp turns as they did. Several wolverines with bottles in paw cheered as they passed, and Lensky thought he recognized a couple of them from their bar sessions. He hoped it wasn't a high-risk incident they were reporting to. He and Isla had scored good grades at the academy, but that was nothing compared to experience in the field. A couple of drunks they could handle, but a full-scale riot was a different case. Proper equipment and another two months of specialized training were required for that.

They pulled up right beside a cluster of scattered patrol cars. Lensky leapt out, Isla following close behind. Many other officers were already there, including the recently graduated cadets. To his surprise, Lensky recognized Staff Sergeant Pasca and a couple of trainers from the academy. Drill Sergeants at the academy were rarely on call for incidents, so they must be really short of manpower. Parked nearby were several military trucks filled with rolls of concertina wire.

"You, go over to that side," said a uniformed Captain to Lensky, gesturing at the badgers to his right. "And you can stand over on this side, Chek." He gestured at the cluster of wolverine cops on the other side.

"With all due respect, Sir, I think Officers Schmander and Racovitch make a good team," coughed Staff Pasca.

"Fine!" the Captain threw up his paws. "Both of you, go to my left! Are these the last of the respondents?" he barked at a Lieutenant.

"Yes, Sir." The badger checked his clipboard.

The Captain lifted a megaphone to his lips. "Alright. All of you listen good," he announced. "We of the United Law are assisting the 2nd Melish Army in setting up an administrative boundary across the entire city. Don't ask why, the orders come from up top." The badger glared back at the assembled officers. "See those two lines opposite from each other? All officers on my right will set up the blockade there. Those on my left will do so here." He pointed at the street they were on. "Go! You will report directly to your Detail Sergeants!"

The officers surged forward to receive the rolls of wire from the soldiers in the truck. Lensky and Isla grabbed two rolls each and started mounting them onto the wooden posts the other officers were putting up. Several soldiers had started arriving by truck and patrolled among strategic points along the fortifications, rifles in paw.

"Isla, something's up," whispered Lensky. He was the only badger working the detail on their line.

"What?" growled Isla. He hadn't gotten over the delay in them getting back home together.

"Don't you find it strange?" the badger looked back at the other officers and soldiers around them. "The Captain separated the work detail into two groups, both of different species. The Mel officers have been sent to work on the fencing on Belhinder, while the Cheks on this side of Tasvous." The badger fidgeted with the wire as a soldier passed. "And look at the way these soldiers are patrolling. None of them are helping with the fortifications."

"That's what we're called here for. To set up this crap while they stand guard," said Isla. "You're overthinking again, little badger."

"I thought so too, but something's off," continued Lensky, gripping the length of wire gingerly. "Unlike the United Law, the two wings of the Army are still separated Chekish and Melish units, each run by the assigned Chekish or Melish Defense Minister. But by law, any joint operation requires troops of both groups to be present. Do you see any Chekish soldiers, Isla?" Lensky jerked his muzzle towards the trucks. "I don't! Even the UL Captain in charge of this gig is Melish. These soldiers aren't here to help us. They're here to stop us from running across the border! The Melish government wants to split the city. Perhaps even the whole country."

"Shit! Alright, I get your point. But what can we do?" answered Isla. "I'm not going over to Belhinder, sure as my name's Racovitch. We're in Tasvous where we belong."

"We've got to go get Ivor!"

Isla's eyes widened. Ivor's university, along with its dormitories lay on the other side.

"When the soldiers turn their backs, I want you to run over to the other side," hissed Isla. "You're a Mel, the other police won't notice anything strange about your being there. When I create a distraction, get as fast as you can to Ivor, alright?"

"I can't leave you!" said Lensky as his fur stood up.

"Ivor's roommate has a car, you can still make it back here before morning," growled Isla. "We'll be together soon enough. Promise." Isla lifted his paw.

Lensky gripped it. "Swear on it?"

"I swear by the Forefathers. Go!"

The soldiers didn't appear to be looking their way, so Lensky carried a roll of wire over to the Melish side. Keeping his head low and cap over his eyes, he looped the end of the wire around a post, stretching it out across the ground. Behind him was the expanse of park he and Isla had played at, interspersed with a couple of trees. Several low hills made up the elevation of the park, and the top of the playground could just be seen, about 80 meters away.

"Hey, soldiers, I've got a problem with this here wire!" yelled Isla. He kicked hard at a post, the wire rattling.

"So fix it!" scowled one of the privates. His comrades turned towards Isla. Their rifles were held at the ready, almost like they anticipated trouble from a Chek.

"Well, fuck you if I'm not trained in wirework like you army cunts!" spat Isla. The soldiers growled, and Lensky sidled his way to the park. Five meters...ten...fifteen...

"Hey, stop that guy!" yelled a soldier behind Isla and it was all Lensky needed to run.

Yells and gunfire rang out behind him, and Lensky kept himself low as he dashed in a route that led past the trees and bushes that would give him cover. Clods of dirt and wood fragments cascaded around him, eliciting a yell. Confusion reigned everywhere as the police officers yelled and ducked, those with pistols drawing them as they did. More than one yelled, having been cut by the wire. Lensky found cover behind a large tree. He could feel the thuds of high-velocity lead on the wood against his back, and knew that his cover was as precarious as his survival. A soldier yelled that he would be moving forward, and Lensky knew he would soon be caught.

"Run, my badger!" came Isla's voice, and there was a yell followed by screams. Lensky chanced a look around the tree and saw that Isla had grabbed a rifle from a soldier, firing several shots at him and the others. Lensky ran, turning his head back as he did. He could see the soldiers and several of the cops firing back at the wolverine, blood and fur erupting from his pelt. His eyes widened as Isla fell against a stretch of concertina wire, bladed barbs snagging his body upright as it fell. The badger turned his eyes back to the front as he whimpered, trying and failing to take in what had happened. It was only when he crossed the park and cut through two blocks that he stopped, leaning hard against a lamppost. At this time of night, there was no one around.

There was no way he was going back to Tasvous, not with the danger that came with crossing the border. Isla was dead, and it was all his fault. Had it not been for his idea, Isla would still be alive, despite the fact that they had been trying to take Ivor with them in the first place.

Ivor... Lensky's back slid down against the smooth metal. How could he ever break the news to the younger wolverine, and tell him that his brother was dead? If he hadn't talked Isla into it, he would still be alive. In fact, the three of them would still be, despite being separated by a barrier conceived by only the most insidious of governments. And he, Lensky, would be able to go back each day to Isla's arms...

Lensky knocked his own head against the lamppost. How could he be so selfish? Ivor was still his little brother, even without Isla. For now, he would have to make sure that he was okay. The younger wolverine needed someone with him, and that person was him. Staggering to a payphone, Lensky made a call to Ivor's dormitory.

\* \* \*

The badger barely made it into the door of his own apartment before he broke down, sobbing uncontrollably as he slid down against the wall of his room. A blurry photograph of a wolverine peered at him, and the badger reached out for it, knocking the frame over in his inebriation. He ignored the sting of broken glass as he seized it, paws fumbling to straighten it out.

It was the picture the three of them had taken in Isla's home two years after they met. Isla had Lensky and Ivor next to him in his signature choke hold, his muzzle open in a guffaw. Lensky and Ivor could be seen vainly trying to break free, bewilderment and laughter on their faces. They were so happy, so carefree that day. If Ivor hadn't stalked off in a huff when they were up on that hill, they might still be together. So near, yet so far...

"You all right, Lensky? I came as soon as you called."

He hadn't heard the door. Ivor stood stock still with an outstretched paw towards him, his other paw on the doorknob. He stepped forward even as Lensky staggered towards him, bawling and wailing as he did. Ivor held onto him in surprise as he shook, paws rubbing uncertainly against him.

"Come on, talk to me, Lensky?" whispered Ivor as the badger sniffed. Lensky couldn't bear to see the pain in the young wolverine's eyes. But as Isla's brother, he had a right to know, not matter how much it hurt.

"Isla died trying to protect me," sniffed Lensky, his heart breaking as he saw Ivor's features change to confusion. "The Melish Army and Police were trying to split the country, so I tried to cross to Belhinder. But the soldiers saw what I was doing and so Isla fought. I saw…I saw him fall. There was nothing I could do. I'm sorry, Ivor."

"But why?" Ivor's muzzle was furious as he pushed Lensky away. Tears had sprung into his eyes, his scent was tinged with anger and fear. "Why did you come back here? To be with your own kind? I hate you!" The wolverine dashed out of the room, and Lensky followed, catching by the arms. Ivor tried to shake him off, striking out at him.

"Please, Ivor, listen to me," Lensky choked. "I was coming to fetch you back to Tasvous."

"Why did you do it?" snarled Ivor. "I'm happy where I am!"

"Because Isla loves you. And so do I."

No more words were needed. The first cracks of despair erupted upon his face, and Ivor choked, kneeling on the ground as he bawled. The two mustelids held each other and shook. They remembered back to when they were cubs, enjoying each other's antics at the playground. They remembered how they would carefully climb to the top of the plastic castle, if only to see who could land best in the leaf pile the gardener had swept up. Many a sore back and bruise had been sustained then, but Lensky wished he could feel that just once more, if only to hear Isla's laugh again. The two mourners looked back at how much they had lost in such a short space of time, each new memory of times past yet another burr against their grief. Was it only an hour ago that he had spoken with Isla? Now he never would again, yet another victim of cruel fate. A fate created not by the Almighty, but by subjugation and the prejudice of those who knew not what it is to love, and have it lost. The badger had never hated his government more, but most of all he hated himself for still being alive while Isla went on his journey to the Forefathers.

Ivor stroked his paws absently against Lensky's back as they leant in on each other and sniffed. "Did Isla ever tell you what happened when I was six?" he croaked.

Lensky held him tighter. "Tell me."

"I was waiting in the park for Isla while he helped Grandpa with an errand. I remembered it was summer, and Grandpa had just given each of us a lolly. We enjoyed them as we couldn't afford more than one a year," Ivor sniffed. "Grandpa didn't get much for his pension, you see."

"Go on." sniffed Lensky.

"A short while later, a Mel brute and his friends came and stole my lolly. I felt like I had nothing left in the world. But Isla gave me his, just as he gave himself today." Ivor shook with the memory.

"Don't worry, little brother. I will take good care of you." whispered Lensky. "Just like Isla took care of us." The badger held onto the wolverine, the warmth comforting against his pelt. He didn't dare let go, for who knew if Ivor would fade from his life if he did? Life was fleeting, and more so were the ones close to you.

Ivor's head rested against Lensky's shoulder, a warm comforting weight against his pelt. The badger pushed his muzzle against the wolverine's face comfortingly, tongue searching and washing off his tears even as he sought solace in his own despair. Ivor tasted and smelled remarkably like his brother, and Lensky realized he could close his eyes and not know the difference. So different, yet so similar. He breathed in, letting every nuance and detail of the wolverine's scent wash through his nose, titillating and ingraining itself in his mind. If he would take good care of Isla who was to be his mate, how could he not with one so similar to the one he so loved? It wasn't like Ivor was a stranger; all those times they had gotten together, closer than he ever was to his parents. How could he not accept Ivor, not just as a brother but also as one he shared his hopes and aspirations with? Dreams that would be more meaningful with someone by his side? Just as Lensky would be the pillar of support for Ivor, the wolverine was his roof and arch, giving purpose in his otherwise meaningless existence. Just as no building existed on its foundations alone, no one could survive alone in a hard and unyielding world, each new challenge a storm threatening to rip apart what held it all together. If pillar and arch worked together, however, they would emerge victorious from the hurricane of fate, cracked but still standing. In time, the two of them would rebuild the foundations of their relationship before the next storm arrived, each new one serving to make them stronger.

Lensky held onto Ivor, lending him the support he needed. As long as he lived, he will take good care of this brother.

* * *

The Grid was set up over the next few days, prefab rebar mesh with concrete bases tilted upright onto the historical limits of Tasvous-Belhinder. What had been the park was now a cleared strip of land, with military and police personnel converging in the area.

The first news was announced during breakfast by radio. The Chief Minister of Belhinder declared that the constituent countries of Tasvous-Belhinder were now separate. Belhinder would henceforth be known as the Independent State of Belhinder, or ISB. All citizens currently on the ISB side of the border were automatically granted ISB citizenship, with no provisions made for negotiation or deportation. The Senior Minister of Tasvous was appalled that such a state of affairs could happen in their once-united country, and had demanded that Belhinder overturn its 'barrier of speciesist hate'.

The shootout at the border wasn't mentioned, and Lensky knew why. Tensions among the two species were bad enough as it was, with thousands displaced from their original halves of the city. Riots had broken out before government institutions in Belhinder, and were quickly put down by the recently-deployed Military. The badger was hesitant in reporting to the station the next day, but it seemed that in the confusion, UL stations at both sides had to revise their records, along with organizational structure. Patrol and guard details were hastily enacted, and it was by a cruel irony that Lensky found himself posted to the new checkpoint at the road leading through the Grid. Most of the recently graduated police officers spent their first assignments by the border, and it was the same on the Chekish side. Whether the officers served Belhinder or Tasvous were simply subject to the fate of where they were on that fateful day, rather than where they had lived. Lensky heard numerous accounts of families separated overnight, including that of a young Melish Private fresh out of the Academy. He had attempted to defect across the border to his family on the Chekish side, only to be shot down by the very peers he had trained alongside. Each incident hit closer to home, and Lensky knew how fortunate he himself was. He could have been killed that night, and Ivor wouldn't know what happened.

The start of the process of Reculturization was enacted shortly after the Grid, displacing most of the Cheks from their previous homes to state-run quarters by the border. Storefronts and Chekish influences were relocated or altogether removed, in order to protect the young from disruptive influences. Having foreseen potential challenges, Lensky had cleared the necessary paperwork with Police HQ for custody of Ivor. Despite suited agents checking on the apartment the wolverine shared with Lensky, the government couldn't lawfully relocate him as long as he kept his muzzle clean. Lensky had convinced Ivor to discard his more sensitive materials, at least for the time being.

The badger would have it no other way. For on this side of the border, they only had each other. He had to be Ivor's big brother, in everything but fur.

* * *

*Ivor sat forlornly among the other relatives of the new recruits on the left of the Academy's hall. On the right sat the recruits, all decked in their newly issued uniforms with caps off. Banners with the Melish and Chekish flags of the United Law stood at opposing ends of the hall, facing off over the intermingled sea of people below. Grandpa would have been proud of Isla. He had died only a few months back, assured that his grandkits would follow in their parent's pawprints. And Isla had proven him right.*

*The wolverine barely heard the Commanding Officer's speech of Justice and Equality, the worries of his own musings running through his mind. Ivor was as independent as the next Chek, but he had always found solace in the fact that when everything seemed hopeless, Isla was always there for him. He had just received his acceptance letter from the local college, and wondered how well the Melish majority would accept him. And now his elder brother would be away for the next few months, leaving him to fend for himself.*

*He didn't realize that the speech had concluded and that the recruits had been sworn in by the Oath of Justice. He looked around in confusion as the recruits and their family got up from their seats, coming together for one last goodbye.*

*"Hey, little one," said Isla and Ivor jerked in surprise. The larger wolverine had come up to him, bending slightly to bring his muzzle close to his level. Up close he looked impressive, his form-fitting uniform accentuating his figure. "I've come to say goodbye." He took the seat beside his brother. "I've been watching you since you arrived. Anything you need to talk about?" he asked gently. At the far end of the hall, Ivor could see Lensky clarifying something with a Sergeant, looking flustered as he gestured at the trimmings on his shirt. Mels; always striving for perfection.*

*Ivor avoided Isla's eyes. "What would I do without you?" he asked softly. Their conversation could barely be heard in the voices of weeping and laughing relatives around them, one voice of many painful separations. Somehow, he didn't feel any better.*

*Isla held his brother's cheek with a paw, his touch so gentle for one so strong. Those who didn't know better would say he was a person of contradictions, but deep down, Ivor knew his brother as otherwise.*

"Bro, you're a Racovitch! In war or separation, we had always made do by ourselves," he whispered. "When the War began, our relatives took up our arms and fought. When Pa and Ma died, we made do with Grandpa's help. Mind you, we helped him just as much. I wasn't the only one who helped support our family; every day you insisted on helping with something. You reminded me what I was doing all this for. As long as you remember what we've been through, nothing is impossible."

"I mean…" Ivor's tongue fumbled. How could his brother understand? "Your training's dangerous, and you will have several deployments in the field during then. What if something happens to you? What will I do if you're gone? I don't want to be all by myself, with no one to understand me…" He started tearing. His brother, strong, confident, Isla must see him weak, a coward who could make it in college, but not in the real world.

Isla drew an arm around his shoulders and leaned against his brother, turning briefly towards where Lensky stood. "Ivor, let me tell you a secret. Ever since we've known Lensky, we have never been alone. If anything happens, he will take good care of you."

"Will he?" Ivor had known Lensky since he was a kitten. But he was still a Mel, and they didn't always understand the concept of brotherhood and family. To them, it was all about seizing the future, whether it be in qualifications or career prospects.

"Yes," said Isla simply. "He's a badger, but he's not like the others. You remember when we invited him for lunch that first time? I saw it in him then. He may be shy, but he's as much a big brother as I am. Whatever fur hue he is, to him, we're family. As long as he's around, you'll never be alone. I promise you that."

"Isla, we've got to get to the parade square!" yelled Lensky, shaking Isla on the shoulder. "Let's go! Hey, glad to have you here, Ivor! We'll see you again during our weekends off, alright? Have fun at college!" The badger ruffled his adopted brother's headfur as Isla joined him. In that moment, Ivor knew what his brother meant. He had never felt so safe, so secure when anybody touched him. And as he watched the two of them march away with the sea of recruits, he no longer felt alone.

* * *

"Lensky, don't you miss Isla?" The two mustelids lay side by side as they watched the first rays of the sun creep through the window, their fur stark against the white sheets. For months Ivor had cried himself awake in the night, and Lensky had held and soothed him, holding back his own remorse. They had brought up the issue of Isla's burial with the Belhinder

Police, but they were hesitant over souring already-tense relations with their counterparts. As the Lieutenant had so aptly put it, they were lucky the two countries weren't already at war.

Lensky was initially reluctant to remind himself and Ivor of the memories they had with Isla, but it had to be done. They revisited all their old haunts on this side of the border, including what was left of the playground after the Grid had split it away. Lensky himself had broken down when he saw the spot Isla had fallen through the Grid, and it was Ivor's turn to remind the badger that if it wasn't for him, they wouldn't have been together. And Lensky would also be dead, the first in a long line of victims. They had then talked for a while about their plans for the future over tea rather than vodka, and realized how much they shared in common. Lensky wanted to eventually become the Chief of Police, so he could speak out on police brutality against Cheks. Ivor, on the other end of the spectrum wished to be a rights activist to speak out against the policies enacted against his people. Being a politician wouldn't be a reality until his people had equal rights.

On that note, Ivor wrote a thesis on Isla's sacrifice for publication in a journal, but Lensky had reminded him that things were already precarious as they were. Someday the country and the world would know of the wolverine's sacrifice for both his brother and lover, but now wasn't the time. Their time spent together had made Lensky and Ivor realize that they were comfortable with going further in their current relationship, and it wasn't long before they progressed to becoming mates. Ivor had proven to be more experienced than what he had let on, that was for sure. Whether it was through his studies in Sociology or unspoken experience, a year later saw Lensky looking forward to their bedtime together.

Lensky's mind returned to the present. "Of course I do, my Ivor," whispered Lensky, his paw stroking Ivor's belly as he sighed. "He may be lost to me, but he was the model of selflessness. He gave up the most valuable thing not just for you, but the both of us. And woe betide any who refuse to honor such a sacrifice."

Ivor nodded in agreement, and for a while they lay in silence, punctuated by the rise and fall of their chests. "You know the photo of us and Isla?" spoke Ivor quietly. "Well, on that day, I told Isla we were lucky to have met you. I still think so."

"Thanks, Ivor. That's really sweet," murmured the badger as he nuzzled his ear. He looked at the clock beside him and flicked his whiskers. "Listen, class starts in an hour and a half; it's time for you to go. Study hard for me, alright?"

Ivor groaned as he nudged Lensky back. They sat up together, and Lensky knew that there was still a lot they had to talk about, but that could wait till tonight. For now, Ivor needed to look to the future, and not the past that never will be. And so should he.

"Lensky?" Ivor tensed against him and the badger turned. "Were you comfortable working your shifts at the Grid?"

"Yes, of course," said Lensky. Ivor stared back in surprise. "The Grid may not be the best decision of my government, but it was through it that I realized how much you meant to me. And for every shift that I stand ready, I am honoring your brother for his sacrifice. Go on, have a great day at school." Lensky pecked Ivor on the cheek.

As he heard the door to the apartment close, Lensky took a deep breath. The strong scent of Ivor still lingered, and he knew just how fortunate he was indeed. He would never smell the same again, but he now carried the smell of someone he loved. Putting his paws together with his head bowed, he sent his thanks up to Isla and the Forefathers. He thought he heard a sigh of contentment next to him, but when he turned, no one could be seen. Nothing there, save for a scent that there was no mistaking.

\* \* \*

Badger and wolverine stood side by side in the once barren strip, the first signs of vegetation sprouting from the soil where countless had lost their lives for the last 30 years. Tourists gawked at the rusted and broken fencing as tour guides ushered them with their flags, their voices lost in the silence of the moment. Cubs frolicked upon the remains of the playground that the three of them had played upon, life finally coming in full circle. Lensky and Ivor each laid a flower before the stone marker they commissioned. The two mustelids leaned against each other, smiling in mingled grief and joy.

They were finally reunited with Isla.

*Build an animal to be a killer, a super-warrior. Then the war ends. What does it become in peacetime?*

# Lime Tiger

## *by Slip-Wolf*

Acetylene bit into grey hide. Freya watched the molten wound grow as another slab of the past was cut away from itself for the lorries waiting below. Her claws pricked the inside of her thick gloves as the steel fragment of the decommissioned battleship swung on the long crane arm. Two steps back ensured that a gust of coastal wind would not send it back her way, and she shouted the all-clear for the badger in the crane's greasy cab to deliver it to the flatbed.

Lifting her helmet for one moment to catch a breeze, the tiger gazed out upon the concrete, cenotaph-like towers of the tenements rising beyond the docks. The bell would ring soon, crowding everyone to the gates. There was not enough time to do another cut-and-mount. Freya beat her own shins with her black and orange tail, took a ladder-well down to the massive blocks holding the hulk in place, and handed in her mask and safe-locked torch before punching her card at the gates. Out where the snarls of late day traffic started, she smelled someone familiar.

"Jack," she named the specter at her shoulder, and the slim suited ferret came away from the gate where he'd waited.

"Surprised to see me?" His lip lifted as he clucked his tongue and straightened his tie. "I've worried about you."

Freya briefly checked the sky for a threat of rain, something of an impulse these days, and grunted. "Worrying's in your nature." She sniffed her broad pink nose as she looked the brown-furred soldier over. "Not that I could blame you. How's the kits?"

"Never see them." He waved a pack of cigarettes as though it cleared a bad smell away. "I expect they're getting into trouble, not that their mother ever tells me."

Freya took one in her leather-gloved paw and then leaned into his lighter, taking a long draw. On her salary she had to stretch her smoking out. "Surprised they have you so busy," she said. "Isn't that a piece of your navy we're taking apart in there?"

The ferret glanced back once at the behemoth being cut on the blocks. "I'm not in the part of the Navy that ever sailed, stupid as that sounds. Got some time for me, Freya?"

The tiger cocked an ear and shrugged. She still found it difficult to smile around Jack, even three years after she'd turned in her papers. "For you I'll make some," she said agreeably. "Buy me a drink?"

Jack knew where she wanted to go, leading her on a pedestrian congested road that wound uphill.

Freya smoked the hand-rolled tobacco with relief, her muscles still aching from pushing steel and climbing derelict hulls, sparing one glance back from higher up the lane.

Seen from a distance, the *Temeraire* was a skeleton now, firefly acetylene sparks from the final shift of the day patiently carving her up for the hungry foundries down the coast. Prior to joining the mid-day cutting crew, Freya had worked for a time as a gutter, reclaiming electronics throughout the spent cruisers and frigates they towed in that could be retooled for industrial use out in the settlements. The deck crane that once hoisted shuttle boats was now erecting a school house down south that had been rebuilt from buzz-bomb rubble. Other parts scrounged from the beached hulks were jig-sawed into car engines or power plants, the obsolete incorporated into the renewed.

Just like her.

But not like Jack. Having moved from the Army to Naval intelligence, he walked in that purgatory between gunfire and diplomacy that held the peace, gathering intelligence on the remains of the Axis powers while they stitched the world back together.

Five years following the armistice, Helene was a city of unquiet ghosts. The traces of what came before were everywhere you cared to look. Alley-sides of buildings bore gunfire scars. There wasn't a hill for two young hopefuls to make love on beyond the core that didn't have a body beneath it somewhere. Freya walked the rebuilt square of this renewed world and saw clear as day that the smoking rubble remained un-cleared in every old mammal's wide awake eyes.

Jack's own face was a storm of business when he sat them down and ordered a pint. Freya took a crisp swallow and quietly awaited the sneak of numbness before she spoke. "I don't see you for nearly four months and you look like you don't want to say anything."

"How's your rabbit?"

"Eiran's fine. Shakes rarely come anymore. He's making us dinner tonight." Freya immediately realized she'd subtly suggested Jack get on with it and held back a wince. She owed him more than that.

Jack just nodded, taking a cautious breath before he spoke again. "You remember Stormhold." He didn't make it a question.

Freya's arm froze as it raised the beer again. Her wet lips felt dry real quick. "Name one other thing in the world I couldn't forget but desperately wish I could, Jack."

He had another cigarette, his mouth skipped it up and down as he muttered, "I know, and I'm sorry. Something came up. ONI reached out to me a week ago, looking for... recruits. Based on select items and *experiences*," he paused for emphasis of that word, "in your personnel file, your name went high on a relatively short list."

"Do I even want to know what for?"

Jack's ciggie and whiskers drooped. "We've intercepted some fugitives moving through Lister in an East-fleeing refugee convey. Four scientists. Ranking, inner circle types."

"Scientists," Freya said. The beer was on the table, forgotten. "What kind of scientists?"

Jack knew Freya knew, but said it anyway, "Geneticists."

They both sat a moment, then Freya plucked Jack's cigarette from his lips and took a puff, keeping it. "Why is this news to me? Beyond the obvious. I mean..." she chose her words carefully. "Did they all get lined up and shot?"

"No."

"Why not?"

Jack fidgeted. "They were captured and sent to the ONI, who've been looking for them for quite some time."

"For war prosecution, obviously."

"Not quite." Jack's fingers wanted another cigarette, but he folded his hands, took another drink, folded them again. "I've been on assignment for three months on a special operation, top secret. I couldn't even tell you until now. It's called Stemclip." He tapped his fingers nervously. "We have had several divisions of border patrols and embassies keeping an eye out for geneticists escaping the liberated territories as the Axis' military apparatus has been dismantled. We're rounding them up. For interrogation."

Jack stopped speaking and Freya sipped her own beer, realizing her heart was beating a little faster. She glanced to the sky for a trace of rain again, but it was grey and featureless. "To what end, Jack?"

He sighed. "I'm sorry, this is hard to hear, Freya. But high-ups in government want their knowledge for several disease research projects that have come in the wake of the war. Scab lung, aggressive leukemias, water supply poisonings that got a lot worse with the war's fallout. There's chemical residues in the soil everywhere, causing all sorts of illnesses and genetic abnormalities."

Freya lifted her beer and chugged it. Her white throat emptied the glass in four swigs and she set it down. "Another," she told the rat server who passed by. "What does this have to do with me? Beyond things you know I don't want to talk about."

Jack sipped his own beer and coughed. "I've been… ordered, to find people skilled in East Axis languages and with, well, special inside knowledge who can help us interrogate these scientists, learn what they know and put their knowledge to good use."

Freya had to set the glass down to keep it in one piece. "And you thought I, of all people, would be right for this? For fuck's sake, are you insane?"

"The ONI has your file," Jack said. "They know of your presence at Stormhold, of the day it was liberated, everything that came since you signed on. They've read your file front to back, including all the parts I helped you with." He let silence hang for a moment. "They think you're perfect for the job, and they were sending somebody to request your help." Jack finished his own beer. "I had to make sure that was me. For old times' sake, let's say."

"No."

"Freya."

"No. I won't do it. I don't care how bad you want what these bastards know. I've seen everything that they've done, Jack. I -"

Freya broke off as their server put another beer down for her and reading the tension hanging in the air, backed away quickly with a curt nod. A glance at Jack's empty glass was met with a shaken head before he slunk away. Freya took a couple fast swallows, fighting down her frayed nerves before speaking again.

"Why the hell would you even ask me, Jack? Why is this even being considered? You remember the rocketeers? Remember Werner Von Maut, who designed all those guided bombs launched from those mobile fire platforms that killed thousands upon thousands? We both saw him during the Westward extraction, after I was commissioned into the unit. Remember seeing that bastard's body swinging from that rope in the Saxon square after they rounded up half the inner war cabinet? That's what happens to mass murderers, both the ones who press the buttons and those who draft the plans. Why is it that suddenly we don't need rockets in the west but we need skin treatments and that means that the chemists get saved from the rope? They should hang with all the rest."

"I knew you'd feel this way," Jack muttered.

"And did you tell them *why*?" Her eyes bored into his.

He met her gaze levelly. "As I said, my superiors read your file. They didn't *need* to ask any questions."

"They know all the horrors we've seen, but they want whispers from the devil anyway."

Jack leaned forward, turning his glass with one hand. "I don't know exactly what they want, but it's important. There are lives to save. Is it possible, just possible, that it would give you closure to get what we need from them and actually fix a bit of this world they've helped break?"

Freya stood up, woozy with the two beers sloshing inside of her, but feeling a burn deep down inside her that was familiar and frightening. She had to go home, see Eiran, and hold him so he could help her forget again. Calm her down. That was the least she did for him. "Thanks for the drink, Jack. Had they sent anybody else... well, they'd of learned a lot more about what I feel than they wanted to."

"How much does your mate know?" Jack asked, sorrow holding his muzzle low.

"Nothing. Even years later he's still fragile, has nightmares. I'm something *good* in his life. That's important to me as it is to him. I'm sorry, Jack. Good luck with the shit they shoveled on you."

Freya made a hasty exit, nearly pushing over a couple seating themselves. For the briefest moment she was reminded of how her sheer mass made her larger than most of the mammals on this street-side patio, how doubly amplified her fury appeared with the black stripes on her broad orange neck and forearms stretching over taut muscles. Eyes met hers and went away, fearful deep down. She could taste the iron in her mouth, smelled the ashes burning in her nose, feel the crunch of soot under her bare paws, and see the skeletal bars of Stormhold holding back the starving masses of consigned and condemned.

Within corridors of concrete she'd heard the howls, the snaps of electric shocks that dimmed lights, the cracks of whips, the whet sharpening of knives and syringes.

They'd lined them up. When the charges blew and the Allies stormed in, they'd lined them up, smartly dressed Axis jackals and cats and wolves with doll eyes long lost to pity or sympathy. They'd shot them all, watched them sketch marionette dances against the concrete as bullets left the monster's bloody shadows against walls beyond the labs, anti-chambers into the most pitiless of hells. Bodies from failed experiments and victims of the successful tests alike lay covered in lime, awaiting entombment by steam-shovelled dirt.

Freya hurried down an alley, bundling her nerves tight, claustrophobic walls on either side. Her hand longed for the cool lacquer of a sub-pistol grip, the heft of a balanced knife. A cough to her left startled her. A rat was leaning against one alley wall, frayed service-man's jacket loose around his bony shoulders, looking dully at the bloody patch he'd coughed onto his olive-green sleeve. Poisoning from agent grey exposure. She'd seen it often enough.

She hurried past, fur crawling with the rising tide of loathing and fury as she bounded up a wider thoroughfare, charging through the crowds, ignoring the squeak of a coyote who she nearly bowled over. Finding an open lane of space, she ran, as she'd trained herself to, giving the cold rush of urgency its fight or flight outlet. Were she in a contained space, she'd be clawing the walls open right now.

God damn Jack. He should have known this would happen. Even plied with drink he knew where these memories took her, what mark she had stamped in her. The account had never settled between her and the things she'd seen and experienced at the tail end of the war when the Axis unravelled and the black layers of its charred heart opened up to the soldiers who pushed forth into the fortresses and camps and labs and chambers of the fleeing bastards.

Those bastards had done this to her. They had made her this way.

She bounded the rest of the way home, covering a muddy creekside mile beyond Helene's bleached walls in less than five minutes. She huffed as she reached the hamlet that she called home, where her triggered senses could smell the inviting waft of stew winding up their slim chimney. The familiar scent of rabbit greeted her beyond the wooden door on their rustic plank-built shack. Freya's gloves were off and her claws were out when she put her great hand against it. She held herself, breathed deep, willed them back into hiding. She drove the anxiety out of her face and bundled it down. Another layer in the mask she'd worn for years fixed itself in her expression. She opened the door to home.

Eiran was at the stove, one long ear rising to her entry, the lame one resting back and limp. "Frey," He said and turned, white fur drawing taut as he grinned. His lip quivered, his eyes a warm pink. "How was work?" His joy faltered. "What's wrong?"

No. She'd buried nothing. She stood frozen at the vestibule. Her jaw fluttered soundlessly, and then closed. So much she had never said, so much she still couldn't. "I had... a bad day."

Eiran let go the wooden spoon he was stirring with, and it floated on round inside the bubbling pot, kept on by its own tide. "It's more than that. Come over here."

He went to her. The rabbit's head nestled against her worker's overalls, his live ear brushing her suspenders and orange hide. She looked at that ear, watched it work against her fur before she nuzzled his forehead. "I've missed you," Freya said honestly. "I wanted to get home fast."

"Was there a problem on the ship today?"

"No." She contemplated lying for a moment. It would be so easy. "Jack came by, my friend from the war."

Eiran looked up at her, light from the kitchen's lone window catching a milky glint of the furless scar that ran from his limp ear down to his chin. "Did he bring back some bad memories?"

Freya rumbled, a storm inside that demanded a voice, "Several of them. They have ranking members of the Axis science corps in custody that they need help interrogating."

"And Jack went to you?" Eiran broke away, recovered himself by moving back to the stove and stirring again. He poked at the fire inside the iron stove one last time before moving the pot to a warming plate by the sink. Freya could smell the root vegetables and mushrooms strongly and saw cubes of beef that Eiran had cooked and placed in a small bowl. Despite his personal revulsion of meat, he was always thinking of her.

"He was ordered to find somebody who could interpret for them. He knows I'm fluent in the right tongues. I came up on a list the ONI has."

Eiran started dishing the stew, and Freya could see his live ear flicking in agitation. She immediately wished she'd kept her mouth shut. "He should have told them no for you." Eiran muttered. The light caught his scar again when he turned the bowls. "It wasn't fair to even ask."

"I owed him my attention, even if it was to say no." Freya said, moving to join him at the table. "Jack's done a lot for me."

Eiran set the stew and meat down before her.

"Did you refuse?"

"Yep."

"Good." Eiran set his meal down and took his seat across from her but didn't lift his spoon. "Six years in the service and they think it's all a tiger's good for."

Freya sighed, seeing the very idea had disturbed her lover no less than her. Why hadn't she just lied to him, made up something about the ship demolition? He deserved no less an escape from what those detainees represented. Eiran picked up his spoon and started on the stew. Freya, her anger subsided, did the same, the last word on that matter spoken.

As she held him later than night, hearing the distant call of night birds in the close-by forests and the thoughtful songs of crickets, she realized she'd brought it all back home to both of them again, their scars sore as though new. She cursed herself when he muttered and jerked in his sleep.

His heart was pounding when he woke with a start in her arms.

"Another dream?" Freya asked soothingly, petting the space between his ears.

"Yes."

"The same?"

Eiran was silent for a long time, just breathing. "I don't know why, it's not even the night of the bombing. It's never the blitz-tanks or the bomb roars or the roof coming down…"

"You know you don't have to talk about it."

Eiran swallowed. "The raiding parties, the ones they sent in ahead of the soldiers. I still see them. It's what those *people* made, the ones they caught. I know. I've seen them. The lab-changed animals that went in naked, empty-eyed, all teeth and claws. They had camouflaged fur in brown and green so the woods concealed them like wraiths until they fell upon you. They were mindless horrors, worth no more to their handlers than those they were sent to kill." Eiran took in a sharp breath. "Those hungry eyes were bottomless. One got my sister. My little *sister*."

Freya loosened her grip on him, then thought better of it and tightened it again, enveloping the rabbit in warmth. "I know. They're gone, Eiran. They and the war machines and everything else."

Eiran got his breathing under control, putting his paw in Freya's. "I always felt sorriest for her, you know. My daughter and my wife were lost to the same bomb that took my ear, taken in an instant. They were my whole world, but it was my sister who lingers when I let myself remember. I think it's because her screams were… clearest. She felt the end. Knew it was inevitable."

He was on the verge of another episode, a fetal curl and crying he would not recover from for hours. Early on, it had been a day. Freya's arms wrapped him tight. "Don't do this to yourself. Please, let it pass. Its years over and you're safe. We're safe."

She held him and repeated the words metronomically, massaging his shoulders and back. Eventually, wordlessly, Eiran fell back asleep.

Freya couldn't join him. She placed the blanket over him, slipping out of bed to fumble in a dresser drawer for the small box where she kept a meager supply of rolled smokes. She leaned away, lighting one with a quick flick of her lighter. She sat naked on the edge, smoked and thought.

She'd told herself that he was right for her, and she right for him. He a skittish rabbit brought to frequent anxiety by memories of vicious idiocies of the world around him and she a fuming mess brought to flashes of anger by the same thing. They'd never married, simply settled in, settled down, an odd couple from opposite ends of a natural order rendered defunct by the struggling march of civilization. They eked out a life together, safe from the roots of their scars.

Freya for her part, kept her own ghosts buried as deep as possible. That was a matter of necessity.

Absolute truth in relationships was ill advised and they both knew it. She'd poured lime on more corpses than she could ever count, friends and enemies alike. With them were buried parts of her life she needed to forget for both their sakes. She turned over that sentiment again and again in her head as the nub burned out and then settled back in with him to await the dawn.

In the morning she woke early, showered cold, went to the privy to check her age-concealing fur treatments in the mirror, and satisfied that the orange and black of her naked form were intact, went back to bed to find him awake, blinking away his bad dreams. They made slow love, nuzzling and licking one another's muzzles, and he snickered. "I could stand to see some grey, you know. Some silver in your fur might look beautiful on you."

Freya smiled thinly. "I need the dyes. They don't hire you for dock work if you look any bit old, trust me. I see folks turned away all the time. And there's no other jobs out there right now." She remembered with a groan. "Well, maybe just one I'm not taking." She got up and went to the telephone outside of their sleeping nook. She wanted to get this closure while Eiran was awake and alert. This call was for both of them. "Hello, ONI station six? Is Jack Keppler there? Never mind. Take this message down for his secretary. I very much appreciate the offer he was sent to make, but I'm not commissioned and not interested. Please give your superiors notice that I've declined." Freya gave her name and disused-serial number from the combat office and disconnected the call. She immediately felt Eiran's arms around her, which startled her.

"Do you have to work today?" he asked.

"Not if I don't want to get paid."

"Will you see Jack again? If he calls, do you want me to -"

"No, thank you. I'd rather you not speak with him. He's an old friend, yes, but that's from a... different part of my life. You understand why, right?"

Eiran slipped around and gazed at her silently, but she could tell he did. Freya thought about Jack as she hugged Eiran goodbye, thought about what he'd tell his superiors about the tiger who would rather cut up decommissioned ship hulls than sit with monsters who conjured nightmares from test tubes. She was struggling to avoid bringing her anger to the fore again when she set out under the dawn's gaze, hoping Jack wouldn't ring that phone, or come and see her.

An hour later, Freya met the rest of the first shift at the gate and noticed a few had been separated from the group. A wolf was snarling in the foreman's face, a sagging, tired looking otter who shook his head and closed his eyes. The wolf turned away and melted into the crowd, sputtering, a pink slip of paper in his grey fingers. "What happened?" Freya asked a dog standing by, slipping his gloves on.

"Took four of us aside, the older, slower hands, gave 'em bad news and slips, with a single day's pay to make up fer it. 'Parently the frigate that we were gonna start gutting next week ain't coming. Some other outfit down the coast under-bid us for the job."

"What?" Freya moved through the sullen group at the gate and over to the otter foreman who'd just sent the last of the unlucky away with an apology. "What the hell are you doing cutting people loose, Gordy?"

The otter craned his neck to look up at her. "The boss ordered it. We have to take some losses now as we're gonna have an empty lot in a week. Might be another week before anything comes again."

Freya fumed. "Even if we're gonna run short of work for a bit, we still need spotters at the key joints and back-up hands guiding the cranes. The structure isn't stable as it is. What if we mis-coordinate? Are we at least slowing the job down?"

The foreman shook his whiskered head. Gordy was always just another cog turning at the pace required. "We have to have this scrap to the foundry before the end of the week or we fail to collect bonus. That happens, we could all get buggered."

She grumbled, knowing he was on her side. The argument was lost hours ago somewhere up town in Helene, where the fool who ran the whole show was counting the slipping away of his post-war lucre. How many ships were left to cut up, anyway? Freya didn't think about the pink slip of paper that could be in her own hand, or the slim prospects that lay past that. She and Eiran were paycheck to paycheck and the rabbit hadn't had stable work in a long while.

The *Temeraire's* remains sat silently as the remaining cutters and spotters punched in, grabbed their torches, ropes, ladders, masks and began to crawl into and upon their victim. Freya felt the familiar cool feel of the steel helmet down over her muzzle, followed by the tinted shield that shrouded deck 3, section B-thirty-four deck in darkness. Her torch lit, blue flame illuminating a chalked off line and she bit flame to steel, setting to work. Twenty minutes later, the familiar routine having finally settled her down, she raised her mask, hooked the crane arm to the hole in the hull sheet and cut the last few tendrils that allowed the plate to swing away, the first of thirty she'd do today. Her gaze wandered down past the crane cab to the tracks of its treads in the lake-side dirt and to a familiar form standing by the lunch table. One ear stood tall, the other leaned and she could see Eiran was scanning the hulk for her.

What the hell was he doing here? Her eyes tracked him up and down and she saw the item in her mate's paw. It was her battered red lunchbox, the one she'd forgotten at home when she'd gone out with Jack on her mind and all his rejected offer entailed. The whole way here she hadn't noticed that she'd forgotten it, and that annoyed her when she realized how deep in her own head she was stuck. Now wasn't the time to be wasting money in town on meals she might not soon be able to afford.

Her annoyance at herself rapidly fell away as she saw Eiran turn and speak to the ferret who approached him, decked in the smart dress of an office worker whose real position wouldn't be betrayed in public by something as gauche as a uniform. Jack looked apologetic as he spoke words to Eiran that Freya couldn't hear, whispered as though conspiratorially.

Red cornered Freya's vision, which narrowed to a point. Goddammit!

"Hold on section B starboard!" Freya shouted and waved down at the crane operator with frantic cutting motions that she needed a time-out. She stormed across the open deck, leaping over two gaping shaft drops before hurtling down a ladder to the boarding deck where the ramp to ground was. She hurried out of the hull, waved to the foreman to ensure he was paying attention, and he cocked his head with a haze of confusion. In the shadow of the *Temeraire*, Eiran hurried up and Jack was right behind him, looking stern and guarded.

Freya put an arm around her mate, "Thank you, bun," she all but growled, her gaze over the rabbit's shoulder on Jack. The ferret's tail twitched in agitation as he read Freya's glare, but looked worried in a way that didn't read as apologetic. He was anxious to speak with her, but kept back while she held Eiran. "What did he say to you?"

Eiran looked up. "He's your friend, isn't he?"

Freya swallowed, battling back the feeling that too many eyes were on both of them. "Eiran, what did he say?"

"He said that he needed to speak with you urgently."

"It's true," Jack said, just in earshot. "Freya we need to -"

"Wait a goddam minute, Jack." Freya couldn't hold back her teeth-baring growl, didn't want to. One thing she had asked of Jack since she'd met Eiran, just *one*.

Freya glanced down into Eiran's eyes and saw that he was afraid, even though he didn't understand why. Afraid of her. That tremble that started in his whiskers and would sink his eyes into the deep glaze of shell-shock if something would make as little as a sudden loud noise.

His head was tiny in her great hands as she caressed him, fingers clumsy as she kept her claws sheathed. Eiran was not supposed to be afraid of her. Not ever. And Jack was ruining it. *Ruining it.*

"Eiran." She lowered her tone, holding control. "I have to speak with Jack for a moment. I'm… I'm unhappy with him right now. We just need to talk for a moment, okay? Thank you again for bringing lunch for me. I was in the clouds this morning."

Eiran stood back, letting her paws slide off his face and hold his arms. His eyes were cautious. "You look pretty upset right now,"

"A bit," she said and then glared at Jack.

The weasel's cigarette was down to a nub. She hadn't seen him light it, much less smoke it completely in no time at all. He had to be worried. Good.

"Right back, Eiran. Jack." She pointed to a space in the hull that was open, but dark. Eiran wouldn't see their lips move, and Freya would keep it short.

Gordy approached, thick finger tapping his cheap wristwatch. One look from Freya shut him up as she led Jack into the shadow of the *Temeraire*.

His mouth was already at work when they were under the shadows. "Look, Freya, it's not what you think. I didn't tell him anything about -"

"You weren't supposed to talk to him at all!" she hissed. "That was the only promise I wanted you to keep. Do you have any idea how fragile Eiran's life still is? I'm all he has, Jack."

"I know, I know. That's why I came." His ears perked.

So did hers. A groaning sound rose, and through her hammering heart Freya realized she had missed its slow rise, deep and primordial, like a great sea creature coming to life deep within the hold of the torch-pecked vessel. She heard a shout from high above, then another and realized the movement of shadow over Jack's solemn face wasn't the result of his stepping back.

A rivet popped off a stanchion and made a bullet ping off its neighbor as a section of badly-cut hull buckled. "Run!" Freya darted back, beckoning Jack forward.

He was confused, unable to process what was happening in the moment.

It was a moment he couldn't spare. Two bounds had him out from under the collapse, and a third would have had him clear of the wreck entirely, but he wasn't fast enough. A thick press of steel came down against his legs as a massive section of the *Temeraire* surrendered to gravity, flattening with the tortured rend of tank hulls in a god's teeth. The ferret was pinned down, shins disappearing under the great trap of ruined steel that just barely missed Freya, the foreman and her mate, all of them scattering. Erian's face went blank, the skin around his scar turning pasty white as he stopped to look back. Freya wanted to hold him, block his vision, but in the chalky dust that settled, she was compelled to turn back, see the squirm of ferret, hear the intakes of breath as he struggled to gain enough strength to scream. The cross brace steel girder atop his shins was itself covered in shorn refuse, piling up and back towards a sunken mess of ship.

The danger sirens were already sounding as the still standing parts of the hull were cleared by gangway, porthole or rope. The rest of the thing could come down any minute. Debris would spread out in an avalanche, destroying the scaffolding and cranes surrounding it. They all had to get clear.

Jack finally screamed, a high pitched shriek that he bit off with a snap of his jaws.

The debris above him shifted.

Freya was already breathing hard, muscles bunching, pulse racing, gathering reserves she hadn't drawn on in years. The adrenaline poured in, rage returning like a hot stain.

In an instant, she was above her friend, grabbing the cross brace, hundreds upon hundreds of pounds alone, more debris crowding above it, and heaved.

The pile shifted, the assembled cutter crew standing back, stock-still in shock, powerless to move in and budge one stick of the broken mass. Freya shifted her grip, put her legs and back into the effort anew and pulled, sinew standing under her black and orange pelt, tinting her hue in the morning light.

The slab loosened and shifted, girders above protesting at the resistance of tiger against gravity. "Grab him!" she managed to hiss.

Welder-gloved paws grabbed the ferret's spasming limbs and pulled. A tortured mewl escaped the ex-soldier's lips as he was extracted from the wreckage, the pulped horrors below his knees leaving runways of red on the sand as they dragged him back to a safe distance.

The site doctor stumbled over a lain pipe, nearly tumbling onto his muzzle as he hurried over with the kit and shouted for someone to ring for a medical lorry. The workers who'd escaped the wreckage counted their number, gasped and shivered. Gordy was a frozen pillar, tail limp, eyes wide.

And Eiran. He'd sunk to his knees, limp ear and live ear alike plastered back, staring at the horror before him and the ruin beyond with knowing eyes, hands over his muzzle.

Freya, for her part, was at Jack's side. She tore strips from her own clothes with efficient claw drags, winding the strips around the ferret's thighs, separating the living rest of Jack from that which surgeon's saws would soon cut away to save him. He screamed and wept and screamed again. A morphine shot took some sense of the agony away.

The wail of the hulk-evacuation alarm was joined by the coming keen of the ambulance siren, workers making way as they hurried in. There was another rend of metal as a hull plate fell against a crane, but everyone was far enough away from the wreck now. Only the equipment was doomed.

And maybe the ferret at their feet. Freya bit her lip and tasted her own blood as the attendants moved in, took her place, checked her ties and Jack's pulse.

The workers gathered around the corpse of the naval battleship *Temeraire* stood like lost ghosts, bereft of sense and purpose as the ambulance took Jack away.

Freya gazed back at Eiran, seeing his terror, scenting his chilled blood. He peered back at her through shell-shocked hands, begging her silently to come back, hold him, banish the fear.

But Freya couldn't. Her claws stood out, dagger-like, gasps swallowing air with an engine's ferocity and rage, bottomless rage, standing every cord on her. The resources she'd drawn on couldn't be extinguished. For minutes they shook in their respective, lonely worlds before Freya found her bridle, cooled the adrenaline cauldron and put her natural weapons away. She gingerly took the rabbit into her arms, unsurprised and yet rent by his fear at her touch, and led him from the yard.

* * *

Days passed without any words of consequence. Neither could find the words to breach the silence as life failed to return to normal, Freya having no place to go. The yard had been shut down indefinitely once the debris had been cleared as no more hulls were coming in. Inwardly, the torrent of emotions had subsided from the accident, but a hollow emptiness had filled it. She knew where it came from. The silence that hung following the horror was borne out of things she'd never reconciled. She'd run, but the past had caught up.

Rain had started, pocks on the roof that became rolling drums and then a crescendo. Eiran had just returned from an expedition to the market and had put vegetables in the ice-box crisper. He'd planned on tending the garden today, but it would have to wait. They were trapped inside, and the wet in the rabbit's fur mingled in the air with the stale dust in hers. Freya realized it had been three days since she'd bathed. Three days since she'd used her fur treatments. The place stunk of tiger and rabbit.

Freya looked out into the downward cascade of water upon their grotto and spoke with resignation. "I'm taking the job."

Eiran's ear went back. "You said you wouldn't."

Freya stared at the telephone that would go dead in less than a month, next to the sparse, crumpled job ads that had taken her nowhere and the bills that would stack up in no time. "I had something to do then. Something that paid. Jack knew what I had wouldn't last, even if he never said so."

The ferret was still unconscious in a hospital bed both times she'd gone to see him. He'd asked for her, they said, when he was awake. His ex-wife and cub had stopped by at some point too.

Eiran tottered over to her, a slight limp returning in the weathered cold. "Why would you want to do this? You told me you wanted to put this all behind you for good. We *talked* about this…"

"And I told you what we both wanted to hear. But this is all that's left for me now, assuming it's even still available." Freya stared at the black plastic of the phone. In the light of the single bulb over their heads, it looked like a waiting insect.

"What we *wanted* to hear?" Eiran took a deep breath. "What should we have heard? That you want to go into rooms with evil people, find out about the monsters they made and how they did it?"

Freya winced. "They want to find ways to take that knowledge and help people." She took a deep breath, feeling the storm coming on stronger beyond the walls. "Maybe… not everything these people know has to be used for…." She trailed off.

Eiran sat on the small chaise lounge they'd scrounged cash together for, bought from a reclamation from bombed houses that had been bull-dozed to rubble years back. He made no motion for Freya to join him. "What else could it be used for? They made killers and monsters. You said yourself you didn't want to see them. I could see in your eyes you wanted them dead if anything. I feel things you don't say, Freya. It's rare that you even try to hide what you're feeling from me."

Freya heard the slight waver in Eiran's voice, knew what the rabbit was getting at. Or feared he was. She swallowed. "Eiran, I -"

"How did you lift that girder, Freya?"

"What are you taking about?"

"That metal you lifted off your friend from the war was as heavy as the ambulance that took your friend away, yet you lifted it."

"Because I had to."

"It's more than that. You didn't want to hold me after they carted your friend away. I was having another… episode. That blood." He swallowed and Freya saw the verge of tears. "You stayed away."

"I couldn't come near you." Freya felt a pit in her stomach. The rain outside was a torrent, the kind of torrent she always feared. Had it been three days since she'd last seen to her needs? She was stinking in this closed room with the rabbit she loved, but was that the stink of lies, or the stink of honesty? Was it finally time?

"I don't understand." Eiran's whiskers curled.

"Do you love me?"

"Of course," words spoken, no hesitation. That should be a comfort.

"What if Jack didn't come to me because we were in the war together?"

"What?"

Freya reached up and began unbuttoning her shirt. She didn't even know she was doing it at first. The humidity was building inside the closed space, but she wasn't hot, nor was there any trace of eroticism as she began to disrobe. She stripped away her shell. "We were in the camps. We killed a lot of people there during the liberation. Axis soldiers and scientists."

Eiran shrunk into the couch as he saw something he didn't like in the tiger's eyes. "You never wanted to talk about this."

"For you, I never did."

Eiran's eyes watched her clothes fall to the floor, one garment at a time until she was naked.

But Freya knew, not entirely naked.

"Freya, what are you doing?"

Freya went to the back door and out. Rain battered her head and shoulders, soaking in, reaching cold honest fingers all the way to her skin. Three days without the grey tiger-fur treatment. Three days without a bonding agent. A pool of orange began to collect at her striped bare feet, leaving the natural black stripes behind. And that which was not natural at all.

She turned back to Eiran as he teetered over to the door, jaw quivering against gravity, eyes blinking frantically. Standing inside, as realization came, his cheeks were as wet as hers.

"I didn't help Jack and his assault force liberate the Axis slave camps, Eiran. Jack liberated *me*." She raised a green and black furred arm, claws curving from her fingertips. "And once freed I helped them kill every one of the bastards who didn't escape."

"You're one - you're one *of them*?" Eiran's heart was pounding now. Freya could feel his urgency, the impulse to run and hide. He'd felt it often enough in their time together, at the sound of distant munitions being disposed of, at the shout of arguments in the street, at the site of Jack being dragged legless from the wreckage of the *Temeraire*. But never, until now, from her.

For so long she'd cultivated this relationship as Eiran's protector, as strong arms he could rest in. She had thwarted the Axis scientists who wanted to make her a war machine, a berserker, a tool of death and destruction. Just a few more brain surgeries would have taken her personhood away from her. With Jack's help, dye treatments and tampered paperwork, she'd escaped her destiny as a slave-made-killer, a monstrous tool for the Breeder-land. Freya had become a nurturer, a lover instead. She had won.

But in all this, she'd had to be a liar, one who promised often that she would tell the rabbit she shared herself about where she'd come from when he was ready, when he was healed.

"I'm not one of them. I'm the one you love, and who loves you in return."

"Why didn't you tell me?" He backed into the kitchen, receding into the shadow of their home. Freya put her palm on the door-frame and took a step back inside.

"Stay back!" It was almost a shriek and Freya felt her own heart rend deep inside her as Eiran scuttled back into the darkness. The single bulb lighting the center of their home had winked and gone out.

The rain raged on. Freya had to raise her voice. "Eiran, I wanted to tell you. Jack helped me put together a different life after I helped destroy the camps and got me enlisted with the Allies. We forged a few papers but I more than proved my dedication until the day I handed in my uniform and rifle. For years after we first met, I had planned on telling you. I was desperate to tell you. Neither of us were ever ready."

"You lied to me. Things like you killed my sister and all these years you lay with me and lied to me!" Something hurled out of the darkness. A kitchen utensil bruised when it bounced off Freya's collarbone. She bared her teeth instinctively, water causing her eyes to blink.

The rising rage she could barely control, designed by gene-splicers and buried deeper than her own bones, gave way and died as she heard the distinctive sound of a knife being drawn from the wobbly cutting block.

There was something painfully affirming in her own sob. "Eiran, please."

"I don't know what you are," Eiran said, voice hollow. "Don't come near me."

"I love you."

Eiran backed out of the kitchen, blade held high as Freya took wobbly, wet steps back into the box that was a home until moments ago. "Maybe all killers are liars, but you're... you're *worse* than-"

"The war is over," Freya said. "If we want it to be. I want nothing more than to put all the violence behind me and be a person again who can laugh and love. That's what I was before they took me." Freya waved a paw at her green and black flank. "This is all they wanted me to be. But the horrors fade and we heal. I want to heal you. I need you to heal me too."

The front door opened and Freya saw Eiran's head in silhouette against the storm, one ear back and the other down as she stayed at the back door's portal, staring through the empty expanse at him.

"Eiran?"

She wasn't sure if she heard him start to cry before he closed the front door behind him, but she did see the shine of rain against the knife blade in one trembling hand.

The bulb blinked back on awhile later, the lime tiger dripping dry in the same empty silent space as the rain slowed, ebbed, and moved on.

She picked up the telephone and heard its droning hum.

\* \* \*

Jack wasn't awake when she went back to see him, but they said again he was trying to reach her. In her conversation with the ONI, she heard that he'd be getting an honorary discharge, the very least they could do after fifteen years of distinguished service between two branches of the Allied forces. She informed them that she would be staying at his place to see to his affairs for a time and would be dividing her government contract fees between his hospital care and the lonely occupant of a little hamlet house down the muddy creek a piece. Her name would not be on the slips, but Eiran would know.

In a windowless room, they sat her down, her concealing orange stripes back in place and demeanor impeccable despite the tempest roiling deep within.

The badger smoothed his striped suit down. "As we have your signature on the Official Secrets Act, we can now brief you on the full scope of this assignment. We have retrieved four assets from Operation Stemclip who have been moved to different locations, one of whom you will be assigned to as a confidant and liaison."

Freya blinked. "Liaison? I thought I was to be a translator and an assistant in their interrogations?"

The badger traded looks with the bowler-hatted wolf leaning against the cabinet across the room. The wolf smoked and shrugged.

"Well," the badger said. "We have taken an… adjusted approach in dealing with these guests of ours. Forced extraction of information would be of limited value based on the complexity of the science involved and the degree of its importance to the nation's long term goals. We did pass the refinements of the task on to agent Keppler who spoke very highly of you, but he told us to hold off on the offer until he had a chance to talk to you again. Did he -?"

Freya could see Jack's apologetic but worried expression in her mind's eye, right before the *Temeraire*'s mis-cut hull had given away. She'd assumed he was simply sorry for speaking with Eiran, but that morning, they had told him what the assignment really was. And he'd come to warn her in case her mind hadn't been made up.

And now here she was, no turning back. "Of course," she lied. "Please lay out the particulars so I can make sure I know exactly what I'm doing. Jack has an interesting way of phrasing things." The smile she plastered on her own face was the kind that could fool a lover for years.

"Well, since the reception is nearby, it may be simpler if we simply show you."

The car they sent for her was blacked out, the ride a half hour through bumpy roads that became far smoother as they left the coast. Nobody spoke, save the wolf who asked Freya in a guttural Axis dialect a couple simple questions about what she did at the port. He seemed satisfied with her answers, which demonstrated her high proficiency with the language.

They let everyone off in a closed garage of what seemed to be a massive country house. Two other ornate touring cars sat unattended as they escorted her through a side entrance, down an oak-lined hall with tall oil portraits of generals and politicians keeping sentry.

A smattering of conversation floated from one pair of solid doors, which were opened by a smartly dressed, stolid looking rat on approach. Freya followed the wolf inside.

A record turned on a platter, jaunty jazz popping the air with merriment. A couple politicians whom Freya vaguely remembered from local papers and a retired Admiral by the ribbons at his breast, joked and laughed around a massive table festooned with bread loaves, shrimp cocktail in concentric rings and glazed ham atop a bed of baked fruits. At the head of the table sat a slovenly, mischievous-eyed jackal, tall ears cirrhosis-veined and pink with the flush of alcohol. He whispered something into the ear of the star-shouldered cat at his left, who laughed long and loud with empty detached eyes.

"Alpine cats know all the best tricks," the jackal added. "You'd think they scale mountains with those tongues of theirs." The table looked up as Freya approached and the small pockets of conversation and snickering halted with a scrape of cutlery.

"Doctor Mengal, this is Freya Smith. We would like her to act as your liaison during your stay with us."

All eyes went to the jackal whose gaze went up and down Freya. For her part, she felt stone cold as she heard the wolf say something emptily flattering about her and then direct her to an empty chair next to Mengal. Freya was vastly under-dressed in comparison to the rest of them, having a simple unisex tunic that was functionally airy but not very decorative. Her muscles rippled under its stretched fabric as she crossed around the table and sat. It occurred to her that the jackal had taken notice.

"Such an immaculate specimen of *panthera tigris* stock you are, Miss Smith. Quite beautiful."

"Thank you."

"You remind me of some people I worked with..." His flushed ears wavered and he chuckled before taking a swallow from his brandy snifter. "... in other places. The strength and power in nature are so closely aligned with the beautiful, you must agree. It's so hard to improve upon what is so very nearly perfect." Lidded eyes took her in clinically and he shrugged. "I did try."

A cabinet minister to Freya's other side tinkled his scotch glass with a claw and laughed in a way that sounded at once insincere. "You'd like to tell her all about how that's done, wouldn't you, Josef?"

The jackal smiled a disgusting smile. "I'd love to show her many things."

"Like what you did in the war?" Freya asked. Her paws were flat on the table astride her empty, white dinner plate. For the first time she could remember, she felt a preternatural calm that was alien to her. "Are you going to show me what you did for your Axis masters? In your labs with the prisoners and witless volunteers they sent you for your tests?"

Silence fell around the table again and it was broken by Mengal's nervous chuckle. He could not meet her gaze when he spoke. "Axis, Allies, mere lines on maps. I was never in this for political reasons. I simply wanted to apply my knowledge and perhaps turn a tidy profit while I was at it. Would that the Western powers have been quicker to knock on my door, I'd have been with you all so much sooner. You all know from your intelligence, the Axis chancellors didn't offer their guests much choice in the matter. I was simply playing it smart through my cooperation. You can't fault me for that."

The vulpine cabinet minister to Freya's left swallowed audibly. "And we're so glad to have you with us Doctor Mengal. We know you'll do amazing things now that you're working for the *right* side."

Mengal nodded profusely, the blush in his ears nearly purpling them. "This war was always such a foolish business, even if it taught us to build amazing things with the natural bounty that is the purest of our stock. If your people are smart and attentive, they will learn wonders in my labs. We'll build a better world together." Mengal raised his glass. "I will be grateful to teach you!"

"Here, here!" Brandy snifters rose around the room and tipped back.

The general with the most ribbons on his breast plastered on an empty smile as he finished sipping his drink. "We're so glad this war is over," he lied, turning his bland feline gaze to Freya. "Aren't we all?"

She nodded mechanically, watching the Doctor devour a cocktail shrimp as she herself gingerly reached for one of the hot dinner rolls in the basket before her and used her knife to spear some of the ham just beyond it. The repast concealed the bone-white face of her plate in an enticing glaze. She put a wan smile on her lips, as empty of joy and mirth as every face around hers. A rumble rose deep within. Another storm it felt like.

Yes. The war is over, Freya thought as she dug a straight deep trench into the dinner roll in her fingers. The war is over.

She could imagine Eiran sitting across from her, hearing those words, testing that promise with hopeless pink shell-shocked eyes. The steak knife's serrated edge caught the dull last light from the ornate window as it turned in Freya's orange-striped grip.

*This and the next story are in a sense a two-part unit. The Ape worlds of the Simian Empire (officially the Getran Empire of United Simians) and the Canid worlds of the Canine Government have been fighting a space war for as long as either can remember.*

*Ismara is a planet. It's a space station. It's also an escape-proof prison of the Canine Government.*

*Destroy the last two!*

# Umbra's Legion:
# The Destruction of Ismara

## *by Geoff Galt*

"What are they hiding?" Skulking, shifty-looking dogs. The Doberman soldier had no idea she was being watched, seen from such a distance that the air seemed to shimmer and shift as if she were a full-bodied mirage, seen from on high. She filled the screen at such clarity that her simian watcher could identify the markings on her uniform. Worn, old battle dress, clunky and cheap weaponry. She was clearly unaffiliated to any official military, but rather some sort of soldier-of-fortune. Every uniformed body down there seemed to confirm the fact that this massive prison facility was guarded by mercenaries. A hodge-podge mixture of bored dogs baby-sitting a bunker-complex labor camp.

She yawned, directing her attention to her prisoners. They were Getran citizens; simians of all walks of life. A finger tapped the brim of his observation monitor impatiently. The scanner waded through the many faces of these prisoners. Humiliated, dirty, avoiding eye contact with the Doberman guard as she paced between their ranks. She sneered as she cradled her rifle. The same finger tapped more forcefully, and its host let out a sigh. "This is disgraceful."

The Olive Baboon had the distinction of being an Intelligence Officer of the Getran Naval fleet. He was from a stealth reconnaissance cruiser designated *Blackdrift* in low orbit above a remote planet within the Canine cluster. The dogs had probably named this planet after a figure in their worthless lore, but to Getran cartographers, this planet's name had been computer-generated centuries ago as CB4L. "C" for Canine, "B" for "Breathable", "4-Low" for being the 4th rock from their lowest star. The planet looked unremarkably dusty. It had been terraformed by the dogs as a mining colony, mostly. This sprawling Ismara prison facility had been kept a secret in any database the apes had seen.

"Where are you…" the Intelligence Officer muttered, sweeping his sensitive camera over the crowds of simian prisoners. There were so many of them; apes of different shapes and sizes, different ages. All of them lugging around mining equipment and navigating back and forth between patrolling guards. The Baboon stopped. His heart sank. The camera paused over a very young Silverback gorilla mopping up a puddle. Quietly, he closed his eyes as he held his emotions in check. His eyes opened with reinvigorated, fierce hatred for the dogs.

"Those fleabags are gonna pay," he seethed. "What? What'd you see?" a voice piped in from the dark control room. "A kid… they got kids down there, Brekan." He rubbed his temples in frustration. Brekan, the Lars Gibbon pilot of the cruiser, jolted up from his seat in the dark bridge. He clambered over empty chairs that he could barely see, wading his way to the only light source in the room. "What the hell, they're slave driving kids now!?"

"He's a tiny gorilla. I think he was born in the facility." The camera settled on the mouth of a tunnel where workers funneled in and out lugging canisters. The prisoner leaving the tunnel handed off a small re-breather to a worker on his or her way in. Guards with batons barked and beckoned the new worker to hurry adjusting the mask, and threw an empty gas canister in their arms. After kicking them into the tunnel, the cycle resumed endlessly.

Brekan shook his head in disbelief. "Just how long has this place been here?" A tinge of worry swept over his face. He pawed the Baboon's shoulder. "You don't think they have more kids in there, do you? You don't think they're having them work in the tunnels, do ya, Pillen?"

Lieutenant Pillen eased back into a more relaxed position in his seat in a futile attempt to suppress his disgust at the notion. "The kid's the first I've seen, and he wasn't anywhere near the lines or the cave. Kid was probably mopping up… blood… or waste, or I dunno." Brekan said, worried, "But our guy… he's gotta be in there! I've identified Getrans that were on the same missing ship as he was, in that tunnel line. Unless he's somewhere inside, far away and safe from the gas. They probably threw him in the tunnel."

Brekan leaned in closer to the surveillance feed. An orangutan ripped off his mask and shoved it into the hands of the next in line. The guards tensed, preparing to beat the ape, but he buckled over and vomited on the floor.

Pillen turned his chair, facing the empty space between Brekan and the monitor. "They're gonna try and get him to develop weapons, but I don't think he's going to help those dog bastards." Concerned for his fellow Getran, the ape that was next in line moved closer to assist the orangutan, but got pushed back by the guards. The sickly slave spewed more at his own feet.

The Lieutenant cupped his long chin, trying to wrap his head around the situation. "It could be a few more weeks of observation, but unless he's inside one of these giant bunkers, he's somewhere in this *expensive* facility."

The orangutan leaned back, looking up to the sky while the sun washed over his face. "They probably shoved him into the tunnels..." Pillen's wandering eyes returned to the monitor. "Trying to force him to change his mi-..." Pillen's jaw slacked open in disbelief. The orangutan in the monitor was the ape he had been searching for. Weeks of dodging patrols high above CB4L, of blackouts, electronic silence, of tension and stuffy air in a cramped and lonesome ship. The tired visage of relief on that orangutan's face validated all of their efforts and hardships.

"ON THE-!" Pillen could hardly contain himself. "B-Brekan! THAT'S! - He's!—Call - get the - CALL HQ!"

Brekan grinned ear to ear, "I'm on it, Lieutenant! Nice and steady." The monkey returned to his seat. Soft red lights breathed to life illuminating his control panels as he flipped switches that lit the bridge several screens at a time until the whole room conquered the suffocating black. Blast shields over the window ports lifted slowly.

The Lars Gibbon peered at the orbiting spaceport, Ismara, geosynchronized above the heavily defended facility. The planet's openly-acknowledged orbiting spaceport (and defense satellite) and secret prison camp shared the same name. Brekan wasn't worried about detection from the prison, but the satellite was another story. One wrong move, one misstep, and that platform would alert the Canine Defense Force. The fragile truce between the Simian Empire and the Canine Government would tip into a costly war if the galaxy learned of this heinously illegal labor camp.

With a magnetic buzz, a panel popped out just long enough to silently but firmly jettison a capsule out the front of the stealth cruiser. The projectile quietly, subtly, was flung in the direction of the simians' space port.

The dogs and the apes had scuffled once before, long ago in the Ragnarok War. The Getran Empire of United Simians now traded freely between all species. Rightly so, considering their innumerable space colonies that wove nets of tightly controlled territory across a vast crescent of the galactic spiral arm. Their numbers grew in every direction, exploring reaches of space towards the outer rim, slowly making their way to the galactic center over centuries of expansion.

As the capsule glided over past the space station, the massive stealth cruiser, *Blackdrift*, pitched its nose in the opposite direction delicately. Should *Blackdrift* be discovered, not only would they be in danger of attack from fighters, but everything they worked for could be undone, with the relocation of the prisoners below. Most of all, with their target lost, they would have once again let their most brilliant military engineer slip past their fingers.

Which begged the question: What were the dogs hiding? Why were they risking all-out war with the largest military force in the galaxy? What was this mysterious gas they were mining, and why use simian slaves to do the dirty work for them?

The capsule drifted closer and closer to the space station as if it were ordinary debris. However, it looked just out-of-place enough to pique the curiosity of someone aboard the space platform. Amid the array of listening outposts and satellite dishes, a small searchlight was activated from the station fuselage. After some small overshooting, it found and tracked the capsule curiously. In an instant the capsule separated into two-halves, connected by a spool of cables unwinding rapidly. The two halves, propelled by rockets, reached their full extension!

As fast as the capsule engaged, a tremendous flash of light burst from Ismara! Blinding flares burned steadily. *Blackdrift* scrammed away under the cover of the disposable decoy. As instruments aboard the station attempted to reset, the half of the capsule pointing planet-side plunged down into the atmosphere. Self-disposing evidence, with not a trace of a Getran ship having ever been there. All in an instant and right under the nose of the space station.

The orangutan finally caught his breath. A stocky pug merc nudged him with a baton. "Well, ya gonna stand there all day!? Get a move on, you nappy lookin' beast!" "What are you going to do?" the ape glared at the considerably shorter guard. "None of you are gonna kill me." He turned and squared his mighty shoulders. The gray jumpsuit expanded with his musculature. With a bark off to his blindside, a larger guard rushed him. The ape turned to swing, but got cold-cocked with a rifle stock! The pug went for his knees, which promptly buckled. This ape was no fighter, but rather an engineer. A scientist. A gentle creature from a gentler place. His arms lurched up to protect his head from further blows. His legs protected his belly from the unrelenting battery.

"You are correct sir; I'd say you're quite correct!" a piercing, tiny voice erupted from behind the crowd of worried Getrans. The mercenaries bared their teeth, but shouldered their weapons as they backed away from the defeated orangutan. The fearful simians parted to make way for a tiny Chihuahua in a suit. The ridiculously tiny dog stood tall with his nose pointed skyward, staring sternly down his snout at his rebellious prisoner. He was known as the terrible Warden Nyx.

He waved a paw at his side. "File." A mercenary who resembled a Boston Terrier promptly handed his boss a clipboard. Warden Nyx wasted no time perusing over the paper as he trotted over to the orangutan. "Let's see, Mister… Mister…"

The battered ape still had not recovered from his sickness in the tunnel. His voice quavered as he struggled to hold his head up to the Warden's height. "You… know who I am…"

"Jaggum! Yes, Marxis Jaggum, of course. Indeed, I knew who you were… it's simply your name I forgot!" Nyx flashed a smug, closed-mouth smirk. "Bad with names, y'know." He frowned at the crowd of simians all around him. "Your… *weird* Getran names. Hmph. But you're absolutely right, Mister Jaggum. We simply *cannot* afford to kill you."

One of the larger guards dragged something behind him as he approached Marxis. With a thud, the full gas canister Marxis had been carrying dropped beside him. He winced from the light-colored dust it kicked up from the ground. Nyx thumbed further through the file. "But if you were to succumb to the side effects of the Ismaragen Gas, then… well… I'd say that would be a waste of a good brain."

Marxis deeply coughed. His eyes strained to focus as he peered over the tiny oppressor's shoulders and to the faces of his comrades. When Marxis Jaggum puked, it was the contents that Nyx expected like bile and food. Some of these apes had been vomiting blood for quite some time. Others had boils and irritation in place of fur. Pocked and diseased skin. Some were too sick to stand. Fewer had yet to get their fill of gas exposure. Nyx locked eyes with the worried, tiny gorilla in the back of the crowd. The only infant among them. Warden Nyx blocked Marxis' view by stepping in front of his face. He locked eyes with Marxis.

"This is all preventable, you know." Marxis focused on the Chihuahua's face. The Warden softly urged the ape with an uncharacteristic tinge of sincerity. "Just work with us. We'll get you out of this mine, get you off-world to a much freer, much more relaxed environment. They're willing to even *pay* you for your work."

Marxis chuckled. "Let's say... hypothetically... I agree to your leader's proposition. What then? I design weapons for the Canids... to be used against Simian kind?"

Warden Nyx scowled, visibly disappointment at the inquiry. "We utilize a militant defense force. The only way the Getrans would find themselves at the tip of our sword would be if we saw them come at us with the tip of theirs."

Marxis slowly lifted himself upon one knee and laughed as heartily as he could. "Is that what, uhh..." with a smirk, he pointed in loops all around himself, "... this is? This... labor camp? This *prison* was a defense?" He stood upright, looking down upon the small Warden. "Was it *defense* that wrenched us from our unarmed transport vessel?"

"*Your kind refuses* to respect our borders! Our walls! Our territorial space! Your kind respects nothing - *no one,* but yourselves!!!" What the enraged canine lacked in height, he compensated for in his posture, baring his teeth, his eyes wide and wild. He relaxed his mouth and furled his lips back down across his white teeth. After collecting himself, he adjusted his disheveled suit from the outburst. "... But if they will listen and respect only their kin... maybe they'll listen to us with our newfound leverage."

The unmoved orangutan noticed a glimmer from just beyond his brow, high above the sky. Without being too obvious, he witnessed the streak of something small burning up in the atmosphere. He knew it could be something ordinary like space debris. But he suppressed a smile. Somehow he knew that friendly eyes had been upon him. Without moving his head once, he glanced back down to the Warden. "You can't keep me here forever."

"It's my job to ensure that, Mister Jaggum... one way or another. We'll either send a useful version of you to home world Cerberus... or we send a useless version of yourself to the *bottom of the mine.*" The orangutan tightened his lips and swiftly punted the Warden like a football. His clipboard twirled harmlessly to the side while the Chihuahua himself rag dolled, arms and legs fully extended making an "X" shape. He cartwheeled over the heads of the awestruck apes, the awestruck guards, the slow-thinking guards, and the guards that had snapped into ferocious focus by beating the orangutan. The laughing, battered and bleeding, Marxis Jaggum.

Wurran stared, still as a statue. He sat upon an ammo crate with his five other Getran Marine squad mates. No one moved, but they were visibly uncertain about what they were seeing. They sat angled in a way to better launch themselves from their seats. To have multiple places to run should abrupt motions come from the ten jungle-cat warriors who were sitting opposite of them in their own hangar.

The cats were calm, but equally transfixed on the simian warriors of relatively equal size across the hangar bay. No one spoke. The air felt stuffy, the silence deafening. The minutes that passed were eternities measured by each rhythmic click of the artificial air generators overhead. To Wurran, this felt like torture. Something inside him boiled his blood, the way these cats unblinkingly stared at him. He was sick of being left in the dark.

While he felt right at home in combat roles, he wished only to rise in rank if nothing else; but he wanted to be kept in the loop. These days more than ever, 'being left in the dark' apparently meant waking up at the crack equivalent of "morning", falling in to the hangar bay unarmed in your casual wear, and only noticing the militarized cats over your shoulder after one of the silent bastards sneezed.

That initial encounter had been an exciting ordeal, with a lot of yelling and screaming. Lutoi, the chimp marine, lugged a wrench over to his side. At this point, it still rested over there. But it was the immediate leaders of each group that had calmed the frenzy. Wurran's stone-like temperance grounded the simians, while the cats seemed to obey their Sabretooth.

There they sat, waiting for a briefing. Each outburst from the Getrans was immediately silenced by Wurran. Every question he asked the Sabretooth had been met with deflection. "Just wait for the Lieutenant, he'll fill you in." These passive statements and the like had been repeated, again and again. So Wurran stopped talking. So did his squad mates. The whiskers didn't say anything to begin with while the apes lost their shit. Just when the sleep-deprived gorilla couldn't stand it anymore, in walked Lieutenant Pillen.

"*Attention on deck!*"

"Ah, 'morning troops. I hope you were friendly to our guests, here." As the long-faced Baboon gestured to the ten-cat squad, he couldn't help but notice the indentation on a metal panel and a discarded wrench on the ground. He frowned, but didn't call attention to it. His files at his side, he briskly marched front and center between the two groups.

Among the Getrans was a cascading spectrum of the squad's experience. The chimps, Lutoi and the Rookie, knew they would get yelled at if they were doing anything but standing at attention. The Medic Silverback gorilla and the Marksman spider monkey were shifty, unable to contain their curiosity by glancing over at him. The Mandrill Chief never stopped eyeballing the cats once, while Wurran locked onto Pillen.

Lieutenant Pillen reached his destination between two heavily armored dropships in the hangar before the two groups. With a quick referral to his notes, he pivoted to face his apes and ordered coolly, "At ease." All Getrans resumed more relaxed stances, except for Wurran who remained at attention. He simmered with irritation as he glanced at the stoic cat warriors.

"Lieutenant... what the fuck are *those*!?" The mighty gorilla popped his arm pointing at the strange creatures while his squad mates silently but clearly expressed their agreement.

Pillen narrowed his eyes, wincing in disappointment. "Honestly, have none of you peanut-brains graduated from school? Can't you tell a Felid when you've seen one?"

Lutoi and the other two green marines chattered in astonishment. *"Those are Felids?" "I thought they'd be bigger..."*

The Chief Mandrill snorted, "We know what they are, Lieutenant. *Why* are they here?" "What's going on!?" Wurran added impatiently. Pillen simmered, clasped his eyes shut, and beckoned his apes to silence. "Just— JUST... settle down, troops. This is a rescue operation. The Canids have enslaved innocent civilians to mine some kind of hazardous gas, most likely used in production of weapons-grade materials." The Chief sat back down, honed on the Lieutenant as he paced around the hangar, addressing the feline Marines as equals. This, in it of itself, made the simian troops uncomfortable.

"Furthermore, they have Marxis Jaggum. The brilliant engineer responsible for perfecting our Spaceclimber technology and inventing Gorger Super Mechas. No doubt, they are attempting to pressure Jaggum into developing weapons for the CSDF."

The squad of Getrans locked into focus. The severity of this situation rippled through their fur. Spaceclimbers were heavily armored mechs used extensively through the Getran military; siminoid machines that housed one or two simian pilots in the chest. Gorgers, on the other hand, were extremely rare, but extremely powerful variants of the same concept.

Gorgers were the size of battlecruisers, but were insanely fast and strong machines. Hulking monstrosities of armor and technology with enough power to decimate scores of war vessels at once. Each machine could orbitally bombard completely on its own. Gorgers were named so for the vast amounts of resources they consumed in order to operate. They were a super weapon used only as a last resort. At the time, only four had ever been made. Marxis had led the development of each.

If the Canids found a way to bridge the gap between their level of military technology to anything close to that of a Gorger, it would be everything the dogs needed to vie for outward conquest. It would be a bloody expansion that would disrupt the balance of intergalactic trade between ALL species, and undoubtedly result in the enslavement of more Getrans. Killing more simian-kind. This could not happen.

The Lieutenant leaned upon the black-armored nose of the nearest dropship, *The Bearhawk*, named after one of the terrifying beasts indigenous to their home world, Getra. Its armor and armaments fit the tribute. The Olive Baboon gestured to the 10-cat squad. "Sabretooth, if you would please speak on behalf of your pride, sir."

The chiseled Cat Marine lifted from his make-shift seat of an ammo crate with mechanical ease and jutted to a snap at attention as he came upright. The proud warrior locked eyes with the Lieutenant for a beat, then nodded once.

"*Smilodon*." His mouth flared rows of sharp teeth at the Getran Marines. "... *Fatalis*."

Wurran felt skeptical about these bizarre creatures, but even more skeptical of the Sabretooth. He towered above his troops, easily the tallest soldier on the ship. But Wurran was transfixed by his odd and seemingly impractical teeth. Were they engineered to be that way? His ability to speak without a lisp was enough of a mystery to warrant a peer-reviewed study. Lots of creatures couldn't help but bare a bit of fang when they spoke, but these were as ridiculous as they were utterly terrifying to the unsettled gorilla.

"S'cuse me, but is that your name?" Wurran shifted in his seat to be more front-leaning. "Or is that a Felid rank?" Wurran furrowed his eyebrow in an attempt to offset his fear by projecting intimidation. The Sabretooth eyed Wurran up and down as he slowly stepped in his direction. Eerily silent, like a bipedal prowl, heel-toe to heel-toe.

"That is my species, Gorilla." He lapped the roof of his mouth and tilted his head to the side. "I am... 'top combat rank' in my squad. A battle-ready two-ton terminator. A veteran of multiple tours." He halted within arms reach of Wurran, looking down at him from the length of his body. Wurran now sat upright repositioning his face away from the cat's crotch.

The Sabretooth snarled, "... and I am your ally for the duration of the mission." His pupils were jet pin-holes amid their golden iris. With ferocious intensity he lingered there, overlooking the dead silent apes. He sized them each up. "... My Hellcats depend on you six for survival. Cast your xenophobic weights aweigh and come to accept that your survival depends on us as well."

The *Smilodon fatalis* popped a precise 'left face' and slowly prowled to the Lieutenant, who was still leaning a shoulder against the nose of the dropship. "I only hoped there would be more of you... six is the most you could spare?"

Lieutenant Pillen shrugged in a way that propped him back up to his feet. "We weren't quite sure how many your leaders were willing to spare. I know for certain that Getran Command wanted this group small and contained, but..." Pillen scratched his head as he looked at the other nine cat warriors loitering around crates. "Ten soldiers?... Can't say you fangs fuck around."

"My name is Obsidiran. If the dirty fleabags are on the cusp of gaining Gorger technology... we don't want that any more than you do." He offered his paw in a friendly handshake. The Baboon only came up to his diaphragm. He hesitated at first, but noted the cat's retracted claws. With a nod, he accepted his handshake. Taken aback that instead of clasping hands, the cats clasped the inside of the forearm, closer to the elbow to rather 'shake arms' firmly. Odd, but Pillen respected the gesture. He looked into the eyes of a creature he could now call friend.

*Obsidiran*, he thought. *The ebon pelt of his fur makes sense of the name.* Wurran stood in place, offset by this diorama of civility with entities he had been raised to believe were threatening alien menaces, just like the dogs. The fact that he was prepping for battle against mutts, shoulder to shoulder with 'backwards laser-chasers' disturbed him. The era he knew was evolving before his very eyes. He realized the times were going to change regardless of how he personally thought of it.

"We'll be there for you," the Chief called out. Wurran had thought the Chief was similarly skeptical of the cats, but there he stood to salute Obsidiran. "We are kin as soldiers. We'll bleed and kill together. We're gonna do this right." The other nine cats stood to their feet. The feline Chief was a ragged and stocky, five-foot-tall Pallas cat. It was their Chief that was the first to shout "Caedo!" The other cat warriors stood tall and sounded off in unison, "*SAEVIS CAEDO!*"

The siminoids were surprised and perplexed by the strange ritual, but recognized it as their rallying cry. Wurran looked to Obsidiran who gazed upon his squad with a radiating pride of his own as they chanted, "Caedo!" "*SAEVIS CAEDO!*" It became very apparent by his body language, the father-like wear on his face, that he cared very deeply for his troops. The gorilla wanted to think it was weak of him but instead, he admired it. No commanding officer ever swelled with more pride over his actions, no instructor, squad mate, or even his ex girlfriends.

The Getran military were disposable in their culture. Seen typically as a dime-a-dozen, disposable end to justify any means that benefitted the greater good. Enlistment was generally considered the right thing to do and some found it cool, but it was an existence that their culture lacked compassion for. The armed forces that spanned the galaxy were so vast and dense that the citizens were well aware these apes knew what they were signing up for.

*Missing limbs? Well, we'll help you out, but you better not complain about it; you should've read the fine print. What's this? Mental anguish? Shouldn't have become a soldier then.* Veterans were bitter, but complacent. They understood that no one else would understand what they went through every day. That was just the way it had always been.

"Commissioner, I'd rather us play it safe than sorry." Warden Nyx's eyes bulged as he handed the report back to the five-foot-tall Dachshund, who towered above the weirdly short Chihuahua despite her lanky slouch. She was no different from the rest of the grunts under his command; loyal, capable, but stupid.

"Pray tail, Warden, Ah dun thought a place like this'here would have th' gangly space ape lock'd up tahter than a fee-murr in STONE." The Warden winced with every punctuation the soldier-of-fortune borked. "Whut if it's just one a them thar false ay-larms?"

"Ugh… this could be really bad. I have a very *very* bad feeling about this. Do you realize what would happen to us, to *all* of dogkind if the apes have discovered this place?" Nyx felt a churning in his gut, the hairs between his shoulders bolstered against the collar of his suit. He strained against the bandages still freshly applied from the injuries he had sustained from Jaggum. He searched his own thoughts over and over again, and each time he tried to justify it as nerves or paranoia. His gut only lurched dread into the forefront of his mind.

"Listen to me. Our prized prisoner is to be relocated immediately. Do we have any ships on standby?" The Commissioner and the Warden stepped up into a brisk pace as they patrolled down the corridors of the dense prison complex. This particular section held mostly dogs, no doubt perpetrators of severe crimes upon the dog home world. "Warden, it was yer own order not ta haf no ships loiterin' dirtside. We'd have ta call it dahn from that geosynctified space station."

Nyx's face twitched. "'Geosynchronized', Commissioner! Tell them to send one shuttle down immediately! Also, patch in with the Navy. We need heavy patrols. I want warships! I want Gladius Squadrons! I want Carrier support! *I want -*" Warden Nyx stopped his frothing for a few beats while he hyperventilated, blinking wildly. The Commissioner stood terrified at the spectacle, cocking her head to the side in confusion. In the years she had worked with him, she had never seen him this riled before.

He loosened his tie, freed up his neck. It was clear by the way his paws shook and his ears drooped that he was extremely distressed. He looked up to the Commissioner and methodically, nearly-pleaded his point. "Commissioner... Keila... please. Boot up the AA batteries. Clear the Central Hub, and load up the monkeys right in the middle."

She scoffed a laugh and looked at him incredulously. "Mistah Nyx..." "All of them, Keila." "I really don't think -" "Do it, Commissioner!" "They said it was just a flash!" *It may've been a dang fluke, Warden!* she thought. "*You don't understand* what's at stake here!" he yelled. The Commissioner let her arms drop to slap her legs as she searched the ceiling while trying to calm him down. "What, yer 'career' or somethin'? Ye think mine ain't on the line for wastin' dog hours tryin' ta -."

"*FUCKING! LISTEN!! TO ME!!!*" The Warden checked his immediate surroundings, where guards and prisoners with perked ears listened intently. His lips tightened as he quieted his tone. "If I'm wrong about... all of this... I will *gladly* take full responsibility for the overreaction. Bonuses all around! Do as I command and while you're at it... pray that I'm wrong about what's coming."

She shook her head slightly, trying to figure him out. She let slip, "What's gotten into ya..." In a moment, with a look while his guard dropped, he flashed a worried sideways glance to her eyes. "I'm going to step outside... please hurry." He walked away, passing the concerned faces of his hired goons. Passing the cells of career criminals.

"This got anything to do with them apes I smell, Warrrdennn?" a prisoner Wolf cackled. "Those monkeys start fighting back, little guy?" Hahahaha," a Hyena sneered. "Betcha they found out, huh! They're comin' for you, Mister Nyx, you're fucked!" "YOU FUCKED UP! YOU FUCKED UP!"

The whole block chanted as they rhythmically banged on their doors and hard plastic windows in unison. Guards cussed them out and tazed them through slats. They sprayed down others to suppress the jeers. But through the rippled yips and the screams, the chant rippled to every cellmate within earshot. The caverns of metal and concrete rung with the song of unified '*YOU FUCKED UP*'s. For once in the Warden's career, he didn't have the stomach to enact cruel retribution on his prisoners. Not this time.

Eight security checkpoints later, the Warden sat alone outside on the upper deck's outdoor activity area. He stared at the geosynchronized Ismara Space Station above. It took him a couple of minutes to find it initially, but the unmistakable speck appeared to be quivering in the center of his gaze. He had been staring long enough at it that he knew it was actually his body doing the quivering.

He hoped it was a fluke. That the obviously flare-like event near the space station had been just some sort of honest mistake. But if it were Getrans, would they go after his government first? Would the Canid government throw him under the bus because the facility was technically privatized? Would they prosecute him to save face? Or would the Getrans rain hell upon the whole prison because of this whole situation with the ape prisoners, which were the orders thrown into his lap by his own government?

One possibility would be legal but would take longer. He snorted, amused at the thought of becoming a cellmate with the prisoners formerly under his watch. That would spell certain doom for him. But the other possibility—what the Getran force would do if they ever found out about the conditions these apes were subjected to. He would be fucked either way. He had to get out of here.

The distinct whine of the rusty metal door creened open. Familiar footsteps followed a familiar voice. "Howdy, Warden…" Her inflection implied that bad news hugged her words.

"Commissioner…" Warden Nyx bruffed sadly. "Are they sending the reinforcements I asked for?" She stepped closer, and sat next to him upon the picnic-like table he sat upon, resting her feet on the platform his tiny legs couldn't even reach. "The pack 'err mighty concerned for ya, Nyx. Say yer actin' a lil' crazy…" She looked at him with still-reserved emotions, hoping that the statement wouldn't set him off again.

His default rage gave way as he locked eyes with her with sweeping helplessness. "I can't explain it… I can't even explain how I feel, but… somehow I know something terrible is going to happen." She recognized the fear. She could smell it. She respected his openness. "Warden… what is it?"

This opening allowed the waterworks to escape as the Warden turned his head away to conceal his tears. "Did we get the reinforcements or not!?" He braced for the news, with enough time for her to clear her throat. Swallowing her own spit, she told him, "Shuttle's preppin' fer launch, sir."

He turned to her, leaning in with trembling, fleeting hope. "The *reinforcements*? Dammit, are they sending *anybody else*!?" He clenched teeth and fist in a chorus of fear and wrath. Keila leaned away. "They've dispatched a modest squadrin' of..." He leaped off of the table and shook with rage as she elevated her voice, hoping the rest of the news would alleviate his anger. "... S-*Squadron* of Gladius Interceptors and Gladius Recon!" As he tightened his eyelids, the tears streamed down and crept into his short-haired fur. He relaxed his jaw only to relieve his grinding teeth.

"Damn themmm..." "Nyx, talk ta me, please. Whut the hell is goin' on!?" Warden Nyx looked skyward and immediately locked onto the distant speck of Ismara Space Station, screaming "*Damn you, you cowards! Petty fucks! It's not enough! - You've left the door open for them - You've killed us all!!!*" He seemed to jump with every shout, at remarkable volumes emitted from a creature so small.

"WARDEN!" She clasped his shoulders and slid to her kneepads where she could be more eye-level with him. Her pleas to calm him down and communicate were overpowered by his frothing as he continued, "*If I could get my claws on you, I'd rip you apart!* RIP YOU APAAAARRRT!!!"

He couldn't hear her. He couldn't hear her if he tried through all of his anger, but especially not now. Especially not after his jaw slacked in terror, his eyes widened to register the sight of Ismara Space Station as it burst into flames. What was one explosion turned into several, and those several combined into a larger concussive plume of what resembled ash. Twinkling particles that he knew were metallic plates and debris spinning wildly, reflecting sunlight. No one could have survived that explosion. It was gone. And then it had hit him all at once. From the surface, he had just watched so many die. Faces he knew, wiped out.

Finally, he gathered himself enough to tell her, "Look!" He pointed skyward. She obliged and gasped at the horror implied by the still-expanding plume at orbit. "*Oh my God!*" After a beat, she proclaimed. "What are... what are those three lights!?" It didn't take long for Nyx to spot the three bright specks in formation.

"Wh-When you talked to Ismara Station... how many were they prepping to send?" She choked through her hyperventilating, "Just - Just one, sir." The Warden, stunned as if in a nightmare, slowly turned skyward at the three fiery entities entering the atmosphere. "Oh shit..." He grabbed her by the sleeve and started scurrying to the door back into the complex. "The AA placements! *Tell me the Anti-Air is up and running!*" She wrenched her sleeve out of his paw. "I'm pretty goddamned shore they up an runnin' now! Ya think they don't know what th'hell just kickt up!?"

Upon the hulking concrete and metal wall threading away from their position, an armored segment opened up its shell. Missile batteries spun out from the retracted armored plates and pointed their array skyward. "There, see? AA batt'ries are on top of it! Let's get back ta comms and git the Navy up on -"

Blinding them first, deafeningly punctuated, the vibration in their bones confirmed the rest. They curled away from the AA battery from the heat alone, but also the shockwave that told their brains that any sense of ground was an unreliable illusion of security. They opened their eyes at the behest of all of their instincts that screamed *'flight'* and saw only a tall skyscraper of smoke, dust, and debris, reaching still-skyward. Orbital bombardment.

"*They're shelling the Anti-Air!!!*" Warden Nyx's voice cracked. "*Ensure the monkeys are gathered in the central block! Converge all non-essential units there! GO GO GO!!!*" The Commissioner was extremely distraught, but training took over. She merely did, and thus followed his order as they sprinted for the door to the complex.

*Bearhawk Alpha* led the three-dropship squadron. Alpha was loaded up with six burly Getran Marines with plenty of room to spare, fully loaded with their rounded armor, and relatively youthful laser tech loadouts. The Getrans had always been a little ahead of the curve with war technology. Recent generations had granted them unprecedented access to finer and rarer raw materials across the galaxy, allowing their innovations to accelerate at an especially blistering rate ahead of other races.

Their portable laser rifles, full-auto variants, sharpshooting variants, were long overdue for real combat test beds. The conditions of secrecy and the minimization of ape eyes were ideal. Wurran, a black-fur mountain gorilla, led the squad. The Mandrill baboon was their Chief. A Silverback gorilla was their burly medic, a taller-than-usual spidermonkey served as their sharpshooter, and Lutoi and the other chimp were relatively green soldiers.

Lieutenant Pillen reassured himself that reinforcements were just a call away, but he couldn't help but wonder why the Getran chain of command wanted to start this mission with the odds steeped so far against them. Five years of service, twelve major combat operations. It seemed that only one thing remained consistent; nobody told him anything beyond what he needed to do, and that mere moments before he needed to do it. This boiled his blood.

He guessed that this time it had to do with these oddly plastic laser guns they were outfitted with, but there had to be more to it. Could it have something to do with the cats they were partnered up with? As far as he knew this had never happened before. It only made him more tense than usual before a mission. He peered out the window and his face lit up from the bright explosion of another orbital bombardment upon an AA battery below. One thing's for certain: this Marxis Jaggum better be worth the trouble.

*Bearhawk Beta* was the Cat squad. Led by Obsidiran, the hulking Sabretooth commander, a Pallas Chief, twin Cheetahs, a heavy LMG Bengal tiger, a Jaguar marksman, and a relatively slimmer pretty-boy Savannah chatted it up with two Cougars and an Ocelot in the back. Typical feline marines were extremely quiet during drops. A little of that was out of necessity because they couldn't hear each other easily if they tried. Their sensitive ears could barely pick out voices amid their own dropships rattling apart during entry unless they shouted.

This drop, however, produced a weirdly accommodating volume. They glanced out the portholes to see an atmospheric sky, indicating they were already past the worst of it. It wasn't going to get much louder than the hum they were experiencing. These Marines had been through so much bullshit that the jitters they all felt before a mission enticed excitement. Aboard a Getran vessel, this seemed like some kind of fucked-up vacation for them. They had fun pretending they weren't scared. They laughed harder than they'd laughed in a long time at the face of eminent danger, as only a crackpot cat Marine would.

Obsidiran recognized this. In the intermediate years of his leadership, he would've chastised such banter; but he had come to know these soldiers long enough to realize they were masking their jitters. They needed this. Sometimes it was the foolish, petty coping mechanisms that served as the glue that kept them intact, ensuring their survival. He looked out the port nearest to him to see the third dropship peel away from the rest. The shit was about to hit the fan, and he took this opportunity to attach his full-faced helmet.

Dropship *Echo* was designated for being empty. That's why it was overloaded with exterior weapons for its early role in the mission. Lieutenant Pillen himself operated the spacecraft, invigorated by the opportunity to deliver upon the fleabags the rightful karma they deserved. What he had seen with his own eyes would be set right from the wings of the craft at his fingertips. He sighed a thanks to his Command for allowing him to no longer be a helpless bystander to the dogs' crimes.

All of his vessel's energy was devoted to shields as he accelerated his plunge into the atmosphere. Fire clashed with the blue energy of the shields into a brilliant white crackling sheet over all of his viewports.

Flying partially blind, his instruments were his only eyes. As his secondary joystick retracted away, varying panels flipped into different indicators to signal atmospheric flight became recently possible. Parachutes first, flaps second. His gut did a somersault as he grunted against his seat harness from the brutal inertia. He heaved the joystick backwards, into his belly.

The sound of the air around him changed its pitch as onboard levels and speed indicators confirmed the craft's obedience. He had to do a double-take to hear the chirps of a missile trying to lock on, only to abruptly stop, eventually followed by the muffled crunchy thump of another orbital shelling. Brekan had his paws full alone above on the sizable stealth cruiser, but without him bombarding these AA placements, this mission simply wouldn't be possible.

Still coming in hot enough to ignite the air around him, Pillen curved his nose upward and began trouble-shooting. Sweeping across, he flicked various buttons from forward-facing rocket boosters to deploying additional flaps in an effort to slow down. Perhaps with the parachute still shaking behind him, the rest was overkill, but it got the task done quickly. Pillen's head slowly pulled back into his seat. He blinked to see the sky of CB4L for the first time from this perspective. The base of the parachute popped off with the help of explosive charges. More armored panels shed away to reveal the wing-mounted armaments tucked away at the dropship's underbelly. His craft flipped over and unfurled its wings as it descended further planetside.

First the two horizontal stabilizers at the main body which carried the explosive payload, then the four diagonally formed vertical stabilizers near the tail, and finally the two that unfurled from the top that took with them additional armored engine pods. Lieutenant Pillen overshot the landing zone slightly in his speedier approach. The other dropships were descending at a more consistent pace.

Pillen's main priority was getting to their landing zone first. He dumped energy from shields into engines and boosted forward. He was low enough to see the complexities of the massive concrete facility that dominated the landscape below. Across the plains, yet another AA battery was obliterated from above. Pillars of smoke scribbled across the sky to indicate the growing number of AA placements that had got hole-punched.

*Bearhawk E* swept across and battered out fully-automated grenade launcher rounds across the rows of concrete fortifications. *Bearhawks A & B* set down and opened their rear hatches to allow their troops to fall out. Their respective pilots, informed by their own cargo-bay camera feeds, knew precisely when to launch off of the ground. They couldn't stay stationary for long in case someone on the dog side of things became wise and hurled an anti-vehicle projectile in their direction.

Not that they didn't try, but as soon as one mercenary set up along the top of a wall or structure, *Bearhawk E* scattered them apart in a hail of dust and hellfire. As fast as they landed, the dropships were up off the ground again. *Bearhawks A & B* lurched forward in a slow ascent and churned their rockets forth into a wall face. With explosive proficiency, they burrowed a hole into the center of the prison by sheer force. Their sixteen troops had eyes in every direction, strained against the dust kicked up around them, and made their way towards the focus point of the barrage.

The dust puffed beneath each stomp they made forward. The heat from the point of rocket fire on the fortified wall was their door into hell. The smell of the dusty shithole tinged sourly with the nearby gas-mines, and mixed with the bouquet of burnt destruction from the *Bearhawks'* assault. CB4L's ground shook with *Echo's* grenade launcher bursts. The concert of fire warmed their faces and shone into their eyes. Their stomachs drummed with each occasional orbital pound into the crust. Piercing through it all was the loud alert siren from the top of each hub structure. It seemed desperate.

The explosions around the concrete formation shifted from the surface to inside the building itself. *Bearhawks A & B* ceased their concentrated barrage, and peeled away to join *Echo* in its top-side strafing runs. The dust settled as the sixteen approached the still-smoldering hole. With a moment's pause to check for debris falling atop them, and carefully scanning the ridge above for enemy troops, they leapt through the heap of concrete and metal into the charred interior of the mess hall.

Wurran honed his rifle towards a likely firing point to find an empty place in an empty room. In stillness, he felt his squad mates sweep the corners of the room. The cats filed in and fanned out across the heavily-damaged floor. Metallic table setups had been blown apart, some of them flung by the blast to embed themselves into the far wall. There were no bodies, but evidence showed that they had gotten people out of here in a hurry. Wurran crept towards the still-shut main hall door and listened.

The distinct rumble of the Bearhawks above streamed overhead erratically, dopplering from one area to another. He felt it letting out a burst of grenade fire to some unlucky mercenary topside. The thunderous blasts of orbital bombardment shook the whole facility, but became less frequent. The alarm shrieked with piercing long-sustained howls. Dust fell from newly formed cracks around the silent soldiers.

"*Be advised...*" the commset in Wurran's ear quietly chirped to life with Obsidiran's distinct murmurs. "*Detaching four of my guys up top. Callsign: Strafer.*" The Getrans eyeballed each other quietly, not certain what they had to gain from splitting up so early in the mission, but nobody felt the urge to question it. Wurran clicked his comms: "Copy that, Bearhawks? We're gonna have four of our cats up top."

"Echo Confirmed," Pillen chimed in almost immediately. The four cats, the twin Cheetahs and the two Cougars, jumped up to a platform on the second floor meant to overlook the mess hall. Through a door, they found themselves at the top of the wall in that sector. They advanced cautiously while Bearhawks zipped around overhead.

"Yeah, Alpha, got it." The squad approached the metallic sliding door between the mess hall and the main corridor. Wurran looked up at nothing, impatiently waiting for the third confirm. "Egh!... Beta copy!" The strain in his voice had incoming missile-lock tones in his backdrop. The cat warriors started laughing. The Panther among them softly chuckled. "Looks like the flyers got their hands full out there!"

As they snickered, the annoyed Wurran heaved the large, cumbersome metal door to the side with one mighty arm. He swiftly steadied his rifle with his other hand downrange. The violent metal shriek locked up the laughter and all guns stared down the empty corridor. Their silence was inadvertently punctuated by a nearby orbital strike and a fast-moving Bearhawk clicking out flares high overhead. The lights flickered and swayed from the shelling, yet successfully illuminated the ventilation and water pipes overhead. A long, cold, sterile corridor was their path to the rest of the facility. Now perfectly focused, six apes and six cats trekked onward.

Warden Nyx shook violently, his comm unit trembling in his paw at his ear. "Yes!... Yes, Getrans!... *They're shelling the place as we speak! Send all the help you can get!*" Two gargantuan mountain dog warriors filled the cramped office with him. A petrified Commissioner Keila stared into the eyes of her reflection at a nearby mirror. *This is it*, she thought. *This isn't just a jailbreak, but this might be war. Actual war.*

"*WE'RE GONNA NEED MORE THAN JUST A COUPLE OF FIGHTERS, YOU MORONIC MUTT!!!* Send in the Navy or *we're all DOOMED!!!*" Nyx let his arm fall to his side and dropped the comm on the concrete floor. He fought to catch his tiny breath before he snapped his attention to one of the two SWAT dogs. "Do you know where they are now?"

With a deep bass voice that rattled the Warden's cabinet doors, one called back, "Breached through Central's southern mess hall. They bored right through the bulkhead, and they're working their way up to Central Hub."

"Dammit! How the hell do they know where they are!? They're heading straight for the rest of their kind… Oh, what should we do… Can we - or *should* we relocate them?"

"In what way, sir?"

"Any way! Can we uh… move them to a different part of the facility? Can we… can we *airlift* them? Can we -"

"Ships'll git shot down, sir…" Commissioner Keila hung her head. "Or captured… either way wouldn't do us any good. And relocate 'em where, with the Canid crim'nals?" She brushed her shoulder with the massive SWAT dog's elbow who gave her what space he could spare. "No-sir. We fight… put 'em down fer good. Shut 'em down, cause we in the legal right. Present the findin's to the higher ups, git our heads in the clear."

Warden Nyx stopped to think of it, if only for a moment. "Keila… I know we're rapidly running out of options, but these are *soldiers* we're up against, not lawyers!"

Keila scoffed, "We're soldiers TOO, sir! We were soldiers before we were reduced ta guard duty, and this's become our turf! We know these halls well, and we outnumber 'em too. 'Ey Chief, how many combatants are confirmed?"

"On the ground? Less than twenty." She growled, "Less than twenty, Warden… we're 300 strong, an' we got the arms." A burst of dropship fire emitted a tremor that shook the lights as Nyx furrowed his brow.

"Those numbers are rapidly diminishing top-side, so you best act fast Commissioner." "Ah don't have the clearances you do. Levy overall command to me, an' I can git this nice and organized." Warden Nyx's eyes were weary from stress. He'd had enough. *"Done.* Done, anything you need. Let's do it."

She was still scared. More terrified than she'd ever been in her life, but duty was more important than herself right now. With her shoulders back and her head high, she saluted with a look of determination. "Patch me thru with whoever's in charge at Central Hub."

The caged dogs screamed and shouted. The siren faded and the orbital bombardments became less frequent, but one noise seemed to be traded out with another as the squads cautiously walked down the rows of jail cells that held canine prisoners. The few that weren't scared shitless were confused. While many receded into their cells, others reached out with their arms to the strange soldiers, begging for answers, begging for help, begging for anything.

"Apes and cats!? What the fuck is going on!?" was the particular sentiment that seemed to come up the most as they strode their way down the block. Everything else was an incoherent mess of shouting and cussing, slurs directed at them, cheers as if they were going to free them. Wurran snapped back to the front when he had to remind himself that the crowd was marking their positions. The shock from one prisoner when they saw a Getran or Felid acted like a wave. The prisoners were like a living beacon, and it put the squads on edge.

The twelve hugged the concrete wall opposite of the cell blocks. On the other side of that wall, a mirrored arrangement of cells. They finally reached the connecting "H" between the parallel corridors, and the leading Getrans signaled the cats to split up. Six apes took one hall, six cats took the other. Nobody questioned it. Obsidiran had been watching their rear carefully, and served as the caboose to the row of cats that stalked their way into position.

The loud crowd of Canid prisoners drowned out so much noise that a few of the cats felt comfortable sacrificing stealth for speed. Nobody could hear anything in this stressful chaos of barks, cries, and shouts. Just as Wurran was about to move on through his lane, he saw a large object twirl at the cats' feet. He spun to face it. He was met with a plume of smoke, the object's bouncing making a barely audible clatter. It was one of the large canisters of gas with its valve all the way open. *"Contact!"* could barely be heard from the Feline Chief over comms!

The two leading cats opened fire down their corridor at the unseen Canine soldiers. With a few loud, echoing pops, the plume of gas that enveloped them ignited into a fiery explosion! The shouts didn't change, but compared to that crunchy gas explosion, seemed reduced to a whisper. The two cats, the Ocelot and the Jaguar lifelessly collapsed in the carnage kicked up by the explosion. Comms went unfiltered with inescapable shouts from one another.

"Cover! Get to cover right now!" Most obliged, except for the hulking Bengal Tiger who handled a large machine gun at waist level. He blasted a hot load of fully auto fire down their range. With the smoke of the blast still at his feet, unignited fumes threaded the air around them like otherworldly wisps of ghostly shreds. The gas had a thickness, its stench unmistakable. Their eyes itched. Their *eyes!*

*"Masks on! Masks on! Gas gas gas!"* Wurran belted out. In seconds, the soldiers had unsheathed and pulled their respective gas masks over their faces. With a checking glance at his surroundings to ensure no mercs were upon them, Wurran turned his attention to the rest of his Getran comrades. Their medic had his mask halfway across his face, the

Silverback's mighty paw held firmly over his own neck. Blood gushed over the gasping gorilla's fingers. His other paw sifted through a kit mounted to his armor, desperately trying to find materials to patch himself up on the spot.

"*Medic's been hit!* Medic, took..." Wurran looked into the desperate Gorilla's eyes, to his surroundings, at the sharp flak of shrapnel from the canister, some large and twisted, some small. "Shrapnel to the neck!" the Silverback shoved a cluster of gauze into the wound, gurgled a cough, and bared sharp teeth already splayed with blood. The cats were furious, angrily sprinting down the corridor where the first canister was thrown, but Obsidiran, still checking both pathways to the rear, snapped a concerned glance to the injured gorilla.

"*Get 'em away from that cage!*" Obsidiran said to the apes. The medic's back was to the cage of a terrified border collie prisoner, who hunkered down at the furthest place he could between the shitter and his cot. "We need a fucking medic for our medic!" Lutoi shrieked, lending a supporting hand to his injured comrade. The continued gunfire from the cats robbed the mob of their spirit in noise-making, allowing Wurran enough time to detect a new noise. Down his lane came running two Canid mercenaries who lugged an open-valved canister in their direction.

Wurran snapped to action, straight to his feet, and swiftly shouldered his rifle while widening a death glare through the glossy curved viewport of his armored gas mask. Time slowed as he howled, "APES, CEASE FIRE." The Getrans looked downrange to see the canister, spewing the thick and spindly gas, arc up near the concrete ceiling towards Wurran who continued to stride forward. "STOW WEAPONS!"

The other four Getrans rose to their feet, sliding their weapons behind and beside by their slings. The felled Medic applied necessary aid to his wound behind the tainted gauze. Just as the gas canister was about to sail over the mountain gorilla's shoulder towards the rest of his squad, he spiked it down with one mighty swing of his arm. With a denting crash and spin, the canister tumbled back the fogged way towards the mercenaries. Though faceless behind their own gas masks, and hiding behind their riot shields, their instinctive steps backwards were all the fearful indication the apes needed.

"Knuckle down..." Wurran's mighty paws slumped to the ground before him, positioning himself in a primal charging pose, shoulders and brow forward to the aggressors. Their bodies quickly faded back into the growing plumage of smoke. "... *Tear them apart.*"

Training came in handy for the everyday life of a Getran citizen. Gorilla, Baboon, Chimpanzee, Macaque, Gibbon, for any kind of ape in the Imperial Militaries. The training was pretty universal, and only sometimes catered to the unique specifications of any particular race or gender. What mattered is they were all apes, and there was a way you do things. For the close-quarter combat Wurran was charging forward into, training would have him do things a little differently.

But protocol, on paper, would have the gorilla soldiers thinking that their natural, primitive rage was more-so a liability than a strategic tool. There was no thought to it. But if Wurran had *really* thought about it, he probably couldn't recreate the disarming technique he had maneuvered on the closest dog Riot Guard. It wasn't strategy that swatted the baton out of his hand while elbowing the shield in such a way that the upper corner jabbed the guard in the face.

Wurran had learned the exceptions to his training; when to know the time and place for terrifying, instinctual, primitive combat. So when Wurran screamed at the top of his lungs through his gas mask, he knew that what little the wide-eyed dog could see. If he tried to couple a face to this terrifying sound he was experiencing, all he would see was a gorilla's furious eyes of death in an ocean of shadowy blackness. It was only for a split second. A soul-withering second before the same arm that disarmed and shield-bashed him, backhanding his whole body and causing him to sail down the corridor.

Training also helped the Canine mercenaries to keep a level head when things didn't go as planned. Now the corrosive Ismaragen gas was being used against them, and these terrifying ape soldiers were practically swimming through it. To get to them and to beat the shit out of them. It was a scary situation that no training in the world could've prepared the riot dog for. His last words were an undignified whimper when the Mandrill Chief grabbed him by the neck of his armor, hurled him into the nearby cage wall, and repeatedly bashed him against the bars with forces exceeding the dog's body-weight.

Lutoi and the marksman spider monkey sprinted ahead up the corridor, closer to where the other dog landed; the fog dissipating and separating in their wake. Wurran regained his breath thanks to his gas mask. He imagined that if he were to stare at his own reflection, he'd observe his pupils widening past normalcy. The Chief continued to savagely beat and thrash the riot guard in his clutches, while the inmates around him coughed and gagged from the gas exposure.

Through their immediate anguish and the horrors they glimpsed, they wept. It began and ended in seconds. The ones most heavily exposed to the gas reeled, vomited, and died quickly. The other unprotected prisoners breathing the gas traveled a longer, more grueling downhill road to death.

The comms chirped to life with the voice of one of the pilots overhead. *"Blackdrift* this is *Bearhawk Bravo.* I'm observing additional fortified anti-air; can we get some more shelling please?"

Brekan manned the Stealth Cruiser alone, high above them in space. "Uh, that's a negative, *Bearhawk*; got my hands full up here."

There was a beat. "… 'Hands full', *Blackdrift*?"

Brekan sounded stressed. "YEAP. Been micromanaging enemy fighters, seem to be scouts! As soon as my bubble's clear, I'll resume."

It was way too soon for enemy space fighters to engage the stealth cruiser. After a stunned pause, the Mandrill Chief let the eviscerated riot guard's body slump to the ground before he ran to catch up with the front. The other chimp rookie was hot on his tail.

"So yeah, if you folks could hurry up and find our prisoners? Now would be uh… a great time for that!"

Wurran turned back to where they had come from and swatted at the strange gas to disperse it quickly. It irritated what little skin it could reach, and he knew he would need an immediate chemical bath once this was over. He marched through the blotches of smoke to the medic, and gasped at the sight before him.

The medic was slumped lifelessly on one shoulder, his back still to the cage. A prison shiv stuck out of the side of his head. There stretched over his body was a mangy canine arm, desperately reaching for the sling to the Silverback's laser rifle. The dog froze when he saw the Mountain Gorilla emerge from the smoke.

The Silverback was a heavy creature, so Wurran huffed when he pulled his fallen brother away from the cage. The armor and equipment at the medic's back had prevented his head from comfortably touching the ground, but it let flow the open wound at the neck caused by the shrapnel. The self-patch had never been completed, and his eyes remained open and vacant.

Even with the bandage, Wurran wasn't sure how much longer the medic would've remained alive. But this vermin, this Canid *scum* decided to take it upon himself to hasten the process when no one was looking.

"… Just kill me…" the dog whispered. Wurran felt like he should've listened when Obsidiran told him to get him away from the cage.

"Just… just kill me," the dog said again.

He thought that he hadn't seemed like a threat at the time. He looped in his mind wondering why didn't he make the call.

"Ya hear me!?" the dog clutched the bars between his face.

The Pallas Chief jeered through comms. "Alright Getrans, the ground level cats made it to a forward intersection… more corridors… Looks like your corridor aligns. Waiting on you."

Wurran collected a few of the medic packs attached to his brother and began affixing them to his own loadout. "Medic's dead" he comm'd flatly.

"Hey!" the dog snapped the fingers of his paw at the gorilla.

"UH, GROUND TEAM," Brekan's voice cracked back onto comms, "Long range scanners picked up a few capital class cruisers that seem to be curving this way. Let's pick up the pace, shall we!? May be actual Canid Navy, repeat, ACTUAL NAVY."

Lieutenant Pillen specifically primed his mic just to say, "Ah shit. *Bearhawk Alpha* here. We're kinda running out of things to shoot. They've been staying out of sight topside."

"*Kill me, you fucking idiot!*" the dog continued to snap.

"Yeah, kill him already!" an unseen prisoner chimed in.

The Mandrill Chief called into comms, "Where are you, Wurran? We met up with the cats."

"I'm on my way," Wurran hastily replied. He unslung the Silverback's rifle, identical to his own, and aimed it at the criminal before him. He stared at the pathetic Canid. "… I want you to know, it's not because you told me to."

The dog let out a single weak laugh, "It doesn't matter to me, you *gangly fuck*. No one gets out of this place alive."

Wurran pulled the trigger of the laser rifle. There was no recoil, but turbines spun rapidly to cool down the barrel. There was no blast, merely the hum of the inner mechanisms whirring away to produce the laser, and the soft whine of the cooling turbines. There was no visible beam, but the super-heated point upon the dog's head immediately lit with flame. It glowed white hot, rapidly burrowing a hole through him and scorching the wall behind.

Wurran held the trigger back, tracing the invisible beam down and boiling the flesh off his body. It separated unevenly, smoldering with the fur burning and peeling away. The jumpsuit caught fire next as what was left of the dog slumped to the ground, steaming. Black and red blood spilled onto the cold concrete floor. Wurran looked at the body of the Medic solemnly and said "I'll be back for you, friend." Even with the trigger off, the cooling turbines continued to work as Wurran double-timed down the corridor.

It was a straight shot, even after the cell blocks had ended. Bodies of dog mercenaries littered the ground. He didn't even consciously register the gunfire amid the chaos he had gone through back there. The claustrophobic corridors opened up vertically into a well-lit clearing. More bleak gray concrete walls stretched skyward to natural light. The rumble of the soaring *Bearhawk* dropships became clearer. They maneuvered more erratically in the hopes of catching more dog soldiers outside. The absence of grenade bursts indicated that the dogs had wised up.

There at the perpendicular intersection of this hall and a wider one, amid the dust and debris, stood the team. The Mandrill Chief saw Wurran approach and addressed his comm, "Wurran's here." Lutoi was scuffed up a bit, dirtied as though he had been dragged. "Did you get the gorilla's medkit?"

Wurran, stunned by the lack of concern for the fallen Medic, bit his tongue and pressed it to the side of his cheek. He glared at the chimp while he patted the kit that he had affixed to his belly. "Yeah... yeah I got your kit right here."

"Oh good. You mind throwin' me a painkiller?" The chimp was bouncy, but ragged. It became clear as Wurran approached that he had been shot but treated.

The pretty-boy Savannah cat stepped between the chimp and Wurran. "He's had enough, I treated him." The cat shrugged a shoulder to right his rifle's sling, and with a free hand double-checked that his corpsman kit was secure.

Lutoi looked skyward in a rush of rage, and shook his oversized Autolaser with frightening ferocity. "C'mon, your pussy shit is weak! First you dig around with your fuckin' litter-crusted kitty claw *in my wound*, and then ya stuck me with the biggest damned needle I've ever seen in my life. *What kind of backwards Dark-Aged shit are you working with!?*"

The Savannah's ears swept back and his lips curled to display his fangs as he spun to face the chimp. "I stopped your bleeding and saved *your life!* You have a proper painkilling dosage, so quit your apeshit!" He rolled his eyes and slinked back to the middle to watch over the corridors, eyeballing the blasted corners where cameras used to exist.

The spider monkey marksman kept his eyes down the hallway he was propped up on, but leaned in to add, "Apeshit's all we know. It's what we do, cat!" His chuckle rippled a laugh from everyone but the injured Chimp and Wurran himself. Wurran was locked onto the fact that they had lost three soldiers already. He got the impression that losing the Getran medic was merely an inconvenience to the rest of the squad.

"Hey team leader, you alright?" the other Rookie chimp called out to him. "Are you fucked up about the Medic?" While his inflection implied his question to be endearing, the audacity of his own soldier chilled Wurran's bones. The chimp continued "It's alright, boss… we got another one," as he casually pointed to the equally stunned Savannah cat. This should've been expected, considering the overall worth of a Getran soldier's life. Maybe that's why they sent six when the cats sent ten. But Wurran couldn't shake the unconquerable feeling that this was wrong.

He hefted a laser rifle in each hand and all he could do was shrug. "Ha, uh… yeah… You're damned right I'm pretty fucked up about it." The cats recoiled away in silent sympathy. "But Wurran," the Mandrill Chief said. "… Did you even know his name?"

Wurran glanced a stunned look at the baboon. He became aware that he actually didn't know his Medic's name. He barely knew any of his squad's names in the months he'd spent with them. He only knew 'Lutoi' because he acted up all the time. Chief was Chief and Rookie was Rookie. He realized he perpetuated the very indifference he grew to despise, so deeply that he wasn't even aware of it. He turned his gaze away, searching for an answer, only to land on the cat squad hanging their heads in sympathy. More sympathy than the Medic ever garnished with his own kind.

Of all creatures, Obsidiran was the first to break the silence. "I'm sorry for your loss." Wurran gasped. *He* had lost *two*. He lost two feline warriors and yet, he seemed to care more for a Getran than they would for their own. Wurran looked to the floor as he thought long and hard about everything that was wrong with his culture, as the comms rang to life. "We found them!"

Obsidiran raised a paw to his ear as he called back, "Say again, Strafer?" It was one of the four cats that left them at the mess hall. The comms chirped back with the voice of one of the cheetah twins. "The Getran prisoners are all corralled at one point. We see them! Looks like they're holing up in the core hub of the facility."

The Chief went to a knee and started rummaging through his own backpack, while the rest of them whooped and cheered. Wurran closed in on Obsidiran, slinging a rifle to his shoulder and clasping the giant by the shoulder. "Hey, thanks. I'm sorry for your losses as well, Obsidiran."

The warrior looked down at Wurran with a nod, through the red pin-camera points in the cavities of his full-faced helmet that was shaped to resemble his own skull. His actual jaw stood out, black fur among the matte black paint of the armor, when he spoke.

"It is an unavoidable hazard of the job, Getran… could've easily been you or me. We must remain vigilant, and get your people to safety."

He punched Wurran's arm for good measure. "It's why we're here."

Wurran wanted to go back to mistrusting the cat, but he fought to tear down the mental blocks built by his own culture. The same xenophobic culture that had taught him that cats were equally as treacherous as dogs. But here now, the warrior resonated with the genuine conviction in his voice. It wasn't charisma, but his gut believed every word in his voice. He now thought of the Sabretooth as an idol in leadership.

After a sniff to offset the obvious emotional swell he exerted, Wurran lifted his finger to his own comms. "Can you give us coordinates based off of *Blackdrift*'s mapping?" One of the Cheetahs in the four-cat squad chirped back, "Stand by…"

A glance at the Chief Mandrill confirmed he had a small portable device to read-out the local terrain on a map. With the tap of a button, a blank interface awaited coordinates to be typed into its program.

*The apes lack respect,* Wurran thought. *I aim to command respect not just to myself, but to impress the value in respecting each other. We're not disposable, we're not merely property… we deserve to be mourned. Not out of pity. Not as a tool of propaganda to prove a point, but as individuals. We deserve… worth.*

Warden Nyx growled, "Hurry up… *hurry up!* How many times do I need to say it?!" The Central Hub was an overcrowded catastrophe. All the ape prisoners, all 42 of them, were huddled in the spacious central foyer of the large concrete dome of the central hub. Many segments of walls that adhered to the curvature of the circular room implied a line between them and the mass of dog mercenaries that scrambled and churned about like headless chickens.

Marxis Jaggum stood upon a chair in the dead middle of the petrified crowd. He watched as dogs in full riot gear continued to funnel into doors at either side, trying to shout information to each other in the deafening storm of yells. This exasperated engineers who were actively attempting to *barricade* said doors.

The crying and stressed-out apes were certainly doing their part to add to the audible chaos. Marxis, battered and bruised from his 'disciplinary correction' outside, watched helplessly as officers of the prison dragged canisters of Ismaragen Gas into the crowds of apes. They were threaded together by a hose the officers held over the heads of the seated ape prisoners.

Commissioner Keila held one ear down, struggling to hear the transmission from her comm unit in hand from her perch on the upper catwalk. "No, *daggummit! Return to yer Anti-Air post, BUT DON'T DEPLOY 'TILL THEY ON THEIR WAY OUT!*" More radio garble continued through the comm unit only to violently, loudly cut out, followed closely by the distinct ground-quaking thud of another orbital bombardment. Keila clutched the comm unit with the intention of crushing it with her bare paw. With a shriek, she threw it into the crowd of Getrans below like a skipping stone.

"ALRITE, THE REST A YA!" Her piercing voice stilled the Canid Mercenaries, commanding their attention. "Grab some canisters! Thread 'em together like Officer Ricknee showed ya, and integrate 'em nice an' good with the monkeys. C'mon, c'mon, don't dilly!" She clapped her paws loudly as most of the dogs began to move with refined purpose. "Don't dally! We got guests to please, c'mon now!" She kept clapping while all of the mercs moved to assemble the canisters into makeshift bombs rigged to blow. The apes screamed in protest, but fearfully huddled away from the surrounding riot units.

Nyx looked sick. He felt his back against the wall, both literally and to the situation. He had always been a cruel manager of the prison, brandishing tactics that evoked fear to get the prisoners in line. He couldn't mentally swim out of the drowning feeling that the decisions he had made with the ape prisoners were going to bring the hammer of many worlds down upon him. For the first time in many ages for the Chihuahua, the internal drag of hopelessness dominated his spirit.

Commissioner Keila wore a lifetime's worth of stress on her face, earned in a matter of hours. She sat next to him. "I sure hope this works, Warden... I got a bad feelin' about this'n."

His voice was raspy from screaming all day, and his fatigue added even more texture to it. "They'll have to listen, Keila. It should buy us enough time for the Navy to come in... it's the only shot we have."

"We're... are we *actually* gonna gas 'em?"

"... If there's the slightest chance they'll kill us all..." Nyx tampered with the remote switch in his hand, normally meant for mining operations, but modified to trigger all of the gas canisters at once. "... Then they gotta fail. Plain and simple."

A loud clang and clatter startled just about everyone in the room. The Warden jolted upright to see where it came from—a shaky, tail-between-his-legs mercenary who had accidentally dropped a loaded canister of gas.

"Hey asshole!" the Warden shouted, "Careful with that thing! You wanna blow us -" all of a sudden, a piercing metallic explosion that prompted everyone to scream.

A *secondary* blast! The double-doors to the further wall of the massive rounded room flew open as five fully armored Getran Marines strode in with their weapons at the ready. They climbed over the ineffective and hastily positioned barricades with ease. The feline marines funneled in behind them, training their weapons in every direction. The armed Canine mercenaries on the upper level aligned on Nyx, with the terrified mercenaries on the ground floor joining them.

Wurran quickly surveyed the situation. The dogs who were just maintenance workers were slowly backing away to flee. One, at his feet, was too close when they breached. He crab-walked away in terror. Many others were equipped for non-lethal riot control duty, the vast majority of them armed with batons, stun prods, and riot shields. Only an astonishing few of them were actually armed, and some even fumbled their rifles in an attempt to aim at the imposing berserkers.

It was quiet enough to hear a pin drop. The ape prisoners sitting on the floor in the middle of the room wasted no time in cooperatively lying as flat on the ground as they possibly could. Marxis Jaggum stood, surrounded by Canine mercenaries. The canisters, and the hoses connected to the still-standing gas bombs seemed to be partially set up, covering half of the crowd in a zone of certain death.

The mercs holding the Ismaragen gas cans froze. The ape prisoners flattened themselves like pancakes, squirming among each other just trying to get as low as they could go. Marxis tightened his arms at his sides, bracing with eyes wide. Silence. Broken by a single laugh. Warden Nyx approached the center of the platform above the apes, remote trigger in hand.

"That's far enough!" He licked his teeth, concealing his fear with pure rage and conviction. He went all out. "What you're doing is highly illegal, you know! You want to start a war? You must first consult the law… And in Ismara Prison, *my word is law!* So if you're willing to talk, I'm sure we could negotia-" That was as far as he got before his throat lit with flame, and a concentrated laser beam streaked from his arm to his hand. The beam absolutely melted his flesh off, possibly liquefying some bone as well, before he reeled backwards tossing the remote charge away.

One of the dog mercenary's shouts snuck in before the eruption of gunfire dominated all senses. The Getrans had an easier time maneuvering their perpetual death beams across, painting the many terrified, desperate canine faces. The smell of burnt fur and flesh became overwhelming. The overall temperature of the room bumped up significantly. The dogs tasked with loading the canisters fell as half melted, charred and burning heaps around the traumatized prisoners. Marxis closed his eyes tightly.

Round after round from the cats eviscerated any dogs that were missed. Ankles were obliterated beneath riot shields that had put up a wavering defense against the onslaught of super concentrated heat. Bullet casings danced and flickered across the ground as the dogs repositioned themselves into whatever suitable cover they could find. Return fire from the canines bounced off the rounded armor of the apes, and kicked dust off the lesser armor of the feline marines. Rounds entered flesh of the Canine warriors, and they let out primal screams as they ran through the fire.

The Commissioner crawled on the upper platform, inconsolably screaming at the ghastly sight of Warden Nyx's fate. She was too far from the remote charge. She desperately called for help amid the chaos. The dogs' Elite SWAT force responded; the twin mountain dogs with heavy shields. They linked up, and slowly strafed to form a covering bridge for Keila, rhythmically making their way toward the remote.

Wurran saw it first, from the cover behind one of the semi-circle concrete walls surrounding the prisoners. The concentrated gunfire between all parties drowned out his voice as he screamed into the comms for help. Upon putting his guns to the task at hand with the numerous canine warriors, his laser rifles quickly overheated into invalidity. Once the barrels were toast, they were useless. He was down to his pistol, and without any angle to address the two SWAT dogs and the Commissioner.

A chunk of the ceiling behind the two SWAT dogs erupted from a explosive charge as concrete rained down upon them. Out of the fresh hole streamed the two Cheetahs and the two Cougars, leaping directly onto them with guns at the ready. The Cougars aimed at the more vulnerable spots of the mountain dogs' armor. The giant beasts fell soon after.

In the most potent panic of her life, Commissioner Keila scrambled on all fours to the remote detonator. She felt like she was trying to run underwater. One of the Cheetahs rolled into a perfect landing, launched off in her direction with one leg, and without blinking once, reached out to her with one paw. She was still trying to crawl forward when his arm swiftly reached in front of her and clutched her throat, with his claws digging into it. Her legs kicked in a futile protest as his clawed paw clenched into a blood-soaked fist. Her trachea became a handle for him to yank out and away as she lifelessly collapsed.

Brekan's voice had become a profound and unprofessional panic over comms. *"YOU HAVE GOT TO GET IN THE AIR—NOW!!!! Our own Navy warped in, and it's ship-on-ship out here! Get the fuck outta there!!!"*

The soldiers could see he was right. They could see it in the sky above. Brilliant dots in the sky that reflected actual sunlight against the backdrop of an atmosphere softly at dusk, traded blows with each other.

Smaller craft among them also battled it out. Somewhere in the chaos was their ride out of here; the stealth cruiser, *Blackdrift*.

The sun faded into a blood-orange hue over the horizon of dust and sparse mountains. The many pillars of smoke began to fade into wisps. *Bearhawk Echo* and *Bravo* were loaded up with fifteen prisoners each, hovering above, glancing around the ruinous nooks and crannies of the prison facility in their immediate area. They were covering as *Bearhawk Alpha* landed and awaited loadup.

Lieutenant Pillen impatiently comm'd in, *"C'mon folks, let's shake a leg!"* The remaining thirteen prisoners, including Marxis Jaggum were already aboard, along with all of their wounded; the Chimp Autolaser gunner, the Tiger, both Chiefs, and the Savannah Corpsman. They took close watch of their dead, the Ocelot and Jaguar that had died from the gas ignition, and the recently deceased Rookie chimp.

Obsidiran and Wurran double-timed as hard as they could while hefting the weight of the Silverback Medic's body. The laser guns hung uselessly by their slings, their plastic bubbled and their barrels warped into invalidity. All of the laser rifles were toast. The Sabretooth and the Mountain gorilla dragged the body past their line of defense, which was the spider monkey armed with one of the fallen cat's guns, and the twin group of Cheetahs and Cougars. Everyone was roughed up, and ready to go home, immediately trailing behind their leaders.

The engine noise was overpowered by the cheers and joyful sobbing from the prisoners. The craft itself lifted momentarily before the hydraulic gate came to a close. The involuntary wobbling of the passengers dissipated as artificial gravity pulled them to the floor at their feet, and in a moment of surreal, gut-flipping bewilderment, the horizon out of the viewport rotated 90 degrees.

The injured soldiers grinned from ear to ear. Those with injuries in their torsos wanted to laugh the most, but couldn't. Most simply clapped. Wurran fell to a knee next to the body of the Silverback Medic. After catching his breath, he thumbed for the tags around his neck. With a smiling gasp of relief, he now at least knew his name. He had trained with him for weeks, lived in the same quarters as him on a ship, and now, too late, he finally knew him to be Den Mutera. He shut Den's eyes, and hung his own head at the realization that he might be the only one aboard the dropship that cared.

With one more jolt of inertia, they swayed hard to the rear of the craft as Exit Jets burst to life with a colossal roar. The sound was like that of an angry gorilla god ripping the world apart. The Exit Jet thrusters were located on either side of the cargo bay, which made communicating to each other face-to-face nearly impossible. But by the vibrations and the pitch of the sky, they knew they were making tons of distance.

*Alpha* particularly climbed so fast they could watch them overtake *Bearhawk Echo* out the viewport. Its pilot was apparently experiencing a missile lock as he streamed flares out the underbelly of his craft. Unless the dogs had some special form of pursuit missiles on the ground, the Exit Jets could outrun them at these altitudes. Without any kind of warning of the abrupt changes of speed, which were constantly pulling the passengers to the rear of the ship, the prisoner apes could only faintly compete with the thunderous engines with their terrified shrieks and screams.

Ears popped and pressure built. The injured soldiers felt it even worse. Wurran scanned the crowded hangar to ensure that everyone was doing alright. He saw Marxis Jaggum attempting to speak to Obsidiran. Even when the mighty Sabretooth turned his head to better hear the orangutan, who was *screaming* as hard as he could into his ear, the feline just shrugged. Wurran watched as the ape clasped his own head as he freaked out, looking frantically around the hold. He lunged for the dead Rookie, pulled the large combat dagger mounted near his collarbone, and disappeared behind the crowd of other prisoners, pulling across the cargo net strewn across the hold's ceiling, one arm after the other. The hue of the sky outside faded as the atmosphere grew thinner and thinner. The horizon of land transitioned into the hazy horizon of a planet ever receding to the rear of the craft. Obsidiran registered that he should do something a few beats too late, and struggled against the thrust of the ship, attempting to wade through the Getran prisoners. Wurran followed suit, taking a cue from Marxis by pulling himself by the cargo net above his head.

Wurran politely maneuvered his way past a mother Silverback rocking back and forth with her child gorilla. He waded past a snow monkey coughing up a lung, covered in boils from gas exposure. He firmly shoved aside a sickly bonobo, and after pawing a macaque aside, he was shocked to witness Marxis frantically digging into the back of his own skull with the knife. Blood flowed down his back.

The atmosphere of the planet CB4L outside faded into the blackness of space. The Exit Jets detached violently, shaking the whole dropship as other engines took over the task. The prisoners who had turned their attention to Marxis when Wurran and Obsidiran rushed him screamed in a panic. Marxis himself couldn't help but to wretch from his self inflicted agony.

Obsidiran had his paws open and out to the orangutan, ready to pounce whenever he could. "What the fuck are you doing!?"

With nothing but shock in his eyes, Wurran pleaded, "Are you trying to kill yourself!? Put the knife down! *Put it down!*"

Marxis screamed *"Stay back!!!"* The saw-like rhythm of his hand quickened, while his other hand parted his fur out of the way and dug into the wound. Obsidiran lunged forward trying to clasp his paws around Jaggum's to secure the knife, but the stubborn orangutan shoulder-checked him in the chest. Marxis swiped his knife wide, flaying a streak of blood across anyone immediately near him.

*"Back off!!!"*

He gritted his teeth, digging his fingers into the bloody opening while wincing with intense pain. Suddenly his eyes widened. As Obsidiran righted himself off the wall, ready to pounce again, Marxis jabbed the knife into the back of his skull and pried while howling a sharp cry. The knife tumbled off of his back and fell onto the floor as his eyes narrowed. With his free hand he flicked a blood-soaked device about the size of a lugnut out in front of him, which popped mere feet from his hand.

**BRRRRT!** A cascade of similar, muffled pops rippled from the front of the ship to the rear. The soldiers flinched, not as much from the noise, but from the warm and wet slap of blood that flecked them from all around. Wurran was transfixed on Marxis in shock as he regained his breath. He didn't want to look, and yet, as bodies slumped against his legs he knew he had to.

The Pallas Chief was the first to shout in exclaimed profanity. The soldiers were just... stunned. Wurran slowly turned around to see all of the prisoners, every single one of them, slumped over on the floor of the cargo hold, fountains of blood sputtering from the fresh cavities in the back of their skulls. Comms erupted with the *Bearhawk* pilots frantically trying to figure out what had happened. Wurran, with tears in his eyes, unhinged his ear piece and let his arm fall to his side. His mouth agape in wonder to the horrors of the world.

The other eleven soldiers were in a similar situation; their eyes wide, mouths agape, and painted in blood. The Savannah covered his mouth, and promptly fell apart. Others in the hold were soon to follow suit, because that's all they could do. But Obsidiran could only stare at Marxis. In the midst of this, Marxis Jaggum tugged at a blanket to free it from beneath the dead body of a nearby ape who pinned it down. He wasted no time in bunching the blanket up and pressing it firmly against the self-inflicted wound at the back of his blood-soaked head.

Flashes of light shone through the viewports from the space battle they rapidly approached. Wurran was tired. He was numb. His emotions had spiked into reaches he had never experienced before. It broke him. He collapsed, his mouth widened to suck in as much air as he could, thinking that would help the hole blown into his heart. Against his better judgment, in conflict with all of his training once again, he wept deeply. Wurran knew there was a time and a place for everything. So he let go. If only slightly. If only for a moment.

He opened his watery eyes to look upon the baby gorilla standing, his tiny paws pressed upon his mother's face. Wurran shuddered and with a gasp, locked eyes as the tiny creature looked at him. An explosion outside lit his little face, with the tears streaming down his cheeks. He bore a look of disbelief, as if to ask what had happened to his mother.

There was no thought. No premeditation, but, as if on autopilot, Wurran slowly and calmly wrapped one of his large arms around the child. He delicately pulled him closer to himself. The lad likely had no one out there. Wurran quietly locked up his kaleidoscope of emotions, his ultimate distress. He closed his mouth and embraced the child. Then he slowly rocked as the little one cried into one of his armor's exterior pouches.

Marxis hissed in pain, but spoke in shock, "I had to - there was no time, I - no one could… hear me, I -"

Wurran was not in an emotional state to utter a single word. His tightened lip quivered as his jaw clenched against his teeth and his head shook. He had to blink an insurmountable amount of times to clear the tears out of his eyes. He viewed the distant CSDF *Notos* out the port window. Canid Gladius fighters were doing battle with Getran Spaceclimber mechs. Missiles and rounds crisscrossed in the chaos outside.

"I was… I'm too important to lose here. I need to… back to work…" Marxis Jaggum continued.

The selfishness of the comment threw rage into the forefront of Wurran's mind. He snorted as he jerked his face to stare at the front of the ship. But he fought it. He fought the anger. The little one seemed too tired to cry, but he laid still against him.

"… Hey…" Wurran whispered. The boy positioned himself to look Wurran in the eye, wiping a tear off of his own face. Wurran was transfixed by the child. "… What's your name?" The bay of *Blackdrift* swallowed the view of the battle as the dropships glided into its hangar bay. As its hatches closed, so too did *Blackdrift* conquer the lights.

*Who are the good guys and who are the bad guys? In "The Destruction of Ismara", the good guys were the Apes.*
*In "Charon's Obol", it's the Canines.*

# Umbra's Legion: Charon's Obol

## by Adam Baker

*"Sing martyr, the call of Fenrir, son of Zeus, they who bring the countless dead upon the Acheron, so that the ferryman may usher them home."*
*- Epicurus; excerpt from the CSDF Marine Scout/Sniper Handbook*

Warm water had accumulated onto the rifle's scope from the brief but recent rain. It beaded down the banana leaves overhead and fused with the existing globules until density would send it rolling off the steel to the jungle floor. Insects bounced and fluttered everywhere, drinking and feasting on the marine-hound's blood from what flesh they could find. His coarse hair and armor provided limited protection from the native parasites as they fed. He could feel their penetrating needle-like mouths occasionally pierce his flesh. Despite the invaders and the hot, sticky barrel of the weapon, Rylan Charon, a young thylacine of slight build, quietly and patiently waited with silent, unwavering intent.

His paws ached from the hours of clutching the barrel within soiled, sweaty gloves. He tried to periodically flex his fingers within the limited grip of the weapon's bulky housing. "No visual. I repeat, no visual," Rylan said, blending prone under a mess of twigs and leaves. He wore no helmet, instead choosing to matt his fur with striped, camouflage paint. He was lighter that way and could at a moment's ready, change his guise to better match the environment. "Stay frosty. Should be any minute now," his ghillie suit clad spotter whispered back anxiously. They had been there for hours now, silent and still in their blind. Yet this was the job. This was his mission. Just one of many towards an uncertain fate. This time it was a tedious and arduous worm-crawling trek through treacherous, alien jungle, evading enemy drones and sentries. Only to take up position in some tiny cubby of earth; only to wait, cramped and pinned for days on end, withstanding the climbing, prickling numbness of any variety of limbs falling asleep. Then came the counting and confirming the number and identity of personnel in and around the site; the guards, their weapons, the timing of their sluggish patrols. All this to end the life of some monkey whose name neither of them had ever heard of and would probably never utter again.

Rylan's spotter, 'Thrower', whispered through the headset again, "Gemini is on the move. I repeat, Gemini is on the move." Rylan's ear twitched as his radio feed buzzed. He heard everything, even when the voice spoke, simultaneously soaking in the various other sounds around him: insects buzzing, water dripping, ants clattering away against logs and the faint, fluttering wings of birds above. Hundreds more yards away he could hear the humming of the base's generator, the clunking of poorly kept jeep engines patrolling the jungle, the invisible Sliprunner drones cloaked from sight in the atmosphere. However, none of these were as important as 'Gemini'.

"Copy," Rylan said. His words were followed by similar acknowledgements from the two other marines through the headset. It was Charlie and Delta teams, the two other scout/sniper units in the surroundings hills. "Be ready," Rylan said to himself "show him death," his trigger finger aching no longer with the sudden rush of blood to each of his extremities.

"He's in a convoy moving south towards us, now. In the second vehicle, brown jeep. E.T.A. three minutes," Thrower continued. Thor-Hermantus, nicknamed 'Thrower' after an embarrassing grenade exercise in basic training, was a mixed breed of pseudo-distinguished descent. Rylan only had a modicum of wolf from his mother's side. Uncommon breeds such as his did not usually have such notable careers. What's more was that his name was not of esteemed decent. Names and their heritage were of great importance to the Canid race, but the *Charon* name had also belonged to his father who, unlike many soldiers, was far from any hero. Rham Charon was discharged from his mandatory military service for a variety of alleged war crimes during the Reach Excursions. He was however acquitted and after returning to Cerberus, one of the Canid twin home worlds, married and found work as a prison guard. His nefarious reputation did not end there, as after he fathered three children, Rylan and his two younger sisters were reportedly prone to varying degrees of domestic violence, drugs and mood swings until his death. The thought struck him just then, that his mixed blood and stigma was the very reason why he was neck deep behind enemy lines.

Despite Rylan being no more than half canine, their exquisite sense of smell and hearing was not lost to him. More chatter filtered its way through the wireless buds in their ears, and Thrower perked up. "Command has confirmed voice recognition. We are go to engage." Like before, his words echoed in the radios of Charlie and Delta teams, who both acknowledged.

"Sonuvabitch is only an hour late," Rylan murmured off comms.

"Would you expect any less? Damn dirty shit slingers," Thrower said, adjusting his binoculars to scan down thousands of yards over dense jungle to a thin, dirt road cut between the trees. Careful not to disturb either of their ghillie suits, he leaned forward and methodically adjusted his viewfinder for a better look at the convoy of shoddy jeeps. "Aaannnd I have visual," he started up again just as the convoy of jeeps rounded a bend in the distance. "Gemini is on the move. E.T.A. two minutes."

"Copy," Rylan and the others said.

Using his scope, Rylan began to peruse the facility. It was a stout, featureless building with high fences and only a few small windows scattered about its sides. The only signs or markings were on the main gate, warning lethal force if trespassed. The only entrances to the building were a personnel door at the front and a large, cargo door on its backside, presumably to move the massive equipment and parts necessary to build their oversized mech-armor. Intelligence had chosen this location over many during the craft's assembly due to the fenced courtyard, making personnel vulnerable. Security was also minimal, thanks to secrecy of the facility and the planet's location, nestled deep behind the Getran Line, some five thousand nautical kilometers from the nearest Orion outpost. The yard was already busy with workers and staff. Among them was a heavyset capuchin monkey that shouted orders at his various subordinates who scurried within the clearing. He was making room for a wide mechanized slab that rolled out from the cargo doors on tank treads. Guards followed it out at each corner, who fanned out to the fence exits after the thing groaned to a stop.

The capuchin was the site foreman, Ehrek Breek, a poorly dressed, rotund individual with a greasy mustache and lanky arms that he liked to throw up and out while directing or giving orders. His flaps of skin would wobble and shake with each hysterical movement, even though he tried to hide them under his stained shirt and vest. Rylan followed the embarrassing character, making any necessary adjustments to keep him in his crosshairs as he traipsed around the yard. Though he could not hear him or the other workers from such a distance, he could smell them. At least a dozen. Each with their own distinct and fetid odor.

All this was transpiring some 4,000 yards away. The extreme range was made possible by the SR-7 "Howler" Deimos Rifle and its magazine of hypersonic scram-rounds, a type of experimental slug developed by the Vulpine agency, RENARD. While the bullet itself fired at incredible speed, the sonic round was boosted mid-flight using a form of scramjet technology, forcibly 'pushing' the shell into speeds rivaling mach 12. This projectile, firing at such speed, would literally tear through a target before it even heard the shot or felt the incredible force that would follow. Seconds later, all those around it would hear the tell-tale 'howl' of the bullet, a fitting trait given the shooters.

The caravan skirted down the covered, winding road. The dirt had become mud from the recent rain, provoking their tires to kick up mud and send it splattering against nearby trees. Rylan shifted to follow the second jeep, making out his target's silhouette through the tinted glass. "Target sighted. I repeat. Gemini spotted." Gemini was the codename for Marxis Jaggum, an elusive Getran engineer behind the Simian Empire's Exomech program. After his escape from a private prison years ago, he had been in hiding, but now he had finally emerged from the shadows to oversee the final touches of his latest weapon. The fairly common Spaceclimbers and their heavily armored counterparts, Gorgers, were the pinnacle of Ape technology. They were massive, mechanized suits designed for combat both in space and in a variety of atmospheres. Now, the newest variation was ready to test, goading Jaggum and his staff to one place.

"Do not let him out of your sights, Corporal" a soft, female voice interjected. "Uh. Roger, Command. Like I was planning to do something else on this shit hole?" Rylan rolled his eyes. It had to have been subconscious, but the more he watched the Apes skitter and hop about, the worse their smell became. "Cut the chatter," she hissed back. It was a fox, no doubt. Rylan could tell from her accent and inflection.

"My audio sucks. How's your lip reading?" Thrower asked, nudging Rylan again.

"Pretty good. I've been practicing watching your sister through her window every Saturday night." The rest of the team chuckles until the fox's voice snaps them short. "Keep it quiet. I want radio silence unless mission critical." Thrower straightened up. "Gemini is entering the base," he said, tensing the muscles of each of the canines on the frequency. Rylan aligned with the convoy as they passed through a series of checkpoints into the base. Thrower's ear bud chirped again with the female voice. He listened for a moment, repeating what Rylan had already heard through his ears alone. "All squads, call for status," Thrower continued, still trying to keep his suit from rustling.

Charlie team's marksman called it first. "Green," he said, his eyes undoubtedly on the fearsome capuchin. Green was code for a good, clean shot. "Red. No shot." Delta team's sniper said, the base's security supervisor nowhere to be found. No matter. The real prize was just arriving. Rylan followed his jeep as it skidded to a stop next to an array of pallets. Thrower nudged his sniper again. "Command wants to talk to you. Alone. She's on two. Says they have updated orders." Rylan scoffed then tapped his wrist against the housing of the rifle. "This is Charon."

"Corporal Charon, you have updated orders. You are to neutralize Gemini as soon as you have a clear vantage, even if the other two teams have not acquired their targets or are compromised. I repeat, you have permission to fire on your target as soon as you are able. If they miss their window, you must take yours. Understood?" Her voice was one he had heard before on previous assignments. Stern and purposeful. It was as if she only lived to give orders to the grunts and fodder of the CSDF. She was a fox indeed, slippery and wily and shifty all at once. Nothing was disrespectful to them. What she was doing spearheading Canid military operations wasn't for him to question. For her to put his squad mates in danger or suggest leaving fellow soldiers behind was not. What seemed like a minute passed. After the long pause she insisted, "Do you read, Corporal?"

"Negative, command. I do not read. How copy? Must be some sort of interference." He knew damn well what she said.

"I see your comms are clear, Corporal. Be advised that this is a direct order from the Fleet Admiral," she said, her voice steeped into condescending anger. Rylan sighed. He couldn't be sure, but if Thrower's hearing was half of his, he could very well hear the entire exchange. It was no use hiding it. Reluctantly, he responded, "Roger that, Command. Clear to engage."

"Excellent, Cor-" Rylan tapped his comms out of her frequency and back to Thrower and the others. On their channel, Charlie and Delta teams were trading variations of 'red' and 'green' as their targets moved about the facility yard. For the first time in hours, Rylan took his eye from his scope and looked back to Thrower, who was already staring at him. His eyes told him everything he needed, probably the same look he was giving back to himself. If he were to fire, killing Jaggum before light and sound could comprehend what had transpired, there would be no time for the other two teams to make their own shots. The surviving apes notwithstanding, Charlie and Delta may not have the necessary time to escape.

Down range, Jaggum and a handful of scrawny simians filed out from the vehicles and fanned out over the courtyard. Breek and the husky orangutan traded some sort of half-handshake, a kind of primitive gesture where they knocked the backs of their palms together. From there they moved to the Gorger, still mostly concealed with a tarp, comparing its features to a checklist in Breek's mitts. Their words were but whispers to Rylan but he could read their lips. "Is the prototype ready for flight tests?" Jaggum asked, smiling as Breek nodded back in approval. Though the orangutan was still miles away, one could still make out the numerous scars on his face and neck. Some were even brands, interwoven with bar codes and prison system numbers.

"Charlie and Delta. Report status," Thrower barked over the comms. Rylan could hear them through his spotter's ear bud. "Red," on both counts. Their targets were either not in line of sight or, given trajectory and wind speed, a kill was not assured. Rylan's finger fidgeted over the trigger. He contemplated the risk of ending it now. Just as they had ordered. Every patriotic part of his mind told him to fire. Maybe the other two teams would still have time? Maybe the order was just a test of his fortitude? What if the other two targets weren't necessary at all and both Charlie and Delta teams would be far enough away not to even be detected.

"Red. I'm red. No shot," Rylan murmured. Thrower covered for his lie.

Breek moved to the tarp covered behemoth and flipped up a corner to show Jaggum. The bulky frame had been completed, a busy skeleton of jutting, black metal. But even without its armor and mounted weapons, it was a terrifying sight to behold. Though the tarp still covered much of the machine, one could still see its menacing claws and sharp edges. "I have visual on the Gorger. You seeing this thing, Thrower? It's huge," Rylan spoke back into his headset. "I'm all over it," Thrower said. Simian ears could only hope to detect it but Rylan's ears easily picked up the faint shutter of the camera as it transmitted dozens of images to Canine Military Intelligence, a branch of the Canid Space Defense Force, or CSDF.

"Green! I got green!" Charlie team's shooter shouted into the radio. His voice was strangely static-filled from some sort of interference. Strange only because they had no such resonance during the entirety of their mission. But Rylan's curiosity was halted by, "Green! I repeat, Delta is green!" Delta's spotter chimed. The jeeps started up again and began to career out of the base, "Come on… come on…" Rylan said, the whirling metal vehicles blocking his shot. Thrower gave the wind speed and trajectory. There was silence for what felt like millennia, a quiet that burned with each passing second. "Come on!" Rylan spat out. The final jeep cleared, but in that moment a forklift parked itself in their line of sight with Jaggum. "Red. No shot." Rylan huffed, tending to a bead of sweat off his snout. "Fuck!"

The static flared up through his headset again. A growing buzz like someone turning up the white noise on a radio. "You hear that?" Thrower said, studying the skyline through his binoculars. Rylan could hear the 'something' as well, but the noise was foreign, even to the vast pitches and tones heard throughout his service. That's when the thought occurred to him, besieged amidst an alien world to stop only the known horrors of Getran science and imagination - what if there was something else? What if the wicked Gorger was only one of the new and malign weapons being tested or used here? What if they were not as alone as they thought?

"We have contact! Contact left! Contact left!" Charlie team's spotter yelped. Rylan broke from his sights for a glance over the valley towards their location. Five Sliprunners were overhead, cascading searchlights over the trees. A drone was even higher, de-cloaking at the very moment Rylan's jaw hit the jungle floor. His eyes had failed him but now he could hear the surging thrusters of the ships and the cacophony of enemy radio chatter. The confusion and frustration of communications relaying information around the planet. Klaxon alarms blared from the facility, the roar of even more ships overhead multiplied. Rylan snapped back to his scope only to find Jaggum in full sprint towards the safety of the building. He tried to hone in on a shot but all the noise and screams from his headset had sent reverberating shock waves through his body.

Rylan ripped off his ghillie suit and lifted the rifle to a tree trunk on his right. Using it to brace the weapon, he zeroed in on the ominous Getran ships. "Some sort of patrol. We didn't see it! Came outta nowhere!" Charlie cried. Rylan honed in on one of the Sliprunner gunships closest to the ground. Like clockwork, its side opened and three gorillas, decked out in shiny silver armor, jumped from either side. He lost them in the trees but then re-zeroed to the Sliprunner. "I'm engaging," he huffed so Thrower could pin his ear plugs tighter.

TWA-KROOOOOOO! The 'howling' hyperscram round breached mach 12 before disintegrating the Sliprunner. Its vacuum whiplashed the trees and, like a crack of thunder, shunted all other sound as it ripped the air in two. There was no time for reaction, only an ear-splitting shriek followed by a vacummous explosion before shards of flaming debris scattered to the trees below. Yet almost immediately, like a hydra regrowing one of its heads, three more ships thundered down from the stratosphere to join those existing.

Comms were still a nightmare of shouts and screams from both Charlie team and command. There was no time for reinforcements. There was no one coming to help. The nearest safe beacon was hundreds of clicks away and even then one would have to signal the retrieval boat for pick-up, if it was still even there. Thrower nudged Rylan with his knee, "They have our position our frequency. They can hear everything and more 'Runners are inbound. We gotta go, now!"

"Delta, come in!" Rylan barked into his headset.

"I read. Go Charon."

"Do you have visual on Breek?"

"What? Are you kidding me? We gotta hightail it outta here, like now!"

"We're not leaving. Do you have him or not?!"

The Delta sniper hurriedly scanned the base. Sure enough, Breek was still in the clearing, shouting at the various workers to push the Gorger and its slab back into the building. He turned just as he spoke, gleaming a unrestricted view of the orangutan target. "Y-yes. I have visual. Dunno for how long though," Delta team's sniper relented. "You are one crazy son of a bitch."

Jaggum had taken refuge just inside the double doors at the rear of the building. Despite the pleas of his subordinates and the veritable armada of soldiers running every which-way, he remained within eyeshot of his baby. He was looking over the Gorger.

"Call your status!" Rylan hissed into his headset. His speech was almost drowned out by the thunderous screeching of two dozen Sliprunners plummeting out of orbit and the hundred-plus infantry climbing and swinging their way up the mountainside. And when Delta's sniper said 'green' his finger tightened down on the trigger.

"Gemini acquired. I'm green!" Rylan said, his barrel aimed at the wall. Thrower murmured the wind and trajectory, trying his timbre in a low growl in an attempt to mask what words he could from the radio. Zeroing for Jaggum's slight movements behind his cover, Rylan whispered, "Let me show you the way home…"

Classified records conflict on which occurred first. Most accounts and audible files suggest that the two Marines fired almost simultaneously. The tell-tale 'howl' of their Deimos rifles echoed out across the vast, green jungles of 'R-26 Blackroot', followed by the sudden rushing vortex that trailed in the scram-round's wake. Others say that Charon fired indiscriminately, first at Jaggum before turning on what Getran soldiers he could before they reached their blind. Whichever transpired, forensics would indicate that his bullet tore through steel and concrete like a hot knife dividing butter, instantly liquefying the orangutan and his immediate entourage. The arm of another lackey and the legs of two others went with it, sending blood and tissue against the walls. With any luck, there would only be fleeting bits of Jaggum's DNA to confirm his death. With further luck, his death hoped to bring about the end of the Gorger program and eventually save the lives of millions of Canines abroad on their homes of Cerberus and Orthrus.

Breek had apparently suffered a similar fate. As he was moving when shot, the round grazed his shoulder, cleaving off a chunk of his torso, arm and midsection. He was still alive when his body was jettisoned across the courtyard and sent flailing into a concrete divider. Later reports would state several bones were broken upon impact and he died minutes later from extreme blood loss.

The churning, tumbling horde of foot soldiers would have rabbled their way up the hill as the Sliprunner drones swarmed overhead. Whether they made it to the lifeboats, held off until extraction or died fighting has been classified for years. But what is now known is that thousands were freed from the evil Simian Empire. There would be no ribbons or medals. Not for the likes of them and certainly not for the thylacine half-breed with a stigma to his name. But what was made public, before communications were severed, was Rylan Charon's last transmission....

"Gemini down. For Orthrus and for Cerberus. Gemini is down."

*Every species has its own supremacists who want to exterminate all other species. Only mankind has been sentient enough to make that desire a reality.*

*Now give all species that intelligence. And some species begin to fight back in organized self-defense.*

# The Call

## *by Lord Ikari*

It was a sunny day. The worst kind of day because that's when the bodies stink the most.

The streets of Irabani were filled with the sound of machine guns and explosions. In the sky, the fighters and the anti-aircraft guns were executing the deadliest dance in the world, with the pilots flying their planes in all directions and the artillery trying to hit 'em. Once in a while, you would hear the sound of an explosion or see an explosion. You got used to it.

I was leading a platoon of 20 men, mostly mice who hadn't joined the nationalists, across an alley. We were going to launch an assault on the Aziz company office to take it back from the nationalists. I told my guys to stop four meters away from the street. I needed time to think.

You see, I had enlisted only four months ago, just after I had learned that the fascists had taken over my native town. They basically took me to the shooting field, showed me how to hold a gun, and sent me to the front. After having been there for three months and still alive, they judged I could be a second lieutenant.

There I was now, dressed in a joke of a uniform and wearing a dirty helmet, leading a bunch of untrained civilians like me against former soldiers and some mercenaries.

The Nationalist Union of Uzikan was at first a party that had been created after the fall of Shatt III. They were claiming to represent the mice, who were 50% of the population. They had come in second during the elections. But soon, they united the different mouse militias that had formed during the war, effectively creating an armed wing for their party. The multi-species Democratic Party that was in power asked them to incorporate those units into the new national army, which had been the revolutionary army. They refused. They claimed they needed to protect the mouse people from the lizard Independentists in the province of Friban, and that only mice could protect other mice. They were supported in our neighborhood by those who didn't want the multi-species democracy. Soon, clashes happened between the new national army, the lizard Independentists, and the mouse-only "nationalist" troops.

Their leader, Alma Shakari, insisted on creating a greater Mouseland that would unite all the mice. But to do that, he would exterminate or expel all the lizards, birds and rats who dared to live in the regions that were mostly mouse-populated.

I looked carefully at the building, 40 meters away at our right, on the other side of the street. It was three stories tall, all made of white granite. Its windows were small, with some of them broken. Intelligence had told us that it was an office and a small warehouse. Most of the fighting was happening in the northern and western part of town. We were in the Fakari district, in the eastern part of town. We didn't expect much resistance, but in war, you have to be ready for everything.

We were part of an offensive that aimed to take control of this part of the city. I later learned that we were only 700 soldiers to secure an area of 40 square kilometers.

No guards nor snipers were in sight. I waved my hand, giving the signal to the boys to cross the street. We would follow the sidewalk, then we would look for an entrance in the back. We acted fast and silently. For the the first time in four months, I felt like we were real soldiers, not a bunch of armed civilians. No one would freeze if his gun jammed. No one would panic as soon as we heard a gunshot.

Soon, we came to the warehouse. I checked to see if the alley next to it was guarded. No one was there. We went to the back where there was the loading dock.

That's when when all the illusion of professionalism disappeared.

While standing in front of the door, I realized that no one knew how to storm a building. How should we enter a room? How to take cover? I put my hand on the doorbell, realizing that ''we will find out'' should have been our war cry, and opened it.

I entered a dark room with only a table in the middle and some lockers. There were two doors. I sent Irami and Bansani to check the one on our left. There was nothing there except some provisions and the air conditioning.

I told another guy to open the second door, with everybody prepared to shoot. I stood to its left, prepared to engage in close combat. He opened it. Nobody shot at us, so I went into the front office, ready to unleash a storm of bullets upon anybody who was not from my platoon.

I looked around carefully. I ordered two guys to stay there, and we went upstairs. Nobody was there either. We went back down and I took out my radio to call the command post. That's when we heard them coming.

The first sound to come to us was made by their caterpillar tracks, then voices. I told my guys by sign to take cover. We did it silently. I took cover behind the receptionist's desk with three other guys. Some took cover behind the walls between the windows while other just lay down on the ground. I risked taking a look, and I saw a god-forbid lot of soldiers running alongside light tanks.

It was great!

We would let them pass, then contact our command center and tell them about it. They would send reconnaissance to see if it was a major offensive or just a diversion (our troops were kind of close). They would be ready to greet them properly and probably by surprise. We would win this battle and I would have played a role in it.

Naturally, one of them came inside to take a leak.

He saw us, froze, and one of our guys shot him. I took cover as a rain of bullets fell on both sides of the windows.

I was hidden behind a desk that was not bulletproof, in the middle of a huge fire fight. I looked at the three guys with me. I pointed at the back door and they acquiesced with their heads. I don't know if I jumped or if I ran so fast that my feet didn't touch the ground. All I remember is seeing this door, and having used it. Of the three guys, there was the Zurvan brothers, and Tarik. A lizard. The species the mouse-supremacist nationalists had sworn to exterminate.

He was so quiet, so small, and so thin that I almost laughed when I saw him for the first time. It was only after I saw him climbing onto a tank and setting its crew on fire with an improvised gasoline weapon that I started taking him seriously.

I told them to lie down on the ground and aim their guns at the back door while I tried to contact the command center.

Then, Tarik's cellphone buzzed silently. He wasn't supposed to have one, but what the hell? He took it out of his pocket while still aiming his gun at the door.

-Pira!

He listened for 7 seconds, then just replied:

-Cuzzi da. Boko boko.

He turned it off, and told us that his wife had given birth to a little boy. We were so focused on surviving that we forgot all the stuff we usually would have said. But I cannot forget the look on his face. This expression of emptiness. It was almost certain he would die today. What kind of life would his wife and kid have? Would they be refugees or would they live normally?

I contacted the CC on my radio and told them the situation. I asked for air support when I saw a guy in the doorway. His body almost exploded as three assault rifles poured into him. I dropped my radio immediately. All of a sudden, a grenade landed in front of me, and I kicked it. The force of the explosion knocked me down, and the whole wall in front of us disappeared. Four bodies were lying in front of us. I expected to see the enemy charging in, or at least a grenade to take us out. I stayed like that for 10 seconds, but nothing happened.

My hearing was coming back, and I could hear the fighting in the front. I grabbed my radio to give them our position, when, above all the gunshots and the shouting, I heard the sound of a cannon. I dropped on the floor as 90 millimeter ammunition flew over my head. I shouted with all my strength into the micro, not knowing if they could hear me or not.

I wondered why they had not used them before, not that it really mattered. I later learned that my guys had destroyed two of their light tanks with grenades.

I had a dilemma now. Either I and the guys here could go to the front, and die like heroes. Or flee, knowing for the rest of our lives that we had abandoned our squad. Many of my friends from the university were here, and I knew I would have to explain to their families that I had fled while their loved ones were dying. On the other hand, it was a waste to die heroically like that. As I was thinking that, the gunshots stopped. I rushed to the front, while the guys stayed there to guard our back. What I saw after I opened the door will haunt me forever. Saddam, the other lizard in our platoon, was lying in the middle of the room with his brain spread in front of him. One of my best friends, Zahalt, had been cut in two, his face showing an eternal expression of terror. I froze there, overcome by my emotions. That's when there was a huge explosion in front of the building. I was thrown again onto the floor.

Another explosion, and another one after that. That's when I understood that we were being saved. I got back onto my feet and told my guys to get out the back right away. The last one to leave was Kazaku. As he ran towards me, he got shot in the back. I grabbed him before he could fall to the ground. I looked at his injury, and realized that his spinal column had been hit. I dragged him with Irani to the back door. If he was lucky, maybe one day he could walk with a cane.

He wasn't lucky.

In the end, we lost twelve men, including all of my friends. The mouse nationalists had lost 120 men and five light tanks. We had slowed down a surprise offensive on the eastern flank. If it hadn't been for us alerting the command center, and resisting one of their four regiments taking part in the attack, they could have done a lot of damage. Also, their northern offensive that happened two hours later was based on the idea that we would be too busy to fight them.

Apparently, a couple of airstrikes can take care of four regiments of infantry and twenty tanks. Finally, the nationalists were forced out of the city one week later.

We all received the medal of courage, including me who I felt didn't deserve it. Tarik was given the chance to leave the army, but he refused. He needed to make the nationalists pay even more now. He survived the war, became a teacher, bought a house, got three other kids and lived happily.

I personally went to the fallen ones' families, to tell them about their sons. I saw so many mothers cry, so many fathers realizing they never would see their son again. I went back to the front after having done my duty.

I lost my right arm in Khuzan two weeks later. After recovering in the hospital, I was mustered out of the army. That was the end of the war for me. But it looked like it was worth it. Uzikan's unity was saved.

The decades-old recording ended there. Adaban switched it off. He couldn't help but feel a bit sad. All those men of different species who had fought to stop the death of their country, and who had managed it at such a great cost. Yet it had been for nothing. Sixty years later, Uzikan had split into four different countries.

He needed to be careful with this recording. This town had ended up in Mouseland, and its authorities didn't permit any pro-lizard media, even old historical recordings. The young historian could be executed just for having watched it. He would hide the digital key somewhere where the next mouse-purity search patrol wasn't likely to find it.

*Suppose that Men and Horses were of equal intelligence throughout history. Men have carried warfare to sea since antiquity. Would intelligent horses have made good sailors?*

# Every Horse Will Do His Duty

## by *Thurston Howl*

The wind roared across the deck of the *HMS Fortitude,* and a black line of French ships thickened against the horizon, advancing through the choppy waters of the English Channel.

"They are here, Fletch," the signal-officer said.

Relishing the feel of the ocean breeze through his mane, Fletch's ears pricked as he stared out at the formidable fleet in the distance. "Is this it, truly? The ultimate battle?"

The signal-officer laughed and patted the horse on the back. "Don't you worry. You'll be protected by the crew." Fletch's ears flattened at the blatant condescension from the senior lieutenant. His hooves pressed against the railing. "Midshipmen like you typically should stay out of the way, and you'll be fine. *Especially* since you're a horse." He had no worries about what would happen in this battle, yet he did not correct his commanding officer. At the Academy, he had learned that much at least. Fletch turned his head to look toward the flag-captain of the fleet, Admiral Nelson. While they could by no means see the admiral from their ship, the flag-ship was the largest one, and its flags communicated orders throughout the fleet. Fletch watched as new flags were raised from the flag-ship, and his mind translated each flag with ease: the white with red fly (*Attention fleet*); the blue and white stripes (*Prepare for engagement*).

He turned to the signal-officer and started, "Sir—"

"Fletch, I want you to go down to the captain's quarters and inform the captain that we could use some blankets up here. I know you do not need one with your thick brown hide, but we humans need a little more than our own skin." In truth, Fletch was also cold. His fur was not as thick as it seemed, and his large seaman's coat was loose as it was the only uniform that would fit on his equine frame without being ripped when he turned his torso.

Irritated at the order typically given to landsmen, the horse walked down the stairs, his bare hooves clopping against the wood. Only halfway down, the signal-officer called back, "Ass!" Fletch whipped his head back around to face the angered officer. "When you leave your post, always check the flag-ship. They have signals there for us presently! Make that mistake again, and I shall have you scrubbing the decks clean after this engagement."

"Yes, sir," Fletch replied with his jaw clenched.

"What was that?" The officer had one hand on his hip and the other at his mostly decorative sword. Officers of his training did not possess exceptional martial merit but were experienced in memorizing and translating the annually released signal-books for the Royal Navy. "I did not catch that."

The horse opened his mouth a little more as he replied with his back erect, "Yes, sir!"

"Excellent." The officer relaxed his stance and shook his head. "It still amazes me the captain let a damned horse on his deck. You beasts are just one step above slaves."

"Yes, sir," was Fletch's snorted response.

"Very good. Get to the quarters and inform the captain of the Admiral's orders."

Fletch saluted his senior and proceeded down the rest of the steps. Even as he stepped across the weather deck, he heard a few able seamen snicker and laugh once he had passed them. His pointed ears caught more of their whispers than they thought he could have. "Look at those hooves." "Since when did we teach barn animals to read flags?" "Now, we know who the biggest ass on board is!" That last comment made Fletch cringe, but he did not address the seamen as they moved ropes across the deck. Technically, he was above them as a midshipman. The rating had been granted to him for his academic excellence at the Royal Navy Academy, the first horse to ever pass the rigor of the examinations. Furthermore, his family was one of the few aristocratic equine families in all of Great Britain. The captain of the *HMS Fortitude* had leapt at the chance of having a real, intelligent horse on board his ship to help the signal-officer translate the flags. However, it was still unclear to Fletch whether or not that alacrity was due to the genuine need for another flag-midshipman for cheap, or to the comic curiosity of having a beast that walks upright on board.

Entering the officer's quarters, he spotted Captain Richard speaking with a lieutenant. Fletch immediately raised his hoof in a salute before interrupting. "Pardon me, Captain. Orders from the flag-ship."

The Captain, in all his blue and white finery, turned and said, "Proceed, horse."

Fletch faltered at being addressed by solely his species, but he regained composure quickly. "Yes, Captain. Admiral Nelson requests that we prepare to engage, sir."

The Captain nodded to his lieutenant who walked past Fletch and began barking orders to the crew outside to prepare to move. "Very good, horse. Did you read that by yourself?"

"Yes, sir. But Officer Briggs ordered me to seek you out directly for the communication."

"Officer Briggs," the Captain started, "is a fine soldier." He picked up his bicorne hat and placed it on his head. "You would do well to follow his orders and not question him. Today is no day to try to be a hero." Fletch was dumbfounded by the reproval, but he remained at attention. "I received a myriad of letters from the Academy detailing your desire to be different—your desire to show that horses can, in fact, be as intelligent or as useful as any human soldier." The Captain approached Fletch, his face merely inches from Fletch's huffing snout. "I shall tell you now that you will not have the chance to be either today. Stay close to Officer Briggs, and you'll do enough." He passed Fletch and went on deck, calling to the flag-midshipman, "At ease, horse."

Relaxing his posture, he turned to follow the Captain, his nose huffing again, now with rage. Officer Briggs came down from the quarter deck and approached the Captain. "Sir, new orders from the flag-ship. They are calling us to engage by fleet division."

"Excellent." The Captain nodded. "We follow right behind the flag-ship then." The first lieutenant barked orders to the crew, and Fletch followed behind Officer Briggs to climb up the foremast to one of the nests, a balcony from which they could read the flag-ship's signals and call them down to the lieutenants.

Officer Briggs leaned over the railing, and Fletch stood back a few feet, his head swiveling as he examined the moving fleet. Together, the ships-of-the-line advanced toward the approaching French fleet. Napoleon was supposedly on one of those ships, possibly the flag-ship. The blue, white, and red became increasingly visible, and Fletch realized that this was going to be the largest-scale battle in naval history. His Majesty's strongest fleet was to defend the Channel from all of Napoleon's finest ships. Today's battle would decide the end of the war. Fletch was by no means concerned with personal accomplishments as the Captain had suggested. He came from a long line of servitude to the King of England, and joining His Majesty's Service had been a decision for Fletch to do his own part of helping the kingdom. He loved life, but he loved Britain more.

The French man-of-war ships darted toward them, dark and looming behemoths that towered over many of the ships-of-the-line and carried Russian cannons in their gun ports. Their bowsprits were wooden daggers that stretched anxiously to maul the British ships. Just as Fletch could make out the scrambling men aboard the first of the French fleet-ships, he turned to examine the rest of the British fleet. He saw the square of yellow from the flag-ship: the order to fire. He turned to face the lieutenant on the weather deck. "Orders from the flag-ship to fire!" As he called out the Admiral's orders, the seamen on the *Fortitude* heard the flag-ship already initiating cannon fire against the French fleet. The Captain called out orders to prepare cannons, and, when Fletch turned around to look back at the flag-ship for more orders, Officer Briggs landed a punch across the side of the horse's head, sprawling him against the foremast.

"*Never* communicate the Admiral's orders to a senior officer without my ordering such to be done. Do you understand me, ass?"

Fletch resisted the urge to rub his jaw and replied, "Yes, sir." In the heat of this moment, he would not give in to instincts. He would remember his training.

"Do something like that again, and I swear to the Queen of England and God Almighty that I will send you over the stern. Then, we can see if sharks like horses better than British men do. Do I make myself perfectly clear to you?"

"Yes, sir" was Fletch's unchanging response.

"Good." Sighing, the officer added, "Now, just sit back and watch me work. I—"

Cannon fire rocked the ship. The opponent's ship was broadside against the bow of the ship and drew open fire against the *Fortitude*. In their argument, both Officer Briggs and Fletch had failed to see the flag-ship's order to turn ship to meet broadside.

The Captain roared from below, "Briggs! What is the Admiral saying?"

Officer Briggs leaned over the railing and called back, "He says to rotate to meet enemy broadside!"

Another cannon blast shattered the mizzen mast, and the rocking sent Officer Briggs over the railing. He bounced off the ropes between the nest and the forecastle and landed, sprawled, on the deck. Amid the chaos of the battle, no one but Fletch seemed to notice the officer's fall. The boat rotated to meet the opponent broadside, and the lieutenant called out the order to fire. Explosions lit up the French man-of-war, and Fletch struggled to gather his senses. The din of cannon fire and men shouting, even screaming, overwhelmed his pricked ears. The stench of burning flesh and gunpowder made his eyes water. But through the clouds of smoke, Fletch kept his eyes on the flag-ship's masts. He saw a new flag being raised beside the yellow: the article 25 flag. He looked back to communicate his interpretation to Officer Briggs but remembered harshly that he was the only other flag-midshipman on board the *Fortitude*. Leaning over the rail, he yelled above the clamor, "Captain, flag-ship's orders to fire at the aft!"

The Captain and lieutenants relayed the orders throughout the crew, changing the ship's direction as well as the positions of the guns. As soon as they started, though, the French ship also turned, stopping the *Fortitude* from being able to aim at the rear of the ship at all. The Captain called to Fletch, "What the Devil is wrong with you, horse? Can you not read basic signs?"

Fletch turned to look back at the flag-ship. The flag was still the same. Definitely article 25. There was no mistaking the Admiral's orders. How had the French reacted so quickly to the *Fortitude*'s change of direction? Then, he watched the flags change again: articles 10 and 22. "Horse!" the Captain yelled again. "Your Captain has asked you a question. Report!"

"Sir," Fletch responded, ignoring the query. "Orders from the flag-ship for the *Fortitude* to quit the line. We need to double around!"

The Captain hesitated. "Are you sure this time, horse?"

Fletch did not turn back to verify. "Yes, sir!"

"Men, fall back!"

Just as before, as they rotated the ship to quit the line, a French ship-of-the-line darted in front of them, cutting off their escape route. Now, they were flanked by two separate ships, although the positions of the French ships prevented any of the three ships to attack each other. Fletch's heart pounded in his brown-furred chest as he pulled a telescope from his coat pocket, managed to extend it with some difficulty due to his hooves, and examined the French flag-ship. He could not understand the large number of symbol-emblazoned flags, although he got the sense that they were using a telegraphic system, similar to Admiral Popham's. That was when he saw it. There was a man in the crow's nest of the flag-ship who was using a similar telescope to look at Admiral Nelson's flags.

"*Horse!*" the Captain yelled, climbing up to the rail himself. "You messed up again!"

"No, sir!" Fletch retorted. Saluting the Captain as he stood in the nest beside him, he pleaded, "Captain, they know our codes!"

"What?"

Fletch lowered his firm stance and offered the Captain his telescope. "See for yourself, sir. At the crow's nest of the enemy flagship."

The Captain snatched the telescope from Fletch's hooves and looked at the enemy crow's nest. "You may be right, horse." He thrust the telescope back into the horse's arms and said, "If you are even slightly wrong about this, I will have you living in the stables the rest of your life as a workhorse. I do not care how intelligent and capable for emotion you are. You will be living off hay and mud, and the only solace you will receive is when you get to graze in your owner's pasture. Do I make myself clear?"

"Yes, sir."

The Captain gave a sideward glance to the French flag-ship. "We need to communicate this to Admiral Nelson. Any ideas?"

Fletch looked out at the attacking fleet for some possibility for relaying the message covertly to Admiral Nelson. He examined the French flag-ship's signals. Most flag-officers could memorize two whole signal-books. Clearly, the French fleet had the main British signal-book. It could have been a spy who gave it to them. However, the new telegraphic signal-books had just been delivered early this week. There was a good chance the French had not managed to snag one of those yet. "Telegraphic flags…"

"What?" the Captain asked.

"I need paper, pen, and five or six quick-thinking men."

Without asking why, the Captain leaned over the rail and repeated the orders as loud as possible. Within a minute, there were men ready to be at Fletch's disposal. The horse asked one to write down a set of instructions multiple times, since Fletch himself could not hold writing instruments. "Alright," Fletch ordered, "set up the code 792 on the foremast and 974 on the mizzen mast."

The men departed as quickly as they had come, looking at their instructions as they moved so they could figure out which flags were which numbers, hardly understanding what the two numeric codes actually meant. Fletch looked out at the flag-ship, hoping they interpreted the message before they delivered any further communications. He saw the Admiral's flag-captain start to raise a flag but then withdrew it before it reached its peak. The *Fortitude* started firing against one of the nearby French ships, now that they were in position to engage, yet still not in a position to quit the line. Although the *Fortitude* rocked with the firing shots, Fletch held a tight grip on the railing, refusing to be knocked off his position as easily as his commanding officer had been. Then, he saw the British flag-ship raise new flags, all blue and white.

The Captain joined Fletch's side at the rail. "Those are the same kinds of flags you had the able seamen use. I have not seen those flags used in a few years. What are they?"

"Telegraphic codes. The codes came out this week. I sent the flag-ship the message, *Code wrong*. They figured out the meaning, and the French have not figured it out, sir. They do not know this code." He pointed with a black hoof to the flag-ship. "Now, they are giving us new orders. *Attack fleet head. Napoleon*."

Laughing, the Captain turned back to the deck. "Everyone, go for the flag-ship! Full power!" He placed an arm on the horse's shoulder as he said, "That dog Napoleon is here after all. The Admiral wants us to make him draw a truce."

Fletch watched as the British fleet acted in unison for the first time in the battle. This time, the French could not anticipate their moves and floundered in the wake of the British ships-of-the-line. Fletch's eyes were frozen in an unblinking state, red and watering from the smoke but staring intently at the flag-ship. With each changing command, Fletch read the orders to the Captain, and the crew responded in turn. With stunning agility, the British ships-of-the-line swerved around the French broadsides and laid waste to their afts, bringing down mizzen masts and sterns across the fleet, until the French flag-ship stood powerless inside a circle of the most powerful British mans-of-war, the British cannons aimed all around the flag-ship but not firing.

As the firing stopped and the smoke cleared, a new flag soared at the top of the French flag-ship, a large white banner. "*We surrender*," Fletch read with a smile. They had saved the Channel; Britain had won the war against Napoleon.

The Captain opened the door from the officer's quarters, and Fletch followed to behold cheering on deck. They were all chanting his name: "*Fletch! Fletch! Fletch!*" His thin tail raised in excitement, and his ears flicked.

"What is all this for, Captain?"

"Your reward."

Fletch's mouth hung as he faced the Captain who now held out a silver medal, a blue ribbon holding it. "But, sir, I—"

"Soldier, kneel."

Fletch did not protest and kneeled before the Captain.

"For your first rate performance on board His Majesty's vessel, the *Fortitude,* I grant you the distinction of Royal Navy Medal of Honor and the promotion from flag-midshipman to Flag-Lieutenant, First Ass." For once, Fletch laughed along with everyone at the poor joke. "Oh, I mean, First Class." With a smile and a chuckle himself, the Captain lowered the medal over the horse's snout and onto his neck. More privately, the Captain said, "I do hope you will consider staying aboard for our next assignment. The crew has grown rather fond of you, I daresay."

Fletch smiled at the Captain as he rose. The Captain offered the decorative sword that is customary of the lieutenant's office. Nodding with a smile, Fletch accepted the sword and replied, "I would love that very much, sir."

*Many stories have humans working with alien partners, the two species learning to work together smoothly. In "Matched Up", they have been too successful. Pfc. Raeke, a drijan, has come to consider herself a human.*
*She is reminded that she is not.*

# Matched Up

## by K. Hubschmid

"Something funny, Raeke?"

Private First Class Raeke spun the scope dial on her M24 sniper rifle, carefully keeping her eye on the crosshairs at all times, losing no time in scanning the roof of the compound below. It was clustered like an assortment of old cardboard takeout boxes, centered in the bottom of a gravelly, sand-blown valley.

"Just that you're so worried," Raeke answered. "There are only twenty of them down there, Krakosz."

"You don't know that. Anyway, that's twenty gun barrels to worry about." Private Krakosz checked their six, keeping his head down; though it was unlikely any of the men at the base would spot their camouflaged heads amongst the myriad boulders speckling the ridges. "And last time, I was out for three weeks."

"That's because you got yourself caught in a crossfire, Private Idiot."

"Don't call me that."

"I'm sorry, you're right. There's nothing private about it."

The earpieces in their helmets crackled.

"Heading in now—snipers hold position and provide cover fire, on my mark," came the voice, from Private Richter, the designated 'secret squirrel'; designated by their squad's training instructor, or T.I, to run today's operation, to call the shots, and the only one to have any foreknowledge of the exercise. It was a chance for him to step up.

Unfortunately for him, Richter was an idiot, too. Usually surrounded by a band of admirers, he navigated the social arena like a rankoon through trash, but tactically (and about every other way); he was about as useful as a box of three-way hammers.

"Cover fire?" Raeke demanded. "What's he gonna do, drive straight in there?"

Someone popped flares from the hills to the south of the compound, drawing Krakosz's gaze to the flickering lights arcing up into the air, hissing and trailing smoke. Raeke was already scanning the compound, looking for rubber-neckers—and she was not disappointed.

"I clock five—no, six in the main building, for sure. They've got— Krakosz, they've got crates." Raeke risked a look to the north, outside the scope. "Really, Richter? A diversion?"

Sure enough, the moment the flares had left the ground, an armored van peeled out from between the northern hills, racing down the ragged slopes and sending fans of sand out to either side like a skier.

"Cover fire!" came Richter's voice. "Keep 'em busy!"

The faint patter of paint bullets bursting on the walls of the compound floated up to them, delayed.

"Crates…" Raeke muttered, her finger on the trigger. "Why would they have crates…?" She saw more shadows cross a couple windows and loosed two semi-automatic bursts, sending one recruit spinning.

No one from the compound was firing on the armored van.

"They've got something," Raeke said.

"Fire!" Krakosz snapped at her. "You're supposed to be laying cover fire!"

"On what?" Raeke retorted. "No one's even poking their head out! They're not—you know what? Screw this."

Flicking the safety on, Raeke de-chambered the rifle and vaulted over the ridge they'd taken as a vantage point, her combat boots sinking deep into the sand as she landed. With each step she covered huge lengths of ground, launching herself down the steep incline, dislodging a growing avalanche of sand behind her.

They had to have a grenade launcher. Why else allow Richter to bring his van so close without defending? Raeke raced across the ground, feet pounding, evaluating as she went—the structure was designed to be impenetrable, walls twelve feet tall, the outside parapet lined with barbed wire. Had there been anyone defending the place, they'd be up there on the roof, taking shots at her right now.

Raeke pelted towards the wall, finally spotting what she wanted— running straight for it, she bounded off the knee-high gas line protruding from the wall, reaching—holding her rifle by the stock, she stretched, catching the rests on the gutter, and hauled—managing to clamp her other hand on the gutter and swing herself up onto the roof, just clearing the barb-wire mesh.

Landing, immediately tucking into a roll to silence her arrival, she located the roof hatch. A ladder awaited her, but she knew that was too slow, and she could hear voices.

She dropped in. Right in the midst of ten camo-clad recruits. Dropping to a knee, she pelted the first five in two quick bursts—rolling as they reeled, she re-aligned—pelting the next five, up and out the door as they began to shout—outside, the scouts turned to look, and she took them out, walking as she fired, keeping the pace up. Speed was essential, now.

Not fast enough. She took cover, cussing, as the remainder of the compound's forces finally got wise, just in time to get to cover. In the shadow of this corner, though, she'd be safe until Richter arrived with his van, if he could manage that. They outnumbered the compound's forces, now.

It was only moments, though in Raeke's opinion, much longer than necessary. Richter brought his troops in, clearing the compound.

"What the hell were you doing!?" Richter demanded, stomping towards her, drawing everyone's eyes. "Running in there like a kamikaze?"

Most people found him intimidating. Raeke found him short—shorter than her, rendering him unable to glare down his nose like he usually did. She thanked her lucky stars she hadn't been born a human female; only the tallest humans outsized her.

"You should talk. What was your plan?" Raeke snapped, contemptuous. "Drive through the front door? You know they had a grenade-launcher, yeah?"

"Bullshit!" Richter retorted, almost reflexively. He glanced at the crate at Raeke's feet. She kicked the top off, revealing two rows of paint grenades on ammunition belts.

"Someone here clearly does." Raeke cast an eye at the twenty surrendered compound forces, hands on their heads between Richter's troops. "Or haven't you searched the place, yet?"

"Mark me, *hund*," Richter snarled, stepping right into her personal space, drawing out the slur as though it would hurt her more. "You step on my toes again, you won't be stepping on anything for a while."

Raeke snorted derisively, aware of everyone's eyes on her. He may be tough, but she was still a half-head taller than him, and a full head smarter. "What's that supposed to mean?"

Eyes flashing, Richter opened his mouth to reply—

Their earpieces squealed, causing a collective flinch throughout both groups.

"Exercise complete; against all probability, you sorry sacks of dung have made it through another day without being sent home—that is, most of you!" came the voice of their T.I, Garrell. "Fall in to base, debrief is at 1600—Richter, Raeke, report to your commanding officer immediately!"

\* \* \*

Interplanetary Forces Base Neilo, nestled in the desert wash of sand outside Svei city, was the only military base on New Earth, and still new. It had been commissioned only a couple years ago, and Raeke was one of 400 recruits undergoing training for the equally new Allied Marine Force—a partnership between First World and New Earth, designed to foster harmony and mutual trust between the species of both worlds— but old habits, and all that. Recently settled (mostly by those displaced by the First World's population crisis), New Earth had no trained military force of its own, and army brats transferred from First World tended to be human—so much so, that she *was* the .25 percent of non-human recruits on base. One in 400, but it had never bothered her. Having been raised on First World (the original Earth) by an adopted military family, Raeke had yet to come face-to-face with another non-human, civilian or otherwise. She didn't care to, either. They were all soldiers first, and she was a damn good one.

"Ma'am, Private First Class Raeke reporting as ordered, ma'am!" At attention, Raeke held her salute, three paces from the front of First Sergeant C. Vogul's desk, centered exactly between its corners, on the spot of shiny floor soon to be worn down by many a marine's boots.

Vogul gave Raeke a look so long, so very patient, it had her wondering when, if ever—

"At ease."

Ah, there it was. Raeke assumed 'parade rest', hands behind her back.

"You killed your team, today, Raeke."

Raeke blinked, "Ma'am?"

"Is your head so fat you can't hear properly?" Vogul got to her feet, fingers tented on the desk. "I said you got your team killed. You were given orders to provide cover fire. You disobeyed."

"Ma'am, with respect, I intervened before *Richter*—"

"No, I *don't* think you are speaking with respect," Vogul snapped stridently. "I think you have lost that ability, sometime between arrival and today, don't you think?"

Nonplussed, Raeke stared at her commanding officer, a building thundercloud of indignant anger stirring in her chest.

"Answer me, recruit!" Vogul demanded. "Can you emulate respect for another person, or can't you? Because you certainly don't seem to be capable of feeling it."

"Ma'am, I acted with initiative because I thought Richter was putting us all at risk, ma'am."

"One ma'am is plenty, recruit." Vogul slapped a clipboard and paper down on her desk, pointing at it. "Next time you pull a stunt like that, I'll have you written up for it. You're not here to be the 'Raeke force'. You're here to work as part of the cohesive unit that is the Allied Marine Force. Copy that?" Sitting sharply, Vogul pulled open a file on her desk, donning her reading glasses.

"Dismissed."

"Yes, ma'am—permission to speak freely, ma'am?"

A beat of silence seemed to freeze the office in time, and finally, Vogul's eyes came up under drawn brows, fixing unwaveringly on Raeke.

"Speak."

"Did I complete the mission?"

The stare remained, still unwavering. "Excuse me?"

Raeke remained at ease, but inwardly she braced like a bull before the charge. "Did I complete the mission successfully?"

Vogul's eyes narrowed almost imperceptibly.

"Dismissed, recruit." This time, the steel in Vogul's voice was sharp enough to pierce through the anger clouding Raeke's head. Snapping to attention, she saluted, and left the room.

\* \* \*

"Fresh fish today!"

"That's chicken, Krakosz."

Krakosz gave her a dry look. "New recruits, I mean." He forked at the chicken in its non-descript cream sauce, grimacing, much like the other recruits seated down the long benches on either side of them. The clatter of forks and cafeteria trays, adding percussion to the rumble of conversation, hid the specifics of Richter's remarks from most human ears. But even over the heads of twenty people, Raeke picked up every word, her tall, pointed ears swiveling. Nothing more than the usual names; Sparky, Jackass Jackal, and frequently, 'hund', a slur for her species expressly banned by the Allied Marine Force. She'd gotten him smoked for that a couple times.

Not that she cared what he said. Sore loser.

"They're coming from Svei, I heard," Krakosz went on, spearing peas. "A busload of them. You think there'll be more of... your type, Raeke?"

Raeke stabbed her chicken. "Probably."

"So long as they don't have poisonous teeth, like I've heard," smirked Setzer, blond-haired with blue-devil eyes, on his second plate of dessert, which he'd wrested from the recruit beside him. "Or night vision. Eh, Raeke?"

"You believe everything you hear, bumpkin?" Raeke sneered.

"Hey—we never worked on takedowns!" Krakosz cried suddenly. "Raeke! Remember, you were going to show me the defense against downward strikes again—"

"I'll show you in class," Raeke grinned slyly.

"Hey—that's not fair—"

"Speaking of class, we'd better get going."

"Raeke!"

\* \* \*

"All right, gentlemen and women, step up if you think you can show me something. You heard me, Finkbeiner! Gentle is what you are, recruit, and it's all you'll ever be, a gentle reminder of the weakest of the human race, when the hordes of the interstellar criminal community come crawling down your throat! Well?! Can you show me something or can't you?"

Assembled in the usual grid formation in the combat training room, Raeke stared straight ahead, expression neutral, and fortified to stay that way throughout any tirade Garrell might care to direct at her. A small man he may be, but he knew how to take advantage of any sign of weakness.

He marched in front of them, eyeing them, his quick, sharp gaze picking for flaws, his acid tongue at the ready.

"I'm here to inform you sluggards that it is the opinion of the powers-that-be that you are no more fit to wear the insignia of the Allied Marine Force, than a brand new recruit! Clearly you have failed to impress the men and women you need to impress! Through sheer ineptitude, you have all gotten yourselves recycled—and! We will therefore be accepting into our fold another suchlike recruit!"

Planting his feet, Garrell shot a glare at the doorway, beckoning.

"Front and center, fish!"

What the room of recruits expected next was certainly not what happened. Yellow-gold eyes darting, the recruit stepped through the door, holding a bag of belongings in front of him, his entire person covered in short black fur, blue-sheened under the lights. His tall pointed ears, twitching uncertainly as he turned his attention around the room, finally fixed, laying backward like a dog someone had just scolded.

Like a dog. That was generally how the other recruits would describe him, and really, his facial structure was extremely canine, long teeth and all, unsettlingly animalistic. Anatomically, he was otherwise extremely similar to humans—he walked and talked and, in general, moved by the same bipedal means. But he certainly wasn't human, and it was far stranger to see one in real life, rather than on an internet search.

"What are you dilly-dallying for, recruit?!" Garrell shouted. "Don't take me for your mother; simply because we'd both rather you stayed unborn! Front and center, NOW!" Fixing the rest of the room in his beady glare, Garrell went on; "folks, this is part of the Allied's new hand-in-hand unicorns and rainbows friendship pact, working with recruits like this fine young gentleman here! Say hello to Recruit S. Anders! For those of you whose eyes are bugging out of your head, yes, he IS a drijan! Did you think they all looked the same?" Garrell's eyes flashed at Racke, smirking at her.

S. Anders, with no apparent hurry in him, had finally reached the place the T.I indicated, and dropped his bag at his feet, his gaze flickering uncomfortably over the faces of the assembled audience.

Turning slowly, Garrell's eyes landed upon the bag.

"Did I tell you to put that down, recruit?"

Looking completely disoriented, Anders blinked at him. "What?"

The lack of 'sir' before and after Anders' words didn't appear to mean anything to him, but the rest of the room let loose an audible gasp.

"You're gonna learn real quick, aren't ya, recruit?" Garrell demanded, pacing right up to him, craning up to yell in his face from about a foot away. "At attention! This is you at attention? You look like you've been caught licking your balls, is that what you've been doing? Smells like it! Straighten up, noob, what kind of sorry-ass, kowtowing posture is that— have you got your tail between your legs on the first day? It's not going to protect you, because you will assume the position any time I ask, is that clear?!"

Anders glanced at the other recruits, correcting his posture somewhat, although he clearly lacked any instruction in it. Every mistake he made riled Garrell further, including the glance, and he circled Anders, looking him up and down. "Why are you looking at them, recruit? Get that dumb look off your face, are you still thinking about the taste of balls? 'Cause

I've got a real nice set, and I like them shiny! Either we retire to my office now, or you can do push-ups till I feel tired! NOW, RECRUIT!"

Looking relieved, Anders dropped to his hands, his breathing the only sound for a few moments, while Garrell percolated further verbal abuse.

"Congratulations, you have successfully completed the only thing you will probably ever be good for. THAT DOESN'T MEAN STOP! I'm not tired yet, Anders, I have a lot of stamina, and if you ever have the misfortune to have it exerted upon you, you will not walk the same again. Faster, recruit, faster!"

Apparently bored, Garrell turned to the rest of them. "Recruits! Partner up and practice takedowns! All three we worked on last session, I want ten of each, then switch!"

Finally released to move, the class split up and commenced, working around Anders, who was beginning to slow down, his arms shaking.

"Did I say to slow down?!" Garrell demanded, circling Anders again as his breathing became more and more labored. At exactly 12:30, the combat instructors arrived, and Garrell chatted with them by the door, letting Anders continue. Eventually, he could barely keep moving, and Garrell swept back towards him.

"I didn't say stop, Anders!"

But Anders' arms were giving out, and he sat back on his heels, heaving for breath. Working with Krakosz, Raeke caught glances of the goings on between rolling on the mats and tapping out.

"You want to impress me, Anders. On your feet, you sorry sack of lazy crite. Your mother should've run away the day they tried to breed her." Garrell spun, facing Anders, looming over him. "ON YOUR FEET, RECRUIT, MY PATIENCE IS WEARING!"

Had someone peed in Garrell's chow? Raeke hadn't seen such intense, focused abuse from Garrell since Week One, and certainly not aimed at her—possibly because she was good at everything, but still.

On his knees, Anders glowered up at Garrell, his long white teeth flashing in a snarl. More disturbingly, he *growled*; a guttural, bestial noise, unsettling Raeke right to the bones, and thoroughly disturbing to the rest of the assembled recruits.

Her mother would've smacked her for that. Soldiers were the epitome of courage, self-control, and intelligence. They didn't growl.

Even Garrell took a moment to adjust to it.

"Are you threatening me, Puppy Eyes?" he hissed. "Pardon me, I don't speak mutt, but I'm guessing you just used a swearword. Are you swearing at me, recruit?"

Slowly enough to steep every movement in defiance, Anders got to his feet, standing a foot taller than Garrell once more, meeting his eye.

He'd be gone by tomorrow, Raeke thought. No one lasted through that kind of disrespect.

"Someone should help him," Krakosz muttered, barely audibly, as he prepared to let Raeke throw him to the ground. "Raeke."

She met his eyes sharply. "What. Me?"

"Who else?"

Scowling, Raeke flipped him, slamming him on the matts so his breath whuffed out.

"Fat chance," she snapped. Like she'd come to the rescue of a drijan. She was on the fast track; everyone knew it.

"Three-oh-two squad!" Garrell yelled above their heads. "I need a volunteer to run an errand! Krakosz—you'll do, get your butt over here."

Snapping to it, Krakosz reported three steps in front of Garrell, and was promptly sent hustling from the room under muttered orders. Raeke thought she must've heard wrong. But when Krakosz returned, a Frisbee in hand, she stared stupidly, along with everyone else in the room.

"Stand beside me, Krakosz, and be ready to throw that." Garrell's eyes swiveled to Anders. "Since you're resistant to training as a man, we'll appeal to the other half. I'll make you a deal, Anders. For every catch you don't make, your squad will not sleep one night. All of you will do drill through until reveille, understand?"

Sharp whispers and muted exclamations flitted through the room, but when Garrell spun to identify the sources, every face had been composed.

"Ready?" he asked, turning back to Anders, lifting a hand to cue Krakosz, and nearly loosing it—

"Oh, and Anders. Hands behind your back."

"You've gotta be joking me."

Everyone's heads swiveled as they looked between Anders, who'd said it, his voice a surprisingly average, male voice, and Garrell, whose temple was beginning to bulge with a pulse.

"Like I said, you'll learn fast," Garrell retorted. "Throw it, recruit!"

Well accustomed to Garrell's orders, Krakosz did so. Anders let it sail past without moving, his eyes fixed on Garrell with a mixture of fury and disbelief.

"That's one night of drill!" Garrell said. "Krakosz—Frisbee. This is good work, Anders, you stay there. Take a good look at your new squad mates, little shysters that they are. They'll love you for this one, I promise."

His eyes did flicker over them. If they looked anything like Raeke felt, it would not be a comfortable sight. An entire night of drill?

"Throw it!" Garrell cried; and it glided past again, but this time Anders flinched as a rustle of dissension ran through the room. Recovering it, Krakosz returned to Garrell's side once more.

"Two nights of drill!"

The third time, a blank look settled over Anders' face, and he lunged, clumsily catching the Frisbee in his teeth.

"Ahah! Bring it here, boy," Garrell said, holding out a hand. Anders, clearly about to take it out of his mouth, froze, watching Garrell with a glittering gaze. Finally, he approached, and Garrell pulled it out of his teeth with a sharp jerk, ignoring the murderous stare Anders was giving him.

"That's enough staring, recruits!" Garrell cried. "Get your butts back in line!" Coming forward, the combat instructors called for everyone to get back in their pairs. Throughout the succeeding hour, they practiced various tackles and defensive maneuvers, and in the last five minutes, while the instructors finished up with the usual slow learners, Raeke grabbed her towel, dabbing sweat from her face.

"You should talk to him."

"Shut up, Krakosz. I'm not talking to him."

"Why not, Raeke?" It came from Richter, surrounded by his usual band. "Show us your leadership skills."

Raeke leveled a condescending glare at him.

"Unless you're worried?" Richter added.

"Worried about what?"

"Worried about him, being a drijan. Threatening your title. Apparently they're athletic."

Raeke smirked. She'd mastered basic combat training quickly, naturally—and it had always bothered Richter that she was unbeaten in their sparring rounds.

"It'll take more than a new recruit to take me down," she said offhandedly, flinging her towel over her shoulder.

"Why don't we see?" Richter crowed, arresting her exit. "Anders, right?" He was addressing the drijan, who looked up from a conversation with one of the combat instructors.

"Fancy a spar?"

Anders looked suspicious. "A what?"

"A sparring session, with her. You know what? I'll warm up with you," Richter said, flashing Raeke a cheeky grin. "Don't worry, I'll go easy on you, show you what she normally goes for."

Anders shrugged. "Fine."

They squared off, both wearing gloves with padded knuckles to soften their blows.

Richter was on his face in ten seconds. He'd started with a couple jabs and a right cross—which Anders grabbed and twisted, putting his cheek on the mats.

"All right!" Richter yelled shrilly, tapping out. "All right, easy…" Released, he clambered to his feet, gingerly rubbing his elbow.

"Lucky—that's my bad elbow," Richter said, rotating it. "Or I'd be…" He cleared his throat. "Well, Raeke?"

Intrigued, Raeke peered at Anders. "Do you have combat training already?"

Shaking his head, he pulled the Velcro on one of his gloves. "Wait."

He looked up, still too different, too weird, for her to be at all comfortable. But.

"Let's go a round or two," she said.

Raising an eyebrow, he shrugged and replaced the Velcro. Making space, the rest of the squad circled up, muttering amongst themselves. Raeke bounced on her toes, already warmed up, ready to move.

"Okay. No face shots," she said with a smile. Anders tipped his head, acknowledging, and teed up in front of her, following her movements. He let her lead, as she'd expected. Boys were always nervous the first time.

She sent him some quick jabs, testing his speed, seeing what he'd slip, what he'd duck. Squaring him up for a sideways slip, she caught him in it, hooking her heel behind his, sending him to the mat with a heavy thump.

Eyes wide, he looked up at her for a second, regaining his breath, before rolling to his feet. "Okay, then."

Snickering, she crooked her hands, egging him to come at her. He did, throwing a few jabs and crosses—she caught one and pulled it, yanking him forward off-balance, and pushing him to the mat, putting a knee on his back.

"Is that familiar?" she asked with a grin, holding his wrist so he couldn't escape. Releasing, she watched his reactions as he got to his feet. This was usually when pride started to kick in, rendering most people worse off than before.

He wasn't particularly readable, but he squared up again, and she focused. Dodging her first few jabs, he stepped back, and she followed, loosing another—

He ducked her fist, hooking an arm around her arm and neck together, trying to lock her in a chokehold. She shoved her hips back, slipping his grip, spinning and sending him a sharp elbow to the face—overdoing it, she realized—he reeled, just ducking her kick; she flung a second one—he moved inside it, taking out her other leg—

Her back hit the mats hard, air shunting through her teeth, as a round of catcalling swelled from the surrounding recruits.

Anders retreated slightly, as though he hadn't expected her to fall so hard. Re-approaching, he offered her a hand to help her up, ignoring the jeers around them. Raeke avoided his hand, getting to her feet on her own.

"The champ takes the fall!" Richter howled. "You should've been worried!"

Raeke was barely conscious of anything as she left the room, but their words reverberated in her head. It shouldn't matter, getting beat once—it wouldn't matter for anyone else. But she... she was different. She was on the fast track. She was a damn good soldier.

"Raeke!"

Hunching, Raeke sped up, rounding the corner of the main compound, heading for the barracks.

"Raeke!" It was Krakosz, she realized, and slowed down as he came jogging up beside her.

"You're gonna be late for P.T!"

"I'll be there, Krakosz, don't worry about it."

"Hey," he began, "Don't listen to Richter, if all drijans are athletic it makes sense that—"

"I'm over it," Raeke snapped. She just needed to change into her workout gear. Did he need to hold her hand for that?

\* \* \*

Physical Training was, like everything else, a group activity. When she arrived, Anders was already there, and he held her gaze for a moment. If it was an apology, she refused it, tossing her head and looking away.

They lined up while Garrell strutted in front of them, beginning the exercise with his usual friendly nitpicking, while the recruits stared straight ahead, still as statues. Before them, looming at various heights, stood an obstacle course built of wood and metal, but infused with the pain and exertion of hundreds of recruits. They called it the Bonecrusher.

Berating their pathetic performance from yesterday, Garrell challenged them to show themselves impressively, and once lines were made they ran the course several times without rest, until people were starting to puke.

Raeke finished, sweat-drenched and bleeding from the shin, returning to attention where she'd begun, alone in her place as she was accustomed to be. Almost.

She broke form to gawk at Anders, who was clearly winded but standing at attention. Luckily, Garrell was otherwise occupied.

"As usual, the men in our company will have to wait another day to prove themselves men!" he yelled over the rapid patter of boots, the gasping for air, the grunts of exertion. "If this pansy-ass performance continues, you will be tying white rope to your heads, henceforth to be known as Team Tampon! Do I make myself clear?"

"Sir, yes, sir!" everyone chorused; everyone but Anders.

"Did you hear me Anders? Or is the inside of your head as fuzzy as the outside?"

As some of the other recruits reached their places and snapped to attention, Garrell strode to stand in front of Anders. "Well, recruit?"

"Sir, I heard you," he answered, albeit in an almost conversational tone.

"Well, I think I just heard a butterfly fart! Anders, I asked you a question! Does the size of your skull accommodate any gray matter, or am I talking to an air pocket between two ears?"

Anders hesitated. "No, sir."

"It doesn't accommodate any gray matter?!"

"Yes, sir!"

"I CAN'T HEAR YOU, RECRUIT!"

"Yes sir, it accommodates gray matter!"

"Dandy, it'll make a pretty splatter when they finally beat some training into your thick skull!"

A flicker of irritation went through Anders' face, "Yes, sir."

As Raeke expected, Garrell rounded on him. "If I didn't know any better, I'd say you don't like me, Anders!"

A long pause. "Sir?"

"Well, Anders, don't you like me?"

"Not particularly, sir," Anders said, and Raeke felt a ripple of tension, however repressed, run through the assembling recruits.

"That's just fine with me, recruit, I'm a very forgiving person. Fetch me that flag!"

Everyone knew the flag he meant; everyone except Anders, whose gaze swept the obstacle course.

"Flag, sir?"

It wasn't a flag, really—it was a tattered red rag, attached to the top of a thirty-foot wooden pole legendary for its slivers, the largest of which were stuck into the bulletin board that notified the recruits of schedule changes, upcoming optional courses, and recreational events, until a T.I noticed and disposed of them.

"I swear you get dumber the longer I look at you, Anders. The flag at the top of that pole! Get it for me, NOW!"

Would he ever learn to hurry? Slow off the mark, Anders trotted off to the pole, surveying it.

"NOW doesn't mean you should stand there scratching your unmentionables, recruit! Get up that pole and show me how your mother made her money!"

From where he was, Raeke knew the splintered wood clearly displayed the marks of many a lacerated palm; close to the bottom, it was stained red between ragged shreds of uniform.

Shooting Garrell a grimace, Anders gripped it, crouched, and leapt upwards. Raeke heard a few sharp intakes of breath, hissing through teeth—almost everyone had been subject to the pole, and less than a handful of recruits had ever made it to the top.

Baring his bright white fangs, Anders clambered up and up, never slowing, making good time—*incredibly* good time. He grabbed the rag, glancing down, realizing now what every watching recruit was thinking. Going down was the worst part. Recruits had been excused from P.T for weeks for the mess this descent had made of their palms.

He shifted his grip, bracing—

And pushed off hard with his feet, releasing the pole, free-falling—landing and rolling out of it, he came sharply back to attention in front of Garrell.

"Sir," he said flatly, and despite its lack of enthusiasm, Garrell took the rag without comment, staring at it.

What followed was the longest pause of silence Raeke had ever seen Garrell allow, when face to face with a recruit.

"Recruits—five laps of the track, NOW!" he managed at last, fighting to elevate his voice to the usual pitch. Everyone popped smoke, hustling off to the track before Garrell could get his bearings.

\* \* \*

"That's like, thirty feet!"

"Well—maybe 27. He wasn't standing right on the top."

"Yeah, *only* 27. No big deal."

Deliberating not to slow down, Raeke strode for the rear door to the barracks, where a passel of recruits was smoking and joking, generally blocking her way.

"Make a hole," she growled, keeping her stride speed up—

"Raeke, tell us you're not impressed. Tell us your interest isn't... aroused."

"I'm not here to join your pool-cue party," she retorted, pushing through.

"I think you're just jealous because *you* haven't made it to the top yet."

One hand on the door, Raeke froze. Don't let him get to you—don't—

Approaching, Richter pulled a posse of oglers with him, the usual sheep.

"You haven't got the flag yet," Richter grinned. "That's why you're mad."

"Shut your face," Raeke snarled, pushing on through the door, but it couldn't swing shut fast enough.

"You two *belong* together, Raeke!"

Hunching her shoulders against it, Raeke strode furiously down the hallway, passing door after door before she reached her own standard, two-bed room, soon to find solace in the quiet—

Only, her mattress was gone. She stood in the door, staring at the empty bedsprings, the open locker void of all her things, the naked space of floor where her trunk usually sat. Outside, the fracas of a couple hundred displaced recruits drew her ear—she joined the growing crowd surrounding a ramshackle pyramid of belongings.

"Room swap, recruits!" The T.I's were yelling. "Room swap! Come and get your new room numbers!"

Sighing, Raeke joined the shifting crowd, reading the labels on everything, finally locating her trunk and most of her belongings before she reported to Garrell. The best of the mattresses would be quickly claimed, and she rushed to her room to drop her armload of stuff off, sweeping into room 16.

Jerking up in surprise from where he had just dropped a similar pile of things, Anders' brows lifted, the silence dragging.

"What?" It escaped from her unbidden, high-pitched with disbelief. "But..." She composed herself. "But this is 16."

"Yeah," he agreed.

"But—you—you're—"

Clearly not interested in whatever she might say, he turned away to continue placing things, leaving streaks of blood on the fresh white sheets he'd been given. He'd get smoked for it, if Garrell saw.

Looking at him, though, she wasn't surprised his bones could support such a long fall. Drijans were, in general, a little taller and a little sturdier than humans; she knew the benefits.

"No, there's been a mistake," Raeke managed finally. "You're male."

"Thanks for letting me know."

"Excuse me."

Off again at her fastest speedwalk, Raeke crossed campus, barely able to think through her conviction that it had to be a mistake. It had to be. Nearly dancing on the spot, she was announced by the door guard at the First Sergeant's office, wringing her hands.

"Enter."

"Private First Class Raeke reports!"

First Sergeant Vogul did not look up from her desk for a moment, her chocolate-hued hair now haloed by the late afternoon sun, surrounded by the golden dust motes Raeke had sent swirling, slowing to reclaim their relaxed pace of descent.

"At ease. What is it you want, recruit? I'm rather busy at the moment."

"Permission to—"

"Permission granted. What do you want, Raeke?"

Having forgotten to pre-phrase anything in her head, nothing acceptably civil came to Raeke's mind, leaving her momentarily dumbstruck.

"Well?" Vogul's practiced gaze strafed her, flawlessly imparting the belief that every second Raeke delayed took away from Vogul's immensely heavy and important duties to her superiors.

"I—ma'am, I have been assigned a room incorrectly."

"Is that so?"

"Yes, ma'am. I've been assigned to room 16, with the new recruit Anders."

Vogul tilted her head. "What makes you think the assignment was incorrect?"

Inwardly, Raeke staggered. "Pardon me?"

"What makes you think it was incorrect?"

"Ma'am, Anders is—Anders is a male."

"Yes."

Raeke gulped for air, trying to form words. It couldn't be right—he was—she was—

"Raeke." Vogul flipped a page, her eyes returning to her work. "I assure you, our staff were aware of that when they re-assigned the rooms. Is that all?"

"No! No… ma'am." Raeke swallowed, bracing herself. "I'd like to request re-assignment; to a new room, First Sergeant."

"No."

"No?" Raeke repeated, not in time to catch it. "But—First Sergeant—he's—"

"What is it that offends you about him, Raeke?" Vogul asked, reading on.

"He's…"

"Is it that he's better than you?"

"Better, ma'am?"

"Garrell informed me on his first few classes. Are you threatened by his performance?"

"No, ma'am," Raeke growled.

"Then, what, recruit? Speak plainly. If you have nothing to say, you are dismissed."

Raeke clenched her teeth. "He's not—I don't think we'll get along, because I've never met a drijan—"

"Drijan?" Vogul snapped, looking straight up into Raeke's face with wide eyes. "I know you were raised with humans, Raeke, but surely you can appreciate why—"

"Ma'am, please, I'm not comfortable with—"

"Do not interrupt me!" Vogul was on her feet, the chair feet shrieking on the floor. "I placed him with you deliberately. He is the perfect solution to your overconfidence, and he will be a daily reminder that you are not untouchable, you are not the perfect recruit, and you *still* have plenty to learn." Pacing round the desk, her eyes flashed with frustration as they held on Raeke. "You have been an exemplary recruit in the past—but you need a humility check, and the Allied Marine Force has provided me with the means."

Coming to a halt in front of Raeke, she stared her down with a fury that cowed Raeke's head, despite being several inches shorter.

"But—ma'am he's a—a drijan—"

"Drijan?" Vogul demanded, shaking her head. "You should be *at least* as comfortable as the other recruits. He is, after all, one of your own species—"

"With respect, ma'am, I'm a *soldier*—"

"*You're a drijan!*" Vogul yelled, cutting her off. "Is that it, then?" She stared at Raeke with disbelief. "If you've got some deep-seated issue with who and what you are, Raeke, you had better get over it real quick. Because the two of you are going to be spending a lot of time together, understood?"

Raeke could barely breathe. It was all she could do keep her hands from shaking. All her life, she'd been groomed to be a soldier. Her species had never been important, or even worth worrying over; she'd learned long ago to push it down. First and foremost, she was a soldier; serving with others, enduring with them, excelling at whatever task she was given...

As hard and as bright as diamonds, Vogul's eyes held her prisoner, baiting her to defend herself, to argue - and then she realized. No one lasted through that kind of disrespect.

Not even her.

The words hurt, but lots of things hurt, "Understood, First Sergeant."

*Ancient warfare between the tribes of the wolves and the reindeer. Which can be trusted?*

*Who within each tribe can be trusted?*

# The Son of Goulon Stumptail

## by NightEyes DaySpring

Bertil panted heavily, trying to pull air into his lungs while he crouched low, round shield and sword at the ready. His gaze stayed fixed on the reindeer before him, a glistening blade pointed at the wolf. Out of the corner of his eyes, he could see four other reindeer, circling around behind to surround him. Blood trickled down one side of his body, seeping into his black fur.

His father, Goulon, always stressed he watch out for his tail when fighting in close combat, lest Bertil end up with a stump like his old man. Even though it was uncomfortable, the aged warrior insisted the black wolf wear tail armor while training. However, in the rush to get ready for this raid, he forgot the plate of armor that protected his tail at home. Hopefully after they killed him, his tail would still be in one piece.

"Lay down your sword, wolf," commanded the stag in front of him. The reindeer stepped over one of the two wolves who had fallen in the skirmish between the war parties, coming closer to Bertil.

Even though he was bleeding, he still stood strong. He knew what was expected of him. "Never," growled the lupine.

"If you surrender, I won't turn your comrades into blankets to keep us warm in the winter."

The wolf snarled. "You wouldn't dare do that!"

The reindeer chuckled and glanced as his compatriots flanking Bertil. If the wolf tried to charge him, he'd expose his back to attack. Considering how quickly the deer had killed Frek and Horter, his odds didn't look good. Two of the four wolves under Bertil's command had fled in panic, leaving Bertil and the others outnumbered two to one. In the pitched battle that followed, Bertil only managed to wound one of the reindeer before they cut down the other two.

"Are all the antlers that adorn the great halls of your people from feral deer? I don't think so," said the reindeer. "You Westmoor wolves are the same, always willing to die for the pack. No wonder you have such big families."

While some of the Westmoor wolves claimed territory in these hills and the mountains to the west, Goulon had been clear that this land had always lain beyond the wolf clans' territory. These raids, he said before Bertil left, were to test the young. "Don't let them fool you with their speeches of honor and glory", Goulon had warned. Still, he was honored when they offered him command of the war party. He realized now that joy would be short-lived.

"I would rather die like my brother before me, on my feet, than be a coward," spat the black wolf. At least they could say he was willing to die fighting.

The deer snorted. "Very well. Who do I have the honor of sending to Valhalla this morn?"

His ears flicked at the casual way the deer spoke. The reindeer was ready to slay the wolf and be done with this incursion.

"Bertil, son of Goulon, Jarl of North Hold," stated the wolf.

The deer dipped his sword slightly. "I was not aware that the great Stumptail had fallen out of favor in the clans."

Bertil snarled. "Out of favor? This is an honor!"

"If you consider the title 'no tail' or 'one ear' an honor, assuming you come back alive, then I guess so." The deer flicked up his sword tip. "Very well, Bertil, my name is Gunhild, Jarl of the Dundor Hills, whose land you trespass on. Are you ready to die?"

Gunhild was only two summers older than Bertil, but already he'd made a name for himself pushing back these raids. Since Gunhild's holdings sat on Iznit's border, the Westmoor wolf clans demanded tribute and fealty when he became a lord. Gunhild had told them only the King could levy such demands, but the Jarls had taken to raiding his holding to get their due. The reindeer had petitioned the King of Iznit to intervene, but he had avoided coming down against the Westmoor clans. Only if the High King put pressure on him, would the wolf on the throne intervene. Until then, the dispute simmered.

Bertil glanced at the reindeer that had flanked him. Already he'd felt the taste of their steel against his mail. "Face me on your own, like lords," he said to Gunhild. "As my father's heir, you owe me the honor of single combat."

"No," said the stag. "If you wish to die this day, you die on my terms. I've killed enough of your kind that I find no honor in besting you one-on-one. You can either put down your sword or die. The choice is yours."

Enough of his kind? How many raids had there been this year? Even now the snow still clung to the valleys and shaded hillsides. The high passes in the distant mountains were still full of snow. Yet the clans had already sent multiple raids against Gunhild this year?

Losing one son had been hard on Goulon. The old warrior was already too hobbled to fight like he used to. Losing his remaining son would leave him a broken man. Bertil's twin sister would be forced to marry to ensure there was an heir for North Hold.

Someone in the clans had set this up. Either Bertil came back a hero or a hold opened up for inheritance. With Bertil's hand already promised to the Sylvi, daughter of a landless huscarl, the inheritance for North Hold would be secure if he survived this test.

"How... how many have you killed?" asked Bertil.

"Since the winter solstice? We've killed a half dozen. A dozen or so more since I became Jarl a year and a half ago. I've lost good men fighting your clans."

Bertil stuck his sword into the soft ground in front of him. He dropped the shield he was holding. There was no honor in dying today. Hopefully disgrace would be better than death.

The deer blinked and lowered the sword. "You surrender?"

Bertil sighed. "Yes." His ears laid back. That was a coward's admission.

Lord Gunhild came up to him, still carrying his blade at the ready. "In better times, we might have been friends you know. You are almost my age."

He gave the reindeer an appraising eye. He was a little taller than Bertil, and up close, he smelled of wood smoke and unfamiliar spices. There was a nutty smell that the wolf couldn't place.

"Do you really skin my kind for rugs and blankets?"

The reindeer frowned. "We have. My father slept under a wolf skin his entire life. I personally favor a good sheepskin. I prefer something that didn't come from an intelligent creature."

The wolf nodded, waiting.

The deer pulled Bertil's sword out of the earth and looked it over, twisting it around in his hand to feel the heft. "It's well balanced," he remarked. "Perhaps someday it will be yours again," he said motioning to the ones behind him.

They came up and grabbed him. "Now we get to find out what a wolf is worth," one of the reindeer sneered into his ear.

"Father won't pay a ransom," growled Bertil, struggling against the reindeer.

"No? Well we'll see. For your sake, I hope I don't have to leave you locked up long," remarked Gunhild.

They forced his hands behind his back and a length of rope was looped around his wrists.

"Surely my honor is worth more than this injustice," he grumbled.

Gunhild turned around. "Your honor? Your clans lack honor."

The wolf squared his shoulders as best he could with four reindeer hanging on. "You don't trust me?"

"Not at all," said the reindeer. "Your kind have fed the eagles with us for far too long."

"Do you treat us wolves any better?"

Gunhild looked at the two dead wolves lying on the ground. "The dead are a part of the natural order. They feed the earth."

"Will you at least let me bury my dead? They followed me here without question. They earned their place in Valhalla."

Gunhild pointed at one of his men, "Woden, treat his wounds and make sure Oystein is okay. We'll bury the wolves. It's the least we can do for our charge."

* * *

Bertil's mail had stopped most of the slashes against his body. He'd been able to avoid any crippling blows on the exposed parts of his arms and legs, with only one bad gash on his sword arm. However, he had been struck on the shoulder with an axe. While the blow only stunned him and did not penetrate the mail, the force of the blow radiated under the armor. The soft pads under the armor he wore beneath the mail were torn and soaked with his blood where the iron rings had cut through the padding.

"You are lucky, furball," commented Woden as he looked over Bertil while the wolf sat shirtless. Most of the dried blood had been scrubbed out of the lupine's fur, but it was still damp. The wind picked up and ruffled his fur, giving him a slight chill. "Lucky we didn't cleave your shoulder off," the reindeer mentioned, having finished looking at Bertil. "I certainly did my best to do that."

The aching in Bertil's shoulder was a testament to the force of the blow. The wolf looked at the dented chainmail. It was the only one his father could afford, and Goulon made sure his son had taken it. The rings were bent around the right shoulder and had frozen together. It would take a blacksmith days to fix it. Next to the mail sat his helmet, staring empty-socketed at him.

"You would sooner I be dead?" asked the wolf.

The warrior shrugged. "Why not? You fought well, and it would be one less wolf to fight tomorrow."

"Thanks," said Bertil as the buck got up and went to check on the wounded reindeer. When he shivered again, it wasn't just because of the cold of the wind.

A few minutes later, Gunhild came over and undid the rope holding his hands behind his back. "Go pay your respects," ordered the stag, pointing to where they'd buried the bodies, "and then we can be on our way."

Bertil got up and walked down the hill. Surprisingly, they didn't follow him, but they watched him carefully.

Gunhild's men had dug shallow graves for the two dead wolves. They took everything of value off of them, but Bertil had made sure each was buried with his water flasks so they could wet their palates on the way to Valhalla. He knelt next to the two fresh graves.

"My brothers, may you find honor with the gods," he whispered. He glanced up the hill, where the Jarl and his men watched. "You fought well. May your journey forth be swift, may yours paws be fleet, and may your nose be sharp." He bowed his head. "May the gods receive you with honor in the great hall of the dead."

The prayer recited, he got up. Honor. Was there honor in this? Was there honor in the fact he was still alive? Would his war party have buried Lord Gunhild with such respect and wished him on his way to Fólkvangr, the afterlife the reindeer believed in, had Gunhild fallen?

He knew the answer. They'd have left him to rot in the sun just like the reindeer would have left him if he'd not laid down his sword. He was a coward, and he had earned no honor in the eyes of the clans.

He walked back up the hill, the eyes of six reindeer upon him. Bertil stopped in front of the gathering. "Thank you for burying them." The wolf walked over to where his damaged armor lay.

The reindeer got up. Bertil reached for the blood-soaked undershirt he'd been wearing.

"I want you alive and well, not mangy," Gunhild said, tossing him a clean shirt out of his own pack. "Put that on. We'll carry your armor."

Bertil just nodded and buttoned up the light shirt over himself. It smelled of reindeer, and he laid his ears back. Any wolf he encountered now would smell his shame.

They at least let him carry his small pack, but everything else of his they took for themselves. They also insisted on binding his wrists before they set off in the opposite direction than the one from which Bertil had come.

\* \* \*

Even with his red and gray fur covered in dirt, Hakon still stood proud. Next to him stood a gray and white wolf, Thorn. When Hakon spoke, he spoke with the commanding authority of his father, Lord Volkner. "We were ambushed. Bertil fought valiantly, but it wasn't enough. We were split up after Frek and Horter were killed, and they were able to encircle Bertil and overwhelm him. After that, we fled in order to escape with our own lives."

Runa squinted at the two of them. There was no dried blood on their fur. "Did you try and rescue him?"

"Of course," huffed Hakon. "Thorn and I did everything we could to reach your brother." He softened a little. "I'm sorry we could not save him. You have my condolences. I would be happy to—"

She held up a paw, the dark black fur of her body interrupted by streaks of white on her arm. "Thank you, but I would like to be alone."

He bowed. "Of course." He turned and when Thorn didn't follow fast enough, Hakon hissed and they left swiftly.

The white wolf Ivar, who was sitting next to Runa got up putting a hand on her shoulder. "I'm sorry Runa, I… I will let you be."

"Not you, Ivar," she said.

He nodded, but his ears drooped low. "If they let me go on that war party, this might not have happened."

"Yeah," she mumbled. "I've never trusted Lord Volkner though. It's too convenient that Bertil didn't come back. I'm not sure they tried to save him."

"Only the reindeer know the truth now."

"They do, don't they?" She got up and dusted off the dress she wore with its embroidered trim. "Do you think they would tell us?"

Ivar looked at her and whined. "You can't be serious, Runa. They will kill us for trespassing on their land."

"Would they kill a lady looking to find her twin brother's remains? For all I know, Hakon killed Bertil, Frek, and Horter himself so he could have them out of his way."

"Your father would disapprove of you going there alone. I also know you have no intention making this a diplomatic affair."

She chuckled. "I bet I can handle a bow better than any of Volkner's warriors. They haven't had to hunt game with their bows. One wolf is harder to notice than two, but I would appreciate if you joined me."

The white wolf shifted his weight. "Runa, our duty -"

"To the clans? You saw them with your own eyes, Ivar! They don't look like men who returned from battle. They look like they fell on the way here running too fast with joy."

The white wolf grumbled. "There is a reason my mother hated when I visited your family. I'd come back limping or with my clothing torn, a big grin on my face. She thinks your clan is closer to ferals than civilized creatures."

"Does Lady Sigrid still hold us in such low regard? She was nice to me the last time I saw her."

"She called you all civilized ferals not that long ago. Take that however you want to."

Runa's ears fell flat. "She does have a sharp tongue, doesn't she? How did she raise a son like you?"

He chuckled. "Father keeps getting the brunt of it. I learned to let him take the licks."

She wagged her tail amused and stood up, walking to the open window. In the distance, tendrils of dusk lengthened as the sun slipped from the sky. "If we slip out of the keep around midnight, we can be on the border between the holds just after dawn."

Ivar grinned. He was two winters older than Runa and Bertil, but he had grown up with them. "We'll have to travel all night, but isn't Goulon supposed to be here tomorrow, looking to welcome Bertil back from his raid?"

"He'll know once they tell him we're missing where we've gone."

He scratched behind his ears. "We'll have to travel light in order to cover that distance so quickly."

Runa smiled. "My father raised me to be a hunter first, and a lady second. I have my gear at the bottom of the trunk."

Ivar smirked. "And you wonder why my mother calls you a civilized feral."

\* \* \*

The reindeer made sure Bertil could not escape, and placed him in the middle of the group as they traveled. Since they had started back late after digging the graves, they camped a few miles from the battle site in a small clearing. During a break to let Oystein rest, the reindeer Bertil had wounded, the others foraged for some tender leaves and moss. Once they made camp they put this and root vegetables they had brought into a porridge they simmered as they went about their business.

They left Bertil to sit and watch as they worked, before removing his bindings so he could eat. He devoured the little bit of beef jerky still in his pack hungrily. It was the first food he had eaten since the battle. While meager, it was something to chew on.

"Do you want porridge?" Woden asked after it had been simmering for over an hour on the camp fire.

Bertil shook his head. "I'm not sure I can eat some of the stuff you put in there."

Lord Gunhild chimed in. "The moss is toxic to carnivores. Give him some of the dried fish. Those two strips of jerky he ate didn't look like much."

"You can eat that?" asked Bertil, ears perking in surprise.

"Just a little. We can't eat much meat or fish, but it is good for when we have to stay on the move," said the Jarl, ladling some of the porridge out for himself.

"I did not know that," said the wolf. Woden rummaged through his pack and pulled out two pieces of dried trout, which he gave to Bertil. The wolf ate them hungrily, the salt tingling on his tongue.

He listened as the reindeer talked. If his feet weren't bound, with his eyes closed, he would have thought he was with wolves. They talked about many of the same things while they threw dice.

When they were ready to sleep, they assigned watches, and insisted on rebinding Bertil's hands together. Afterward, he lay in his bed roll staring up at the stars thinking. These were his enemies, and yet they were in a way like him. That didn't ease the fact they meant to ransom him, but it wasn't just the ransom that bothered him.

They spoke like wolves when they talked of war.

\* \* \*

Getting out of the keep proved easier than they expected. They were able to slip into the town of Shorn by simply saying they were going out for a late night drink. The lone guard gave them a look suggesting he thought it was a liaison, but they hadn't tried to dissuade him. The fact he smelled strongly of stale beer made the task easier.

"I don't think he realizes we've known each other since I was four and you and Bertil were two," Ivar whispered, as they walked down the main street of Shorn. It was already past midnight, and the cold air of winter bit into their traveling clothing. Spring had come, but it had yet to warm the land. With the chill and the lateness of the hour, the road was deserted.

She sighed. "I would like to dispel that thought, but if that's what he wants to think the rumor is at least useful. Who goes out to hit the hay or drink armed, though?" she asked.

The white wolf shrugged. "I think he was too drunk to notice. I thought we might have to bribe him to look the other way. With Bertil dead, they will put pressure on you to marry now."

She growled low. "I would never marry one of the lot here if they were the last wolves alive."

"Well, North Hold will be yours someday, Runa. You have a holding to pass on now."

"I don't want to think about that," she said. "My brother's body is barely cold, and I can already see the ravens coming. When I went to get those supplies from the kitchens, I ran into Hakon. He wanted to 'make sure' I was doing okay."

Ivar stopped and turned to the female wolf. She was a half head shorter than him, and they were both dressed as warriors. She had traded in her dress for padded leather armor and a traveling cloak. The pack with their food sat on her back. Underneath she had hidden her bow, quiver, and a dagger. Ivar wore padded armor also, but he hadn't bothered trying to hide his weapons. On his back he had a shield; his battle axe hung at his waist.

"I have been thinking about it, and I believe Hakon let Bertil die," he whispered, looking to see her reaction

Runa's ears flicked, and she frowned. "I think so too, but only he and the reindeer who killed him know." She resumed walking and they passed the tavern in Shorn. Light streamed out the door, but inside it sounded quiet. The last drinkers of the night were finishing up.

Beyond, the road headed out into the rolling hills on the border of the Westmoor.

\* \* \*

They walked through the night, first down the road. Later, they turned west to head over the hills in the direction the war party had gone. Once they left the road, they passed few farms. The ground became rougher as the hills grew bigger, and the open moorland gave way to forested foothills.

Dawn found them on the border of Gunhild's and Volkner's holds. Ivar had a rough idea where the war party had intended to camp, but they still had to search for it. After an hour, they were able to find the campsite nestled in a ravine. There was no mistaking they had the right camp; their noses told them Bertil had been there.

"I think we can track where they went," said Ivar, pointing at the trampled path through the woods. He stooped low to pick up the scent.

Runa had pulled out her bow, and had an arrow at the ready. "It's enemy territory from here out," she said.

Ivar yawned. "Perhaps we should rest for a bit. We've been walking all night."

"I want to find where the battle happened while the scent is still fresh. The tracks through the woods will fade."

The white wolf nodded. "Fair enough."

They set off through the brush. The trail was faint, and snow still clung to a few parts of the woods. They had to carefully track the passage of the warriors. A few times they lost the trail and had to backtrack to find it.

Eventually, they reached a clearing on a hill side.

"I don't know if we can follow them across this," Ivar said looking at the rock-strewn land. It was still too early in spring for the grass to cover the hillside in green.

Runa pointed to a spot a way up the hill. "We may not have to," she said. "Look."

"Graves?" he squinted. Two small patches of raised dirt sat on the hill.

"I think so," she said, taking off with a trot up the hill.

"Wait!" he called after her, but she didn't stop. She ran straight out into the open. Ivar glanced nervously to the edge of the trees before he followed her up.

By the time Ivar caught up to her, she'd knelt between the graves to inspect them.

"I'm surprised they'd bury them, but what is really interesting is the fact there are only two graves," he panted.

She flicked her ears while thinking. "I can pick up Bertil's scent."

"Which one is his?"

She leaned down and sniffed the ground. "I think he's alive, Ivar. It's not coming from the graves."

The white wolf blinked. "Let me smell," he knelt next to her and sniffed. He then walked over to sniff at each grave. "I think you're right." His tail wagged, "but why?"

"They might want to ransom him?" she glanced around. "It must have taken time for them to dig these. They might not be that far away."

"Runa, we can't take on an entire war party. They'll be well rested, and we've been traveling all night."

"Ivar, Bertil could be wounded. Even if we can't get him back right now, we'll know if Gunhild has him." She got up and started walking toward the top of the hill. "I need to know that he's alive."

The white wolf followed her. "Probably they took him back to Jarl Gunhild's hall; he has a walled town under him."

"Yeah, but how far is that?"

"I don't know the area well. I know the hills are lightly settled, but the town is down in a valley."

Runa reached the top of the hill. "They were supposed to raid a small village, weren't they?"

Ivar nodded. The view it commanded wasn't great, but they could get some bearing of their surroundings.

"What's that column of smoke over there in the distance?" she asked, pointing.

Ivar squinted. "That looks like the village, I think I can see multiple plumes." He scanned the horizon. "What about there?" he said, pointing to a faint shaft of smoke. "That's in the direction of the valley."

Runa glanced at it and nodded. "That looks promising. Let us be swift, and hopefully we can pick up their trail," she said, taking off in a jog.

\* \* \*

In the morning, the reindeer had stoked their fire and cooked a good meal before they got ready to break camp.

"We'll be back home by the afternoon," commented Gunhild to his men. "Then we can send a messenger to ransom the wolf."

"North Hold is poor," said Oystein. "I'm not sure we'll get much for him."

"Oh, I plan to make Goulon pay, even if I have to send him half of Bertil's tail," joked Gunhild. They all laughed. The black wolf's tail curled instinctively under him.

After breakfast, they set out through the woods, and soon intersected an old road. They turned south on it. Bertil idly watched the trees go by as they walked down the road, thinking about what Goulon would say when he found out his son was alive.

"You know, for the son of a great warrior, you slouch just like any other prisoner."

Bertil turned. It was Gunhild, who had come to walk beside him.

"There isn't honor in this," mumbled the black wolf.

"If you want, I can break a few of your ribs and we can drag you back like a fresh kill. Is that what you wolves find honorable?"

Bertil's ears flicked. "How would you follow the coward's path then?"

The reindeer huffed. "Is choosing life over certain death cowardice?"

"That depends how much of me you mean to send to my father."

The reindeer chuckled. "You wounded one of my men," he said, pointing toward Oystein. Even now, he walked slowly, bringing up the rear.

"You sent two of mine on their final journey."

"No matter how many wolves I send on their way, your jarls have continued to raid my lands, and the lands of the Einheart clan. Two dead wolves don't replace the burned farmsteads. Is it only the wrath of the king that keeps your clans from preying on the merchants who cross my hold? I am in my right to kill any wolf I see on my land."

Bertil sighed. "The cycle continues then. A tit for tat?"

The reindeer laughed. "You know, your clans used to hunt these woods for us to keep the game down, so we could farm our fields in peace."

"You let the High King bring his men through your hold unopposed to clamp down on the wolf clans. Your clan betrayed Iznit, and for that the wolf clans will not forgive you."

"The independence of Iznit was a lost cause when the rebellion happened. The wolf King of Iznit in Toreaken did not support your own cause, yet the Westmoor clans blame us when we stayed loyal to your King, the same King you tried to betray."

"Forgive me, my liege, but were you both not born after the rebellion?" interjected the reindeer Woden.

The Jarl shot the warrior an icy growl, but Woden shrugged. Gunhild spoke to the black wolf softer. "It seems we fight the war of our fathers."

\* \* \*

Only coals remained at the fire in the camp when they located it, but they followed the trail through the woods, Runa always running ahead. Ivar had to do his best to keep up with her. When they reached the road, they followed it south from the tree line. It didn't take them long to find the reindeer. There were six of them, with Bertil in the middle.

"I think that might be Lord Gunhild himself," panted Ivar, next to Runa. They'd pushed ahead of the group so they could observe the war party.

"The one in the back is limping. I can probably take down two or three of them before they can catch us," whispered Runa. Her eyes were fixed on the lead warrior.

Ivar frowned. "It wouldn't be a fair fight."

"I know," she said notching an arrow into the bow. Two others were held in her hand.

"Runa, are you mad? I know you're good with a bow, but there are six of them, and only two of us," he hissed.

She grinned, showing her fangs. "I can cover you so you can cut them down."

"Runa," said Ivar holding out a hand to try and still her. "We can't just take on a war party."

She looked at Ivar, with steel in her eyes. "There will never be a better chance, Ivar. You think I can't take them down from here?"

The white wolf blinked. "An archer only has the advantage when they have cover."

She brushed him away and stood up. "Let me show you."

Ivar shook his head. "We need to get down by the road before we can launch a surprise attack. The trees are too dense here for this to work."

She let the bow string go slack. "Very well," she said. "Tell me what spot looks good to you for our ambush."

\* \* \*

Gunhild had lapsed into silence, still walking next to his captive. Bertil thought about what they discussed. These skirmishes were the jarls' prerogative, and while Goulon had fought in the rebellion, he'd already paid for his pride with one son.

Bertil would have stayed in a silent musing if there hadn't been the telltale whistle of an arrow through the air. It struck the lead reindeer in the group.

"Archer!" shouted Gunhild reaching for his shield.

The reindeer scattered toward the woods, leaving Bertil and Gunhild in the middle of the road. Another arrow whizzed through the air striking the lead warrior in the back as he tried to seek shelter. He fell with one arrow sticking out of his back and one out of his chest.

"Find the archer," yelled Gunhild, as he raised his shield up in front of him. A third twang was heard, but he managed to catch this one with his shield. Two of Gunhild's men grabbed Bertil from behind and dragged him into the woods, while one went to pull the stricken reindeer from the road.

Woden headed down the side of the road, shield up seeking the archer, when a blur of white emerged from behind a tree. He danced back as a battle axe sliced through the air. A second slice followed quickly, and while Woden deflected this with his shield, the fury of the blow knocked him down. Another arrow shot out, but Bertil could not see the intended target. His eyes were fixed on Ivar.

"Wolves!" yelled Gunhild, stepping forward quickly. He drew his sword and charged, forcing the white wolf to change his swing from finishing off Woden to parrying the incoming attack.

They traded blows, sword against battle axe, and Ivar had to step away from the fallen Woden as Gunhild closed in. The reindeer managed to draw Ivar off balance after forcing him to parry with his shield.

Without hesitation, the reindeer took a back swing at the white wolf, hooking his sword against the back of the axe head. With a grunt, Gunhild forced the axe down against the ground. Ivar cursed and tried to get his axe up, but the stag slammed him hard with the shield, and Ivar lost his grip on the axe. With a swift kick Gunhild knocked it away.

Ivar tied to backpedal from his attacker, but he tripped, falling to the ground. The white wolf tried to protect himself with just his shield. With a practiced ease, Gunhild made short work of the shield and knocked it aside. He pinned Ivar's shield arm with a hoof. Ivar looked up at the reindeer, the tip of Gunhild's blade at his throat. The reindeer shook his head.

"Let him go or I'll put this arrow right in your skull." Runa had stepped out from a nearby tree and had her bow pointed straight at Gunhild.

The reindeer looked up and glanced around. "There are just two of you?" he asked.

"Let him go," she repeated.

"Surely you don't think you can walk out of this alive," he asked her. Woden had gotten up and with two of the other reindeer, were waiting behind her, weapons at the ready.

"All we want is Bertil."

Gunhild glanced back at the black wolf and then to Runa. "No," he said. "These are my lands, and on these lands, my word is law."

She growled. "Give me my brother."

"Ah, now it fits," he mused. He glanced down to Ivar. "And this one?"

"Ivar, son of Lord Brand," the wolf offered, eyes still focused on the sword against his neck.

"Why do you wolves keep sending your young to die here? I don't understand the point of it."

"Look, give me Bertil, and we will be gone."

"You may have just killed one of my men," he said with a nod toward the fallen reindeer. Oystein had propped up the wounded reindeer to inspect his wounds. The stricken reindeer was gripping Oystein's arm tightly, wheezing. "Tell me why this wolf's life is not worth Ake's life, and I will let you have them both."

"I -" she laid her ears back and loosened up on the bow a little. "I don't know."

Gunhild's ears flicked and he stepped off of Ivar, letting him scramble back against the ground. He turned toward Runa. "You are like every wolf I have ever meet: arrogant and speciesist."

Runa let the bow string go slack. She was surrounded. "I wish only to have my brother safe and sound."

"Then why did your clans send him?" asked Gunhild.

"Father warned there would be a test before I could join the warriors at their table during feasts," offered Bertil.

Gunhild gave a sardonic laugh. "You do this for preferred seating?"

"The clans test each warrior to prove their worth," said Runa.

"What of the other two who ran when we engaged the war party? Will they sit in disgrace with the children until they can come back?"

She shook her head. "I knew it! They wanted Bertil dead so I would be forced to marry."

"You may have the black wolf back after you pay a ransom. If Ake dies, I will also expect compensation for his family," said Gunhild, sheathing his sword and walking over to check on his wounded warrior.

"Our clan is poor," Runa said softly.

"That isn't my problem. Have the people who sent him here chip in."

"I implore you," she begged. "Have you no honor?"

Gunhild looked up at her icily. "Have you any yourself?

"Our clan has honor," interjected Bertil. "The quarrel with you is not with us, but with Lord Volkner. He is the one who calls for these raids. I would happily propose to Goulon that we seek a peace deal. I am sure for his son's life Ivar's father would do the same."

The reindeer stood up. "Would Goulon and Brand honor an agreement like this, and would the warriors under them agree to such terms?"

"My father has three daughters, but I am his only son," said Ivar. "He will honor it."

"Yes," added Runa.

Gunhild considered for a minute. "If they will sign such a treaty under the laws of the King in Iznit and the High King in Sendal, I will be happy to let that be your ransom. The question is, can I trust you?"

"We will give you our word," offered Runa.

"The word of wolves has not been an honorable one."

"You will have me as collateral until the treaty is signed," said Bertil. "My life against the honor of my father."

"And if they refuse the treaty?" Gunhild asked.

"Then my fate is yours to decide."

"He won't refuse," interjected Runa.

Ivar nodded. "He was heartbroken when his eldest son died."

"I will accept and Bertil may return with you, but you must first prove to me you are not savages. Ake is badly wounded, and it is still over two hours walk to my hall. Help us carry him there, and tonight we will toast this new beginning on the last of the summer mead. In the morning, my men will take all three of you to the border."

The wolves looked at each other and nodded.

"It is agreed," confirmed Bertil.

"Woden, can you run ahead and tell the steward to prepare for our guests? Let the fox know to prepare meat for the wolves. He will be pleased to have a chance to cook a roast."

"Yes, my liege," said the reindeer bowing before he took off.

\* \* \*

They made a litter and together, they carried the wounded reindeer to the great hall. Each took a turn at litter except for Oystein. Their efforts were not for naught, either. Ake lived through the night, and in the morning the healer said he would recover.

The feeling in the morning was one of relief. After breakfast, Woden took them to the border. Shortly after noon, they crossed into the hold of Lord Volkner and followed the old road back to Shorn.

Near dusk, they reached the town. There was a murmur of the guards at the keep's gate when they arrived, but the three only smiled as they were led to the great hall.

The first person to emerge from the hall was Goulon.

"Bertil!" boomed the old wolf coming up. Even though he was only in his late-forties, the scars Goulon had earned in battle made him look older. One ear had been torn badly, the tip of it lost, while the remaining base was mangled. His other was notched on each side, and he had a scar below it that crossed his cheek. A ferocious warrior in his prime, his strong frame was now carried with a limp, the legacy of many battles. He could still swing a word, but age had started to catch up to him.

"Praise the gods you are both safe," he said, coming up and grabbing Bertil and Runa each with his arms.

"Father," they greeted him, ears splayed.

He squeezed them hard. "Runa, where did you find your brother?"

Runa looked over her shoulder. Lord Volkner and his son Hakon had exited the hall and were now talking softly together.

"Lord Gunhild took him prisoner, but Ivar and I were able to negotiate for his return," she said carefully.

"Negotiate?" asked Goulon.

She nodded and tilted her head toward Volkner.

"I see," said Goulon. He then he dropped his voice, "Did Hakon leave you out there to get killed, Bertil?"

The black wolf nodded.

Goulon scowled. "They did seem more concerned that Runa had gone off with Ivar than making funeral arrangements for you. Ivar, if I would be so kind, please see Runa into the hall. Let them know that she did what they could not."

"Yes sir," said the white wolf as he led Runa away.

Bertil squared his shoulders. This was the moment of truth for him. "For my release, we made a promise to Lord Gunhild, on our word, you and Brand would sign a peace treaty with him."

"A treaty?" asked Goulon. He looked older than Bertil remembered in that moment, his scarred muzzle looking tired.

"Yes," Bertil said.

"With a reindeer?"

Bertil nodded.

The old warrior scratched at his ruined ear. "You dishonor the clans by making a treaty with a Jarl we are hostile with."

"Our kind tried to have me killed, father. I know they set me up to fail. Hakon fled so I wouldn't have the chance to survive."

Goulon looked toward the other wolves. Lord Volkner's father and his son were talking with some others, and they didn't look pleased. Goulon leaned close to whisper. "Hakon is his younger son. It makes sense his father would want to find him a holding of his own."

"Do not the clans dishonor themselves then?"

Goulon chuckled and patted his son on the shoulder. "That they do. I will be happy to sign this treaty. You and Runa did well this day."

Bertil's tail wagged. "And about Gunhild?"

The old wolf shrugged. "I have no qualm with him. Our holdings do not border his anyway, and neither does Brand's. Brand has always been an ally to me as I am sure Ivar will be to you. Neither of you are Jarls yet, but already you are showing leadership. The clans will not like it, but I don't care. Volkner can rot for what he's tried to do. This may be the leverage we need to extricate ourselves from these pointless, petty raids."

"What of Hakon?"

Goulon sighed. "For now, we can only wait. The sooner you and Sylvi are married, the sooner you can ensure his greedy paws stay off of our land. We will need to be careful going forward. His time will come."

The old wolf turned. "Come," he said, letting his voice carry. "Let us celebrate your return!" His voice boomed and the others perked their ears. He gave his son a sly smile and walked over to the other wolves.

Goulon smirked at Lord Volkner who frowned at him. "I think a toast is in order," the old warrior said, "to old friends and to new friends. Especially to new friends."

"New friends?" asked Volker.

Goulon patted the gray and tan wolf on the back. "Yes, new," boomed Goulon to the other wolves. "Now, let us drink, and none of the cheap stuff. Bring out the finest wine in honor of my son."

Volkner's ears drooped. "Of course," he said to the assembled jarls and warriors. They cheered, and followed Volkner and Goulon into the great hall.

Bertil waited for the others to enter the hall until he and Hakon stood outside alone.

"You fight well," offered Hakon.

"You fight like a coward," spat Bertil.

Hakon growled, showing his fangs. "I will show you how well I fight, if you want."

Bertil walked up to the other wolf, putting his nose against his. "I know you ran," he whispered.

The red and gray wolf twitched his muzzle and then smirked. "I assure you, I did no such thing."

"It's okay," Bertil sneered, "you don't need to tell me. The reindeer told me. They are very gracious hosts."

Hakon's muzzle twisted, half way between shock and fear. "What?"

Bertil brushed past the other wolf. Hakon did not follow him inside. In the center of the hall, Runa and Ivar waited for him by the fire, in the place of honor. Goulon was in conversation with one of the other jarls, and Volkner sat off to the side scowling.

As he walked up, Ivar handed him a mug of beer. "The beer is good, but our host does not seem happy to see us," whispered Ivar.

Bertil raised his mug and smiled at Volkner across the room. Their eyes meet for a brief moment, and Bertil could feel the ice in the lupine's gaze. The gray and tan wolf looked away, the spell broken.

The black wolf brought the mug to his lips to sip before he sat down. He looked at Runa, who smiled amused. "He'll have to deal with it. It's only for one night anyway. We won't be coming back here after tonight."

*This story features a more modern setting than the previous one, but it asks the same question—*
*Who within each side can be trusted?*

# Noble

## *by Thomas "Faux" Steele*

*Screech.* Tires complain as oversized brakes bring our vehicle to a halt just inches from the back of the burqa-clad woman on the back of a weathered moped. I can feel my claws piercing the leather of the steering wheel, but I'm irritated enough that the damage doesn't bother me.

"Do the locals always drive like that?" the wolf in the passenger's seat asks.

The woman and her male companion nonchalantly putter away, though she does give me the finger for my trouble.

"Yeah, fuck you too," I mutter under my breath.

"I've been stationed on enough of these backwater worlds to say that's par-for-the-course. Hell, even Mombasa back on Earth isn't much better," the officer replies. She chuckles and takes a sip of her soft drink, one of the new Coke variants, its silver can glinting in the light of binary suns streaming through the panoramic sunroof.

"So you've been around?" the wolf asks, turning around to halfway face her.

"Yes, pup, I've been around," she replies, shaking her head. "Do I look like I'm a fresh hire to you?"

The wolf snorts, narrowing his eyes as his ears perk up. "Hey, lady, you do not get to call me pup. I'll have you know—"

"Riemann, is it?" she interjects, her eyes drifting down to the name patch on the right of his chest. Her stare is intense, the sort that cuts right through you like the wind of a frigid desert night.

"What's it to you?" he spits back, baring a few razor-sharp teeth in a wicked grimace.

Unfortunately, I was not gifted with the genes of a chameleon, so I have to split my attention between the traffic ahead and the drama behind me.

"Oh, nothing," she replies, crushing the aluminum can flat with an audible crunch. "I'd have thought your boot camp instructors would have taught you better than to talk back to your superiors, pup."

I swerve into a roundabout, deftly avoiding a herd of goats already blocking half the road. If I didn't enjoy the relative lack of government presence that an assignment on a backwater entailed, I'd already be long gone. I've debated going out to try and make my fortune on Ilysis, a rugged rainforest world, or perhaps Krios, home to the tallest mountains in the explored universe. Of course, then I'd have to deal with the thousands of species of poisonous creatures or the risk of falling off cliffs so tall I'd have time to watch a feature film before I hit bottom, but one can dream.

"I'm not taking this shit from a civ, especially not some human who thinks she can talk down to me just because I have fur." I haven't known anyone in this SUV for longer than twenty minutes, but I can already tell Riemann has some anger issues.

"You're going to take my shit because it's your job. Suck it up, buttercup." She rolls her eyes and pulls out another soft drink from the minifridge in the center console.

"You think this is funny?" Riemann looks like he's about to have an aneurism, the wolf half-baring his teeth now. As amusing as I find this whole pointless argument, I should probably intervene before it escalates into something more than sarcastic remarks.

I sigh and tap the brakes firmly enough to capture everyone's attention. "How about both of you play nice, huh? Riemann, I get you have a bone to pick, but save it." I step on the accelerator, letting the SUV surge forward as I make a tight maneuver around an ox-drawn cart broken down in the middle of the street.

"Oh, ha, *bone*. Because I'm a mutt, right?"

I feel like bashing my head against the steering wheel a few times. Duh. I probably should've caught that before it came out of my muzzle. Well, too late now. "No, I'm sorry; it's just a colloquialism—"

"Can't you take a joke?" the officer says, rolling her eyes. "It wasn't meant as an insult to your species, or at least I didn't see it as one."

"You do not get to determine what is and isn't an insult. I'll have you know—"

"Okay, I'm now seriously annoyed." I give Riemann the stink eye. "Right now, you're on the clock. Deal with your species-inferiority issues when you're not my problem."

I see wheels turning in the wolf's eyes, trying to think up a clever retort, but he suddenly thinks better of it and shuts his trap. His ears remain perked, but at least he's no longer baring his teeth at me, not exactly submission, but a small concession nonetheless. There's a soft hiss as he cracks open a can of standard-issue Rip It, the energy drink everyone seems to have become addicted to, and proceeds to immediately chug its contents.

I glance back in the review mirror to note the second guard, a sinewy otter, has fallen asleep again. I know this backwater—Amerathia—doesn't exactly attract the cream of the crop, but I didn't expect it to be quite this bad.

"Michaels! Wake the fuck up!" I shout, apparently loud enough to snap him out of whatever dream had enthralled him.

"I'm awake, I'm awake," he mutters, sitting up just enough that I can see his eyes. They're an artificial blue, a deep cerulean, one of the few remaining genetic oddities of my kind. I should know. My eyes glow a luminescent violet in the reflection of the rearview mirror. While the possible genetic defects of the first few generations were... extreme, by the time my mother conceived me through artificial insemination, most of the bugs had been worked out.

All except for the eyes, apparently.

"Good, and you better fuckin' stay that way." I scan the road again, looking for anything out of place. It's been mostly quiet out here, but there have been insurrections on other colonies, and being a symbol of Earth's governance makes you a target. I'm part of the Colonial Security Authority, a private security contractor that provides a significant bolster to the Colonial Military, but that's arguably worse. I've heard what rebels do to C.S.A. prisoners.

"Yeah, yeah, whatever," Michaels remarks, grabbing a can of Sprite from the minifridge despite my stare of disapproval. "You need to relax. There's no rebel activity on Amerathia. You worry too—"

My ribs creak as my seatbelt suddenly tightens, keeping me secure as we lurch to the left, the rear of the SUV kicking out until we slam into the side of a concrete domicile. It takes a moment, but my biological responses immediately shift into overdrive. The Suburban is still running, and for the most part intact. There's a rusty agricultural truck with a crumpled front end a few feet from where we've come to rest, probably what just slammed into us. I see a few shrouded figures climb out of the rear cargo area, but I don't stick around long enough to get a clear look.

For once, my luck holds out. The impact doesn't seem to have done significant damage to the drivetrain, and aside from a few shudders of reluctance in first gear, the electric motors still seem as capable as ever. A few gunshots echo off the closely-packed buildings, but they go wide.

"Overlord, this is Heartless, requesting Quick Response Team to my position ASAP. I've been broadsided by a truck, and there are hostiles with rifles after us." I dodge through the crowd as fast as I can without plowing pedestrians down.

"We copy Heartless... reports are flooding in from all over the city, bombings all over the market district. We think they've also hit the Provincial Government. It seems like dozens of simultaneous, coordinated attacks. Get to a safe position and hunker down. We'll get out to you when we can."

I glance back at the officer. She's middle-aged, just old enough that skincare products are still keeping most of the visible wrinkles at bay. She's overweight but not fat, and her blondish hair is flecked with gray. Her body armor is the standard-issue gear for higher ups, layers of carbon ceramic that look like lizard scales. Otherwise, there are no identifiable markings on her armor, so I peg it as spook-grade.

"Well? What do you want me to do? The city's in flames, like they've hit everywhere at once. I've seen personnel logs; we have nowhere near enough troops out here to contain this."

"There's a safe house in the Malakasis District. It's C.I.A. If we can reach it, there are enough weapons, ammunition and supplies there that we can wait this out." There's a firm resolve in her chocolate eyes, "Emphasis on if."

"Ma'am, you're talking to the best driver in the entire C.S.A.," I retort, slamming the transmission down a gear as I weave through a series of tight back alleys. The high-displacement hydrogen-fueled V-8 more than compensates for the additional weight of ballistic and plasma protection. As I half-drift out of an alleyway and on to an open stretch of highway, I let it breathe until the speedometer kisses triple digits. The engine lets out a pleasant snarl, eager to be unleashed on the empty straightaway.

Beside me, Riemann's grabbed a sleek, pump action shotgun from inside the inner door pocket. He's fumbling with a box of eight-gauge shells, clumsily loading them into the receiver. Behind me, Michaels is struggling to figure out how to load a compact submachine gun.

"Uh... is it a stupid question to ask where I stick the magazine?" the otter asks, cringing slightly. Michaels lets out an awkward chuckle, but it does little to diffuse the tension. If this is the level of competence I have on my squad, just kill me now and let it be over with.

"Yes," the officer replies, roughly grabbing the SMG and quickly flicking a lever just above the trigger guard, before sliding the magazine in. She tosses the hapless otter a compact Glock pistol. "If you can't load your gun like a big boy, you don't get a big boy gun."

"Am I going the right way?" I ask, as I catch a pair of sleek black sedans approaching in my rearview mirror. "I don't exactly have an exact address."

She nods, glancing behind us. "Yes. You'll take the next exit, and then it's a straight shot."

I steady myself, keeping a close eye on the progress of the sedans. As they get within a few hundred feet, I see figures with the same shrouded garb lean out the passenger's windows, rifles in hand. Just a few moments later, bullets start pinging off the tailgate.

"Do not return fire," I mutter, cranking up the volume on the integrated infotainment system, some electronic number with a rapid beat by an artist I've never heard of.

There's a sound like the crunch of gravel being tread upon by a large boot. Their aim has improved slightly, though the pane of transparent armor that serves as a rear window holds up. The wolf glances back at the leading sedan, playing with the safety on his rifle.

"If you roll down the windows, you're going to get us killed." My eyes flick over at Riemann, who looks like he's aching for a shootout.

I grimace as one of the sedans slams into our rear. "Come on, I'll take out the driver, easy-peasy," Riemann says, as I can see his paw going for the window switch. I sigh and activate the child-proof window locks.

I glare at him, baring my front fangs slightly. Unlike other big cats, cheetahs don't have massive fangs. However, mine are still large enough to give him pause, and I can see his ears fold in a sign of submission. "I don't want to tell you again. My word is law. If you can't follow orders, I'll let Mrs. Spook deal with you and I'm sure—"

Before I can say more, another shunt, harder this time. I grunt, keeping the rear controlled as it tries to slide like a New Tokyo drifter. So this is the game they want to play. Well, if they're expecting me not to retaliate, they've made a big miscalculation.

I brake and downshift, using the combined force of mechanical and engine braking to drop down thirty miles an hour in an instant. I can't say I don't get a bit of satisfaction as I flick the wheel to the left and send the sedan careering across the median. There's a row of buildings ahead where the exit takes a hard right onto a boulevard, but I've got plenty of time to brake.

Right as I cross the point-of-no-return though, I see the line of improvised mines laid across the road. I slam my foot down, but it's no use. There's a boom like a wave of thunder, and then I feel the steering go dead. I'm slammed forward into the steering column as the car careens out of control, and the last thought I have before it all goes black is: shit, isn't that building approaching kind of fast?

* * *

I come to slumped against the steering wheel, muzzle buried in a mostly deflated airbag. I catch blindingly bright white LED lights shining through the rear window, probably whoever was after us come to finish us off. I don't even get a chance to peek around to check the condition of my passengers before one of the advancing lights is shining directly in my face through the driver's side window. I hear the exterior handle click, but it's still locked.

I could just wait here. I'm sure they're after the officer. The rest of us are just incidental, the chaff surrounding the wheat. They'll just shoot us, leave us here to rot. I'd be okay with that, I think. No more running, no more hiding from my past. I haven't known peace in a long time.

*Get up.*

The voice is dulcet with a hard edge, like a well-aged whiskey. Mother? *Everything will be okay in the end. If it's not okay, it's not the end.*

I gasp as my body comes alive, fire coursing through my veins. One thought fills my mind, though it's not my mother's voice this time, it's mine.

I'm not dying on this shithole planet.

I grab the interior handle, and with as much force as I can muster, drive the door into the shrouded figure outside. I hear a yelp of surprise as it tumbles into the cement wall. In one fluid motion, I quickly slit my seatbelt with a diamond-edged claw and draw my sidearm, pivoting around to fire two shots into the head of the second figure. I step out, relieved to find that I haven't fractured anything important, and walk around to where the other figure is pulling himself up.

"I'm going to try and enjoy this," I mutter under my breath, as the figure takes a swing at me. I sidestep and drive my elbow into the side of the figure's cloak, which seems to muffle at least some of the otherwise debilitating blow. He stumbles into the wall, panting.

"Get up," I say, giving it a moment to recover its composure. Again, he opens with a punch, but I effortlessly deflect it with my forearm. My retaliation is brutal, several upward punches to his ribs that leave him coughing on his knees.

"Pathetic. This is what passes for an assassin?" I flick back the cloak, revealing the forest green eyes of a lynx. Not exactly what I was expecting, but life is filled with surprises.

"Not what you were expecting?" The lynx lets out a soft chuckle. "I can see it on your face. You thought I'd be human, didn't you, Mark?"

I narrow my eyes and bend down, firmly grasping the front of his garment. "How do you know my name? I'd start talking, if you don't enjoy the application of high-voltage electricity to your intimate areas."

"So many questions," he says, a wild grin appearing on his face. "Good luck getting answers." In an instant, he goes limp, his pupils so large I can barely detect an iris.

"Fuck!" He's dead before he hits the ground. I take a deep breath, stand up, and kick at the SUV's shredded tires in frustration. I came here to escape from my problems, not to encounter new ones. Is a quiet, uneventful tour of duty too much to ask for? The universe seems to love kicking me while I'm down.

"I see you've met one of them," the officer calmly states, suddenly standing next to me, having appeared like a wraith from a ghostly fog.

"Fuck!" I shout again, shuddering slightly with surprise. "Do you have to be a literal spook too?"

"Yes, it's part of the mandatory training when you're kidnapped from your parents at age five," she says, sarcasm practically dripping off her tongue.

"Who is them?" I ask, squatting down to inspect the lynx's body more closely. Upon second touch, the shroud feels smoother than the finest natural silk. Definitely nothing like you could get at a street market out here. I'd guess it's some sort of—

"Spider silk? You'd be right." The Officer nods. "And no, it's imported. There are species on Ilysis that make silk many times stronger than any spider found on Earth. It's a painstaking process, but the silk can be woven into a lightweight cloth that can stop nearly any bullet you can throw at it."

"You didn't answer my question," I reply, standing. My inspection is rather fruitless otherwise. He's wearing standard-issue military surplus garb that can be found at any number of outlets, even out here. He's got a pistol, but it's also a standard-issue Glock, nothing extraordinary about it. Ditto the knife, a KA-BAR that could've seen action in any war for the past two centuries. In short, other than the weird shroud, there's nothing to mark him out from any of the other numerous rebel groups out there.

"We're not entirely sure what they are. They call themselves the Children of Aranyani. They're elusive, but as best we can tell, they're connected with an escalating series of attacks on both the outer and inner colonies." She sighs, looking over the other body, a wolf missing the left half of its—it's difficult to tell gender at first glance—face, thanks to the effect of high-explosive rounds.

"Can you tell me more? I need to know what we're up against." The officer turns the body over, but aside from the key to the car that had pursued us earlier, it's the same story as with the lynx.

"There isn't much more to know. Their existence is highly classified. We're not sure of their leader, though we assume it's a military defector, and thus far they haven't made any official demands nor released the goals of the organization."

"So they're just killing to kill? I don't understand. Terrorists should be logical. There should be a purpose."

She shrugs. "We're not sure, and I can only speculate. Insofar as I can tell, it's a separatist organization for the uplifted. Unfortunately, we haven't managed to capture any members alive," she says, gesturing to the dead lynx. "All foot soldiers are issued a suicide pill concealed in a compartment in their muzzle, an overdose of a street drug called Blyss. It literally cooks your central nervous system with serotonin. Symptoms are like you saw, ecstasy and pupils so dilated the iris is difficult to see."

"So, where do we go from here?" I ask, just as Riemann stumbles out of the passenger's side. He's got a nasty gash across his forehead, although he otherwise seems fine.

"The safe house is about a click west of here. I think we've crash-landed in one of the parking garages for a neighborhood near the Grand Mall. We can either go around, or push through."

"Safe house? Are you fucking kidding?" Riemann says, with a confused laugh. "We're never going to make it. I say we set up camp with the car, and wait to be rescued."

The officer sighs, shaking her head. "There's nothing on all frequencies but static. Check for yourself if you like. It seems they've taken out Sahara Base. I'm not sure what else they've hit, but it's safe to presume that everything in this sector is down. We'll starve here before we're rescued."

"What about other options? Any chance of a Colonial Military ship stopping by?" I head around to the rear of the SUV, popping the lift gate and grabbing a sleek plasma rifle from a hard case pressed against the back seat, along with a heavy backpack, emergency gear and personal effects.

She shakes her head, the lines on her face made more distinct by the sunlight streaming through a hole in the tin roof. They make her look older, though her stance conveys the sort of hardness that makes me doubt she's been enfeebled by age. "No, there's nothing scheduled for at least another week. If we stay here, we die. It's that simple."

Finally, Michaels emerges, though he looks to be in tough shape, sporting a head wound that's been bandaged with the emergency med-kit under the center rear seat. Riemann's content to bleed. It looks relatively shallow, so it's not a major threat. Scalp wounds always look uglier than they are.

"What'd I miss?" the otter says with a bemused chuckle, before noticing the bodies. "Oh... shit."

"Yeah, oh shit," I retort sarcastically, tossing him a sleek flechette shotgun. "Can you use one of these?"

He nods, "Point and shoot, right?"

"They're meant for suppression and crowd control. Wide-spread. The individual needles contain a powerful convulsive and neurotoxin. Technically non-lethal, but I sure wouldn't want to be hit with one. I've heard it's quite the experience."

The officer gently feels around the hard inner plastic of the cargo area until her closely-cropped fingernails hit a concealed lever. "Gotcha," I hear her mutter, as she withdraws a weapon of unusual design, certainly something I've never come across.

"What the hell is that thing?" It's a sleek silver pistol, with a few dark gray lines running down the length of the barrel; innocuous enough, but if she went to the trouble of having it installed in a secret compartment in the cargo area, I can only assume it's of some value.

"It's need to know," she replies, winking as she slides it into a holster in her belt. "Emergencies only."

"Come on! Why can't we get some of that firepower?" Riemann glances down at his standard-issue personal defense shotgun. "If we're going to be fighting our way through the city, I don't want to have to depend on some *human* to bail us out." I see his eyes dart between us, thinking. "Right, guys?"

"Riemann, I'd shut your goddamn muzzle right now before I shut it for you." Her voice is more intent now, with a cold edge that drops the temperature in the room twenty degrees. "If you think the Colonial Military gives a single fuck about your lives, you're delusional. I'm the only reason any of you would be rescued at all. They'd rather glass the city than let it become a stronghold for -" she gestures to the body of the lynx, "whatever organization these creatures belong to."

"You know, this has been a long time coming. I am sick and tired of you fuckin' humans—"

It takes all my energy not to cuff Riemann across the muzzle like a petulant cub. "Both of you stop it," I say, letting out a feral snarl to capture their attention. Michaels is quietly leaning back against the dented fender of the driver's side door, smoking a contraband cigarette and pretending not to notice anything out of the ordinary is happening. "We're stuck out here, and if we're going to make it through this, we have to work together."

I toss my personal rifle, Mjolnir, a custom chimera of different weapon parts I'd scavenged up from many years of service, over to Riemann. "You want firepower? Take it."

"What makes it so special?" The wolf turns it over in his paws, looking it over. I see his eyes focus on the crest painstakingly engraved on the side, a grim, hooded figure with the motto *Mors est ad nos* underneath, but if he recognizes it, he doesn't give any indication.

"It's a hybrid tech. Fires a magnum variant of a 7.62mm projectile followed almost instantaneously by a plasma charge. The projectile damages body armor, and the plasma causes lethal soft tissue trauma." I see him nod in approval.

"You designed that yourself?"

"Yes. I've been around," I reply. I don't in particular feel the need to inform them of my background, especially with the spook around here. There are things about my past that are better left there, where they belong.

Riemann seems to relax a bit. I grab the last weapon from the back, a variant of the Kalashnikov family of rifles that's seen action in one form or another for a few centuries now. This one is designed for close engagements, with a compact body of durable polymer and HUD interlink.

I glance at my motley squad, a shadow of the armies I once had at my command. I sigh and shake my head. Right now, they're the best I've got. Outside, the binary suns shine overhead, one a similar shade to Earth's, the other a red like dying coals.

"Come on. We need to move."

*Cowards die many times before their deaths; the valiant never taste of death but once.*

Great advice, mother. Death comes for all, I suppose. The question is only when.

* * *

"Looks clear ahead," I mutter, scanning the horizon with the optical zoom embedded into my helmet's visor. "If there are patrols, they're well-hidden."

"You sure? We've already run into a few units clearing house." The officer raises a pair of old-fashioned binoculars, something of an antique, scanning the expansive parking lot. This mall had been recently constructed when I'd arrived on planet a few years ago. Apparently it caused an absolute uproar locally. The developers basically demolished a good portion of a historic—relatively speaking—neighborhood. This colony isn't all that old, but it's one of the first in this sector to be inhabited, so it does have a bit of history behind it.

That doesn't make it any less of a backwater, but there are worse places to live, especially on the outer lip of the inhabited zone. Lots of company planets out there. They offer good paying jobs, at the cost of a lonely multi-year tour of duty. I thought about heading out there, after the incident, but the C.S.A. was willing to take anyone who could hit the broadside of a barn with a rifle, so here I am, in the middle of an apparent revolution.

"There's no such thing as one-hundred percent sure of anything," I retort, slowly standing from my crouched position. "But I'll bet the mall is mostly clear. I'm not sure where the hell everyone is, but I'd wager they're probably not anywhere public, not after the bombings." While it wasn't a particularly long journey from the wreck of our SUV to the outskirts of the mall, it had been long enough to witness the aftermath of the attacks. Whoever the perpetrators were, they aimed for maximum chaos.

The officer nods. "I guess that's as good an answer as anything." She glances over to Michaels, tapping around on a smartwatch. I see her eyes narrow, but she holds her tongue.

"C'mon, we're moving out." I grab my shotgun from where I'd tucked it behind the sandstone wall of the roof, and sling it over my back. "I'd like to make it to the safe house before dark."

Riemann takes a final puff on his contraband cigarette and grinds it into the imported tile with his boot. "Right behind you." He grabs my rifle off a patio chair and keeps it held low, ready for action.

"I'll take point." I draw my sidearm and hold it low in my right paw, extending the claws of my free paw. "Michaels, you guard the VIP. Riemann, on the rear, and make sure nothing tries to come up our asses."

I cautiously open the door that led onto the rooftop patio, a solid teak that took two shells to blow open, but the stairwell is clear. We'd met a few patrols in the area, but they went down quickly, as if they weren't expecting resistance.

Moving down the open, wrought-iron spiral staircase, I don't see anything on the main floor either. Whoever lived here was obviously one of the better-off inhabitants. My eyes catch astronomically expensive imported mahogany crown moldings, a grand marble-faced fireplace, and luxurious greenhouse grown fruits on the granite countertops. I hold up a fist. Something's not right. The front door is firmly shut, and I'd left it just slightly ajar when we'd come in. I scan the floor ahead, and catch the faint glint of a tripwire, probably attached to some sort of claymore. I take a deep breath.

In an instant, I'm moving. I hop the railing with enough velocity to knock the fox that pops up from behind the counter back into the full-height wine fridge. While I'm down, I hear a few shots of gunfire exchanged, but it's over before I can pop up. The officer's standing right in front of Riemann, holding a smoking revolver, while an otter with a shotgun is slumped over the leather couch. I glance back, and the fox is out cold, but I put two shots in his head anyway. Yes, it's technically against the rules of civilized warfare, but out here, you do what's necessary to survive.

I turn around and holster my sidearm, giving her an appreciative nod. "Nice shootin', Tex."

She nods, wincing as she pats the front of her vest. I think she took a slug, but it doesn't look like it went all the way though. The bottom layer probably stopped it. "That's gonna leave a bruise," she mutters, examining the hole.

Riemann nods appreciatively. "Hey… thanks for taking that hit for me, uh…"

"My name isn't important," the officer replies, shrugging. "But thanks. It's the least I could do."

"But aren't we supposed to be your meat shields or somethin'?" The wolf shrugs. "I thought you said nobody gives a shit about us."

"Just because the Colonial Military treats the uplifted like shit doesn't mean everyone does," she says, deftly walking over to me and liberating a bottle of wine from above the fox's head, one with a pretentious, foil-embossed label. *Egon Muller-Scharzhof Scharzhofberger*, it reads, in what I think is German. "Seems a shame to let it go to waste," she says, casually smashing the neck against the counter until it cleanly breaks. "Care for a swig, gentleman?"

I nod, taking a muzzle-full despite knowing jack shit about wine. Even back when I had the wealth and influence to acquire whatever I wanted, I preferred whisky and cognac. The wine is pleasant and goes down smooth, which is about all I need at this point.

Riemann nods, smiling for once. "Thanks, lady. I needed a drink," he says, as I hand the bottle to him.

"Consider it an apology. I'm… sorry, about earlier." She looks away, but I see something in her eyes. Regret, perhaps? It's hard to say.

"Don't mention it," Riemann says, handing the bottle to Michaels. "You know, there's going to be danger ahead. I'm sure these guys didn't just stumble across us. They were waiting. We're playing right into the paws of whoever is running this whole scheme." The wolf snorts. "This could get us all killed."

I nod, loading a fresh magazine into my pistol. "Well? If we're fucked, might as well get it over with. I'd rather make my final stand behind the barrel of a gun than die in here like a cornered rat." My eyes dart between the three figures, Riemann's gunmetal eyes pensive, Michaels, nervous, but not shutting down, and the officer, her gray-flecked hair just a bit out of place.

Riemann nods. "There's honor in that, at least." I see his paw brush over my crest.

The officer sighs. "I only regret that I have but one life to lose for my country," she mutters, flicking out the cylinder for a reload. "Let's move. We're losing daylight."

I nod. "One final effort." I grab the wine bottle off the counter where Michaels had set it, and polish it off, letting the soft taste of spring fruit linger on my tongue. Time to move.

* * *

"Keep them pinned," I shout, slamming another magazine into my scavenged submachine gun. The officer nods, leaning around a faux marble planter to empty the remainder of her AK-47 at the two soldiers taking cover behind a smoothie stand. Stupendous Smoothies, definitely takes my vote for the dumbest store we've run across thus far.

"We're never going to make it at this rate!" she shouts, ducking back behind cover for a quick reload. "There's too many of them. We're going to run out of ammo soon if we keep running into ambushes at this rate."

I nod. "Let me handle these punks. Make sure they don't pop their pretty little heads up in the next few seconds," I reply, peeking around the corner. A bullet pings off the edge of the planter, and a second later, I feel a bit of detritus sting my cheek like an angry hornet. I briefly tap the wound before drawing my paw away, and it comes back flecked with red. I narrow my eyes. They're going to pay for that.

"Now!" I roll out of cover and sprint, covering the fifty-odd feet in slightly over two seconds. Just as the ferret with a shotgun pops up to blast me, I deliver a roundhouse to his jaw with the full force of my momentum behind it. Something cracks and he goes down hard. At the sight of the second, though, I hesitate for a moment. There's a distinctive scar along his jawline, an ugly pink mark around his brown mustelid fur, one that I recognize from a field op during my African campaign.

He doesn't seem to recognize me, though, and my hesitation gives him enough time to blast me point-blank with a shotgun. I grunt as my chest-plate absorbs the impact. It saves my life, but that's going to leave a mark. Before he can pump it and get off a second shot, I step forward and slash my claws across his forearm. Titanium tipped with a diamond cutting edge, they slice through fur and flesh like rice paper. He screams. The shotgun clatters to the floor like the tolling of a funeral bell.

"I recognize you," I say, watching coldly as he applies a paw to the wound, the pain displayed plainly on his face. "You served in the Africa campaign, back in '54. Operation Dingo II."

He doesn't reply, blood streaming down the back of his paw. It's not a fatal wound, but I'd imagine it hurts quite a bit. I see him glance up at me, and there's a spark. Perhaps he does remember.

"You darted in front of my Jeep. My driver nearly plowed you down." I sigh. "You're not going to die; I didn't slice your radial artery."

"General Voisin?" he asks, eyes widening.

"All clear?" I hear the officer shout, as a chocolate eye peeks out from behind the planter. "Riemann and Michaels are getting antsy."

"We fuckin' good?" I hear a gruff, canine voice add.

I ignore them, keeping my eyes on the ferret. "Once." His fur is neatly-groomed, and he seems well-fed, hardly like the scruffy human rebels I'd fought back then, desperate people fighting a losing war. "Who is it you're working for? What is this all about?"

"I… I can't say," he says, looking away. "You have no idea what she's capable of."

"She? Who is she?" I see the rest of my ersatz squad marching towards me, weapons raised.

"She… she…. s-she…" I hear him stutter, as his body suddenly starts to tremble. Fear flits across his face, and then it suddenly becomes a vacant smile as his pupils go wide.

"Fuck!" He's already gone by the time I manage to roll his sleeve up and get a finger on his radial artery. A small rivulet of red-tinged saliva flows out of the corner of his mouth. "God damn it!" I stand and take my anger out on the row of blenders in front of me, reducing them to shards and electronic detritus until I regain my composure. I stand there, panting, as the officer slowly lowers her rifle.

"You're bleeding," she says, frowning. I don't feel it, but there's a large slash across my left paw where a jagged piece of glass pierced the thin upper of my glove.

"It doesn't matter." I sigh. "We need to keep moving."

"Either you bandage it or I do it for you." She detaches a hard-pack off her thigh and tosses it to me. "I don't need you bleeding all over everything."

I shrug. "Patch me up, doc."

The officer rolls her eyes, but closes the distance between us and examines the wound. "This will need a few stiches. You really should exercise more restraint. I don't want to see you hurt, soldier."

"How sweet." Another voice, female, intones, "A human taking pity on a wounded animal." Behind us, an imposing figure, clad in armor like a demigod of Greek myth, a maroon cloak fastened around her collar. Beside her, two more in slightly downgraded armor sans cloak. "Isn't this a touching moment?"

I turn and snarl, though her guards don't react. I can see they're well-trained though, like a jack-in-the-box waiting for the final turn to spring out. "What do you want?"

"Oh, nothing," she shrugs, her chuckle harsh and metallic through the amplifier. "I just thought I'd introduce myself." She draws a pistol and levels it at the officer. "Hello, Catalyst. Long time no see. Do you remember me? Because I certainly remember you."

The officer narrows her eyes. "Whatever the fuck you think this is about, I want no part of it. It's been a long time since I used that name."

"Seven years. It's been fifteen years, one-hundred seventeen days, to be exact. I've been keeping count."

The officer doesn't seem intimidated. "Whatever you want, I'm not giving it to you. It is official policy not to negotiate with terrorists."

"Oh, you think I'm here for information. How naïve." She shakes her head, her guards still as marble statues. "No, I already ransacked your little black-ops hideaway under that base on the outskirts of town. Good effort though, it took me a whole fifteen minutes to torture the location out of the base commander." Without warning, she fires the pistol twice. *Crack. Crack.* Two red rings blossom outwards on the exterior of the officer's vest. "No, this is personal."

"You bitch! She was the only human that ever showed me even an ounce of kindness!" Riemann raises a rifle and opens fire, but it's a Sisyphean task. Powerful energy shields deflect the bullets and absorb the plasma, and when it clicks empty, the figure is no worse for wear.

"How noble," she says, shaking her head. "Such a waste."

*Crack. Crack.* Riemann drops like a stone. She looks at the otter. "Well? How about you? Do you want to do something noble too?"

Michaels shrugs. "Hey, if it gets me out of ending up like that guy, I'll do whatever you say. I don't want to get my head blown up." I'm sure he sees the hatred in my eyes, but it doesn't faze him as he walks away.

"Fuckin' traitor!" I yell, but I'm met only with silence.

I squat down, looking over the officer's wounds. Whatever ammunition this figure loaded, it was more than enough to cut through ceramic-plate armor. We exchange a look, and in that in a silent acknowledgement that she's about to earn a star on the Memorial Wall.

Cold steel presses against the back of my temple. "And then there's you. General Mark Constantine Voisin, identification code I-045-29-343C. Hero of the Scrimischar campaign, conqueror of New Cairo. Status: Deserter, effective July 6, 2255. Call-sign, Heartless."

"If you're going to kill me, do it. That was another life. Mark Voisin died a long time ago." I laugh, harsh and biting. "He died along with my mother and boyfriend, in a musty warehouse in the meatpacking district of Mombasa."

I remember that day, watching the pixelated footage, African Liberation Front soldiers torturing them both, for no other reason than for the sheer hell of it. I'll never forget their screams, how they begged. They were the most hardened soldiers I know, but everyone breaks. At least they died without pain, a gunshot to the temple after the soldiers had their fill.

What I did afterwards... even God could never forgive. I won't repeat the details, but it's sufficient to say that I deserted shortly afterwards. Something inside me had broken, and like Humpty Dumpty, all the king's horses and all the king's men couldn't tape me back together.

I stare at the officer's face, deathly pale, and gently rest my paw on her hand. There's a moment of connection there that transcends the bounds of species as I watch her pass. I fight to hold back a sob, but a few tears still find their way down my cheeks.

I'm reminded of who I used to be, before all this. "My name... is... Noble," I say, closing my eyes, taking a deep breath and muster my energy, like a cheetah about to give chase to an antelope.

In a flash, I pivot, knocking the pistol away as I spring to my feet to face her. Inside, all my turbulent emotion has fallen away, replaced by a deathly calm. I flick the plasma blade strapped into my right wrist on. It glows a violent red, and I can smell the harsh tang of ozone through my helmet filters.

She backs away, and her guards raise their rifles. "I'm going to enjoy cutting your fucking head off, cunt," I mutter, closing the distance between my position and the left guard almost instantaneously. Two bullets to my chest plate don't even slow me down. It's over in an instant. It barely got its arms half up before I drive the plasma blade through the center of the visor, slashing it side-to-side to ensure a fatal wound.

"A noble effort," she says, shaking her head and the body clatters to the floor. "But I'm afraid you are outgunned."

The second guard pulls a rifle from where it's been slung over his back and brings it up to his shoulder. I recognize the model instantly, a grim legacy of times long-past. Designated the M-5480 by the United States Army, it was banned for being inhumane. It used 'smart' ammunition that could detect when it had entered flesh and would then trigger a secondary detonation, causing massive and agonizing tissue trauma. I thought they had all been destroyed.

"Who are you?" I ask, my blade dissipating. "I'd like to at least know who bested me."

She chuckles, popping the seal on her helmet. "Oh, you already know who." My heart stops for a moment as I catch the piercing violet eyes, a perfect match for my own, the scarred muzzle, the right ear with a small notch. "Hello, son."

"Oh, fuck no." I scour her face, trying to prove it belongs to anyone other than my mother. "I saw you die. I watched as they put a bullet in your head."

"Amazing what can be faked," she says, chuckling. "I needed a way out, so I took one."

"What about my boyfriend? Where the hell is he?"

She shrugs. "Oh, I'm not sure. We were separated when they captured us. I offered them a sum that they couldn't turn down, and so they staged the torture. What you saw was quite real, but who those uplifted were, I haven't the faintest idea."

Something inside me shatters like a wine glass being gripped too firmly. "Do you know what I did to those soldiers?" I ball my fists so tight my claws start to dig through my palm, but the pain only makes me angrier.

She snorts. "Oh, please, stop being so melodramatic. I thought I taught you better than that. Besides, their lives were worthless. They would've died anyway." She gestures to the bodies scattered around us, those I'd killed, those she'd killed, and those that had died in the attacks. "Death comes for us all, cub. *Mors est ad nos.*"

"I can't justify what I did to those men," I say, my lips drawing back into a snarl. "But the least I can do is to make sure you understand exactly what they suffered."

"Oh, please, what do you think this is, some sort of space opera?" She laughs, but there's no humor in it. "I'm not telling you all this so you can take revenge on me." She turns to the guard. "Kill him."

"Wait," I say, my paws trembling slightly with white-hot fury. "At least tell me why you're doing all this. For fuck's sake Miranda—mother."

I see her expression twitch slightly. I've never had the courage to actually use her name before, for various reasons.

"Power, mostly." She chuckles. "You see, a lot of uplifted are tired of being treated like shit. I offer them a home, a better life. Everyone likes a good cause, and there's plenty of foot soldiers ready to join up. Don't blame me, I'm not the cause, just a symptom."

"I'd like to pipe in!" Michaels interjects. He's clutching the officer's sleek pistol, cutting a heroic figure, for an otter at least. "I like a good cause too, but you're just a power-hungry bitch." He glances over at me. "Right, Heartless?"

My mother narrows her eyes. "And kill him too, for having a big mouth."

The last thing I see before it all goes black is Michaels shooting me a wink, and a flash of light that catches the remaining guard right in the chest. A concussive wave throws me back, a lightning bolt of pain shoots through the rear of my skull and then, nothing.

* * *

I wish I could say I could wrap this story up nicely, with a bow and a little gift tag on top, but life doesn't work like most of the time. I skip over the briefing papers haphazardly spread out over my desk and go for the mostly empty Styrofoam cup perched on the corner. There's barely enough stale coffee to get my tongue wet, and I toss it towards the corner wastebasket in disgust. It lands just short.

There's not much to say. My mother is gone, along with a few terabytes worth of classified intel and the rest of her revolutionary army. Michaels disappeared into the ether. Only I remained on-planet for the Colonial Military to retrieve.

I brush the officer's pistol, neatly holstered at my waist. Perhaps it will come in handy, whatever comes next. Michaels left it. I guess he wasn't so bad after all. I'm not sure if I can ever be fixed, or redeemed, but that doesn't matter now. All that matters is bringing this to an end, stopping her.

There's no window in my cabin for obvious reasons, but as I gaze at the bare titanium wall, bearing the scuffs and scratches of the dozens of enlisted who've had it before me, I imagine I can see the stars, and perhaps amongst them, I can find my peace.

"Noble, please report to the bridge. I repeat, Noble, report to the bridge immediately," a voice announces through a crackling, dated speaker.

Noble. It has a ring to it. I look down at my uniform and gently tear the Heartless badge away, tucking it away in a drawer to be forgotten. From my bag, I withdraw a purple silk cloak, still as beautiful as the day I'd received it as a symbol of my rank, along with a snow leopard plush my boyfriend had given me for our anniversary.

Holding him in one paw, standing proud, I let a smile cross across my muzzle.

Noble, reporting for duty.

*Reportedly Edward A. Murphy (1918-1990), the man whom the "law" is named after—"Anything that can go wrong, will go wrong"—was very displeased with the quip. He was a quality control officer working on the USAF's high-speed rocket sled experiments in the late 1940s. Quality control at the time consisted of testing something until it broke down, fixing it, and then testing it further. Murphy pointed out that they couldn't do that. The experimental rocket sleds had live human test pilots in them who could be killed if anything went wrong. What Murphy really told his engineers was that they had to figure out in advance everything that could possibly go wrong, and make sure that it didn't happen.*

*This is similar to the situation that Sea Bee Chief Petty Officers Loutran "Tor" Rivers (river otter) and Caster Banks (beaver), stationed in the South Pacific, find themselves in. Extend and beef up an improvised island landing strip until it's strong enough. Long and strong enough for what? That is a Military Secret—just do it!*

# Trial by Error

## *by Jaden Drackus*

Day 1: 0800 Hours, Springfall Atoll (Piax Ocean Theater).

"God damn it! Not again!"

The profanity rolled across the camp of the 23$^{rd}$ Unified Territories Naval Construction Battalion (Sea Bees), awaking any members of the unit that were still asleep. One of those was Chief Petty Officer Loutran "Tor" (short for Torpedo) Rivers. The river otter was startled out of his doze and came to his senses on the floor next to his bunk. He grabbed a thin khaki work shirt and some "borrowed" Army pants that were too large as they had been cut for canines, dressed quickly, and then headed out into the warming Springfall morning. Given the time of the tirade, Tor could guess what it was about. A moment later Tor's guess was proven correct as a large mass of beaver waddled past him, muttering under his breath about "tanuki bastards."

Tor turned to his left and stood on tip toe to see the end of the row of Quonset huts. Sure enough, the laundry line was empty. Once again, the remaining Araigumase on Springfall had managed to steal the Sea Bees' underwear. Tor sighed, shook his head, and silently thanked the Good Lion that he had the foresight to keep a stash of underwear in his duffel. Something had to be done about this. The otter's thoughts were interrupted by a shadow falling on the ground in front of him. Tor looked up to find that the irate beaver, Chief Petty Officer Caster Banks, had returned.

"We need to fix this, Tor." Banks slapped his tail on the ground in frustration. "We don't need five hundred guys running 'round in this heat with no underwear."

"Yeah," Tor agreed, looking around to make sure no Seamen were close enough to overhear. "No offense, Cas, but you get smelly enough as is. Even to me. Not sure I could stand you with all your musk gettin' out through just your shorts."

Banks let out a short laugh that whistled through his larger front teeth. "Be glad you're not the boss. Poor wolf bastard must hate being around us all day with that overactive sniffer of his."

"I'm glad I am not the paddler," Tor nodded sagely.

The otter fell into step with his superior as the pair headed towards the commander's office. Commander Lycon was a good CO. But there was no denying that the wolf did try to keep his nose out of what to him must have been the reek of the enlisted men; which explained why he usually called his chiefs with less sensitive noses to a meeting in the morning and then let them handle the direct supervision of the battalion.

This particular morning, the chiefs arrived to find Lycon already deep into his daily paperwork. The wolf barely looked up at the two noncommissioned officers, and then pointed at the coffee pot, set on a lower table for their convenience.

"Grab some coffee and a seat. This one's going to be a doozy."

Tor's whiskers twitched in curiosity. Like most of the Sea Bees under his command Lycon was an older individual, depending on one's view of 40 as "old." To the teen and early twenty-something Marines and Army infantry, Lycon seemed ancient. Of course, that was typical of most of the Sea Bees - like Banks, they were mostly over 30 and had backgrounds in construction before the war. Tor himself split the difference at 25 and was a career navy man, recently transferred to the Sea Bees from destroyer duty. So what could get the former construction foreman so riled up that even an otter could tell?

Soon, the otter had his muzzle in a wide mug of coffee which covered up the scent of canine irritation that was spread around by the four fans that the wolf had going in the office. Banks climbed onto the other stool in front of the commander's desk. The wolf shuffled the papers on his desk, selected one, and then glared down at his two senior NCO's. Tor swallowed nervously and put his muzzle deep into his mug to avoid the wolf's wrath. Banks, more familiar with his commander's moods, took a swig of his coffee and met the big wolf's gaze without concern.

"So, what's going on, boss?"

"New top secret, drop everything and do this *now* crap," Lycon huffed and let out a low growl. "No real information other than what we need to do the job."

Lycon tossed two pieces of paper in the general direction of the two aquatics and slapped his paws on the desk. Tor picked one up and began to study it while Banks clicked his tongue against his prominent front teeth and continued to meet the canine's blue-eyed gaze. Lycon bared his teeth and Tor shrank a little deeper into his stool, despite the memory of Banks telling him that the act was one of frustration, not of threat.

"They need the north runway on North Field extended. The 'A' one, if you're using the official designations."

"No big deal. Been doing that for over a month now anyway," Banks sipped his coffee. "Least no one's shootin' at us much anymore. How much longer?"

"They don't know," Lycon growled.

Banks choked on his coffee, spit the last mouthful back into his mug, and rocked forward gagging. Tor let out a quiet chatter of frustration of his own.

"How the... How can they not know?" Banks coughed, surprising Tor with his self-censoring. "It's not like those big chrome Army birds have changed at all."

"Apparently they have," Tor murmured as he continued to study the sheet of paper. He looked up in time to see Lycon staring at him - Tor was usually silent during these meetings. The otter quickly pulled the paper back in front of his face.

"What?"

"No real details," Lycon waved his paw in dismissal. "Scuttlebutt is that they have modified some Leviathans to carry some new payload. All they provided was that the new takeoff weight is heavier than normal. They think."

"And the Army can't do this on their own?" Banks's tail smacked the floor in agitation.

"The unit flying them is going to be assigned here," Tor put in, his own thick tail swept behind his stool as he reached back to scratch the base of it.

"Damnit," the beaver swallowed the last of his coffee out of the wide mug. "And when do the Army morons expect us to have this done?"

"Yesterday," Lycon grabbed a pen and scrawled something Tor couldn't read on a notepad. He ripped the sheet off the top and repeated the process and handed the papers to Banks. "So I'm putting my best Chiefs on it, with written permission from me to acquire anything they need to get a Leviathan of the weight specified into the air a-sap."

"A-sap means PSP and crushed coral," Banks took the paper with a huff. "Thought the Army mechanics said that screwed with the engines."

"Not going to be our problem." Lycon handed Tor the other copy. "Just get it done."

"That's impossible." Tor put the orders back on the wolf's desk. His tail twitched in agitation that overrode his nervousness. "How're we supposed to build anything with only the briefest of information? And what do they need it for so soon?"

"You don't even have the hard part," Lycon glared down at the otter. "Corvin is going to be putting in the weird stuff they want for this new payload. But that's not your problem. Get the damn runway finished by the end of the week or that big rudder tail of yours is going back to destroyer duty."

With that, Tor swallowed nervously and the wolf waved them away and returned to his paperwork. Recognizing the dismissal, the two chiefs slid from their stools and headed back out into the tropical morning. On Banks' suggestion, they headed to the aquatics' mess and got breakfast while they considered what to do about their new problem.

"So, where do we start?" Tor finally asked as he finished his last fish stick.

"Well, as my Pap always told me," Banks swirled the wider mug meant to accommodate his tall muzzle and large teeth. "Start at the beginning. Whadda we know, and whadda we need?"

"We have sorta guesses that might represent the added weight of whatever modifications plus the payload," Tor ticked off on his paw. Banks had the gift of bringing out the otter's confidence. "We don't know about the runway, 'cuz the Army told us how long to make them in the first place."

"So we know how long it needs to be for a regular Leviathan. All we need to do is figure out how much longer to make it."

"Right. Lotta math there, lotta unknowns."

"So we don't bother," Banks smiled broadly. "Let's just extend the runway as much as we think we need, say another fifty yards, then load up a Leviathan to what we think the new weight is and see if it takes off. If it doesn't, we extend it some more and try again."

"Which means we need to get paws on a Leviathan and a pilot crazy enough to try and take off with no guarantee of making it," Tor rubbed his whiskers. "Might be difficult to get those."

"Com'on, Tor," Banks laughed. "You know how ta get things done. Between all the ice cream makers we've 'borrowed' and the other things we can do for them, we've got plenty 'o stuff ta trade for a plane and a pilot."

"I know. I just wasn't sure if the boss would want us spreading the word around that we have those."

"He did say to use everything we had," Banks waved the paper. "Just don't offer them explosives. I'm not rebuilding the pier cuz they want to go dynamite fishing again." Neither of the aquatics could understand why the army mammals found fish so exotic and obsessively tried to get them, but they did.

With that the beaver pushed back from the table, got to his paws, and shoved Lycon's orders into his pants pockets.

"Well. I'm gonna round up the crew and get starting on building the runway. Hopefully we can get it done before any rain comes in. You head over to the Army boys and get us a pilot and a plane."

"Me? They'll listen to a chief?" Tor scratched the base of his tail. He preferred the weight of his borrowed Army issue pants (or rather the lack of weight compared to Navy khakis), but the rarity of otters in the army meant that in addition to being too large for him, the tail slit was sized for thinner canine tails. He'd had to modify the opening, and it still pinched and the hem itched sometimes.

"That paper from Lycon says anything you do is with his authority," Banks smacked the ground with his broad tail, a sign of finality to beavers, before Tor could protest that he had never handled a project on his own before. "Just flash that, be ready to bargain, and you should be good."

"Hopefully the bomber boys haven't run out of crazy pilots," Tor nervously swallowed the last of his own coffee.

\* \* \*

0945 Hours

"Let me get this straight, Chief." The cougar in a colonel's uniform stared down at the otter. Even seated behind his desk, the cougar towered over the standing otter. "The Navy wants us to provide them with a bomber and a pilot, just so they can see if the runway that they have already constructed is good enough for our planes."

"About the size of it. If you boil it down that far," Tor nodded with the characteristic bob of an otter. He couldn't really tell what the cougar (Col. Noble according to the name on his desk) was actually thinking, as felines were naturally good at hiding the signs of their emotions. But unlike his dealings with Lycon, Tor had known a couple of cougars and bobcats back home in Boston, so he was slightly less nervous around the bigger feline then around the wolf. The otter knew to look at the tail and ears for clues to feline reactions. Col. Noble's tail twitched slightly and his ears were fairly still, which meant that the feline was relatively calm. Still, Tor was around a larger predator and fidgeted nervously. He rather preferred talking to fighter pilots since they all tended to be on the otter's level: smaller, less threatening predator species like foxes, weasels, and bobcats.

"Why should I do this?" Noble kneaded on the desk, his fingers occasionally clicking as his claws extended with the motion. His tail gave a quick twitch and Tor knew that meant that the cougar was ready to negotiate.

"I'm sure that we can come up with something to convince you," Tor smiled knowingly, glad he could finish the exchange before his Banks inspired confidence could leave him.

Half an hour later, the otter hopped up on the running board of the bulldozer that Chief Banks occupied while directing the Sea Bee work crew. Tor waited, protected from the sun and bullets by the piece of tank armor that the unit had welded onto the side while Banks called out orders to the crew. Most of the crew was leveling the coral that had been piled at the end of the runway while a few massive horses and rams began to stack planks of PSP near the end of the runway to be easily accessible when the time came to put them into position. The entire crew was violating modesty and scent consideration laws by wearing as little clothing as possible - save for those from desert climates, who followed them a bit more stringently. For the enlisted construction crew, that mostly meant shorts that had been cut off just below the pockets and boots. Boots were usually an odd item for most mammals, but working with heavy steel planking, heavy machinery, and on blisteringly hot pavement demanded them - only the horses and rams were not wearing them. Only the two chiefs were wearing shirts, both of them open to the stomach, and solely for the purposes of being easily identified as those in charge.

Tor frowned suddenly as he studied the makeup of the work crew. Like most Sea Bee crews, there was a wider selection of species than one usually saw in the military. That wasn't surprising, considering that they had been selected specifically for having careers in construction before the war. But there was something bothering the otter about this specific crew. His tail slowly swished as he considered it. Then he got it: the crew was all squirrels, mice, a groundhog or two, the occasional otter, plus those towering horses and rams. There were no foxes, wolves, cougars, or other species that were predisposed to being nocturnal.

"First test is tomorrow," Banks explained when Tor finally got to ask him about it. "So we're going 'round the clock. In fact, you need to go hit the hay after this so you can supervise the night shift."

"I thought you liked working at night. And I've never run a crew on my own."

"I do. But someone had to get started on this while you were off talking to the army boys," the beaver slapped his tail on the bulldozer's engine cover, which someone had had the foresight to pad. Banks took a drink from his canteen. "You'll be fine. Just do what you think I would do. So whada got for us?"

"I got us *The Reluctant Dragon*," Tor pointed to a revetment where one plane of the dozens of chrome bombers stationed on the island was parked. "She's ours, even when we're done with the tests. Plus we got a pilot. A captain named Tanner. He's a buck. Seemed willing to try anything, but not crazy like the fighter jocks. Only took a quart of juice for him to get on board."

"And what about the rest of the Army?"

"Two ice cream makers and a fifty-five gallon drum of special blend," the otter's tail went still and his tiny ears vanished into his head. Banks wasn't going to like the price.

He didn't. The beaver almost choked on his water, spitting a good deal to flash to steam in the tropical sun.

"How many stars does this Tanner guy have?" Banks sputtered. "Cuz you know we don't give but a couple o' quarts of jungle juice for squadron commanders."

"He's just a captain."

"Look, Tor…"

"Lemme finish, boss," the otter ticked points off on his paw. "We got the plane. We got the pilot. We got the copilot and crew chief. We got no other requests until this is done. We got a ground crew for the plane. And we got permanent guards for the laundry lines."

"Might be worth it," Banks clicked his front teeth with his tongue. After a moment of contemplation he stuck his head out of the cab. "Pavsen! You're off the hook! Report to me for special assignment."

The beaver shook his head and turned back to the otter while they waited for the groundhog with stains in his fur from his chemical engineering days to trot over.

"I just wish I understood what all the damn fuss was about."

"All the orders said was something about specially modified Leviathans that will be arriving," Tor shrugged. "Claimed they would be using some new weapon system or some other hush-hush bureaucratic nonsense, then just stated that the take-off weight would be heavier than a usual Leviathan and a guess of how much to load it up to. All they were telling."

"Militaries and their secrets," the beaver huffed and smacked his tail again. Pavsen was slowing down his trot to stop a respectful distance from the discussion. Banks waved him forward. "Get some rest, Tor. Let's get this done."

"We have to," Tor replied as his nervousness from Lycon's threat returned. "I don't want to go back to destroyers."

\* \* \*

0130 Hours

A runway of PSP was a fairly simple affair. Once the ground had been properly flattened, the mat, consisting of ten-foot long, fifteen-inch wide planks of steel with holes punched in them to lighten them, which give them their name of perforated steel planking. They were still heavy, though, requiring a lot of smaller mammals or a couple of big ones like horses, bulls, or bears to move them. To create a mat of the stuff, the planks came with hook-like extensions on one long edge (which the scars on the webbing between Tor's fingers could attest were rather sharp sometimes) while the other long edge had slots cut into for those hooks to slide into. That action was repeated until a mat of the desired length had been reached. If the work crew was feeling ambitious (and the chiefs had decided that they were), the planks could be welded together for extra stability. That done, the whole mat was covered in coral dust to allow some sort of traction: Tor had walked across frozen ponds back home that were less slippery than PSP, especially when it was wet.

During the heat of the day, Banks and his crew had gotten most of the heavy lifting done by getting the area at the end of the runway dug up, leveled, the mat stacked, and the few remaining trees removed. That left the actual placing of the mat to Tor and the night shift. Compared to the day crew it was a smaller crew, both in number and size of the members. The crew was all typically nocturnal species: foxes, wolves, otters, beavers, and some big cougars and a massive bear or two for heavy lifting that were still mostly clad just in shorts. With blackout procedures still in effect at night for fear of marauding Araigumase planes (something that was all but unheard of in months) and the few remaining Araigumase forces on Springfall, it was essential for night work crews to be composed of species that could see in low light conditions.

Tor, feeling confident again once he had something to actually do, undid the last button on his shirt in surrender to the still warm night as he got to his paws to stretch his back. For the past twenty minutes he had been down on his knees checking the alignment of the mat before he had the crew level and weld the planks together. Tor motioned to the leveling crew, a quartet of beavers with metal plates and harnesses on their broad tails. The chief moved back as the crew began to slap the seam, pounding it flat. Tor had been skeptical of this system when Banks had first introduced it to him, but had to admit that the beavers did an admirable job of leveling the mat without the waves left by using a steamroller or the smaller dents of sledgehammers. Behind them came the welders: a pair of ferrets that wore heavy denim solely to protect them as they welded. Tor watched the sparks fly into the starry night while the beavers pounded down the next seam and the rest of the crew set another plank into place. Things were going well. They should be ready for the first test by morning.

\* \* \*

Day 2: 1000 Hours

"Are you sure this is going to work?" Captain Tanner cast a dubious glance at the water dripping out of the drums hanging in the bomb bay of *The Reluctant Dragon*, and then looked down at the two chiefs. "Those don't look like they're held in there real good."

"We'll make sure they're in there good and tight," Banks reassured the big pilot.

Tor yawned as he walked beside the beaver and the buck as they inspected the large silver bomber. His crew had finished up just before dawn, so he had actually managed a few hours of sleep while Banks had supervised the preparation of the *Dragon*. The bomber had been loaded with cement blocks, dummy bombs, drums filled with water, and anything else the Sea Bee crew could find and secure in the massive airplane. Tor remained outside the aircraft while Tanner and Banks climbed the ladder into the *Dragon's* cockpit, still discussing the safety of the additions, and studied the outside of the plane.

The Leviathan was the largest aircraft that the otter had ever seen. The general shape of the aircraft was a massive chrome tube with flat, four-engine wings and a massive tail. The blunt nose of the aircraft was a Plexiglas cap, along with many small windows in the top of the fuselage through which Tor could see Tanner looking down at what Tor assumed was the beaver he was still talking to. The rest of the fuselage was broken by mushroom shaped caps that housed the defensive machine guns. The square tail housed another pair of machine guns, plus a larger caliber cannon that looked for all the world like a bee stinger. Tor walked around to the other side of the aircraft where the name and art of a dragon covering its eyes, holding a machine gun, and wearing one of those old style helmets that looked like an inverted dinner plate was painted under the cockpit windows. Tor chuckled as he studied the art, but the smile vanished from his muzzle as a scent hit his nose.

His nose twitched as he turned around and faced the engines on the left wing. He sniffed and approached the inboard engine. He stared up at the slightly oxidized metal of the engine cowl, looking for where the smell of oil could be coming from. He failed to find any visual sign of an oil leak, but the odor persisted.

"You're not gonna find anything," a tired, cynical voice came from behind the otter. Tor turned to find a hassled-looking weasel (perhaps annoyed at the fact that he was wearing coveralls in the morning heat) walking towards him. "Once the engines get used enough they just start to reek of oil."

"Odd," Tor sniffed again as the mechanic got close enough for the otter to read "Yanson" on the left breast of his coveralls.

"It's a quirk with these damn engines," Yanson huffed and rubbed at something on his paw. Tor was struck by how still the mechanic was compared to the other weasels he had known. Perhaps Yanson too had been kicked from his bunk with little sleep. "Always leaking a little sumtin' from somewhere. They made them so complex that you need a stateside level maintenance facility just to keep 'em running. Luckily, we got that here now. Heard in Shinona the things would catch fire all the time."

Tor was about to question this claim, which was in direct conflict with what he knew about engines, but any further comment from the navy otter was put off by a cockpit window opening high above them. Tanner thrust his head out it.

"Yanson! We're ready to give this a try! Can you shake Ace and Konner from the mess for me?"

The weasel replied in the affirmative and scurried off, leaving Tor to wonder how a bomber crew member could end up with the nickname "Ace."

Fifteen minutes later, the drone of engines signaled that *The Reluctant Dragon* was ready to begin the test. Tor and Banks sat down at the west end of the runway, ten yards north of the seam between the asphalt and the PSP extension, under one of the last remaining trees on the north end of the island. Both mammals watched the silver aircraft as it taxied out of her revetment and out to the runway, shining brightly in the sun.

"You think this is going to work?" Tor watched the bright spot of the *Dragon* as it stopped at the end of the runway. His whiskers twitched nervously and his broad tail dug little trenches in the coral.

"Honestly?" Banks shifted the stick he'd been chewing on from one side of his mouth to the other. "Tanner wasn't sure."

"So that's why we've got another pile of mat ready to go?" Tor pointed, even though it was unnecessary.

"Yup," Banks spat out a mouthful of shavings. "You'll take the day crew this time. Do another fifty yards and I'll get the mat welded down tonight."

"Right," Tor let out a nervous squeak. "Hope we're close. Kinda running outta island at this end."

The stick in the beaver's muzzle snapped. Tor turned to find Banks glaring at him.

"You say that again, and I'm gonna tie you naked to the bar sign as a warning to fools."

"Aye, aye, boss," Tor swallowed and turned back to the plane as the roar of engines grew. He understood the beaver's reaction. He had no desire to do any major earth-moving, either.

Both turned back to the east end of the runway as the *Dragon*'s engines reached full song and the plane began to roll down the runway. The plane picked up speed and Tor heard Banks hiss through his front teeth as the bomber rapidly grew larger. The roar of the engines pitched up to almost a scream as they strained to get the overloaded Leviathan into the air.

But two-thirds of the way to the chiefs, the roar suddenly died. The bomber briefly drooped down on its nose as two engines cut and the remaining two slowed to almost idle. Both chiefs jumped to their paws, ready to call their crew to attempt to assist with any problems. The plane continued to roll slowly down the runway as the two mammals rushed to the tarmac. As the bomber began to turn onto the taxiway, Tanner stuck his head out the window and shook it sadly.

"Too short," the stag mouthed to the chiefs before the plane turned and passed them. Banks swore in response and turned to Tor.

At that moment, both chiefs flinched as an explosion rocked the island. Above the retreating *Dragon*, a massive waterspout rose into the sky. Banks wheeled on the otter.

"Damnit, Tor! I told you not to give them any dynamite!"

"It wasn't me!" Tor waved his arms in protest.

"Damn farm wolves and their obsession with fish!" Banks sprinted off in the direction of the dock, leaving Tor to assemble the Sea Bee crew to get back to work on the runway.

\* \* \*

Day 3: 1330 Hours

Tor looked on nervously as the *Dragon* began to taxi into position once again. He scratched tiredly behind his small ears. The test was somewhat delayed today due to a series of rain squalls that had come through during the night and the early morning. Banks didn't look too bothered about working in the rain, but some of the canines on the crew had returned to the huts looking rather bedraggled and upset.

The last squall had blown through about two hours ago, and the tropical heat quickly dried out the tarmac while the Sea Bees managed to grab lunch. At lunch, Banks informed Tor that the Army had managed not to damage the dock while they were fishing. Tanner wandered by as well and let the chiefs know that he thought that the added length would be enough. Tor was glad: they only had about fifty yards of island left on this side. Despite the pilot's optimism, Tor had spent the morning getting earth moving equipment into position while Banks had been wrapping up putting down the mat. After the rain came in, the nervous otter had actually begun the process of extending the island, just in case.

The *Dragon* reached the east end of the runway and paused to run her engines up to full song. Tor briefly wondered if his pup self would have recognized the sound of the engines as the roar of a dragon. He wasn't sure and he couldn't turn and ask Yanson what he thought about the matter, as the weasel was mumbling to himself as he listened to the engines. Tor cocked his ears to try and make out what the mechanic was saying.

The *Dragon* began rolling down the runway towards the two chiefs and the sergeant. Yanson chittered as the aircraft picked up speed. Tor held his breath and Banks chewed on another stick. The drone of the engines became a scream as the massive chrome bomber rolled down the runway and for a moment, Tor thought it was actually going to make it into the air. Tanner must have thought it too, because the buck kept going past the point where he had aborted yesterday. But it wasn't to be.

Just as the *Dragon* reached the turn off for the taxiway, Tanner must have realized that he wasn't going to make it into the air. The scream of the engines cut out as the pilot throttled down to idle. Normally, the bomber would have slowed to a stop with plenty of the mat runway to spare. But the rain washed the coral dust coating off the mat leaving bare, wet metal exposed.

Tor winced as the plane's tires hit the mat. Walking across wet PSP (or rather, attempting to walk across it) was a hazing practice in most Sea Bee units. Even an experienced hand like Tor himself, or even Banks, often wound up on their tails: the *Dragon* had no chance.

With no traction, the bomber refused to slow down and continued to speed down the runway with the same momentum. The *Dragon* slid by the two naval mammals and the mechanic, and Tor was surprised to see that Tanner wasn't panicking. Instead, the buck was glaring out the cockpit window at them as he went by. Yanson let out some combination of a squeak and a snort. Tor winced and braced himself.

Sure enough the *Dragon* slid right off the mat, tore through the coral soil of the island, went off the embankment the Sea Bees had piled, and into the water with a massive splash. Tor winced at the crash and the ear-piercing screech of metal meeting water. The wave created by the airplane easily cleared the embankment and splashed onto the mat. Silence fell as the two chiefs looked at each other in horror. Yanson broke the moment with a cackle.

"Well. Looks like *The Reluctant Dragon* turned out to be an *Eager Whale!*"

"We need to go fish her out," Banks glared at the Army mechanic.

"Don't bother," Yanson waved the beaver off as he wiped his eyes. "She was WW any way."

"What?" the Sea Bees shouted in unison.

"She was war-weary," Yanson clarified patiently. "Too much effort to keep flying. We were going to scrap her for parts soon. Her engines were pretty weak, turrets kept jamming, and the control surfaces were unresponsive."

"What?! 'Engines were pretty weak?' You lied to me about that oil! And we loaded her past capacity!" Tor shouted as Banks glared accusingly at the weasel and smacked his tail on the ground. Over the mechanic's shoulder, rescue crews swarmed over the foundering airplane.

"Yeah, well. Whadd'a ya think we were going to do?" the mechanic huffed. "Give you a perfectly good aircraft? Look what you guys did with it."

Tor's mouth opened and closed several times as the otter desperately tried to find a way to suitably express the view that if they had been given a plane with properly working engines, this wouldn't have happened. But it was clear that the weasel's indifference could not be breached by reason. Next to Tor, Banks thumped out a steady rhythm with his tail.

"No. Booze," the beaver finally hissed. "That was for us getting a damn plane in the air."

Yanson gave him a hurt expression and the twitch of the whiskers that weasels did that came across as nervous to everyone else.

"Yeah, sure," he squeaked. We'll get ya a plane. No worries."

"A *working* plane," Banks snarled, exposing his big front teeth and pulling himself up to his full height. Tor shuddered as the memory of what a beaver could do with those teeth in a fight went through him. Yanson apparently had similar memories.

"A workin' plane," the mechanic agreed with a swallow. Before another word could be exchanged, he scurried off towards the Army offices.

"I'll get the groundhogs together," Tor said into the sudden quiet.

Banks spat out the shavings from his stick, nodded, and swore. Both chiefs looked up as the soft but distinctive sound of hooves on asphalt approached. Tanner, looking rather bedraggled, unamused, and still dripping strode towards them. He stopped an arm's length away and pointed a shaking finger down at them.

"One of you," he declared coldly, "is coming with us tomorrow. That's an order."

Before either of the naval personnel could respond, an explosion rocked the island. Behind Turner a waterspout shot skyward. Banks swore loudly and ran off at the surprising speed that an angry beaver was capable of, leaving Tor to look up at the unhappy aviator.

"Nice of you to volunteer, Chief," the stag huffed as he went off in search of dry clothes.

Tor frowned, trying to think of how to explain to the pilot that he had never flown before. The otter realized that it wouldn't make a difference. Instead, he kicked at an imagined rock and trotted off to get the earth moving groundhogs collected and started on the island extension.

* * *

Day 5: 1100 Hours

It took the entire day and night to properly extend the runway the desired seventy-five yards into the ocean. The wreck of the *Dragon* was no issue, as the quick thinking Tanner had angled the plane southward so that it splashed down out of the line of the runway. Tor and Banks had grabbed every piece of earth-moving equipment on the island and every able-bodied worker they could find to move the massive amounts of coral required. Tor didn't know if the island extension would last in the tides around the island much beyond the intended use of the runway, but that probably wouldn't matter. What did matter was that they were running out of time. Tor couldn't go back to destroyers after the UTS *Orca* had ended up on the bottom of the Piax, almost taking him with it. The otter had spent every moment he wasn't doing something pacing nervously.

In spite of the otter's growing anxiety, the day gave Tor, Banks, and Tanner time to pick out a new bomber. The pilot picked out a plane named *Special Delivery* which featured nose art of a pin-up vixen straddling a bomb. Tor spent most of the time that Banks, Tanner, and Yanson were inspecting the plane trying to figure out if the vixen's top was actually clothing or just tasteful censorship. He couldn't decide, and wandered back to the construction efforts after assuring himself that Yanson actually was inspecting the engines on this plane.

Earth moving lasted into the evening, followed by yet another routine night of laying PSP. Tor and Banks took turns supervising the construction, while Tanner took personal charge of seeing to the preparations of the *Delivery*. The Sea Bees finished the last weld just as dawn turned the cloudless sky rose. Tanner walked the runway and took special care to kick just a little more coral onto the mat. With the inspection finished, the buck took Tor to get fitted with flight gear. Tor did not look forward to trying to cram his tail into a rat's pants. To the otter's surprise, there was very little additional gear required - just a jacket over his khakis. Tor was used to the bomber crews of Gryphons and Rocs who had to bundle up against high altitude freezing temperatures, but Tanner explained that the Leviathans had a new feature called a pressurized cabin which made such extreme measures less necessary. They wouldn't even need to use oxygen masks.

With his gear picked up, Tor trotted quickly out to the boarding ladder leaned up against the side of the *Delivery*. Already the tarmac grew uncomfortably warm under his paws. He quickly climbed up the ladder and into the cockpit.

Tor climbed into the cockpit and looked around. He was surprised to find that the Leviathan interior wasn't the yellow-green of the interiors of other bombers, but had a definite blueish-green tinge. The otter paused to take the huge interior in, but was interrupted by a deer head thrusting into the door behind him.

"You're going to be a bombardier today," Tanner pointed past the pilot and co-pilot positions into the almost completely Plexiglas nose. "So you'll have a great view of all the action."

And be the first in the water if things went wrong, Tor knew. The otter nodded and picked his way across the cockpit and down into the nose, right between the pilot stations. He reached the seat and looked back to see the big buck hunched slightly making his way to the pilot's station, followed by Ace (who proved to be a coyote) the copilot and Konner (the thinnest raccoon that Tor could remember) the flight engineer. Tanner lowered himself into his seat and looked up at the otter while Ace fiddled to position his tail in the slot of his seat.

"You get one question before we do preflight, Chief." The pilot seemed to read Tor's mind. "After that: sit down, get your rudder in the slot, put your helmet on, and strap in."

Tor was about to inquire how he was supposed to communicate with them once the engines started but Konner had leaned over the pilot console, clearly waiting to assist the otter in getting set up. So the otter chose the other question that had been on his mind.

"So what do you do in the fall, sir? I mean. Do they not let bucks fly while their racks are in? I don't think I've ever seen antler scratches on the ceilings of Army planes."

There was a pause that was just long enough for Tor to realize that he had hit on a sensitive subject. The otter swallowed and chittered nervously as the big stag's whiskers twitched in thought.

"I trim them, Chief," he finally answered quietly. "Now strap in."

"Oh," the otter breathed as he complied. Belatedly, his mind flashed back to school and how the stags whose racks hadn't come in or were small had been teased by the bucks with big antlers (and the times he had almost gotten crushed in their fights). He winced as Konner assisted him with getting strapped in and his helmet on. The raccoon hooked him into the intercom and demonstrated how to use the throat mike. The otter did a quick check, got confirmation from Ace that he'd been heard, and then put his paws in his lap and stared nervously out the nose. His tail didn't quite fit in the allotted space for it and lay between the pilot consoles which it bumped into as Tor swished nervously until Ace put his paw on it. After that, Tor focused on keeping his tail still while he listened with half an ear to the Army crew going through their preflight routine and then looked up see Banks standing on the side of the tarmac. The beaver tossed him a salute before heading off in the direction of the bar. Any thoughts Tor might have had about what Banks' actions meant were curtailed by the bundle of an otter-sized life vest landing in his lap.

"Put your life vest on, Chief. I saw you drop it in the doorway."

"I can swim just fine without it. I'm an otter, after all."

"Well, you learn something new every day. Hey Ace, you know that otters can swim when they're unconscious?"

"News to me, boss."

"Me too. So put the damn vest on, Chief. I bet your rudder would be hard enough to pull out of here even if it wasn't drowning."

Tor tried to shrink into the seat. The stag had a point. He put the vest on without any further protest.

A few moments later, the engines rumbled as Tanner sent the *Delivery* rolling down the taxiway. The buck paused the plane on the runway proper before he asked the question.

"Ever flown before, Chief?"

"No sir," Tor replied, his eyes glued to the tarmac visible through the nose. He felt the pressure of a paw on his right shoulder, but didn't look back at Ace.

"Well, just tighten your belt and try and relax," Tanner reassured him. With that, the pilot returned to his preflight checks. Tor did as ordered and tried not to think too much about how this was their last chance to get this right.

A moment later, the rumble of the engines grew to a roar and the bomber began to roll down the runway. Tor watched as the unmarked pavement of the runway slid under the nose. Behind him, he heard Tanner mutter something that was lost in the throaty rumble of the four engines at full song. Out of the corner of his left eye, Tor saw the half circle shapes of the Quonset huts of the Sea Bee barracks flash past. The bomber was approaching the end of the paved runway. Underneath Tor, the black of pavement gave way to the pink and gray of PSP covered by coral dust with just the slightest bump of transition.

And then, suddenly, the otter became aware that there was a shadow underneath them. The shadow grew larger and to Tor the holes in the PSP grew smaller. The otter let out a squeak of surprise as he realized that they were actually airborne. Then they were over the water and the wreck of *The Reluctant Dragon* flashed by, completely visible in the shallow water. Tor became aware of odd mechanical sounds: a whine, a hiss, and a clunk that he guessed was the landing gear coming up. Below the otter, the white-tipped waves that surrounded the island grew smaller and smaller as the plane gained altitude.

Tanner winged over to take an easterly course and everyone in the cockpit let out the breaths they'd collectively been holding. Ace yipped, Konner laughed, and even Tanner chuckled.

"Nicely done, Chief," the buck complimented. "Your crews did good work."

"Thanks, Cap," Tor returned. "I'll be sure to pass the word."

It was a good job, Tor thought to himself. A week ago he'd been the new chief, content to be nothing more than Banks's shadow. Now he'd negotiated with two large predators by himself, led his own work crew - even taking initiative on getting the earth-moving going, and was taking his first ever flight. Not bad for a slightly shell-shocked sinking survivor who'd been content to serve out the war hiding behind a beaver.

"Think we'll ever know what this was about?" Ace asked.

"Probably not," Tanner answered. "Heard they're flying in special crews with the new bombers. Commander is some hot-shot colonel from Eurain. Supposed to have led the first big bombing raid over there."

"What about you, Chief?" Ace inquired. "What's next on the Navy's agenda?"

"Dunno really," Tor's nose twitched as the relief that he wouldn't be going back to destroyers fully hit him. But that also meant that he would have to become more of a leader in the Sea Bees - Banks couldn't come up with every project on the base. "There's always the chaplain's jeep."

"It'll keep, Chief," Tanner assured him as he guided the plane back over Springfall. "I want to burn off some fuel before I try and land with all this weight. For now, just relax and enjoy the flight."

Tor settled in and did just that, though he had to ignore the waterspout that sprang up beneath them as they flew over the docks. Damn fool wolves.

*In our world, historians have marveled at how 500 men could conquer an empire of about 500 million people. (Well, European diseases helped.)*

*In "The Night the Stars Fell", KC Alpinus shows what might have happened in an anthropomorphic dimension.*

# The Night the Stars Fell

## by KC Alpinus

"Steady the mast there, Miguel! Don't want any early morning crashes!"

"Aye, Captain Diaz!" The young bull wrapped the frayed cord around his burly hand and pawed at the deck, straining to keep the heavy mast from coming loose. The salty water sprayed his face, but he held tight. He didn't have to hold on for too long before other young bulls joined him and they could safely navigate the rough seas. The Captain nodded, surveying the land through his spyglass as the ship plodded towards the shore. After so many months with an endless ocean view, seeing the horizon and the faint scent of fresh grass made his eyes water.

"How long before we make land?"

The Captain turned to see a gruff, weather-worn bull striding towards him. His beady, brown eyes were narrowed as he stopped beside the Captain, a hooved hand out for the spyglass. The Captain didn't dare protest for the Commander was not one to be trifled with. The Commander stroked his well-groomed beard for a moment while surveying the coastline and then handed it back.

"Not long, sir. Seems like we could pull right up to the shore if the water remains deep," the Captain said, pocketing the spyglass and nodding to the First mate regarding the wheel.

The Commander flared his nostrils and flicked his ears, keeping his gaze on the approaching coast.

"And you're certain of this?"

"The only way to be certain of that would be to keep going and we'll find out there, eh?"

"I'd rather not endanger the fleet. We might need the ships in case this is yet another island. In fact, I have another idea. Slave!"

His gruff shout made a nearby rat squeak and tremble before it backed against a wall.

"Y-yes sir?" the rat said, crouching low onto the deck. His whiskers twitched and his muscles were tense, as he was ready to run should the Commander swing out with a hoof large enough to break him in two.

"One of you recently whelped, did she not?"

"Y-yes sir. It was hard and long, but she came through with a litter of seven."

"Seven," the Commander said, fingering the golden ring in his nose. "That would be seven more mouths to feed, would it not, Captain?"

"Aye, it would, Commander. It'll be rough with rations being as low as they are, but I think we'll be able to-"

The Captain was silenced by the Commander, who motioned for two soldiers. One held a struggling dam rat in his hooved hands while the other had a bundle that held three squeaking rat pups. When the soldier brought them near, the Commander curled his lip and waved him away. The soldier edged to the side of the ship, holding the squirming bundle over the edge.

"One thing that I will not tolerate on this mission is insurrection and impropriety. You have sinned against me and therefore sinned against our Lord and incurred a debt. Captain," he bellowed, "what are the wages of sin, especially aboard this ship?"

"Commander, you can't mean-"

"Sir," the rat pleaded, squirming in the grasp of a third soldier, but his small frame did little to dissuade the burly bull. "Have mercy, m'lord! Don't-"

"Death."

Before the Captain could react, the soldier dropped the bundle into the ocean, where it floated before it was overtaken by the waves. The Captain could only mutely stare at the Commander, the screaming of the dam rat blocked out by his shock. The soldiers then dragged her back below decks, ready to carry out the second half of the punishment. The buck rat wept, his tears leaving sooty trails on his fetid, grimy fur.

"I expect to be obeyed at all times by all who serve me, including slaves. Take him below deck and give him a lash for each remaining waste of rations."

The Commander made to head back to his quarters, but stopped and looked over his shoulder adding, "You'd do well to thank the Lord for his grace, slave, for Commander Eusebio Ávila isn't known for his mercy."

Ávila stomped off, leaving a horrified crew and a weeping rat slave in his wake. The Captain, too mortified to speak, crossed himself and lifted his eyes to the heavens, hoping that the shooting star he saw was an acknowledgement of his silent prayer.

\* \* \*

Two years later.

"I cannot believe you decided to do this, Father."

The yellow jaguar grunted and crossed his paws over his chest, looking away from his ebony daughter. The younger jaguar sighed and applied a poultice to her father's knee, tsking as she did. In the corner, a second jaguar shuffled and flexed his spotted tail, his eyes fixed on the pair.

"I tried to dissuade him, Arrow Stars, but your father was most obstinate. He didn't want to believe the omens I had foreseen."

"Omens?" She looked from the speaker to her father, who was now grooming the fur on his chest, ignoring the discussion. "What omens, Chief Xipili?"

"The one showing the falling of the heavenly bodies and the coming of great change as brought by strange beasts," Xipili replied, scratching under his jaw and shifting again. "A few weeks ago, I saw a great flash of light against the sky; there were so many dazzling, burning lights that it seemed as if the Sky Goddess were leaping down from the heavens to fight against intruders once more. I couldn't believe my eyes, so I took the matter to your father, but he disagreed-"

"I refuse to believe your drunken prophecies!"

"I allowed you to see for yourself, sire. I have checked and confirmed with my other priests, and they all agreed."

Arrow Stars held out her paws, interrupting both males. "Honored Star Chief Xipili, thank you for sharing your findings with us. Emperor Xiuhcoatl treasures the tributes and gifts from the people of Topoxte. Please allow our slaves to see to your every whim until the end of the *Flower Wars*." She snapped her fingers at the frail slaves, who flinched at the sound before shuffling to the Chief.

The yellow jaguar nodded and was led out of the emperor's common area to his own borrowed rooms. When they had left, Arrow Stars turned to her father and sighed.

"Did you at least win?"

The Emperor snarled, banging his heavy paw against the armrest of his chair before hobbling outside to the balcony. Arrow Stars flattened her ears, but she knew arguing was futile. Her father was as headstrong as she was and she'd have better luck negotiating for tributes with the Chontal-Mayans than changing his mind. Nevertheless, she padded to the balcony after her father.

He was leaning against the railing, his tail flicking back and forth as he tossed his beloved obsidian knife in the air before deftly catching it in his paws. He narrowed his eyes when Arrow Stars approached and after a final catch of the blade, he turned away, his fierce eyes gazing out on the bustling waterways that provided transport through the city.

Arrow Stars straightened her sleeveless blouse and brushed her skirt, plucking a gold thread from the material. She wanted to make sure that she was impeccable before she approached her father, but he ignored her. Huffing, she came to rest beside him, her paws dangling off the balcony.

The day was beginning and there were many merchants preparing their wares for market, while slaves and those of the lower classes scurried about. The wind from the lake danced upon his long whiskers, sending a shiver down his spine as he closed his eyes.

"I lost."

"You what?" she asked, flicking her ears back.

"I lost," he repeated, flaring his nostrils and curling his tail downwards. "Xipili told me the news and I disagreed, so I challenged him to a game and lost."

"But-but how, Father? You haven't lost a game in my living memory," Arrow Stars said, her mouth hanging open.

"The Gods didn't agree with my defiance of their will. I have never lost a match against him, but the prophecy couldn't be real. How could I have lost a small game when the Gods have uniquely blessed me?" The Emperor snarled, baring his long teeth. Arrow Stars lowered her eyes and looked away, not daring to move for fear of her father's volatile temper. For a time, no words were spoken between the two, until Arrow Stars sighed and looked up at him.

"What will we do?"

"Nothing, or at least nothing that you should be concerned about," Xiuhcoatl said, looking down at his daughter. "Your focus should be on today's Flower War and watching over Obsidian Fang as he proves himself, not on stars and omens. Your unique skills as a Healer will be prized by such a skilled warrior and maybe future husband."

Arrow Stars crooked a smile at her father and rubbed her face against his shoulder, smearing her face paint on his coat. "Yes, this is true. The Flower Wars are always a perilous time for us, but Obsidian Fang is a good warrior and a shrewd fighter. I'm not sure if he's worthy of me."

Xiuhcoatl looked down to see his daughter's smirking face staring up at him. "As my beloved daughter, I don't think any Mexica is worthy of you, but he seems well-bred and strong."

"Do you think he'll make *Cuāuhocēlōtl* like you did?"

Xiuhcoatl looked away towards the gleaming sun and sniffed the air. "He's found favor with Huitzilopochtli, King of the Rising Sun. But only Tezcatlipoca, the Night Lord, can be certain of his becoming a high warrior and following in my paw prints. I will say that I'd be surprised if he didn't."

"Then let us hope that Obsidian Fang gains the blessings that he needs. I won't stand for a mate that is clumsy and wayward in battle. He will bring back many slaves and tributes for the Sun God," Arrow Stars grinned, looking out towards the horizon. She didn't see her father nod his head solemnly before turning his eyes out towards the coast.

"It is a good thing that you are a girl, Arrow Stars, for I'd hate to be your enemy in battle."

"It's a good thing I am a female, Father, or I would bring home many tributes from my fighting. My arrows would lay waste to many of the Totonac, Chontal-Mayan, and not even the sinister, suffocating cowards of Kowoj with their strong coils would stop me," she said, twitching her tail and lifting her head higher towards the warmth of the sun.

"I know you would. Let's drink to Obsidian Knife's prowess in battle and the Night Lord's blessings."

Arrow Stars growled at a slave to bring them some of the treasured wine-infused chocolate, *xocolatl.* When the slave served it to her, she flicked her paw and dismissed them, sending them back to work. Before she brought the drink to her muzzle, she looked around, admiring how the morning sun gleamed off the gold of the buildings, setting her world ablaze. Someday she would be co-ruler of all she surveyed.

"War is life for we Mexica, Father, and in death, there is rebirth."

"Yes, Arrow Stars, war is life for we Mexica."

\* \* \*

The combatants faced each other, their chest muscles heaving from exertion. They were in the center of the stadium, their backs facing thousands of spectators as they eyed each other. The one on the left hissed, the sunlight glinting off his scaly pelt, as he waved the blunt club in front of him. He snapped his long snout and smiled at his opponent, motioning him closer.

"Why not rush me, Mexica Warrior? Afraid you'll meet your fate between my jaws, like the others you threw at me?" He swished his long, green tail and snapped at the jaguar before him. "If they were the best that Xiuhcoatl had to offer, then his empire will crumble before the year is out. I, Prickly Pear, will laugh as I crush your head between my jaws!"

The jaguar flicked his ears, his body attuning itself with the wind that batted at his loin cloth, but otherwise was immutable. His eyes surveyed the earthen stadium floor, taking in the scene around them. Five warriors lay on the ground, groaning and bleeding from various wounds, while a sixth was sprawled in a heap, his eyes glazed over in death. They had been foolish indeed, misjudging the power and strength of the Totonac prince, and it had cost them.

He swung his club, a massive piece of carved wood and deadly obsidian, as he paced in front of the caiman. Like all Totonacs, Prickly Pear's scaly hide provided him with an impenetrable armor that the others had taken for granted. That temerity had cost them their health and possibly their lives.

Obsidian Fang snarled, swinging the club again, his topaz eyes focused on his opponent. For a moment, he could hear nothing but the roar of the crowd and the thundering of blood in his veins. Taking a deep breath, Obsidian Fang clenched the thick muscles in his legs and leapt at the Totonac prince, his jaws gaping in an ear-piercing scream.

Prickly Pear growled at him and swung his weapon, catching the jaguar across the chest. Obsidian Fang had anticipated this, so he wrapped his body around the club and clung to it, thrusting out with his own weapon. The sharp obsidian scraped off the caiman's hide, but did little to slow Prickly Pear down. As the wind was pushed from Obsidian Fang's diaphragm, he could hear Prickly Pear's roaring laughter as he was thrown across the ground.

Sucking in air and gasping from the pain, Obsidian Fang watched the world spin as he rolled before coming to a stop and dimly he could hear jeers and booing from the crowd. As he struggled to focus, he could make out the dark outline of the caiman as he hefted Obsidian Fang's club and snapped it in two with his powerful jaws.

"Is this the best that the Mexica have to offer?" Prickly Pear taunted, spreading his arms wide at the scattered warriors. "Are these all that the mighty Xiuhcoatl can offer? You're not worthy to be gifts for Huitzilopochtli, merciful God of War and the Rising Sun of Victory! I will bathe in your blood, you-"

The caiman stopped and looked down, his eyes wide before a loud scream rent the air of the stadium. The jaguar had sunk long fangs into his legs muscles and was twisting his head back and forth, tearing at his flesh. The caiman screamed and tried to slam his club into Obsidian Fang's chest, but the nimble jaguar let go and scuttled between Prickly Pear's legs, his long, spotted tail giving him balance. Prickly Pear tried to turn and catch the jaguar, but he lacked the speed and strength of his opponent, so he only grasped at air.

Obsidian Fang climbed onto the back of the caiman and clung to him, digging his sharp claws into the spaces between his scales, biting and clawing at him. Prickly Pear swung and grasped at him, but the jaguar was too close to his body. He sensed what was happening and used the club to swing it at him. It missed and at the last moment, he released all the tension in his body and fell back, hoping to stun the jaguar. Just as his knees buckled beneath him, he felt those sharp teeth sink into the base of his skull and the edges of his vision began to darken…

"Lift him! We need to work quickly while he's still alive!"

Obsidian Fang felt the massive weight of the caiman lifted off him and his chest swelled with life-saving air. Gasping, he curled onto his side, coughing as he watched the Priest recite the ancient incantation as he held an obsidian blade above the exposed chest of Prickly Pear. He turned away as the blade plunged into the chest of the struggling prince, tearing him open as they sought their most precious prize.

"Sons and Daughters of the Rising Sun, we offer the heart of the enemy, taken unwillingly!" Xipili's glorious headdress bobbed up and down as he held up the heart to the cheers of the stadium. Someone pressed a dagger to Obsidian Fang's shoulder, drawing blood and presented it to Xipili as well. He nodded and then held the dagger up to the cheering crowd.

"Blood of the warrior, offered most willingly!" The crowd cheered more and Obsidian Fang noted the dancing and chanting of those around him before he was lifted to his paws and presented with the warm heart of his opponent.

"Eat, Brave Warrior Obsidian Fang, and ensure our safety for the next fifty-two years!" The heart was pressed against his spotted muzzle and as he lifted his eyes, he could see the smiling gaze of those around them. Winning this battle ensured the safety and longevity of his people for years to come; consuming Prickly Pear's heart had earned him the Night Lord's favor.

Wheezing, he sank his teeth into the tough, warm flesh and chewed, feeling strength and life flow back into his body. Xipili nodded and walked off while attendants applied salve to his wounds and turned him.

One trickled a bitter broth down his throat, making him gag before he swallowed it.

"Ugh." Obsidian Fang laid his head back against the dusty floor of the stadium and closed his eyes, the stomping of padded paws filling his ears. He tried to lift a paw to lift himself up, but a bolt of pain flashed through his shoulder, making him grimace and bare his long teeth.

"It's best if you try not to exert yourself. You've done a great deed for your people, Brave Warrior, and deserve to be catered to."

The warrior looked up to see the glorious plumed headdress of Emperor Xiuhcoatl swishing above him. The emperor's spotted face beamed down at him and he spread his arms wide before turning to face the sun and the crowds.

"Who among the Mexica will honor themselves by caring for this brave warrior of Tezcatlipoca?"

Obsidian Fang's eyes closed and he groaned from the effort, but didn't have long as the hands of servants lifted him into the air and made to carry him out of the arena. As his tail dragged along the ground, his eyes caught the gleam of a dark pelt and a bright smile before he was carried away. As they traveled, he could hear the chants of "War is Life!" wafting behind him.

\* \* \*

"Lay him on the table."

The slaves nodded and placed the muscled warrior on a table, taking care to not give him any unnecessary jolts. Arrow Stars padded around the room, opening jars and mixing herbs together. The fragrant aromas wafted through the air until it filled Obsidian Fang's leathery nostrils, making him stir in his sleep. Arrow Stars's ebony face brightened as she watched the warrior groan and writhe on the table.

"Shh, now, don't want you to hurt yourself,"

Golden eyes rolled up to gaze into hers and a pained smiled crossed his face. "No, never that."

Arrow Stars hugged him around his powerful neck, drawing a gasp and a groan from him. "Oh! Sorry!"

"I just fought the Totonac Prince, a little tenderness is warranted," he smiled, pressing his powerful limbs against the table to raise his upper body. "Not that I really need it."

"Sure, you don't," Arrow Stars chuckled, pressing her palm into his chest to lay him back down, "I thought he had you for a moment."

"Me? Never! He was far too fat and besides, I fought Fire Snake during my training with no big deal, and he's as big as that dumb caiman. I'm too tough to let that happen." Obsidian Fang fixed Arrow Stars with a glare, but when he flexed the muscles of his chest, they both burst out laughing, though the warrior grimaced and laid his head back down.

"If you're in one-piece to accept your promotion, I'll take a few lumps and bruises on you," she replied, liberally applying some of the poultice she had been mixing onto some of his deeper wounds. He winced and growled under his breath, but the gentle licks on his ears caused his whiskers to relax. The silence that settled between the two was welcomed, broken only by Obsidian Fang's infrequent growls and grimaces, until Arrow Stars stepped back, nodding her head.

"Yeah, I think you'll be good enough to show off tonight,"

"Good," he said, swinging his legs over the side of the table and flexing the muscles in his shoulder. "I just want to be able to stand before everyone at the feast and accept the honor. I hope the tributes I captured were enough."

"I'm certain they are more than worthy. You've ensured that we won't have to use slaves as sacrifices for the feast. Father will certainly give you praise for your feats," Arrow Stars said, her green eyes sparkling as she dressed the area, "among other things."

Obsidian Fang pulled her around to his front and wrapped his large paws around her full waist, his eyes glowing from the afternoon sunlight. "You think he'll finally announce me as his successor then?"

"He doesn't have a reason to deny you that; you brought down one of the most formidable tribes in the area. Father says that you've made it possible for us to offer a mighty sacrifice of slaves to Huitzilopochtli for months to come and even quelled a possible rebellion."

"It was nothing," Obsidian Fang said, lifting the corner of his mouth and smiling, "the Totonac are stupid, boastful water creatures; they brag about their feats, but on land, their strength and speed leave something to be desired. Now if we were in the water…" He tilted his head back and laughed it off. "I'm just glad that we were on land; capturing him in the water was no small task."

"I know," Arrow Stars purred, wrapping her arms around his neck and resting her head on his shoulder. "I thought I almost lost you during that battle. When he swung that club down at you, I-I don't even-"

Obsidian Fang placed a clawed paw against her ebony lips and laid his head against her chest, sighing and flaring his nostrils to take in more of her sweet scent. "The Gods won't have me, at least not yet. I have come too far and sacrificed much to win your heart; I won't be swayed when it comes to winning your father's respect, not even by death."

They remained there, their breaths synchronized and their eyes locked until someone scratched at the door. Both cats jumped, their ears swiveling around while their hearts beat out a sharp staccato.

The door opened and a young deer, a Yokot'an captive, with her head bowed and her eyes lowered to the ground, entered. She closed the door behind her and waited until she was acknowledged before speaking.

"Mighty Emperor Xiuhcoatl, His Noble Anger, He Who Fights Alongside Tezcatlipoca, and He Who Is Honored by Huitzilopochtli, requests the presence of you both at dinner. He says that we have very special guests dining with us this evening and doesn't want you to be late."

"That'll be all then, Soft Grass," Arrow Stars said, waving a paw to dismiss the deer, who nodded in return and backed out the brightly colored door. Arrow Stars turned backed to the warrior and pressed her head against his once more and sighed.

"Let us prepare for the feast then."

* * *

"Welcome, People of the Sun! We are honored to have our beloved Emperor, He Who is Praised by Huitzilopochtli, He Who Hunts Alongside Tezcatlipoca, and He Who Watched the Stars Fall! We honor him and his triumphs with this sumptuous feast! We who are not worthy offer our Life Water to the Sky Lord and hope our paltry gifts can slake his mighty thirst! In return, we accept the fruits of the earth, sea, and sky!"

Tendile walked in a grand circle, clapping his massive paws summoning the servants who removed the palm fronds from the food, revealing the mouth-watering dishes. On one table, there was pepper-roasted haunch, ash-baked river trout, glazed suckling pigs, and a myriad of soups, sauces, grains, and other savory dishes from the bounty of the forest. Arrow Stars huffed and licked the fur between her paws. Though long-winded, Tendile was well-versed in the art of captivating his audience, but must he do it at this banquet and before her father announced Obsidian Fang's new title?

Arrow Stars fought the urge to groom her dark coat (the taste of the brilliant blue and green dyes would ruin her already frail appetite) and waved off a slave who tried to refill her cup. This wasn't the time for long-winded speeches, or at least Arrow Stars's swiveling ears and short growls at the wait staff hinted at this. This was a time of action and of commendation, but as well as the fruition of her long plans. Surely, some could claim that she was being a tad spoiled by being impatient at Tendile's flowery speech and presentations, but she wanted this to be over. She wanted to be with him after so much anxiety and waiting.

Her eyes scanned the lavish banquet hall until she found Obsidian Fang. She could feel the tension ease from her limbs when emerald eyes aligned with topaz. He ran his tongue along his muzzle while shaking his head ever so slightly before looking away.

"You know, if I hadn't given up betting so long ago, I'd place a lot of coinage on that warrior having caught more than just a passing interest from you."

"What?" Arrow Stars jumped and turned, her gaze lighting on the striking figure of a strange feline, who also had spots but lacked the ringlets that were prized by her people. He also had tufted ears and a short bob for a tail, instead of the nimble weapon that gave her people balance in the trees. She had not met him, but she knew of him. He had only recently come into their realm from someplace far away.

"Steady Knife," he said, holding out an oversized paw and tossing the magnificent ruff of fur around his head. "Pleased to make your acquaintance."

When she didn't shake his paw in return, he laughed and licked his whiskers. "I have to remember that my customs go over your heads. No matter, my comment still stands. You seem charmed by that warrior over there."

"And why shouldn't I be?" she retorted, splaying her ears and narrowing her eyes, "Obsidian Fang is a good warrior and has won many battles; he will make any female a fine mate and head of a new lineage."

"Aye, you Mexica and your love of lineage and social standing. I thought going to an entirely new world would help me escape it," he said, leaning back in his chair and propping his oversized paws on the table, drawing a few hisses from nearby guests, "but alas, I did not. Can't ever escape it, huh?"

"Escape what? And I'll ask you to keep your dirty paws off our banquet tables. I don't know where you're from, but it's a wonder the Gods haven't killed you outright for your disrespect of feasting tables!"

The strange feline shrugged and drank from the glass, but took his paws down, winking at Arrow Stars. "The Gods won't have me because they aren't ready for me just yet. I was born during a time of great turmoil and I will return to them during a time of great turmoil. Being killed at a banquet for being a dirty lout won't quite cut it. But I see that I've disturbed you some and for that, I apologize. It wasn't my intention to upset someone as comely as you."

Arrow Stars lifted her head higher and flared her nostrils at Steady Knife, but allowed him to continue his inebriated rant.

"Nevertheless, he has a good eye for beauty; I envy him for it. I've traveled to so many new worlds, but the women of your world have a certain beauty and freedom that I'm not used to. I wish the females back home enjoyed the same freedoms. Ah well, here comes the roasted boar!"

Steady Knife grinned and turned to the great tray full of meats, fruits, and sumptuous wines, his loud, braying laughter scaring some of the cubs, who scurried away on their awkward paws, only to scamper back to inspect this curious stranger.

Arrow Stars twitched her tail back and forth, mulling over Steady Knife's words. If he had seen that they had more than a passing interest in each other, then who else had noticed? It was forbidden for Arrow Stars, as one of Xiuhcoatl's First Daughters, to show an interest in any of the High Warriors before the results of the Flower Wars or Huitzilopochtli's Feast Night was observed. She would be sent to the Wailing Place, her very blood seen as unfit to fuel the Gods and sustain the world for her treachery.

"The Gods be praised! I am but a humble servant, subject to the whims of my betters!"

There were more than a few hearty laughs and chuckles as Xiuhcoatl stood and stretched his arms wide to welcome them. His booming speech and flowery words flowed down from the dais that he was seated upon, bringing Arrow Stars back to the world around her. They were clearing the tables for the Presentation of Gifts, the time for her father's announcement drawing near.

"I hope that my brothers and sisters under the sun have eaten and drunk until their bellies sagged with the bounty of the forest; I know that I have had more than my share. So, it is on a full belly, that I may present our newest High Warriors. Bring them in front of me so that we may honor them!"

There was the scuffling of paws on the stone-slab floor as more than a few warriors stood and rushed to line themselves up in front of their Emperor. Some were wearing various slings and bandages, evidence of their earlier trials, but they refused to show any weakness of fatigue. Standing at the center of the line was Obsidian Fang, his neck adorned with his golden warrior's collar and his club hanging from the leather strap along his waist. Seeing his proud figure, Arrow Stars lifted her head a little higher and shook herself, the shells and feathers of her own headdress tinkling in her ears.

"Ah yes," Xiuhcoatl said, clapping his paws in front of him and dipping his feather headdress, "these are the best that we could ever hope to be blessed with. Tezcatlipoca would be pleased at the skill and shrewdness that you all showed during today's Flower War. No lives were taken unnecessarily, but no warrior showed more strength and prowess than Obsidian Fang!"

The elder jaguar stepped down from the dais and stopped in front of the younger, yet more muscular cat. Xiuhcoatl placed his large paws on Obsidian Fang's shoulders and nodded.

"No finer a fighter could we Mexica have asked for; I see why the Gods have uniquely favored you. Praise Obsidian Fang because his teeth sliced through Prickly Pear better than our blades!"

The room erupted in cheers and Emperor Xiuhcoatl nodded for the Priests to come forward. They covered Obsidian Fang's broad chest in dazzling red and black war paints, tattooing his spotted pelt with symbols of power and authority. When they had stepped away, he looked as fearsome and as proud as the Emperor, who bared his long fangs in a grin and clasped his paws against Obsidian Fang's shoulders.

"Behold Obsidian Fang! The Gods have shown you much favor and have seen fit that you will serve them and our people well when I travel to the Land of Mists. They have chosen well, so all that is left, is a mate worthy of your strength and power."

Arrow Stars's ears splayed and she could feel the heat rushing to her face as she rose from her seat and padded towards her father's other outstretched paw. As her ebony paw was joined with his spotted one, Arrow Stars tried her best to feign surprised and excitement.

"Have my daughter, Arrow Stars, and may you both reign well when my time on this plane has come to an end." Xiuhcoatl nodded and stepped back, the thunderous applause of the room filling their ears. Obsidian Fang averted his eyes for a moment, but when Arrow Stars hugged him around his neck, he rumbled out his happiness from deep within his throat.

"I knew it would come to pass. I am yours and you are mine," Arrow Stars purred into his ear, which he returned by rubbing his cheek alongside her face. When he pulled back, there were more roars and streamers were thrown about, along with the nimblest of acrobats performing, but Xiuhcoatl waved them down, calling for calm.

"Peace everyone, I have yet to present the gifts for this young couple."

With a slow wave of his tail, he ushered in many more slaves and servants, who pulled and pushed carts carrying mountain of jewels, spices, sacred wood for scratching, and more precious obsidian weaponry. These were standard fare for engagement gifts, but the last two caught Arrow Stars's eyes.

They were unknown, muscular creatures who had rings in their noses and long ears that flopped as they tossed their powerful necks. They smelled of sickness and sweat, causing guests to cover their muzzles and back away.

"Where did you find these men?!"

Heads turned to see Steady Knife coming towards him, his ears laid against his head and his eyes narrowed. Every hair stood straight up on his body and Arrow Stars swore that if the short cat had a long tail, he would have assuredly been twitching it behind him.

"There should be no more of them! Only I and another survived our expedition; no one else should be here!"

While the others murmured, Steady Knife stopped squarely in front of the Emperor and pointed at them. "How did they get here?"

"You'd be amazed at what can happen when you do not forsake our Lord and Savior, Gonzalo."

The Mexica feasters parted to allow a tall, broad-shouldered creature to pass through. His leathery nose twitched in the cool night air and two identical horns that ended in sharp points, sprouted from his forehead. He strode through the doors of the banquet hall, flanked by two massive and similar looking creatures. They all carried long swords at their waists and wore strange clothing.

Following beside these strange creatures with hooves, was a feline, similar in make-up and markings to Steady Knife, but he seemed more haggard and fatigued than her colorful dining partner. He licked his whiskers and nodded at Tendile and her father, before waving a paw to indicate the strange creatures.

"My Lord, may I preset Eusebio Ávila, a Commander of far-off Spanÿän. Commander Ávila has heard of the feats of your..." He paused, licking his whiskers again and swallowing, "kingdom. He wishes to-"

His speech became unintelligible as he lapsed into a strange language that grated against Arrow Stars's ears. There were murmurs and various whispers, her Mexica flattening their ears and twitching their tales in agitation. The slaves that these strangers brought looked indistinguishable from their captors, but rarely did the tributary villages turn over slaves of their own people, not unless they had suffered unbearable shame during the Flower Wars.

"He wishes to pay proper tribute to a worthy Emperor such as yourself."

A Yokot'an female stepped forward and placed a hooved hand against the shoulder of the large male and nodded at the strange feline.

"Aguilar's command of the master tongue is rudimentary at best," the doe nodded and waved at the feline, who sniffed and turned his head. "Forgive my intrusion, I am Malinalli and I can speak where he cannot. He wishes to present these slaves during this honored festival of Huitzilopochtli. They are bull warriors who have heard of the Sun God's feats and wish to die in the master's service."

"Commander Ávila wishes to-he wishes to-"

"He wishes to discuss his conquest of the lesser tribes and how to share in the glory of our Sun God with others, as well as his plans for the subjugation of the Tlaxcalans," Malinalli interrupted, her soft eyes flickering to the largest bull.

Tendile looked at Xiuhcoatl, who raised an eyebrow but inclined his head, his crown of feathers and gold rustling. Tendile lifted his head and gave a bemused smile, his golden eyes wide and glittering.

"We are honored to receive their sacrifice and it won't be forgotten. Emperor Xiuhcoatl would like for you all to gaze upon his wealth and the bounty of the Sun God, so he wishes to open his home to them. We shall show them a feast and festival that they have never seen before and would never see again!"

There was much clapping and agreement, but while Emperor Xiuhcoatl looked pleased, Steady Knife hissed and scowled. Arrow Stars turned to Obsidian Fang, whose face flashed concern, but shifted back to his usual stoicism. When Arrow Stars's eyes found his, he nodded his head slightly but then didn't move. They would discuss this later, but for now, they would be patient and watch. Tendile was speaking again as he waved in more slaves, who plodded along, the weight of the massive silver and gold disc weighing them down.

"Our Lord wishes to welcome you with proper gifts, so he presents this to your Master as this gift. May we have a wonderful new ally within our empire!"

There was more clapping and whopping as the slaves presented Ávila with the massive disc. His men took it eagerly, their floppy ears flapping as they moved to flank the dark bull. Despite the celebration, there was something about Ávila that disheveled Arrow Stars's fur. She wasn't alone in her unease, as she could see Steady Knife growling and spitting before stomping out of the room.

As she lifted her wrist to groom her dark fur she couldn't help but notice the deep, sad eyes of the doe following her. When she reached out to accept the paw of her new mate and future emperor, those same eyes stalked her through the banquet hall, the wanton hunger causing her flesh to writhe beneath her pelt. Even hours later, as the deep rhythmic snores of Obsidian Fang filled their marital chamber and the rest of the palace slept, she couldn't shake the feeling of unease that she had viewed from Malinalli's eyes.

* * *

"I can't believe how much you've let your archery fall by the wayside."

Arrow Stars released the string on her arrow and rested the arrowhead against the stone marker. Obsidian Fang crossed his paws over his broad chest and smiled at her, his long, dagger-like teeth gleaming in the early morning sun.

"You know I'm right," he said, walking up behind her and tapping her arm.

"I know," she sighed, raising her arm to lift her ornate headdress out of her eyes, "but it's been more than taxing these past few weeks trying to accommodate these foreign warriors and their insufferable friends from lower castes, all while briefing father on how things are going with the lady nobles of the city. Some things have fallen to the wayside and the slaves are demanding more lands and more mobility within the city-states. If Father didn't spend so much time drinking and pouring gold onto these newcomers, I guess I would have more time."

"Hmph," he grunted, lifting her shoulders and correcting her form, "that's no excuse to let something this important lag, beloved. I work hard and train the younger warriors every morning before daybreak and have endured the same. What empire would allow their next empress to have a bad archery form and neglect her fighting skills?"

"The same one that allowed their next emperor to bite through the back of an enemy's head," she shot back, drawing the arrow back and releasing it. The arrow flew some 250 feet before embedding itself in the limestone of a building. Yet another arrow that had missed its mark.

"Bah! Another one, Sprouted Blossom!"

A slave stepped forward and placed an arrow into her outstretched paw. As she notched it in her bow, she looked back over her shoulder and huffed. When Obsidian Fang lifted an eyebrow, but nodded for her to continue, she let the arrow soar through the air, landing square in the center of the target.

"See? It was only a matter of getting back into the habit. It just took a little bit of practice," Arrow Stars smirked, placing the large bow on the ground and leaning against it, her tail curling and uncurling as she preened in front of her mate. She nodded to Sprouted Blossom to retrieve the arrow and licked down the soft fur on her chest, the cheekiness of her actions clear.

"Bragging is unbecoming, dear," Obsidian Fang sniffed and after stringing his own bow, he notched an arrow and released the string. The arrow landed squarely in the middle of the target, quivering beside hers. He gave his toothy grin and Arrow Stars snorted at him before she was enveloped in his powerful arms. "I'm glad your beauty more than makes up for your haughtiness."

"Very funny," she replied, cuffing him under his jaw and drawing a chuckle from him. For a moment, they stood there, enjoying the warmth and comfort of the other until Obsidian Fang began lapping at her face, smoothing her dark, sleek fur down and eliciting several chuffs from her. As she looked up to gaze at his sturdy jaw and strong features, a piercing scream cut through the air. Jumping away from her mate, her head swiveled around the courtyard, looking for the source of the scream, until her eyes landed on Sprouted Blossom.

The slave girl was crouched on the ground, crying out as one of the bulls bellowed at her and pawed the ground. He raised his fist to strike her again, but before he could, Obsidian Fang was barreling towards him. Arrow Stars had already strung another arrow and let it fly, the obsidian tip slicing some of the hairs of his beard off before embedding itself in the ground. As he turned around to identify his attacker, Obsidian Fang was there, his spotted arm clenching the fist of the bull's. The bull bellowed but Obsidian Fang wouldn't be dissuaded, so he released his own ear-piercing scream in response, rising to the challenge.

"How dare you raise your fist to me, cat?" the bull spat, his black eyes boring into those of the warrior's. He moved to punch the jaguar, but soon found a sharp blade pressed against his neck.

"You-stranger!" Obsidian Fang spat, his words faltering with his unease of the language, but the intent remaining. "No...hit...Flower! Protect!"

"I'll strike whomever I want! She is beneath me, like the rest of you savages, and she got in my way!"

"This not what we agree to," Arrow Stars panted, skidding to a stop behind them, her headdress forgotten in the dirt. "Slaves have spirit, not just dead limbs. You no treat them like this!"

"Out of my way, female! I do not parlay with savages and those who worship false gods, but I will be damned to the hottest pits of hell before I let a woman dictate my actions!" The bull bellowed again and tossed his head, aiming his large horns at the warrior. The jaguar had anticipated this and closed his jaws around one of the bull's horns, his claws scratching at the bull's face. His powerful jaws twisted around it, making the bull roar in anguish. Arrow Stars tried grabbing her mate around the waist to pull him off, but he rolled his powerful limb and sent her flying.

As she lay dazed and disoriented, the sweet scent of grass filling her nostrils, she could make out Obsidian Fang and the bull scuffling, the jaguar male seeming to gain the upper hand. Just as he was about to sink his powerful canines into the neck of the bull, Malinalli galloped into the area and fired off some of the rapid language of the bull's. The bull bellowed at her but backed off, facing Obsidian Fang. His eyes blazed in the afternoon sunlight and he promised retribution, but stormed out of the courtyard.

"Are you okay?" The concerned muzzle of Obsidian Fang came into view. He cradled Arrow Stars's head in his lap while the doe came over, offering a cup of water to her.

"My sincerest apologies, warrior. Ignacio has a horrible temper and an even fouler disposition. He didn't mean to hurt her."

"You need to get your lord to enforce some discipline among his men," Obsidian Knife growled. "Had he have been among my warriors, I would have sunk my teeth into his throat and given his blood as a gift to the gods."

The doe's eyes flashed, but she pressed a cloth to Arrow Stars's face and shook her head. "I'm sorry, it won't happen again."

"Are you sure? Those bulls do not respect our ways. They expect everyone to cater to them. This is not *our* way, Yokot'an," Obsidian Fang hissed, nuzzling Arrow Stars who clutched a paw to her head and sat up. "If she had been hurt, I would have poured my wrath onto all of you."

"Obsidian Fang, no," Arrow Stars said, touching the tense shoulder of her mate. "We don't need that. I'm not hurt, just a little stunned, but I'll be fine."

Malinalli's face brightened and she eagerly offered a flask to the jaguar. "Here, drink this. It'll help the head pains go away."

While Arrow Stars drank and Obsidian Fang ran his rough tongue over her velvety fur, Malinalli sighed, her shoulders slumping. "It's been pure hell dealing with those beasts."

"So why do you stay? You could have run away long before now and lived among the Empire," Obsidian Fang snorted, his eyes narrowing. "You picked a horrible side to root for."

"It's more than that, warrior; I was promised my freedom in exchange for helping them understand you. I was taken from my family when I was small and forced to live among my *people*. I was taught how to think, speak, act in favor of the nobles, lest my nose be cut off and my face disfigured for any defiance. You all claim that we're of one people, united under the Sun God, and yet you decide who is superior to whom."

Arrow Stars opened her muzzle to speak, but no words would come. The Yokot'an wasn't wrong, but having their customs for demanding obedience from their lessors laid bare lit a fire within the black jaguar.

"It's so easy for one who was born into a life of luxury and privilege to dictate what others should do," Malinalli added, her long ears turned pointing behind her. "Funny how you rebel when others make a mockery of *your* customs and a slave seeks to defy *your* laws to survive."

Obsidian Fang growled under his breath and even Arrow Stars found herself grasping at the right retort, but how could she have responded? The doe was correct: slaves *were* traded throughout the empire with little thought for their feelings or opinions, so why wouldn't this one leap at the opportunity to gain her freedom, even if it were at the hand of invaders?

"You're right," Arrow Stars sighed, struggling to her paws, "it's easy for me to suggest what you should do without having gone through your circumstances. I don't agree with your choices, but I can't blame you for them. Still, I do not like these invaders and how they treat our slaves as nothing. Our ways of life may be brutal and demanding, but our slaves are given great honor and respected as members of our Empire. I'm going to speak with my father."

The doe glared at Arrow Stars before turning around and heading towards the soldiers' quarters. Before she got too far, she looked back over her shoulder. "It must be nice to hand out the truth that you see as absolute; I hope that works out well for you."

Before Arrow Stars and Obsidian Fang could call her back, Malinalli had bounded over a garden hedge and darted out of the courtyard. The jaguar pair looked after her for a moment, until Obsidian Fang flicked an ear backwards and sighed, the blasting of a horn summoning him.

"I'm needed for afternoon training; are you going to be okay seeing to your father without me?"

"I should be fine," she sighed, rubbing the spot on her head, "as long as I don't do anything overexerting."

Obsidian Fang gave a short nod before speaking. "Just make sure that he understands what has happened here. Guests or not, we don't abuse our slaves or show such disrespect to hosts."

*  *  *

Arrow Stars straightened the elaborate headdress that sat atop her head, fluffing the fur around her neck out in the cool, evening breeze that circled the hall way. She sniffed once, grimacing from the noxious odor that emanated from beneath the door. It stank of stale sweat, dirty fur, old vegetables, and *xocolatl.*

She pressed her ears against her head and curled her lip at a soldier who leered at her while making an obscene gesture as he stumbled out of the banquet hall. These "visitors" were abusing guest privileges and no one had corrected them. Her father had to have been aware of this, because she remembered his slaughter of a visiting noble who'd disrespected the patron lord of the city. Why was he so oblivious now? She would see her father and bring this disrespect to his attention.

She lifted her paw and knocked against the heavy, wooden door and was greeted by a bull with bloodshot eyes.

"What do you want?" he belched, drawing a hiss from the Mexica princess.

"Father...I see him," Arrow Stars demanded, her eyes narrowed as she flexed her claws within their sheaths, resisting the urge to use them.

"Father? That would make you some sort of princess, right?" The bull reached out to touch her soft pelt with a grimy hoof and was rewarded with two swift strikes across his leathery muzzle. He bellowed in pain and raised a hand to strike at her, but someone called him back.

"Tomás, let her enter. We can't be rude now, can we?"

The bull snorted and tossed his neck, but allowed her to enter. She growled under her breath and pushed past him, her jaw dropping when the entirety of the room came into view.

The ornate carvings, so lovingly crafted into the wall, had been smeared with chewed grass, food, and other unmentionable muck. The floors had been scuffed by countless hooves scratching over them and in more than a few instances, the glittering jewels that represented the eyes of the beloved Gods had been plucked out, leaving vacuous holes in their wake.

"What have they done?" she gasped, clasping a paw to her muzzle, willing the tears that welled up in her eyes to not spill over. Had they no morals, no fear of the terrible and awesome powers of the divine?

"Arrow Stars, welcome! Come to see your father and greet our visitors, yes?"

Arrow Stars flattened her ears, the coarse language of the foreigners sounding like the baying of coyotes, turning her stomach when she saw that the language came from her father's own spotted muzzle. He lazed about, his muscular body sprawled across the armrests of his golden throne, his ornate headdress askew on his head. His words were slurred, as if he had grown too lazy to put effort into pronouncing his words.

When she approached, Xiuhcoatl held a goblet of xocolatl out to her, beckoning her to drink. She curled her lip at him, pushing the chocolaty wine away.

"Is there somewhere that we can speak, alone?" she asked, the sound of their native tongue comforting her and providing a layer of protection.

"What for, daughter? We are among friends!" He raised his goblet to hearty bellows and snorts from the gleeful bulls.

"There are some things that are for Mexica ears only, Father. I know that you love these newcomers and the gifts that they bring," she said, motioning towards the mounds of fire sticks and glass, "but I need my father's words now."

Xiuhcoatl nodded his head, his hazy eyes seeming to focus on his daughter, but as he made to stand, the largest bull stood, the females that had been lounging around him hissing and slinking away at being disturbed. He stroked his beard and sauntered over to the dais, interrupting the conversation. He had countless pieces of gold adorning his horns and his face. Atop his head was a crown like her father's, complete with the sacred feathers of sovereignty.

"Is everything okay, Sir Xiuhcoatl?" His voice seemed placating, but it made the fur on the back of Arrow Stars's neck and spine stand on end. "It seems as if something is bothering your daughter. Perhaps I or my men can be of some service?"

Arrow Stars's eyes flashed and she pressed her ears against her head. He was the cause of all of this and she told him as much.

"You! You and-and bulls bother! Disrupt us! No...no respect for Gods! No respect for slaves!"

"My apologies. It seems that my men have upset her. I know that your females are allowed a little more freedom, but perhaps some time laying down will calm her. I, Commander Ávila, will see to it that she is protected. Being around so many males may have startled her delicate sensibilities and caused her to give in to hysterics."

Most of Ávila's words were too complex to translate with her limited grasp of their language, but what she did understand made her lunge at him, her claws unsheathed. How dare he disrespect her, the daughter of the mighty emperor and sworn sovereign of her people? She would shred his flesh and char his heart for the offense!

Powerful paws and hooves grasped her before she could sink her claws into his smug face and held her. Her father had leapt to his paws and bounded down the dais, his eyes blazing.

"Arrow Stars! You have shamed your father and our guests! Out of my sight until you have learned to respect our guests and the words of men!"

Arrow Stars struggled against the warriors and soldiers that held her, but despite the fire that blazed within her, she was no match for them. As she was removed from the room, she saw her father clasp Ávila on the back, the pair laughing like old friends while a bull pulled a statue down and removed some of the gold that adorned it, sending the entire room into uproarious laughter.

After she had been tossed in her room like a rag, she could only lower her head and cry, the tears that slid down her muzzle doing little to ease the hole that had been in her heart. Her father had always made time for her and would have gladly killed for anyone who dared disrespect her, but he had cast her aside, like so much rotten meat. What had these outsiders done to him and why was he allowing this?

Tossing off her headdress and removing the golden collar, she went to the small altar in her bedroom and kneeled, the pale light of the moon frosting her fur and illuminating her green eyes. She bowed her head and whispered a small prayer to her namesake, the proud goddess of the stars.

*Please, Beloved Goddess, help me in this sinking sand. Help me to help my father see these men are no good for our people. Help them see...*

As she opened her eyes and looked up, she watched the twinkling stars above her, hopeful that her prayers had been heard and that she could free her father from this sickness that had confused and blinded him.

\* \* \*

"What say you, Arrow Stars?"

The ebony jaguar stopped, the arrowhead that she had been fiddling with falling into the bowl of water. She looked up to see the quizzical faces of Obsidian Fang, Tendile, and a few of the other Mexica nobles. They were seated in a room that was across from one of the water ways and displayed a magnificent view of the city to those who cared to look.

"Wha-I'm sorry, my thoughts are swimming. What did you say?"

"I was asking about how you would like to deal with these intruders," Tendile sighed, splaying his paws wide on the table, "and their treatment of you in front of your father, as well as how we should approach your father. He hasn't listened to any of our counsel for weeks now; he has Totonac, Tlaxcalan, even Yokot'an scum surrounding him! These coyote-tongued intruders must be stopped!"

There were a few snorts and hisses as the others chimed in. Her father's dismissal of all Mexica nobility had caused dissension and frustration within the city, with Obsidian Fang and the other warriors being dispatched daily to quell tensions between the Mexica and their "guests".

"I think we should go before him," Obsidian Fang suggested, his deep voice resonating within the room. "He may be our Emperor and absolute ruler, but he isn't above the will of we Mexica. If we gather an emissary of all of us, he can't turn us away. The Gods wouldn't allow such blasphemy."

"Nor should they!" Tendile banged a paw on the table in front of him, knocking his gilded bowl over and sending a slave scurrying as they tried to clean up the mess. "He'll have to answer us and banish them!"

"Yeah, but what if they don't?"

The cheers of agreement subsided as they turned to look at the lynx who had his large paws propped up on a table, his platted collar tinkling as he filed his claws with an obsidian blade. Steady Knife, feeling the captive glares of his audience, continued. "Hells below, they didn't listen to me when I tried to say something about them."

"What do you mean? Why wouldn't Xiuhcoatl hear our concerns and banish them?"

"Because they've whet their appetites on the gold and jewels of the city; they won't leave until they've swallowed the wealth of the entire Mexica empire, not much unlike a Tlaxcalan who has suffocated their prey, or they have been forcibly removed," Steady Knife sighed, twitching his tufted ears. "They're insatiable for gold and conquest."

"How would you know?" Tendile asked, folding his arms across his chest and curling the tip of his tail.

"Because I used to be one of them," Steady Knife said, turning away from them. "Under the name Gonzalo, I, along with Aguilar, Ávila's chief translator, used to be a scout for the Spanÿän army. We were sent by the King and Queen of my home world, Spanÿän, to investigate the lands and report back to our Governor about any riches or resources we found. Once we gave our reports, the armies would come and overrun the native peoples there, looting, killing, and enslaving people who had only shown us peace."

There were more than a few gasps and breaths that were caught in throats, but when no one moved to stop him, Steady Knife continued.

"We soon met our match. The Tetzcocatl overwhelmed us and Chief Falling Eagle gave our Commander the chance to ransom our freedom. Well, the cowardly bastard balked, saying that 'the Lord gives and takes away', leaving us to our fates. I had never hated someone so much, but I resigned myself to my fate. Aguilar was sold off to a neighboring village, but I stayed and learned from Chief Falling Eagle and in time he granted me my freedom to live as a Tetzcocah warrior. I haven't looked back since, but I haven't forgotten their barbaric ways. I have heard tales of this Ávila; they say that his brutality is second only to his thirst for gold."

"So, what do you suggest?"

"We go to see Xiuhcoatl," Arrow Stars stood, adjusting her skirt and looking around the room. "He may be able to have his new friends escort me out, but he can't ignore the entire city if they're gathered before him. We can't allow this any longer. We will see my father tonight."

"We will need a new leader then," someone shouted from the back of the room and after several moments, one of the slaves, Sprouted Blossom came forward, holding a plumed headdress pull of crimson and purple feathers. She knelt before Arrow Stars and lifted her bright eyes towards her.

"You are one of the last ones with the blood of the Gods flowing through your veins, so it is fitting that you should lead us. We are in troubling times and a stubborn, audacious leader is needed."

"I-I-this isn't what we- "

"Why not? You showed great courage when it came to seeing this butcher Ávila and standing up to him," Tendile said, crossing his paws and sticking out his chest. "More of a leader than your father."

The others purred and chuffed their approval, until Arrow Stars finally looked down at Sprouted Blossom, and placing her paws underneath the slave girl's chin, Arrow Stars raised the slave to her paws.

"If you will accept me as your Empress, then I must grant you your freedom. We will need all the help that we can get and if you all are willing to fight against these invaders, then we should respect you as full Mexica!"

Tears glistened in Sprouted Blossom's eyes as she placed the ornate headdress on top of Arrow Star's head, and stepped away. The gathered nobles and former slaves nodded in agreement and crossed one arm over their shoulders in respect before standing, with some bowing before her.

Obsidian Fang dipped his head and Steady Knife raised an eyebrow but pushed back from the table, his eyes blazing.

"Back home, we don't have women who are as brazen as yourself; pity, though. I think we'd be a lot further along in life if we did," he chuckled before slinking out behind the others.

\* \* \*

Arrow Stars walked down a line of warriors, nobles, and even slaves of the empire, the lights from their torches showing her the way. Her bow was clasped in her paws with a quiver of ornate arrows resting in the quiver on her back. Following close behind her was Obsidian Fang, his obsidian knife at his hip and his club slung over his shoulder. Steady Knife padded after him, his knives the only sound he made as his large paws crossed swiftly over the cobblestones of the courtyard. A burning, unquenchable fire blazed through Arrow Star's body as they marched in front of Xiuhcoatl's balcony. A sleepy-eyed bull placed a hooved hand on his sword hilt and peered over the edge.

"Who goes there?"

"Arrow Stars, She Who is Blessed by the Night Lord, She Who is Bathed in Darkness, and First Daughter or the Mexica!" Arrow Stars shouted, her heart thundering in her chest.

"What do you want?"

With a nod from his mate, Obsidian Fang stepped forward and roared at the bull sentry. "We wish to speak with Xiuhcoatl!"

"He's busy! He will see to you all later," came the gruff reply.

"He will see us now," Arrow Stars said, stepping up beside Obsidian Fang, "by the laws of our Gods and the muscle beneath our pelts, from an Empress to an Emperor, lest we come for him."

The bull sneered, but retreated behind the balcony. He returned a few moments later with Ávila, who snorted and leaned over the balcony.

"He is busy right now, but if you have any messages, I can take them to him."

"You will take him nothing! He will come to us and hear our words!"

The bull snorted, but disappeared, only to be replaced by the Emperor himself. His words were slurred and he wobbled on unsteady paws, a far cry from the proud creature Arrow Stars had seen only days before.

"Wha-what is the meaning of this? What do you all want?"

"We want these intruders gone from our city. We don't believe that you have our best interests at hand, Father, and so I will rule in your stead until your head isn't so cloudy with strong drink and flattering words!"

375

"Arrow Stars, is that you?" Xiuhcoatl mumbled, his eyes narrowing and his ears perched forward on his head to hear through the cheering. "I thought you had been banished to your room. Why are you out here, causing such a scene at this hour?"

"Because we, your people, have grown tired of these 'foreigners' and want them gone from our home. Because your people have chosen me to serve in your stead and lead them to what is right. If you will not do it, we will!" She shouted back, to a chorus of roars and hissing from the citizens. They pressed in close to her and held their torches up in the darkness, illuminating the Emperor's face.

"You-you have no idea what you wish. These men were sent by the Gods to help us for the coming season. The omens foresaw it," he shouted back before turning his back on them. "Go home, all of you. I will see to this in the morning."

A stone whizzed past his shoulder, causing him to stop in his tracks. "What is the-"

Another stone struck the Emperor on his shoulder, causing him to spin around, roaring in pain. "What is the meaning of this? Who would dare strike their Emperor?"

"We would dare! You are no Emperor!" came the resonating roar from beyond the balcony. As Xiuhcoatl peered over the edge of the balcony, he stared down into the gleaming eyes of his people, their spears, daggers, clubs raised in defiance, demanding to be heard.

"We don't want this, Father, but you're leaving us little choice! Either remove these intruders," Arrow Stars said, narrowing her eyes to thin slits and twitching her long tail back and forth, "or we will do it for you!"

She raised her bow and arrows above her head, and she was followed by assenting roars of the Mexica behind her. By the end of this night, they would be rid of these intruders.

\* \* \*

Xiuhcoatl chewed his lip at he paced in front of the ledge. His ears twitched at the sharp clip of hooves on the stone floors. Turning around, he saw Ávila, flanked by his bull soldiers.

"Good, you're here! Help me! Tell them that you've been sent by the Gods to help me usher in a new era!" Xiuhcoatl's eyes were wide and the color had drained from his nose and face. He grasped the front of Ávila's uniform, his claws digging into the fabric.

Ávila snorted and pushed the pleading jaguar off. "This is most unbecoming, Xiuhcoatl. I don't think this will do. Your people need you, but they can't hear you. That speaks about your ability to rule, I would think."

"I-I have always been a good ruler, an unworthy servant of the Gods who I know have sent you. You could help me reason with them and maintain my rule." Xiuhcoatl nodded, his eyes darting from the Commander to the other bulls gathered around.

"Hmm, well, perhaps we may be able to make out a deal...for payment." Ávila murmured, stroking the coarse beard under his jaw.

"Yes, anything to calm them and from becoming angrier!"

The bull grinned, his dull, yellowed teeth glinting in the lights from the torches. "Well, this will take some convincing of my men, but I'm sure they could be persuaded to change their minds, if the price were right."

When the Emperor nodded, Ávila huffed and two of his biggest bulls came forward, lifting Xiuhcoatl up and helping him to the balcony, despite his paws slipping on the stone tiles. They stood beside him as he addressed the rowdy crowd, sneering and displaying rude gestures just out of his line of vision.

Ávila watched, his broad face a mask of concern as he watched the impotent Emperor try to placate his people and failing miserably.

"How goes it, sir?"

"The people are fickle," Ávila said to Aguilar, who stood beside him, watching the Emperor dodge fruits, vegetables, and bits of cloth that climbed over the battlements. "But, they are useful, unlike this puppet Emperor."

"How so?" Aguilar asked, looking up at the bull.

"Well, we've packed a ship full of gold, with more coming. We'll need all of their labor to send all of the treasure back in the new ships that the Totonacs have built."

"That is what the slaves are for, sir. They're just useless workers; they idle when they aren't instructed on the Word or on hard work."

"All who are not under the crown of His Majesty, are slaves; they just don't know it yet. Each as expendable as the last and so few worth their weight in gold."

"Sir?" Aguilar looked at Ávila, who nodded at towards the ledge. The lynx pressed a paw to his muzzle as one of the bulls removed a knife, just as a stone struck Xiuhcoatl on the head. As the Jaguar Emperor fell, the bull snatched the obsidian knife from the Emperor's waist and drew it across his spotted neck, releasing bright, red blood all over his luxurious pelt. When the Emperor's golden eyes had glazed over, they hefted his body off the battlement and clapped their hooved hands, chortling between them.

"Like I said, Aguilar, they're all expendable. I want soldiers at every port and the guns and cannons ready. I want this palace looted and every jewel, cup, and plate placed on our new ships. Leave nothing valuable behind. We shall leave at dawn and may the Lord help any of these heathens that would get in my way."

\* \* \*

Arrow Stars watched as her father's body somersaulted through the air, bouncing off a stone block before crumpling on the unforgiving ground. His plumed headdress landed beside him, obscuring how broken his body was.

The Mexica drew in close, their eyes darting from the balcony to the lifeless, spotted body as they drew in close. Their murmurs raised in pitch until a fierce wail pierced the air right as the obsidian-coated female broke through the crowd, low moans leaping from her chest.

Arrow Stars sank to her paws, her paws grasping at her father's shiny pelt. She clutched at him, her mouth struggling to find the words that threatened to spill from her muzzle like spoiled meat. How did this happen? What were they going to do? What could she do?

The Mexica didn't give her an answer as they morphed into an angry, amorphous mass, full of roaring, screaming feline lungs, unsheathed claws. Nobles and merchant flowed against one another, taking up torches, tearing into the Spanish barracks, sinking their weapons, their claws into any Spanish ally or slave that they could find. They surged into the alleys and byways of the stone city, heading towards the doors of the palace, seeking to drive out the intruders and avenge their Emperor. Meanwhile, Arrow Stars rocked and clutched at her father, wondering what to do. She buried her face in his limp shoulder, oblivious when her Obsidian Fang came and held her close, staying with her. The others had tried to pry her away, but the swipes to their noses had been warning enough. They left her there to cling to her father until she heard a click and the smell of something burning. Arrow Stars looked up to see the bulls standing on the ledge, their weapons aimed at her, while their Commander paced and pawed at the ground.

"We know that you heathens have more gold, so we will strike a deal: load our ships up with gold and make your unruly mob to allow us to leave, or we will slaughter you like the scum you are!"

Arrow Stars glared up at them with bright, green eyes while her people surged around her. Some of them fired arrows and slung stones from slingshots, hitting a few bulls. The bulls bellowed in return and fired into the crowd, sending several jaguars to their knees. Those that survived the initial impact groaned and howled on the ground, clutching bloody stumps or staring blankly into nothingness. The bulls fired their weaponry once more until piercing screams stopped them.

"Enough!" Arrow Stars screamed, her back arched and the fur on her spine standing on end. "We will give you what you want!"

"Arrow Stars, no!" Obsidian Fang growled, squeezing at his bloody stump of a tail.

"Get down, they'll kill you!" Steady Knife yowled, leaping in front of her.

"No, this must end," she said, shrugging the lynx off and standing in front of the ledge, defiance emanating from her body. "I want no more Mexica lives lost because of these monsters. If it is more gold that they want, we will give them all the gold they can handle and then some!"

The crowd slowed and settled, but they dropped their weapons as the bulls opened the doors to the palace and flowed out, bringing their own slaves and traitorous tribe members with them. As Ávila paraded past, Malinalli leaning on his shoulder and laughing scornfully at them, he stopped and using the tip of his sword, lifted Arrow Stars's head, a hard smile plastered on his thin lips.

"In most matters, I get everything that I want. If you come with me, I will have everything I came for."

Arrow Stars snarled and snapped at him, leading to her being jabbed with the butt of a sword and a few tense moments as the crowd surged forward. They were pressed back by the bulls, but not before Ávila tossed his head back and shook his long horns.

"Very well then. We will see you at dawn. Have our ships loaded or else we will burn this city to the ground."

Ávila laughed, leaving a sneering Malinalli behind him. The Yokot'an doe laughed and jeered at the battered Mexica, going so far as to snatch at Arrow Star's headdress. The Empress' paw caught the doe's hooved hand and pulled her in close, snarling in her ear.

"The Gods will not forgive you for this treachery, *malinche*,"

The doe's eyes widened as she was shoved back, only to be caught and shoved aside by a bull staggering under the weight of a golden disc. She turned and ran towards the front of the line, her frantic bleats trailing behind her.

The Mexica gathered around their Princess, their golden eyes gleaming in the dimming fires of the city as they watched their "guests" leave.

* * *

"Are you ready?"

Obsidian Fang shielded his eyes with a heavy paw and peered out over the ramparts of the city. The wooden canoes were filled to the brim with gold and precious stones, waiting on their new owners. Below him, the people watched the lead warrior, waiting for his next move.

"I am," Arrow Stars replied, stepping up beside him, placing her arrows on the ground watching the sun creep over the walls of the city, casting them in an orange glow that gave the appearance that the city was on fire. She looked around, her eyes lighting on the blood-stained sheet that had been draped over her father, drawing a small sob from her. It felt like months since she'd watched him fall from the balcony that night and in that time, she'd aged by years.

"They're here," Steady Knife shouted at them from the walls, and indeed, the hoof beats of a few hundred bulls drummed on the lush forest floor, heading towards them. In the lead was Ávila, with Malinalli bounding in step beside him, her face the picture of glee and satisfaction. When they approached the boats, Ávila cleared his throat and shouted up at her.

"Ah, I see that you've held your side of the bargain. Glad to see that the heathens can be taught."

As his words were repeated by Malinalli, there were several growls and shuffling of her people, but she hissed at them. Now wasn't the time.

"Well, if this is everything, we'll be off!" Ávila bellowed, waving his bulls towards the boats, which they loaded themselves into, marveling at the gold and clapping themselves on the backs. Arrow Stars, Obsidian Fang, and Steady Knife looked down at them all, their faces tight, with Arrow Stars clutching her bow, but they let them steer the boats away from the roadways, towards the center of the great lake.

"Such a shame that you all didn't learn of our Lord's mercy and grace; if you had, I would have told you to go with God. Ah, well!" Ávila turned around, his eyes gleaming with desire as he chewed feverishly when looking at the gold. It had a strange smell emanating from it, but as was the case with all things from the native tribes, it carried a foul stench that could be easily removed.

With his back turned and the boat winding away, he didn't see the line of archers stand up from behind the balcony. They touched the tips of their arrows to a torch and took aim at the ships, their bows tight.

"You're right, Ávila," Arrow Stars shouted, drawing their attention, "I don't believe in your impotent god, but I have faith in mine, especially He Who Walks by Fire!"

Drawing an arrow from her quiver, Arrow Stars lit her arrow and took aim at the stack nearest Ávila, her eyes blazing and a smirk on her muzzle as the arrow connected, setting fire to the kindling under the mound of gold, which spread to the wooden boats. There was much screaming and shouting as the bulls struggled to leap from the boats, but they didn't expect the Mexica to be waiting for them.

The moment the bulls connected with the water, the Mexica warriors rose from the depths of the lake, their black blades clenched between their teeth. Like angry, watery revenants, they grabbed the hapless bulls and slew them. The waters turned a strange orange color from the blood they shed and still more came.

Ávila tried to escape, but he found that the bottom of his luxurious cape was caught on the arrow, pinned to the boat. As he tried to climb out, he could only bellow in horror as the boat began to tip over, taking Malinalli over the edge with him. As the boat dragged him down, he could only shout curses at Arrow Stars.

"Female! Save me! We can talk!" he screamed, trying to escape from his fate, but as the gold dragged him down, he could only watch in horror as Arrow Star's lips moved, but no sound came to his ears as the orange waters had already filled them.

"I'm just a female," Arrow Stars said, her face grim and her muzzle drawn into a tight line, "being surround by males such as yourself has damaged my sensibilities."

\* \* \*

A Mexica cub darted past a column of long legs, making its way towards the gates of the city. As he placed his paw in his mother's, he could hear the voices of those he had run past, drifting into his ears.

"So, this is it? We're going to abandon all of this?" Steady Knife yelped, his eyes widening, swaying as the cub ran by. "I mean all of this?"

"That's the idea, yes," Obsidian Fang said, giving a curt nod to a few warriors, who padded off to help a former slave who struggled with a basket of corn. "She thinks it's best."

"Yeah-but-but"

"But we must," Arrow Stars said, as she placed a paw under Steady Knife's sputtering jaw. "More will come, of that we are all certain. It would be best for all of us to be far away from here before they get here. We will head to the forest and greet the tribes there and prepare for them to come to us."

"I liked it here," Steady Knife said, flicking his ears backwards. "I mean what will they have that I don't- "

A pair of Mexica female trotted past him, swishing their hips and casting quick glances at him.

"You know," Steady Knife said, grinning and cleaning off his whiskers, "I will have to continue this conversation later."

As he darted off, Obsidian Fang shook his head and hefted his club onto his shoulder, nestling it beside a pack of dried fish and meat. "That lynx never misses an opportunity, does he?"

"No, not at all," Arrow Stars agreed.

"Are you ready?" he asked, looking down at her.

"Give me one moment, I'll catch up to you," she said, walking towards the edge of the lake. Obsidian Knife nodded and headed towards the gates and ensure the exodus was moving smoothly.

Arrow Stars kneeled at the edge of the lake, her green eyes peering down into its dark, tranquil depths and sighed. Somewhere down there, her father kept watch, his piercing eyes keeping the invaders at bay.

With trembling hands, she removed the elaborate headdress and placed it on top of the waters. As it began to sink beneath the waves, Arrow Stars felt her lips moving, a familiar refrain passing over them.

"War is life for a Mexica and in death, there is rebirth. May you win all your wars in the afterlife, Father, so your spirit may come back to us."

*How was the Earth created? Why do we have warfare?*
*This is the Creation Myth of the hyenas.*

# Tears of the Sea

## by MikasiWolf

This was told by my grandfather's father, and those others before him. Long before war existed, the waters of the sea tasted as fresh as the stream you now partake of. Every stream had been tainted by the blood of war, that is true, but only when it communes with its many brothers and sisters is the salty tang of blood, sweat and tears apparent.

You see the rosy color of the very soil you tread upon? That's right, my son. It is blood. The blood of our countless ancestors simmer beneath us, reminding us always of their sacrifice. Through rain or shine, they have been immortalized where they had fallen, never far from us.

Why are the frost caps of our world free of red, you ask? Well, sonny, many a war was fought neither on bleak glaciers nor freezing peaks. Since the dawn of time our ancestors had chosen to fight in the relative comforts of warmth and pain, their own comfort unbefitting of their enemies. Deserts, you say? Yes, though the sand is paler than the soil of your envisioned ground, much more has been fought over the scorching desert than the frozen icelands, giving it its more… creative hues.

When the Earth was formed, it was like flawless quartz, untouched and undefiled. She Who Makes All, Creator of All That Is, made the world as such, sculpting and shaping it as she knew she should. During this great undertaking, she rested in twelve intervals during the time she took to complete it. These became known as the Months. 365 and a quarter days later, the world was complete. This became known as the Year.

Aiag, as She is known to us, admired Her creation. Despite Her masterpiece looking a lot more varied and unique than Her siblings', She felt that something was missing.

"What have you created, Big Sister?" asked Siera, her one of many brothers. Siera was by far the nosiest and most chaotic, though Aiag, being as tactful as She was, never told him that. We see him as the red star in the sky, though his world is nothing more than a red gaseous planet, as full of hot air as he is.

"A planet, little brother," explained Aiag. "I have taken much time into its making, but I feel that it lacks something."

"All our brothers and sisters have a planet of their own," said Siera thoughtfully. Secretly, he resented the many colored hues his sister's world had. "You are by far the last of us to create one. Why the disappointment?"

"We have lived for eons, my brother, far many beyond that of memory," said Aiag. "Always have we lived in the ether, creating and influencing events as is our right. What if there are other beings just like us, but in this world?"

"You are always one for trying new things, Big Sister," said Siera with mock admiration. "After all, you built the very rings that encircle the planet of Sister Sainu's. Go ahead, play by your rules! How many beings will you create? Seven? Fourteen? Shall they bear any resemblance to us?" Already he was grinning to himself.

"There shall be a total of fourteen beings similar to me by way of appearance," declared Aiag. "They shall hail from the hottest region of the Earth, just as how we were all borne of Mother Sun. As we had come from fire, it is only fitting that my children awaken to the very rays that had given us life. They will be of opposing genders, so that they may have cubs of their own. They will not be alone in the world I have created, but live alongside others who will bear the image of you and our siblings."

Siera nodded, pleased that there will be creations in his image. But then, Aiag had her favorites.

And so it was done. From the very essence of earth itself, fourteen of each species came into being.

Machik was one of the first Hyenas, perfect in every aspect. Her fur billowed with an almost otherworldly sheen, spots as defined as stars in the night sky. Around her was the fast blowing sands of a desert, the sun beating down upon her and her brethren. They stretched their bodies and paws experimentally, testing out the new vessels of their souls. As far as their eyes could see, only land greeted them. Then, there was only one continent, and the Ancestors were born right in the middle of it. Vegetation and life sprouted slowly from the land, coaxed into place by Aiag's presence.

"My children!" resonated Aiag, her voice echoing within the consciousness of The People. They stumbled upon their earthly frames in surprise. "You have been created from my very flesh, and borne of my essence. As you take on my image, you shall be the favored people of my world."

"Whatever do you mean, Mother?" asked Machik, looking about her. The First People did not need to learn to speak, they already knew. "We do not know where we are, or even how we came to be. What is our purpose here?"

"Just as my mother had breathed life into us from her rays alone, so shall I unto you," said Aiag proudly. "You are the Yakhi-Nah, proud rulers of my kingdom. You will beget children of your own, and shape the world as you see fit. Know that other than you and your brethren, there are many others different from you in hue and stature. In every direction they may be found, and you are destined as my offspring to lead them. And I trust you to do it well. The world you are in is still young, and it is up to you, with the help of your brethren to help it grow into your home."

"We will, Great Mother," replied Machik, her chin and ears held high. "Where your mother the Sun had rallied you and your siblings, so will I the Peoples of the Earth." And so Aiag began her long slumber. For making a world took a lot out of a Divinity.

The Yakhi-Nah travelled miles across the lands, settling down where they could. The world was vast, and as different throughout as Night and Day. In the plains they met the Wolf People known as the Tishkare, created in the image of Siera, and in the tundra they met the Bears known as the Ursari. And in the many other lands yet more others could be found, too numerous in type to count. All these beings were different from them in height and stature, but being borne of Aiag's essence, were similar in way of speech. They taught them the ability to build and farm, to hunt and gather, all the many life skills we now take for granted. They taught them the best manner of foraging, and the direction to build the entrance of one's home towards. During then, no one grew old and expired, for being made in the image of the Divinities ensured immortality.

But all this was watched in interest by Siera. Where he only had a world to swirl the reddish-hued gases within for his viewing pleasure, his Sister's world had living and breathing figures to play with! Not just in Aiag's image, but that of Her siblings! With the Tishkare borne of his image, shouldn't he have a say in their lifestyle as their Chief Father? Wouldn't that also mean that the rest of the family have a say in what went on in Aiag's world? Within barely a millennium, Siera made his decision. He went before his brothers and sisters, laying out the misdemeanors of Aiag. Who was she to play mother to those not of her image? Had she even asked permission from her brothers and sisters to do so? And why should the people not in Aiag's image be subservient to those who were?

The Divinities listened and argued, but there was only but one common consensus. This affront would not be tolerated.

And thus Siera and his many siblings of the universe intertwined their essence into Aiag's creation, involving themselves with The People.

For the first time in history, the other Peoples became independent of their teachers. From the seeds of discord from their new masters, they realized that they had no need of the Yakhi-Nah to teach them how things were done, but to derive their very own methods of doing them. Where the Yakhi-Nah taught that the right way to build huts was from mud and twigs, the Ursari and Tishkare started building them out of logs. Where the Yakhi-Nah gathered water with pots, the Ursari and Tishkare did so with buckets. The Yakhi-Nah knew something was amiss when this happened, for the other People had always followed their teachings. They didn't yet know that this was the start of different cultures.

The Yakhi-Nah complained to Machik a month later. The people they were supposed to civilize were developing identities and cultures of their own. Surely this was not what Aiag would have wanted, for wasn't it She who tasked them with this endeavor?

"The other People are resisting the will of our Mother!" screeched the Yahki-Nah to their leader, their crests and hackles bristling. "Who are they to go against the very teachings that made us what we are? Surely it is our duty to set right this heresy?"

Machik nodded slowly, her curved ears flicking to the cries of her people. To go against the ways of the Earth Mother herself was like spitting her in the eye. As Her favored, the Yakhi-Nah will have to give the Peoples a show of strength.

"We will force the ways of our Mother upon them," declared Machik. "For though their numbers may be many, so are ours. To arms!"

Siera and the other Divinities saw all this from the ether. With their children's independence threatened, they imposed their will upon their Sister's world. With feats capable only by the Divinities, they started separating the land their People lived upon. But as this was Aiag's world, their influence on the Earth was limited, causing the land to shift ever so slightly. By the time the Yakhi-Nah reached the borders of the other Peoples, a gap of some hundred feet was formed between them, the blue of the sea not yet deep enough to prevent crossing. The People of the Divinities gathered on the shores, glaring back at their previous mentors.

"As the children borne of our Mother's essence, you have gone against Her very ways of living!" snarled Machik to the defectors. "In disrespecting your betters, you had begotten Her fury! Return the land to what it was, or you shall be banished!"

"We are not borne in your Mother's image, so we take no orders from her!" challenged Bajok, the leader of the Tishkare. "If we must fight, so shall it be." Sticks were sharpened and rocks were chiseled, and it was the first time tools were turned into weapons.

The battle lasted a total of seven days and nights. This became the Week. For the first time since the Earth's creation, blood spilled. The Yakhi-Nah and the defectors fought in the steadily deepening water between their lands, blood and sweat pouring into the sea as countless waves after waves of their people died. When the fighters thirsted and stooped to take a drink, all they could taste was the blood and suffering of the fallen. The water undrinkable, many soon fell not from battle but thirst, till only the strongest were left. By the seventh day, the fighters realized the sea was too deep to fight within, and padded back to their own sides. Snarling at the defectors across the expanse of the sea, the Yakhi-Nah were cut short by a voice; unheard for so long it was almost forgotten. Only this time the voice held no warmth, only disappointment and sorrow.

"Children of my flesh!" resonated Aiag. At this, the Divinities fled, leaving their children to Aiag's mercy. Roused from her slumber by the sounds of death and fighting, Her voice boomed around the survivors of the battle, resonating against the very atmosphere. With their hold on the Earth released, Aiag did not realize what her siblings had done. All she could see were The People carrying out vicious acts of war on their own accord. The sight of blood soaking the land into a reddish hue saddened her, the once pristine sea She had created for her children's survival now a cesspool of death.

"Upon bestowing the gift of life upon you, I have been more proud than I was creating your home," spoke Aiag. Her voice carried nothing but disappointment, sending a shiver down everyone. "Yet the very life which you have been given, taken from my very essence, is thrown as carelessly away as excretion. Yakhi-Nah, you most of all should know better, being the missionaries of my teachings."

"But Mother! We are merely enforcing the ways you had tasked us to protect!" protested Machik, her pelt stained guiltily with the blood of her brethren. "Would you hold that against us?"

"Enforcing the Way does not justify the deaths of your flesh-kin!" snapped Aiag, the anger of her consciousness cutting through everyone. Their ears and tail lay flat, and their hearts and their bones chilled. "As different as your other brethren are, so shall their ways be so. That you will remember your paws are not meant for fighting, you shall now walk upon them! As the instigators of your world's defilement, you shall never again walk the same as the others. Forever will you remember your greatest mistake. So shall it be!"

And since that day, the Peoples of the Earth walk on fours. Even though their paws were no longer capable of violence, that hasn't stopped them from harming one another. Nothing is easily forgotten, the fire burning within each being the testimony of that great battle. The lands that had been separated exist today as the continents. Within them, their People live in relative harmony, developing their own cultures and traditions. And over in the lands where they hailed from, hyenas today have higher forelegs than hindlegs, reminding us who started the first battle of the world.

And from that day on, war after war had been fought upon the many continents of the earth, the salty sea and red soil a reminder of all that was. Which is why, Sonny, we must take good care to respect the Earth as it is. Much had been sacrificed for all who live today, even as we tread the ground beneath us.

*Levi used to be a solitary feline hunter. Now he is a member of a mixed-species Pack.*

*What are the differences? Which is better—alone or with teammates to watch over him—but who might also get him caught?*

# The Pack

## *by Argyron*

No matter how much the frosty air burned going down the leopard's throat, Levi maintained his slow and gentle breathing. He hated the cold the most, but his training had taught him that keeping calm breaths were more important than his naturally anxious inclinations.

His eyes narrowed onto the target, the slits of a deadly hunter as he pulled the knife from his sheath and prepared to pounce. Fast, his first move a blur in the tundra storm as his weight came down on top of the other fur. They both fell forward onto the ground, his mass pushing the other into the snow, paw pressed against the back of his head as the knife pierced into the side of his neck. He could feel the guard beneath him struggling, but the leopard waited patiently for him to bleed out. And except for the lashing of his tail, he stayed relatively calm until he could drag the lifeless body away from the fire's light. A moment later, the storm would cover up the remainder of his bloody tracks.

Hopping down from the campsite bluff, he moved forwards towards the compound a distance away. Had it not been for the lights keeping the structure's walls well lit, he would not have been able to see the building in the dark of the night. Exhaling slowly, he closed his eyes as a flurry of snow wrapped around his form.

With the world gone black and his whole body numb, all he was left with were the gusty sounds surrounding him. He listened closely to the wind's howling, but the voice of the wind sang to him the only tune she knew: That he was alone, left out in the tundra to freeze in a desolate isolation, and abandoned by all those that had come to this frozen land with him. Those words comforted the naturally solitary predator as his thoughts drifted back to the last time he had hunted by himself.

* * *

Like a piece of film catching on fire, the darkness of his memories burned back to a bright sun peeking through hazy clouds. The flames of the film rustled, forming the brightly colored autumn leaves at the tops of trees. The remaining darker patches, untouched by the blaze, turned into the branches and trunks all around him. He breathed in deeply that woodland air and purred as the breeze gently wafted his golden, spotted fur. The wind had sung to him then as well, comforting the feline in much the same manner.

He could still feel the rough wood under his paws, claws extended into the bark, keeping him perched on one of the larger branches. The big cat let his sight drop down towards the ground, looking at the forest floor a mere twenty feet or so below him. From up here, the small dips and hills of the terrain looked nearly flat, giving him a better chance of spotting his prey. His eyes darted about, looking for movement or any indication at all that someone was approaching. He saw nothing.

With nothing in sight, he changed his attention to one of his other senses. His ears swiveled about, monitoring the surroundings for any noises out of the ordinary. Birds were chirping all around him and the wind continued to speak to him, but nothing that called for his attention.

His heart raced as he stayed focused on the task at paw. Backing up towards the trunk of the tree, he set himself up in a small alcove that left very little of his body exposed. The price of such protection was obvious to the feline, his vision now blocked on most sides by the surrounding bark and the smell of wood surrounding him. He paid the price willingly for the extra cover, but knew he would need to rely on his sense of hearing for the time being.

Pulling his tail up towards his chest and brushing the soft fur, he waited. The time seemingly passed slowly, but soon enough, a twig snapped from the ground below that caused his ears to turn towards the sound. The leopard's tail flicked in his paws with anticipation.

The big cat cautiously poked his head out from his hiding spot, looking toward the ground where he thought the snapping might have come from. His ears stood tall, focused in that general direction until the crunching from other steps gave him an exact location.

While he could not see exactly what was approaching him, he was able to find a few additional clues elsewhere. The scents that drifted in the air told him that canines were approaching. He could also tell there were at least two based on the smells of their furs. But most importantly, by their careless footsteps and regardless conversation he could tell they were coming closer.

"Where the hell did they go?" huffed a first voice, out of breath. "I mean… we just saw both of them run this way a minute ago."

A second voice responded, much deeper than the first. "I already told you to keep quiet and eyes on the lookout." There was frustration in his words, but the second canine quieted down before adding, "They have to be out here somewhere."

The feline's eyes narrowed onto a pile of large rocks several yards away. From around a large boulder three well-armed canines came into view. He flatted his ears and stayed attentive as they walked almost straight towards his location.

His mind became a jumble of thoughts as the leopard wondered what he should do. His natural inclination was to push his body back into the tree and hide until they passed, but that would leave him unaware of their actions. He needed to know what they were up to in case he needed to run. Of course, he felt uncertain he could outrun their gun and knew they would not miss every single shot. Without another course, he listened to the only thought that stayed in his mind and took each breath slowly.

His eyes concentrated not on the canines themselves, but on the barrels of their guns. He had learned long ago that just because a fur looked in your direction did not mean he had seen you. The only warning he could trust for sure was when the cold end of that gun pointed right at him. But the three failed to notice their overhead watcher as they passed below him. He breathed out in relief and closed his eyes, shifting to look over the other side of the branch to take mental notes while allowing some distance to grow between them.

The front canine was clearly a grey wolf and the leader of this group. He held his gun at the ready and stayed fairly tense as they moved forward. Every one of his movements was well-defined, made for efficiency and to maximize his alertness. He had even trained himself to always keep his attention forward, something Levi barely noticed as he watched a lone ear momentarily tick backwards to listen to a bird chirping. His shoulders looked stiff, his posture similar to that of a wooden board, and even his tail hung straight down. Every now and then he would motion off to one side, a sharp signal for one of the others to quietly divert from their path and check around a tree or another boulder.

An ash colored coyote followed behind him like a second-in-command, though Levi felt uncertain about his exact ranking. He followed orders diligently, proceeding in the directions signaled by the wolf with a cautious eye. His movements were calculated and swift, tail flowing for balance, and each step placed with clear precision to dodge the twigs and leaves. Yet upon returning to the lineup, his guard and gun would both lower.

The final canine, another coyote but with deep auburn fur, brought up the tail-end. She was less deliberate with her actions and followed almost none of the front lupine's orders. But she added value to the group by staying cautious, taking a few seconds to check behind them every so often. The feline took great note of this, because she would need to be the first one taken out.

By this point, the three canines had all progressed far enough away from him that the leopard felt ready to proceed with his own plans. He looked over the edge, his claws extended into the branch as he shifted his weight. With the cracking of bark, he swung down from the tree to land silently amongst the leaves. As his paws touched the ground, he let the momentum of the fall pull his body close to the earth. If they had heard anything, the uneven landscape would hide him perfectly from view.

He let his fur settle while pieces of the branch landed on or around him, eyes closed as he checked which direction the breeze was blowing. Since he had smelled them, the wind had changed direction as he caught the scent of the canines flowing towards him. He opened his eyes and let the natural predator come out.

Quietly, he crept along the forest floor. His spotted fur camouflaged him well with the deadfall, foliage, and shadows. Over the exposed roots and around trees, he crawled on all fours towards the group. His approach was swift, gaining on them fast while locking his sights on his targets.

Time slowed down for the cat, for without much notice, the female coyote's ears flicked backwards and stayed locked on him. Her sensitive hearing must have caught something that left her uneasy. She stopped without telling the other two, her head slowly turning to look back.

His reactions were all instinctual as he rose up behind her. He watched as the fear grew in her eyes, as she saw his frame rise from the ground, and his own reflection shone back at him from those dark pupils. One paw clenched her muzzle shut while the other pulled a knife from the sheath. He held tightly onto the blade as his arm swung forwards, stabbing in the middle of her chest.

He followed through with the moment of his attack but twisted at the last moment as they both fell back to the ground. He aimed for a soft patch of dirt and rolled across his shoulder blades as quietly as possible. In a moment, the two of them would disappear into the surrounding landscape and thick brush.

In her eyes he could see the powerful fire of his own killer instincts reflecting back at him. His short snout bumped against her cold nose, exhaling slowly before gently whispering, "One down," to his victim. He pulled the knife from her chest with a surprising amount of effortlessness, wiping the blade out of habit before re-sheathing it once more. Levi finally let go of her muzzle, closing his eyes while slowly inhaling. "Two to go," he purred.

\* \* \*

When he opened them again, he found he had returned to the cold, dark tundra with a small layer of snow covering him from the recent flurry. Shaking his body gently, he brushed off most of the snowfall before refocusing his sights on the brightly lit structure in the distance.

His headset buzzed to life as a light hearted voice called out. "Foxtrot One Romeo Three, I'm tracking several tangos patrolling this area. Sending their coordinates to your HUD. Over."

The leopard looked up to the corner of his goggles where he had a map of the surrounding area. Above the rectangle there were numbers indicating his estimated latitude, longitude, and elevation, while at the bottom spun the small letters and tick marks of a compass. In the very center of the map he could see a blue arrow across a series of grey contour lines. There were four blue dots close by, but he paid little attention to them as several amber dots appeared on the screen.

Over his headset came a different, deeper voice than before. "Roger, Wifi," responded the second fur. "Pack members are to take note of their surrounding tango locations and adjust their position as needed. Do not engage until clearance has been granted." The second fur paused, most likely to allow pack members to move before he continued. "Control, do we have clearance to use deadly force? Over."

The com went dead, leaving the feline once more with only the howling of the wind. He watched as a pair of the dots moved closer to his position on the map. Instead of relocating to a safer area, the leopard lowered his head and waited. Another small flurry from the storm blanketed his body, hiding him from view. His tail had long since gone numb, folded back ears frosty, and a chill seeping through the thermal suit to the fur covering his stomach. Still, he waited until a third voice spoke up.

"This is control. Use of deadly force has been authorized for this mission. Over."

"Roger that. Pack members are to move towards the objective and proceed as necessary to complete the mission. Stay frosty, over and out." With that, three clicks ticked off one after another to signal the pack had been switched back to local communications only.

With focus still on the two dots moving closer, he felt a growl building in his throat. Levi held back, suppressing the sound by breathing slowly as he had been taught. He watched as the dots came to a halt right in front of him with their lights shining down on him.

Guided only by the constant movement of their flashlights over his snow-covered visor, the leopard was uncertain if they had seen him. He wondered who they were, what their species was, and why they were patrolling so far away from the structure. Most of all, he wanted to know where they were looking and if he could come out from under his frozen cloak.

They started talking and he listened, and although their words were in a foreign dialect, he was able to pull something from the conversation. By the calmness with which they spoke, he could tell that they had not seen him; and from the roughness of their speech, he knew they were of eastern decent, though he was not exactly sure where. Shifting his ears cautiously forward, he tried to pick up more of what they might be saying.

A moment passed with his vision blind, listening to their general chatter and soft shuffling of feet in the snow until a gust of wind uncovered a portion of his goggles. His heart skipped a beat as he glanced through the clear plastic. Their chatter continued without pause.

In front of him he saw two illuminated silhouettes created by the reflection of their lights on the snow. He could see one was clearly turned away from him, but the other was harder to tell. Even still, they both were constantly turning and moving to stay warm. Glancing down, the cat felt lucky when noticing their pools of light on the ground ended right in front of him.

His eyes locked onto a moving paw, watching patiently as the fur on his left lifted a cigarette up to his short muzzle. He breathed in deeply, the end flaring up in red and orange as he sucked on the cancer stick. Based on the shape of his ears and the length of his snout, Levi guessed he was some sort of feline, which left him little worry since he had a wealth of experience with cats from training. He observed the other feline exhaling smoke for a moment before looking towards his partner.

The other soldier had a very clear cervine form, identifiable by his large antlers and elongated snout. With eyes on the side of his head able to see almost everywhere and ears made to twist at the slightest of sounds, he would be troublesome to sneak up upon. Additionally, the leopard needed to consider where the buck swung those antlers. While he doubted they would be powerful enough to deliver a lethal blow, they could still break a rib and place him at the mercy of a bullet.

Calculating the odds, the wisest choice would be to eliminate them from a distance with his weapon. Gradually, he moved his right paw through the fresh powder on the ground, though his eyes remained locked on his targets with narrowing pupils. His fingers touched his hip, grasping the handle of his pistol as he pulled the silenced weapon free from its holster. In this position he paused one final time, exhaling into the cold snow at the end of his muzzle.

As a gust of wind rushed over them, he pushed up to the kneeling position. His armed paw swung forward, thumb flicking the safety off while his free paw wrapped around the other. Taking aim, he pulled tightly on the trigger.

\* \* \*

Blinded by an unexpected second flash, the world around him disappeared. His ears were ringing, the sound of the wind's cry long since gone as a mellow tone continuously overpowered all other noises. He put a paw to his ear, the side where the flash had come from, and listened to the resonating note as the light dissolved.

The forest from his past appeared in front of him, the surrounding just as he remembered, and where the silhouettes of his tundra enemies had previously stood there were now the two canines from before. But the cat's eyes were still adjusting, the blurred lines of the woodlands sharpening while the dull tans and greens brightened out of an otherwise grey world. Only after a few seconds did he begin to see other colors such as the deep reds splattered across both of the canines' chests.

Levi needed a moment to put what he was seeing and what had happened together, his head pounding from the still vibrating sound in his ears. They had been shot, that much he could see, but he only remembered pulling the trigger once and yet both had been taken out. There must have been another shooter.

\* \* \*

The leopard jerked his head backwards towards where he had seen the second flash, but the quick twist made him lose sight of the memory. What had once been forest turned to a whirlwind of ash and dusk. He watched as the specks from his past floated up into the sky before getting lost in the storm.

A flashlight from one of the dead soldiers had gotten stuck in the snow, pointing upwards to illuminate the flakes he so carefully watched. From out of the darkness appeared the figure of a rabbit dressed exactly like him. He observed that figure calmly walk over next to him before settling down onto one knee. "Just like old times."

Levi groaned his reply, eyes examining the lapin's dark mask in annoyance. He knew who this rabbit was, and he knew him quite well. Even with the black mask on and in the dead night, he could still see the face that was looking dead at him. The cottontail was smirking, his lips cracked upward in a smile but only on one side, and with amber eyes that held the same potential passion of embers on a fire. He looked away from that mask before adding, "I would have had them both if you hadn't fired."

Over his communication he could barely hear the rabbit snort. "You keep telling yourself that, kitten." The lapin put a small paw on the much larger feline's back, patting gently before moving forward to examine the bodies. "Now, let's see if we can pull something off of them and get the hell out of this snow."

For a moment, the leopard hung behind to watch the rabbit return to his work. As his eyes followed the form of the little bunny, he thought back to a few years ago when he had always imagined himself as a lone hunter. Back then he was always a solitary predator, stalking his prey alone before making the kill. He relied on and trusted no one with his life, but that was because he did not need to.

He wondered how much his younger version would recognize him now. Sure, he had the same spots in all the same places and he was still a strong hunter, but he knew he needed another fur to watch over him. This rabbit had become that other animal, and in the last few years they had slowly learned how to cooperate with one another. Even these slight jabs had only come with time and respect for each other, and no one else was ever allowed to pat Levi on the back. Still, he cringed to the touch and had to remind himself not to bite back.

Getting up from where he had been kneeling himself, he followed suit and started searching the dead patrol unit. The leopard pushed the larger, deer-like form over, taking the flashlight out from the snow and got his first good look at the enemy's face. The guy was a reindeer, colored with light and dark brown fur with a few patches of grey here and there. Yet the most striking feature were his still open eyes, which in death had started to cloud over in the iris. His pupils stared out, alone in an empty shell that sent shivers down the feline's spine

He shook off those feelings, returning to his task by letting the light drop down towards the uniform. Slowly, paws opened and searched pockets for anything useful. A cigarette pack in the left breast, a picture in the right, and so on and so forth. If the items were of no use to him, the cat paid his respects by placing all of them back where he had originally found them.

Before he could search the buck's pants, his partner called out, "Found something!" The cat's head looked up to see a red keycard at the end of a lanyard in the rabbit's paws.

He nodded towards the lapin before clicking off the flashlight, then the two worked to hide the bodies under some snow before checking their map to see if anyone else was coming. The path looked clear as the duo stalked off towards the well-lit structure below.

They moved slowly in the snow, each step forward sinking their feet in up to the waist, which gave the feline some time to reminisce. He looked up at the glowing silhouette around his partner from the large structure lights ahead. The longer he stared, the brighter the light became until the bright illumination enveloped his rabbit-shaped form before washing him into a memory.

\* \* \*

They were walking out of the woods and back into the compound, and seeing that small rabbit in front of him frustrated the large cat. The final kill of their session, stolen from him by a little bunny that appeared out of the brush. He had robbed the feline from shooting the alpha wolf, a thought that made Levi's tail naturally lash about.

His anger was building, his paws clenched tight, but before he could say anything his name was called by their training officer. Growling deeply in frustration, he jogged over to meet with the uniformed lion.

"Yes sir," he spat, coming to attention in front of the officer.

For a moment, the lion just stood there and looked him straight in the eyes, as if digesting the other cat's thoughts without words. "You're probably one of the best candidates we've ever seen in this program," he confessed, thought keeping a paw held up to inform Levi to stay silent. "In every training exercise your group has completed, you are always the last one on your team alive and you always manage to take out several of your targets before being taken down."

The other large cat paused, his tail flicking up behind him while his eyes narrowed. "However, you have also proven to be incapable of working with any of your teammates." There was thunder in his voice now, a crack that rolled off the tongue as he spoke. "Don't think we haven't noticed." His nostrils flared, his agitation building, and then the lion paused to look at something else.

Levi turned his head to see what had pulled the other feline's attention away from their discussion. Behind them casually walked the wolf and two coyotes from the woodland training grounds. They were laughing and talking with one another, discussing how they could improve next time and what had gone wrong this time, as well as reliving the more exciting moments. He even caught the trio saying a few things like, "that darn leopard," and, "we'll get him, just wait and see," though anything other than that falling hushed or outside of earshot. He growled under his breath before turning his attention back to the officer.

Those narrow eyes were back on him, a curl on the cat's lip that now showed frustration, but the leopard spoke first. "Sir, my teammates are holding me back and are keeping me from my full potential..."

"Your team is your full potential, solider." He pushed a single claw against the leopard's chest, making sure there was more than enough force for the cat to feel it through his training gear "If any single one of them fails, then you all fail." And as he spoke, his voice increased in intensity for a second time while his mane fluffed-up like he might just roar. "Do I make myself clear?"

Levi held his ground, his nose wrinkled in a bit of a snarl. "Then what would you call that out there today, sir?" Even as he spoke, he could feel the lion's gaze begin to singe the ends of his fur.

The commanding office growled under his breath, clearly agitated as he thought his words out carefully before speaking. "I would call that one hell of a dumb cat catching his last bit of luck." He gave one final push with his claw against the other cat before lowering his paw. "None of us are lone hunters here, none of us go out onto the field with our backs uncovered. We work together, we fight together, and we hunt together." He let the words sink in before slowly saying, "That is why each group is called a pack.

"Those three over there," he barked as a paw snapped up to point in the direction of the canines that had just passed. "They may have lost today because you are better than them now, but as a unit they are growing stronger. Soon, the three of them will be more tactical and cunning than a lone cat hiding in a tree ever will be.

"I suggest you find a friend here and fast, or else we might need to recommend you for a different program." With that, the lion's paw lowered as he turned and started to walk off. "Why don't you go and talk to the recruit that saved your lucky ass out there today." And then the other feline was gone.

He remembered staying outside the compound alone and angry, thinking about the training and everything the lion had told him. He had wanted to be a pack member since he had first joined the forces, for the stories that came back were always ones of heroism or valor. Each pack was known for being a small tactical group that would go into the heart of the enemy's territory to do unbelievable things. They possessed a sort of courage or bravery not found in your average soldier, and he easily could relate to that.

And yet here he stood on the brink of failure because of his inability to work with others. In his own mind he was the pack, a full unit made to go in and get the work done. Somehow, he had created this false image that they were the action heroes for his entertainment, animals that single handedly took out entire armies, and not a well-trained group working together.

Standing alone, he listened to his only friend as she sang to him once more. The wind called out, wrapping around him with a gust of dead leaves and debris. He listened and heard the trees rustling her tune.

\* \* \*

As he looked down towards his feet with an expectation of seeing concrete, he was almost surprised to see the snow. Glancing back up, Levi could see they had almost arrived at their destination.

The lapin next to him spoke up, opening his communications channel to reach out to all pack members. "Foxtrot One Romeo Three, this is Coal. We are in position to enter the compound; can I get confirmation that all security cameras have been hacked? Over."

The two got on their knees, huddled up close with backs to one another in the darkness while they waited. Over the communication came a crackling before an out of breath voice spoke up. "Closed-loop security cameras have been hacked and are now running continuous feeds of five minute recorded video. You are clear to enter. Over."

Not long after they were at the front door, sliding the keycard through the reader and watching as the indication light blinked green. A lock cranked as the door slid open to reveal a small room inside. "We are entering the compound. Over."

Over their headset came the deeper voice from before. "Roger that Coal, you have permission to enter and proceed with the plan." There was a second's pause, not hearing the familiar three clicks to end full broadcast, before the voice spoke again. "All pack members are to meet at the rendezvous point by oh-two hundred. Over."

The two looked down at their watches one last time in the bright overhead lights at the top of the monolithic structure before moving inside. The rabbit shut the door behind them while the feline called out, "Setting a timer for forty-two minutes." On both of their goggles appeared a clock in the center, counting down as the fluorescent lights in the room flickered on.

They spent very little time examining the small entrance room, both quickly moving up to the steel door across the way. Levi looked over at the lapin, watching as his partner detached his front mask while swinging a small backpack off of his shoulders. He clipped the mask to the top of the pack before unzipping one of the side pockets. His little, lithe paws dug through that pocket for a second before pulling out a small scope, one with a camera at the far end that synchronized with his goggles.

Already down on his knees, the rabbit bent the scope before sliding the camera end under the door. Hitting a small button attached to his side, his goggles lit up with an image.

The leopard turned around and watched the other door, tossing his own pack down on the bench before taking out what looked like a rectangular box. As he unfolded the plastic and metal and snapped pieces into place, the box turned into a small, automatic weapon. Reaching back into his bag, he twisted on a suppressor to the end while asking, "See anything?"

"There's a separate security room in the middle with two guards inside not paying much attention," the rabbit softly informed. "Can't see their weapons, counter in the way." There was a small clicking as he adjusted the camera before continuing. "We've got two long hallways going past the station. I'm uploading the digital reconstruction from the scope now."

After pulling a loaded clip from his backpack and snapping the magazine in place, Levi slung the pack back over his shoulder. He put his back against the lockers, looking over at his partner while still keeping his position at the ready in case anyone tried to enter their room. On his map he watched as the hallways appeared with two amber dots, recreated digitally from small ultrasonic pulses and infrared readings taken from the front of the camera. "Bullet proof glass?" he nonchalantly asked.

Putting the camera back into his bag, Coal looked up at the leopard. "Affirmative on the glass, what are you thinking?"

The feline's lips curled into a smile as he purred, putting the automatic weapon into his side sling. "Black window," he replied while grabbing something else from his gear, "or is that plan too simple for you?"

The bunny grinned back, nodding in approval before putting his mask back on and slinging the bag over his shoulder. He hopped across the room, landing with one paw on the light switch, as he looked back at his partner.

The cat was holding a canister, smoke already pouring out at a quickening rate. He set that on the floor underneath the bench in front of him and took hold of the door handle. With a nod, the lights went out as he twisted the handle.

The guards looked up as the front door creaked to a full open, black smoke pouring out from the frame and covering the floor. The fumes flowed down the hallway a good several feet before dissipating enough to be ineffective, but nothing else followed out of the room. The two looked at each other, uncertain what to do before looking back at the building fog.

What they failed to see were the two mammals hidden beneath the smoke screen. Low to the ground and crawling like feral beasts, they snuck up to the window front before following the wall around to the security room's door.

Levi turned back after passing the frame, waiting intently. He could see his lapin counterpart's visor for only a brief moment before once again disappearing in the ever moving fog. The dark mask and black goggles were haunting to look at, especially with the front filter, but the leopard saw past that to the mammal beneath. He could see the rabbit's grey muzzle, the three white spots around his left eye, and the dark stripes on his forehead.

The door opened inwards, but the first thing to pass from the frame was the cold steel barrel of a gun pointed down. The guard raised his gun before stepping one cautious boot out into the hallway. The boot wafted the smoke screen cover, and for a precious second the leopard and rabbit became barely visible. He took no notice of the two at his feet, but gave them a perfect view of his canine muzzle.

The timber wolf looked in one direction before twisting to the other, his ears standing tall with his black nostrils expanding and contracting quickly. He was trying to detect an enemy, but the smell of the smoke screen was purposefully made strong and the two furs were deathly silent. He easily failed to notice the danger lying right next to his feet.

While neither could speak to the other without giving away their location, they knew each other well enough to guess what the other one would do. Levi was always in the front, the first into battle, and the one getting in trouble. Coal was the opposite. He followed up behind the cat, keeping him in check and using his smarts over his brute force. So when the feline saw that boot appear in front of him, he took action and knew that Coal would clean up whatever he missed.

As the wolf walked into the hallway, he tripped and pulled the guard right into Coal's deadly paws. The fog pushed up around them, granting the wolf a second's notice to see the feline's terrifying gas mask before death.

But the cat was already on the move, his tail flowing behind him as he went into the security room. A dark cloud followed him as his boots tapped on the ground, alerting the other guard of his presence. He watched as a young canine turned around, eyes growing big as a paw clamped down on his long muzzle. The feline used his grip on the lupine's snout to twist his head up and to the side of his body, snapping the neck efficiently. "Clear."

An unmasked rabbit pushed past him toward the main security console, looking at all the camera feeds around the building as well as the older computer in the center. "I think I can pull a map out of here and disable most of their security system," he said, putting his backpack down on the chair near the console and pulling out a small thumb drive. "Can you get the guard's body back in here? I can't lift him."

The leopard gave an affirmative nod before unlatching his own mask, snapping it onto his side before stalking back over to the door. He looked down at the timber wolf on the ground, reaching over to pull the body into the room.

With a couple of clicks on his headset, he heard the lapin speaking to everyone in their unit. "Foxtrot One Romeo Three, this is Coal. We have entered the compound and are working on uploading a map from the security console. Over."

Static poured through the headset for a moment before clearing up. "Roger that. See what other information you can pull from the console. Over and out." Three clicks and communications went dead.

Passing back over to the monitors where his partner was typing furiously, he scanned the hallways around them. All of the halls were pretty much empty, which felt strange to the feline who was not used to entering such heavily guarded facilities. "Why aren't there guards roaming the halls?"

The rabbit's eyes were glued to the screen, his paws moving quickly over the keyboard as he downloaded information from the building and hacked into other parts of the system. "Most likely because we're on the unrestricted levels." He took a breather and looked up at the large cat. "I was able to quickly access the information for this floor and all the floors above us, almost like they weren't trying to protect it. It's mostly just sleeping quarters, training halls, a cafeteria, and such, but it's obvious there's an underground portion of the building."

With a paw pointing at the screen, he showed an image of the inside of an elevator on one of the security cameras. "Notice the number on the elevator's level? That's a subterranean floor."

The leopard glanced over, looking at the red 'M' on the level and four little lights lit up underneath it. "I take it that those are security clearances," he asked without really needing the answer. "Well, get what you can and then let's get moving quickly. I don't like being this exposed."

"I know, I know." His partner tapped his paw pads on the counter in annoyance. "I'm going as fast as I can." He started typing on the computer again, but stopped to quickly add, "Why don't you call this in while I keep searching?"

Nodding, the cat touched a paw to his ear while walking towards the other end of the room. "Pack leader, this is Pyre calling in. We've got substantial evidence pointing to subterranean floors in this base. Over."

The headset clicked to life with a bit of static before the pack leader came on in his usual, deep voice. "Roger that, Pyre. Your new objective is to find out where that elevator goes and call back with any intel.

"As for your original object, Smoke and I are almost done with clearing the third floor and will work our way downwards from there. Call in if your team runs into any trouble. Over and out."

After hearing the com click off, Levi dropped his paw from his ear and looked back towards the console. He could see the rabbit was still typing away, trying his hardest as usual. The feline rolled his eyes before passing back over to the door, pulling his gun to the ready while looking out into the hallway.

Above him buzzed the fluorescent lighting, which were disturbingly loud in an otherwise quiet environment. The more he thought about it, the more he felt as though something about this place was not right. For being such a high security complex, there were almost no guards or defensive systems. He also noticed that Smoke and Scorch, the other members of their pack in the building, had nothing new to report on their end. The whole situation was making him uneasy and unable to contain his anxiety as he glanced around.

He pushed the timber wolf's body with his boot, making sure the dead soldier was well within the room, before proceeding back over the rabbit. "You've searched long enough; we've got to get going now."

With an audible sigh, Coal pulled off the computer and unsnapped a drive from one of the side ports. "Fine," he added before shoving the piece back into his pack. "I couldn't find any useful information on that computer anyway." Motioning with a paw towards the door, they both left the guard station and ventured down the hall using the map Coal uploaded from the security station.

They stayed quiet, save for the tapping of their paws on the tile flooring, and listened for anything that might tell them that they had been spotted. Rounding the corner, they heard voices coming from down the hall and decided to enter the closest door, a large cafeteria.

The room was empty at this time of night, and convenient given their current situation. With large, glass windows on one side, they had a perfect view of the hallway. The light coming through those panes lit up the room well enough for them to see.

The two quickly wandered into the center of the room, past long, linear tables and benches to hide behind a large column near the center of the space. Coal was small enough that he ducked under one of the tables, getting on his knees and looking out past the bench at the windows. He picked one close to the column Levi was behind so that they could communicate quietly, but even so he still used paw motions instead of words to say what was going on.

Muffled by the glass, the leopard could hear that several soldiers were standing just outside. He looked over to the cottontail and held up a paw, thumb motioning towards the noise.

The rabbit nodded before looking over, holding up his own paw flat for a second before curling the fingers. He opened his mouth, visibly counting off each enemy before turning back. Lifting his second paw, he held up seven fingers. A moment later, he quietly whispered, "They've stopped to chat."

Levi kneeled down, knowing he would have to wait a minute for the group to pass, but he stayed ready for anything. In this large, open room and against so many individuals, their best defense was to go unnoticed. While he waited, he looked out at the dimly lit, empty benches and tables around them. He wondered how many conversations had gone on here, friends joking and laughing, and the sound managed to form in his mind the more he thought about it.

\* \* \*

The vision in his mind became surreal as the fluorescent lights above flickered on, causing his eyes to adjust to the sudden brightness. When they did come to he was back in their training camp's mess hall. Furs at all different levels of training and several different packs all crowded around. They were talking to one another, laughing and enjoying their small amount of free time as they ate. He could even hear the clatter of silverware against plates and smell the different furs that had been there before.

In his own paws was his lunch tray, though exactly what the meal was that day he could not remember. He clicked his claws on the back of the plastic lightly while looking around. Though the room was filled with happy faces, he felt unwelcomed amongst all of these different animals. His eyes gleamed over the crowd, but he knew he would not find a friend anywhere, for Levi had managed to stay solo since he had joined. Spotting a free table, he went to sit by himself.

His solitude did not last long though, for the grey and white rabbit from before came to sit down across from him. Levi looked up, studying those three spots on his face and the twitching of his nose with caution.

"Well, they gave me trash," the bunny ranted as he pointed a finger down to the meal on his plate. "Don't they know I'm not a meat eater?" he added before looking up with a friendly smile.

The big cat growled from deep in his throat, not in any mood to talk to Coal after their morning session. He was still ticked off that the lapin had stolen the final kill and was not really looking to make friends with him. Flicking his tail, he brushed off the other fur's presence by looking at his own plate.

But the rabbit seemed determined to have a conversation, pushing the meal to the side. "Good teamwork out on the field today!" He continued to smile with two ears straight up, trying his best to hold his good intentions. "I thought I was a goner for sure when I saw the three of them approaching."

"I didn't take them out to save you." Levi's tone was deep, almost a snarl in his undertone. He let his eyes and ears drop, eyebrow furrowing in frustration.

"Oh." Coal's own ears fell as well, drooping behind him as he put his paws on the edge of the table.

A silence built between them, Levi using his fork to mash up the food on his plate. He did not feel like eating anymore, but he also could not bear to look up at the rabbit. He exhaled before letting the fork drop to his plate. "Was there something you wanted?"

He could hear the rabbit quivering, or at least he thought he could, and that got his head to slowly lift back up and look the lapin in the eyes. His nose was twitching, his eyes like saucers of water in the light, and yet he kept his composure strong. "I just thought you needed a partner…"

"Well I don't want a partner," the cat spat back.

Again, silence built between them as this time the rabbit stood up. With one paw still on the table, he pulled his tray over and looked around the room. "We all need a partner out there sooner or later." The little bunny took a few steps away before looking back over his shoulder. "I guess I figured the only leopard in this group might not mind working with the only herbivore." With that, he left the feline to eat in peace.

Levi's stomach turned over, twisting his gut while his eyes followed that teardrop tail out of the room. When the cottontail had left, he looked back at the slush pile on his plate in disgust. He had forgotten that herbivores were a rare commodity in this outfit, the work they performed daily not something instinctual to their nature. Yet here was a small rabbit, out there fighting with the rest of them, and probably better than many of the other furs in the cafeteria. In a fit of anger, he tossed his tray across the room and roared, "Damn it!"

The sounds of laughter and small talk died all around him as the mess hall went dead. For a moment, he could feel everyone's eyes digging into him, staring at his form like an enraged beast at the zoo. As if on cue, the farthest fluorescent lights went out to the sound of a heavy, metallic switch, only to be followed by the next row. Each row clonked off to the incessant pounding, until finally the dark abyss that had once been so distant was all around him.

Above him buzzed the last of the cafeteria lights, which cast a greenish glow upon his fur. He felt sick, a chill sweeping through his nerves that made his stomach turn. The feline closed his eyes and breathed in deeply, but the illness that he felt did not leave. Neither did the feeling of all those eyes watching him underneath that final light. In his mind, they glowed maliciously, as if waiting for the last light to finally go out.

With a loud clonk, the last light died out and plunged him into the unknown. The leopard immediately opened his eyes, taking ragged breaths and looking for anything in the darkness. His ears flicked about, but all he heard were the dying echoes from when the light switch had been flipped.

\* \* \*

After some time, his eyes readjusted to show he had returned to the empty mess hall. The large cat looked out among the mess of tables until he found his partner at the far end of the room. He watched as the bunny lifted his head up, gazing back in the big cat's direction before giving him the thumbs up to let him know they were good. He breathed in slowly, calming himself, before the two of them left the room once more.

Venturing back into the hallway, the two pack members took a moment to look around for more hostiles before moving quietly towards the elevator. Had Coal not stolen the map, they would have been lost in a labyrinth of white walls, diverse rooms, and endless corridors.

They ran from one door nook to the next, progressing down the halls one after the other in a sort of limping fashion. Levi would take the lead, crouching next to the wall with his paws on his gun, ready to fire. When he arrived at the next door nook, he would motion for the rabbit to follow behind, a swift wave trailed by the soft tapping of the rabbit's light steps.

They reached a corner by this method, and Levi stopped at the edge of the wall. Giving a wave to signal his partner to join him, he leaned around the edge to get a quick glimpse. He could see the elevator at the end of the hallway. Right in front were two guards chatting.

"Two tangos in front of the door," he whispered back, "armed with assault rifles." Pulling back from the corner, he pushed up against the wall and looked over towards the rabbit. "Both are wolverines."

Coal showed his understanding before pulling out his scope and pushing the small camera around the corner. "Such nasty looking bastards," he whispered mostly for himself. Pulling the scope back and putting the device away, he looked at the feline with calculating eyes. "I think we should tap and tug."

Tap and tug was one of the first maneuvers they had devised as a pair, which made it easy to remember. The ploy was pretty simple, one of them creates a distraction made to draw an enemy towards their location, the tap. The second fur would then take out the enemy forcefully, the tug.

Levi felt confident that this would work against most animals, such as wolves or tigers, but wolverines were another story. They were vicious, known to carry tempers that made them shoot first and ask questions later. And even if they managed to draw one of the guards close enough to forcefully attack, wolverines were known to have sharp claws and the strength of a small bear. These were not mammals to try and wrestle with.

He shook his head in disagreement before making his own suggestion. "We need to take them out from a distance."

The bunny listened to each word, but at the end of the sentence he dropped both his ears and rolled his eyes. "There's no way we can kill them before they get a round off and wake this whole damn place up." Brushing a paw over his head before tugging on one of his ears, he went on to say, "We need to do this silently."

Levi flicked his tail as his own ears dropped in annoyance, but before he could say anything back a new threat presented itself.

Two more guards rounded a corner behind them, their conversation dying as they laid eyes on the pair of intruders. Lifting their guns, they shouted out loud in a foreign language that neither Levi nor Coal could understand, but their gesture was clear. They wanted the leopard and rabbit to raise their paws and be captured. They had no plans on doing such a thing.

Coal reacted first by placing his feet against the wall and pushing off. His body slid across the floor, twisting about until he found himself facing his enemies. Meanwhile, Levi took a second longer, his own firearm snapping upwards as he aimed down the sights.

Then both sides fired.

While the rabbit had used his extra second to get out of the way, the leopard did not have the same luxury. As the guns lit up, time seemed to slow down for the feline. Each flash was like a slowly bursting fire from the ends of his enemy's guns, each bang sending a piece of metal his way. He thought he could hear the bullets whistling by his ears, or even feel one or two singe the fur near his face, but the reality was that a few had hit him in the chest. They knocked the wind out of him, and by the time he had registered anything, the firefight was over.

The cat fell backwards, knocked against the wall he had previously been leaning on as his vision blurred. In the far distance he could hear someone mumbling, calling out, but the words were too muffled to understand.

\* \* \*

Levi blinked, dazzled by how the blurs in the distance began to move in a swaying motion. They danced as though in a light breeze, swinging back and forth until some of the hazy shapes started to fall towards him. And behind all those obscure forms he saw the sun every now and then.

Two large figures appeared over him, staring down at his body as he blinked and tried to recognize who they were. For a moment, his eyes focused and he saw the wolf and coyote from his past.

"Fuckin' cat. I can't believe he tried to sneak up on us again," spat the coyote, giving a good kick with his boot. Levi coughed as pain shot up his spine, but stayed down.

The wolf threw a paw up on his teammate's shoulder. "Hey! You know the rule, Smoke." He let go of his buddy before leaning over.

With his face right next to the leopard, the canine spoke softly and slowly. "Let this be a lesson, kitten. Your time stalking us is over." He stood back up, pointing the barrel of his gun right in the feline's face. "Next time I see you in these woods, you better be fighting me like a real predator."

The lupine stepped over his body, heading off to hunt down the remaining members of their team. But before he did, he turned back and shouted. "Oh, and can you relay that message to your bunny friend?"

With that, the two left him.

\* \* \*

He blinked, but as he did so the blurs of the distant trees were no longer moving. A small paw began prodding his body, lifting his arm and tugging him as best the other animal could. He could even hear someone calling his name, but his senses were still coming back to him.

Then the words broke through, crystal clear like his vision as he saw the dull white walls of the corridor. "Come on Levi, I can't pull you!"

He looked over and saw Coal trying to tug him back down the hall to where they had come from, only managing to get the feline to fall over onto his side. Putting a paw on his chest, he felt where the rounds had hit. Each hit that had landed on his vest had left a mark, and underneath all of that protection and fur he could feel the sore pain of bruises.

As his heart started beating again, he looked past his partner towards where the guards had been. Seeing the two bodies on the floor got his adrenaline pumping again. "God damn."

The two had no time left to spare, each one darting down the hall as fast as possible towards a pair of door alcoves. They could hear the calls of the wolverines behind them leaving their post to come see what was going on, but again could not understand them. Both of them got inside just in time.

They both dipped down low and crunched up against the wall, an easy task for a small animal but more challenging for the leopard. He looked across the way at the rabbit, who peeked his scope around the corner before letting the camera just sit there. The bunny held up a paw telling him to wait, then counted down with his fingers until the wolverines would pass.

The two beastly mammals walked by them one at a time, claws ticking with each step. Levi aimed his gun appropriately at their heads, waiting cautiously to fire. As they passed, he could hear them whispering to one another in their own language.

When the two had completely gone by, he eased up from his position and looked back at Coal. Jerking his gun towards the wolverines, he nodded his head to try and communicate what he wanted them to do next. The bunny understood, nodding in agreement before aiming his own. Levi then turned back, took aim, and fired.

Two suppressed shots went off, one right after the other, only to be followed by the sound of bodies landing on the tile floor a second later. With no way to clean up the bloody mess, they left the bodies where they landed and quickly ran towards the elevator.

There was no button to call the elevator, just another slot for a keycard. Coal slid one that he had picked up earlier, though where exactly this one had come from was unknown to the leopard. He watched as the little indicator light turned green and the elevator doors opened.

But the inside device was different, a touch screen with all sort of gadgets that required both a password and a couple scans for authentication. A simple keycard would not work this time around. "Got a plan?" he asked the cottontail.

"Sort of," smirked the bunny before smashing his knife into the seam of the metal panel and pulling the whole touchpad off. "Let's hope this works." The rabbit put his backpack on the ground and pulled out the drive from before. Taking a moment to examine the circuit board on the other side of the panel, he disconnected a few wires before inserting his drive into one of the service slots. The small, blue light on the side ticked to life.

Lifting up the front face of the panel, he watched as a loading bar came up on the screen, the skull of a rabbit with some crossed bones shown above. In the background played out different pieces of code, each one executing quickly as the portable computer worked.

"I figured they'd have better security here, so hopefully that program works." He tapped a paw on the metal panel, watching as the bar slowly filled up. "If it's using an algorithm similar to the front desk, my device should be able to hack it in a few minutes."

Letting the screen hang by its wires, Coal dipped both paws into his backpack and began digging around. "This is definitely a high security zone," he informed while pulling the butt of a gun out of his bag. Being a smaller animal, carrying fully assembled weapons became cumbersome. To get around this disadvantage, he brought them in pieces and assembled them on the battlefield if necessary. Placing the part on the ground, he dipped back in to fish out the other parts. "I've got some prep work to do, can you call the others?"

Levi groaned in response, but still pressed a paw to his ear. "Pyre to pack leader, we are now descending on the elevator. Over." Releasing his paw from the button, the large cat leaned against the wall.

The bunny glanced over his shoulder with a look of annoyance, frustrated by how vague the leopard had been. Putting a paw to his own headset, he added, "Foxtrot One Romeo Three to pack leader, we have good reason to believe we are entering a hot zone. What is your ETA? Over."

Static poured through the communications for a few seconds until a panting voice finally came through. "Smoke here. We're a little busy right now, but we'll meet you down there in a few minutes." In the background, they could hear the sounds of suppressed gunshots and shells landing on the tile floor. "Just remember to leave a key. Over and out."

As the conversation ended, the elevator jolted to life. The lapin stopped his weapon assembly for a moment to lift up the metal panel and look at the screen. "Not quite there yet, but it's still working."

Unmoved from his wall, the feline watched as his partner returned to assembling his weapons. Examining his own, he checked for any faults before asking, "So what do you think they've got down there."

Locking the barrel of his weapon into place, the rabbit responded with a simple, "Don't really know." He clicked a latch that pulled the two largest parts together tightly before glancing over. "Gotta be something pretty good to put it underground, right?"

Levi thought about that for a little bit before nodding, but by then the room had already gone fairly quiet. Deciding not to pester the rabbit while they waited, he stared at the wall and let his mind drift.

\* \* \*

But it was the wall that started to drift away, the elevator seemingly expanding outward as the room enlarged. He looked out across the newly formed space, only to realize he had returned to one of the training rooms at their base.

Coal had not left him. The bunny now stood at the ready with a combat knife clenched tightly in his paw. He jumped forward, taking a good swing at a practice dummy that had been set up in the middle of the space. The knife hit with a good amount of force, but the blade barely scratched the surface of the armor.

The leopard had come here for one reason, to make an ally of the rabbit. Taking a few steps into the room, he could feel his heart beating loudly in his chest as a wave of emotions washed over him. Uncertain of what to say, his muscles tensed as if to tell him to turn around. And then he remembered the wolf from the woods leaning over him. "Let this be a lesson, kitten," echoed the words in the canine's deep, southern voice. "Your time stalking us is over." Levi clenched a paw tightly, claws extending into his fist, as his other muscles gradually relaxed. He knew what he needed to do now, and he knew what he wanted to say.

"You won't land a kill with a blow like that," he called out while nodding towards the fake body. "These guys have been made to represent real body armor, so you're going to need more force."

"I already know that," the cottontail retorted. He turned and paced in a small circle, clearly agitated now. "I was kind of in the middle of practicing."

Levi rolled his eyes, pulling out his own knife as he walked an arm's reach away from the practice dummy. "Then let's practice." With unprecedented speed, the cat attacked. He grabbed onto the body armor, using the protective gear to his advantage as he pulled the dummy into his attack. His other paw jabbed the knife into the armor, the blade smashing through until the gear depressed inwards.

He glanced over at Coal, who stared with astonishment at the act. Without turning back, he pulled the knife free and took a few steps back. "Now you do it."

The rabbit watched as the blade cleanly cut out of the practice manikin. His eyes followed the metallic shimmer before looking back at the perfect hole. He approached the dummy, ears dropping down, and put a paw onto the newly made cut.

Pulling out his own blade, he examined the metal as a paw traced over the shark teeth. He slid down to the tip, pushing the point gently into his paw pad for a moment. He breathed slowly with an open mouth, licking his lips as they dried. "I can't do that." The blade dropped back down to his side.

Levi re-sheathed his blade, uncertain of what he was supposed to do next. He had never really interacted with another fur on this level before, which left him feeling slightly uneasy. He flicked his tail, both ears splayed flat. "It's not as hard as it looks."

The words fell flat and silence filled the room as they stood there.

Letting out a sigh, Coal looked back over his shoulder at the big cat. "Why are you even down here?"

The feline did not know how to answer. His gaze shifted between Coal's amber eyes, tail flicking as he thought through what to say, except he already knew the only thing to say was the truth. Dropping his guard, his eyes fell towards the floor as he spoke. "I need your help."

The cat listened to the words as they bounced off the walls, making him feel as though the room was closing up on them. "Last time we were out in the woods was the first time I was ever shot. Fell out of a tree after one of those stun rounds hit me in the back. When I woke up, Scorch and Smoke were standing above me. Even gave me a good kick in the side." He stopped for a moment, paw rubbing his ribs to the reminder of the pain. "There's no way I can beat that group alone, not anymore."

With a quick breath, he looked up towards the cottontail, searching for a response. When none came, he continued on. "I'm not good with others, never have been, but it's like you said: I'm the only leopard and you're the only herbivore." He again waited for the rabbit to say something back. When the bunny kept quiet he took that as his cue to leave. Rubbing a paw behind his neck, he started to leave.

"Hold on," the bunny commanded, "we're still practicing."

The feline turned back to a smirking rabbit, blade lifted in his paw. Bouncing off the ground and twisting backwards, he stabbed at the training dummy with all his force. The blade sunk into the protective gear a little way before getting stuck, clearly not deep enough to pierce through.

Putting both of his foot paws against the mannequin's chest, he pressed off the body until his knife came out. "I've been trying all morning, but I can't get through."

For a large animal, such as a wolf or a big cat like Levi, getting the force to break through the armor required nothing more than a purely muscular attack. But for someone small like Coal, directly stabbing an opponent would never work. Instead, the rabbit would have to create momentum in his thrust from somewhere else, and Levi knew where.

Marching over to the dummy, he asked, "I'm sure when you were on the playground as a teenager you saw a couple of deer get in a fight, right?" He waited for the rabbit to nod. "Okay, well when two bucks fight one another, they don't throw down their fists. They run at each other and butt their antlers.

"Now, I'm not saying that you should be trying to head butt the enemy, but you can learn something from them. They turn their momentum into a much more powerful attack.

"You've got to do the same. This time try running and jumping at the manikin directly to stab."

Coal looked down at the knife in his paw while rubbing his chin with the other. He looked as though he were calculating his next move, figuring out exactly what to do. When he was satisfied, he dropped both paws and proceeded to the other side of the room. Getting in a ready position, he took off running straight at the practice dummy.

\* \* \*

There was a rather loud beeping sound that made the cat blink, but as he opened his eyes the training room had disappeared. Instead, he found himself back in the elevator, his gaze still upon Coal as he jumped forward. The lapin flew through the air, knife in one paw, as those two elevator doors slid open.

On the other side was a guard that had just turned at the sound of the elevator. His eyes went wide as the blade sunk into his chest, the canine exhaling his last breath as the full force of the bunny pushed into him. The lupine started to fall backwards.

Adrenaline pumped through the feline's veins, the sight of his partner's attack returning him to the present. He grabbed his own knife and rushed out to tackle the second guard. The two met at an awkward angle, the enemy having only partially turned around when the leopard collided with him. Levi stabbed the other fur in the side, putting a paw against his muzzle as he threw the unsuspecting animal into the wall.

Snarling, the leopard pushed down the corridor towards the other enemies in the room. He purposefully dodged the next animal knowing that his partner would take him out. As he passed, he could see blood gushing out of the animal's head from a shot fired from behind him. He did not stop.

He had his sights set on a big brown bear at the end of the hall, the ursine having turned around and almost pulled his gun up to the ready. As the cat reached him, he curved past the barrel of the gun and pushed the bruin's aim towards the wall. He put his weight forward as their bodies met, bringing up his knife to let the blade sink in.

Even with a knife in his chest, the grizzly was still standing. He grabbed Levi by his gear and held him tight, roaring spit and saliva directly into the leopard's face as an act of dominance. When the bear stopped, he smashed his head against the cat's before tossing him effortlessly across the room.

With a loud bang, Levi slammed into the now closed elevator doors. His vision blurred and the world began to spin. Unable to move, he watched as the ursine in the distance aimed his weapon to fire. The grizzly growled, only to freeze before dropping onto his knees and falling over to his side.

Levi breathed a sigh of relief while closing his eyes, the large cat wanting nothing more than to rest for a minute or two. He could feel a weight climbing into his lap, but kept his eyes closed. Two paws grabbed his shoulders and shook.

"Levi… Levi… You have to get up."

He opened his eyes to a blurry rabbit nose twitching in his face, paws leaving his shoulders. "What?"

The bunny in front of him started looking around before leaning down and grabbing something off to his side. A moment later, a flashlight was shining in one eye while a paw held the lids open. "You don't look too bad," he noted while switching to examine the other eye.

Putting the flashlight back from where he had taken it, Coal got off the big cat and pulled on his paw. "Come on, we have to get going before someone else comes."

The leopard put his other paw against the elevator's door frame, using the cold metal to stabilize himself as he stood back up. His world was still moving, just less so than previously. He took a cautious step, eyes following the rabbit in front of him. "Give me a minute," he called out.

Looking back over his shoulder, the rabbit could see the big cat still needed help. Slinging his rifle onto his back, he came back over to his partner and put a paw around his waist to help him. They both moved slowly to the first door.

Levi looked through a window in the upper half of the door to see what was inside, but quickly ducked back. "There's a lot of fur in there; scientists from the looks of it."

Helping put the cat up against the wall, Coal held up both paws as a signal to stay. "Okay, I'll dip inside and see if I can find anything out. You stay here and get your bearing again." Handing his gun over to the feline, the little rabbit dipped into the room.

Levi leaned up against the wall, holding the unfamiliar gun close to his chest. He closed his eyes and let his body slide down, feeling his backpack drag upwards as he did so. Hitting the floor, he breathed slowly and waited. It was times like these that he liked to imagine he was back home in the forest again, listening to the world around him as the warm summer's breeze shook the trees.

*　*　*

There was a crack, the sound of a twig snapping in the distance that got him to open his eyes. A forest surrounded him on all sides, including the large branch of a tree underneath him. He looked out towards where he thought the sound had come from, even picking his rifle up out of his lap in case he needed to quickly fire, but caught nothing in his sights. His ears stood tall and searched for another clue, because he was being hunted.

Out of the corner of his eye he saw a blur moving as quick as the wind. His head swiveled, snapping his gun up only to watch as the last bit of a canine's tail disappeared behind a rock. Getting to his feet, he stood at the ready with both eyes glued to that rock.

Another blur moved to his left, a second figure that also dodged out of sight the moment his head turned. He could feel the moment coming.

"Kitten climbed back in his tree," shouted a voice from the direction he had seen the first figure go. "I thought he would have learned by now."

"Maybe he needed a second lesson," laughed a second one.

Levi had but a moment to remember exactly what happened last time he was in this position. Without a warning, the two coyotes dashed out of their hiding spot, running as fast as they could towards his position. Neither had their gun set and aimed on him just yet, for both were trying to get a little bit closer.

He paid little attention to them. Instead, the leopard focused his eyes on the forest in the distance as he searched for something in particular. With a glint of sunlight, he found what he was looking for, the wolf.

Grabbing onto the trunk of the tree and digging his claws in, he swung down to the ground. Although he could not see it, several rounds passed through the space where he had previously been. Nearly dodging that attack, he came down to the forest floor and rolled into cover. Tapping the side of his headset, he calmly said, "Alpha is about a hundred feet away behind a rock and both pups are coming up on either side. I've got right."

Placing his arm on top of the boulder, the leopard stabilized his aim as he looked just over his sights into the distance. The coyote was coming at him still, his blurred figure seen passing from one tree to the next as he approached. Levi looked through his scope, the barrel of his gun now following that blur back and forth. He waited for the right moment to make the perfect shot.

When he had his chance, he fired.

The familiar, loud sound of gunfire erupted only to be followed by a second shot not long after. Levi did not falter from his stance, weapon raised and ready to fire again in case the first shot had missed. He waited patiently for any movement.

After waiting what he considered to be more than long enough, the cat looked over the top of his scope. The forest presented itself as he had always remembered, quiet and empty. He sluggishly stood up, eyes tracing the terrain as he peered over the boulder until he spotted his enemy. The coyote had fallen less than twenty feet away, knocked out by the powerful stun rounds.

Levi smirked, but the smile vanished as a paw grabbed hold of his side.

* * *

Rolling away from the paw, he flipped over and immediately aimed towards the other fur. With ragged, nearly growling breaths, he looked through the scope. He could feel his digit on the trigger, shaken but still ready to pull. As he looked down the sights, the feline stopped himself.

"It's just me, kitten," calmed the rabbit. Coal had both paws up, eyes wide as he starred down his own gun towards his partner. "Put down the weapon."

Tension eased off the leopard as his paw backed away from the trigger and his muscles relaxed. "Sorry," he apologized while holding his paw out to give the firearm back. "What did you see?"

The rabbit took his weapon back and looked towards the room. Both of his ears had dropped, eyes fixated on the room with a sterile gaze. "There's a reason this place is underground." He breathed in, holding everything in like this might be the last one. Slowly, he raised a paw and touched his headset. "Foxtrot One Romeo Three calling control, this is Coal with an update on this facility. Over."

Crackling flooded their headset, the layers of earth and concrete above their head preventing a perfect signal from getting through. After a while they could make out a voice trying to talk to them, but not what was being said. A minute later the headset went dead.

With his partner still staring intently at the door, curiosity got the better half of the cat. Levi got to his feet and sidestepped along the wall until he was right up next to the door. He turned his head towards the door's window, his breath fogging up a small portion of the glass. Cautiously, he looked inside the room.

He could see the scientists from before standing at the far end of a long, metal table. Almost all of them were chatting with one another, jotting down notes and exchanging information. A few others were on computers, typing up their own sets. His eyes gleamed over each of them with no particular interest, say for one.

In the back of the group, the farthest from him, he spied a lynx in a lab coat. The other cat's long ears twitched, a paw on his facial fur as he gently pulled. He was neither partaking in their conversation nor watching them, his concentration glued on the large window in front of him. Raising a paw, he tapped the glass.

Levi followed that paw into what looked like a small and what appeared to be empty room. A door opened and two guards entered, each one moving as though watching where he stepped. They picked something up and left.

The scientists' chatter died as the guards appeared in a door at the far end, but exactly what they had grabbed was still to be seen. Slowly, the other furs moved aside for them as they lifted up their prize onto that cold, metal table. The feline's eyes went wide as the body of a snow leopard was placed onto the table, a child no less.

"Foxtrot One Romeo Three calling control, this is Coal. Do you read me? Over."

The room in front of the cat seemed to elongate as the scientists started their work. They were drifting away from him, or maybe he was drifting from them. Either way, the horror in front of him seemed to slowly become more and more distant as Levi unknowingly backed away from the door

A crackling hiss came through his headset again before stabilizing. "This is pack leader to Coal, we're going to boost your signal with our headset. Wait until you can hear control before you speak. Over." The crackling returned.

Levi could barely hear them, his eyes locked on the window. Even if he looked away from that pane of glass, the image would remain in his head. He could see the scientists as they moved around the body. They were pulling their gloves tight and picking up scalpels. And they prodded on the lifeless corpse and took notes on what had happened to the body.

What sent shivers down the feline's spine was the body of the snow leopard, lifeless and cold on the table. There was terror in those blue eyes. Even though he had never heard the cat's voice, Levi could hear his cries.

The other voices all sounded distant now, echoes far away from the leopard, but still there. "This is control. What have you found, Foxtrot? Over."

He could hear his own heartbeat better than his partner in the same room. "Control, we are in a biological weapons facility…" The voice of the rabbit was distant, almost lost.

But those eyes. He could not let go of the horror still locked in those sapphire eyes. They had looked right at him, piercing into his soul and bringing out memories he had long since forgotten. A chill swept his being as he continued to step backwards.

Without looking at where he was going, he tripped over the body of the bear. His heart raced, mouth open wide, and paws grasping at air. Time seemed to slow as he fell, crawling by in a similar way to when he had first taken out the coyote in the woods during training camp years ago. Except he was in her place and fear had overcome him.

\* \* \*

As his body hit the ground, he bounced on the soft dirt. The wind had been knocked out of him, but he had sense enough to get up onto his elbows to try and back away. Ears splayed flat, he looked up at the wolf in front of him.

The canine stood above him with his pistol pointing down at Levi's face. He looked larger from the cat's point of view, and his lip was curled up on his muzzle in a snarl. "Now I told you to stop stalking and start fighting like a real predator," he barked, "but maybe I didn't make myself clear."

The lupine took a step forward, watching as the cat backed up to stand against a tree behind him. He snorted out the front of his nose as if disgusted by the sheepish display in front of him. "Listen, kitten, if you plan on being anything in this outfit then you better start working with other members. I mean, they don't call us a pack for nothing."

The lupine clicked the gun's safety, his tail wagging behind him. From the joy visible in his eyes, Levi could tell he took pride in his dominance over another animal. With an arrogant smile, he added, "Then again, I guess not all of us were made to be pack animals."

The leopard had a second to think and all he could wonder was what had happened to Coal. He wondered if the wolf had already taken him out or if the cottontail simply decided to run. He hoped it was neither as he breathed in, ready to take the sting of the bullet.

\* \* \*

Bright light appeared in front of the cat as he opened his eyes. He could feel two paws shaking him gently, and as he looked over he saw a familiar bunny standing there. "You okay?"

"Just fell over." There was a bit of silence between them as the cat laid back down to stare at the lights above. "You tell control?"

The rabbit let go and walked back towards the door to grab his gear. "Yeah. They want us to make this building go up in flames and make it look like an accident."

For a moment, the air between them went quiet again as they both thought. The leopard had no idea how to get the building to explode, much less how to make the explosion look like an accident. He sat up against the wall and looked at Coal. "So what's the plan?"

The rabbit turned around, rifle in his paws as he looked at the cat. "Well, we're supposed to wait for the other members of the pack to get down here," he groaned while detaching the magazine. He checked the clip's remaining rounds before snapping the ammo back in place. "Except I know a certain kitten that's gonna do his own thing and I'm just gonna have to tag along." He aimed his rifle down the hallway, ears back in a final check of his weapon. "You know, to save his ass."

A tank is wrecked in a battlefield during a war. Its five-man team—a coyote, a fox, a pronghorn antelope, a hare, and a mouse—are forced to try to return to safety on foot.

Which of them—if any—will succeed in Going Home?

# Going Home

## *by Miles Reaver*

There was always a feeling of relief that came after surviving yet another battle—a reminder that others who fought by your side weren't as lucky. You've gained another few hours, perhaps a day or two, and then it was time to push your luck once again. Maybe this time, it wasn't going to last. You think to yourself, 'it can't happen to me', and then it does.

The platoon of tanks rolled away from the battlefield, leaving behind a graveyard of fire and steel, a terrifying image of the kind of power they held. Amongst the wreckage was a single functioning tank still left for repairs. Four out of its five crew-men lingered around their armored vehicle in dead silence, following the example of their Commander, a short coyote named Sergeant Anderson. He was leaning onto the back of the mud-fouled tank with a freshly lit cigarette in his muzzle, idly staring off in the distance. After the battle came the tedious necessity of making quick repairs before the vehicle was in a condition to be driven anywhere. Their original plan was to make a quick repair before catching up to the rest of the tank platoon, but after a long and frustrating hour, they were beginning to realize that they might not be able to.

The young fox fiddled with the tank's track links, trying to make them fit back together again. The tank's loader and gunner, Grigs and Pell, hovered over the fox impatiently.

"Is it done yet, JJ?" asked Pell, a soldier who was only a few years older.

Julian's ears flicked and he turned his head to face the hare.

"Does it look like it's done?" he asked with a sour tone, wiping the mud and grease away from his muzzle.

"I'm not a mechanic," said Pell, "and neither is Grigs. We're from the city." He exchanged glances with the pronghorn antelope who nodded in return.

Julian rolled his eyes and turned back to the tank, his dirty paws struggling to keep a firm grasp on his tools. "No, it's not done. It wasn't done when you asked five minutes ago and it won't be done anytime soon if you keep asking me all the time."

Pell scowled at the fox, clicked his tongue and said, "Someone's grumpy. We're alive, at least. I think you need a good vixen to help you unwind." The hare and antelope grinned at each other.

Julian's ears fell flat against his head and squeezed the wrench tightly in his paws. The downfall of spending nearly every hour of the day with your crew is that you eventually get to know everything about them—everything.

"Alright, that's enough," Sergeant Anderson's gruff voice boomed over them. "Pell, cut the crap. We're still in enemy territory." His tail lashed behind him as he reminded them of the situation.

Pell adjusted the strap of his rifle across his shoulder and backed away from the fox, twitching his whiskers at him.

Anderson continued to assume command, his own patience wearing thin. "Jackson, what's the situation on the track?"

Julian hesitated, doing a quick check of the spare parts at their disposal. He swung his tail across his lap and dropped his gaze.

"I've already used up most of the spare parts we've had," he began to explain. "We could do without one support roller, but I don't think we have enough track links."

Pell swung around on one foot and planted the other in the mud. "What the hell does that mean?"

"It means we're stuck here," Julian answered, wiping his paws against the bottom part of his uniform.

The hare dragged his own paws across his trembling ears. "Great." His voice shook.

"Great." Grigs echoed.

Sergeant Anderson got the message loud and clear. He pounded the hull of their tank with his paw and shouted: "Zio!"

"Sir?" A small-framed mouse popped his head out of the hatch, the signal receivers still strapped around his ears.

"Try reaching the other tank platoons. Tell them we need one of them to come back. Tell them it's urgent."

The mouse shook his head briefly and readjusted the straps. "I don't think that's possible, sir. The tank squadron left roughly an hour ago and they may be out of range."

"I said try, damn it." the coyote barked his order at Zio, who quickly ducked back inside the tank.

Sergeant Anderson quickly finished off the rest of the cigarette and then began to rub his muzzle. He was thinking through the situation while Grigs and Pell made their best attempts at holding it together. The fox knelt by the broken tracks of the tank, thinking of ways to make the repairs but always coming to the same conclusion.

They waited in anticipation for what seemed like an eternity, until the radio operator slowly rose through the hatch shaking his head, removing the straps from his ears.

"No use, sir. I get static, but that's about it."

Anderson growled at nobody in particular. He moved a few steps away from the tank with his paws at his hips and said something under his breath. The crew was his responsibility. They were a pack that followed his orders. His decisions would make all the difference to their fate. The coyote turned back, looked at them one by one, and sharply exhaled.

"Alright," he said with a nod. "Destroy the radio and grab the guns. We're moving in five minutes."

The crew exchanged glances before turning back to the coyote. Pell spread his paws widely, one of his feet trembling against the ground.

"Move?" he asked the Sergeant. "We're in the middle of nowhere. Where are we supposed to go?"

"Home." The coyote growled quietly "We're going home."

\* \* \*

Besides being burned alive, one of the worst nightmares of a tanker was having to move on foot. It was dangerous, reckless, and more often than not, it ended in death. The way tank schools picked their soldiers had been divided into species and height. If you were small enough to fit into a tank, you were it. The crew was only trained to operate and maintain the armored vehicle, not to fight without it. Each of them carried a sub-machine gun called a paw-greaser and an extra sidearm. Their equipment had been humble enough that all they could hope for was that they wouldn't have to use it.

Sergeant Anderson drew a basic map in the dirt and gave them instructions to follow. They would make a beeline through the woods on foot and meet up with the rest of the tank platoon on the other side by sundown. It all sounded a bit too simple.

The forest bordering the battlefield was engulfed in darkness and fog, a dark presence lurking somewhere in the shadows. It was thick with trees, and deathly quiet as they moved in arranged order through the dirt. The coyote led the pack in front—his canine senses of smell and sight would prove more than useful along their way. Zio as the radio operator walked next to him. His hearing had not been the best given his species, but it had been the least damaged. The crew wasn't taking any chances. They knew the situation they had been thrown in.

Grigs and Pell walked together right behind them, with Julian taking up the rear. The hare and pronghorn kept on guard, their twitching ears and tails showed apparent anxiety. None of them besides Sergeant Anderson had any previous experiences on foot. They knew he had fought in the trenches before being stationed as a tank commander. A coyote small enough to fit into a tank was seen as shameful, and the crew knew better than to ask him about it.

The tank crew passed a small creek in the forest where the water ran through moss-covered rocks and dropped down the hill. Since the moment they had entered the forest, Julian noticed signs that he couldn't quite piece together. The fog they had been in was different than usual. It dragged behind them as they walked. Those with bushy tails would push it out the way like it was smoke. It was only paranoia, Julian thought to himself as he marched behind his crew. Paranoia would keep him on his guard. As Julian looked up, he noticed the hare up front glancing back at him. He let out a sigh when Pell fell back to walk besides the fox.

"You scared, JJ?" Pell grinned and tried to hide the nervous gesture of his ears. His body betrayed any attempt he had made at appearing smug.

"I think we're all scared," Julian responded. He locked eyes with the hare. "We're on foot, and I think it's useless to pretend that we're trained to be infantry. We should have stayed behind."

Pell smirked as if he had been expecting such a response. "You don't have to be such a downer all the time, you know," the hare said, shaking his head. "Maybe the rest of the team would like you better." Grigs up in front swiveled his ears backwards at them.

"I don't care if you like me," Julian snapped. "Besides, they're saying the war is almost over. If it means working together a bit longer, that's fine by me, but I don't have to put up with your smugness."

"You don't really mean that," Grigs chipped in before Pell could reply. "I like you plenty, Jackson. So does Zio, and I'm sure the Sergeant does, too."

Pell clicked his tongue and looked away. "Yeah, I bet he does."

Julian stopped in his tracks and grabbed Pell by the shoulder, who in return shook the paw off and shoved the fox.

"For god's sake, Pell," Grigs raised his voice and stepped between them. "This is what I mean. We've all been through a lot together. I think it's high time you stopped being such an asshole."

The two soldiers glared at each other in silence, ignoring Grigs' words. Julian bared his fangs at the hare, his temperature rising, but Pell refused to be intimidated. There was tension all around, and it was apparent that the driver and gunner didn't actually like each other.

Sergeant Anderson's voice suddenly boomed over them: "If you two are done with your stupid argument, I'd like to get this crew to the base before sundown."

Nobody responded right away. They knew sundown was soon and that time was not on their side.

"Wasn't an argument," said the hare.

"We could hear both of you." Anderson's tail lashed behind him, and Pell noticed all eyes were on him. "We won't get anywhere with that attitude of yours. Front with me, Pell." The Sergeant barked his order, and before the hare could argue, the coyote took a step towards him, claws extended. "Don't make me drag you up here."

Julian knew the Sergeant's tendency to snap, especially when it came to following orders, so he had remained quiet. Pell felt the need to wrinkle his nose at Julian and wipe down the spot where the fox had grabbed him before joining the Sergeant and Zio up in front. They had broken formation, but under the coyote's orders they would make the best of it. The only way to make it work was to separate the hare from the fox.

"Shouldn't let him provoke you like that," said the pronghorn quietly enough for only Julian to hear as they continued on their way. "You know he only does it to get a rise out of you."

"I know," The fox confirmed. "But I don't need that *right now*. My fur is on edge as it is."

The pronghorn nodded his head. "We're all on edge. We're exposed out here."

"I wanted to stay behind. I think leaving our tank was a mistake." Grigs made a grunting sound. Julian shut up, feeling that continuing to talk about it wasn't going to help their situation.

The October clouds blocked the sun's rays above the forest, making it darker the farther that they progressed. The forest had started to get wilder, more thick with large bushes, making it more difficult to see far in front of them. While the coyote had been under a lot of pressure, the crew trusted his instincts and his skill to guide them through. Soon enough night would fall, and their chances of safe passage through the forest would drop by at least half. Wind whistled through the leaves and bushes, pushing the fog with it. Julian's paranoia returned when he had noticed the coyote sensing it too. He sniffed the air trying to get some kind of scent. The fox mirrored his movements, and yet could not locate a single scent—not even those of his crew.

When you spent enough time in a closed space with other soldiers, their scents became easy to recognize and pick up. With time it became almost unbearable. It stayed in your nose. Often you begged for fresh air. The coyote raised his paw indicating a stop—his body posture stiff.

"Anyone smell that?" he asked nobody in particular.

"Smell what?" Pell took a few whiffs around him. "I smell nothing." Then his eyes widened. Even with his own nose not as good as that of a coyote or fox, he was still able to notice the difference.

"Exactly," the coyote confirmed. "This isn't fog. It's gas."

Trench warfare had advanced far enough to discover new ambush tactics. One of them was the release of a neutralizing gas that would poison the nasal passageway, making any attempts at picking up an enemy's scent impossible. The gas had mixed in with the fog, something Julian thought had just been natural. Due to the wind, the gas could have come from anywhere; but due to the fact that it was yet unsettled, it had to have been released only recently.

Sergeant Anderson gave them further orders. They were to use the trees as cover and move accordingly, switching from one to the next in order to be less visible.

"Remember," said the coyote, "they can't smell us coming, but they can still hear us. They don't know we're here, so let's not fuck this up." He glared at Pell and Julian, both of whom only nodded in return.

The forest itself grew even more wild and uneven as they went along. Julian kept shifting his eyes and ears, hoping to spot any signs of the enemy before the enemy could spot them. It wasn't long before they started noticing discarded items. Pieces of metal that looked like they used to be a rifle lay underneath a bush. An old and torn jacket was laying by a tree on the opposite side. Julian thought he could see what looked like a suitcase a bit farther away from them, but with the gas and fog, he couldn't be sure.

They had all seemed to have slightly dropped their guards. A small dry ditch appeared. Following their previous instruction to move from cover to cover, they crossed the ditch one at a time. Anderson placed his weight alongside a tree to help himself across, extending a paw for Zio to grab onto and follow. Grigs was the tallest and didn't need as much help as Zio and Julian, but it was Pell that took the initiative to jump across the ditch by himself. Branches cracked bellow his weight and something beside him fell over, a snapping sound following a split-second later. They all but jumped in place—all eyes had been on the hare. They were quiet, listening. Nothing happened.

"Just a suitcase," said Pell and waved his paw. "Glad it wasn't a grenade, though," he chuckled and quickly added, "but I'll be more careful," when he saw the coyote turn and scowl.

"That's the second one I've seen," Zio commented after they'd made a good few steps ahead. "Lots of things left behind at random."

As if on cue, the Sergeant suddenly stopped, making Pell nearly walk into him. The coyote's tail froze, his ears flicked nervously. Slowly, he looked left, right, and then shifted his weight, turning his head around and licking his muzzle.

"Don't touch anything," he said in a low grumble. "In fact, don't even move."

The crew exchanged glances and remained still. They had been walking a long time, and were all tired from being under pressure and being extra-cautious. The coyote was clearly being paranoid.

"Touch what? There's nothing around here but junk someone left behind," said Grigs, taking a step toward a big rock.

"Grigs, I told you not to move." The coyote swung his head around, growling through his fangs.

"I think you're just paranoid, Sarge," the pronghorn complained. "There's nothing here," he added as he idly kicked what looked like a discarded helmet near the rock. There was a high pitched buzzing sound as the helmet fell into one of the bushes; then a sudden snapping sound. The group went quiet, fur prickling all around. Julian broke from cover and stepped closer to the Sergeant, readying his rifle, but the coyote waved for him to stop before he got too close.

"God damn it, Grigs!" Anderson raised his voice. "I told you not to touch anything." There was another sound in the distance, like a click or a buzz. Being inside a tank, there came a time when you temporarily felt invincible, and that's when it was easy to make a mistake.

It came too fast to see, too fast to react or do anything about it. There was a sound of a thousand angry bees before it hit. Sergeant Anderson was the first to fall. The bullets hit their mark and a splash of blood sprayed out, his body dropped to the ground like a puppet with no strings—and then it was raining bullets.

\* \* \*

Leaving their tank behind had turned out to have been a mistake. They had ventured into the unknown unprepared and under-equipped, and now they were paying the price for it. It sounded like a deep thunder, only it wasn't. The sound of the machine gun echoed through the forest like a monster—the roar seemed to have come from all around them, closing in.

Over the volume of the barrage, Julian found himself on the ground, kicking and shoving while screaming at the top of his voice. He was disorientated, panicked by the shock he had just experienced. He could feel his blood seeping into his fur, running down his ears and muzzle—the ground beneath him shook violently. He struggled and yet he couldn't move. Something was on top of him, pressing him down with all its weight. There were voices he couldn't quite make out, shouts he couldn't understand. It took only a few seconds before the voices became clearer.

"Stop fidgeting!" Julian could recognize Pell's voice. The hare had been holding Julian to the ground, keeping his head low and out the way of gunfire. He could see the bark splintering away from the trees. To his right, the Sergeant's lifeless body lay face down, his blood seeping from the back of his skull. He was dead and there was no question about it.

Zio and Grigs had jumped down into cover, each behind their own tree, shoving their heads as close to the ground as they could. Once Julian had stopped trying to fight Pell off of him, the hare tapped the fox on the shoulder. "Stay low and don't move," he said before sliding off, dragging himself away just enough to face the other two tankers. They had to get out of there or else they would end up like the coyote.

"I can't see anyone," Grigs shouted to Pell. The enemy wasn't using tracers but they could tell where the bullets were coming from.

"Stay under cover!" the hare cried loudly. "He'll have to reload and that's when we run. Do not hesitate!" He put his own head low behind the rock he and Julian were hiding behind, and held his long ears down with his paws.

Breathe and focus, Julian reminded himself. He had been in battles before, and this was just another one that they would have to survive. Pell had been handling the pressure well enough to put himself in charge. The others would have to follow his lead. Sergeant Anderson didn't deserve to die in some forest in a far away land. He deserved better than that, deserved to be remembered. Julian knew what he had to do. As the crew waited anxiously for the gunfire to cease, the fox managed to turn himself around to face the rock in front of him. He braced himself against it. His tail had tightly curled between his legs and all he could do was hope it wouldn't slow him down.

The final bullet rang out a moment later and the tankers jumped to their feet, bolting into the opposite direction. Pell had been the fastest. As he looked behind him, he saw both Zio and Grigs running close by—but no fox. He swore under his breath, stopped and turned back. He shouted at them to keep running while he quickly backtracked. Julian had been at the Sergeant's body, reaching for the tags around his neck. He had managed to separate the two tags just as the hare caught up to him.

"We don't have time for this!" he shouted at the fox as he grabbed him by his paw, pulling him up. "He's gone, Jackson."

"He deserves to be remembered," Julian argued and grasped the tags tightly in his paw. By then it had been too late, and the window of opportunity had nearly closed in on them. Shots rang out closely enough for them to hear them being absorbed by the trees, followed by distant shouts. Out of the fog, the duo could see enemy soldiers in long blue coats quickly approaching.

"Run!" Pell shoved Julian forward. Together they dashed up ahead to catch up with Grigs and Zio. There was the sound of bullets whistling past them, popping noises as they hit the wood and dirt. The two tankers ran in a zig-zag, swearing and jumping over bigger branches and rocks, panic making them feel their enemy's eyes on their backs. Back at the ditch, the mouse and pronghorn garrisoned the position with their rifles aiming down the line.

"Christ, does anyone ever listen to me?" shouted Pell. There was no time to lose, no time for questions or arguments. Julian and Pell had enough momentum to jump across the ditch with ease, then all together they made haste to disappear into the forest.

Fear had guided them back along their previous path. Their primal instinct, the desire for survival had been severe. There was nothing wrong with being afraid. Fear had been a double-sided sword that pushed you forward, adrenaline that kept you through danger. You moved like never before by pure instinct. Despite them knowing that it was time to run away, being in unfamiliar territory did not help their situation. They knew that enemy soldiers were hot on their tails. They heard their bullets fly past them. They heard shouts from all around them, but were unable to pinpoint their exact location anymore.

While Pell as the hare had been the fastest runner, it was Grigs that was the tallest. With his long legs he made decent progress up ahead. The rest of the team followed his lead, trusting him to guide them out of danger. Pell could have outrun him easily, but being in the position of the current commander, he could not let Zio and Julian fall behind. Once more they reached the small hillside in the forest where the small creek ran down farther away from them. Grigs had decided to change directions. Unanimously they agreed that the best course of action would be to change the direction where their enemy expected them to be. Grigs turned left at the creek and ran uphill. While the hill did slow them down, it also gave them hope of losing the enemy in the end. The pronghorn was nearly leaping up the hill without much effort while the other three followed behind. Once he had made it to the top, he descended down the other side and disappeared.

They quickly paddled their way through the mud and dead leaves, reaching the top just a few short moments later. The pronghorn was gone. Julian did a quick scan of the area, but through the trees he could see nothing. He shouted for the antelope, but there was no answer.

"Shut up," Pell hissed at the fox. "Don't give away our position." Julian bared his fangs but remained quiet.

"Which way did he go?" Pell looked around furiously. Zio watched their backs with the rifle firmly in his paws.

"He ran," said the mouse, trying to catch his breath. "We need to move and we have to stay together."

Pell nodded. "Agreed," he said and assumed the lead.

While the creek side of the forest had been mostly wild and uneven, the section right over the hill had been divided into a series of smaller hills. The trio went up one side and down the other, maneuvering from cover to cover. They ended up climbing a third, much steeper hill. Their tiredness had them moving a lot slower, and their guns bumping against their backs suddenly increased in weight. Now the forest had been relatively flat. They had made a beeline in heavy hopes of somehow spotting Grigs ahead, hoping he had already made it out of the forest. Their hopes ended up having different plans, however, as after only a couple of feet the hilltop ended in a steep slope.

"He didn't come this way," Julian pointed out as he stood at the very edge of it. "There would have been some kind of marks in the dirt."

Before either Pell or Zio could respond, their ears perked up when there was a rustling of leaves. A nearby shrubbery shook.

"Grigs?" Julian raised his voice and Pell quickly nudged the fox in the chest, hissing at him. The rustling stopped for a brief moment and heavy footsteps approached them. They appeared as shadows behind the bushes. They didn't reveal themselves before starting to shoot.

Out of the corner of his eye, Julian saw Zio return fire just before his body went limp and fell to the ground. Once again they had been too slow to react. The hare shoved Julian backwards and out of the way. The fox fell down the slope and the rest was a blur.

\* \* \*

The momentum had carried Julian down into the unknown, spinning him uncontrollably. He stopped when he had reached the bottom. The fox laid motionless on the ground, his vision blurred and his head feeling ten sizes too big. He took his time before he managed to pull himself to his feet. He looked around his surroundings in a daze, before his tail jerked him off his balance and he backed up into a tree, grasping it tightly with his claws—it would keep the world from spinning as he focused on remembering what had happened. He lost his sense of time. He didn't know how long he had stood there. After a while his mind came back. His senses slowly turned to normal, leaving him sore.

Pell had pushed him down the slope, saving his life for the second time that day. For the second time, Julian felt completely useless. He grasped his rifle close to his chest, too afraid to look behind him, afraid of what he might see. He felt lost, confused about what to do and where to go. Despair clutched him like a shadow. If the enemy got their paws on him now, he would be shot on sight or worse, interrogated and tortured. They told stories in camp about what had happened to captured soldiers, although those were just rumors as nobody really knew what really happened - and that made it worse. Then a thought daunted him. What if he was found by his allies while walking around in the woods by himself? Would they believe what had happened, or think of him as a deserter? They shot deserters, didn't they? The walls were closing in around the fox. He was running out of time and options. He couldn't think clearly.

Julian felt the weight of his sidearm on his thigh—he had completely forgotten about it. Was that really the answer? Julian let his weapon dangle off his shoulder by the strap as he pulled the sidearm out of his holster and held it in his paws. His chest was tightening as he slowly raised the gun up to his temple and closed his eyes. Could he really do it? Was this really the only way this could all end? The fox stood frozen with bared fangs and his tail tightly between his legs. He was unable to bring himself to pull the trigger. A snapping sound from behind brought him out of his daze, followed by the rustle of leaves. Julian's body quickly tensed and he turned around, ready to pull the trigger. A dirt covered soldier approached him with fire in his eyes, and before Julian could react properly, the hare swung around a stick and smacked him across the shoulder with it. It didn't stop there. Pell released his anger at the fox, who tried to block it as best he could. Julian opened his muzzle to speak, but the hare quickly cut him off. "Shut up!" he snapped. "You incompetent idiot, I risk my life for you and all you have to show for it is trying to kill yourself?" He swung the stick backwards again for another hit when Julian quickly grabbed onto it and stopped it. Pell nearly fell backwards before using the stick to balance himself. The fox's muzzle was partially open and yet he couldn't come up with any words. Was he really about to end his life?

"Forget it," groaned the hare. He used the stick as a kind of crutch. Julian's eyes widened when he saw the big red stain on Pell's knee, and his teeth pressed together in agony. The fox quickly grabbed onto Pell's arm and supported his weight. The hare didn't fight back.

"You've been shot." Julian pointed out.

"Nice of you to notice." Pell clenched his teeth and struggled to use the stick as a substitute for his leg. Julian hesitated for a moment, noticing now that Pell had been alone.

"Zio?" the fox asked quietly.

Pell didn't respond, instead he reached into his pocket and pulled out a small tag, shoving it at Julian's chest. The fox's ears flattened on his head. His chest hurt, but he had to keep it together.

"I got one of them." Pell reported, short of breath. "I think I wounded the other one, but he still got away. They'll be back for us, Jackson. We need to move."

"Move," Julian echoed with a nod. He wrapped his paw around the hare's lower back, grasping at Pell's paw when he slung it over the fox's shoulder. Pell didn't complain about the fox putting his paws on him anymore.

They moved in a beeline. They made slow progress, Pell groaning from agony all the way through. The bullet had pierced his knee, and while neither of them had said it, they both knew that Pell would never walk again. As they slowly made their way through the forest that they had grown to hate, the tree-lines grew thinner. Rays of sunlight passed through. The fog had mostly cleared up. and for a moment it looked almost peaceful; but they knew the enemy would search for them and they were running out of time.

"Wait." Pell slowed down and turned into the direction of a stump. "Set me down there." Julian helped the hare sit. He could not imagine the pain he was in.

They took a moment to rest, neither of them speaking. The two never saw eye to eye, and it was an odd turn of fate that they had ended up having to rely on each other. Pell had extended his foot and his head along with his ears hung low. Julian had managed to relax enough where his tail didn't bother him when he walked. He shifted his weight and asked, "How long do you think we have?"

Pell slowly raised his head to look at Julian, holding his gaze on the fox with his ears held to his head. His eyes trembled as he clenched his muzzle together. Anger, Julian thought and he couldn't blame the hare for it. Pell closed his eyes and hung his head again, letting out a deep sigh.

"Not long," he said quietly. "The camp is up north and it'll be sundown soon." Pell indicated where north would be with his left paw.

"We better move then," said Julian. He approached Pell to help him stand.

"No," the hare waved his paw at the fox. "Not me, just you."

"What are you talking about? I'm not leaving you here."

"Yes, you are."

"No." Julian growled, clenching his paws. As he took a step closer, Pell reached for his sidearm and aimed it at the fox, making him stop in his tracks. "Yes, you are," he repeated. "Or I'll shoot you where you stand and then myself."

Julian slowly raised his paws up and licked his muzzle. They didn't have time to fight between each other, but the hare's threat had seemed genuine.

"I'm only slowing us down. They'll follow the blood trail and know exactly where we are. You know I'm right." Pell shook his head. "You can't save us both."

As much as Julian hated what Pell had been saying, he hated to admit that he had a point. It was only a matter of time before the enemy soldiers would catch up and then it would be over for both of them. But could he really leave his last crew-mate behind?

"How can I leave you behind?" Julian started to raise his voice. "How can I live with the fact that I left my own crew-mate behind?"

Pell stomped his good foot on the ground and tightly clenched his free paw into a fist, his gun still pointed at Julian.

"Do you ever think of anyone else but yourself?" Pell spoke through his teeth. "I'm a hare, Jackson. What good is a crippled hare to anyone?" Julian opened his muzzle to speak but when he didn't, Pell went on. "If someone offered me a chance to live, I'd take it and be grateful for it." He spat the words at Julian who grew more frustrated by the second.

"Then let me help you," He dared to take a step closer. "You're still alive and we can still get out of here."

"I don't need your help," Pell argued. "And that's different. I don't want to live the rest of my life like *this*. It was over the moment we got caught off guard. I'd rather go out on my own terms."

The fox tested his luck once more by stepping closer and forced Pell to pull the hammer back on his gun, his paw lightly shaking.

"So you're just going to sit there and let them shoot you?" Julian nearly shouted.

"No," said the hare and reached into his side pocket, pulling out a single grenade. "I'll take them with me, so help me god." Pell must have gotten the grenade from the Sergeant's compartment as the coyote had left them behind.

Julian remained speechless. He didn't want to make or even think about the choice laid out for him. Pell was stubborn and determined to have it his own way. He had already made his decision. The hare had saved Julian's life and now he was laying down his own as a full stop at the end of his story.

"That's suicide." The fox said quietly.

"My own terms," Pell responded "Better than a burning tank."

Pell had made his final choice and that's how things were going to be. He was offering to buy Julian some time, or to shoot him where he stood. It was madness, insane and suicidal. It was war.

Sunlight crawled across the sky, its rays passing through the forest. For a moment it was almost warm. Pell had been looking up towards the sky, through the branches and somewhere beyond. There was a just a hint of a smile that appeared on his muzzle.

"I knew I'd die in this war." The hare's smile weakened as he looked at Julian, locking his gaze for a moment. "But I never thought it would be for you," he added as he shook his head. His shoulders slumped down tiredly. Julian stood in silence as he watched the hare slowly die inside. He should say something, apologize, make him reconsider, jump at the gun and hope that Pell would miss. But he couldn't do any of it. His chest tightened into a knot.

"Pell, I'm -"

"Don't," the hare cut him off and shook his head. "Don't say anything, just—go home, Jackson. Go home." Pell reached down his shirt and pulled the chain that held his tags. He separated one from the other and tossed it to Julian. There was a shout in the distance, followed by another. The two could only assume that the enemy trackers had found Zio's body and that they were close by.

"Go home, Jackson," Pell repeated and closed his eyes. "I need to make peace." He pulled the pin from the grenade and grasped it tightly with both paws. Julian watched him a moment longer and felt sick. He muttered that he was sorry. Although Pell's ears twitched, he did not respond. The fox turned around and ran.

* * *

Julian rushed through the forest as fast as his feet could carry him, gritting his fangs and keeping his eyes focused. If he could only make it out in the open, then he could find a road or some kind of sign to show him the shortest way to their camp. There was no clear path, but as the tops of the trees began thinning out, more of the sun was able to shine though. Julian followed that light, hoping it would lead him to safety. It was either by luck or faith that he could see from a distance, a sea of green basking under the autumn sun—grass, he thought, which meant a field and possibly a sign of solace.

He jumped over gaps and dashed through small bushes, hurrying as if afraid it was going to get away. He paid no heed to anything along his way or anything that he might be stepping on. As he jumped over a small boulder, he did not see that there was a small but muddy path there. He landed on it and slipped, losing his balance, and falling knees first into a shallow puddle of mud. It had been another strike against him. He was covered in blood, sweat and tears, and now he could add mud into the mix.

Julian tried to hold it in, baring his fangs and squeezing his eyes shut. And then he broke. The fox let out a scream, a frustrated, angry cry and he didn't care who heard him. He pounded the ground with his paws until they began to hurt and then he pounded some more. He thought that perhaps it should have been right for him to die. Perhaps he should have been the one to stand in front of Anderson and take the bullets, or that he should have fired into the bushes before the enemy fired at Zio. Perhaps he should have been the one left behind, instead of Pell. Slowly, he got up from the mud and fiddled with the strap of his weapon, before growing frustrated with it and tossing it on the ground, then slumping against a nearby tree.

A deep and terrible fear had clutched itself around him.

Just for a minute, he thought. He would rest for only a minute and then make his way further. Julian squeezed his eyes shut and shook his head, thinking that he was about to go insane. His chest had begun to hurt again and he shook uncontrollably. This was war and you couldn't save everyone no matter how hard you tried.

Just then, a distant memory came rushing back to him—a memory of his father when the war had started. Why now of all times did he have to remember it? He remembered how he had received the letter and his father's words strict and haunting, "You will go," he said "and you will come back a war-hero, or not at all."

"No." Julian hissed through his fangs, covering his ears over his head, wanting to make the voice go away. He took a few deep breaths to try and focus, as he was taught to. He slammed his paws into the cold dirt and pushed the memory to the back of his mind. He swore to himself that he would make it back alive, reminding himself of what was most important. Others had died so that he wouldn't have to. Perhaps it was fate or luck that was on his side, but he would see until the very end that he and the memories of his crew-mates made it home.

\* \* \*

The sea of green Julian had seen from a distance turned out to have been one of the rarest pieces of land untouched by war. It stood out from the rest of the countryside. The road to sanctuary was anything but lively. Although still dangerous, Julian walked along the edges of the concrete road with his back to the sun, glad to finally feel something other than cold dirt below his feet.

The road bore mud marks from tank tracks, though it was impossible to tell in which direction its platoon had gone; impossible to know if it had been friendly or not. Julian knew that he should head north and meet up with the tank platoon based there. With the tragedies that had happened, they had missed their chance of arriving there by sundown. By the time Julian made it to his first road sign, the sun was already shaded a dark orange and fading by the minute. The fox realized he wouldn't make it to camp that same day, and that his priority was to find a safe haven for the night. Anything would be better than the forest, he thought to himself as he approached the outskirts of a town. The sign on the road read 'Padno'; a faded yellow, rusty thing bearing three bullet-holes.

The majority of the town lay in ruins. Crumbling bricks were a part of every structure Julian passed. Nearly all the roofs had collapsed, with broken shards of glass and bullet casings lying on the streets and parts of the grass. The place was a ghost town; the wind echoing and howling as it bounced off the old bricks and whatever else was left.

There had been a battle there not too long ago. The distinctive smell of smoke and casualties lingered in the wind and tickled Julian's nose. It seemed that his sense of smell had become functional again. He almost wished it hadn't been. There must have been at least a dozen bodies somewhere close by. The fox followed the main road deeper into town and eventually found an improvised resting place, if it could have been called that. Maybe not too long ago it had been a patch of garden in the heart of town, surrounded by a white picket fence where cubs played and vegetables grew, but now it had been turned into an improvised graveyard. Its occupants had been of larger species; two tigers, one lion, two bears and one boar. Bigger species also meant bigger guns, the kind that made Julian's paw-greaser rifle look like a toy.

The dead soldiers had once been a brute force infantry and now they were just dead. The fallen soldiers wore long blue coats, the kind Julian recognized seeing back in the forest. Morbidly, the grave gave the fox some comfort, reminding him that it wasn't just the allies who were losing friends. Julian kept his paws around his nose. It was a terrible stench and an even worse sight. Bugs crawled all over the bodies, separating fur from skin. The sight alone made the fox's fur itchy and irritated. Blood ran from the garden patch onto the road and formed a puddle that flies gathered around. There were other puddles that split from the main one, and one of them was still wet. Someone had died there not too long ago. But the other marks didn't make sense. It was as if they had all died in the same spot.

Paranoia or not, slowly but surely, Julian started piecing it all together. He looked around curiously. There was nobody in the streets, nobody at the windows or on the roofs. Besides the dead bodies, he was alone; and yet it didn't feel like it—his fur prickled and something just didn't feel right. Julian turned his back to the sun. In the opposite direction he saw a glare facing him. He froze when he connected two and two together. Quickly, he threw himself to his left. He scraped along the cobblestones until he had managed to stand up and dash to the corner of a nearby building. His heart raced, and he nearly had to swat himself for the stupid mistake he had made.

The enemy soldiers all died in one place because the shooter had the perfect position to take them all out from a distance. Kill one, leave him as bait.

Carefully he approached the corner and pressed his muzzle against the brick building, only allowing one eye to see onto the street for a quick peek. The glare was still there, placed on top of the church. It seemed to be the highest building around—the perfect sharpshooter spot. Julian slid back into the alleyway when a thought occurred to him. Why hadn't the sniper shot him when he had clearly been standing out in the open? He shook his head and discarded the thought as soon as he came up with it. It was obvious. The dead soldiers had all been the enemy, after all, and so the shooter had to have been a friendly. Paranoia, he told himself once more. He decided to break from cover. Once he did, that was when the shot rang out. The bullet missed his head by inches and struck the wall besides him. He quickly jumped backwards into cover and swung his rifle around, trembling. Perhaps he had been wrong after all.

Nevertheless, he decided that he wasn't going to fall victim to a single shooter after what he had been through. With his weapon firmly in his paws, he followed the wall to the other side of the building that led to a backyard. He scouted from the corners for more intruders and saw no one. The positioning of the houses would keep him safe from the view of the church as long as he stuck to the walls and wide roofs. If he could just get as close to the church as possible, then the shooter couldn't spot him.

He moved up half a block before he came to a stop. In front of him was a clear path that would bring him to the side of the church, but there was no longer any cover. He would have to run for it. He had been running all day long and though tired, a bit farther up wouldn't have made any difference. Just as Julian prepared himself to run, he saw a shape from the corner of his eye.

Julian spotted him hiding behind a corner of the run-down building that had been nearest to the church—in the opposite side that Julian had aimed for. He was definitely wearing a longer coat, and in his paws he carried what looked like a long-ranged rifle. From that angle, Julian could see pointy ears and slender muzzle equal to his own. Fox vs. fox it was, then. As the shooter concentrated on Julian's last known position, his side was left completely exposed. Julian would have to relocate to the church, circle around it and catch the fox off guard. He was going to have to be quick if the fox would never see him coming.

Julian made haste, dashing confidently while he was still unspotted. It was either him or the enemy. At the end of the day, Julian had still been a soldier—he too could kill.

As quickly as the tanker approached the corner of the house just before the church, he was taken by surprise just as fast. Just before he turned, a shadow moved into sight. Another soldier, a hyena appeared before him, shoving the butt of his rifle towards Julian. He was too close to stop, but his reflexes remained sharp. Julian lifted his paws and used his weapon as a shield, absorbing the initial blow that would have otherwise hit his chest. However, the soldier's reaction had been just as quick. He stepped forward and with his foot, kicked Julian in the ankle to break his balance. It worked, and as Julian stumbled to the side, a foot planted itself into his ribs a split second later. He felt a sharp pain as he dropped backwards as if he was drunk. He just barely had enough left in him to move his tail and avoid falling on it.

His weapon had been thrown to the side and he laid on the ground, gasping for air as the barrel of a rifle was aimed at his head. The bravado that had pushed him forward evaporated. It felt a lot like drowning. It didn't make sense. Julian had been sure he saw a fox, but standing above him now was a hyena. He watched Julian struggle on the ground. He didn't shoot, didn't say a word. He took his time, nice and calm. The shooter kept Julian in place by pressing his weight down onto the fox's ankle with his rifle aimed at him. Finally some air managed to break into Julian's lungs. He gasped and coughed loudly, feeling relieved to being able to breathe again. But his ankle and chest hurt, the hyena easily outweighed him. As he stared at Julian, the fox returned the look. He noticed that the soldier wasn't wearing a blue coat, but instead the olive green uniform that marked him as an ally.

The hyena remained completely still, even as Julian struggled underneath. Not even his tail moved, unlike Julian's that nervously thumped against the ground. The shooter brought one claw to his muzzle to indicate silence and waited. The hyena's ears twitched as he carefully listened for upcoming danger. A short moment later there was a sound of squeaking wood from inside the building. Both soldiers focused their ears in that direction. It was quiet, but not impossible to hear. Floorboards were gently creaking, and here and there a piece of glass cracked or furniture got shoved out of the way. Somebody was going to a lot of trouble to sneak up on them, keeping as silent as possible.

Julian knew to keep still and quiet as the hyena held his rifle idly towards the fox. He thought it would be best not to give the hyena any reason to squeeze the trigger. Slowly, the soldier reached for his sidearm and aimed it at the wall just to his left, under the window from which they heard movements. For a moment, Julian was afraid to breathe when everything had gone still. There was a clicking noise as the hammer was pulled back. The enemy must have heard it as well because there was a sudden commotion inside. The hyena wasted no time in quickly emptying his magazine through the window and wall. Julian covered his ears and turned to his side to shield himself from the ricocheting bits of brick. Things fell over inside until there was a loud bang at the wooden door and the enemy was gone.

They took a moment to breathe and reevaluate what had just happened. Had the hyena just saved Julian's life? The fox coughed, unable to think of anything to say, still not able to take deep breaths. The soldier looked at him curiously before finally moving his foot off of Julian and replaced his sidearm into his holster.

"You got a death wish, fox?" the hyena's voice started out flat. "Walking in the middle of the street like that is how you get shot." He stared down at Julian laying on the ground, not bothering to help him stand up or even apologize. By instinct, hyenas and foxes didn't like each other very much. It was the same with hares; a good reason why Pell disliked Julian to begin with. It was a species thing. Julian slowly stood up and tried to match the hyena's size but ending up a head smaller than him. The hyena's round face and black tipped ears stood out—his eyes of dark brown remained unsympathetic to the fox.

"I was looking for a safe place, actually. The sun's about to go down," Julian answered.

"I'm aware of that." The hyena was careful of Julian. Although his rifle was lowered, his finger remained firmly on the trigger. Julian coughed again as he picked up his paw-greaser. "Why did you hit me?" he asked and looked over his shoulder.

The hyena's ears flicked and he diverted his eyes. "Thought you were with the other fox," he indicated to the broken window with his head. "Guess you got lucky."

Julian's tailed lashed behind him. He gritted his fangs. Species usually stuck together and favored their own, but being on opposite sides didn't mean that they were working together. The military frequently reminded its soldiers of species prejudice. Some soldiers simply did not want to work with others. If the enemy has a squadron of foxes, for what reason would you trust the foxes on your side?

The hyena must have remembered the warnings against making enemies within allies. He said, "If you've got food, I have a safe place for the night." He sounded reluctant to do so, perhaps hoping that Julian would turn down the offer. But the sun was fading and shelter was primal.

"I'm willing to share," said Julian and added, "For shelter and safety."

The hyena nodded, agreeing to the deal.

"First things first," he pointed out and extended a paw towards the fox. "I'll need your weapons. Safety reasons."

As desperate as Julian was for some rest, handing over his only means of attack and defense didn't stand well with him. Without them he was useless. While the hyena was fighting for the same side, there were more than a few apparent trust issues.

"Sorry," said the fox and adjusted his grip on the paw-greaser. "I can't do that." He didn't move an inch, returning a threatening glare towards the bigger soldier as best he could. The hyena needed food as much as Julian needed shelter, or else he wouldn't have made the offer. Julian was prepared to spend the night in a deserted house if he had to.

The hyena lowered his paw and nodded in return, edges of his muzzle turning into a grin. One thing you never do in war is to let go of your weapons.

"Smart move, fox." he commented and indicated for Julian to follow.

The hyena had been bigger than Julian, with his fur a brownish-gray. His muzzle, tips of ears and tail had been fully black. Julian was tense, despite the hyena's sudden ease. The bigger soldier carried himself confidently though Julian hadn't decided if he really trusted him or not. Julian had been through enough in one day to end up trusting the wrong soldier.

The hyena led Julian around the church. Because of the fox's long tail, he had to tell him to keep it off the ground before showing him the reason for it. There were mines buried underneath the patches of grass surrounding the church. Home defense, the hyena had called it. The church had been the only building in town left intact from the ravages of war. Most soldiers on both sides shared the same religion, and considered firing upon such a place sacrilegious and strictly forbidden. Though the hyena didn't seem to mind planting mines around it.

The two soldiers went around the tower to the back door that led up to the steeple. The door was made of plain wood and left unlocked. The only thing inside was a set of wooden stairs that creaked under their weight as they made their way up into the tower.

Julian's assumption had been correct; it had indeed been a sniper's nest. The very top of the steeple had been made nearly entirely of white stone, emitting cold and that stuffy church-like smell. Besides that, the nest had smelled almost entirely of hyena.

"The name is Hale, by the way," said the hyena as he lighted an old oil lamp. "Alec Hale." The dark room lit up, light reflecting off of its polished surfaces.

"Julian Jackson," the fox introduced himself. He looked around. The place hadn't been big, but it had enough room for the two of them. Right before the stairs was a small stack of cartons, previously containing food but now presumably empty. The wall to the left of that had been where the hyena had collected ammunition and weapons. There were at least two different rifles propped up against the corners with a small sized ammo box placed in between.

"So they call you JJ? That's a riot. That corner is yours, by the way." Alec tried to hold back his hyena laugh as he showed Julian the empty space near the stairs.

"Sometimes," Julian answered with a flick of his ears. He wasted no time in settling down.

As he promised, the fox took a small packet from his side uniform pocket; the only bit of food he had been able to bring with him when he left his tank behind hours ago. He slid the small packet over to the hyena, who wasted no time in tearing it open and beginning to devour its contents. Julian didn't feel hunger as much as he felt tired. In the weak light of the white room, Julian closed his eyes and faded off to sleep.

\* \* \*

When Julian slept, his dreams were nightmares. Death appeared in his head over and over. He saw images of his fallen crew, telling him it was all his fault, grabbing his paws and dragging him with them. He found himself in a forest that was engulfed in darkness and twisted into a limbo. Pell was there, his white fur coat covered in blood. He called Julian a coward, the unpinned grenade still in his paws. The hare released the explosive and then there was a flash.

Julian awoke with a jolt and fumbled to his side. Squeezing pain washed down his legs as they had fallen asleep. He shifted about and tried to move them, feeling a tingling sensation like puncture marks all over them. He remembered he was in the church steeple. The oil lamp sat by the corner, set to its lowest light.

"They're only dreams," he heard Alec say. The hyena had been lying on his chest with the rifle pointed through a small opening in the wall. Night had fallen. While Julian was aware that hyenas were nocturnal, he found it impressive that Alec could scan the area in nearly complete darkness.

"Who's Pell?" the shooter asked. Julian hesitated to answer. He feared about going into any details.

Julian shifted in his place and instead asked, "Was I talking in my sleep?"

Alec's ears flicked towards the fox. "Screaming."

Julian sighed and leaned his head back against the wall, staring into a dark corner. His chest had begun to tighten once more, and he knew he wouldn't be able to fall asleep again. He curled his long bushy tail around and placed it on his lap, placing his paws on top of it.

"You're a tanker, aren't you?" Alec asked a moment later.

"Yeah." Julian confirmed with a nod.

"I recognized the uniform. Where's your tank, then?"

"Out of commission." he answered and closed his eyes "My crew is dead."

Alec made an agreeing noise along with a nod, and that was it. This was war, Julian reminded himself. He shouldn't go looking for any sympathy. Everybody loses friends. Alec was quiet and mostly still as he looked down the barrel of his rifle, peering into the darkness of the town below. Julian saw the hyena shift uncomfortably in his spot from the corner of his eye, probably feeling like he should say something.

"I know," he said after a long while, "you smell of death." Alec wrinkled his nose as if trying to get rid of the stench. The hyena was by no means clean, but compared to Julian he might as well have been. Julian's olive green uniform had been tainted with blood and mud, and his pants were torn at the knees where he had fallen. His red fur and the patch of white running from his muzzle down his chest had been anything but clean. The fur was matted and stuck together where it had been wet, and the mud began to crumble as it dried up. Old stains of oil had long settled in.

"What about you?" asked Julian "Why are you here all alone?"

"Team is dead," Alec answered nonchalantly and shrugged. "We came to take back the town." Alec left it there, but Julian asked what happened next, making the hyena sigh.

"We were outnumbered, out-gunned. I hid in the church and played dead until the tanks left," Alec explained, and then his black muzzle twisting upwards into a grin, revealing his white fangs, he said, "I shot those that stayed. Only one left is that damn—the fox." He caught himself at the last moment.

"So why not just leave? This place is in ruins."

Alec lashed his tail and his head quickly turned to Julian. The fox's ears pointed backwards towards his head. It didn't make sense to Julian why someone would continue to fight when everything had been lost.

"Until we are clear of these vermin, we will always be at war," Alec stated in a low grumble. "These people need us. This country needs us. They need heroes."

There was that word again, 'heroes'. It's what everybody in the old garrison had talked about; it was what they had mentioned in tank school. Everyone wanted to be a hero. Everyone was expected to be, but the only ones who were named true heroes had been those who had fought and fallen for their country.

"So you won't quit," said Julian with a nod. "What about the other guy, then? The sniper."

"The same goes for him," Alec pointed out. "He fights for his own side, the same as we fight for ours."

The hyena started opening up, beginning to describe what he himself had named 'The Battle of Padno'. Day in and day out, the two sharpshooters would hunt for each other. The town lying in ruins had been their playground. Only one of them would have the final victory.

"We are fighting for what we believe in, just as he is. The better will win in the end, and I am content with that. I've held my own against a heavy infantry before." Alec leaned onto his side and from his inside pocket fished out a paw full of the patches that enemy soldiers had sown onto their uniforms. He made sure Julian saw his collection before replacing it back into his pocket. They were his trophies.

"Whoever wins this battle, we both will be regarded as heroes that had fought for what they believed in."

For a moment, Julian admired the hyena's display of bravado and heroism, but he recognized that there had been many flaws to his logic.

"If you die," Julian said, shifting uncomfortably by the wall, "nobody will remember this so-called battle."

"You're wrong," Alec growled and pointed a finger at the fox. "Maybe not right away, maybe not until we're long gone, but someday they will remember us and we *will* be heroes." When Julian didn't respond, Alec asked, "Don't you want to be a hero?"

The question hung heavily in the air. Julian's shoulders felt even heavier than before. He was aware of the chain around his neck that held his tags. He felt them tugging at his furry chest.

"I'm no hero," Julian responded tonelessly, feeling heat gather behind his eyes. "I let everybody down. I was useless when they needed me, and they died so that I could live. They're the heroes, not me." His voice came out as strained.

"Heroes aren't meant to survive," Alec preached. Julian couldn't agree, but who was he to say what was true? He remained quiet, thinking it over. He kept coming to the same conclusion.

"I ran so I could live. So why would I waste that being a hero? A hero nobody remembers." Julian wasn't sure Alec was still listening, but it felt good to get things off his chest. He reached into his pocket and fished out the three tags belonging to his crew-mates.

"I'm a coward," he added quietly. The hyena shifted in place before slowly getting up from his prone position and pushing himself up against the wall. He reached for a nearly crushed packet of cigarettes and silently lit one up. It had been the longest that Julian ever saw a soldier who smoked go without a cigarette. Alec's eyes had a distant look, thinking and remembering. His tail shifted back and forth across the floor.

"If I'm honest, I never liked Pell," Julian admitted, even if he was speaking only to himself; "though I guess I had some sort of respect for him. He ended up saving my life, three times in fact." Julian lifted up three fingers, nodding to himself. "Yeah, if anyone is a hero, it's him."

The tags Julian held in his paw brought both comfort and sadness. For a moment he wasn't sure what to do with them.

"Yeah," the hyena finally said as he licked his muzzle. "Maybe you're not a hero, and maybe you don't have to be. Heroes aren't meant to survive." He roughly blew out cigarette smoke from his muzzle and pointed at Julian. "And you don't get to be a hero. You get to live. You have to. Somebody has to bring those memories back home." The hyena managed a tired smile. "So, go home, Julian Jackson."

The weight didn't exactly lift off of Julian's shoulders, but the thought did hit close to home. 'You don't get to be a hero, you get to live,' rang heavily in his mind. Could he really discard something that had been crammed into his head that easily? Julian saw another view of the whole situation. Alec would fight this battle until he would eventually win or die—by gunshot or starvation, but he would die a hero. His obsession kept him going. Up until now, Julian's own goals were to survive day by day. He would make tally marks on his side of the tank for each passing day, but he didn't make one before it was over.

He could have left the war behind like other soldiers did. He could just disappear or he could get shot, injured or crippled. Soldiers did it to themselves even, and then they were sent home. But Julian had no home. His father had sent him away, forced him to join the army. He had told him he wasn't welcome back until he would return as a hero—a hero his father could never become.

But how could he bring the memories back home, when home wasn't there anymore? A place where he wasn't welcomed or needed.

Just then, as the two soldiers sat in the glow of the oil lamp lit room, the answers started falling into place. Silence filled the room between the two soldiers. Alec had given Julian the answer that despair made him overlook. What both Alec and Pell had said started to make sense—the fox knew what to do.

* * *

Morning had approached slowly. The fresh fog that crept through the town below them had tickled their noses. From the steeple, the town of Padno was wrapped in a white void that was nearly invisible from the tower. Despite both shooters being nocturnal, they could not see past the thick fog. They both knew it, so they didn't even try. The enemy fox would have to get close enough, and since it was now two against one, Alec doubted that the fox would dare.

The fog brought back his memories of the previous day. It reminded Julian how a thing like that could become deadly if you walked in it blindly. This was war, after all.

"If you head down south," said Alec as he accompanied Julian behind the hill that circled the town of Padno, "you should reach your destination." They used the morning fog to disguise their movements. Alec doubted that the enemy shooter would stalk them while he was at a disadvantage. While he didn't trust him, he knew the fox well enough by now to predict some of his movements.

"I'll tell them to send help," said Julian. "I'll tell them your story." The hyena didn't answer, but Julian thought he could spot the edges of Alec's black muzzle curl up in a smile covered by the fog.

"Go home, soldier," said Alec. "Bring your crew home."

Before Julian had a chance to shake Alec's paw and thank him, the hyena disappeared into the thick mist. The sounds of his footsteps on the morning grass quietly withdrew before they disappeared entirely.

Maybe it was the night of sleep he had gotten, or perhaps just the safety that he felt when he needed it the most, that made Julian realize what kind of fool he had been. Maybe it was even the fact that someone was able to talk some sense into him. He had endangered others, and had even thought about taking his own life when the heat of the moment had brought despair upon him. Remembering that made little to no sense to him as he followed the river's stream down south—listening to water washing over the stones. Maybe he wasn't a hero, or had gotten any terrible war injuries; but his crew's actions had been heroic enough for all of them. He was proud of them for it.

The river led Julian back to the muddy path that he had trampled over just the day before. He was careful not to slip and fall once again. He made a beeline across the path, noticing how everything had changed. The forest was the same, with fallen leaves and crushed bark, but he was no longer afraid of it.

The final goal had been there all along, waiting for his return. Typical for a tanker, he felt a moment of invincibility and he savored the moment. He would be invisible to planes and other tanks. With the war nearly won, he felt as though he had nothing more to fear. He survived, he lived.

Passing through the forest out into the opening, he imagined passing through the gates of hell onto a giant battlefield where heat had burned everything in sight, and the cold had come along to freeze the images in place. The air felt a lot heavier and it tasted like ash. Julian could feel it settling down into his fur and bushy tail, making it heavier, but he wouldn't let that stop him.

The scorched field now lay in a ghostly silence. Dead armor and the remains of soldiers laid motionless around him. He followed his nose and let his instincts guide him through the rubble. On the far side of the field he could see the blackened forest that bordered the battlefield. From his perspective it seemed to be miles away still. He would have to push himself just a bit longer to get there.

One foot in front of the other, paws firmly on his weapon, he kept his tail lifted proudly as he stepped through the field until he could hear voices. His ears flicked towards them. He could recognize the language, but to him it seemed so far away, so unimportant at that moment.

They appeared out of the fog, shadows moving animatedly like puppets. The closer he came, the more they revealed themselves. First one group and then another, and another after that. Julian could see them in color now and they were definitely real. They were investigating the area around the tank with the broken tracks—his tank.

Finally, one of the soldiers had turned and noticed Julian. He shouted something at the others and pointed at the fox, making the rest turn their heads. Two soldiers in particular, wearing Red Cross armbands ran towards Julian. One of them, a weasel offered Julian his paw, but the fox shook it away, keeping his eyes on the brown tank.

The other soldiers stared at him. He knew he looked like hell. He'd been through hell. The medics examined him from ears to tail. They asked him a thousand questions he couldn't begin to answer, so he didn't even try to. He stared past them at the only thing that had made any sense for the last two years—the brown tank covered with marks, dents and holes.

He was determined to fulfill his promise. For Anderson and Zio, for Grigs and Pell. Julian thought of them as he reached for the chain around his neck and fished out the tags he held close to his heart. He hung them on the gun of the tank, letting them jangle back and forth in the autumn wind. Maybe he wasn't a hero, but he could tell you stories of those that were. He closed his eyes, his muzzle curling up in a sad smile.

"We're home," he told them and thought about heroes.

# About the Artist

Teagan Gavet

Teagan Gavet is a professional illustrator, graphic novelist, and freelance rambler. Find more at: http://www.teagangavet.com
http://www.furaffinity.net/user/blackteagan

# About the Editor

Fred Patten

Fred Patten (1940-current) joined the Los Angeles Science Fantasy Society in 1960 while in college, and has been an active s-f & fantasy fan ever since. He began writing for and publishing fanzines in 1961 (see http://www.zinewiki.com/Salamander), and has written over a thousand reviews of anthropomorphic literature since 1962, irregularly for s-f fanzines in the 1960s, 1970s, and 1980s; for *Yarf!* from 1990 to 2003, for *Claw & Quill* in 2004-2005, for *Anthro* from 2005 to 2008, for *Renard's Menagerie* in 2008, for *Flayrah* from 2011 to 2014, and for *Dogpatch Press* since 2014. He has written three non-fiction books and edited twelve anthologies of furry fiction. He wrote a weekly column on animation, *Funny Animals and More*, from 2013 to 2017 for Jerry Beck's Cartoon Research. He founded the Ursa Major Awards and has been on its administrative Anthropomorphic Literature and Arts Association since 2001. He is a member of the Furry Writers' Guild and the Furry Hall of Fame. He co-founded Japanese anime fandom in 1977, and was awarded the Comic-Con's Inkpot Award in 1980 for introducing anime to America.

A stroke in 2005 has left him hospitalized. He carries on his fan activities via a MacBook Pro laptop.

www.ingramcontent.com/pod-product-compliance
Lightning Source LLC
Chambersburg PA
CBHW071341020726
47502CB00001B/200

# About the Authors

## KC Alpinus

Kirisis "KC" Alpinus, is a graduate student of Florida State University and a happy-go-lucky dholf who likes to spend her weekdays reading, writing, and providing social commentary on her Twitter. Her weekends are usually spent swimming, traveling, or playing Magic the Gathering. Her favorite foods include fresh-picked peaches, barrel pickles, kimchi, and sushi, the later being something she'd eat three times a week if able. KC prefers to spend most of her time reading philosophy and zoning out with world mythology and urban legends, but she's always open for enlightening conversation.

Her works can be found in the Cóyotl Award-winning anthology *Inhuman Acts*, the sci-fi horror anthology *Bleak Horizons*, and the upcoming *Fur to Skin: Ladies First* anthology. When she's not sleeping, she can be found getting into various forms of trouble with a certain purple-striped tiger creature or traveling to exotic locations with him, like the mythical land of Canada. Even though she lives in a fantasy world, these will always be true: she likes board games; the New England Patriots are her favorite team (the Falcons blew a 25-point lead); she's an adrenaline junkie and aloe drinks might just make her the happiest, little dholf ever.

## M. R. Anglin

M.R. Anglin is a YA author who was born in Jamaica in 1980 and moved to the U.S. while still young. Despite her initials, she is in fact, female. She started writing in middle or high school and has not stopped since. All of her books, including those starring humans, have some sort of mythological, alien, or anthro creature featured in them.

She has self-published five books in her ongoing *Silver Foxes* anthro series—*Silver Foxes* (April 2008), *Winds of Change* (June 2009), *Prelude to War* (October 2013), *Into Expermia* (July 2015), and *Interlude* (August 2016); all published by CreateSpace and Kindle; has a traditionally published Middle Grade novel called *Lucas, Guardian of Truth* (Lamp Post, May 2012) available; and has written several other stories that are available to read online.

## Argyron

Argyron is an engineer, writer, and coffee connoisseur currently residing in the wonderful Seattle, Washington area. He took-up writing in High School to fill his free time, but continued when he learned others enjoyed reading his work. While writing is not his main focus in life, he does believe the act has saved him from the jaws of depression.

Outside of his literary work, he spends most of his free hours sleeping, exploring, or working towards some other crazy life-long goal. He has previously lived in Southern California, Colorado, and Texas. Feel free to contact him on his FurAffinity profile of Argyron, or his Twitter, @Argyron69.

## Adam Baker

Adam Baker is a dedicated screenwriter currently residing in Texas. He was born in 1985. Inspired by whiskey and influenced by the likes of H. P. Lovecraft and Stephen King, he has created such works as the found footage short film *Angler* (writer/director) and his screenplay adaptation for the infamous Lovecraft 1928 story "The Call of Cthulhu" (no relation to the 2005 movie adaptation).

In his spare time he enjoys watching and creating films, writing and podcasting. Contact him at adam.baker214@gmail.com

## Cairyn

Ronald W. Klemp, a.k.a Cairyn, was born in 1964 in Northern Germany and became acquainted early on with science fiction and fantasy literature. Despite these leanings, he chose computer science as his professional career; the starving poet firmly in mind. As one of the first German furries, Cairyn has been actively (not to say obsessively) involved with anthropomorphic characters since the early '90s. He is one of the founding members and main staffers of Eurofurence, the European furry convention held in Germany.

As an author, he has been writing several short stories and the novel *Khiray of the River*, serialized online during the 1990s and published in both German and English since then. He is currently working on a new novel and a too-slowly growing array of CGI character designs.

## Jaden Drackus

Jaden Drackus, or Jay Dee is a foxdragon from Baltimore, Maryland. Born in 1983, he has been writing furry stories since officially stumbling into the fandom in 2010. Since then he has written in his spare time to remain sane while pursuing his bachelor's in military history, which he achieved in 2016. A video gamer, builder of model airplanes, reader, and keen observer of Life's little ironies Jay Dee lives with his boyfriend and 4 cats, when he isn't writing while waiting for games to load.

His work can be found at http://www.furaffinity.net/user/jadendrackus/ His silly observations on life can be seen on Twitter: @ JadenDrakus

## Alice "Huskyteer" Dryden

Alice "Huskyteer" Dryden's stories have been published in anthologies including *Inhuman Acts; A Collection of Noir,* edited by Ocean Tigrox (FurPlanet Productions, September 2015), *The Furry Future; 19 Possible Prognostications,* edited by Fred Patten (FurPlanet Productions, January 2015), and several volumes of *Heat* and *ROAR.* Born in Dorset in 1977, she now lives in southeast London near a pizza place called 400 Rabbits, where she first learned of the drunken Aztec rabbit gods. This is the first and only time a pizzeria has provided her with a story idea, but she continues to eat a lot of pizza in the hope that it will happen again.

She can be found at huskyteer.co.uk, or as @Huskyteer on Twitter.

## Dwale

Dwale is a genderless abomination/houseplant who lives in the Mojave Desert. Producing works at once abstruse and aggressively pretentious, it has nevertheless managed to dupe its way into publications such as *Allasso* and *Hot Dish*, in addition to various journals of poetry.

When not writing, Dwale can be found wrenching noises out of a guitar and caterwauling in a way that some have construed as "singing." It enjoys reading and is also an anime enthusiast. Its influences span across different forms of media and include such names as William S. Burroughs, Mamoru Oshii, Satoshi Kon, Dead Can Dance and many others. The truly masochistic can peruse more of its work by visiting http://www.furaffinity.net/user/dwale/

## Geoff Galt

Geoff Galt started creating at a young age with the Newgrounds animation community. Now working full time with *Cyanide & Happiness*, he has partnered up with two of his friends collaborating on the Umbra's Legion saga. Together, they hope to share more exciting adventures with interested readers in this expansive universe they've created.

## Thurston Howl

Thurston Howl is the editor-in-chief and founder of Thurston Howl Publications. He is also the editor of *Furries Among Us*, the recipient of an Ursa Major Award in 2016. He was born in 1992 in Jackson, TN, but has lived all across Tennessee. With a Bachelor's in English from Vanderbilt University and a Master's from Middle Tennessee State University, he now teaches animal literature and current affairs at the college level.

When he is not writing or berating students for comma splices, he is enjoying the mountains of Knoxville with his faithful trans-species dog (dog-to-cat) Temerita, his artistic lover (a panda), and his ever-furry tarantula Venaticus, who wants to eat everyone in the household.

## K. Hubschmid

When she's not writing, KHub works in the film industry on T.V. shows like the supernatural Western horror *Wynonna Earp* and the black comedy/crime drama *Fargo*, or on commercials in her local town as a videographer. Her debut novel, *The Meddler*, is coming to the world in 2017, featuring idealistic freshman Reo, who strays into a criminal underworld, where only a quick wit and courage will get her out alive.

Check out khubswindow.com for more!

## Lord Ikari

When he's not procrastinating or busy finishing high school, Ikari likes to write furry fiction in his room, surrounded by his collection of stuffed animals and military helmets. He currently lives in Longueuil, Quebec, and will soon start a formation to become a nursing assistant.

"The Call" is his first published text. He was born in 1998 and can be reached here: http://www.furaffinity.net/user/lord-ikari/

## MikasiWolf

MikasiWolf (1990-current) started his journey through the labyrinth of prose and wordcraft since 2007, months before discovering furry fandom. He has never been without inspiration since. Though he occasionally dabbles in the wetwork and complexity of art, he considers himself more of an artist of words. His stories have appeared in *The Furry Future; 19 Possible Prognostications,* edited by Fred Patten (FurPlanet Productions, January 2015), VancouFur 2015 conbook, What The Fur 2015 conbook, Anthrocon 2015 conbook, and *Claw the Way to Victory*, edited by AnthroAquatic (Jaffa Books, January 2016), as well as in this here anthology. ;)

Despite the sweltering heat, he currently resides in the midst of an urban jungle. He spends his time picking up the pieces after his dog codenamed Taro, writing, and enjoying video games with a good premise. He can be found on: https://twitter.com/MikasiWolf, and http://www.furaffinity.net/user/mikasiwolf. Feel free to DM him with any comments you may have! Or if you just wanna talk. He doesn't bite…yet.

## NightEyes DaySpring

NightEyes DaySpring is a known troublemaker who is rumored to have a penchant for coffee and an interest in dead, ancient civilizations. His stories have appeared in *The Furry Future*, edited by Fred Patten (FurPlanet Productions, January 2015), *FANG 5* and *6*, edited by Ashe Valisca (Bad Dog Books, January 2014 and July 2015), *Trick or Treat 1* and *2*, edited by Ianus J. Wolf (Rabbit Valley, September 2013 and October 2014), and other anthologies. Currently he resides in Florida with his boyfriend. In his spare time, he masquerades as an IT professional.

More information about NightEyes can be found at: http://www.furaffinity.net/user/nighteyes/ and https://www.weasyl.com/~nighteyes. For day-to-day nonsense, follow @wolfwithcoffee on twitter.

## Miles Reaver

Miles Reaver is a writer, originating from the southern part of Europe. He has an immense love for coffee and anything noir related. While others sleep, he spends his time daydreaming, talking to cats and writing deep into the night. With a wild imagination and a tendency for procrastination, he is determined to find a fitting middle ground. While his writing preference is focused on noir, he is not afraid to add a touch of rainbow into the mix and explore other genres inside the furry fandom.

Outside of his writing, Miles enjoys hour long conversations about the Power Rangers, reading works from authors that have influenced him, both in and outside the fandom, and catching up on his favorite shows whenever time permits him.

## Slip-Wolf

Slip-Wolf (1975—the moment he least expects immortal wrath) has been wandering the furry realms of the western world for a scant three years, spooling tales for the publishing houses who control all writers' destinies. When not reconciling legends from lies for coin and drink, Slip convenes with other writers in the digital ether and the panel shrines in conventions where the writerly arts are worshipped, flaunted and sinned against. He has burned offerings in the halls of Sofawolf with *Heat* issues 11-13, FurPlanet with tales in *ROAR 6, FANG 6* and *7, Will of the Alpha 2* and *3*, and the *Inhuman Acts, Dungeon Grind,* and *Gods with Fur* anthologies, and with Rabbit Valley in its *Trick or Treat 2: Historical Halloween* anthology. He most recently placed an offering in *GoAL*, issue 2.

Slip occasionally leaves word of his doings on: http://www.furaffinity. net/user/slip-wolf/ He also can be marked on twitter: @Slip_Wolf

## Thomas "Faux" Steele

Thomas "Faux" Steele was born in 1997, and began writing fiction in high school after being inspired by a 9th grade writing assignment. He's an Arctic Fox whose works have been published in multiple conbooks, most recently in Anthrocon 2016's *Roaring Twenty* and *FANG 7: Vegas through Time.*

He enjoys fast cars and travel when not studying foreign affairs. In his free time, he enjoys reading furry, fantasy and science fiction, gaming, and playing clarinet in the university band. He would like to dedicate "Noble" to those who serve without public recognition, for "Ye shall know the truth and the truth shall make you free."

## Televassi

Televassi currently lives in south-east England, but secretly wishes to move back to the south-west, where he studied for his degree in English Literature, and can resume exploring the beaches and woods there. He is fascinated with imagining the world as other animals see it and combining it with our own human perspective—naturally leading to his participation in the Furry Fandom. Televassi writes both poetry and prose, and has a 'slight' obsession with Beowulf, The Elder Edda, Celtic La Tène culture, and Germanic cultures. Considering these interests, it is ironic that his nickname is TV. Yes, as in a television.

You can find Televassi's work in *Civilized Beasts, 2015* edition, edited by Laura Govednik (Weasel Press, December 2015), *Gods with Fur,* edited by Fred Patten (FurPlanet Productions, January 2016), Sofawolf Press' *Heat #13* (June 2016), and *Wolf Warriors III: Winter Wolves,* edited by Jonathan W. Thurston (Thurston Howl Publications, September 2016). You can also find him on Twitter regularly talking about writing, history, and rock climbing; or bring him to you by collecting lots of books on the Celts.